DATE DUE

#47-0108 Peel Off Pressure Sensitive

THE
War
Memories
COLLECTION

Includes *Winter Passing*
and *Blue Night*

Cindy McCormick Martinusen

Christian Jr./Sr. High School
2100 Greenfield Dr
El Cajon, CA 92019

T 22532

TYNDALE HOUSE PUBLISHERS, INC.
WHEATON, ILLINOIS

This special edition combines the following titles:

Winter Passing

Published in association with the literary agency of Janel Kobobel Grant, Books & Such, 4788 Carissa Ave., Santa Rosa, CA 95405

Scripture quotations are taken from the *Holy Bible,* King James Version.

This novel is a work of fiction. Names, characters, places, and incidents are either the product of the author's imagination or are used fictitiously. Any resemblance to actual events, locales, organizations, or persons living or dead is entirely coincidental and beyond the intent of either the author or publisher.

Blue Night

Published in association with the literary agency of Janet Kobobel Grant, Books & Such, 4788 Carissa Ave., Santa Rosa, CA 95405.

Scripture quotations are taken from the *Holy Bible,* New International Version®. NIV®. Copyright © 1973, 1978, 1984 by International Bible Society. Used by permission of Zondervan Publishing House. All rights reserved.

Scripture quotations are taken from the *Holy Bible,* New Living Translation, copyright © 1996. Used by permission of Tyndale House Publishers, Inc., Wheaton, Illinois 60189. All rights reserved.

This novel is a work of fiction. Names, characters, places, and incidents are either the product of the author's imagination or are used fictitiously. Any resemblance to actual events, locales, organizations, or persons, living or dead, is entirely coincidental and beyond the intent of either the author of publisher.

ISBN 0-8423-3245-6

Printed in the United States of America

07   06   05   04   03
 7   6   5   4   3   2   1

winter
passing

Cindy McCormick Martinusen

TYNDALE HOUSE PUBLISHERS, INC. | WHEATON, ILLINOIS

To David,
my beloved and kindred traveler

For, lo, the winter is past,
The rain is over and gone;
The flowers appear on the earth;
The time of the singing of birds is come.

Song of Solomon 2:11-12

AUSTRIA
August 11, 1941

Her eyes weighed heavy, but Tatianna could not sleep. Time ran too quickly against her life for one moment to be wasted in rest.

A movement disrupted the silence. She waited, but nothing. Someone in another cell must be stirring. But soon the footsteps would come. Then Tatianna would hear soldiers' boots beyond her door, the clang of a cell opening, and the scrape of shackles against the floor. A frantic plea for mercy would descend into the prison, or more often, an eerie stillness. Tatianna would sit unmoving, knowing unseen strangers in their cells listened with her. She imagined they held their breath as she did, until the sound of bullets erupted.

They would come again. Yet today would be different. It wouldn't be the cell down the hall or the cell beside her that would open. Today Tatianna's door had been chosen. No lamb's blood covered her doorpost. The death angel in SS uniform would find his way inside. Today her shackles would scrape the tile floor. Today the bullets would burst into her chest.

God, will you not send me a savior even now as I go to my death? I chose your way, but I'm afraid to die.

Tatianna folded her hands and winced in pain. That was good—to feel pain in her stiff and broken fingers. The throbbing up her arm reassured her that life survived within her. The gaunt and tattered body, though foreign to her eyes, continued to breathe and move. They'd tried everything to make her speak, but, thank God, she didn't have the information. Through their torture, Tatianna knew she would have cracked. But she didn't possess the answers they sought. And the one piece of the puzzle she did know, they'd never asked.

Tatianna sat on the floor and drew her legs to her chest. Fleas scampered away as she leaned back against the thin mattress. She smiled, feeling her lips crack. For Tatianna had one victory over them—one they would never know. They saw her as useless now, so she could take her secrets with her. But could there still be a way in her final hour? Miracles always happened in the books she read. At the last instant, the heroine was rescued. But there was no one to save her. No one near enough to help.

A stream of light shot through the high bars of the cell. The beacon of morning would have meant warmth and security if shining through the glass panes at her home, but today it signified her approaching death. Her time drew to the end as rapidly as light gathered and crept along the top of the cement wall.

Tatianna closed her eyes. Her mother would say, "Keep your jaw set and your way clear. Everything will work out." *Will it, Mother? Will everything work out today?* Her mother and thoughts of home brought doubts that clouded out hope once again. Hope, then fear; hope, then fear. Tatianna had made the right choice, hadn't she? Hope, fear.

A creaking noise rang down the hall. Tatianna jumped. The first gate opened and footsteps approached, then stopped at her cell. Keys jingled in the lock and the door opened.

Tatianna didn't look into the faces of the two soldiers as she walked between them. The thud of their boots and clang of her shackles echoed through the stone corridor. She knew the other prisoners sat and listened. Did they hold their breath?

A guard bent and removed her shackles. As they entered the open courtyard, a chill of morning cold grasped her body.

Next it was down stone steps and out of the execution area. She looked at the wall where she had expected to die. Should she feel hope? Were they releasing her instead?

They crossed the roll call area but did not turn toward the main gate. And then she heard the music: a Mozart tune, one she'd played on her own violin a hundred times. Tatianna knew what that music meant. And she knew where she was being taken. Today she would die, but not alone.

Bits of gravel cut her bare feet as they moved down the roadway between blocks D and E. What would it feel like? How much would it hurt?

Panic seized Tatianna with a frantic desire to escape. Could she somehow jump or fly beyond prison grayness into the colors of life: green trees, yellow flowers, purple mountain peaks? Today couldn't be her day to die. Not today. The sun shone too brightly. She knew people strolled the streets beyond the cinder-block walls. In the village below, they shopped, laughed, and picked flowers in their gardens. Surely a family packed for an afternoon picnic. A mother held her child in her arms. A girl read a book on a park bench, perhaps nearing the end when the heroine against all odds and challenges would finally get away.

They made their way between barracks. Tatianna saw eyes stare from behind warped glass. She'd escaped what the other prisoners were granted with intense work and starvation: a slower pace toward death. Instead, she'd been the honored guest of the camp's prison where torture, a quick bullet to the neck, and a mass execution were the gifts of hospitality.

Tatianna looked again toward the faces behind barrack windows. She recognized fear in their open stares. *Please, let that girl's death not be mine*, they thought.

She turned away, and with each step toward the open gate, the "I'll nevers" came flooding back. *I'll never wear a bridal veil. I'll never experience a man's love. I'll never hold my child in my arms. I'll never hug my kindred friend again.*

She must stop. These thoughts had tormented her for days. Tatianna must fold the remnants of "I'll nevers" and banish them to some darkened crevice in her heart. *Remember you promised to be strong. Go to your death with dignity. Keep your jaw set and your way clear.*

She saw her place in line. The open gate revealed a row of several dozen breathing skeletons. There had to be many thousands more in the barracks and jailhouse behind them. A few skeletons dared to peer her way as a soldier pushed her against the wall. Hollow and haunted, their eyes reflected fear—an old man in tears, another with prideful defiance, a father and son clinging as one being.

Her fingers trailed a crack in the wall, touching the granite, feeling its coldness in the shadows. She filled her lungs with the cool freshness, savoring its flavor in her mind. She glanced again at the strangers who were now her family as they stepped into eternity together.

Tatianna turned her eyes to the stiff column of marchers lined up before her. Here were the witnesses, and the executioners. She searched the eyes of every face. Ten soldiers, twenty frozen eyes. Wait—she knew that face. The last soldier in the line. His blank expression mirrored the others. She had known that boy at one time, but she did not know him now.

She forced herself not to look below the men's shoulders to the guns they held. She waited, jaw set. Something caught her eye. Above the wall, a bird glided on the morning breeze. It rose and danced above the prison wall, above the distant treetops. The sunlight caught the sheen of black wings before it dropped from view.

A soldier shouted. Guns raised. Tatianna's eyes jerked toward ten barrels.

Someone cried out; a child screamed. Where was her savior? Today the heroine would not get away.

Her body jumped as ten rifles cocked. The sound resonated through the courtyard, echoing within her body. Suddenly the winged creature rose again to soar high above the walls. Tatianna's eyes lifted to the bird as her body exploded in shaking. Her Savior had come, and he brought freedom on his wings.

Tatianna had chosen well.

CHAPTER ONE

Sebastopol, California
Autumn, Present Day

Tatianna! Tatianna!"

"It's okay, Grandma. Calm down."

"Tatianna!" Grandma Celia's frail cry rose to a shriek.

"Grandma, wake up!" Darby Evans tried to hold thrashing arms and shoulders. Her grandmother was slow to calm and return to her pillow. The woman's eyes did not open, but her mumbling quieted.

"*Hilfe*," she whispered, and Darby remembered it was German for "help." But her grandmother never spoke her native tongue. Why now?

Darby put her hand on Grandma Celia's warm forehead.

"*Machen Sie schnell!*" The older woman's expression turned fearful again. "Tatianna!"

Darby held her grandmother's shoulders. "It's okay, Grandma." Her grandmother's hands grasped and fought unseen devils; her features contorted with inward struggles.

"I'm here, Grandma. It's Darby. There's nothing to worry about." The old woman calmed once again. Darby opened the fingers clutching her arm and held them within her own. She brought the bony hands to her lips. They felt like tissue paper drawn over bone and blue veins.

Darby moved a chair close and rested her arms around the old woman. She hummed a Mozart tune, one her grandmother had hummed to her in the late-night hours of her childhood, and watched Grandma Celia slowly slip into a peaceful sleep. After a while, Darby tenderly pulled the covers up and smoothed strands of gray hair from her grandmother's face.

The dim lamp cast shadows along the top of the bedroom walls, creating dark eyes that followed every movement, listened to every word. This house of her youth had never held the presence of shadows, at least none Darby had known. But tonight it seemed that a secret had slipped from the lips of her dying grandmother. It was the name of a stranger. Tatianna. The callings in German had quickly turned to frantic cries that sent a shiver down Darby's spine. It frightened her to think that, although flowery body powder—a familiar childhood aroma—scented the room, and her grandmother's personal items appeared in proper order, there were secrets in this house. And now the shadows, like a pack of jackals, circled their prey. She could almost hear their high-pitched laughter and leering words: "There are secrets here. We know them, but we won't tell."

Her grandmother stirred, and Darby could see the name on her lips before breath brought it to life. "Tatianna."

She waited for another rise of panic, but Grandma Celia slid more deeply into sleep. Darby stood and walked toward the window. The moonlight brought an ethereal glow to the back-yard. Even the rosebushes around the gazebo looked ghostly, with silhouetted fingers pointing skyward. The dim light exposed stray weeds twisted along the stone pathway. She shook her head to cast away the fears. This was home. Even though she now lived a few hundred miles north in Redding,

California, Grandma's home in Sebastopol always welcomed her back. How could her grandmother's cries for a stranger bring such darkness here?

Darby could see herself from the age of five until she left for college, growing, changing, all here in this house. Had hidden secrets stalked and crept while she, in childhood oblivion, laughed and played unaware?

Perhaps she was making too much of this, and there was a simple explanation. Maybe her grandmother was reliving wartime memories. Or could the elderly woman be hallucinating from the myriad of painkillers and medicines? Yet Grandma Celia's anguish appeared real, not imagined.

Darby extracted a letter from her jeans pocket and smoothed the envelope. Another secret, but this one Darby would keep. She probably should have followed her first reaction to burn the letter. How dare this man, Brant Collins, write such words to her grandmother? The stamp and return address were evidence of its European origin. Her grandmother would have eagerly checked the mail each day in hopes of receiving this letter if her illness hadn't progressed so rapidly.

Darby reached to touch the top of her grandmother's head. She held her hand an inch above her skin, not wanting to disturb her, but wishing to hold the woman against all pain.

I don't care about some inheritance. I only want you, Darby thought, tracing her grandmother's face without touching her cheek. Her grandmother had begun searching for the family inheritance, hoping the recovered treasure could be a gift for her grandchildren. "I want to pass on what belongs to our family," she'd stated firmly. Grandma Celia had written Holocaust organizations and even learned to use e-mail and the Internet.

"Can you believe your old grandmother is surfing the Web?" she'd asked Darby on the phone. It hadn't really surprised Darby. Grandma Celia was always involved in something—country and western dancing at the senior center, volunteering in the local kindergarten class, sending letters to congressmen. The notion that Nazis had confiscated her family inheritance wasn't new—only Grandma's sudden search. Why now? Perhaps terminal illness and the reluctant opening of Swiss banks? Darby usually tried to encourage or help her grandmother, but this time she was involved in the remodeling of her photography studio and she thought the pursuit of fortune a bit far-fetched.

Darby examined the soft lines in her grandmother's face. Her cheeks revealed sharp bones beneath; her eyes had sunk deeper into their sockets. It had only been a few months since Darby's summer visit. The cancer had progressed more rapidly in the last months than anyone had expected—except, perhaps, Grandma Celia. Darby had found a paper on the table when she'd arrived that evening from the local hospice care. The information gave signs for patients who had one to two weeks left of life: "Agitation, talking with the unseen, confusion, pale and bluish, sleeping, but not responding." Many were the signs she'd seen in Grandma Celia. The list moved down to the signs for patients with only days and hours left: "Surge of energy, irregular breathing, glassy eyes . . ." The list went on and on, but the last sign, "fish-out-of-water breathing," terri- fied Darby.

Darby's anger rose as she thought again of Brant Collins and his letter. The most endearing, honest woman rested before her, and that man had actually accused her of illegal activities. He wrote that he knew the truth about the Lange family, and if Celia continued her pursuit, impersonators would be prose- cuted. Darby would keep that secret from her mother and grandmother—she'd deal with it herself.

"Where are you, Grandma?" Darby whispered. "I want my fireball grandmother who'd call this Collins character and give him a piece of her mind."

She could picture it now. Grandma got stirred up when she

believed in something. It had only been a month ago that Grandma had declared to Darby over the phone, "Those Nazi pirates aren't keeping what belongs to my family!"

Darby had laughed. She'd enjoyed the story about one of her grandparents being an archaeologist and finding two rare Celtic coins. Her favorite part of the inheritance story was the relative who had helped an Austrian empress, receiving the empress's personal brooch as a gift. Yes, she'd enjoyed the story, especially as a child, but that was as far as Darby had taken it. It was simply another story. The family inheritance, if it had ever existed at all, was certainly long lost or forgotten in some museum or personal collection. Darby had been surprised by Grandma's fierce determination. The dear woman certainly would have been upset by Mr. Collins's words.

Darby blinked as she sat in the recliner beside her grandmother's hospital-style bed. Her eyes wouldn't stay closed. Sleep wouldn't come. Were there many things she didn't know?

Footsteps sounded down the hall. Darby's mother peered in from the darkened doorway. "How is she?" she called softly.

"She's fine—now," Darby answered as she tiptoed into the hall. "You're supposed to be sleeping. Tonight's my watch."

"I know. But I heard her call out and couldn't go back to sleep," Carole Evans said. "I'm so glad you came."

Darby rested her head against the doorjamb, the collection of family photos catching her eye on the opposite wall. Though the dim light hid the faces, she knew each picture by heart. The top three portraits displayed her all-female family: Mother, Grandma Celia, her younger sister, Maureen, and herself. Uncle Marc and Aunt Helen's photos were below. Beside those was Darby's favorite. The framed photograph captured her mother sitting beside a window with Grandma Celia brushing her hair. The lighting had been perfect, and the expressions on their faces depicted an older version of mother and child. Darby had won an award in college for that photograph.

As Carole peered into Grandma Celia's room, Darby noticed how the late-night shadows heightened the circles under her mother's eyes.

"You should have called me sooner. I would have come, you know."

"I know, but you have a life too, and I didn't want you to cancel that photo trip."

"Grandma's more important. Have the doctors said anything more?"

"Well," her mother admitted, "they say she's at the two-week stage. I try to prepare, but even though I see her decline, I'm not ready. There are so many things I still want to do with her. Things I want to know about her. I'm not ready to lose my mother."

Darby looked over her mother's shoulder toward her grandmother. *I'm not ready to lose her either.*

She wanted to pull her mother into her arms. Instead she placed a hand on her shoulder. Even that slight touch seemed to break something within the older woman as a quiet sob erupted. Darby patted her awkwardly, as if her hand was out of rhythm to the beat of a song. This was not her mother's way. While love had always been given freely in this house, sorrow and tears were kept to the privacy of their hearts. Darby fought her own grief and fear, remembering the only other time, outside of a romantic movie or a memorable event, that she'd seen her mother in tears. While playing hide-and-seek with her younger sister, seven-year-old Darby was under her mother's bed when she heard sobbing. Her father had left that morning, but Darby expected him to return. He always had before.

"Mommy, why are you crying?" she asked as she slid from under the bed. "Is it 'cause of Daddy leaving?"

"Yes, honey." Her mother had turned away.

"I'm sad too. But Daddy said he'd write lots and lots of letters while he's working in Texas."

Her mother wiped her eyes. "I just wanted you raised with a daddy. Not without one like I was. . . ." She'd wrapped her arms around Darby, and the tears broke out again.

Darby hadn't known her father was more than just working in that place three states from their Californian home. He'd found a new woman to build a family with. Darby received a few letters, but eventually they stopped. Soon after, Darby, her mother, and sister had moved into her grandmother's home in Sebastopol, a stone's toss north of San Francisco.

Somewhere over the years and conversations with her mother, Darby surmised that much of her mother's sorrow wasn't from the loss of her husband, but from the loss of a father for her children. Her many comments about never knowing her own father emphasized that point.

Now Darby's mother cried again. Darby's father had disappeared almost as if he'd only existed in a dream. But this time it was Grandma, the solid rock of the family. The anchor that kept everyone grounded. Darby had never lost a loved one to death, especially someone so close to her heart.

"Oh, for pity's sake," her mother said as she cleared her throat. "I'm sorry, Darby."

"This is Grandma we're losing. That's reason for tears."

Her mother breathed a long sigh and smiled. "Grandma would say, 'Look, you've gone and watered the carpet.'"

"She's right. And tomorrow we may find a bean stalk here. I never did find those magic seeds of mine."

Carole chuckled. "I'm so glad you're here. You could always handle hardships better than your sister. Maureen tried to help, but she was so emotional and with the kids running around, well, I'm afraid she was more of a burden than a blessing."

"I'm here for as long as it takes." Darby nodded toward her grandmother. "Clarise can handle everything at the studio, and I'm caught up on my deadlines for a while. I'll take night watch. After all, you never were a night owl. I don't know how you've handled it these last months."

"I'm simply thankful for some help now." Her mother patted Darby's hand, then took a step down the hall.

"Mom?" Darby hesitated. "Grandma keeps calling for someone. Who is Tatianna?"

The hallway had little light, but Darby could see the weariness in her mother's expression. "Honey, I don't know. Grandma has called that name during her bad spells for weeks. She also says words in German. I've started to ask a dozen times, but I haven't. She has so few good moments."

"Grandma's never mentioned her before?"

"I've never heard the name *Tatianna* until last month. And Grandma has never mentioned her except in her sleep."

"Okay. Now *you* need to sleep."

"Good night, honey."

When her mother disappeared into the darkness, Darby turned back to Grandma's bedroom. She stared at the shadows that now hid her grandmother's face. After a lifetime of family and love, why were Grandma Celia's last thoughts possessed by a stranger?

Darby leaned over the edge of the bed and touched her grandmother's skin-and-bone arm. She remembered how Grandma Celia would pat the mattress and gather Darby into her bed whenever Darby had a bad dream. It was Grandma who always soothed away her troubles with a story during a tea party or while brushing Darby's long, brown hair.

"Princesses didn't have dirt-colored hair and eyes," Darby had whined at age five.

"No, but our princess has dark gold strands that look like sunshine on the mountain. Our princess has eyes like a tender doe in the meadow and a pretty heart-shaped face."

Tonight it was Darby who lowered the bed rail and gathered her grandmother in her arms. "I love you, Grandma." She closed her eyes to the shadows surrounding them while one question returned to her mind: *Who was Tatianna?*

--===◎===--

HALLSTATT, AUSTRIA

His wooden cane slipped in the loose rocks and the flashlight's beam made a wild dance as the man caught his balance and limped onward. The shuffle of his footsteps along the road harmonized with the mournful song of a cricket. One sang and another more distant joined the tune.

He tried to keep his steps quiet as he trudged along the narrow lakeside road. At the end of a cement wall, he found familiar steps leading up the darkened mountain. Higher, through blind turns and covered walkways, he headed toward the church spire that was silhouetted against the moonless night sky. He was almost there. His chest grew tight with the raspy breaths that fought the frozen air. The last turns up the mountain, the steps he once could run up with stealth, now stole his strength. He rested at the wooden gate, leaning heavily against his cane. When he pushed the gate open, its familiar creak welcomed him to the sentry of headstones and soft red candles that lit his way.

He moved forward, past names he didn't need to read. He knew them all by heart. With great care, he climbed the steps to the upper level of the cemetery and plodded toward a large, white structure. The graveyard and church were cut into the mountainside just like the village below. When autumn leaves crunched beneath his boots, he stopped abruptly and bent before the grave, looking for any weeds. None. He'd made sure the rectangular patch would be well cared for in his absence. He sat on the edge of the concrete border and laid his cane on the ground.

"I—" His voice caught, and he cleared his throat. "I've come again."

He examined his work and smiled. Such passion of youth
had stirred him to spend hours on the wrought-iron headstone. Other headstones were iron or wood, but he could not
purchase her marker. He had to do it himself, to feel the metal
turn in his hands, to sweat, to cut his hands and bleed as she
had—though so much less than she had. He'd needed to carry
the finished work on his back—his cross to bear forever.
Though friends believed the war had turned him crazy, he'd
needed the work to survive the day and the day after that,
until he stood here now all these years later. For his work was
more than a headstone; it was his memorial to his young wife.
It was the closest thing he could have of her. For no, she
wasn't here. Her body didn't rest beneath the earth. That had
tormented him in the beginning. For there was nowhere he
could go to find it, except to take a bit of ground from the
place where she'd died. That was all he had left of her and so
he brought only dirt to where he could visit and feel close to
her again.

The old man removed his tweed hat and set it on the edge of
the cement. He strained to rise and limped toward a stone
faucet capped into a mountain spring. He turned the handle,
and water gushed loudly into the tin watering can. He closed
the valve and carried the can to the grave.

"Let's give those flowers some water," he said to himself,
glad that the pansies and fall daffodils appeared healthy. The
man reached to yank some dead petals from the rosebush that
grew around the base of her headstone, and a thorn pricked
his gnarled finger. He opened the iron cover plate to see her
name. His fingers traced the neat letters on the metal, leaving a
smear of blood around the curve of the C.

"I feel this could be my last visit," he told her tenderly. "No,
it's not our anniversary already. I just needed to come tonight.
You've been in my thoughts so often lately. But it won't be
much longer until I can't hike this trail. I won't have to

wonder and fear. I'll know everything for certain. And we'll be together—at last. And, my dearest, I'm very ready to be with you again."

In the red candlelit night, the man studied the last blooming rose on the bush. Its petals were perfect. The pale yellow roses continued to blossom well in the early autumn days. It seemed they knew this would be the last chance for him to see them grace her grave. So for one last time, he'd see his final offering of love.

The man bent to place his lips upon the cold metal nameplate. Just one more look at her name before he closed the cover. That name he loved so well, even after all these years. If he suspected correctly, soon he'd speak her name, and they'd be together again. Forever.

CHAPTER TWO

The window shade jolted upward and morning pierced the room.

"Wake up, honey."

Darby groaned and squinted in the brightness. "Mom, I just closed my eyes. Do I *have* to go to school today?" She grinned with her hands shielding her eyes.

"You probably did just go to sleep. I didn't want to wake you. . . ." Her mother's features came into focus. "But Grandma's having an exceptional morning, and I knew you'd want to talk to her."

Darby kicked off the quilt. "Can I see her now?"

"She's waiting."

Darby hurried from her old bedroom back into Grandma's down the hall.

"My Darby. Finally, you are here." Grandma Celia sat up slowly. Daylight heightened the sallow coloring of her skin. "You've kept an old woman from her grave so you could traipse the mountains for weeks at a time."

Darby smiled. This was the Grandma Celia she knew, though the name Tatianna still echoed in her mind. Grandma's lively expression kept away her questions. At least for now.

Darby moved to the chair beside the bed. "Who hooked me on the mountains with years and years of her Austrian Alp tales?"

"Not me." Celia looked at her innocently. Darby always loved the woman's soft German accent, though Grandma Celia denied she even had one, saying, "I w-worked too hard to sound American." Darby would try not to laugh. Grandma sometimes tried so hard to sound American with her proper English, emphasizing slangs and especially accentuating the *w*s in an effort not to pronounce a *v* sound, that she actually sounded more foreign in her efforts.

"You're just jealous that I found a way to make money hiking among the pine-scented forests." Darby reached for her grandmother's hand. "And what's this about keeping you from the grave? It looks like you have enough spunk to chase the Grim Reaper away for the rest of eternity!"

"W-well, let me tell you." Grandma pointed a trembling finger at Darby. "Mr. Reaper and I have developed a nice relationship. You know, he's been misunderstood over the years. I've found him a pleasant fella once you get to know him."

"Are you giving my daughter a hard time this morning?" Carole entered the room with a bottle of pills and a glass of water.

"I wouldn't want to disappoint *my* granddaughter." Grandma winked. Darby, who was watching her carefully, perceived an underlying weakness in her tone.

"It's time for your medicine!" Carole said loudly, putting two pills in her hand.

"I've told you before, Daughter, I may be dying, but my hearing is just fine!"

"Oh, hush, and open your mouth."

Darby watched her mother hold two tablets and a glass of water before Grandma's mouth.

"I'm not a child either. I can take medicine all by myself, thank you." Grandma Celia grabbed the pills and swished them down with the water.

"Grandma, you're as feisty as ever."

"What did you expect? That I would get docile in my last days? Goodness, no! I'm ready to march up to those pearly gates and give Jesus the biggest w-whomping kiss he's had in the last millennium."

"You mean *whopping*. Here, give me the glass." Carole took the cup and walked out.

"No, a w-whomping kiss," Grandma Celia called after her, then turned back toward Darby. "I like the sound of that better—no matter what it means."

"Well, Jesus can wait awhile longer for whatever kind of kiss you give him," Darby said, crossing her arms. "You aren't leaving us yet."

"Quit that nonsense talk, my dear. Look at me. I'm as thin as a pencil."

Darby didn't want to look at the arms she had stared at the night before.

"You young whippersnappers believe you must pretend life on earth does not end. But it does, and that's certainly the way it is. A time to be born and a time to die." Grandma Celia patted Darby's hand and sighed. "But I must say it's an odd place to be, on the threshold of death's door. You look back and see it all, your whole life. The mistakes, sorrow, joys, triumphs. Then you look ahead and wonder what's really on the other side."

Darby leaned closer in surprise. "Grandma, are you doubting?"

"Mercy, no! God has w-worked enough in my life for me to know that he is real. But I think it'll be more, so much more—

w-what's the w-word?—immense or spectacular, than I ever imagined. It's very exciting, with maybe a hint of scariness mixed in."

Darby wished she could argue with her grandmother. She wished she could promise a longer life, but Grandma Celia spoke the truth. Celia *was* dying. But how could her grandmother speak so casually about death and seem almost excited about the prospect? Even with Grandma's body waning before her eyes, Darby could not imagine life without her.

Grandma fumbled with the pillow, and Darby noted how even such small movements caused her breathing to labor. Grandma Celia squirmed into a comfortable position, took another long breath, and addressed Darby again.

"Tell me all about your latest work. Not the boring stuff you do in town, pictures of weddings and snooty-nosed children. I want to hear the mountain adventures! Did the group go to the Trinity Alps like you suggested?"

"Yes, and it was wonderful!" Darby exclaimed.

Grandma Celia reached over to move a few brown tendrils of hair behind Darby's ears, just as she'd done for years. That touch and the excited light in her grandmother's eyes caressed Darby's entire being.

"You remember it was that same hiking club from San Francisco? They told me the photographs have been all the rage in the office of the hiking club's president. He's the CEO of a San Francisco insurance company and a hiker in his spare time."

"Is he married?"

"Yes, Grandma. His wife came along and is a wonderful lady. I've told you, the good ones are taken."

"Oh no. Your man's out there waiting. He's a nice fellow, too. I pray for him all the time. He's sick of you hiding beneath your work and ready for you to meet him."

"And who is this man?" Darby tapped her finger against her cheek.

"I'm not certain. But I know he's out there."

"Anyway, let's stick with my story. The club wanted more photos this year and chose a more adventurous expedition with eight days and a forty-mile trip with some face climbing. It's a good thing I joined the gym over the summer. The elevation is over eleven thousand feet." Seeing her grandmother's smile, Darby tried to conjure up the storytelling vividness that her grandmother always used. "The best part of this trip was this one total city boy."

"This isn't the CEO guy?"

"No. This guy is in insurance also, but you could tell he only did the trip to get some photos in his office. He wanted me to take his picture like he was hanging from a rock when really his feet were on the ground!"

Grandma's laughter brought a smile to Darby's own face. She felt like a little girl, telling her grandmother about her day's woes or adventures. After she told her story, Grandma always had a similar tale or story of encouragement. Darby remembered being more enthralled with these stories than with her favorite television shows like *Scooby-Doo* or *The Bloodhound Gang*. Nothing compared to Grandma's vivid tales of the Austrian Alps. Those mountain tellings had bred Darby's own love for the wilderness and a desire to see the towering peaks of her grandmother's childhood. Darby had never made it to Europe, probably never would, but the scent of pines and the crisp mountain air tugged at something within her. It was a feeling she could never quite explain— because of the stories. Grandma's stories lived within Darby now. Yet in all those countless tales, Grandma Celia had never mentioned the name Tatianna.

"Oh, I wish I could have been there!" Grandma's laughter broke into a low, rasping cough. "I'd—have pulled a few pranks on that city fella!"

"Well, just wait till you hear the rest!" Darby continued

with a chuckle. She ignored her grandmother's condition and pretended she was telling just another story on just another day. "We reached the crest of Siligo Peak, overlooking Deer Creek Canyon hundreds of feet below, when something catches my eye."

"City Boy?"

"Yes! He's clinging to this rock, scared to death, with his eyes shut! So, since I was assigned to take pictures . . ."

"Oh, you naughty, naughty girl! Did he even know you took pictures of him?"

"Oh, yes! He heard the camera clicking and opened one eye. Then he starts yelling at me to stop. Of course, I didn't. For the rest of the trip, this guy was begging to buy that roll of film from me."

"I've never been so proud of you!" Although Grandma's tone was light, her eyes appeared glassy, and Darby wondered if it was from the laughter or the coughing.

She continued to describe her trip but noticed her grandmother's eyes blinking heavily. Grandma sagged back against her pillow and squirmed deeper under the covers.

"Well, I can see my stories just don't hold your interest anymore."

"It's this horrible medication. I can't stay awake for long with it, but it pains me too much to live without it. We have a real love—" Grandma burst into another coughing fit—"hate relationship." Darby propped her forward as her body was racked with uncontrollable spasms. "W-wa-ter," she sputtered. Darby grabbed the glass and placed it to her grandmother's lips. Droplets flew across the quilt as Grandma Celia struggled to drink. Finally the cough subsided, and Grandma leaned back. She closed her eyes, then her smile came in slow motion. "I've got to hear the rest of your story, my dear. You know it's not fair I got stuck in this hilly country. You're lucky to be in the real north of Northern California near all those mountains."

Darby stared at her grandmother for a minute. How she loved this woman. She didn't want to be part of this game of telling stories, joking while disease consumed her grand-mother before her eyes. But she swallowed the tears that threatened—there would be plenty of time for crying later. These last moments needed smiles, stories, and joy. And below it all remained the unanswered questions.

"I guess you'll have to wait to hear about the cricket in City Boy's sleeping bag. I'll let you rest." Darby forced a smile and rose to leave.

"Wait." Grandma Celia grasped Darby's hand. "I need to talk to you about something."

"Okay. How about as soon as you wake up?"

Grandma Celia's grip tightened around Darby's hand. The intensity in the older woman's gaze startled her.

"Yes, it'll have to wait. But it's very important."

Darby could feel her heart beat faster. Maybe she'd discover the secret the shadows held. She had fought the desire to ask, fearing, like her mother, what the mention of that name would do to her grandmother. Darby wanted the real Grandma Celia this morning.

"What's it about?"

"I couldn't explain it to your mother. She w-worries, and she couldn't do anything. Besides, it's something you should do. I've known that for a long time."

"What do you want me to do?"

Grandma Celia's eyes were shut for so long that Darby thought the older woman had fallen asleep. But when Darby drew closer, a second later, Grandma's eyes fluttered half open.

"I need you to do what I can't do."

"Anything. What is it?"

"I need you to make things right with Tatianna."

"Who is Tatianna?"

As Grandma Celia gazed toward the ceiling, an age-old weariness poured into her features. "Tatianna was my best friend."

Sensing their time together was short, Darby wanted to hurry her, to ask question after question, but she held her tongue to give her grandmother space to open at will.

"I have a small safe that Fred is keeping for me."

"Fred Bishop, your lawyer?"

"Yes . . . you'll find some answers in there. I'll tell you more when I wake up. But Darby—" Celia held her granddaughter's arm with two hands. "You must make things right. Make them right for me, please."

"Make what right?"

"You'll know when you get there."

"Where?"

Grandma's eyes flickered shut, then opened slightly. "Tatianna needs her name. I'll tell you later. I need some rest first."

"Her name? What do you mean?" Darby asked, startled.

Grandma's hand motioned *not now, not now,* then she fell asleep.

◦—≡◦⊂≡—◦

SALZBURG, AUSTRIA

The rain slapping Brant Collins's face was neither felt nor acknowledged. The drops streamed like tears from his jaw, nose, and chin. His legs walked without direction across wet streets. He even crossed a busy intersection without looking. A loud horn and the *whoosh* of a bus focused his thoughts. He stepped onto the bridge and finally stopped at the crest.

Resting against the railing, Brant glared into the gray fingers of the Salzach River below. He noticed the newspaper clenched in his hand. It had long ago turned limp and now dripped like a leaky faucet. He wiped rain from his face and unrolled the paper where much of the black ink had worn off against his wet hand. The faces in the photo were now contorted images, quite suitable for the people they represented. The man had been captured with his eyes toward the ground, but the woman stared straight from the page into Brant's eyes. Her smile was a twisted sneer—the person she really was. Her eyes still met his defiantly beneath the headline: COUPLE ACCUSED IN HOLOCAUST SURVIVOR FRAUD.

Brant had given much of the past year to the Aldrichs. The woman had begged his help to find her family's lost paintings. They were the last link to her father, who had not escaped the Nazis. More than oil and canvas, they were the only portraits of her childhood. "Please help," she'd pleaded. "I want to die with those paintings on my wall." So, of course Brant had helped—that was what his work was all about. More than papers and research and digging into the past, his work at the Austrian Holocaust Survivors' Organization was for people— for making a difference in the individual lives that had been tormented by war, incarcerated in camps, and tortured. He longed to see Frau Aldrich's expression when he told her they'd recovered her dream.

And Brant had done just that. He did find the art in a small collection in the United States. He did see the joy in Frau Aldrich's face. But he also saw the torment of the rightful owners.

It had all been an act. The Aldrichs—brother and sister, they said—had come to his office door after another newspaper account reported a victory for one of Brant's clients, a French woman survivor. They'd told their sad story and walked from his office surely laughing at his concern and commitment to help. Not only were the Aldrichs not Jewish, nor brother and sister, Greta was actually an ex-Nazi camp guard. Her information about the art had come from one of the inmates under her guard. It was suspected that Frau Aldrich had even selected her victim for the gas chamber because of the information she'd obtained. Greta Aldrich had been unable to find the art after the war, but with Brant's help she'd almost gotten what she wanted.

He couldn't believe he'd been duped. Brant tore the soggy paper into several pieces and released them over the railing. The river's ripples gathered the pieces and carried them away.

This had not been the first attempt at a fraudulent claim, especially since the opening of Swiss banks. Brant had immediately identified a recent claim as false—an American claiming to be Celia Müller. He had prided himself on the fact that he could not be deceived, and now the Aldrich story had shattered that illusion.

Angry, Brant turned away from the river. He moved quickly, suddenly aware of the cold that clutched him. When his pager sounded, he paused beneath the eaves of a weathered white-stucco building. Brant was about to turn it off when he noticed the number. Why would she be calling? There could be only one reason. He found his phone in his coat pocket and punched in the number.

"This is Brant. What happened?"

"We think he had a stroke," the woman said.

"No."

"You better come."

Brant was already running.

D arby saw death in Grandma Celia's face. It wouldn't be long. As Grandma's breath grew more labored, Darby's day was consumed with watching that breathing. Her mother seemed to accept that this was the end, though her expression shifted from the weariness of waiting to the clinging hope that Grandma's life wouldn't slip away quite yet. But Darby couldn't accept it. She even prayed for the first time in years. *God, don't take her, please, don't take her.*

Darby's childhood in an all-female home had been with an example of strength in both her grandmother and mother. She tried to maintain that strength on the outside but felt herself weaken as her grandmother walked closer to death's door.

Death is part of life, she reminded herself throughout the week. *Everyone loses loved ones. Everyone dies. I need to be ready. But how can I prepare?*

Grandma had been her cheerful self only a few short and treasured minutes. Although she continued to call Tatianna's name in the late-night hours, there was less urgency in her voice. Yet no opportunity had arisen for Darby to ask about her grandmother's mysterious friend.

Darby waited until her mother went grocery shopping, then found the number for her grandmother's lawyer.

"Is she gone?" Fred asked before saying hello.

"No, not yet."

"Oh, thank goodness. I see my share of lousy people in this profession. It's an honor to know someone like your grandmother."

"I agree. But I'll get to the reason for my call." Darby propped her elbow on the counter beside the telephone. "Grandma told me about a personal safe she has left with you."

"Ah, yes. She brought it to me about a year ago. I don't normally keep such things and encouraged her to get a safety deposit box, but you know her thoughts about financial institutions."

"Yes. In high school, she'd let me leave an IOU note for every ten-dollar bill I borrowed from her mattress. Does she have her savings in the safe, or should we check under her bed?"

"Actually, I'm not at liberty to tell quite yet. Besides, I don't know the complete contents. My instructions are to wait for her passing, then we'll move to those details."

"Grandma didn't tell me anything except that you had a safe, and I'd find some information she wanted me to have inside."

"I understand, but those were the instructions."

"That's all I needed to know. Take care, Fred."

"You too, Darby. And take care of our lady."

"I promise." She hung up the phone and sat back in her chair. Whatever was in the safe, it wouldn't help her at present. Soon, too soon, the safe would be opened, for her grandmother would be gone.

Darby spent the nights in Grandma's room, in case anything happened.

The days and nights blurred until their borders appeared as one continuous fog, only distinguished by the house lights being turned on or off. In the middle of a night, a voice stirred Darby. Fatigue held her as she struggled toward the surface of consciousness. Suddenly, she sat upright, seized awake.

The voice traveled its own journey, moving backwards along a near-forgotten path as Darby's eyes sought through the dim light to where her grandmother sat up in bed.

"Perhaps in another time or place it would not have felt so intense—but we were there, in that troublesome time. People fear hard times, but challenges usually make strong bonds stronger. We found great love in the midst of turmoil."

Darby strained forward, mesmerized by Grandma's voice. Its rhythm was like a midnight hymn rocking her back and forth.

"Would our love have changed if given the chance to be together all these years? I've wondered, can't imagine it, but we only had six months as husband and wife." A chuckle escaped. "We cherished every moment of that time." Her voice seemed to drift away to memory.

How welcome this dreamlike spell was compared to the coughing fits or troubled callings. Grandma Celia reached for Darby's hand. Darby moved forward and grasped the outstretched fingers, surprised to see her grandmother's eyes shining lucid and full of comprehension in the reflected light. "Darby, will you open the window for me?"

"Of course." Darby leaned awkwardly over the bed to pull the window up an inch. Cool air swam into the room, and moonlight filtered through the parted curtains.

"That box on my dresser, the one Uncle Marc made me. Bring it to me, please."

Darby moved toward the lamp switch.

"My dear, please don't turn on the light. The moon is bright enough. I don't want to lose this—this magical night. I have found your grandfather in my memories here."

"Yes, Grandma."

Darby retrieved the miniature carved box. She turned and stopped, seeing Grandma Celia with streams of moonlight flooding the bed. She was beautiful. Her rumpled gray hair glowed like an angel's cloak down to her shoulders.

Celia's hand trembled as she reached for the wooden box. For a moment, Darby wondered if this was real, or if perhaps she was still asleep. Even the questions she'd been holding all week vanished while she watched her grandmother search inside the carved box.

Grandma Celia's voice again broke the aura of silence in the room. "I haven't spoken about him in a long time. It was easier for me, and for your mother. She wanted to know him so badly. Even when my hope had died, your mom's continued. I had told too many stories about her daddy, though eventually her hope was crushed by reality. That's why I quit speaking of him, since we had to leave him behind. But he's been locked inside all these years, always near." Grandma patted her heart.

A sharp cough interrupted the stillness. Grandma Celia placed a tissue over her mouth, then crumpled it in her bony fist. Her weak smile reappeared. "Perhaps it would have changed if your grandfather and I had been given a life together. We might have become like some couples who have grown old together. But in my mind, he's still that wonderful man who swept me off my feet. You would have loved him, Darby. You've reminded me of him. You both were full of life, laughter, and adventure. Ready to tackle anything that comes along."

Darby had never heard her grandmother talk this much about her grandfather, and for some reason, she'd never asked many questions about him. He was long dead sometime during the war, and there was little else she knew. The way her grandmother spoke of him brought such curiosity, and Grandma Celia's voice had never sounded the way it did now. She seemed to spin memory on her lips, like she tasted each thought, kissed each moment.

The moonlight touched a tiny object Grandma withdrew from the box. "And here it is."

Darby looked closer.

"It's too late for the two of us in this life, but there is something that must still be done—" Another cough seized Celia. Darby leaned Celia forward, groping for the water behind her. Grandma's thin frame jolted into slower coughs until they died away. Darby reached for the tissue over her grandmother's mouth and offered the glass. Even in what Celia called the magical moonlight, Darby saw bright red splotches on the tissue she tossed into the trash.

"I want you to have this." Grandma's voice was hoarse, her hands shaking.

"A ring?"

"Only half a ring. This is the engagement part. The wedding half is gone. Do you see the diamonds on top?"

Darby saw where, in place of the usual setting, there was another ring of gold with diamonds attached around the rim.

"Your grandfather designed this ring." Grandma cleared her throat and sat up a little more. "When joined with the w-wedding half, that circle becomes two small rings locked together, surrounded by lasting treasure."

"It's beautiful," Darby whispered, looking at her grandmother's face. *She should rest now.* But the expression on Grandma's face, tired and weary though it appeared, held a sense of purpose. "What happened to the other half?"

Grandma Celia smiled. "So many stories I have told you, my Darby." Her fingers caressed Darby's cheek. "Since you were a child, so full of wonder, I have told you my tales. But I kept hidden the real stories because I didn't want to steal the joy I saw in your eyes. When your mother was a child, I stole many moments from her because I was consumed with my own sorrow. I tried to protect you, but other forces have taken the wonder from your eyes. I see an empty place in you—one I recognize from experience. And you run from it, afraid to face your own heart."

Darby stared at her grandmother for a long time. How had the past so quickly turned to focus on Darby's life? "Grandma, don't worry about me. I'm happy, very happy."

"But you've lost your joy. It's taken years for me to see it. I saw your spirit wounded as a little one when you finally understood that your father was not returning. I also don't think you've ever gotten over you and Derek breaking up. I see it most clearly through your work. You hide behind the camera, where once you danced with it. Yes, I see the change most in your work."

Darby sat back in the chair. What could she say to these words that cut so deep, even as she denied them?

Grandma squeezed her hand and breathed deeply. "Don't be afraid. Don't hold me so tightly. You must know that you can't put your faith in people—they fail you, break your heart, die on you. You can love them and receive love, but don't put all of yourself in another human—we are too imperfect of creatures."

"So what can I do?" Darby asked. "How can I let you go?"

"I will be with you always—don't let me go. But you need more than me inside that heart of yours. I couldn't really find God until I lost my husband. Not that I think God wanted me to lose Gunther—I still don't understand all the workings of God. Of course, I couldn't. Though soon, I will know him, even as I am known." Grandma smiled, though her voice grew raspy. "I do know that when I was weak, the Lord made me strong. People are for loving and for loving you back. But God is the place to put your heart, soul, and mind. He'll never let you down, I promise."

Grandma closed her eyes for a long time. Her hand weakened its hold on Darby's. Her voice was low and labored, barely above a whisper. "This ring is part of my last story for you. And my story now becomes yours. But, my little one, I'm not going to finish it. You must."

"Do you need your oxygen?" Darby asked while reaching for the mask on the nightstand and turning the valve on the tank. Grandma accepted the mask and took two or three breaths before setting it on her chest.

"Can't explain now. Trust me. You'll know when you get there." Her eyes opened as she took several more breaths, and she smiled weakly. "You'll discover more than I can imagine. And it becomes your life after mine—new journey, unraveling past secrets, and making injustices right." Grandma inhaled a long, full breath. "Your future will change. I pray you will choose the right path when the time comes. I'll go soon. I'm ready. Then you'll find your start in the safety deposit box. Your mother has the key."

"Grandma, I don't understand any of this." Darby's body trembled.

"I know. I know, my dear."

Darby could see her grandmother desperately needed rest. Yet there was so much she needed to know. What did her grandmother want from her? How could she finish a story she knew nothing about? And what had her grandmother meant about Tatianna needing her name?

Darby grasped her grandmother's hand. She opened her mouth to allow the flood of questions, but Grandma Celia held up a hand to stop her.

"Not now, little one. In time. It will all be revealed in time. For now, this is all."

"But, Grandma . . ."

"Trust me?"

"Yes."

"Then, trust me. You will know. Step-by-step. Very soon."

Darby wanted to argue and to stop the motion of time for just a little while—to pause this moment.

She knew they would not speak like this again.

⋅➤▭◖▭⋅

Sometime in the morning, voices reached her. Darby awoke in her own room and tried to remember when she'd moved there. Her feet shuffled along the carpet in weary motion, stopping at her grandmother's doorway. Her mother was holding Grandma Celia's hands. A tear dropped from Carole's face. Again, her mother was in tears. Darby's legs felt like cement blocks of fear. But then she heard her grandmother's voice—so slow and labored between breaths. Darby remembered the hospice list and "fish-out-of-water" breathing.

"I must say sorry," Grandma Celia was saying, then a breath and a slower breath. "No matter w-what you say."

"I love you, Mother."

"I wish. I wish I had done better by you." Grandma's eyes were closed and only lifted now and then. Darby knew she should leave them alone in their moment. But her feet wouldn't move, her hand wouldn't release the doorway. She knew little of her mother's childhood. What had it been like in a postwar world with an immigrant mother and a father lost across the sea? And what had later led her mother to drop college for a man who ended up dropping them?

"It took long—too long—for me to be strong," Grandma said in a whisper. "I leaned too much on you."

"Mother, you had to reinvent yourself. Even your language wasn't the same." Carole drew closer. "I wondered what you lost by giving up your native tongue. Words in English that took too long to think up. Stories that could never be translated correctly. I saw you make your change and grow into something new."

"At your expense."

"No, I admired you—even if it took awhile to realize it."

"You wanted a father. And I made you hate Austria, our home."

"You didn't make me. I hated it because it took everything. I didn't want to hear about Alpine sunsets when all I could see was the missing face of my father and the grandparents I'd never have. It wasn't you. It was reality that makes me still turn cold at the thought."

"But God gave more—more than I had. Though I was very slow to find it. But you—my daughter. You don't need to live your life that way. Embrace God, and he will help you find healing, so you may be spared some of the hardness I faced. I don't want Darby to go through life that way, either. That's why I've made the special request of her that I talked with you about. . . ." Saying the words seemed to drain all of Grandma's energy. Darby stepped forward, but her mother saw it too. She shushed her gently.

"Rest now. Just rest. If it helps, know that I forgive anything you feel you're sorry for. But I think you are a wonderful woman, and a wonderful mother."

⋆⇒◦⇐⋆

For the next few days, Grandma Celia remained more unconscious than awake. The hospice nurse stopped by daily, and Darby and her mother kept watch—every missed breath brought fear. But her grandmother rested soundly, her medications helping with the pain and coughing fits. Several times she wrestled, fitfully mumbling words in German—the language she'd forbidden from her life long ago.

One morning as the light began to touch the darkness, Darby wearily glanced toward the bed. She bolted upright and looked at Grandma's chest. Her grandmother's eyes were closed; the painful sound of struggling breath was silent. Grandma Celia was gone.

CHAPTER FOUR

Darby produced a smile at the appropriate times. Words of comfort to family and friends somehow came to her lips. The checklist she'd prepared with her mother had lines drawn through it—words like *Lincoln Funeral Chapel, visitation times, Deb's Florist, burial clothes.*

Conversations with relatives she hadn't seen in years, arrangements with the funeral parlor, even the stories she told her two nieces, all seemed to take place somewhere outside her being. She could hear herself speak and her mind registered, but everything seemed distanced and misplaced. Inside, Darby kept a surreal hardness to bring herself through that first week after Grandma's death.

Tatianna, what about Tatianna? The question weighed on Darby's mind, while the greater sense of loss made her withdraw into a shell. She wanted to question her mother about Grandma Celia. She wanted to discover the contents of the safe. But the mysteries would have to wait, at least until the details of the funeral were completed and the visiting family departed.

During the funeral dinner, Grandma Celia's closest friend, Maisie Hansen, pulled Darby aside. Darby looked across the room at the empty punch bowl, wanting to fill it, but she knew she should take a moment with Maisie. The elderly woman had been a friend of the family for years and would soon be returning home. Darby pried her eyes from the drink table in an attempt to give Maisie her full attention. There was just so much to do.

"Darby, I'm so sorry about Celia. A blessed many years she lived, though." Maisie placed her hand on Darby's arm. "She was the sister I never had."

"I know, Maisie."

"Life passes you by. Take my word, your days of youth should be cherished."

"Yes, I know." Darby thought about the two casseroles she had left in the oven. Hopefully Mother had gotten them out.

"This may sound petty, but . . ."

"What, Maisie?"

"There was a mistake in the pastor's eulogy and in the obituary. I wanted you to know."

"A mistake?" Darby heard the words while looking at her two nieces trying to scrape a last scoopful of punch from the bowl. "I checked everything myself."

"It's Celia's place of birth. She wasn't born in Vienna, Austria, but in Hallstatt."

Darby's eyes flickered back to Maisie. "That's not what her papers said."

"Well, I'm certain she was born in Hallstatt. She told me herself. All of her mother's family was born in Hallstatt. Your great-aunt even traveled in her last month of pregnancy from Salzburg to deliver your cousin Henri in the family birthplace. It was tradition, well, at least until the war changed everything."

Darby's mind spun with Maisie's words. Grandma Celia had

told her many stories about Hallstatt, the village she had grown up in. But when she read in Grandma's personal papers that her birthplace was Vienna, she assumed they had moved to Hallstatt when Celia was young.

"Thank you, Maisie, for bringing this to my attention." The older woman appeared relieved. "I'll check into it, okay?"

"Good. I was hoping maybe the newspaper could print the correction or something."

"Yes, maybe." Darby moved away, back to the busyness of the funeral plans. But her mind kept returning to Maisie's words.

⋆═◉═⋆

Eventually the phone calls slowed, and the relatives said their good-byes. Darby's sister, Maureen Lamont, and her twins left for Sacramento. The refrigerator still overflowed with the food prepared by friends. Darby had been surprised by the people Grandma Celia had influenced over the years as they came to bring food comfort—though Darby hoped never to eat another casserole again. With the funeral over, the silence in the house seemed to shout, *What now?*

Darby observed her mother and realized they were alike in one way. Both tried to keep busy when tragedy came. But what would her mother do now?

"You know you can move up to Redding with me." Darby brought up the subject as she helped her mother unload the dishwasher. "I'll have that extra room in my apartment when the school semester is over and Clarise's niece moves out."

"Thanks, honey. Maureen offered for me to move to Sacramento. And Aunt Helen and Uncle Marc invited me to Southern California for as long as I like. To tell you the truth, I don't know yet."

Darby glanced at her mother, who'd never looked so vulnerable and frail. Darby felt a sudden urge to wrap her arms around her but continued, instead, to put the plastic bowls away.

"It's not like this was unexpected," Darby's mother said, staring outside past the tree-lined street to the sloping vineyards beyond. "I've thought about this. But now that Grandma is really gone, I don't know what direction I should take. It's a strange feeling having your mother die. No one loves you like a parent. Well, except for the Lord. I guess it's time for me to ask God about my future."

Startled by her mother's words, Darby almost dropped the bowl she was holding. Though they all attended church fairly regularly, only Grandma spoke about her faith. To the rest of them, it was just another part of their lives, like grocery shopping or going to the movies. Well, maybe more, but then maybe less too. Darby remembered the words she had spoken so long ago. *Forgiveness. Surrender. Come into my heart.* But somewhere along the way, the words merged into her being and became a hidden part of her life. Hearing her mother talk about God left a strange sensation within her. How many times had she heard Grandma speak in such a way? *My prayers are surrounding you, Darby. God's not finished with you yet.* Darby had heard her mother say religious words a few times prior to Grandma's death, but not like God was part of her daily life.

The dishes were finished without further talk. Mother stacked the clean cake pans and casserole dishes, then set them in a box to return to friends and family. Darby decided now was the time to ask. The questions had waited long enough.

"Mom, Grandma Celia told me some things before she died. She wanted me to do something." Darby watched her mother stop and turn toward her.

"I know. Grandma and I discussed it before you came down. I guess today is the day. I'll call Fred to see if he's available. He said he'd like to make a house call to go over the will since Grandma was such a good friend. And I have the key."

"To the safe?"

"Yes." Carole patted Darby's hand. "I wish Maureen could have come back for the reading, but this will have to do. Could I have until this afternoon?"

"Okay, this afternoon."

⋯⊶═⊙═⊷⋯

Darby paced the house. She wanted answers, and she wanted them now.

She wandered the rooms of the home she'd spent much of her life in. Little had changed on the surface—Grandma and Mother's Victorian décor remained the same, and Maureen's room still had a Bryan Adams poster on the wall, though it was currently the sewing room. Darby's room had been converted into neat guest quarters with her same violet-and-white comforter. Everything looked normal, like any other house on rural Poplar Way. But now it felt different. How could such a normal appearance hold so many hidden secrets? Darby knew that, like specters, the ghostly questions had been lurking, waiting to be answered.

Unable to stand the thoughts any longer, Darby knew where to go. Through all the busyness of the funeral and company, she had veered away from saying good-bye to Grandma. Now it was time.

In the back shed she found the clippers and walked straight to the neglected flower garden. Grandma had designed the garden in a circular path with her favorite bush in the very center. Darby stood before the rosebush and cut the best flower the autumn bloom had given. She stripped away the lower leaves and left their remnants on the ground as she walked toward her car.

The gate to the cemetery driveway was closed when Darby arrived. She parked and went through the walk-in entrance.

Grandma's grave was easy to find. The plot she had chosen years ago rested beneath one of the few great oak trees.

Darby stared at the mound of green sod with fresh, black dirt along the edges. It seemed unreal that her grandmother rested somewhere beneath that plot of earth. The fingers that had caressed her cheek since childhood now were cold and dead. How long until flesh returned to the earth? That thought pricked a chill from her scalp down her back. Not Grandma, not my Grandma Celia. But death was as natural as birth, right? The body was just a shell for a spirit that would live on. Next came heaven, angels, God. For Grandma's sake, Darby willed it to be true, truer than life. But heaven was so distant and far away as she stood there, staring at the place where soon only a headstone would mark an entire life.

Celia Rachel Müller. Beloved Grandmother and Mother.

The woman she loved so deeply would be another name among the long rows of granite stones, in just another cemetery, in just another place.

I hope there's more after this life.

Darby knelt in the grass to feel closer. The cold dampness pressed round, wet circles through her pants and around her knees. She scooted forward to run her finger along the dirt edging. Grandma Celia's ring tumbled forward, suspended in the air by the gold chain around her neck. As Darby held the ring, tracing the circle of warm metal with one finger, a few oak leaves drifted down.

Is my life drifting apart and away like those leaves? she wondered. She'd built a wall that was nicely kept around her life. Now that wall was crumbling. What had Grandma said the last night they talked? Something about this last story becoming part of her future too—about Darby needing to make certain decisions—hopefully the right ones? It shook her to the core, touching inward places she'd never dared to think about because if she did, she didn't know what she'd find.

Maybe she didn't want to move into this place of mystery and the unknown. Darby had always planned her own course, and as a result, things worked out perfectly. At least that's what she continued to tell herself whenever the doubts arose. And now this. Tatianna. Secrets. Shadows. Perhaps the truth would destroy everything she knew, everything she was. But there was no turning back. The first step would be the safe. From there, she didn't know.

Darby placed the single flower on the new sod.

"I came to say good-bye. Yet even now, I can't stand the thought that you are gone from me. But I know and vow, whatever you want of me, Grandma, I'll do my best. I promise you that."

She stood and began to walk away. With one last backward look, Darby thought how pleased Grandma would be with the flower on her grave. Her favorite, a pale yellow rose, shone in the late-morning light.

Brant stared at the black-and-white photograph. In the many years he'd known Gunther, his mentor had never shared this picture with him.

He settled back in the leather wingback. Gunther's chair. Just sitting here made Brant feel closer to him. The light scent of apple pipe-smoke lingered in the soft leather and further reminded Brant how much he missed spending time with the old man. He knew this would be one of the last times he would sit in Gunther's study. After today, the room would never be the same without his dear friend's presence. And once it changed, Brant would not often travel from Salzburg to his old summer home next door to Gunther's. With Gunther gone from this place, there was nothing but memories to bring him back to Gosau. How he hated changes—especially ones this severe and permanent.

Brant's gaze returned to the aged photo. "So this is your long-lost love," he muttered, looking at the two faces.

"Yes, and his only love too."

Startled, Brant turned to see Ingrid, Gunther's wife, in the doorway. He started to speak to somehow take away his words. He wouldn't have spoken had he known she watched him.

"Don't look so surprised." Ingrid moved into the room. She walked up beside Brant and gazed at the beaming smiles worn by the young man and woman in the picture. "Gunther only married me because I needed his help. Postwar Europe wasn't exactly a safe place for an unwed mother of two. Gunther took pity on me, which was enough at the time."

"I'm sure he grew to love you," Brant said quickly. When he slid the photo back into the manila envelope, he felt something at the bottom. But with the ever-watchful and acidic Ingrid in the room, he ignored it.

She laughed. "You never were a good liar, Brant. Even as a little boy, I could always tell. You look away and start doing something when you lie."

Brant gazed at the sharp contours on her wrinkled face as she propped a hip against the chair across from him. Was that pain in her smile?

"Gunther didn't love me like a wife. For a long time I thought it was because of my past. It's hard to respect an ex-breeding cow for Nazi officers."

Brant clenched his jaw. These were things he had no desire to hear. He sought words but was left empty.

"I should have known the reason. It was her." Ingrid pointed at the envelope beside Brant's chair. "He never got over her. I knew them both when we were younger. I'll always remember how they looked at each other. I wanted him to look at me that way. But she had his heart, even in her death. He made his trek up that mountain to her grave at least once a year for their anniversary. We never once celebrated ours."

Brant watched Ingrid. What could he say to her? In all the years he'd known Gunther and Ingrid, she'd never spoken so openly to Brant. He was the little brat who she was glad only came to the neighboring cottage in the summer. She had called him that when her kitchen window had been shattered by a rock. Little did she know it had been her grandson, Richter, who had thrown the rock.

"We lived under the same roof all of these years, but we never shared each other's lives. So Gunther told you about her?"

"A little."

"What did he say? He never spoke of her after our marriage."

Brant hesitated. He didn't want to reveal too much, even such long-dead secrets. "Only that the Nazis got her. They were trying to escape Europe and had to separate. She got caught, went to Mauthausen, and was executed. I'm sure you know that."

"Yes. She came from a well-known family and was half Jewish. That's why the Nazis took her."

"He didn't tell me much." Brant averted his eyes and picked up Gunther's pipe from the desk beside him.

Ingrid didn't speak for several minutes. Her eyes pierced Brant with such intensity that he shifted self-consciously in the chair. Ingrid had always frightened him when he was a child, and some of that fear remained. While Gunther exuded warmth with his many rough hugs and slaps on the back, even in Ingrid's smiles there was a coldness. Though she had probably been a beautiful woman in her youth, there was a look in her eyes he'd never liked. Gunther had once told him that Ingrid had, like everyone else, been through hell during the war. But Ingrid hadn't been freed from the demons that trailed her path.

"If you knew more, you wouldn't tell me anyway. I know that." Ingrid rose. "If you could move everything into the attic, I'm going to store it all there until I decide whether to sell the cottage or keep it for summer use. With Gunther's health, he won't be back."

"Don't get rid of Gunther's things."

"I won't, Brant." Her voice sounded condescending. "But I'm going to get my use from this room. I've always loved the deck and French doors and thought it a waste to be a smoke-filled study. I may make it a knitting or tea room. I'm staying in Munich over the winter, then I'll decide. How long until you'll have his things boxed up?"

Brant stood. It took everything in him to bite his tongue. And Ingrid wondered why Gunther could never love her? "I'll have everything moved this weekend."

Brant didn't enjoy the idea of packing up this room. But, after all, he was closest to Gunther. Ingrid had called him in Salzburg every week for the past month to remind him that the job was his. Brant didn't want anyone else going through Gunther's books and papers, yet he still avoided the duty until Ingrid threatened to call the movers and ship everything away. He wished the room could remain forever. The idea of Ingrid turning it into some flowery tea room churned his stomach. No, he wouldn't return to this house of so many boyhood memories. He'd probably even sell or rent out his cottage next door.

"I have dinner waiting for you. It's probably cold now."

"You didn't have to. I brought some food to my house." Brant didn't relish the thought of spending dinner alone with Ingrid.

"No, you can eat here. I'm making you do this work. Richter should arrive soon. I asked him to come for the weekend."

Brant kept his expression the same, for he could see Ingrid was looking for a reaction. He wondered why she'd invited her grandson to Gosau. Richter and Brant had always disliked one another. Ingrid's grandson stayed with Gunther and Ingrid many of the same summers Brant and his mother stayed in the house next door. Brant knew Richter resented the close relationship between Gunther and himself. Ingrid had to know the boys, now men, had never gotten along.

She was up to something. He sensed it. Did she suspect he

knew more about Gunther's secrets? Brant knew only a little information. Gunther kept the most important details to himself. But Ingrid didn't know how much he knew. If Ingrid suspected anything, perhaps she'd invited Richter to keep an eye on him. Yet why not go through Gunther's things herself instead of insisting he do it? There were too many questions and too many suspicions.

"I made that recipe your mother gave me." Ingrid's eyes searched his thoughts. "Fried chicken, isn't it? An American dish for you."

Brant wondered about her thoughtfulness in fixing a meal from his birthplace. Was this Ingrid's peace offering?

"Thank you, I'll be right there," Brant called as Ingrid headed toward the kitchen. He picked up the manila envelope, walked to the bookcase, and placed the books back on the bottom shelf. It had been a surprise to find the envelope hidden behind this tall set of books. He decided to return it to its hiding place until he had more time to look through it. But when he felt the object at the bottom again, he couldn't resist a peek.

Just as he opened the top to look inside, Ingrid's voice sounded down the hall. "Are you coming?"

Brant shoved the envelope back into its hideaway. As he flipped off the light, he wondered if Ingrid already knew about the object and the envelope. The lovely features on the face of the woman in the picture returned to his thoughts. He hoped he was making the right decisions. He was determined to protect Gunther's secrets, even if he didn't fully know what those secrets were.

He'd have to be careful.

⋄⊷⊜⊶⋄

That is the mysterious safe? Darby thought as Fred Bishop, the family lawyer, set it on their dining room table. Any Wal-Mart or hardware store carried a similar kind of steel "fireproof home safe." Darby hadn't expected a wooden treasure chest with a rusty lock, but this seemed a bit too commercial for the secrets inside.

"Let's open it," she said, rubbing her hands together.

Fred Bishop and her mother looked at each other, then back to Darby.

"First, I'd like to go over a few things." Fred extracted a folder from his briefcase.

"Am I the only one in the dark about the contents?"

"Neither of us knows," her mother said. She carried three cups of coffee to the table.

"What do you know?"

"Patience, honey," Carole said with a laugh. "You act like it's Christmas Eve."

"No, this is worse." Darby sat at the table. *Why the wait?*

"First we'll talk about monetary assets." Fred shuffled through the papers. "We'll look at her life insurance policy and investments."

"Grandma had investments? She was afraid of banking systems."

"Yes, for what she considered her base money—money she wanted to hold on to, whether inside the house or in the safe. But she enjoyed a bit of investing with her 'extra money,' as she called it. It wasn't much. But in fact, she made some good choices in her finances. For one, she invested in Microsoft. Always said she had a good feeling about that Bill Gates."

"What?" Darby and her mother said in unison.

"As in computers?" Carole asked.

"You have to be joking." Darby stared incredulously at the papers.

"Yes, computers, and no, I'm not joking. In fact, she sold those stocks several months ago and made a fifty-thousand-dollar profit even with the drop in stocks."

"What?" Carole and Darby said again in unison.

"She was one sharp cookie, ladies."

"You didn't know this?" Darby asked her mother.

"I knew she played around with stocks and invested a bit. When she bought her computer, I never even learned how to turn it on. But she was on it all the time. Well, you knew that—she e-mailed you constantly. But I never expected this."

"She never mentioned a word of it to me, either."

"I think she wanted to surprise you both." Fred took a sip of his coffee.

"She succeeded." Darby shook her head. Grandma Celia investing in Microsoft? The woman never ceased to amaze her.

"Now, her life insurance was not particularly high. She always did fear the companies would fail, especially in the new millennium, so she had a medium coverage, also of fifty thousand. But since she paid for her own funeral expenses, this is a nice sum also."

"Grandma knew how to prepare," Darby said. She imagined her grandmother making all these plans and provisions for her family, knowing they'd be sitting here with Fred someday soon.

"Now, your mother gets the house, of course, and twenty-five thousand cash. Darby, you and Maureen were given several heirlooms that are detailed on page 18. And Maureen will also receive twenty-five thousand. But the rest of the money, as your mother already knows, goes to you, Darby."

"To me? Why?"

"That's what Celia wanted."

"But that's, what, fifty thousand?"

"Yes, it is."

"I don't understand. Why didn't she give me the same as Maureen?"

"I think there are several reasons," Fred replied. "First, your grandmother told me she was asking you to accomplish a task she was unable to complete. Perhaps because of that, she felt she owed you some help. Those are my words; Celia really didn't specify why. But she also knew that both your mother and Maureen are already taken care of."

"Did Grandma tell you what she asked of me?"

"No." The lawyer settled back in the chair and adjusted his tie. Fred seemed ageless to Darby. The patch of gray in his sideburns had grown larger and his stomach now filled out his dark suit jacket more fully, but other than that, he was the same Fred she'd always known. "Your grandmother wanted the details of her request kept private until she could speak to you. However, she was concerned about any hard feelings arising with the money. I wanted some precautions against family lawsuits—I've seen that happen quite often. So your grandmother and mother discussed this, and your sister has a letter of explanation."

"Honey, I also don't know what Grandma asked of you," Carole said. "But whatever it is, you don't have to do it. I respect your grandmother's wishes, but she's gone now. I don't like the idea of you digging up the past when you have your own life to lead. Don't feel pressured to put your life on hold to figure out what happened a long time ago, especially now with this financial backing. You can go back to Redding, put the extra money into your studio, and there'll be nothing tying you down. Grandma would understand if that's what you choose."

Darby nodded. She couldn't help but consider what that kind of money could do for the studio. She could pay her half of the business off and buy new equipment. But she'd made a promise to her grandmother.

"I agree with Carole." Fred closed his folder. "There are no stipulations with this money. Your grandmother knew your mother has sufficient retirement and her real-estate investments. Maureen, John, and the twins will receive some stock she still has invested. So accept this as a gift, free and clear."

"I'll think it over."

"Can you tell us what Grandma asked of you?" Carole queried.

"To be honest, I'm not exactly sure. I hope there's something inside the safe to tell me. She told me about Tatianna, her best friend, and that Tatianna needed her name. She asked me to give Tatianna her name—but I have no idea what that means."

Fred looked at her strangely. "Really? That's not at all what I suspected. I assumed your grandmother wanted you to take up the search for the Lange family inheritance."

"Tatianna?" Carole queried. "That's the person Mother's been calling for during her bad spells. I too thought she wanted you to search for the lost heirlooms."

"The Lange heirlooms were real?" Darby asked.

Fred shrugged. "I have no idea. Celia's been on a crusade to find them, especially in the last year. I think she's written to every organization on the planet."

Darby remembered the letter from Brant Collins of the Austrian Holocaust Survivors' Organization that she'd kept from everyone. "I know, but she didn't ask me to continue that search. We had little time to talk before she passed away. Perhaps that was part of what she wanted and never asked."

"Did Grandma tell you who Tatianna was?"

"No. She gave me no last name or any information—only that she was Grandma's best friend. I hope the safe will have more information."

"Whatever we find inside," Carole said, putting a hand on Darby's, "as I said earlier, you need to live for today, honey. Don't get too wrapped up in yesterday that you miss out on that."

"Can we please open the safe? The suspense is killing me."

"Certainly." Fred closed the folder.

"I have the keys." Carole went to a desk drawer and took out two keys on a wire ring. "Here you go."

Darby moved the safe over in front of her. It was heavier than it appeared. The key turned, and the lid opened easily. She peered inside and carefully removed papers and folders, lining them up on the table. Fred and Carole drew their chairs closer.

Darby took a rubber band from a pack of envelopes. The postmarks were from the late forties and early fifties—addressed to different people. One was addressed to Tatianna Hoffman.

"Now we know her last name." Darby opened it. "Anyone know German?"

"Your Uncle Marc does, but he won't be here until Christmas." Carole reached for the letter. "I'm shocked Grandma would write something in her forbidden native tongue."

"It's written November 1945, perhaps before her vow?" Darby pointed to the date at the top. She examined the words that might hold all the answers she sought. "I think we need to find someone who can translate for us."

"What else is there?" Fred asked. "Oh, I guess this isn't any of my business and I should be going."

"You can stay—please do." Carole lifted his coffee cup. "I'll fill you back up."

"I have been staring at that safe with curiosity about killing me. If you both don't mind?"

"Not at all," Darby said. She handed him a pile of papers wrapped in a plastic bag. "We'll put you to work."

"Thanks. This does feel like Christmas Eve." And Celia was Santa Claus.

Darby flipped through several photographs. She didn't recognize the faces, and nothing was written on their backs. The documents she found also were written in German.

"What is this?" Darby moved around the table beside Fred.

Carole returned with a coffee filter in hand and looked over their shoulders.

"It looks like travel documents—a passport would be my guess."

"Look at the name." Darby pointed to a line on top. "These are Tatianna Hoffman's documents."

"The issuing date says 1939."

"So this is Tatianna." Darby studied the black-and-white passport photo of the young woman. By her birthdate and the 1939 stamp, Darby knew the girl was about nineteen at the time. She was pretty with dark eyes and hair. There was no smile on her face, but humor glinted on the edges of her lips and within her eyes. Darby had seen that expression a dozen times when she'd taken a serious photo of a client and someone beyond the camera was trying to make the person laugh.

Carole bent in close. "Why would my mother have this person's passport?"

"I don't know." Fred stroked his chin in thought. "Unless they came to the United States together. Perhaps some of these other papers will tell us that. Darby, here's a letter addressed to you."

Darby set down the passport of Tatianna Hoffman.

The letter wasn't weathered by time like the other papers. Darby carefully opened the envelope, read it to herself, then aloud.

> My dearest Darby,
> I have given you a lifetime of stories and words I'm tempted to repeat, for I know these are my last words to you. The rest are already in your memory. But you don't need a Sunday school lesson, and I'm far from perfect enough to give you a life map to follow. God has his own course for you. But my many prayers for my Darby-girl have helped with the boldness I'm about to express. I know I'm asking a lot of you. But sometimes the past cannot be buried. Sometimes the past must be put to rest for the future to be clear. I

*cannot tell you for certain what you must do; you must
decide. There is so much right beyond my vision that I do
not know. But I feel one thing so strongly, and so this I ask.
Go to Austria.*

*I can see your shocked expression. I can really see your
mother's. Yes, Darby, go to Austria. I send you on a mission.
What I hope I was able to ask before I died was that you give
my closest friend, Tatianna Hoffman, her name back. That
will make no sense until you get there. Then you will know.
Also, if in your search you discover our family heirlooms,
guard them well. Many have died because of them. I hoped
to retrieve them myself, but I cannot ask you to take up that
search, for I do not know the danger behind such an
endeavor. But Tatianna deserves what I ask you to return to
her—her name. Yet in all of this, I know you are going for
more than the quest I send you on. I feel so deeply that God
has something for you there. He wants you to find him
again.*

*Take your time. Discover who you are. My heart goes on
this journey. A journey we should all make.*

> *Forever,*
> *Celia Rachel Lange Müller*

Darby set the letter on the table.

"Whew." Fred was the first to speak. "Celia is full of
surprises today."

Carole sat at the table with the coffee filter still in her hand.

"It looks like I'm going to Austria," Darby said. Her mother
didn't look her way.

W e have a problem." Richter stretched back against the chair and put his feet on the table. He exhaled a stream of cigarette smoke into the night sky.

Ingrid wrapped her sweater tighter and half sat on the porch railing.

"We waited too long with the old man," Richter said.

"There's still Brant." She turned toward him. "I know Gunther told him something. We need to find out exactly what that is."

"And how do you suppose we'll find anything out?"

"We'll watch for an opportunity."

"Waiting gets us nowhere, and I'm not a man of patience. We need action."

"No, we must wait. Then we act."

"What if Brant doesn't know anything?"

"Brant may not be our last chance."

Richter's feet hit the ground as he faced Ingrid. "Another person who knows something?"

"Perhaps. Be patient. We'll know what to do soon enough."

"I'm leaving, on a jet plane."

The tune hummed from Darby's lips as she rolled her clothing into neat stacks and put them into her suitcase. As a child, she'd mapped her path through the Alps from Vienna to Switzerland. As an adult, she'd long since put the map away and left the dreams behind. Reality didn't leave room for fairy tales. But the plane tickets, round-trip with three weeks between arrival and departure dates, were proof that Darby was at last going to Austria.

She carried her luggage toward the front door, pausing by Grandma's room. Neither she nor her mother was ready to start boxing things up—it could wait. They had made the bed with Grandma's white embroidered bedspread and dusted the dresser with its perfume bottles and jewelry boxes. Everything appeared normal, as if Grandma Celia had simply gone to the store or was in the backyard with her flowers. Darby hated the images that told her differently—the headstone that had arrived and the newspaper obituary on the refrigerator, the one with its possibly wrong birthplace.

When Carole had set the safe key on the kitchen table a few weeks before, Darby had been sure the shadows she felt every night would finally be vanquished by truth. But that didn't happen. The documents, papers, and photographs only resurrected greater secrets. And with them came two paths—bury the past and concentrate on the present, or seek the answers from yesterday.

When faced with this decision at different stages of her childhood, Darby had turned away from the past. She had her own life of volleyball tryouts, new makeup, hairstyles, "What are we doing this weekend?," and "What do you want to do when you grow up?" Only once did Darby look toward the questions that sometimes arose.

She'd watched the TV mini-series, *War and Remembrance,* on her bedroom television. Before Darby's eyes, the beautiful character Natalie, played by Jane Seymour, was reduced to a starving animal with fear alive in her eyes. Natalie endured a concentration camp. Darby knew that word. Part of her family had died in places like the one shown on the screen. Finally she asked her mother about it. But Carole was angry she'd stayed up late for the entire week, even grounding Darby from her bedroom television—that act alone showed something more in her mother's anger. Darby was rarely grounded and never from the TV. Grandma Celia took her aside and told her it was good she now understood what family members had endured, but they would not speak of it again. Only the Austria of Grandma Celia's childhood was told. The good, adventurous stories, not the terrifying ones that marched in time with Nazi boots. And so Darby discarded her questions, her curiosity abated. Something terrible had happened, but she didn't want to know, didn't need to know. She wasn't any different than her friends. Tammy Dodd's dad had fought in Vietnam. Michelle Ingalls had a grandpa who died in Korea.

In high school, Darby had received a *C-* on the Holocaust unit of history, though she usually received *A*s and *B*s. She'd forged her mother's name on the report card and also performed her one and only act of skipping school the day her class watched a documentary with real footage of a concentration camp. Years later, when a friend invited her to watch *Schindler's List,* Darby had other plans. It wasn't exactly that she was avoiding the subject. But after the intense reaction from her mother and the silence of her grandmother over a television mini-series and simple questions, Darby had received the unconscious message that looking back was not good—until Grandma Celia's letter.

So she picked up her luggage and said good-bye to

Grandma's empty room. She was leaving on a jet plane. And though Darby knew she'd be back in three weeks, the next line in the song kept echoing through her thoughts: "Don't know when I'll be back again."

-->===o(===<-

San Francisco International Airport was like a city in itself. She had to carefully follow the right exits and get in the correct lanes without being run over by a shuttle bus or taxi. Her mother gave advice as they looked for a parking place close to the international terminal and Lufthansa Airlines.

Darby had been there a few times to pick up friends, but she preferred the smaller airports in Redding and Sacramento for any trips that required air travel. The farthest she'd gone was New Mexico for a photography conference and Montana to visit a friend. Darby suddenly wondered about her old friend Tristie Grant in Columbia Falls, Montana. She'd received a nice sympathy card from the Grant family, and though distance in both miles and lifestyles had pulled their friendship apart, Darby knew she could always call her college friend and have a ready ear to listen. If only someone like Tristie was traveling with her, then perhaps the knot in her stomach wouldn't be growing so quickly.

Darby's mother listed everything to beware of as they entered the airport. Darby tried not to laugh as her mother handed her a list of "be carefuls."

"Mom, did you write my name on my socks and underwear too?"

"I should have," Carole said as they stopped at the baggage check-in.

"I can handle it from here. Thanks for coming down with me, Mom."

Carole hugged Darby. "Okay, this is it, then."

"I'll be fine. It's not like I've never traveled. I'll call when I get there."

Darby wanted to make a quick escape. Good-byes were hard enough without long hugs and her mother dabbing her eyes on a tissue.

"I'm praying for you and still trying to believe this is somehow the right thing. But I'm just going to leave now. Call me."

Darby hugged her mother one more time. "See you later, Mom."

As she left Carole behind, Darby began to feel the doubts growing. The last time she'd allowed any of her old Europe dreams was with her ex-boyfriend Derek Hunt. He was an avid cyclist and wanted them to ride across the countryside. They'd made plans, checked airfares, and studied maps, but it never happened. None of the dreams she'd had with him ever happened. Life became cameras, good lights and flashes, appointments, and faces on 8 x 10s. Now she'd volunteered to rip herself away from what had become familiar—even safe. Why was she doing this again?

The doubts turned to pricks of fear after she boarded the plane and stowed her luggage in the overhead bin. She was really doing this, really going to Austria. But it didn't feel like a magical and grand adventure. Suddenly Darby felt like she was clinging to the side of the swimming pool, and her fingers were being pried away. Would she sink or would she swim?

As the plane taxied away from familiar land, Darby wasn't quite sure.

CHAPTER SEVEN

I'm alone. *Alone, alone,* Darby's mind whispered as
she followed a crowd of people toward the baggage area in
Salzburg, Austria. For the first time, she understood being a
stranger in a strange land. Sure, she took wealthy executives
on backpacking expeditions, but that somehow seemed safer—
back in the good old United States.

She paused in the smoky terminal, which bustled with noise
and movement. She felt trapped, surrounded by people speaking different languages, and uncertain in a country she knew
little about, beyond Grandma's alpine trails and the smell of
the trees. Would she get lost in the airport or once she stepped
outside? Where exactly was customs, and would they rifle
through her belongings like in the movies? Had she forgotten
anything?

Darby touched her passport in the front zipper pocket of her
purse for the third time since they landed. The line around the
luggage wheel was packed. Finally, her two black suitcases
arrived, and she squeezed in to grab them. Along with her

camera case, carry-on duffel, and purse, it was a job organizing and carting everything toward the next checkpoint. Darby's eyes burned, and suddenly she was thankful for California's strict no-smoking laws. The customs sign was the next stop, and she moved to the Non-EU line for non-European citizens. She slid her passport to the young man behind a glass window.

"I'm sorry. Your passport is not valid," the customs officer stated.

"What?"

"You have not signed your name," he said with a large smile. He set a pen in front of her.

"Oh, sorry," she said, not finding his humor funny. She quickly signed her name and watched him stamp a blank page. Darby continued through, realizing she'd just survived her first customs.

People hurried around her, some toward families for excited reunions. Other people waited near walls, eyes searching the crowd, with names written on papers. She thought of the six thousand miles separating her from anyone who would race to enter her arms.

The Austria of Grandma Celia's romantic and adventurous stories was not the Austria she entered. Though she allowed little time to give it a fair chance, Darby felt a foreboding, down to her bones. *Get on the next flight to the United States, back to English and baseball and apple pie—back to home,* her mind said frantically. Why had she come in the first place? All her reasons were instantly blurred by the desire to go home.

Darby continued to follow lines of people and signs toward the airport exit. Rain poured upon the historic city of Salzburg. Taxis waited outside the airport doors, so Darby hopped into one and gave the driver the name of her hotel. Angry clouds and an annoying drizzle made it hard to see beyond the windows as the car shot from the parking space. But once she was in the taxi, she had no interest in the city except for surviving the ride. The cab lurched forward, then slammed on its brakes behind a truck, narrowly missing it, then jerked forward again. It reminded her of the New York cab stories, something she'd never cared to experience. The driver was friendly enough, greeting her with a hearty "*Grüß Gott*." She wasn't sure what that meant but said it back anyway.

"Zee," he said, pointing to a tall church.

Darby barely glanced away from the road. The cabbie spoke what she thought was a history of the city, but his broken English was beyond her distinguishing except for a Mozart reference. She remembered that this cold, wet city had birthed the talent of the great musician, and probably every corner shop would have Mozart memorabilia as a marketing scheme to prove it.

"Here, your hotel." The cab came to a hard stop. He hopped outside and opened her door. "Eighty schilling, *bitte*, uh, please."

"Schillings?" How could she have been so stupid? Of course, she couldn't pay in United States dollars. She'd meant to change some currency at the airport, but with the bustle of customs and getting her luggage and finding the exit, she'd forgotten. "I'm so sorry, I don't have—"

The cabbie's expression changed, becoming thunderous.

"I have money, but it's American dollars."

"No, no American dollars," he said, his face stern. "Eighty schilling, or you has euros?"

"No, I don't have euros or schillings. Is there a bank or exchange or something?"

"There, you get schilling or euro." He pointed to what appeared to be an ATM machine at the end of the block. Darby hurried toward it, checking behind her to make sure her luggage didn't disappear from where the cabbie was stacking it at the doorway of the Salzburg Cozy Hotels International. The

green-and-yellow cubby was an ATM. An English version
helped, but how much should she get out? She punched in
three thousand schillings since cab fare was eighty. With a few
pushes of the button, Darby had Österreich schillings from her
United States bank, hoping she hadn't just drained her
account.

"*Danke*," the cabbie said before hopping into the car and
speeding off.

Darby wiped a wet strand of hair from her eyes as she
picked up her bags on the hotel doorstep and walked inside. A
young woman dressed in the traditional Austrian *dirndl*
greeted her at the front desk. "*Grüß Gott.*"

"*Grüß Gott*," Darby replied. "I have a reservation. My name
is Darby Evans."

"Yes, here you are. Breakfast is included, you know. Your
room is number 14." The woman smiled and handed Darby
the room key and some papers. "Payment is when you check
out, and please let us know if you need anything or if your
room is not to your approval."

"Thank you," Darby said, relieved that the woman's voice
reminded her of the soft German accent Grandma Celia had
tried to hide. It calmed her frazzled emotions—a little.

She balanced her luggage and peered around for a hallway
to the first-floor rooms. The simple yet elegant lobby was
connected to a restaurant and sitting room.

"You can take the lift to your room, if you like," the woman
continued.

Darby noticed the elevator, or "lift," the woman pointed
toward. Aware of the woman watching her, she thanked her
again and entered the elevator. The doors closed, and Darby
examined the buttons. When she pushed the 1 button, the
door opened without the lift moving. She was still in the
lobby. The woman saw her and smiled.

The doors closed again. Rechecking the room number on

the card, Darby guessed that the first floor must actually be what was considered second floor in the United States. As the elevator rose, Darby realized how much she'd been assuming during what should have been a simple journey from airport to hotel. Europe was much different from what she'd expected, in the littlest ways that made her feel uncomfortable and shaken. *If today has been a challenge, how will I ever get any information from this trip?*

Darby hauled her luggage up several marble stairs, its weight seeming to increase with every step. She found room 14, yes, on the second floor. The room in the old building was neat and simple. There was no flowery wallpaper or brass fixtures like the Cozy Hotels she had stayed at in the United States. It was low on fluff, but high on efficiency. A white down comforter lay folded sideways at the bottom of the bed atop crisp, white sheets. A small mint sat in the crease of an extremely fluffy-looking pillow. She dropped her belongings in the entry, locked the door, and flopped across the inviting bed. "Safe at last."

Streaks of dull sunshine filtered through the blinds as Darby's head sank into the down pillow. She hadn't slept on the plane. Too many thoughts had swirled inside her head. Every time her eyes closed, she'd thought of the enormous gravitational force pulling hard on the jumbo plane with the cold Atlantic waters waiting to swallow them up. She'd listened to every word of the flight attendant's instructions—even checking for that life preserver under her seat. The person next to her mocked her inexperience with his smile. But Darby figured she'd be the one laughing when he sank to the bottom of the Atlantic while she floated.

The ten-hour flight from San Francisco had felt longer than she had anticipated. The book of essays a friend gave her, *A Dose of Medicine for Travelers*, had quickly bored her. She had already received *A Dose of Medicine for Single Women* and *A*

Dose of Medicine for Photographers. There was only so much medicine a reader could take. Darby planned to read *The Lonely Planet Austria* guidebook she'd bought to be prepared for her arrival in Salzburg. But the international flight allowed only one carry-on bag, and she had accidentally checked in the bag with her in-case-your-luggage-gets-lost outfit and her travel guide.

Darby's next airplane mistake was the two cups of coffee she'd drunk, then regretted when four times she had to hobble over three people to go to the bathroom. Later, she'd attempted to sleep right when turbulence began to jar the plane nearly into pieces—though more experienced travelers continued to sip drinks and tap on laptops. Right then Darby connected with the ominous feeling that had lingered the entire day. She made a plane switch in London and finally arrived in Austria. The flights distanced both time and miles. She had flown into the next day. While home prepared for bed, Austria was grumbling for lunch.

"If you want to beat jet lag, you have to stay awake, stay awake!" Clarise, her business partner, had instructed. "Get on your current time schedule, no matter how tired you become. Get on their schedule, get your work done, and get back to the studio."

Clarise's reminder opened her eyes. She dragged herself from the embrace of the down pillow and comforter. Her shirt stuck to her back and felt like she'd worn it for a month. Her hands cried out against the millions of germs they carried—airport germs, taxi germs, doorknob germs.

She went to the blue-and-white-tiled bathroom and washed her hands. What had happened to her childhood hours dreaming of Europe—hours that took more time than adult hours, for they held her hopes along with her dreams? That little girl had planned to explore every nook and cranny. She'd rent a moped and putt around, because at ten years of age, the idea of a driver's license was more frightening than traveling to Europe. Grandma Celia's Austrian stories had coincided with Darby's first viewing of her favorite movie, *The Wizard of Oz*. Darby would change the few letters in her name to spell "Dorothy" as she imagined herself flying away to the magical land of Oz, the place somewhere over the rainbow where all her dreams would come true. Europe became that magical place with castles beside every alpine lake and kings and queens who would bow to her highness.

"You aren't in Kansas anymore, Dorothy," she told herself. With all the hubbub at the airport, the fright of getting to the hotel, and not being able to speak the language, Darby could almost believe this Oz was the habitation of the wicked witch—not of the west, but of the east.

She walked to the window and opened the shade. Beneath her, a muddy river flowed under a bridge and past tall church spires. The water's surface was pecked with raindrops. Up the mountain, the Hohensalzburg fortress stared at her as if she were an intruder invading the land. When would she be brave enough to venture beyond the hotel window? Not today. Weariness sank into her bones. Her shoulders ached from hauling her luggage from airport to hotel. A headache formed on the rim of her temples and moved outward. No matter what Clarise said about the jet-lag cure, she needed rest. After all, there were lions, tigers, bears, and witches to face in this land far from home.

⊷⊨◉⊫⊷

Brant unlocked his door and met the familiar musty scent of his third-story apartment. Late October brought a deeper cold to the corners of every room, forecasting the coming winter even earlier than the leaves on the surrounding mountains donned their autumn coats. Brant awoke each morning to stale air and came home to it every night, even though he'd bought plants that were now dead and several room deodorizers. These mixed scents only made the smell worse. He promised himself a year ago he'd look for a new place. But with most of his life spent at the office, he hadn't taken the time.

Brant tossed his briefcase onto the leather couch and scoped out the refrigerator. Nearly empty racks reminded him, as they had every day that week, that he needed to go grocery shopping. He picked up the end of a salami stick and a lone apple, smelled the cheese in deli wrap, left it there, and headed back for the couch.

After a day of noise, the stillness of the apartment echoed in his ears. Every other sound—the rumple of leather as he rested his head, the hum of the furnace, the evening sounds of the city behind the single-paned windows—intensified the vacancy of the room. Usually Brant felt unnerved by silence. He'd turn on the TV or some music. But tonight he needed the quiet to think.

For three years now, he'd juggled double careers. His technology advisory company had helped at least thirty Austrian companies make advancements into the age of technology, enabling them to compete with dominant European markets. And his work with the Austrian Holocaust Survivors' network had helped numerous families, in many ways—except for the Aldrich fiasco. His work was important, essential—wasn't it? At the end of the October evening, nothing of his work felt important, let alone essential. The financial world dipped up and down, often crumbling even strong businesses. And the Holocaust survivors—they were at the eve of an ending era. In the near future, not one would remain alive to tell the story. And Brant grieved that his work moved too slowly to help the majority of them.

But tonight something else added to his musing. Richter and Ingrid. Since Brant had spent the weekend boxing up Gunther's things a month earlier, Richter had decided they were now friends. He came down from Munich to Salzburg nearly every week and invited Brant to lunch or a soccer game. It felt obvious to Brant that nothing had changed between them, no sudden bonding had occurred. He didn't feel Richter liked him any more than before, so why the continued charade? Brant suspected the two were up to something—yet since the Aldrich fraud perhaps he'd become too suspicious. He'd keep his eyes open until this all blew over. Then maybe he'd get back to normal life—whatever that was or whatever that needed to become.

Brant tossed the heel of the salami onto the coffee table. What kind of a dinner was that? He rarely had a home-cooked meal or much social contact. Perhaps that was it. When he had first arrived in Salzburg, he'd dated, attended social events, and been considered one of the most sought-after bachelors in the area. But then he'd dived into work, way too deep.

"You need to find yourself a good wife," Gunther had told him on his last visit to Brant's apartment. His old friend had looked into the refrigerator, shaking his head. "Yes, a good wife will keep your belly filled with warm food and your nights with warm love." The older man had winked slyly.

Brant would have loved to hear Gunther say those words tonight. He'd love to have an ear to help him wade through all the things bothering him. But the night Gunther had told him to "find yourself a good wife," Brant hadn't been amused. It had been an especially stressful day with the death of Avia Gerstein weighing heavily upon him. Her only wish, to receive her father's Swiss bank funds, would never be granted. They had worked hard, but time had worked harder against them.

"You say I should marry and what, then be as happy as you?" Brant had immediately regretted his harsh words. Gunther didn't respond; he simply closed the refrigerator and turned toward him.

"Gunther, I didn't mean to make such a judgment. I'm sorry."

"Oh, but you speak what you perceive to be truth. That can be a good quality at times, but honesty tempered with grace is a greater quality."

"I know."

"Do you? And yet, you speak of my marriage to Ingrid. But after all these years, Ingrid isn't my true wife. I was married once and will be married to her until I die. I did Ingrid a favor because we were friends at one time. And in grief and for her, I spoke vows I have done my best to follow. But she has never been my true wife."

Brant stood, speechless.

"I am not sorry. I was granted more love in a short time than many people have in a lifetime—and that is a gift."

Brant shook his head. Gunther held no anger or bitterness, even though all he had left of his wife was a grave on a mountainside.

Gunther always seemed to read his mind. "Listen to me. You fill your life with work—worthy work, don't get me wrong. Much has been accomplished for survivors due to your dedication. And Austria will be a stronger nation as it enters a new age. You are taking our country there. But though this work is worthy, don't forget to live. Cherish each day as a blessing, no matter what God opens or closes in your life. People want to thank God for the good days, then accuse him for the bad. Everything in life is for a reason, to fulfill a purpose, even when it's beyond what our mortal eyes can see. But you need to live, to breathe, to love, even when it hurts and causes pain. But to have love for a moment is greater than never to have it at all. So don't forget to live, to breathe, to love."

Those words haunted him tonight. He was supposed to be figuring out what Richter was up to, or at least consider what to do with his careers. Perhaps he needed to choose between his dual roles. Either he could keep the lower paying and highly stressful job of helping Holocaust survivors reclaim their heritage and record their stories, stories that would soon be lost as the survivor list dwindled. Or he could resign from his CEO position at the Austrian firm that helped the emerging country compete in the age of computer chips and megahertz.

Tonight Brant wished more than anything to have his old friend sitting beside him. He missed the man who'd helped with every major decision since his mother's death when he was in high school. He missed the one person he loved the most, the person who loved him the most. Instead, Brant heard Gunther's words again: "Don't forget to live, to breathe, to love."

The problem was, Brant had forgotten. And he couldn't remember how to get another chance.

CHAPTER EIGHT

Darby awoke to darkness and reached to turn the clock face toward her. It took until her hand grasped for the lamp to remember she wasn't in her Redding apartment or in her grandmother's home, but in a Cozy Hotel International in Salzburg, Austria.

It was midnight, and her body was refreshed and ready to go. The streetlight outside shone foggily through the closed blinds, and Darby heard the occasional slush and fade of a car on wet roads. She dug into her purse for the pack of airline pretzels. The salty snack did little to placate her stomach.

After a hot shower, she sat on the bed in an oversized T-shirt and flipped through the TV channels. At last something resembled home, a *Magnum, P.I.* rerun. But then handsome Tom Selleck was oddly matched with a German-speaking voice. She continued through the round of channels, then returned to the German *Magnum, P.I.*

She still wasn't sleepy and finally picked up the telephone. It took several tries to use her calling card with the international access code before she finally got her mother.

"I'm here!" Darby said in a cheerful voice that sounded strange in the quiet of the night.

"Darby! I was just thinking about you. It must be late over there."

"Actually, it's early. 12:30 A.M. I wanted you to know I arrived safely." She noticed a slight delay between their voices.

"I've watched for airline crashes or terrorist activity. So what do you think?"

"About airline crashes and terrorists? I don't like them at all."

"All right, smarty-pants." Carole chuckled. "I meant, what do you think of our family's homeland?"

"It was raining when I arrived and I haven't ventured out, so not much to tell. I'll have many stories soon enough and a ton of postcards."

"I'll look for them. But don't talk too long—I'm sure these are expensive calls. Just please be careful. There are men who prey on young women, you know."

"How was today—or the last few days? With the time change I'm confused as to how long ago I left you." Darby tried to sidetrack her mom from her fears.

"It was just yesterday, though it seems longer. But I'm fine, thank you. Maureen checked on me and the pastor called too. I somehow volunteered to get more involved at the church, which actually sounds nice. I may even start working on Grandma's room this week. But with you so far away, that's keeping my mind busy enough."

"It's only a place, Mom, like L.A. or New York. Well, those are bad examples because Salzburg is small for a city—only 144,000 people. It's not all that far from home, really, just a hop in the plane. And I read tonight that the greeting here, 'Grüß Gott,' means 'Greet God.' So I'm safe in a country like that."

The line was silent for a moment. "I just don't like my girl there all alone. If you weren't an adult, I would have grounded you home."

"I'll be back, I promise. Clarise only gave me three weeks to return to the studio or she'll be completely bald from pulling her hair out."

"That Clarise needs to take a chill pill."

"Agreed." Darby paused, feeling so very, very far from her mother. "I wanted to say, I'm sorry, Mom."

"For what?"

"I never asked about your father and never even thought to wonder about him. Grandma told me a little before she died, but I'm sure it was hard having a hero father you never met."

"He was always a legend." Then, after a slight hesitation, Carole continued, "Now your bill is really getting high. Be sure to check in every four or five days, so I know you're okay. And call collect next time."

"I'll call."

"Take extra precautions. I heard that train stations can be dangerous if you act like an inexperienced traveler."

"Me, an inexperienced traveler?" Darby bit her lip to keep from laughing. She sat on the bed and bunched up a pillow behind her neck. "Any other travel tips?"

"Keep your wallet deep inside your purse or in the inside pocket of your jacket. Don't walk alone after dark—"

"I was kidding, Mom."

"I know I'm overreacting, but you feel so far from me. I look at the globe and can't believe my daughter is way over there. And I'm reading too much of the newspaper with all the terrible things that are happening—terrorists, kidnappings, disappearances. I miss you already and wish Grandma would have left this alone and not involved you."

Darby smiled. How often had she heard her mother say this in hints or nuances since the day Carole gave her the key to the safe and Darby had decided to come here? Perhaps she should have backed out after all. Her mom wanted to leave the past buried probably because of her own years of relentlessly pursuing her father, finding only disappointment time and time again. But it was different for Darby. She was seeking answers for her grandmother, not trying to fill in the pieces of her own life.

"Here are my suggestions. Put the globe away and quit watching the news. I miss you too, and it won't be long until I'm home. Clarise will hunt me down if I don't return in a few weeks. And Mom, if you aren't ready to go through Grandma's things, wait till I get back."

"Thank you, honey. Remember I'm praying for you."

"Okay." There it was again—newly religious Mom.

They said their good-byes, and Darby hung up the phone. She snuggled down against the pillows, her eyes watching a fistfight between Magnum and the "bad guy." No matter how much she told her body to sleep, she was wide awake.

If she wasn't going to sleep, she could refine her strategy. Once Darby had decided to come to Austria, she'd been so busy preparing for the trip that she'd had little time to figure out what she'd do when she actually arrived. Clarise was her toughest obstacle. Her partner in the photography studio did not encourage her decision.

"You've missed three weeks because of your grandmother's illness. I understood that, of course, but why do you have to go to Austria now?"

"I'm trying to get there before winter settles in and I have to worry about storms and driving in the snow. Or I could wait till spring when we have our wedding assignments."

Clarise finally agreed, though not happily. Darby ignored her comments in the following weeks. After all, she never took vacations, while Clarise took time off every month to do things with her family. It seemed the unspoken rule that since Darby wasn't married and didn't have children, she naturally should work more than Clarise. She thought of mentioning this, but at the time she hadn't minded the extra hours. Darby dated sporadically, hadn't had a boyfriend in years since she and Derek had broken up, and she worked most weekends. So why not make the studio her life? But since Grandma Celia's death, Darby had been seeing things differently—and Clarise wasn't looking for change.

The weeks before the trip evaporated quickly with long hours at the studio and driving the four hours down to her mother's on her Monday and Tuesday days off. Now here she was in Austria with hardly a plan. Well, there was no time like the present, she decided.

She'd made copies of the documents from Grandma Celia's safe. She'd put one copy back in the safe at home, and another set was safely tucked into the inside pocket of her suitcase. The originals were carried at her side in a long, black purse. She'd almost left the originals at home, but many of the letters were still unopened, and she hoped to find an expert who could examine and translate them.

Grandma had said the safe would give her information. Instead, the contents brought more questions. Darby now knew what the coins and brooch looked like by documents she'd found. She had the engagement half of a ring, enough money to live abroad for a long time if necessary, and other documents that didn't make a lot of sense.

She parted the window shade and looked at the dark, deserted street below. Over the bridge, spotlights shone on the church spires and toward the white monster fortress on the mountain. How could she open and run a business and backpack into the wilderness, but feel so intimidated by foreign travel? People did it all the time. Grandma had escaped this country during the Nazi occupation, and she was alone, pregnant, and facing real danger. If Grandma could do that, then Darby could play tourist and ask a few questions in the process. But perhaps that was part of it. Sure, it was the Nazis who had sent her grandmother fleeing for her life to the States. But this was still the same country.

I came here to seek answers for Grandma Celia. I'm not giving up. This isn't some Third World country. Austria is developed and cultured with many English-speaking people.

She sighed and turned from the window. *Even if I don't know a soul for thousands of miles, I can do this.*

Darby spotted the letter she disliked the most—the letter from Brant Collins. He worked here in Salzburg, perhaps even slept somewhere nearby. He had accused her grandmother of being an imposter when the elderly woman lived thousands of miles away. It would be different now that Darby was here. Corporations easily shrugged off individuals as if they were wiping mud from their shoes. But she wasn't so quickly scraped away, not when it came to defending Grandma Celia. Yes, she could face Brant Collins. Darby awaited the chance. And in the process, perhaps, she'd find out why her grandmother had contacted him in the first place.

"Well, Mr. Brant Collins, you may write your letters to old women, but I'm not letting you get away with it."

CHAPTER NINE

Brant turned away from the computer
screen. He'd spent the morning staring into the humming
business world via e-mail and videophone that lived and
breathed within the computer. After weeks of working with
Österreich Forest Products, the company had entered the tech-
nological age with full capacity to compete with other European lumber companies. One more down, and only a few
thousand Austrian companies to join the new millennium.

Brant stretched in front of the window. His shoulders felt
tight though it was still morning. Sleep came hard for him
these days. He looked toward Hohensalzburg, resting confi-
dently above the city in a mass of gray clouds. The fortress
had spent seven hundred years staring from the mountain.
It reminded him that some things endured long past
today. Such success gave him a slight hope for his own
work.

"Herr Collins?" a voice crackled from the small speaker on
his desk.

Brant turned in his leather chair toward his desk. "Yes, Frau Halder."

"You have a call from a woman named Darby Evans. And she speaks only English."

"What company does she work for?"

"No company—she says it's a personal matter."

"A personal matter?" Brant was stumped. He didn't know anyone by that name.

"She said it concerns a woman named Celia Müller."

Brant paused. "I'll take the call." Frowning, he waited a second before picking up the line. "This is Brant Collins. What's this about?"

"My name is Darby Evans."

"I know that already."

"Okay. Well, I'm calling because I received the letter you sent my grandmother, Celia Müller—"

"Celia Müller died over sixty years ago. I don't know what you want, but like I wrote to whoever that was—"

"What are you talking about? She didn't die sixty years ago!"

"Listen, I'm not playing games."

"Perhaps *you* could listen for a moment, Mr. Collins, without interrupting me."

"All right," Brant said, clearing his throat.

"Thank you. First of all, my grandmother never received the letter you wrote. I picked up the mail and never showed her because she was very ill at the time. But I have some things we need to discuss, and since I'm here in Salzburg—"

"You're in Salzburg?" Brant stood and turned again toward the window.

"May I finish, or are you going to interrupt every time I open my mouth?"

Brant didn't respond.

"I'd like to discuss this with you. In person."

His eyes felt drawn again to Hohensalzburg. The fortress had watched the comings and goings for hundreds of generations—protecting, eyeing, always knowing. Brant remembered that the woman who claimed to be Celia Müller was trying to locate information on the Lange family inheritance. Gunther had told Brant little about it, but he knew the inheritance was worth millions—if someone found and claimed it. If he met with Darby Evans, perhaps he could find out what the two women wanted.

It was better to have an enemy below your gaze than out of view.

"When would you like to meet?"

⊷⟫○⟪⊷

Darby pushed back from the small desk in her hotel room. Their appointment set and her notes in order, she was ready to face Brant Collins.

A gurgle rumbled through her stomach. At least one part of her was on schedule. Darby's eyes were bloodshot and finally she was tired, but at nine o'clock in the morning. The day had just begun, and she was ready for food and a long night's rest.

After a quick shower that helped wake her up, Darby hooked the electrical converter and blow dryer to the bathroom outlet in the slight fear she'd fry the hotel fuses or blow herself up. She sighed with relief when the dryer hummed alive. As she dressed in jeans and a long-sleeved shirt with the black scarf and boots Maureen had sent her, she remembered the note from her sister: *You'll look like a beautiful European in these. Remember, no tennis shoes or sweat suits— that's a dead giveaway you're an American tourist. Dress nicely.* Maureen and John had spent three weeks in France and Switzerland on their honeymoon. Her younger sister was the trendsetter of every new fashion so Darby listened to Maureen's advice, except for the faded jeans she couldn't live without. With hair semi-dry and makeup mostly on, she grabbed her purse and headed downstairs before breakfast was over.

She followed her nose to a cozy sitting room with a dining area at one end. It looked tidy in soft burgundy and white with perfect table settings, as if she were the only person who'd come to eat, ever. The food was just like home—pancakes and bacon, muffins, and whole-grain breads.

A woman entered wearing a neat Austrian *dirndl*. "*Guten Morgen. Wie geht's?*"

"Uh."

The woman waited.

"English?"

"Ah yes." She smiled. "I say good morning. How are you?"

"Oh. I am very good, and good morning to you."

She nodded. "Vould you like coffee or tea?"

"Coffee would be very nice. Thank you, or *danke*."

The woman nodded graciously and left the room. Darby picked up one of several different-sized plates from her table. She was probably doing everything wrong but was too hungry to care. The woman returned to set a cup of coffee on the small table, arrange some food on the buffet, then left once again.

Darby sat in the quiet of the white-plastered room and took a couple of bites of the whole-grain pancake. Then a thought struck her—*my curling iron*. Had she left it plugged in? She often did at home and would call her neighbor to check. In fact, the woman had her own key to Darby's apartment, it happened so often. The hotel brochure said the building was over five hundred years old, and it would be just her luck to burn the entire thing down.

Darby left her food, hoping it wouldn't disappear into perfect cleanliness before she returned, and hurried up the stairs. She put her hand on the door to unlock it. Instead, it pushed open.

Hadn't she locked her door? Yes, she was sure of it. She peered inside, but no one was there. She was tired—perhaps she hadn't locked it. Or perhaps the maid? Darby spotted her suitcase on the bed and knew something was wrong. She clearly remembered returning it to the wood cupboard.

The squeak of wheels made her pivot toward the hallway. A maid came from another room.

"Excuse me."

The woman looked up.

"Have you or anyone else been in my room?"

"*Nein. Kein Englisch.*"

"You don't speak English? No English?"

"*Nein.*"

Darby motioned to her room. "My door was open." She pointed to the door and opened and closed it. "Was someone in here? A person?" She tried to think of any German words or something from her high school French classes that might help. "A woman or man?"

"Ah. You *Mann.*"

"My man? Oh, *Mann* means husband, right?"

"*Ja. Mann.* Husband." The woman grinned and nodded. "*Ja,* you husband."

Darby stared at the woman. "But I don't have a husband."

The woman continued to grin. "You husband," she said and made a movement like she opened the door for someone, obviously Darby's husband.

"No. I don't have a husband. Me, no *Mann.*"

The maid's smile disappeared.

"We need the manager. Your boss. Manager." Darby pointed toward the stairs until the short woman hurried away. She touched her purse, to reassure herself that the packet of origi-

nal documents was present, then stepped toward her room. A
shiver raced down her back. Perhaps the man was still there.

⋯═◐═⋯

Brant checked his watch. He'd kept his eyes down the approaching street for over twenty minutes now. Every time a woman
walking alone approached, he expected it to be her. He could
see her hotel down the street. Brant had chosen this café in the
Old City as the meeting place. She couldn't get lost with only a
block to walk. So why hadn't she arrived?

A woman stepped quickly along the narrow sidewalk
toward the café. Brant stood up, but she didn't hesitate as she
continued past. That was it. He wouldn't play these games.
The woman had called him. His work at the office was piling
higher every minute he sat here. Brant paid his bill, then
decided he'd drop by her hotel to see if there had been a
mistake or if, perhaps, there was no Darby Evans.

Brant pushed the lobby door open and headed to the front
desk.

"Darby Evans's room, *bitte.*"

The woman looked at him with a strange expression. "Are
you the man who was here? Are you her husband?"

"No, I'm not her husband."

The woman stared over his shoulder. "Please wait here a
moment."

"Is something wrong?"

"*Nein, nein.* Just wait here, please." The woman hurried
around the desk and through the entry to the sitting room
where Brant could see a group of people and one police officer
standing together. The desk clerk approached and spoke to a
dignified, older man from the group. Brant wondered what
would call a police officer to the five-star hotel. A short, older
woman was speaking to the officer in rapid German, but Brant

was just out of range to understand exactly what was said. Another woman, probably in her late twenties or early thirties, stood with her arms crossed. Probably a maid caught snooping or stealing a patron's jewelry. Then the younger woman spoke to the officer, and Brant caught a few words in English. He took a curious step forward. The young woman had long, dark hair and appeared, from his profile view of her, to be unhappy about something. She wore jeans and a shirt that was a bit rumpled in the back.

Brant saw the desk clerk and the older man look his way. The man spoke to the policeman and the three of them walked toward him, leaving the young woman and maid behind.

"Is there a problem?" Brant said as they approached.

"You asked to see Fräulein Evans?"

"Yes. That must be her."

The young woman, obviously Darby Evans, came up behind them.

"It seems she's had some trouble today."

"Could you please speak English? Is this the man?" Darby asked the officer.

"I'm Brant Collins. You know, the guy you had an appointment with this morning."

She looked surprised. "I didn't forget. Someone broke into my room."

"That is not exactly certain," the man in the suit said quickly. Brant knew he must be the manager of the hotel.

"I think it's pretty certain. After I came down to breakfast, I returned to my room for a moment and found my door open. This woman said a man asked her to open the door—he'd lost his key. At least, that's what I think. He told her he was my husband, or he acted like my husband. I'm still unsure what she said about that either."

The hotel manager motioned for the maid and pointed to Brant. "Is this the man who was in the room?" he asked in German.

"What?" Brant said.

"*Nein, nein.*"

"Okay. You may go back to your work," the manager said to the maid.

"*Danke, danke.*"

"Yes, *danke,*" Brant said and glared at Darby. "I get stood up for a business appointment and suddenly am a suspect in some woman's break-in."

"I apologize but must check all options," the manager said. "This does not happen at Salzburg Cozy Hotel."

"Well, it did," Darby said. "And where is that woman going? You aren't going to do anything?"

"Fräulein." The policeman spoke in slow, broken English. "Nothing missing from your room. We keep contact with you and hotel and see what happen."

Within a minute, the hotel manager said a quick apology and hurried to the front desk, where concerned patrons watched and questioned the desk clerk. The officer also left after giving Darby Evans a business card, an apology for her difficulties, and a promise to find out what had happened. She stared at the card after he left. A long strand of hair fell across her cheek. Darby pushed it behind her ear and looked up at Brant just as he wondered why he was still there.

"This wasn't exactly the meeting I had in mind," Darby said. "I'm sorry for making you wait."

Brant didn't like this either. He'd been prepared to find out what this woman wanted and who she really was. The woman in front of him was nothing like he had expected. Her soft brown eyes with the dark circles beneath them appeared tired from deep within. She bit the side of her thumbnail, then seemed to realize it and dropped her hands to her side. The woman took a breath and attempted a brave look, but she appeared near tears—God forbid that. How could he be shrewd and hard against her?

Brant had to look away from her eyes. "Why don't you call my office tomorrow and we'll reschedule?"

"Sure."

"Fine." He began to walk away, then turned back. Her gaze hadn't moved. Was she wondering what to do? Or was this all a ploy to get information from him? Brant hated that he was so suspicious, but lately it seemed he had to watch every strange occurrence. And Darby Evans was one of them. But the maid did say she had seen someone in the woman's room. "So what are you going to do now?"

She shook her head slightly. "I'm not sure."

"Perhaps you should go lie down or something." He knew as soon as he spoke that his words sounded uncaring, even condescending—more so than he had intended.

"Thanks. That should make everything better."

"What do you want me to say?"

"Nothing. This has nothing to do with you. I apologize for missing our appointment. I'll call your secretary tomorrow. I don't need or expect anything else, is that what you want me to say?"

"I just asked."

"Don't you understand, Mr. Collins? Someone broke into my room whether you, the police, or that manager believe so or not. And what a charming pleasure it's been meeting you. Everyone in this horrible country treats me like an idiot or a criminal. I know I closed my door. I'd know if I had a husband or boyfriend. I don't have one friend or acquaintance for six thousand miles—and I know it's that far because I checked my map last night! I keep asking myself what I'm doing here."

"That's what I'm wondering."

Darby stared at him, anger burning in her eyes. The rims turned red as tears gathered.

"Oh no. Don't you dare cry."

She turned away. "Will you just leave? Forget I contacted

you. I'll find out what I'm looking for on my own." He heard a sniffle.

"You better not cry. I can't have a discussion with you if—"

"I am not crying." He caught the strain in her voice. She was crying, though fighting hard not to. "Just leave me alone, okay?"

"Listen. Just stop that. Why don't we go get something to eat and talk? I'll quit being a jerk, you can quit crying, and this will all work out fine."

"No thanks."

Just then the hotel manager stepped forward. "Fräulein Evans?"

Darby quickly wiped away her tears. The man glanced at Brant with an accusing expression.

"Yes?" she asked.

"I want to apologize. Our hotel has never experienced something like this before, and I promise you are safe here. I sincerely hope the person who entered your room did so mistakenly. We have many guests this week, so we are checking to see if we can find any additional information. We gave strict instructions to our housekeeping staff so this incident will not occur again. I sincerely hope you will continue your stay with us?"

Darby seemed to consider for a moment. "Yes, I suppose I will for now. Thank you, Herr . . ." She looked on his bronze nameplate. "Herr Braucher."

"*Danke,*" the man said, relief spreading across his face. The onlookers were dispersing, and the manager was obviously happy to have his hotel back to working order.

Darby still looked uncertain as to what to do. On impulse, Brant took her arm and said, "Come on, let's get you out of here for a while. We'll get coffee or, or something."

Nearly before he realized it, they were walking out of the building.

Why had she agreed to come with Brant Collins? A stranger had entered her room and what had she done? Left the hotel with another stranger to go for coffee.

They walked without speaking, though Darby's thoughts wandered loudly through her mind. Had someone intentionally entered her room, or could it have been an accident like the hotel manager indicated? Nothing was missing. Her suitcase was open, but nothing had been moved. Darby had run straight for her camera case in the wardrobe, but not even a roll of film had been taken. Then she thought of the spare copies in the suitcase pocket—but they were there. The originals hadn't left her side. Perhaps the man believed her room was his, then realized his mistake when he opened Darby's suitcase and left. Yet despite her attempts to calm her thoughts with logic, she felt as unsettled as when she first felt the door open at her touch. The only person in Austria who knew she was here was Brant, and he had been at his office. Or had he? The maid had not recognized him. Was she now walking into a dangerous situation by leaving the hotel with him, or was this an opportunity to find some information for her grandmother's quest? As long as they stayed among other people, Darby would continue with him. If he led her away, she'd run and cry one of the few German words she knew: *Hilfe!* meaning "help."

"Your first time in Salzburg?"

Darby jumped at the sound of his voice. He was making small talk, she knew. And something in his voice betrayed that perhaps he was regretting his decision to invite her out of the hotel.

"Yes."

"So how much are you paying to stay there?"

"Excuse me?"

"No, let me guess, about eighteen hundred Austrian schillings, or did you use euros?"

"I figured it out to be about one hundred and fifty United States dollars."

"Yeah, that's close to what I said. Figures."

"What do you mean by that?"

"Inexperienced travelers can be so gullible."

"I'm not gullible." She didn't mention the inexperienced part, but her unmistakable blush told all. "I paid exactly what it says in my travel brochure—they didn't raise the prices for me."

"Don't you realize this is off-season, between summer and winter peak? And now after the break-in, I bet I could get them to drop forty dollars a night."

"No, thank you. After today, I'd rather leave well enough alone." Darby glanced at Brant from the corner of her eye. Who did this guy think he was?

"If you want the Austrian experience, stay in an Austrian hotel, *Gasthaus,* or *Pension.* You'll pay maybe three times less a night. Or look for a sign that says *Zimmer frei.*"

"A what?"

"There are many varieties. Most often the owner of a private home rents out a room or two for a little extra cash. Almost all include breakfast, an Austrian breakfast. Some include dinner. What did you have this morning—American pancakes?"

Darby didn't answer.

"Why travelers stay in a clone of the country they came from I'll never understand."

Darby wanted to hit him. And this man had actually made her cry, something she very rarely did, and never in public.

A drop of rain hit her on the head. Darby had left her umbrella in her room. More drops began to fall on the newly dried sidewalks.

"Take my umbrella."

Up to then, she hadn't noticed he carried an umbrella and satchel. He extended the umbrella.

"I'm fine." A drop hit her in the eye, and she blinked it away without looking at him.

They continued to walk another half block as the drops increased.

"Just take the umbrella." He opened it. "I insist."

"No, thank you."

Brant stopped. "Look, I'm sorry about the hotel thing. I've been rude since I met you. But take the umbrella, will you? Please?"

Darby sized him up. His dark eyes did look apologetic. And she'd either accept his offering or soon be drenched. "Okay." She took the open umbrella and began walking.

"Thank you," they said in unison. Darby didn't look his way.

Pit, pat. As the rain increased against the umbrella roof, Darby noticed Brant's dark hair was getting wet.

"We could share it." She lifted one side as an invitation.

"I'm fine."

Stubborn man. He wiped a streak of rain from his cheek. The street was now slick with wetness as the rain pelted the ground.

Darby stopped. "Just get under the umbrella, okay? Please."

Brant's jaw clenched, then relaxed. "All right."

A couple passed, snuggled together under a shared umbrella. It made Darby feel all the more awkward as they both tried not to touch or get too close under one umbrella top.

"Where are we going?" she asked to break the silence.

"There's a restaurant I like another few blocks away. Very authentic Austrian."

"Sounds good," she said, trying to think of what else to ask or say. She'd forgotten the list of questions and comments she'd outlined in her room and nothing came to mind, or at least nothing that seemed appropriate beneath a shared umbrella.

After several blocks along the narrow cobblestone street, Darby realized she'd undertaken her first trip out of the hotel. Their footsteps echoed up the walls of the tall, straight buildings.

"Is this your first time in Austria or just Salzburg?"

"My first time in Europe, actually." *My first time outside the United States.*

"Well, this is Kaigasse. Several streets over you'll find Getreidegasse, a famous shopping street for many centuries. When you see *straße* at the end, like Franz-Josef-straße, that means Franz-Josef-Street. If the name ends with *gasse*, like this one, it means small street, often one-way since they're so narrow."

"Okay."

"I'm sounding like a tour guide." Brant shook his head and smiled slightly. The rain bounced harder on the black cloth above their heads.

The buildings opened to a square with cobblestone streets leading out from its corners. A large fountain bubbled at one end, and arched walkways led to another square on the other end. Darby tilted the umbrella to see the top of the church with its green domes. Raindrops hit their faces, and the points of the umbrella poked Brant's head.

"Oh, sorry. Maybe you should hold it since you're taller." She knew he didn't want to be under it with her, but it was raining harder.

"We're almost there," Brant said, taking the umbrella from her. "I've taken the roundabout direction so you can see the city."

A sign on a building read *Residenzplatz*. The fountain gushed water from horses' mouths and nostrils like bubbles of froth after a long, hard ride. Darby wondered about its history but didn't ask. She suddenly saw beyond her fears of being in a foreign country and her hotel troubles to the wonder of Old Salzburg. The clouds hung low against the towering Mönchs-berg mountain, where the Old City nestled beneath the fortress's gaze.

"That's St. Peter's Church," Brant said. "It has a beautiful dome ceiling you'll have to see from the inside."

"I will." Darby felt drawn back in time. Salzburg certainly had charm with this old section ancient compared to her Californian heritage. It smelled of wet stone and breathed of age chiseled from hundreds of years of dreams, work, and sweat.

They had found a comfortable pace beneath the umbrella, and though she disliked this man for his hard letter to her grandmother, it felt good to have someone with her, to not be alone for an hour or so. She just wanted to walk in the rain with him, even if she struggled with the thought that she might be betraying Grandma Celia. But her grandmother always gave people the benefit of the doubt.

Brant had a look that told of his love for the city. Darby observed that he was good-looking in a quiet, withdrawn sort of way. Probably the kind to be careful of because you never really knew what he thought. She glanced down and didn't see a ring on his finger, which figured. He was probably controlling and domineering. She already knew he was stubborn. Soon she'd strike hard and get the answers she sought, but for now the rain on an umbrella and a little companionship lured her questions away.

They passed stone archways, a line of horses and carriages, and artists sitting with their Salzburg watercolors under the eaves of buildings. They arrived at a two-story restaurant that had white tables and chairs on the second-story balcony.

"We'll have to eat inside with this weather," Brant said. "This is Café Tomaselli, probably Salzburg's most famous restaurant."

Darby noticed the specials menu as they passed but didn't recognize anything. Her stomach reminded her that she'd missed her breakfast, and it wasn't happy at all.

"Have you eaten?"

"Almost, until the guy-in-my-room incident." The cheery dining room was warm, and inviting smells surrounded them.

"Hopefully it was a mistake." Brant walked to a corner table for two and pulled out her chair.

"I hope," she said, grateful that he was a gentleman.

"*Guten Morgen.*" The waitress handed them menus and spoke in rapid German.

"Would you like coffee and some breakfast?" Brant asked.

Darby suddenly wondered if this was supposed to be the meeting they'd missed. She had planned that encounter to be formal as she addressed his response to her questions. But right now, she was hungry and not prepared to interrogate her tour guide.

Her eyes scanned the menu on the table and recognized only one thing. "I'll take ham and eggs. And some hot chocolate sounds really good. Do they have that?"

Brant asked the waitress, who nodded and smiled. They

spoke a little back and forth, and then the young waitress smiled only for Brant, glancing back at him as she walked away.

"What did you say to her?"

"Nothing. She made a reference to you as my breakfast date, and I told her it was business."

"Ah, I understand." Darby chuckled.

"What?"

"Nothing. I just wondered about her smile toward you, and that explains it."

"I missed something here."

"You say I'm a gullible traveler. You're a bit naïve, I'd say."

"I'm not naïve."

"She was flirting with you. Couldn't you see it?"

"No."

"Oh, here she comes."

The waitress set the cups of hot chocolate on the table. As she stepped back a handful of napkins fell at Brant's feet.

He picked them up for her, and the woman smiled widely. "*Danke.*"

"And so early in the morning," Darby said as the girl walked away with a blush on her face.

"What are you talking about? She dropped . . ."

"Exactly. Oh, so gullible."

"She needed assistance."

"Gullible."

"Okay, okay. You got me back. Can we call a truce now?"

Darby shook his outstretched hand and settled back in her chair. The bright room was cozy. Her eyes focused on Brant. He was handsome enough for a waitress to make an immediate pass at him, but Darby also measured him up as a rigid neat freak by the perfect crease in the collar, smooth wrinkle-free slacks, clean shave, and dark hair with only one place a bit messed up where she'd almost stabbed his head with the umbrella spike. His closets at home were probably as perfectly composed as he looked.

But who was she to judge on appearance when she must look a fright? Her hair had been only half dry and uncurled when they left the hotel and now felt limp and flat from the weather. Her eyes were likely bloodshot from so little sleep. What would Brant think he knew about her by today's appearance?

Darby knew she should be more concerned that she was facing Brant Collins—the man she'd planned to interrogate, stand strong against, press for answers. But the room was warm, food was on the way, and two hot cocoas in short, wide cups were on the table. Now the idea of her great concern over the stranger in her room seemed a bit foolish. Her paranoia over being in a foreign country had gotten the best of her. But at present she was away and able to look at it objectively.

Darby watched Brant take his first sip of the steaming cocoa. "I haven't had this in years," he said, wiping a drop of whipped cream from his upper lip. "Austria is a coffee country."

"You speak perfect English."

"I should. I was born in the States and have dual citizenship. My mother and I spent summers in Austria so it was my second home. Now it's my home."

"You're an American?"

"Yes. I was born in Portland, Oregon. My father was American, my mother Austrian. They compromised by living in the States except during summer."

"Portland is a beautiful city. I was there a few months ago at a photography conference."

"My father still lives there. We don't see each other as often as we'd like."

Darby thought of her own father, the man without a face. In the sparse memories she had of him, his face was never there.

"When did you settle in Europe?"

"I attended two years of university here in Salzburg, then decided to stay."

"And what about your mother—still in Portland with your father?"

"She died." Brant took a quick sip of cocoa.

"I'm sorry."

He met her eyes and for the slightest second Darby saw her own reflection.

"Ham and eggs for you." The waitress stood in front of them. They leaned back as she set the steaming platters in front of them. The eggs sizzled above a layer of ham on the hot plates.

"*Danke*," they replied in unison.

"Enjoy," the waitress said, looking only at Brant.

The eggs weren't completely done, but as Darby moved them around the sizzling platter they quickly cooked through. As they ate, she searched words for more small talk. She could mention the weather or ask about the sights in the area. Brant certainly liked the tour guide role. Then Darby recalled the last image of Grandma Celia, eyes closed, hands stilled in her coffin. Sure, Grandma gave people the benefit of the doubt, but could she so easily ignore the fact that this man she chatted so amiably with was the same person who had accused her grandmother of being an imposter? That was a pretty strong charge. Yet here she was chatting and eating ham and eggs with him. Darby couldn't eat the last bites.

"We were meeting to talk about my grandmother."

Something changed in Brant's expression as if he too suddenly realized their roles and the fact that they had crossed an invisible line. He crumpled the napkin in his hand.

"That's right. We've wandered from the intended topic." He glanced at his watch. "The lure of a Salzburger morning . . ."

"We can reschedule."

Brant seemed to reconsider. "No, this is fine. Let me just check my phone for a second." He reached into his black satchel beneath the table. Darby noticed his frown as he stood up. "My secretary called three times. Please excuse me for a minute."

"Of course." Darby watched him walk out of the restaurant. At least Brant wasn't the type to chat in a restaurant on his cell phone—that always annoyed her. She drank the last chocolate-rich sip in her coffee cup, then looked toward the doorway, wishing she'd insisted they reschedule. Darby could barely remember the questions she'd prepared and all at once felt like crawling back beneath the down comforter in her hotel. The cozy ambiance of the restaurant didn't blend well with the type of meeting she'd envisioned. Perhaps she'd meet him at his office the next day.

Brant returned moments later and sat back down.

"Is something wrong? If you need to go, I'd rather . . ."

"No. I have someone at my office waiting for me, but—well, it's someone I'd rather avoid. Let's talk about your grand-mother." He rubbed his chin, waiting.

Darby realized she needed to collect her thoughts, and quickly.

Brant leaned back in his chair. "We've taken a bizarre trip around our meeting. But let's get back to the subject. I assume you are here because your grandmother continues to claim to be Celia Müller."

Something in the way he said her grandmother's name and "continues to claim to be" stirred her anger.

"My grandmother *is* Celia Müller, or rather, she was."

"Was?"

"She passed away last month."

An expression flickered across Brant's face. His tense jaw relaxed as he stared down at his plate. Both were silent for a minute.

"What I'm wondering is why you don't believe my grandmother is Celia Müller, and why she wrote to you in the first place."

"She didn't write to me, in particular. She wrote to the Holocaust Survivors' Organization I work for. Our Salzburg office is not large. In fact, I run two businesses from the same office. Your grandmother wrote us last summer. I brought the letter with me for our meeting."

"You did?"

"I keep records of all correspondence, whether we believe the claim or not." He reached into the black satchel and pulled out an envelope. He looked at it once, then handed it to Darby.

The letter was basic and formal, and thankfully in English.

> *My name is Celia Rachel Lange Müller. My father and brother, Simon Lange and Warner Lange, and aunt, Milda Lange Bergmann, were taken by the Nazis and all sent to KZ Dachau and/or later KZ Mauthausen and Mauthausen/ Gusen, where they perished. I alone escaped Austria. I am writing in regard to a family inheritance that was lost during the Nazi occupation. It consists of two coins and a priceless sapphire brooch. I hoped that you could have possible information on how I can seek these items or what would be the next step in my search. I believe that the Nazis stole these items from my family after I escaped the country. Please call, fax, write, or e-mail me with any information you need or how I should proceed next.*
>
> *Thank you for your time and work. I eagerly look forward to your response.*
>
> *Sincerely,*
> *Celia Müller*

Darby read the "eagerly look forward to your response" twice. "That's a pretty basic letter. Your response was pretty harsh."

"I'm sorry, I don't recall."

"I have the letter with me." Darby opened her pack and handed Brant the letter. He read it, then handed it back with a frown on his face. "I imagine if this was to my grandmother, I would think the letter harsh. But you have to take it from our viewpoint. My organization helps Holocaust survivors. If you knew these people, saw their faces—you can only imagine the horror these people endured. It's a miracle anyone survived. But then after liberation, when they should have had freedom and time to rebuild their lives, they received instead another slap in the face. Their homes, property, assets were unavailable for redemption. For example, a bank account in Switzerland or a life insurance policy—the recipients were turned down because there were no death certificates for family members, no proof of their death. How do you prove or disprove that a relative died at a particular camp? We may have a record of them being sent, but did they arrive? Did they really die there? That's what makes our job difficult. So our organization and other groups try to help, but only in the last ten to twenty years. These people have been brutalized again and again and have come to the end of their lives. Groups such as ours try to offer them and their families hope—or at least a bit of closure before their deaths. So when someone attempts to cash in on that suffering, it provokes some anger. I did respond to your grandmother in this manner."

"I can understand your strong emotion toward fraudulent claims."

"And unfortunately, there are many."

"But what I don't understand is *why* you believe my grandmother is not Celia Müller."

"I look into each claim. And I know the town of Hallstatt quite well. That's where Celia Lange Müller was born."

Darby's thoughts went back to the day of the funeral and Maisie's insistence that Celia was born in Hallstatt, not Vienna as her papers said.

"My mother's summer home was in Gosau, just over the mountain from Hallstatt. I learned to scuba dive in Hallstattersee—Hallstatt Lake. It's not that big of a town. I check out all claims such as the one your grandmother sent. And the papers were very clear, unlike others I've dealt with. I had the birth record and found the death records at the camp she was sent to. Now I don't know you, Ms. Evans. You seem to genuinely believe your grandmother. But understand my position. I have a hard time believing anyone when I have hard facts stating otherwise."

"So what you're implying is that perhaps I'm an imposter also?"

"I didn't say that. But really, I'm not sure what to think about this. What I do know is, Celia Lange Müller died in 1941. She was born in Hallstatt and died at Mauthausen Concentration Camp."

"Mauthausen? You have information that Celia Müller died at Mauthausen? My grandmother told me we had family members who died there, like the letter said. It's a camp here in Austria, right?"

"Yes, it's near Linz. Mauthausen was the largest Austrian camp and ran the many satellite camps here."

"Maybe the records show another Lange, but not Celia. Or perhaps a relative with that same first name?"

"No. I'm certain."

"You can't be. I know who my grandmother was. I know she lived many years in Hallstatt, where her father was an archaeologist in the Celtic diggings there. She met and married a man named Gunther Müller."

Brant jerked his head up and stared hard at her.

"She escaped from Austria in late 1939."

"No," Brant said firmly. "Celia Müller died in 1941 at Mauthausen. I'm not saying that your grandmother was a bad person. Perhaps she really believed she was Celia Müller. The war did strange and horrible things to people's minds. In that era people didn't seek psychological help like practically half the world does now. I don't know about your grandmother, but I know for certain that Celia Müller died a long time ago."

Darby shook her head. Brant thought Grandma Celia was insane or mentally warped? But then, if she saw the facts on paper and didn't know her grandmother personally, perhaps she'd feel differently too. "Can I see these records?"

"My records are confidential. But you could try Hallstatt or Mauthausen. Many camps are establishing on-site records with victim lists."

Darby wondered how she could convince this man, and if she really needed to at all. She had her answers and under-stood his letter to her grandmother—she didn't need him to believe Grandma Celia. But she wanted him to, and she wanted him to believe her.

"You've come a long way for me to tell you that."

"It's not like that at all. I knew my grandmother. I know what she believed in and who she was. She wasn't a liar."

"So then, you'll take up your grandmother's cause to find the Lange family inheritance?"

"What do you know about the inheritance?"

"Nothing." Brant took a bite of his ham. "It was in your grandmother's letter. I know it adds to the motive of your grandmother seeking a claim that wasn't hers."

"Well, the Lange inheritance is the least of my concerns. I'm not here to get rich or find some items I'm not even sure existed. My grandmother had some last wishes. . . ." Darby wondered if she should mention Tatianna. Brant seemed to have his mind made up, but she decided to risk it, in case he'd know how to get information. "My grandmother had a friend. Her name was Tatianna Hoffman. I'm actually here searching for what happened to her—that was one of my grandmother's final requests. Grandma asked that I give Tatianna her name back."

Brant's eyebrows lowered as he leaned forward across the table. "What does that mean?"

She wished she hadn't said it, for the words sounded strange. Even she didn't understand. "It doesn't matter. I don't quite know yet. You are the first person I've sought because of the letter you sent her. But I didn't contact you to pursue the Lange inheritance."

"Tatianna Hoffman? Your grandmother sent you here, searching for this other woman, but she was also interested in the Lange inheritance?"

"And you find that suspicious."

"I find most everything suspicious. Unfortunately, in my profession I've become low on trust."

"That's too bad." Darby looked at his hands on the table. "I don't understand you. In all your work, you know how rumors and mistakes abounded during the war. Why is it completely out of the question that my grandmother could be Celia Müller? People thought to have escaped were killed and people believed to be killed actually escaped. I remember hearing that about the Anne Frank story. Neighbors and friends believed the Franks had escaped from the Nazis years before, while all the time they were hiding in their attic. How can you be so sure this didn't happen to my grandmother?"

"I'm well aware of the Anne Frank story. I know hundreds of stories as tragic as that one. But I have documents that prove Celia Müller died at Mauthausen Concentration Camp. I'm sure this isn't easy for you to accept. I can understand that. But, if you need proof . . ." Brant rested his head on his hand as if considering something. "Go to Hallstatt and look in the cemetery. Go to Mauthausen and see the ovens. Then you'll have your answers."

"You certainly think you know a lot about Celia Müller," Darby mumbled, more to herself than to him.

"It's my job. It's what I do." He crinkled the napkin into a smaller ball. "I looked up Celia Müller's information when your grandmother wrote." He paused for a long time, and Darby could see his mind working. "This friend of your grandmother's. Did you say Tatianna Hoffman? Have you ever considered that perhaps your grandmother is Tatianna?"

She stared at Brant. The idea should have angered her. But Brant's words were the spoken fear Darby had tried to reject every night since she'd found Tatianna's documents in the safe—while the records of her grandmother's immigration to the United States were not found.

Could Grandma Celia actually be Tatianna Hoffman?

CHAPTER ELEVEN

Where would you get the ridiculous idea that my grandmother could be Tatianna Hoffman?"

"For many reasons. It seems strange your grandmother, who has searched for the Lange inheritance, abandoned her search before she died, and instead asked you to give Tatianna her name back. Perhaps your grandmother spoke of herself."

"My grandmother was Celia Lange Müller."

"Darby, she wasn't. If you need further proof, go to Hallstatt. Go to the cemetery and see if that doesn't change your mind."

"What do you mean?"

"Just go see for yourself."

Darby was ready to leave. "I guess that's all I wanted to know. Perhaps, if you have time, you could look up Tatianna Hoffman's name in your accurate files and see if any information appears on her also."

"I'll do that—"

A man stopped in front of their table.

"Richter." Brant's voice didn't seem happy to see this man.

Richter raised one eyebrow. "*Guten Morgen.*"

"Speak English, Richter."

"Do we have an Englishwoman among us?"

"No, an American. I told Frau Halder I was in a meeting and I'd catch up with you later."

Richter portrayed a mock expression of hurt. "Is this the welcome I receive? You are a difficult man to track down, and this doesn't exactly look like a meeting. More like pleasure." He smiled at Darby, then spoke to Brant without taking his gaze off her. "I get no introduction to your beautiful friend, only accusations. I came into Salzburg to see you, have been waiting for hours for this meeting to adjourn—but I now see why it takes so long."

"What did you need?"

"It's not what I need, but what I give. I have two extra tickets to a ballet at the Landestheater and wanted to give them to you. You work too hard and date too little. This is my gift to give you a life back. Perhaps you and your American friend . . . I still have yet to be introduced."

"Darby Evans, Richter Hauer."

She reached for Richter's extended hand. Both men were handsome in completely different ways. Brant might not turn heads at first glance, but Richter exuded a savvy charm that was noticeable at once. He seemed confident, even extremely conceited. He reminded her of a college classmate who liked to use Rhett Butler lines while seeking the affections of Darby and her friends, all at the same time.

"Nice to meet you." Darby noticed how Richter held her hand longer than necessary, while evaluating her with hard, gray eyes.

"So, an American." He added another chair to the table. "The two of you are then perfect for a night together—two

Americans in Salzburg. What songs are written about. Or if Brant will not take you, perhaps I'll take you myself."

"I have not come to Salzburg to have songs written about me," Darby said insistently.

Seeming surprised, Richter replied, "Brant, this woman is not easily charmed. Good for you, but good luck also." He winked at Darby.

"Here are the tickets." He set them on the table. "I will leave the two of you alone. Brant, I'll catch up with you later. And Ms. Darby Evans, it has been a pleasure."

Both Brant and Darby watched Richter's departure.

"You don't like him, do you?" Darby said.

"I don't trust him." He studied Darby.

"You don't trust many people, do you, Mr. Collins?"

"A habit learned through experience, unfortunately. But I do apologize for Richter. He—there's no one quite like him." Brant looked at the tickets. "We don't have to go."

"Of course we wouldn't."

Darby insisted on paying the bill since she had the right currency and had originally initiated the appointment. But Brant paid the tip. Darby noted that he gave the extra money to the waitress instead of leaving it on the table like at home. That detail would come in handy for future dining.

The rain had stopped, though dark clouds continued to hang low over the city. Darby drew her coat tightly around her and tasted snow in the air as they stepped from the restaurant. She turned to say good-bye, hoping she could find her way back through the labyrinth of streets.

"I'll walk you back."

"It's not necessary."

"I don't mind. I won't allow a fellow American to get lost."

"It's not far."

"Really, allow me."

"If you insist."

Again silence walked with them. Darby didn't feel compelled to think of small talk. Instead, she listened to the sound of their footsteps on the pavement. Cyclists on old bikes with wire baskets jingled past. It was a favorite mode of transportation, she noticed. They passed a vendor selling something that tantalized the air with a warm, nutty smell.

"Have you tried *Maroni*?" Brant asked, stopping at the end of the line behind the vendor.

"No, what is it?"

"Roasted chestnuts."

"I've heard the Christmas song—'chestnuts roasting on an open fire.' " She chuckled, then felt foolish. "But no, I've never had them."

"You can't experience autumn in Salzburg without *Maroni*." He waited in line and bought a paper bag of the round, dark nuts. He offered Darby one, then showed her how to open the shell.

The meaty texture reminded Darby of the acorns she'd peeled and mashed as a child with the neighbor kids. She hesitated before taking a bite, remembering how she'd accepted the dare to try an acorn and immediately spit out the bitter nut to the laughter of her friends. She took a breath and popped the white meat into her mouth, determined not to spit it out, whatever it tasted like. To her surprise, the warm nut wasn't bitter, but had a subtle taste that somehow reminded her of autumn woods. "Wonderful."

"My favorite this time of year."

They walked, sharing the bag of chestnuts until they reached the Cozy Hotel. Darby noticed as they passed other hotels how Americanized this one appeared.

She stopped in front of the door. "Here we are. You didn't lose a fellow American."

"Good thing. I don't need anything more on my conscience."

He smiled, a nice smile, but Darby wondered about the

words. She almost asked what things bothered him—perhaps writing angry letters to old people?—but she held her tongue.

"I do know someone who may help you. A professor at the university, a short distance away. He may be a good source if you need more research."

"That would be great." Darby wrestled a pen and paper from her purse and handed them to Brant.

"His name is Professor Peter Voss, and here's his phone number." Brant handed her the paper. "And I'll check for a Tatianna Hoffman."

"Suddenly so helpful?" Darby grinned.

Brant examined her thoughtfully. "I do hope you find what you're searching for, and that the truth doesn't hurt too much."

Darby shook her head. He didn't understand and couldn't believe. If their roles were reversed, what would she believe? What did she believe now?

"We better just leave it at that so we don't start arguing." Brant smiled. "Good idea."

Darby extended her hand. "Good-bye, Mr. Collins."

"Can we forget the proper names?"

"Sure. Good-bye, Brant."

"Good-bye, Darby."

He held open the door as she walked in. At the stairwell, Darby looked back. He waved, then disappeared. She watched for a minute, then looked at the phone number and hurried upstairs. Brant could not be right. She hoped.

--==◦==--

Frau Halder had a stack of messages when Brant finally returned to the office. He had returned slowly, taking back streets and strolling along the river before arriving at the second-story office.

"You missed your friend," Frau Halder said as Brant arrived.

"What friend?" Brant picked up his messages. "Do you mean Richter?"

"Yes. He waited and waited. Such a nice young man he is."

Brant glanced at his secretary as he flipped through the messages. "Actually, I did see him."

"Really? I'm glad." She smiled. "You know, he thinks of you like a brother. The two of you should do more things together."

"Is that what he said?"

"Oh yes. We talked for quite a while. He worries about you, just like I do. We think you need to work less and have more fun." Frau Halder gave him her classic mother-hen look.

"When did Richter get here?" Brant asked.

"Right after you left. I told him you had an appointment, so he just sat down and chatted with me for a while. Then he got hungry and went to breakfast, even brought me back a pastry. Such a nice young man."

Brant wondered why Richter had come and gone and come again. Frau Halder was a kind woman, though not always the most astute. But she'd always been caring and concerned toward Brant. On his walk to the office, he had planned to make sure Frau Halder never revealed the location of another meeting to Richter again. But as he stood before her, Brant knew she had no idea she'd done that. He sighed and glanced through the mail basket.

"Thank you for covering while I was gone so long," Brant said.

"I'm going to lunch now, if you don't mind. I'm meeting my grandchildren at the park if the rain holds off."

"Tell the boys to call me, and we'll play soccer again."

"They've been practicing the moves you taught them. I'll tell them you're ready to play." Frau Halder went into the back room and returned with a lunch basket.

Brant watched her leave. How good it must feel to have

lunch with children. To not wonder about every person's motives. How freeing to simply live life. To meet a pretty woman and actually have romantic thoughts about her, instead of questioning who she was.

He closed the door of his office and thought about Darby. He found her interesting, intelligent, beautiful—especially when she tried her stubborn act. He almost laughed, remembering the expression on her face when she refused to use the umbrella of the enemy. She was too stubborn to even wipe the raindrop that hit her forehead. But she also could make him laugh, something Brant rarely did anymore. It felt good to be with Darby Evans, perhaps because she reminded him of the States—his other home. A few years ago, perhaps even six months ago, Brant might have pursued her. But now he felt rusty, not knowing what to say or how to act. And still, he battled the motives of every person around him—especially of someone who claimed to be the granddaughter of Celia Müller.

Brant set the messages on his desk. It would take the afternoon and evening to get back on schedule, but first he wrote down the name of Tatianna Hoffman. He promised he'd check. What Brant did know beyond a doubt was that Celia Lange Müller died long ago in Mauthausen Concentration Camp. Gunther hadn't spent sixty years mourning his wife for nothing.

Brant wondered how Darby would handle the truth about her grandmother. It had hurt him to discover the Aldrich deception, but the betrayal of a loved one would be even worse. He couldn't imagine the pain he was forcing Darby to face.

⊶⊷◉⊰⊷

Darby shut her door, locked it, and rested her head against the wall. She closed her eyes, then turned to look around the room, remembering that a stranger had been here. The stranger's fingerprints seemed to glow around the room.

She considered changing rooms, but would that help? Darby went through her luggage and investigated her belongings closely. Her hands felt dirty after touching her suitcase. Someone had picked up her black suitcase and unzipped it. How long had he looked inside? What clothing had he touched? She organized her clothes and hygiene supplies and slowly began to reclaim the room and her things as her own. The man had made a mistake—there was absolutely no other explanation.

The white curtains swayed slightly from the window she'd cracked open, and the cloudy sky outside brought a soft light that drew her weariness deeper. Tired through every part of her body, Darby wished to roll up in a ball beneath the down comforter for a year or two until her strength returned. There inside her feather womb she wouldn't feel the presence of a stranger or hear the words that had haunted her since her meeting with Brant: *Could Grandma Celia actually be Tatianna Hoffman?*

Instead of the escape into sleep she desired, Darby forced herself to focus on her strategy. Rest would not come with the upset of her questions. She organized her information into neat stacks on the desk: letters in one pile, information on the Lange inheritance in another, photographs and miscellaneous papers in another. Brant, her first contact, had yielded three more leads: Professor Voss, Hallstatt, and Mauthausen. Darby found Hallstatt on her Austria map and marked the highway route, then continued it on to the Linz region in Upper Austria near the Czech border. She'd rent a car and go there in a few days, but first attempt a meeting with Professor Peter Voss.

As Darby made her list and plans, she noticed the Austrian passport. The yellowed pages worked to form doubts in her mind. Inside, the name said *Tatianna Hoffman*. Place of birth: *Vienna, Austria*—the same city Grandma Celia's records indicated, though Maisie insisted all family members were born in the village of Hallstatt. Though Darby had defended her grandmother to Brant, now her inklings of doubt turned to fear. A scenario grew. Tatianna Hoffman and Celia Müller were best friends when Tatianna escaped from Austria. She came to America, changed her name to Celia Müller since she knew her friend had been sent to a camp, then moved in with Uncle Marc and Aunt Helen, who'd never seen her or the real Celia before. Uncle Marc was Grandma Celia's brother, Darby's great-uncle, though only a few years older than Celia. He had moved to the United States when they were children, and though they wrote for years, the two never met until Celia's immigration. When her grandmother said Tatianna needed her name, perhaps she *was* speaking of herself as Brant suggested. Perhaps Darby's grandma couldn't admit the truth in life and wanted Darby to discover it. Maybe that was why Celia wrote in her letter how Darby's own future would change as she found the truth.

The more Darby thought of it, the more she believed in the possibility. Didn't everyone know how a small lie could wrap itself around an entire life? Could this have happened to Grandma Celia—or was it Grandma Tatianna?

Darby remembered decades of little moments with the woman she knew as Grandma Celia: Band-Aids, gardening lessons, bicycle races, marshmallow roastings, and late-night stories. Darby shook her head. If her grandmother's name wasn't Celia Müller, but Tatianna Hoffman, she was still the woman who loved Darby, and whom Darby loved back.

She put the passport in one of the piles and found a picture of her grandmother in the photograph pile. It had been taken when Maureen had the twins. Darby gazed at the face she knew so well. This woman was the truest, kindest, most sincere person Darby had ever met. This woman could not be a fraud or an imposter. That would shatter everything Darby believed in.

"I believe her. I believe she was Celia Rachel Lange Müller, just like she signed her name in her letter. She didn't sign simply 'Grandma.' Wouldn't she do that if she weren't really Celia?"

If her grandmother was Tatianna, Darby would confront it when she had solid proof. But no matter what name her grandmother went by, Darby knew who the woman had been.

The streets of Salzburg drew Darby from her
hotel that evening. After an afternoon nap, she'd made a quick
call to Professor Peter Voss. He'd agreed to meet her at his
university office the next day.

Hunger and curiosity alike escorted Darby along the city
streets. The main roads bustled with taxis, electric buses, and
cars as she made her way back into the heart of the Old City.
Here only a few cars wound their way around pedestrians and
cyclists with baskets on the front or back of creaky bikes.
Darby noticed that both residents and tourists were drawn
outside while the rain was held within the dark clouds above.
Though most of the shops were closed, people were everywhere. They walked at leisurely paces—elderly couples, a
group of teens, people of all ages and races. The outdoor cafés
brimmed with lively customers who laughed, smoked, and ate
platefuls of food that made Darby's mouth water. She walked
past a musician playing his saxophone beneath a stone archway and an artist drawing a beautiful chalk mural on the side-

walk. She wound down cobblestone streets that opened into different squares, finding Getreidegasse, the famous shopping street Brant had told her about. There she looked up at one of the tall, flat-fronted buildings to see Mozart's birthplace. Her hands reached for her camera—her faithful manual Nikon—that usually hung around her neck. "Old Nikki" had gone on every trip Darby had taken since Grandma Celia and her mother had presented her with the gift for high school graduation. Though she'd bought new equipment, her Nikki camera forever stayed her favorite. But so far on this trip, her camera had been safe in the tan case, well hidden in her room. For the first time in her adulthood, she was completely without it. So as she walked, Darby simply enjoyed what she saw instead of clicking away at it with her camera covering her eyes.

Darby continued down the skinny street, peering in the windows of perfume, shoe, and specialty shops. The buildings towered above and were connected in rows a block long. Ahead she could see the end where sheer rock rose above a church steeple. Darby bet she could have walked here hundreds of years ago and found the place exactly the same—until she spotted the golden arches of McDonald's. Her hunger drew her toward the quaint building that suddenly transformed into an American fast-food restaurant as she opened the door. Though it was fun paying sixty-three schillings for a meal, Darby felt a little guilty buying a Big Mac when she should instead try Austrian cuisine.

The street was still lined by late-night strollers when Darby found her way back to her hotel. The palm of the bed cradled her into a long, deep sleep without dreams or interruptions.

⊷⊰◉⊱⊷

Morning shone above the buildings and through the window coverings that Darby had forgotten to close. She awoke refreshed but wary about the day ahead—the day she'd meet another man who would most likely not believe her story. But Saturday lifted sunshine above the mountains onto a freshly cleaned city, a sign of better things, she hoped.

She pulled on a cream-colored wool sweater before leaving the hotel. Once outside, she discovered that Salzburg awakened early on the weekend. A family in traditional Austrian attire pedaled past on squeaky bikes as she wandered the damp streets. An intense blue sky grew brighter as the sun awakened behind the mountain fortress. The sunrise brought contrasts of light that caught her photographic eye. Darby saw a picture in a woman carrying a bundle that smelled of warm rolls into a hotel, and another in a man reclining on a bench with a plume of cigarette smoke rising in the morning air. But her Nikki had been left in the room once again.

She continued to explore Salzburg's streets with her cheeks stinging in the morning chill and hands rubbed together from time to time. Around a corner, Darby was certain she'd stepped back in time. An open market stretched through a narrow *platz* beyond the stone archway of a building. People carried baskets and bags while waiting in lines before vendors who sold baguettes and rolls, meats and cheeses, arts and crafts, and giant pretzels in barrels. The only evidence of the twenty-first century, besides a few people in modern clothing, was a soda vendor selling Coca-Cola— America comes to Austria.

Instead of returning to the hotel for breakfast, Darby waited in a line and bought a warm, round roll from a vendor. She walked away feeling proud of herself. She'd said the greeting, "*Grüß Gott,*" bought the food, and left with a "*Danke*" and "*Auf Wiedersehen*" like any resident of the city.

After checking her watch, she followed the signs toward the university building. A whistling song nearly slipped to her lips, but she caught it with a smile. Pigeons flew from the shoulders of Mozart's violin, fluttering into the friendly sky, as she walked past.

The lights were out when Darby pushed open the door to the university building. Her walking boots echoed loudly on the marble floor as she tried to walk lightly up to the second story. The entire building seemed deserted as she squinted at room numbers. She turned a corner and noticed a doorway with light shining from within. Darby hesitated. Was she prepared for another rejection? If Brant did not believe her, why would this man?

She slowed her steps and heard the scrape of chair wheels on the tile floor.

"Is that Darby Evans?" A head poked from the doorway.

"Yes."

"Oh, so sorry I forgot to turn lights on for you. We are the only ones here. Come on in."

Professor Peter Voss met her with hand outstretched. He was younger than she had expected. A man in his early fifties, he was handsome and smiled easily. Darby instantly felt at ease in his presence—not at all like some of the professors she remembered from college who seemed to enjoy a self-proclaimed sense of power.

"Welcome. I am happy to meet you. This is my humble and not always so organized office."

Initially, the room appeared like any history professor's office at any university: stacks of papers around the desk, a couch, and bookshelves bursting from two walls. But small objects gave remarkable uniqueness—an odd sculpture that resembled hands reaching upward sat on the corner of his desk, a bright finger painting on a bulletin board, and a framed yellowing newspaper on the only bare wall with a headline reading: GERMANY QUITS. Darby walked closer to see the American paper announcing the end of the war. The professor chuckled as she noticed a box of toys and a child's easel behind the door.

"They are my daughter's, I promise. Sara enjoys coming to the university when my wife has to work weekends. But I will admit, I sometimes find myself playing with the Slinky—what a great invention. Please do not run from the office, thinking I am a crazy professor."

Darby laughed. "I've been known to enjoy a Slinky myself."

"Then we will get along just fine. Here, have a seat." His smile invited while his eyes sought hers curiously. Darby instantly perceived something about Professor Voss. He was one of those people who found everything fascinating because everything had something to teach. While Darby's mind looked for photographs, this man's sought knowledge.

The professor motioned toward a vinyl chair. She sat down, noticing how the window framed the fortress on Mönchsberg. "Great view you have."

"Ah, yes. Between the Slinky and my wonderful window view, I should be inspired toward great things—at least that is what you would think." Professor Voss chuckled, showing laugh lines around his hazel eyes.

"Sometimes great things can distract instead of inspire."

Now he grinned. "Yes, we will get along just fine. Now, tell me a little about yourself before we get started."

"Well, there isn't a lot to tell."

"Oh, come now. Do not be humble."

Darby laughed. "Believe me, I'm not. But let's see . . . I'm a photographer, and I live in California. I don't have a cat, dog, or children—not that I include children in with the others."

"Oh, but at times you can," the professor said with the grin that came easily to his lips. He sat in the chair behind the desk. "Go on."

"I'm pretty much a typical person—nothing extraordinary.

No Pulitzers for photography, but I take pictures at the studio I co-own."

"That sounds interesting."

"It can be. I much prefer my occasional work outdoors. I go on expeditions with groups—hiking clubs, mountaineers, things like that, to get in-action photos. But I'm just establishing myself in that area. Now tell me about yourself."

"Nothing as exciting as that, I must say. I am an indoor man most of the time. I teach several history courses here at the university and sometimes teach at conferences in other countries. I am married and have an eight-year-old daughter, so my traveling is not exciting as it once was. I miss home when I am gone." Professor Voss rubbed his chin. "Now on the telephone, you said your grandmother was from Austria and you were searching for information about her."

Darby took in a breath. *Here we go.* "Actually, my main focus is for information about my grandmother's best friend."

"If you are searching for people, Brant could give you the names and telephone numbers of several organizations, or he could possibly help you himself. Why did he direct you toward me?"

"Brant is looking for information about my grandmother's best friend, Tatianna Hoffman. But . . ." Darby hesitated. "But Brant isn't giving me help in the area of my grandmother because he doesn't believe she was the person she claimed to be."

"What do you mean?"

Darby focused her eyes downward, toward the desk. "Brant believes my grandmother was attempting to impersonate someone else to claim a family inheritance."

"Really?" Darby saw immediate suspicion in the professor's eyes. "And how does this connect with your search for . . . did you say, your grandmother's best friend?" The professor extracted a pen and pad of paper from inside the desk. "Let us have some names also."

"My grandmother, Celia Lange Müller, wrote to Brant before she died, asking for information about her family inheritance. He wrote back claiming she was an imposter—I have that letter if you want to see it."

"Perhaps. First continue."

"I'll start from the beginning."

"That is always the best place." His open expression encouraged her to continue.

"My grandmother began searching for her family inheritance in the last few years, after she saw the Swiss banks opening and artwork being returned to the original owners. I never believed in the existence of a family inheritance in the first place, though I wondered about it when I saw my grandmother's determination. But I lived several hours away and my photography kept me busy, so I never helped or found any real facts. Those are lousy excuses, I know, especially when she found out she had cancer and . . . well, I'm getting off the subject."

"That is fine."

"My grandmother was diagnosed with cancer, and it had progressed too far to save her. For a long time, it seemed she didn't have it because her energy didn't lag. During that time, she wrote to many organizations looking for information. Last summer, she wrote to Brant, and that's when he answered the letter."

"Why did Brant not believe her claim?"

"He says he researched and found the real Celia Lange Müller with records of her death at Mauthausen Concentration Camp."

"But you do not believe him."

"I don't believe the records."

"So you are searching for the inheritance and the best friend?"

"I'm searching for the best friend. Confusing, I know. I only contacted Brant because of his letter to my grandmother. I hoped he'd perhaps give me some lead into finding Tatianna, the best friend. As of now, I'm not interested in the family inheritance like my grandmother was. Perhaps I will be later—but at this point, my main objective is to find Tatianna."

"Why?"

"Before my grandmother's death, she asked that I give Tatianna her name."

"You give Tatianna her name?" The professor set his pen down. "What does that mean?"

"I'm not sure, but that was my grandmother's dying request. She didn't mention that I pursue the inheritance, simply that I give Tatianna her name. Since I don't know how to do that, or what that entails, I'm first attempting to find Tatianna or some evidence of her. Then I'll go from there."

"So Tatianna is the key to everything."

"Yes. If I can trace her, then perhaps I can figure out what my grandmother meant. But I've wondered if Tatianna may actually be in the United States."

"Why would you think that?"

Darby opened her black bag and brought out her folders. She set one folder on the desk. "I hesitate to show you this, for it's actually evidence against my grandmother. After seeing this, my only true defense is that I have faith in her. She was a woman of her word and believed strongly in God, truth, honesty, and morality."

The professor didn't respond, but opened the folder and riffled through the documents. "These are United States immigration papers and an Austrian passport from 1939. Where did you get these items?"

"I found them in my grandmother's safe."

"Did you find your grandmother's immigration papers and passport?"

"No."

"These are Tatianna Hoffman's."

"Yes, I know."

"Yet you do not believe your grandmother was Tatianna Hoffman?"

"No."

"Why?"

"Because I believed her. She told me who she was. Her last letter to me was signed with her full name. I know it sounds unbelievable, but there has to be another explanation. Why would Celia ask me to give Tatianna her name, if she was Tatianna?"

"Did you show these papers to Brant?"

"No, because they would only confirm his belief. And he was very unwilling to discuss any possibility that Celia Müller was alive—he was very adamant."

Professor Voss strummed his pen on the paper. "Brant's response is not surprising. He encounters many attempts at fraud. We have been friends for many years, though we see each other only a few times a year. But only a month or so ago, some clients he had invested a lot of time and faith in were discovered to be frauds. Brant believed the story and risked his reputation by pushing the claim. Then the entire case fell apart. I have not spoken with Brant since it occurred, but I am sure it has been devastating. Brant is a fine man who gives himself completely to his work. So do not take his suspicions personally. You learn to be careful once you have been burned."

"That better explains his attitude, but . . . ."

"But it does not help you much." The professor nodded.

"That sounds selfish, I know."

"It is natural. But perhaps I can help."

"You're still willing to help even after what I told you?"

"If she was Tatianna Hoffman and not Celia Müller, we will find that out. I have nothing to lose here. An historical mystery is always of interest to me, and this one is intriguing."

Darby smiled and sighed in one breath. "Thank you."

"First, tell me what you know about your family. Then let us try to re-create it all."

Professor Voss wrote as she spoke, sometimes looking at papers she handed him. He'd circle one note, then cross out another. After an hour, he sighed and looked at the mess of notes on several pieces of paper.

"Let us go over what we do know." He turned the papers around. The scribbles made little sense until he spoke and pointed to diagrams and connecting lines. "Here is Gunther and Celia who are married, and Celia is expecting a child. Celia and Tatianna are friends. Do you know if Tatianna was married?"

"I don't know anything except her last name and that she was my grandmother's friend."

"Then we will keep Tatianna alone here." He pointed with the pen.

"Most of your grandmother's family were sent to the camps?"

"Her mother died when she was young, and one brother left for America before my grandmother was born. Her father, aunt, and younger brother were sent to concentration camps."

The professor drew another circle, connecting a dotted line to Celia. "Why has the escaped uncle not tried to locate the family inheritance?"

"I don't know. My Uncle Marc has never mentioned it in my presence. I'll ask when I see him over the holidays."

"Your great-uncle cannot help us prove your grandmother's identity if he left the country before she was born."

"Right."

"Why did he leave Austria?"

"I don't know that either. He must have left when he was very young, because he doesn't seem much older than my grandmother was. I don't even know if he went with family members or not, but it must have been twenty years before the war."

"I am assuming the family was Jewish."

"My grandmother's mother was an Austrian Jew."

"That was a difficult time for mixed marriages." The professor scratched his chin in thought. "Here is what I imagine. The Langes have this valuable inheritance." He picked up the information on the coins. "Two Celtic coins from Hallstatt. I wonder why they were not put in the Celtic museum in Hallstatt instead of made to be part of a family heirloom?"

"I didn't even know the Celts had coins, Professor."

"That is not my area of study either. But Lange. That sounds familiar. I will do some checking." He scribbled on the paper and picked up the other papers. "Then, this other item. A brooch—wait a minute, what is this? Could this be possible? The brooch was a gift from Sissi?"

"Who?"

"Empress Elizabeth, called *Sissi*, is probably the best-known Austrian empress, or Austrian woman, in our history. You must have seen pictures of her in the storefronts."

"I think I did see some candy with a princess or queen on it."

"Probably Sissi. She was an amazing woman, deserving of the popularity she continues to have over a hundred years after her death. There have been several movies and plays about her. She would be like . . . whom could I compare her to? Most often Sissi and Princess Diana of Wales have been compared because both were great beauties, lived healthy and active lifestyles, were strong and determined women, though rebellious and uncomfortable with royal traditions, and both experienced unfortunate deaths. It is quite astounding to consider that this heirloom could have been hers. But you know, I believe I heard a rumor of such a story—that must be why Lange sounds familiar to me."

"How did Elizabeth die?"

"She was stabbed in 1898 by a young anarchist beside a Swiss lake, though the man actually planned to kill another dignitary."

"I don't remember much about the story my grandmother told me. She said a great queen gave it to her grandfather when he helped her after a riding accident."

"Yes, let me translate this paper for you. It was written by Herbert Lange in 1887 and must have been handed down by family members since that time. Herbert was visiting Bad Ischl and, while on a walk, he claims to have seen Empress Sissi fall from her horse. He helped her up and caught the horse for her. He says she asked him to promise not to tell anyone about the fall."

Professor Voss stood up with the paper in hand. "This is plausible, for Sissi was an avid rider even as she aged. She was an excellent athlete in a time when women rarely did such things. This paper says that Sissi asked Herbert not to tell anyone she had fallen, because Emperor Franz Joseph did not want her riding if she continued to fall. A few months later, Sissi invited Herbert and his wife to the Kaiservilla in Bad Ischl, where she presented them with her personal emerald brooch for keeping her secret and for his chivalrous help. Herbert and his wife never told anyone until after Sissi was murdered eleven years later."

The professor whistled in awe. "You know, I am certain I have heard something of this story, which I assumed was only a legend. If I remember correctly, Herbert Lange claimed the heirloom after Sissi's death, but most people did not believe the authenticity. Supposedly, and this paper concurs with what I have heard, Emperor Franz Joseph himself gave a written document confirming to the family that the brooch did belong to his wife. He gave authenticity to the story that the brooch was given to the family, evidently the Lange family, as a gift. He wrote this paper after Sissi's death when Herbert

Lange claimed the story. But I do not see a copy of the letter from the emperor here."

"I haven't found it."

"Then the entire story and Franz Joseph's letter could all be legend, perhaps the existence of the brooch also."

"My grandmother said she saw it when she was a child."

"Interesting. And why would your grandmother try to search for the brooch if she did not believe it existed? I believe it could all be true. This record, written in 1887 and amended in 1900 after Sissi's death, appears accurate. And I am certain I have heard the same story, though I must go back and discover from where."

Darby sighed and rubbed her eyes. "We're getting more rabbit trails than facts."

"Rabbit trails?"

"More questions."

"Yes. But, Darby, you do not realize the magnitude of this story. The story is only a hundred years old, which is fairly young for European history. We do not know whether the legend really involves your family or if the brooch actually was a gift from Empress Sissi. If it is true, this piece would be extremely valuable. Anything associated with Sissi is worth a lot, but especially jewelry from her collection and given as a gift. Something like this, even as a rumor, would have been fascinating to the Nazis, or to anyone seeking wealth. And there was probably a lot more information sixty years ago. We now have a war to lose any evidence, including your family. But this is amazing—you could be the rightful heir. Or perhaps your uncle would be. My advice, either way, is not to spread this information around. Even today, the story could spawn a media frenzy or treasure hunt crusade, or even worse, possible danger. These coins and especially the brooch could be priceless if found today. It is possible that your family was sent to their death because of it, and we know there are greedy men and women in every generation."

Darby hadn't considered any danger besides her mother's list of warnings, such as "watch out in train stations." She had considered the story as long ago, and her focus had been on finding Tatianna, not the Lange heirlooms. It also shocked Darby that the story involving an Austrian empress, ancient coins, and a mysterious brooch could actually be factual. When Grandma Celia would tell the story, Darby always said the appropriate *oohs* and *aahs,* but that was all.

"We are finding pieces of the puzzle. Let us return to your grandmother."

"My weak link."

"Possibly, but there may be other options. If Brant investigated, then we know there was most likely an actual Celia Lange Müller. It would be quite a convenient fact for a Nazi interested in the Lange heirlooms to know that Celia's father married a Jewish woman. After the Anschluß, German law became Austrian law. It was illegal to have biracial marriages. Now his wife was dead, but still this man's children were half Jew. If someone wanted the Lange treasures, here could be a perfect opportunity. So perhaps they take Celia's father into custody. Perhaps Celia and her husband, Gunther Müller, realize that, for her own safety, Celia must leave the country. And here, yes, this could be the answer." Professor Voss looked up from the papers and smiled. "Perhaps Celia uses her friend's papers and escapes the country as Tatianna Hoffman."

Darby stared at the Professor and spoke slowly, "That could be it. That would explain her coming to the United States and having Tatianna's papers. Though it still doesn't explain the birthplace mix-up. Remember that all my grandmother's papers say she was born in Vienna."

"That is to be expected."

"Why?"

"If Tatianna were born in Vienna, and your grandmother came to the United States using those papers, she would be able to change her name, but not her birthplace, right?"

"Probably not. So she always held to the record on any paperwork."

"Also, let us think about this. Countries were very tough on immigrants at that time. Many, many people were trying to flee from Nazi Germany and Austria with the flood increasing as the Nazis conquered most of Europe. It would be difficult enough for a young, pregnant woman to come to America. Even harder if she admitted the papers she held were not her own, and that she was half Jewish. If Celia had said, 'Please let me come to your country, but I am not who my papers say I am,' she most likely would have been denied."

"So she kept the false name of Tatianna until her immigration. Then once in the United States, she changed her name back to Celia Lange Müller, but—"

"She could not change her birthplace," they said together.

"But wouldn't Tatianna need her papers if she remained?"

"Yes, she would need them, but if she was not Jewish, then it would not be too serious. Tatianna could apply for new copies, saying her old ones were lost or stolen. And we know she was not Jewish or it would say so on these papers." The professor held up the worn passport and looked through it again.

Darby sat up in the chair. "If Tatianna is alive, we can discover the truth."

"And that is a possibility and where we need to look next."

"Grandma's comments about Tatianna needing her name— she may have meant returning these papers to her. Grandma told me that I'd find the information in the safe and that's where I found these items."

"That seems to be stretching it a bit, but then your grandmother was dying. She might have wanted you to find Tatianna if they lost contact over the years. Giving the papers back may have been Celia's way of saying thank you for saving her life. That might have been her desire."

"Yes, that would be like Grandma. She'd want to thank Tatianna and show her what her gift produced—another generation of people."

Professor Voss touched his fingertips together, deep in thought. "One life for a new generation of lives. Quite amazing."

"How do we find Tatianna? Do we check phone directories? If she married, her last name would be changed."

"There are several routes available. If Tatianna had been Jewish, we could have looked through the World Jewish Congress—they have done amazing work locating people and connecting families. But there are other organizations, including the International Red Cross, that have lists of displaced persons and refugees."

"And we have Tatianna's birthplace and can contact Vienna for records, perhaps a marriage or death certificate."

"It looks like we have our work cut out for us." The professor glanced at the clock on his desk. "The morning has escaped us, and my wife and daughter will be arriving home from visiting family."

"I didn't realize I'd kept you so long. I'm very sorry." Darby stood up.

"Please, do not apologize. I am enthralled by this story."

Darby began to put the papers in their rightful folders. She placed one into her satchel and noticed the bundle at the bottom.

"The letters."

"Excuse me?"

Darby extracted the yellowed envelopes, wrapped in plastic—treasures she couldn't read. "They were with my grandmother's things, and I noticed one addressed to Tatianna. They're in German, and I didn't have time to find someone who could read them. Perhaps there's information that will help us find Tatianna."

She held them for a moment. They were a part of her grandmother's heart—the part Darby knew nothing about. Slowly she handed them to the professor. He accepted them reverently.

"If you don't mind, you could take them with you and read them."

"You would allow me to take them?"

"Yes."

"Thank you. I will take excellent care." The exchange of letters was a pact of trust. Darby knew Peter Voss understood that also.

"I will make copies of the letters and translate them. My wife would be interested. Do you mind if I share them with her?"

"Not at all. I could use all the help I can get." Darby put her purse on her shoulder. The professor shook her hand.

"Then we will meet again. How about Monday evening?"

"Monday evening would be great."

"Perhaps you can come to dinner. I will discuss it with my wife and call you at your hotel. I have the number."

"Great—I'd love to meet her, and the daughter who draws such beautiful pictures."

Darby's eyes caressed the letters once again. She was putting her complete trust in this man she had just met. Yet she knew he understood and wanted to find the truth. Finally, there was someone on her side.

That night she couldn't sleep. The letters were being read, maybe at that very moment. Darby flipped through the TV channels, looking for a diversion. She found it in a Brad Pitt movie, *Legends of the Fall*, though it was so odd seeing native Americans and rugged Pitt speaking German that the drama turned comical.

The late-night insomnia caught up with her in the morning

as she slept in. Darby hurried down the marble stairs the next morning, sure that breakfast was over. As she hopped to the bottom, she heard her name spoken at the front desk. A man and woman stood at the counter, talking to the clerk.

"Professor Voss?" Darby asked.

The couple turned toward her, and she noticed their worried expressions.

"We almost came last night, but it was late." The professor took a step toward her. "We have translated the letters."

"What's wrong?"

CHAPTER THIRTEEN

Let us go somewhere," Professor Voss suggested, with a nod at the desk clerk who kept looking in their direction.

"We could go into the sitting room or somewhere else?"

"The sitting room will be fine."

Darby led the way into the small, private lounge. She sat on the plaid couch, and Peter Voss and his wife sat across from her.

"Hello." Darby extended her hand to the woman. "I'm Darby Evans, and I assume you are Frau Voss?"

"Forgive me—I behave rudely," Professor Voss said.

"When Peter gets something inside his mind, manners and etiquette go away." The woman was younger than the professor, not much older than Darby, with beautiful olive skin and dark hair. She smiled warmly, then she seemed to remember why they were there. "I am very pleased to meet you, Ms. Evans."

"I am pleased to meet you, though call me Darby, please."

"I am Katrine."

Darby studied Professor Voss, whose restless hands moved as if they balanced an invisible Slinky. "You have me worried. What did you discover? Is it something terrible? Do I need to prepare myself?"

"It is good you are sitting down, as they say." Peter Voss looked at his wife and back to Darby.

"Is it my grandmother? Is Grandma Celia really Tatianna Hoffman?"

"No, I believe in your grandmother."

Darby felt a load lift from her shoulders.

The professor set a folder of papers on the coffee table between them. "The letters confirmed to both of us that your grandmother was Celia Müller. I have written the translations so you can see for yourself. I am going to give them to you in the order we read them."

"Just tell her." Katrine nudged him.

"No, let her read first." Professor Voss handed Darby an envelope and a sheet of paper. The envelope was the letter addressed to Tatianna Hoffman. The paper was the translation. Confused, Darby looked at the Vosses, then read.

22 November 1939

My dearest Tatianna,

I write to a blank page and hope my words and heart will reach you. I know many others will read these words before you, but hope it will eventually find you, my dearest friend. I pray for you with my every breath. You gave me so much, but I hope not too much. The baby kicks furiously, especially at night, and often gets the hiccups. If not for this coming child, I would not want to go on. I fear for you all. How can one be separated from her best friend and her husband? I owe my life and my child's life to you. I believe in my heart that we will all be together again.

There is a beautiful park here in New York and I imagine us here, pushing the baby carriage, and dreaming of all that the world has to offer us. I hope we will grow old together, still reading our books and telling our stories. I pray God will let it be so.

With all my heart,
C. Rachel

Darby didn't speak as she set the paper down. She thought of her grandmother as a young girl with an aching heart, yet clinging to a hope that would never bring happiness. For Darby knew the rest of the story. Grandma was never reunited with her husband or best friend. She never shared her child with either.

"You gave me permission to share the story with Katrine," Professor Voss said. "And we have spent most of the night translating and making our own hypothesis."

"And what do you think of this?" Darby asked, bringing her mind back to the facts within the letter that would help find Tatianna.

"We discovered several things from this letter." Peter Voss bent forward eagerly. "This line here, 'You gave me so much, but I hope not too much.' That indicates what we considered— that perhaps Tatianna gave her passport so Celia could escape, but Celia fears this could cause trouble for her friend. See, 'I hope not too much.' "

"So this evidence gives us hope of finding Tatianna."

"Read the next one and we will discuss that." Professor Voss shifted in his seat.

Katrine put her hand on his arm. "Should she skip to the last? It has the real information."

"No, she should read them as we did. This one your grandmother wrote to her husband, Gunther Müller."

Darby took the paper.

3 April 1940

My Gunther,

    I've waited for months and months now, but you have not come. We have a daughter. I named her Carole Marlene Müller.

    I try not to believe the worst or let myself get down. I had such faith for the longest time, but now my faith wavers. You have not come. I've waited and waited. I see you on the street and call out, but it is not you. I know somewhere on this earth you are moving and breathing, or maybe you aren't and your spirit longs to tell me. Have I not really listened?

    Where do I send this letter? Who is still there? What has happened to our home in Salzburg and my childhood home in Hallstatt? I will write this letter a hundred times, but know I will never send it. It is for your eyes alone. But I will send letters to others, and I will search until I know for certain. I will seek every address I can remember, for I must find you. I do not believe I can endure this life without your love. I do not want to try.

    We need you, Gunther. Carole and I need you. Find us, please, my love.

Forever I give my heart to you,
Celia

Darby stared at the letter and read it again. This was Grandma Celia—separated from her closest friend and husband and in a new, unfamiliar country, sending letters with hopes of finding answers and a link to her life. The girl who wrote these letters had died before Darby was even born. Darby had never had the chance to know her.

She glanced up to concerned expressions. Tears pooled around her eyes as the professor stood and walked to the window. Katrine patted her knee.

"It's like I'm reading the words of a stranger. I had no idea what she felt or how badly she hurt."

"Children never do," Katrine said softly. "I never knew my parents' love until we had our own daughter."

Darby nodded and looked at the last letter. She could see the anticipation in Katrine's eyes but almost didn't want to read it. Darby was surprised to see the letter was written not *by* Grandma Celia, but *to* her instead.

> *6 January 1942*
>
> *Celia,*
>
> *By miracle, I am able to send this letter. I have terrible news. Tatianna is dead. She died at a labor camp near Linz. Also, I am deeply sorry to tell you, Gunther is also killed. He did not make it across the Sudetenland border in time, though I do not have all the details. I am so sorry to give you this news. But please, you must not send any more letters. Others have said you have written them also. Are you so foolish not to know there are eyes everywhere? A letter from America will obviously be read. I have been questioned twice and have only escaped suspicion because of my friendship with a Nazi officer.*
>
> *I understand your desire to find Tatianna and Gunther, but you put us in danger by such foolishness. I ask you not to write me again unless this war someday ends. I have created safety for myself. I may even marry my Nazi friend. I know that must disgust you, but you escaped from this place, and I must look out for myself. If I hear any more actual information about Gunther, I will attempt to write the details. Know that I am sorry to give you such terrible news.*
>
> *—I*

"Who wrote this one?" Darby asked.

"We do not know. There was no signature or name on the envelope, just that 'I'."

Darby set the letter in her lap. "Tatianna is dead."

"Yes." Professor Voss returned to sit across from her.

Sickness rose in Darby's stomach. "I guess that ends our search."

"We will not find answers from Tatianna, yet, in a way, we can," Katrine said, trying to sound hopeful.

"What do you mean?"

"These letters give us good information. We can seek Tatianna's family and look for records of her death. What do you know about Gunther and his family?"

"Very little. Rarely did I hear any information about my grandfather. My mother had searched for him when she was a young woman. She hoped he'd somehow escaped the war, and I think Grandma Celia even had hidden hopes for the search. It was painful for both of them to find nothing. I know his name, and that they met in Hallstatt one summer and fell quickly in love. I believe he was an orphan or adopted. My grandmother once told me her aunt wasn't happy to have someone without a family past."

Professor Voss folded his arms. "That does not provide much information. What kind of a search did your mother conduct for her father?"

"I'm not sure, but I can find out. It looks like I need a list to remember all the questions for my mother."

"Your mother will answer them?"

"I hope."

"There is something else that Katrine noticed and we found very interesting." Professor Voss pointed to a sentence in the last letter. "The writer in this letter says Tatianna was killed in a labor camp. Brant told you that Celia Müller died at Mauthausen Concentration Camp. The camp is located near Linz. During the war, the public was told that people were sent to labor camps, which were often labor death camps. If we know

Celia Müller escaped to America, but Tatianna Hoffman died in a labor camp, then . . ."

"Tatianna Hoffman died with the name Celia Müller." Darby said the words, but it took a moment for them to fully reach her mind. Could it be? "The letter said that Tatianna died in a camp near Linz. That must be it! That must be what my grandmother meant. She knew from this letter that Tatianna had died and perhaps she knew Tatianna was thought to be her. So that's what she meant about giving Tatianna her name back."

"Yes, yes," Professor Voss said, sitting beside his wife again. "Either Tatianna gave Celia the papers and then, because she had none to prove who she was, she was arrested as Celia, or perhaps they switched papers."

"It makes perfect sense." Darby stared upward, her eyes trailing the coffered ceiling. Relief pulsed through her—finally she knew what her grandmother's allusive words meant. Yet at the same time Darby felt sorrow for a woman she didn't know, a woman who had not only saved her grandmother, but provided Darby's life as well. And still there was the question: how could she give Tatianna her name back if the woman was dead?

"Thank you for coming so quickly," Darby said.

"We knew you would want to know. I am curious about the writer of the last letter."

Darby picked up the paper. "Yes, it would help to know who it was. Obviously, a woman."

"Your grandmother was never reunited with anyone from Austria?"

"Not that I'm aware of. I'll check with my Uncle Marc about that one." Darby looked at the three letters. "I wish there was more actual information in the letters. Names, places, exact events."

"Understand that your grandmother knew every word

would be looked at and could possibly be endangering someone's life. She had to write with very limited information."

"There are still many unanswered questions, but we know
so much more now." Darby's mind was racing over the information.

"We will do a bit of investigating of our own, right, Katrine?
Perhaps we can find some information about the Lange inheritance, if you would like, of course."

"Yes, we want to help very much," Katrine said. "I can do
some Internet research while Peter looks through the university library. Are you staying in Salzburg?"

"Actually, I plan to go to Hallstatt in the morning. Will I be
able to look at birth certificates and things like that?"

"Try the administration office in Hallstatt," Peter said. "I
wonder how accessible the information will be since you are
an American with no proof yet about your grandmother. And
then there is the language barrier. I have classes tomorrow and
a conference to prepare for, but—"

"Professor Voss—"

"You must call me Peter, please."

"Peter, then. I can take this trip myself. I brought along a
handy German phrase book that I need to try out anyway.
You have helped so much and I know you both have your
own work. Thank you, both of you. I feel much stronger
simply knowing the two of you believe my story."

"We are on your side, yes," Katrine said. "I feel we are
already friends."

Darby looked at her beaming brown eyes and shy smile and
knew she did have a friend, not thousands of miles away, but
sitting a few feet from her.

"Call if you need help, with anything." They shook hands.

"Thank you, both."

Darby held the letters and translations to her chest as she
watched the couple leave the hotel. The answers were close;

she could feel it. She'd leave in the morning for Hallstatt, then Mauthausen Concentration Camp. Were the answers simply waiting to be found?

CHAPTER FOURTEEN

The highway was a ribbon twisting gently through sharp peaked mountains that sprouted straight from the valley floor. Darby had never seen such a beautiful place. It reminded her of northwestern Montana, where her close friend had moved after college. Darby had flown up to Columbia Falls for Tristie's wedding and found herself struggling to attend the indoor wedding obligations of bridal showers and rehearsals while feeling the lure of green, rolling valleys beneath the jagged mountain tops of Glacier National Park. The Salzkammergut Lake District of Austria looked similar, but as if the single Flathead Valley had magnified and multiplied into many mountains and valleys in every direction, growing quaint European villages on their edges. What her eyes discovered seemed unreal, like a fairy-tale world come alive. The ranges of mountains looked like blue giants sleeping in haphazard mounds on carpets of green.

The rent-a-car topped a hill to the sight of a sprawling lake with a tall church tower silhouetted against the deep blue waters. Darby instantly pulled off the road and hopped out of the car. Perhaps it was simply a Hollywood painted backdrop, not really an Austrian village with a lake reflecting sky, clouds, and mountains. Her camera waited inside her car, but Darby again didn't retrieve it. Her breath frosty in the cold air, she clicked shot after shot into heart and soul instead. Bare trees with a handful of clinging autumn foliage framed crystal waters with jagged, whitecapped mountains rising above. The mountainside burned with sienna reds and yellows. Darby knew she could never gather the images into a two-dimensional photograph. Usually, that would pose a challenge and she'd search filters and angles to get the best shot. But as on the rest of this trip thus far, she kept the moment for herself and felt no desire to capture and share it with others. Grandma Celia had been right. Darby did hide behind the lens she manipulated to shape her world. Only in the last month had Darby been unable to keep her life in a tidy framed photograph. Suddenly, all her images were shattered.

Standing before an Austrian lake with nothing left to blind her vision, Darby could almost see God and not fear a world beyond her making. In college, the religion du jour was her belief. She'd moved from Christian to atheist her first year. But out in the wilds of the mountains, she'd found belief in a God again. The wonders and amazing design of the natural world, how every part fit together, were proof of a greater hand. Just as the winds and rain could not carve a da Vinci sculpture, despite a million years trying, so Darby knew the intricate weaving of life and land did not happen by accident. The sight before her was like an outdoor cathedral inhabited by the God of creation. But was it all made by the God of her youth? Was the same God who designed the land she loved available to her as an individual?

A gentle breeze stirred her hair. Days earlier Darby had never seen this land; now it was hers. With an immediate sense of belonging, she knew this. From Salzburg to the Salzkammergut Lake District of mountains, lakes, and villages, Darby had found a home.

⋆⇥◉⇤⋆

The drive from Salzburg to Hallstatt didn't take much over an hour, but at every turn a new lake and fairy-tale village appeared. At the Bad Ischl exit, she glanced ahead to see a town along a crystal river with a backdrop of another range of white-capped mountains. The "Bad" meant "bath," meaning that this was a spa town. This village held the famous summer villa of Emperor Franz Joseph and Empress Elizabeth. Darby determined to return and explore the city where Herbert Lange might have helped the Empress Sissi after her riding fall. The Kaiservilla where Herbert had supposedly received the emerald brooch was the same palace from which Franz Joseph had declared war on Serbia in 1914, commencing World War I. Although Darby was drawn to these facts, today she was going to Hallstatt.

She passed the town of Au, wondering how to pronounce such a name. She tried to practice a few variations aloud until the car rounded a bend and rose to a view of another lake ahead. Hallstattersee—Hallstatt Lake—mirrored in its calm waters the tall peaks that surrounded its shores. A sharp turn pointed one way to Hallstatt, the other to Gosau. As she followed left to Hallstatt, she remembered Brant telling her how he'd spent his summers in Gosau and Hallstatt Lake.

Darby caught sight of a church steeple on the edge of the lake before it disappeared as the road hugged the mountainside and entered a long tunnel. A sign announced *Hallstatt* as the car exited the tunnel, but the town didn't look the same as her first glimpse before the tunnel. Darby slowed and peered back to see little Hallstatt clinging between the mountain she'd driven through and the lake that stretched toward another range of mountains.

She whipped the car around, pausing on the shoulder. If any of the sights of the day appeared unreal, Hallstatt appeared much more so. Wisps of smoke rose from lines of houses and buildings dressed with thick autumn trees and bushes. A light fog danced inches above the black lake, though everything else was crystal clear. A narrow steeple pointed heavenward from the lakeshore and another rounded steeple jutted upward higher on the mountain. Hallstatt, a modest storybook village that could be missed in a blink, had a history dating back to ancient times. Grandma Celia had told Darby how this tiny village that clutched the side of a mountain for centuries had been a mecca of trade during the Celtic age.

Darby opened the door, stepped out, and rested an elbow on top of the car. She stared, finding every detail her grandmother had described in the stories of her childhood. Upward, she could see a tram to the salt mine where Celia's brother had worked. The tram now took tourists straight up a thousand feet to the oldest salt mine in the world, which continued to produce forty-five hundred years later.

She was there, at the setting of evening stories. The place that was interchanged with Snow White's woods and Hansel and Gretel's adventures. Darby had entered imagination and found it as magical as her mind could envision.

Darby finally returned inside the car to search for a place to park. A gate barred the street that took her toward the towering steeple and city center. She turned the car around several times before finding a place, then finally parked, grabbed her brown leather jacket, and left the car.

Seestraße was a paved road that wandered along the lakeside. Darby walked along, feeling the ground was almost holy, not only because of the tiny village's alluring beauty, but at the thought that this was the place where Grandma's stories had been created. Right on these very sidewalks, her grandmother's feet had trod. She'd spent her summers swimming and boating on that lake, climbing the surrounding mountains in all seasons, skiing to the south in the winter, weaving her hopes and dreams, and falling in love with her future husband.

Darby zipped her coat and put her hands in her pockets. The air felt colder beside the deep lake than it had in Salzburg. A man walking his dog nodded as he passed. A gathering of black waterfowl dove near the shore. She looked up the mountain and remembered her grandmother telling her about the houses built on different levels up the steep mountainside. Somewhere, hidden in the trees, were the connecting walkways where Grandma Celia and her friends once played hide-and-seek.

Darby passed a restaurant and several wooden docks, then approached the heart of the town. She wondered about this place that had lived a thousand generations. Darby had always associated the Celts with Ireland. In her guidebook, she'd been surprised to discover the Celts had settled throughout Europe. She was further surprised to discover that this tiny village had a large place in history. An entire epoch of the history of mankind had been named after it during the Iron Age. The British Museum had a wing dedicated to the Hallstatt Age. Though the Celts were the first to find precious salt there and establish a community, they were by far not the last. Salt, the gold of a past era, was later discovered by the conquering Romans.

Darby had read in her brochures how Hallstatt was thronged in its summer warmth by herds of tourists. Thankfully, today she found the streets empty.

She propped her elbows on a cold railing and watched a white ferryboat move slowly across the lake. It had to be the ferry that picked up train passengers from the station on the other side. Darby watched the white *Stefanie* with its bubbling wake, wondering how often her grandmother had done the same.

"Your grandfather drove the ferryboat one summer," Grandma Celia had told her in one of the rare moments she'd mentioned him. "He wanted to be an archaeologist like my father and had come to work a summer in Hallstatt to pay for university and to see the work in the village. I think he also hoped to meet my father, which he did, of course." Her grandmother had smiled like a schoolgirl.

Back and forth, back and forth across the lake—they'd discovered one another. What a wonderful companion her grandmother must have made during those trips.

"My father knew we couldn't get into trouble with me riding the ferry with Gunther. What he didn't know was that it provided the opportunity for us to know each other well in a very short time. All we could do was talk. But when the last ferry took people across, we always managed a little time alone."

Darby perused the waters of her heritage. But, she reminded herself, this journey had not been simply to see Grandmother's hometown. She was seeking answers here. She allowed herself some chilly time on the lakeside road, imagining Grandma Celia taking her hand and showing her sights. Then Darby returned to her mission. She followed the narrow straße as it turned away from the lake and into a gathering of straight-fronted houses and shops, then through a dark roadway between towering buildings and into the village center. The pale buildings of pink, yellow, and blue surrounded the cobblestone square with a tall statue of the Crucifixion in the center. Red and pink geraniums billowed from window boxes and green vines climbed several storefronts, despite the coming winter. Above the buildings a waterfall rumbled down the mountain and disappeared from view.

Darby spotted the Gasthaus Gerringer sign on the corner. She opened the door of the plain stucco building to find the rustic room greeting her with the snap of a warm, crackling fire. The neat breakfast area had fresh flowers on each table, and she noticed a long wooden desk with keys hanging on the wall behind it. Darby felt like she'd intruded into someone's private home without knocking, even though she'd called for reservations. She jingled the bell on the counter and heard footsteps from above. A moment later, a woman appeared on the staircase in front of her.

"Hello! You must be Ms. Evans—the American." Darby was taken aback by the bubbly woman in her late thirties, who shook Darby's hand with enthusiasm.

"Very nice to have you. My name is Sophie Gerringer—please call me Sophie. You are our only guest so far today. Would you like to see your room?"

"I left my car and luggage down the road. I didn't know how to get through the gate."

"I should have told you on telephone. You need resident card, and I give you one. You may park just few buildings down."

"Good. And you live here also?"

"*Ja*—yes. My mother, grandmother, and I live on the first floor and we have our guestrooms upstairs. Of course, breakfast provided for you. Please, let me show your room and make sure it acceptable."

"I'm sure it will be."

"Come," Sophie said, smiling. "Let me show you."

Darby walked beside the woman up the wide, wooden staircase. She noticed a tangle of fishing poles in a corner and snow skis in another as they stepped into a hall. Sophie chattered about the weather all the way up in good English.

"And here we are. Your room."

Darby stopped before entering. It was exactly what she'd envisioned. The hardwood floor creaked beneath her feet as she entered. Red-and-white checkered curtains covered the doorway and windows that looked out toward the lake. The antique bed, soft and inviting, had a fluffy pillow and down comforter folded Austrian style, sideways at the bottom. The hand-carved headboard matched an antique vanity and armoire arranged in the corners. Sophie opened the curtains, then the French door. The balcony hung over a garden area and gave a magnificent view of the lake and mountain on the opposite shore.

"It's perfect. Absolutely perfect." She walked onto the balcony.

Sophie spoke softly. "Come down when you are ready, and I will give you key and parking pass."

"Thank you." Darby listened as Sophie's footsteps echoed away. Again she was alone with the stories of the past, stories linked closely with the answers she sought.

"Well, Grandma, I'm really here," she whispered, looking toward the black lake. But would this place of ancient lives and histories hold the answers she needed?

CHAPTER FIFTEEN

The morning grew warmer as the sun opened its eye over the crest of the mountain. Darby parked the car near the guesthouse but felt too eager for exploration to unload her luggage. She discovered quickly that Hallstatt took Mondays off. Many offices, shops, and restaurants were closed for the day. But those places could wait until tomorrow. Darby wanted to discover the streets and houses. She wondered which house her grandmother had been raised in. Why hadn't she paid better attention to the details when given the chance?

She assumed Brant wanted her to see a grave when he sent her there—a grave that matched the name of her grandmother's grave in California. Darby had discovered that most cemeteries were found beside churches. So toward the church towers she went. The lower church with the tallest spire, the Evangelical church, had no cemetery. She found a road up the mountain and hoped it led to the other church she could see above the lake-level village.

More people were on the streets now, walking dogs, carrying baskets. Darby found a stairway leading from the road. She began to ascend the steep stairs between tiny houses with miniature landscaped yards.

She climbed until her legs ached. Suddenly she wondered why there would be a grave for Tatianna or Celia here. If Tatianna had died at Mauthausen, her body would not be buried here. Darby thought of her grandmother's still and lifeless form. Even though the essence of Grandma Celia no longer remained, that body was still part of her grandmother and not easy to let go of, not easy to put into the ground. But bodies were not items of value for the Nazis—only waste to be disposed of.

She continued up the switchbacked and winding passageways until she reached the Catholic church with its open gate to a cemetery. She'd never seen headstones like the ones in Europe. They were wood or black wrought iron with tall stands holding the nameplates and topped with small, arrow-shaped roofs. While grass covered the cemetery grounds at home, here gravel provided a walkway to the cement-bordered graves. Within the cement rectangles was dark soil with a profusion of colorful flowers planted inside. Darby wandered back and forth, looking at names and dates. Close to a concrete retaining wall, she peered out across the great expanse of sky overlooking the lake. Far below were the parking lot and market square.

Which one would be her grandmother's? Darby wondered. Few of the graves were older than ten or fifteen years. Perhaps she was in the wrong area. The cemetery was in two tiers up the mountain. On the upper tier, Darby heard a noise behind her and saw she was not alone. A woman sat in a small covered area beside a cylinder-shaped building only steps from the graves. Darby walked past, but the woman didn't look up. Was that a cash register on the table beside her?

"Excuse me, *sprechen Sie Englisch?*" Darby asked.

"*Nein.*" The woman shrugged.

"Uh, what—*vas est*—this?" She didn't know if she had French or German in her mixed-up sentence. Darby pointed to the building.

"Twenty schilling."

The woman shrugged again. Darby dug for the coins in her pocket and was handed a brochure. She hesitated as she looked at the photo on the paper and approached the door. Down the thick double doors were squared pictures of leering skulls with crossbones below. She recognized the symbol for Alpha and Omega above the door as she opened it. Darby peered inside and jumped in surprise. Hundreds of hollow eyes stared back. The heavy door closed her inside a window-less crypt. If she ever wanted to avoid shadows, this was not the place to be. The floodlights shining in the cold, dank room made shadows on the walls and especially within the eyes and open jaws of hundreds of human skulls. Three walls had long wooden tables packed with skulls, while beneath were the stacked and organized remains of the skeletons.

Darby read the history with her back close to the exit. She remembered her grandmother telling of the Bein Haus but had forgotten it was in Hallstatt. She'd experienced many night-mares of this place, but the reality felt even more frightening than a nine-year-old child's imagination. This was a place of the dead.

The brochure told how residents had been exhumed from their tiny graveyard after ten to twelve years of peaceful rest. The remains were then bleached in the sun, painted, and placed for the rest of eternity inside the white *karner* bone house.

Darby took a step forward to see the paintings across the skulls. They had each person's name and date painted on the forehead along with vines, flowers, and other adornments. Some even had a snake weaving through an eye socket.

A short gate kept her a few feet away, but Darby leaned close to look at one delicate painting of flowers and vines. The gaping eyes and jagged teeth looked back at her. This had actually been someone, just like herself. Breathing, thinking, with dreams for tomorrow. Now that person, an empty skull, stared at nothing.

Darby felt a mixture of reverence and fear for these people whose once vibrant bodies slowly decayed into dust before the eyes of all who would come and see.

There was laughter outside. The door opened with fresh light and air spilling inside as a chattering German-speaking family pointed and exclaimed before even making it into the crypt. Already the camera was out, with its flash warming. Darby walked out, relieved to be free from the hollow stares as the door closed behind her. It seemed a strange tourist site.

She walked away from the woman with her cash register and the tourists enjoying their show. The gravel crunched beneath her feet as she trailed around the upper cemetery. She didn't find the name of Celia Müller. So why else would Brant tell her to come to the cemetery?

A wooden stairway inclined above the last village house. Darby pulled out the town map and found that the stairway led in a series of switchbacks to the waterfall and onward high above to the salt-mine entrance. Partway up the stairs, she found a wooden bench. Darby gasped at the view. The village, churches, and cemetery were below and she could see for miles across the lake to different mountain peaks, another village to the south, and a small castle on the opposite shore. Darby sat on the bench and gathered the view inside. As yet, Hallstatt hadn't offered any clues, but she felt a change within her, a touch of a deeper peace that she hadn't known in a long time. Her life had once been characterized by horizons, exploration, and tomorrows. Somehow along the way, it was consumed into work. But she'd seen a gentleness in certain people that didn't disappear with busyness—Grandma Celia, for one. And suddenly, Darby knew that was what she wanted most. Instead of her imagined life, she wanted the real thing.

She watched wood smoke rise from chimneys and wisps of fog lift from the silent water like morning spirits greeting the afternoon. Perhaps there was nothing about Tatianna in this place. Perhaps she had come here instead to find some of what her grandmother had possessed. Wasn't this where it must have been born and grown in her? But how could Darby bottle it up and take these feelings with her?

There was a noise she'd heard for some time but only now wondered about. Rhythmic movement—the *scrape, scrape* of rake against a concrete sidewalk—brought her eyes toward an old man raking leaves in his miniature yard at the bottom of the stairs below her. He didn't see her above. His back was hunched with the burden of years, but he pressed on against the wet, autumn scatterings of the night before.

Darby guessed he was older than her grandmother, due to his worn body. She wondered about his life. Had he lived in Hallstatt through the war? Suddenly she saw a story in every person older than seventy. *What were you doing during the war? Were you victim or predator or bystander? Did you save someone? Did you kill someone? What story can you tell?*

How she wished she could ask. Yet how could she approach someone and pose such questions out of the blue? Most likely, the old man didn't even speak English. Head of white, hands beaten by time, eyes turned downward toward his task, he was a mystery to her. He had a story. In ten to fifteen years at the very most, he'd be gone and his story with him. In that time or less, all their stories would be gone. Someone else would rake the leaves.

The sleepy town yawned and stretched below her. Then the sound of a distant chain saw interrupted the silence. No other noise reminded Darby of autumn more than that high-pitched sputter. Lawn mowers were spring, and chain saws were autumn.

Finally she stood and brushed off the back of her pants. Her cheeks stung in the cold air. She had come for a purpose—one other than to find an elusive peace. She might not find any answers here, but she at least had to try.

Darby returned to the village center and found the "I" sign that meant information office.

"*Guten Morgen,*" she said to the woman behind the counter. "I need some information. You speak English?"

"*Ja.* How may I serve you?" The short, full-figured woman examined Darby from behind spectacles. "Do you have a map of the town?"

"Yes, I got one in Salzburg."

"There many tourist sites in the town and in the area. What you looking to do?"

"My grandmother lived here as a child and young woman. I was hoping to find records. Birth and death certificates? Is there an administration office?"

"*Ja.* The municipal offices would be helpful for you. They located here." She pointed on the map with a plump, manicured finger. "Just across from here."

"They are closed today, correct?"

"*Ja.* Tomorrow, they open."

"Do you have any information about Hallstatt during or before World War II?"

"Uh. No, I do not. Perhaps municipal offices help, or museum."

"What about the cemetery? There isn't one for Protestants, only Catholics?"

"Hallstatt has one cemetery for all people. The first level you enter is Catholics' area; the upper level is Protestant."

"What about someone who was Jewish or with Jewish heritage, but she was perhaps Protestant?"

"I do not know. Maybe buried somewhere else or else in Protestant section. I help with tours, not much of history."

"Okay," Darby said. At least she knew there wasn't a cemetery she'd missed.

"There many activities available still in October in Hallstatt. I can arrange reservations for hotels and boating. Or you may go to salt mine."

"Thank you very much. I'll come back if I need anything. *Danke.*"

She turned back to Gasthaus Gerringer to unload her luggage and settle in.

For a second, she heard the *scrape, scrape* of the rake that had followed her down the mountain. It reminded her to stay focused. Some stories would fade away if not captured in time.

＊━━━◯━━━＊

Darby carried her luggage into the dark dining area. The walls were cozy with cedar siding, and antlers hung above the fireplace. Sophie Gerringer appeared from a hallway around a corner.

"Are you enjoying our village? This first time, *ja?*" Sophie smiled as she stepped behind the front desk. Darby liked the sparkle of blue in the woman's eyes. Her dark hair was in a wild, full style that framed her clear skin.

"Yes, this is my first time, but my family is from here."

"Your family from Hallstatt?" Sophie Gerringer looked at her in surprise. "This like a pilgrimage for you to learn more about them?"

"Yes," Darby said in thought. "In a way it is."

"I live here only for last three year. My grandmother live in Hallstatt since she was a child. She maybe knew your family."

"And your grandmother lives here, right now?"

"*Ja.*"

"Could I ask her about my family?"

"Oh." Sophie stopped. "I not know. She is my grandmother but do not like foreigners much, especially not like Americans. This was American Occupation after war, you know? Maybe my mother could help instead?"

"I'd like to talk to either of them. Do you know why your grandmother doesn't like Americans?"

"She not tell us. I do not ask. But we take her to city for summers when many tourist here. She not nice to American or British tourist."

"My grandmother was eighty when she died, just last month."

"My grandmother age eighty-four. *Ja,* she must have known your grandmother and family."

Darby heard footsteps from a room down the hall. A woman walked out, but she wasn't old enough to be the grandmother.

"This my mother," Sophie said, introducing Darby. The woman gave a smile that matched her daughter's. She wore an Austrian-style apron, and her hair was neatly pulled into a bun. "Darby's grandmother lived in Hallstatt same time as Grandmother."

"Really?" the woman said with interest.

"She want to meet her."

The smile disappeared. As the two talked in German, Darby's heart raced. This woman would know Grandma Celia, even Tatianna and Gunther perhaps.

"You know about Hallstatt during the war?" Sophie asked after the volley of chatter.

"No, nothing."

"Hallstatt was about 90 percent Nazi. You see, it was a political party and gave good economics here. People had jobs. That what people in small village most concerned about—they must feed their families. They not know of Auschwitz and other camps. They have work after hard times. So they be

Nazis. My grandfather was Nazi—my mother not know if we should say that to you."

"My grandmother was half Jew."

Both women stared at her, their eyes large.

"My grandmother had family die in camps, but she escaped to America."

The two Austrians seemed embarrassed by their family past. But Darby at once felt old judgments vanish by an internal mirror that reflected her own life. Her political concerns in democratic America were over the economic growth in her own country. She didn't care what happened in Washington unless it involved taxes, small business interests, or the national, state, and local economy. "I can understand people joining a political party for economics. And I'd still like to talk to your grandmother if I could. She may know what happened to my grandmother's friend, whom I'm searching for."

The mother and daughter again conversed in German.

"I will ask her, but must translate if she say yes. She refuse to learn English. But remember I tell you about her and that she not like outsiders."

Darby listened to every creak in the wooden floor after Sophie and her mother left, expecting them to return from somewhere down the hall. After fifteen minutes, she heard a door open and footsteps. If she claimed to be Celia's granddaughter, would she receive a similar response to Brant's? Would this woman also believe Celia had died in the war? If she did, she'd probably not believe Darby or give any information.

"She will see you," Sophie said as they returned. "But she not happy. Are you certain?"

"Yes."

Darby followed Sophie down the hall. How could this old woman be that bad? As soon as she walked into the room, Darby knew. Grandmother Gerringer sat in a chair by the window with a scowl carved like marble into her face. Darby wondered if a smile had ever broken through the frown lines. The older woman sized her up in a glance and *hmmped* with disdainful satisfaction. *Yes, my perception of an American woman is correct,* she seemed to say. For the first time in her life, Darby faced a tiny glimpse of what a minority felt against the eyes of a racist. But her race wasn't in question—only her homeland.

"*Guten Morgen,*" Darby said softly, as if she were a schoolgirl sent to the principal's office. "*Danke* for speaking to me."

Sophie translated as they spoke.

"My family is from Hallstatt. The Lange family?"

The old woman *hmmped* again, shaking her head.

"Did you know them?"

Sophie translated Grandmother's answer. "She said, yes, she knew them, but they are all gone now. Said they were part Jewish family."

"Yes. Did she also know a young woman named Tatianna Hoffman?"

"She did," Sophie said.

"Could you tell me about them?"

The woman burst out in a torrent of harsh words.

"She wonder why she tell you anything." Sophie looked at Darby apologetically.

Darby swallowed and continued. "Before my grandmother died, she asked me to seek our family past."

Frau Gerringer responded angrily. Sophie tried to slow her down, speaking with her rapidly. "She is not happy with questions from yesterday. She say that everyone want to know what happened with their family after the war. Too much time passed for it now."

"Tell her that I have been raised as an American, but now I want to learn more about being Austrian."

"She say you still American, not Austrian."

"I am American and Austrian and others."

The old woman spoke only to Sophie, then turned her face away.

"I am sorry. She will not talk any longer to you." Sophie shook her head. "Please wait for me outside, and I will speak with her alone."

Darby told the grandmother thank you and left. She wandered the hallway that connected bedrooms and a private kitchen and living room, eventually making her way to the garden in the backyard. Wet leaves stuck to the walkway as she found a bench in the sun. It felt like the longest time before Sophie found her.

"She is sleeping now. I again must apologize for her. My grandmother is a very good woman, but the past is not good for her. She not want to talk to you, but this she told me. The Lange father, your great-grandfather, digged for ruins here."

"Yes, he was an archaeologist."

"And then, the girl, Celia, your grandmother, she was age of my grandmother, but a little younger. They went to the school here and at Bad Goisern—you go to grades one to eight here, then to the larger school in Bad Goisern or Bad Ischl. Our grandmothers were not good friends, but she say your grand-mother was younger and had friend for many years."

"Tatianna Hoffman."

"*Ja,* that her. Grandma Gerringer say that Celia married a young Austrian boy, not Jewish. She say the girl and young man married and moved away—she thought Salzburg or Vienna. The friend, too, go away to school for her violin in Salzburg at the Mozarteum."

"Tatianna was a violinist?"

"That what my grandmother say."

"And what about the family?"

"Gone—before the war. She say all family left before Anschluß—when Hitler came to Austria."

"And does she know what happened to Tatianna Hoffman and her family?"

"All gone, she say. Tatianna have only mother; her father die long before in salt mine. That all she told me."

"I wish she would talk to me, but I don't want to upset her. Thank you for your help, Sophie."

"I hope you find what you seek," Sophie said earnestly.

Darby looked at the woman who seemed to understand her struggle. "I hope so too."

⊶══◉══⊷

The next morning, Darby watched the figure skim across Hallstattersee in his black boat. It looked like the head of the Loch Ness monster with its smooth wake trailing behind. She rested against the balcony railing, fascinated, as if this same man had been there for a thousand years, pushing gently through the water, dropping his net in search of his morning meal.

Darby found herself ready for breakfast and decided on the way down the wooden stairway that she could live in this village for the rest of her life. But first, she must answer the questions that would not let her make serious plans for a future.

She carried down a thick paperback, *Hitler's Austria,* that she'd brought from home, though she had yet to crack its cover. Sophie brought coffee and a morning greeting as Darby set the book down along with a plate of food. She was about to bite into a warm roll when a voice interrupted. Grandmother Gerringer sat in a dark corner. Her German was decidedly unfriendly.

"I'm sorry, I don't speak German. No *sprechen Deutsche.*"

The woman continued in a low voice, shaking her head with contempt.

Sophie reentered the room with a plate of sliced tomatoes and almost dropped it when she heard Grandma Gerringer. She turned quickly and spoke to her in German. But the old woman wouldn't be quieted.

"What is she saying?" Darby asked Sophie.

"Forgive us. I will take her to her room."

"No, I want to know what she's saying." Darby stood and entered the dark corner, sitting across from Grandma Gerringer. "Tell me."

"No, she offends you."

"I want to know, Sophie."

"She is an old woman and does not mean her words." Sophie set the plate down and hurried to the table.

"I think by her tone she does. Please."

Sophie sat at the table and covered her grandmother's hand with her own. She spoke to the older woman, whose words quickly flowed back. Sophie hesitated; Darby waited. "She say you are like all other Americans."

"Why?"

"She say Americans are arrogant. They come to foreign soil and demand answers when they not understand what they asking. She say, 'What would you do?'"

"What would I do?"

"Yes." Sophie translated as the old woman spoke. "She say you live in your home with only few Jews here. One is your neighbor, someone you know your whole life. We say we are Nazi for work and better Austria, then someone write and ask about Jews in village. We write and say yes, a few, but this is a good friend in Linz, and we think nothing of it. Later, another letter come and say all Jews must go to Linz. My husband know what happened and Jewish neighbor is his friend. He want to help, but I do not. We have own family to protect. Own family is first responsibility. It is not your own life you risk—it is your children. It is your elderly grandparents who live with you. Would you put them in danger, place them in death's grasp to save your neighbor?"

By the way Sophie was responding to her grandmother, Darby knew Sophie was hearing this for the first time.

"She say that none of us can understand. We only hear stories in books today. But she lived that time. One friend in Linz she knew hid Jewish children. Her old grandfather and grandmother were beaten with a club until dead. The rest of the family sent away and never return. She say there was no choice. It was suicide."

The old woman continued. "She ask you what you would do. What you do now? Do you have beliefs and not follow them? Do you see wrong in your government and say nothing? She say then you too guilty. As guilty as us who sat and did nothing. Do not judge me. I did not kill your family. They were gone by that time. Her neighbor she could not help when they came for him. She had to turn away or kill her family. Would you have done anything different?"

Frau Gerringer glared, and Sophie looked away. Darby needed an answer but didn't have one. She could see into the old woman's narrowed eyes. For her entire life Darby had had a set idea of what a Nazi was or had been. She'd see skinhead rallies on the nightly news, with their messages of hatred. Grandma Celia's family was murdered by the evil Nazis. Darby didn't want to sympathize or understand or even consider anything different than the image she had. The SS and Gestapo were men of evil and hatred. The Germans and many Austrians were pathetic in their attempts to protect themselves and not help the innocents. Right?

"She's right. I *am* an arrogant American. I have not understood." Darby stopped to face Frau Gerringer, then hurried toward the stairs as Sophie's soft voice told the old woman her words.

Darby rushed to her room and locked the door behind her.

She didn't want to know these things, to feel sympathy or understanding for those who allowed the terrors of the Nazis. Grandmother Gerringer taught her what she didn't expect. In a flash she also realized there were probably many Nazi sympathizers, Nazis themselves, still alive and well in this beautiful land. Of course, how could she be so naïve not to know? Many would not like the sins of the past resurrected—even and especially for the sake of truth. And here Darby had come with her swastika-covered *Hitler's Austria* book under her arm, practically proclaiming an attitude against these people.

I have judged people like that all my life without even knowing it until now. Yet, how different are we today?

The old woman's words frightened her. Darby had opinions and beliefs, but yes, she only did what was convenient for her own life. And did she do anything to help anyone else? She'd barely kept her trust in Grandma Celia when faced with the idea that the woman could be someone else.

Darby fell into bed, dragging a pillow over her head. This was a search for the past, not a digging into her own life. The shadows were stronger in this place, even stronger than the ones who had laughed from her grandmother's deathbed. And they wouldn't be satisfied until they took all of Darby with them.

CHAPTER SIXTEEN

Brant rested his head against his hands. He rubbed his eyes and looked at the door, wishing he could leave his office and never, ever return. Why had his work affected him so profoundly lately? He'd seen a hundred taped interviews of survivors. Yet now they came upon him like demons possessing his soul. He had several reviews to complete for the computerized Holocaust Survivor Library. But after today, Brant considered cutting reviews from his job description. It was taking too much from him, and he had plenty of other work he could do. He'd never enjoyed watching the tapes, though the work was preserving something essential for the future. But now it was all he could do to let the survivors' words enter his mind. He felt like an old, old man who had too much knowledge of the world's terrors.

Or perhaps it was because of Gunther. Because of Gunther's waning health, Brant couldn't simply run to his mentor at every turn or theological challenge. It wasn't that easy anymore.

Brant tried to focus on the computer screen. The man on the

frozen frame had an almost apologetic smile on his face. Brant clicked off the Pause button, determined not to let himself get too wrapped up in this.

David Weisman spoke, looking from the screen right into Brant's eyes.

"My brother, Henri, and I were liberated from Buchenwald. We were the only survivors in our family of eight children. I was sixteen and my brother fourteen. We were still very thin, under one hundred pounds, when we decided to make our way from the refugee camp toward our home. Our hope was to find any relatives or friends in our hometown. We were at a railway station in Poland waiting for our train when two Polish officers approached us. They began to ask us many questions. 'Who are you? Show us your papers.' We were surprised and showed our ID cards. My brother, though younger than me, had more bravery—I had lost mine long before. He said, 'We are Polish and survivors from the camps. We are going to our home.' This did not change their attitude toward us. We were ordered to go with them. My brother said, 'We will miss our train.' The officers did not care. We were naïve, believing there was nothing to fear because Hitler and his evil men had been destroyed. We were only upset to miss our train. But we believed that the world was better and would take care of us after we had endured so much.

"The officers led us away from the crowds and down streets that were dark and deserted. Our suitcases and belongings from the Red Cross quickly tired us, for we were still very weak. My brother asked how long it would take. 'Our train,' he said. 'It won't take long,' one replied.

"We turned a corner and it was a dead-end alley. I heard the sound of a trigger being cocked. We turned

and faced the cold eyes of the officers, the same look I
had seen so often at the camps. They both had guns
pointed at us. One hit my brother on the side of the head,
and the blow knocked him to the ground. 'You stupid
Jews. Why couldn't you die in the camps? Now we have
this job of killing when the job should have been done by
the Germans. I am tired of this work.'

"My brother and I were stunned. After all we'd endured,
how could we not have seen this? I could not move, I
could not cry or run or yell out. It seemed inconceivable
that we'd survived the most horrid of conditions and
endured the worst of man's evils to die in this empty alley.

" 'Please, please, why would you do this to us?' my
brother asked. I noticed the blood running down his face
after he spoke. 'We are Polish like you and have suffered
so much as we know you have. The Nazis were both of
our enemies, not one another. See my blood—it is red
like your own.'

"As they moved us against the wall, my brother continued to plead. I believe he wanted them to feel some human
touch, to see us as people. I could not speak, only accepted
that I was now dead. I was resigned to it. The SS and
Gestapo I escaped, but my own people I would not. But
somehow my brother's pleas made the officers waver. He
spoke about being my younger brother and how we
helped one another live through the war. Perhaps these
officers were brothers, for this seemed to have the greatest effect. I know Henri sensed this, for he continued to
speak about the two of us. He put his arm around me and
pleaded, 'My brother is the only person I have left. We
want to go home, to the place we grew up.'

"At last the officers looked at each other. 'They are
only boys. Not worth our time,' one said. They put their
guns away. Before they left us alone in the darkness, one

turned back and said, 'You better get to your home. There are many like us, and we don't let people like you live. You are the first of many.'

"We were saved by my brother. But the hit to his head had been harder than I thought. We were so weak that we had great difficulty returning to the train station and abandoned our belongings. Our train had left, but we crept onto another. It was very cold that night, and Henri and I warmed each other. But in the morning, Henri was dead.

"This was our welcome home."

Brant clicked off the video. He sat back in his chair with a sigh and noticed evening shadows had moved into the room. He'd been reviewing the stories for hours without thought of time or reality.

A quick knock rapped against his door. "Come in," he said, clearing his throat. The sound of his voice was amplified in the room.

"Mr. Collins, I'm leaving for the night." His secretary peered into the room. "Would you like me to order you something to eat?"

"No, I'm not hungry."

"Are you sure? You didn't have lunch either." Frau Halder looked concerned.

"I'm sure, but thank you. Have a good evening."

"You too," Frau Halder called as she exited.

When Brant's stomach rumbled, he realized he was hungry. But the thought of eating sickened him. He imagined what it would feel like to be actually starving. The faces he'd seen today knew that feeling. They knew true coldness, survival, and death.

Brant heard Frau Halder's laughter outside his closed door. Someone knocked twice, and the door opened before he responded.

"Hey, there's the man. Working late, as usual." Richter glanced over his shoulder. "I'll catch you later, Frau Halder." He walked into Brant's office and shut the door.

"What brings you to Salzburg again?" Brant asked, peeved at the interruption.

"Some business for Grandma. And what are you up to?" Richter rounded his desk and stared at the frozen image of David Weisman on the computer screen. "A survivor, I assume."

"That's right."

"What stories those people have to tell us." Richter shook his head as he sat on the edge of the desk.

Brant didn't respond but resented Richter's flippant attitude.

"I'm finding how important it is to discover the stories from our past. I've had Grandma Ingrid tell me quite a bit—what a time that woman had. It kind of explains why she's the way she is now, don't you think?"

"What do you mean?"

"I always thought of her as a cold, grouchy person. My parents hate her, and if I didn't hate them, perhaps I'd be more on their side. But in the last few years since my parents and I have been noncommunicating and I've gotten to know Ingrid, I've found out she's not so bad. Been through hell, that woman has. Used by the Nazis, doing whatever it took to survive and build a decent home for her boys, then they grow up and don't have any gratitude at all. I feel sorry for the old bat."

Brant thought of Ingrid. She didn't have it as difficult as Richter said. The Nazis took good care of her with parties, nice clothes, and jewelry—until the Allies shoved them out and Ingrid had to revise her story. She certainly hadn't experienced even a taste of what people like David Weisman had endured.

"It's a good thing Ingrid found Gunther," Brant said, closing the files on his computer.

"I don't know. That wasn't exactly a marriage full of love."

"Well, at least she was safe and had security. She never wanted for anything."

"But imagine not feeling love from your own husband. I've seen photos of Ingrid, and she was a good-looking lady. Wonder why Gunther never fell for her . . . what's his story behind it all?"

Although Richter sat relaxed in his chair, behaving as if this were a light conversation, Brant saw red lights flashing.

"You never asked Gunther about his past?" Brant asked.

"Not really. I knew he was married before Ingrid and that he was involved in the underground. But I don't know much more. I'm sure you asked. You always loved to hear those old stories, while I thought they were boring. Until now. Age is taking the playboy out of me, and I'm seeing a wider view of life."

Brant wondered about the validity of that—Richter no longer a playboy? Richter interested in history? The history of Gunther and his first wife in particular? "I don't mean to be rude, but I've got several more hours of work tonight. Did you need something?"

"Not in particular. Thought I'd stop by and see what you were doing—knew you'd be working late, as usual. Hey, we could catch a bite to eat. You could invite that good-looking American to come along." Richter adopted his most charming smile.

"Losing the playboy for history, I see."

Richter laughed. "No, I wouldn't move in on your prospect."

"She's not my prospect. I haven't seen her since the day you met her." Brant thought Darby probably now knew the truth about her grandmother—that she could not be Celia Lange Müller. She would have found the evidence at the cemetery and know. He wondered how she had taken the news, and whether he'd ever see her again.

"What? I expected great reports after I gave you the tickets. Saw a blooming relationship there."

"Not even close. I gave the tickets to Frau Halder."

"Ah, Brant, Brant. You have some lessons to learn. So you missed out on a great opportunity—you haven't even spoken to her since?"

"I don't even know if she's still in Salzburg. I believe she was going down to Hallstatt."

"Too bad. But I'll have to set you up with some women who won't let you go so easily. You need a social life. What's that old American movie say? 'All work and no play makes Johnny, or Brant, a dull boy.' Come on, take a break, live a little. Let's get something to eat. Frau Halder told me you haven't eaten all day."

Brant opened his mouth to decline.

"I insist." Richter picked up Brant's coat from the coat tree and handed it to him. Brant was hungry but wary. Richter liked to portray the best pals image, but Brant still wasn't buying it.

⋅⋗══◎══⋖⋅

"You are doing a great job, Darby," Professor Peter Voss said over the telephone.

"It doesn't feel like it." She closed the phone booth door behind her. Darby had stayed in her room most of the day after her encounter with Frau Gerringer that morning, finally venturing out in the evening to call the professor at the phone booth. Her room at the old house didn't have a phone, so she found one along Seestraße. Only locals and a few cars moved along the cold street after the sun dropped behind the Alps. "From the information I gained from Frau Gerringer, I wondered if perhaps my grandparents moved to Salzburg after they married so my grandfather could attend the university there. Do they have an archaeology department?"

"Actually, the university was not open then. The school closed down for a period of time."

"During the war?"

"Actually, for one hundred and fifty years."

"What?"

"Amazing, yes. We have an interesting history starting in 1617, but then it disbanded in the early 1800s until 1964. So your grandfather would not have attended here."

"Then that's a dead end."

"I will check and see if a Tatianna Hoffman was enrolled at the Mozarteum."

"Yes, I forgot about that. I'm glad you're listening."

"I think you have done excellent work. I am amazed the old woman would confess so much to you. Most people are very closemouthed, even with their own families. There are many adults who would be surprised at the Nazi past they have in their family. After the war, it was not often information passed to the children."

"I haven't talked to any of the Gerringer family since the grandmother gave me a good chewing out about being American and stupid. She probably would never have spoken if I didn't insult her with my swastika-covered book."

"You have a difficult job. You see, the people you wish to speak with lived in a time when America did not abide so abundantly here."

"What do you mean?"

"A colleague of mine has done intensive studies on the Americanization of Europe, particularly Austria, since World War II. You can not imagine how much World War II was a catalyst toward changing Old European culture—much of that due to Coca-Cola, rock and roll, and Hollywood. As you have seen, English is becoming the neutral language in most of Europe. But prior to wars, especially the first World War, Europe was the greatest influence on the world. And the

Austro-Hungarian empire was one of the greatest in Europe.
So the elderly were raised with their parents' pride and patrio-
tism for their great nation. The young people today live very
much like Americans. Yet it is the elderly who will help you in
your quest. Few will know the language. Few will trust you."

"I'm seeing that."

"The older generations feel their traditions are attacked by
conquering Americans—no longer with troops, but with music
and culture. And it is true. Imagine a foreign culture surrounding your children and grandchildren as you cling to the
old ways."

"I can understand a little. In California, people protest
schools that fly both the United States and Mexican flags.
Others complain about the foreign cars on the highways and
the influx of Asian and Hispanic people with Spanish often
spoken more than English in certain counties."

"Imagine turning on the radio and having 80 to 90 percent
of your popular music be German songs, sung in German.
Also the majority of your movies and television shows are
produced by Germans with dubbed-in English. Then two-
thirds of computer software is in German, not English."

"I'm getting the picture. So what do I do?"

"Be sensitive. Respect their beliefs."

Darby thought of how she'd read the Nazi book at the
breakfast table. That wasn't exactly respectful of Austrian feelings.

"It can be difficult for Americans to understand. Austria is
an old place. Your America is a new land. Our heritage has
been war and changing hands. In my parents' generation, this
nation had been taken over, torn apart by differing beliefs,
taken over again by the Allies, who were Soviets, British, and
Americans, and divided among them, then given our freedom
again. America is a land of discovery and settlement that has

never been occupied by anyone other than itself. Unless you are Native American, you can find it hard to understand."

"I've been quite in the dark about all of this," Darby said regretfully.

"You are learning quickly. Are you returning to Salzburg soon?"

"Not for a few days or even a week, though I'm running out of time. There's much to look for—time has become my enemy."

"The secrets are not going anywhere, unless they are in human form. And then, yes, time is our enemy. What is your next move?"

"I may drive to Linz and maybe the concentration camp at Mauthausen. It wouldn't hurt to check records in these places after I look here in Hallstatt."

"Did you remember that I leave for a conference in Dublin in several days?"

"I didn't. How long will you be gone?"

"Until 17 November."

"I return to the States on the sixteenth. Unless I stay longer."

"That is unfortunate. But if you return to your home, I will not stop looking. You have e-mail?"

"Yes, at my office. I'll call or write you."

"Katrine will be coming with me to this conference. I am sorry, but you are back on your own for a while."

"And just when I was getting used to you two."

"I know. I want to tell you—to find the answers you seek, think with an Austrian mind, not an American. You must discover what we are like, what we have endured. War had split our country. Evil triumphed, not for a short time but seemingly for an eternity. We have been hurt because of that, scarred forever."

Darby paused, feeling the impact of his words. "I think that's exactly what my grandmother would have wanted."

⋆⟞◉⟝⋆

Her luggage waited by the door. Darby stood on the balcony and said good-bye to Hallstattersee. As she turned away, she spotted something white upon the dark waters. A large swan floated along the edge with curved neck and pure white feathers glowing in the morning light. She hoped it was a message from above, telling her that everything would work out. The administration office had been helpful, proving that Celia Lange *had* been born in Hallstatt. There were other records that could be found at the church about family members who were either buried there or now the residents of the bone house. But Darby didn't want to know that information. It was time to leave, to seek the next piece in the fragmented puzzle. She was hopeful, for she was finding some pieces, though the puzzle grew larger with every discovery.

Darby hauled her luggage down the stairs and rang the desk bell to check out. Sophie hurried toward her with a large smile on her face.

"I am so happy to see you. My grandmother told me something for you today."

"She did?"

"Yes, she very thoughtful all yesterday and this morning she ask if you here still. When I say yes, she tell me some things."

"What?" Darby didn't know if she wanted to hear any more from the old woman.

"My grandmother saw your grandmother one more time after Anschluß, after the other Jews were gone from village. Your grandmother and Tatianna Hoffman came to Hallstatt. My grandmother not know why she come. Her family was gone and house occupied by different family. My grandmother was married and had a child already, and she did not talk to Celia. But they stay only one night in the village and came by train. But when they leave, a young woman pick them up in her car and they go with her."

"Did your grandmother know the woman?"

"No. This last time she see your grandmother, but she hear that all family went to Mauthausen and not returned."

"That gives me more to wonder about, but tell her I said thank you very much."

"One more thing. She say one man might have information, but not know if he still alive."

"Who is he?"

"He was a boy lived here in Hallstatt. He joined Nazis and was guard at Mauthausen."

Darby grabbed a pen and paper from her purse.

"My grandmother say this man maybe know about Lange people who died there."

"A man who knew Celia and Tatianna and was a guard at Mauthausen."

"His name is Bruno Weiler."

※──◎◎──※

Darby drove from the village south around the lake. Had her grandmother taken the same route so many years ago? While Darby turned back toward Linz in Upper Austria, Celia had turned the opposite way, deeper into the Alps and Tirol region toward Switzerland. But in fleeing her homeland with Tatianna beside her, Celia had made a quick stop at her childhood village. Perhaps she had said good-bye to the place of her innocence, the place of first love.

Darby envisioned the girls fleeing the sleepy village with eyes turned in fear that someone followed. The sound of Nazi boots hid behind every crevice, in every corner. Would they make it out alive? Would they see one another again? Did they have any idea that these were their last moments together?

And who was the other woman? Perhaps the one who had written and told Grandma Celia of Tatianna and Gunther's deaths. Darby also wondered why Gunther had chosen another route to escape—through the Sudetenland, which was now the Czech Republic. A completely different route.

Darby spent the morning driving winding roads through mountains and hidden lakeside villages. Ebensee was a lakeside village that had been a subcamp of Mauthausen. Traunkirchen. Gunskirchen. Traunsee. Darby had heard these names from her grandmother and tried to recall the stories.

By early afternoon, she entered the *Autobahn* highway, expecting masses of cars driving over a hundred miles per hour. Yet, though cars sped along, it felt like a comfortable rate. She was never quite sure how many miles per hour she drove on her way toward the industrial city of Linz with the speedometer in kilometers per hour, not miles. Sophie Gerringer had helped her find a place to stay in Linz and had told her a brief history of Austria's second-largest city. Hitler had spent his childhood in Linz—a fact that surprised her. She hadn't realized the German Führer was a native Austrian. Unlike Mozart mania, however, Hitler was not a claim to fame for the country. Perhaps if he had won the war there would be Adolf candies and delicacies. When Hitler returned to his hometown with his German storm troopers, he already had great visions for Linz: to recreate it as the Jewel of the Danube. He'd hoped to retire here, if permanent retirement hadn't been forced upon him.

Darby followed the directions to the hotel and drove into the parking lot. The rural hotel sat on a green hillside with a view of the famous blue Danube River.

Only a few miles of bends downriver was Mauthausen Concentration Camp and its subcamps Gusen I, II, and III.

Suddenly, as if struck in the face, Darby realized where she was going. Her carefully planned list with its connections and leads included the name of Mauthausen. And not just any concentration camp, but the one that had held and stolen the lives of members of her family, and most likely Tatianna's life also. Number eight on her to-do list had once been a place of hell beyond hell, and for people with her same blood.

KZ Mauthausen. A place that stole tomorrows. Darby would be there tomorrow.

CHAPTER SEVENTEEN

Brant jumped awake. His chest and back were beaded with sweat, and the sheets were damp and twisted beneath him. The screams from the nightmare continued to echo in his ears. He saw the images that tormented his sleep— black figures with children and babies clutched within their grasp. A monotone voice spoke above the carnage.

"My baby had dark hair and brilliant green eyes. He would smile and laugh when he looked at me. As I patted his back and rocked him at bedtime, he patted mine and snuggled close to my chest until sleep overtook him. My baby was torn from my chest by a soldier. They threw him into the air and used him like a clay pigeon. I embraced death to escape insanity. But by another evil, I lived. After the war, I married again and had two more children. But never do I stop hearing my first baby's cry."

Brant tried to shake the story from his mind. But unlike a nightmare his own mind concocted, this was a true story. One of the many he'd witnessed on tape. Brant had always been haunted by the stories, but evermore he was becoming consumed. It seemed his future was to be forever crippled with the sufferings of others. No one understood, except those who survived. Yet Brant did not belong with them either, for he had not lived through it—only witnessed their stories.

How Brant wished to talk to Gunther. How Brant wished things hadn't changed. In other downtimes, the old man had words to help Brant through, allow him to see the value of life and living once again. He tried to resurrect the words, but the sound of Gunther's voice eluded him. He could only hear the cry of children.

Brant kicked the sheets and blankets from his ankles and sat on the floor, the metal sideboard cold against his bare back. The room was more than silent. It was empty—just like his life. Suddenly he couldn't take another day of it.

He turned onto his knees as he'd done when he was a child. "God, help me."

At that instant, Gunther's voice returned from a fold of memory. "Everyone asks how God could allow such a terrible thing." Gunther's voice resounded with spirit in each word. And tonight Brant listened again. "Why does man blame God? For I want to know how *man* could allow such a terrible thing. God gave man dominion over the earth. If we simply can't care for one another or stop evil from breeding and growing—"

"But Gunther, I hear their voices," Brant had said. "I dream about them."

"I've struggled as you are."

"I'm sorry, Gunther. Of course you have. I lost my mother to a disease, not by man. Why should I complain about hearing the sufferings of others? It should make me appreciate my life, not come to you complaining."

"You struggle because you truly care. You don't merely listen; you feel the words and hurts of others. That's a good thing, though more painful for you. It's easier to close your heart to others. But keep it open, Brant, despite how you bleed."

"So where is God in all this—if we can't blame him? You tell me he's active in individual lives. Where was he?"

Gunther had faced him then, kindness in his eyes. "And you want to ask, where is he now?"

"Yes."

"I do not know all the answers. But I know some things from my own life. I know God is quiet at times, but not absent. He hears our cries but allows man's business. He allows man his own course."

"And evil takes over."

"Only the evil that man warrants. That goes for yesterday and today. But still in individual lives and as a collective world, God allows choices. He doesn't want puppets to seek him. He wants man with a free will. Perhaps he is silent so that man's work without his involvement can be seen. I do not know. But because of the choice God allows in man, innocents do become victims. While I don't believe God wants this, he does heal all things and punishes all wrongs."

"I doubt everything. I don't know if I believe God exists."

"I must believe in God because I've known both evil and love. I've tasted evil within myself and by what's been done to me. This evil is alive, breathing, destroying. Yet I also have known the opposite of evil. I lived with an incredible, enduring love and found truth and hope in ashes. The good is often harder to find. Evil is easy. Love is hard. But one leads to death. The other to life."

"How have you survived it all?"

"My faith in Christ. I see what is not in our vision. I hear what few are willing to listen for. I feel what most would say is not there."

"I could never have such a faith."

"Do you believe?"

"I think I do, but my doubt is as great. Sometimes it's too much for me. How can I live with these stories in my head? How do they live?"

"I do not understand how the telephone works."

"What? What are you talking about?"

"I do not understand how the telephone works. A few days ago, I made a call and really took a look at the telephone. I've been told about a huge wire under the ocean or satellites that transmit sound, but still, I cannot fathom how my voice can be spoken and delivered across the world in one moment. Yet I use the telephone regardless. I cannot understand the telephone, or the computer, or a thousand things that are made by man. How can I claim to understand everything about God? Yet can I give up on God because of my ignorance?"

Gunther had put a hand on Brant's shoulder then. "One thing I must say to you. I think of you as my son and implore you. You must live, Brant. Live because you can. Live because others cannot. And in that, live for God."

The words faded away, and Brant was alone again with only past moments. He wanted the old times he'd had with his mentor, when they'd meet for coffee and sit for hours talking. "Who will help me, Gunther?"

A breath of answer entered his thoughts. *Come to me, for I know all the answers.*

Brant felt like Jacob in the Bible wrestling with God. But he finally had reached the end. He could not live as he was, and so he put his trust in the one he did not understand.

As Brant bowed his head, he still heard the stories. But a new strength arose in him that told him to live, to love, to breathe.

✦═◉═✦

The day dawned with glorious greeting. Life breathed in hillsides of green, in clusters of trees adorned with their leaves of many colors, in a windless day of warmth. And Darby was driving to a concentration camp.

She wanted to tell the day to be ugly and sad, that an eternal cloud of stark weather should cover the land south of Linz. The sun should no longer warm the earth; geraniums should no longer bloom in window boxes. But the design of nature with its tearing and healing of seasons didn't mind her desire or her destination.

Darby followed the signs, exited the Autobahn, continued through towns, passing a McDonald's and a gas station. A wide, clean bridge crossed the Danube, reminding Darby of her grandmother singing the words to "The Blue Danube," Austria's unofficial national anthem.

When Darby turned the car toward Mauthausen, a hillside community, a sudden chill prickled down her back. The sign for the village shared the name of its concentration camp.

The KZ Mauthausen sign pointed the way. The road wound upward past houses, a beautiful tree-lined curve, open fields, up and up. The road was a perfect place for a Sunday drive until she reached the top. There it stood—a walled fortress stretching across the horizon. Guard towers with pointed tops, a straight concrete wall surrounding it, and a red chimney silhouetted against a brilliant blue sky.

She maneuvered the vehicle between the white straight lines of a parking space. A few other cars inhabited the paved lot along with a tour bus with advertisements for its other excursions—Danube Tours. Darby shook her head at the irony: *One of its stops took camera-happy tourists to a concentration camp.*

With her arms still on the steering wheel, Darby leaned forward, letting her eyes trace the length of the massive blocked wall with five rows of barbed wire on the top.

It's big. As big as I should expect, but bigger than I actually imagined. Tatianna, are you here? My family, are you waiting?

It was time to go in.

Darby carried her camera bag without the intention of taking photos, but for companionship. She stopped at the iron doorway. The structure towered above with a walled courtyard ahead. She felt small in the shadow of the massive stone walls.

No signs led her now, only blind direction.

I feel alone, Darby thought, though she imagined the cries of thousands who hadn't been alone, only dreamt to someday be.

She paused in the center of the courtyard, surrounded by the barbed wire–topped walls. Her entire life she'd denied that this place was part of her family heritage. She denied it from entering her life or thoughts. Now she was here. An instant thought told her to run, run, run.

"I feel a part of me has died too," she whispered to the shadows watching from every crack and crevasse. "Perhaps that's why I can't find love or peace. Part of me died here also—is that it? Not body or soul, but heritage and past."

Darby stood a moment longer. She heard voices from the parking lot, and a couple entered the silent courtyard. Holding hands and a tour book, they'd come to learn and remember. Wasn't that what this place was for—to help people never forget? The interruption brought her back to the place and her mission.

I'm here for a purpose, she reminded herself. *I've come to search for information, facts, answers. I'm looking for Tatianna, maybe my family too. Information is all I seek; nothing else.*

Darby moved toward the end of the courtyard, where wide concrete stairs led upward. Beside them was a plaque in both German and English. She paused to read while the couple passed.

> In remembrance of the members of the Second
> Armoured Division of the US Army who liberated the
> camps of Mauthausen, Gusen, Ebensee, and others

nearby in Upper Austria in May 1945. Their deeds will never be forgotten.

She climbed the steps and stopped at the top. To her left, monuments stretched away toward what appeared to be a massive gorge, which broke off as if the hillside had been eaten away. Darby assumed it must be the granite quarry with its "Death Walk" stairway. She wondered if any of her family members had died on that stairway. Had they stumbled under the weight of granite slabs as Nazis bashed clubs against their bodies? Had Celia's father, brother, or aunt died this way? Anyone against Nazi policy could have been sent here. What did those faces look like? She didn't know and wasn't sure if she wanted that knowledge even now.

Darby turned away from the memorials and quarry and walked beneath another set of stone archways with buildings beyond. A man in a booth sold tickets, tickets to a concentration camp. She understood the need for payment, since the place needed upkeep and financing. But still it made her shiver—she was paying to see where her family was murdered.

Darby handed the man the schillings and asked for a guide or map.

"Bookstore," came his simple reply. She considered asking for more information, if only she knew German.

Darby entered the main area of the camp, which stretched across the top of the hill. She spotted a bookstore sign beside the structure. When she stepped inside the small room, she saw that several other people were there, perusing books and videos. Darby glanced through the resources, too, picked out a few in hopes of finding more information, and bought a guide. On her exit back into the sunshine, Darby held the door for an elderly woman in a wheelchair. Their eyes locked for a moment. Was that sorrow she saw?

"*Merci*," the woman said as she passed. A French woman.

What's your story? Darby wondered as she watched the frail woman gaze around the little store. Darby wished she could have Grandma Celia with her, or someone to hold her hand and share this experience.

Guidebook in hand, Darby tried to refocus on facts. First, get a general overview of the camp, then look for the information needed.

She glanced from map to buildings and walls. The barbed wire atop the granite wall stretched around the camp on three sides. Another barbed-wire fence, once electrically charged, marked the back. Behind her was the entrance gate, while in front was the camp's main roadway with the roll-call area—where she now stood. Housing or "blocks" lined the left side of the road. At one time these buildings had been the first in several rows of blocks that housed prisoners. Upraised foundations marked where the now-missing blocks had stood. A kitchen unit, laundry building, sick quarters, and brothel—everything the Nazis needed—were in the front. Behind were the inmates from all over Europe—political prisoners, gypsies, criminals, "anti-socials"—with the farthest from the front being the Jewish block. Darby plodded down the long row to the last foundation. A headstone stood in the center with the Star of David and individual rocks covering the top. Darby reached for a stone on the ground and put it on top of the headstone with the others. She paused, feeling the heaviness of the moment, then moved back to the roll-call area.

On a granite wall near the bookstore entrance several plaques caught her eye. This was called "The Wailing Wall." Darby found the irony in the name. The famous "Wailing Wall" in Jerusalem, built next to the last-standing remnant of Solomon's temple, was a place of prayer for Jews. This wailing wall was for tears and death during long hours of torture.

Darby breathed in slowly. What did she feel? Was this even real? She moved on, walking in and out of buildings, looking at photographs and reading the guide. For minutes, she forgot where she was, as if she'd entered a library or museum. The next minute she again heard the deafening silence of a death camp—a scream that yelled, "I was murdered here, right where you stand and hold your guidebook. They murdered us all, and here the world ended."

Darby entered a grassy area surrounded by shorter granite walls. The manicured lawn was covered with stone crosses and headstones with the Star of David. No markings rested above individual bodies, since the entire site was a mass grave. Did Tatianna rest here, her body twisted together with Darby's other family members? Or was she in the ash pile behind the camp, dumped down the hillside slope where grass and flowers and trees now grew?

An aunt who'd rocked Grandma Celia, her daddy who'd wiped tears from her cheeks—somewhere like this they died. People, real people—parents, teachers, lovers, woodworkers, travelers, photographers.

Why had Darby never thought of them? In school, her class had done family trees and reports. Several of her friends were fascinated with their pasts and studied at great length. Darby hadn't had the interest. She did the work required, learned the basics of what had happened, but that was all. History was history and not a place for her to look. You couldn't take a picture of yesterday, only of today.

One of her worst school experiences was when her teacher learned she had family who perished in the Holocaust. He was fascinated and wanted her to do a family study for her final report. "You're a child of Holocaust survivors and victims. Which camps? Were they Jewish?"

She'd never been embarrassed about her Jewish blood until she met a friend's surprised questions.

"You're Jewish?"

"A little, just like I'm Austrian, Danish, Cherokee, and a bunch of other things."

Darby hadn't noticed many racial tensions or prejudice in her small town. She'd never quite understood it and became even more confused when she was the victim.

"Well, I'm glad I don't have Jew in me," the girl said.

"When did I become a Jew?"

But that was only a passing scene in the myriad of high school and college events. Darby buried it and hoped her classmates did also. She had many friends and was involved in student government, French club, the yearbook—as photographer, of course. Yet as she stood in the place where her own flesh and blood had died, she finally wondered and wanted answers. Was it simply self-absorption, or a partial reaction to the unspoken silence within her home about past events? Or had Darby herself somehow resisted, knowing the steps she now took were the requirement for such interest?

She wished she could travel back in time and help the ten thousand individuals in each mass grave. That she could tell them, "Stay alive, stay alive. In sixty more years, you'll see that Mauthausen and all the other camps are only museums. Tours will walk through and point to your grave unless you can keep living." And then make it happen.

After walking the length and width of the camp, Darby entered the museum. Two exhibitions were displayed in the long, narrow building. She sat with several others, watching the Mauthausen film that played every hour with different languages in different rooms. The images and information numbed her as she wondered if one set of those hollow eyes that stared from the black-and-white screen would recognize her as their descendant. Did they point and say, "There's my great-granddaughter. She's come to save us a few decades too late"?

Darby left the dark viewing room for the exhibit "Austrians in the Nazi Concentration Camps of Auschwitz, Buchenwald,

Dachau, Ravensbrück, Sachsenhausen, and the Theresienstadt Ghetto." After that, it was the exhibition on "The Mauthausen Concentration Camp and its Sub-Camps."

All of a sudden Darby wondered not about the victims, but about the men in SS and Gestapo uniforms. Germans, Austrians, farmers, banker's sons, poets, and woodworkers—they were men just like their victims and yet not like them at all. Darby stared at the photographs. Frozen eyes stared back.

Where are you now? Are you burning in some kind of hell? Did you finally see yourself before you died? Or are you still living, still hating, or still hiding? Maybe you there are the old man in Hallstatt raking his leaves. Or maybe instead he's the one you didn't get to kill.

Desperate to find something in their eyes—an evil or darkness, or even a glimpse of shadow—Darby moved closer. But the photographs—what she trusted to capture the moment—failed her. For there was nothing to be found. Nothing to distinguish an SS from Gestapo from soldier from civilian. Nothing to show a higher or lower degree of guilt or hatred. One man waved at her from the back of a truck; a mischievous grin sparkled from his face. In life he could be someone who'd flirt and ask her for a date or throw a football with the neighborhood children. In the photo he sat in the back of a truck brimming with human corpses.

Numbers, statistics, and maps depicted the facts, but the faces in the photographs argued it couldn't be true. They were just men and boys. They couldn't have experimented with that man's life or tortured that poor woman's body. Darby read a quote by a United States colonel, Seibel, about the camp's liberation: "Mauthausen was a reality . . . as was the brutal and inhumane treatment of human beings by human beings."

Examining each photo, she read in her book the English version. When she saw a display titled "Guard file cards," she stopped, remembering the information Sophie Gerringer had given her. She took the paper from her purse and searched the chart.

There. Darby couldn't believe it. There was the name. Bruno Weiler. It was difficult to understand what must have been guard information, and she could not find an English version. But she did find his name and "Hallstatt, OS," meaning he must have been from Hallstatt. There were several dates on the file, including 1940 and 1943. Did that mean he'd been a guard here during that time?

Darby left the museum, wondering what to do next. Should she seek to discover what happened to this man after the war? Bruno Weiler could have seen Tatianna before she died. He may also have seen her other family members. But would he still be alive today?

Once outside, Darby noticed a stairway leading downward. A group moved down it, speaking in hushed tones. If it was an English-speaking group, perhaps the guide could help her. Darby took the steps to the bottom, into an unlit room. The group had moved into the next room, but her feet stood still. There was no need for a guide or tour book to know where she stood. The tiled walls were clean, though the grout had been scrubbed till crumbly. Above her head piping crisscrossed the ceiling and faucets hung, faucets which had never felt water push through the spouts. Darby noticed the thick doors, one behind her, one at the other end. She stood in a gas chamber.

At this realization, her heart began to pound. The doors felt like they were closing. She had to force herself to breathe slowly and deeply. She saw hands clawing the tile walls, children crying, and men and women screaming. Her head said to run, but her feet wouldn't move. Darby wanted to vomit, but not even tears would come. Finally, her feet did move. She went numbly toward the opposite door, only to find a labyrinth of other shower rooms and then the ovens.

She stared into the open mouths of two black ovens. A

bouquet of silk flowers rested on a long, iron basket that pushed corpses into the ovens to turn flesh into ashes. Darby imagined the systematic machine, cooking, removing, cleaning, devouring. One human had lovingly buttoned a young man's sweater and brushed his hair—and someone else had put his body into that oven.

I feel you are still here.

Memorial plaques and photographs covered the oven room's walls. One had several toy cars and a plastic doll on the floor in front of it. Darby read the French words *Enfants morts*. A French community's plaque for their children who died at Mauthausen.

The horror was so intense that she had to look away from the plaques, but she was drawn to the wall of photographs. The smiles and faces of men and women, young and old. It seemed she could take an SS guard's photo upstairs and easily replace it here, for they were all flesh and blood, men and women. Only one had chosen to mutilate his brother, and the other was mutilated.

I have to get myself together. I need to focus on my purpose for coming here.

But Darby couldn't shake the sense of blood beneath her feet. And not just blood from veins alone. But the blood of hope, love, dreams, tomorrow—the blood of life poured into this ground. And that blood was her blood also.

She turned back toward the plaques on the walls and read each memorial in search of names. And there she found it, written in English: *Remembrance of the Lange family. Loved for all eternity.* Darby touched the engraved writing and hurried out.

The roadway moved too slowly beneath her feet. Through the stone archway, an echo chased her quick passage down the wide stairway to the last courtyard on the lower deck, then across the high-walled courtyard and out the iron door. She breathed more deeply but didn't halt her pace. She was free to leave—a simple act not granted to thousands of others.

Darby knew from the horror of this place she would never be the same. She also knew that SS guard Bruno Weiler, who had known her family and been their captor, must be found. Whether he was dead or alive.

CHAPTER EIGHTEEN

Mauthausen stayed with Darby. It followed her like a cloud around a mountain, covering, blocking, shielding rays of light. What she'd left with was an increased determination to find answers, and to find Bruno Weiler. But as days turned into more than a week of searching in Linz and back in Salzburg, Darby's determination wavered. Her newfound love for Austria grew weary as her eyes turned toward documents, museum information, book research. She returned to Salzburg with more untied ends than when she'd left. She didn't return to the Salzburg Cozy Hotel, but instead found a quiet place on a back street in the Old City. Time clicked toward her departure home and she found little success, some due to her language inability, some to lack of knowledge in seeking her answers. How could she find a man sixty years after he was last seen? Her biggest help had been Professor Voss, but he was in Dublin and wouldn't return until after she was due to leave for home.

Darby considered staying longer. She felt so close, but so

close to what? What she'd come for now seemed unclear. Her focus had been to find Tatianna or a way to fulfill her promise to Grandma Celia, but now she wanted more answers than that one.

She wondered about Celia's family, her family, and what their exact fate had been at Mauthausen. Darby also wondered about her grandfather, Gunther Müller. Where had he died in Austria? Was there a grave for him?

Inquiries into the Mauthausen Camp did yield some information. She learned that a woman named Celia Lange Müller, along with a group of other prisoners, had been killed by firing squad on the date of August 11, 1941. Then she'd been put into the ovens.

A few days before going home, Darby called her mother to pose the idea of remaining in Austria. Instead, she found the old life drawing her back. Her business partner, Clarise, had called in hopes that Darby had returned early. Her mother was marking the days on the calendar until her return. It looked as if her time was up. Darby consoled herself that in a way she'd done as her grandmother wished. She was certain Tatianna had died at Mauthausen. She had taken Celia's name and her place. Sure, there wasn't any hard evidence. But without solid proof, she couldn't get any records changed to Tatianna's name. And was that what mattered? She knew the truth and so did Grandma Celia and Tatianna. And Grandma's God knew. Did the actual names really need changing? Suddenly, Darby felt tired throughout her body, mind, and spirit. Home sounded even better than when she'd gone to youth camp and cried every day until they let her go home early.

With her heart turned toward home, Darby made a final phone call in Salzburg—one she'd avoided for weeks.

"Hello, Darby," Brant said when he picked up the line. "I've wondered how you are doing."

She didn't like the jumble of emotions she felt when hearing his voice. "I'm doing well, how about you?"

"Very well." He was quiet for a moment. "Would you like to meet?"

"No, but thank you. I'm leaving in the morning, but I have a question for you."

"You're going home?"

"Yes. I went to Hallstatt but didn't find whatever it was you wanted me to see. Will you now tell me what it was?"

"You didn't go to the cemetery?" He sounded surprised.

"Yes, but you didn't give me any more information than that."

"You didn't find her headstone?"

"Are you saying there is a headstone for Celia Müller?"

"Yes."

"But she was killed at Mauthausen. There would be no body to bury."

Brant hesitated. "I know that. But there is a headstone, for the memory, I suppose."

"Was this information in your confidential files? I didn't see one with her name on it."

"Perhaps my files were wrong. I must apologize."

"Well, it was a good trip anyway."

"So have you discovered anything?"

Darby paused. "Yes, but nothing that can prove or disprove who my grandmother was. And now it's time for me to return home."

"I wish you the best, Darby."

She caught sincerity in his tone. "I wish you the best also, Brant."

On the morning Darby left Austria, she felt no better than the day she'd arrived. As the plane lifted from Austrian soil, she watched the mountains rush away below her. Since no one was there to tell her good-bye, Darby left as she'd arrived— alone. Her heart turned toward home, to her grandmother's place and her own apartment in Redding. The things so familiar made her homesick and ready to be there. Once back, she'd discover if the shadows could be buried.

"Good-bye, Salzburg," she whispered. "I'm going home."

CHAPTER NINETEEN

When Darby's feet touched United States soil, relief washed throughout her entire body. America— home of the free and the brave. America—the Statue of Liberty, television in English, and no-smoking airports. Darby wasn't a foreigner here. She didn't have to ask anyone to "*Sprechen Sie Englisch.*" The feeling of home beamed strong and good, for the first few hours.

Her mother hugged Darby tightly as they met in the airport and said, "I'm so happy you're home safe," about ten times before they'd even left the San Francisco city limits. Not that they moved very quickly. The throngs of cars moved like a continuous line of ants; the traffic hadn't changed while she was gone.

They drove Highway 101 north with the world unchanged except for the vineyards and trees turning toward winter barrenness. It surprised Darby to realize how easily life continued on with little change, even though she was completely changed. The grasp on life she'd hoped to reclaim by returning home was quickly running like water through her fingers.

Every mile closer to Grandma Celia's, Darby felt more like a stranger, even in her hometown. It must be fatigue, jet lag, she told herself, and the overwhelming relief from the last month of stress. Surely she'd awaken the next morning renewed and happy to leave Austria and its mysteries behind. She couldn't live forever as a displaced person wherever she went. Perhaps some buried secrets were right where they belonged.

"I'm so glad you're home safe," her mother said again as she unlocked the front door.

Darby smiled wearily.

"I have dinner in the Crock-Pot, some new Mr. Bubble, and the heating blanket will be warmed up in no time."

"That sounds wonderful. Mom, why don't you come to Austria and take care of me like this?"

Her mom stopped in the kitchen. "You're going back to Austria?"

"Did I say that?" Darby rubbed her eyes and sat on a bar stool. "No, I'm not going back. At least, I'm probably not."

"How could you consider it? I thought you'd gone, done your work, and now you're home."

"I didn't finish anything, only found more trails. But you'd know that if you'd asked. I noticed you had a dozen questions about my flight, but not one about what I found there."

"You're tired," her mother said as she turned away, "so I didn't want to grill you. I figured you'd tell me if there was really important news."

"It's all important news, I think. But there's so much I don't know and have no idea if I'll ever know. Aren't you curious? This is your family and heritage, even more than mine. Both your parents were there. One never made it out."

"I'm well aware of that. Why do you think I don't like my daughter going?" She yanked two bowls from the cupboard and closed the door loudly. "Can we argue on a different day, Darby?"

She watched her mother shield herself in activity, putting

Darby's luggage near the hallway, getting a tray and spoon from the cabinets. "I'm sorry. We'll talk later. What's in the Crock-Pot?"

Her mother lifted the lid. "Ragout stew, of course."

"And my favorite baking-soda biscuits?"

"Yes." Carole smiled.

"Thanks, Mom." Darby wrapped her arms around her mother from behind. "I'm happy to be home safe."

"Go wash up, young lady," Carole said, laughing. She grabbed a dish towel and flicked it at her. "I'm glad you're home too."

Darby carried her luggage down the hall toward her old bedroom. She paused at Grandma's doorway. Everything looked the same as when she'd left, except for a few boxes in the corner. She walked to the dresser and touched the carved wood box. The lid to the Pond's cold cream bottle was askew, so she unscrewed the top and smelled the white lotion inside. One bottle of moisturizer was turned upside down to retrieve every last drop. "Every seed of waste can grow a tree of poverty," Grandma would say, her voice almost real inside the room. If her grandmother had been there, she'd have ushered Darby inside and demanded every detail of the trip. As tired as Darby felt, she'd share all the discoveries and new questions she had and sort it out with someone who cared and wanted to know. But Grandma Celia wasn't waiting anxiously to hear her stories today, or any day. Darby hadn't quite understood that until now. Throughout Darby's travels, Grandma's presence had been with her. Now Darby had returned to the fact that her grandmother was gone, forever gone.

-→=◦═→-

Darby was jarred back to reality by an early-morning call from her business partner. She was still in bed when her mother brought the phone.

"Welcome home, and now get back here! We're flooded, and we also got contracts on the Christmas Show at the Civic Auditorium and on Hartley's Thankgiving Party. It's time to come home, girl—mentally and physically."

"I'll be there later today."

"Thank God you didn't get stranded in an airport some-where. I've been so stressed. We'd have had to cancel on the Hartley's Thanksgiving Party or something and that would never have been forgiven and I've been so worried, and . . . well, I'll whine and moan about all our woes when you get here."

"Good-bye, Clarise," Darby said with her eyes closed.

"Hurry! We're desperate up here."

⊷≈◉⊜≈⊷

The four-hour drive to the north end of the long Sacramento Valley gave Darby time to remind herself of who she had been before flying off to Austria. Her life in Redding revolved around the photography studio, and not much more. And this was one of the busiest times of year, time for her to put her shoulder to the wheel despite the dust of her journey still surrounding her. Jet lag clung hard with nothing sounding better than cozy sheets and her mother's stew, but she was a co-owner of the business and needed to fulfill that obligation. She'd left her responsibilities for her grandmother's quest, and home had called her back.

Darby topped a rise on I-5 north to see two familiar volcanic mountains surrounding the Redding Valley. Mount Shasta resembled an ice cream cone on the northern horizon, while smaller Mount Lassen sparkled with white snowcaps in the east. As she turned into her apartment complex overlooking the wide Sacramento River, it felt like years had passed since she'd been home. Then the inside of her apartment appeared so changed, Darby wondered if she were in the right place. Her furniture looked familiar but the décor was far from her own with a fuzzy sheepskin rug, East Indian blankets, and carved wooden sculptures dressing the room. Darby had been thankful for a temporary roommate to water her plants while she was gone, but she hadn't expected Julie to become permanent. Her home was her solitude, and Darby shared that sparingly. However, since she was single, everyone thought Darby the perfect target for any college-aged girl in need of a place to stay. Julie, Clarise's niece, was finishing her semester at the local college before transferring to a university. Her roommate had moved out, and Julie couldn't afford the place on her own. Clarise had said the usual line: "Only for a short time, and then you won't be so alone."

Darby walked inside, stepping over a shoe and some laundry in the hall, and opened her bedroom door. She peered inside, glad to see her Ansel Adams black-and-white photos still on the wall along with her flannel comforter atop the pine four-poster bed. Darby only had time to dump her luggage on the floor and walk out.

Five minutes later, she pulled her tan Jeep into the parking lot of the small shopping center. It seemed a hundred years had passed since she'd last stood in front of "Hanrey and Evans Photography," but she didn't feel the rush of excitement she once had upon seeing her name on the window. This was her world, her big dream. Yet suddenly it appeared insignificant in the wake of losing her grandmother, walking the grounds of Mauthausen, and peering into the past. Coming back to normal life might take some time.

Darby stepped into the cozy showroom and paused. No one waited on the sage green chairs or paged through their portfolio binders. Today must be one of the scheduled workdays Darby had implemented the previous year during their busy seasons. It worked better to schedule shoots three days a week and leave the rest for full work days; their production increased this way. Darby took a breath in the calm of the showroom, then walked toward the back work areas.

Clarise popped up. "Oh, I thought I heard the bell. Thank goodness you're back. Come on, come on, let's get you in here."

Darby was surprised to see her partner with auburn, curly hair. When she'd last seen Clarise, her hair was straight and blonde. The auburn appeared more natural with Clarise's olive skin, but the puffed-up hair would take some getting used to. Darby barely had time to look at her partner before Clarise began updating her and delegating their commitments. The holiday crunch had descended. Clarise chose the Hartley's Thanksgiving Party because, after all, she could take her husband and they needed a date night. Darby got the Christmas Arts and Craft Fair—sticky kids, noise, and probably the same grouchy elf as every year—for after all, she *had* been on vacation for two months.

⋯═◉═⋯

Thanksgiving came and went with Darby's mother volunteering at a shelter, dishing up mashed potatoes and gravy, while Darby worked all day except for an evening stop at a friend's house. At least she didn't have to worry about her mother or feel guilty that she hadn't spent their first holiday without Grandma Celia together.

"Say Santa Claus," she found herself repeating behind her camera lens days later. "Don't cry, honey. What do you want for Christmas?"

While Darby usually loved kids and Christmas and capturing the perfect shot on Santa's lap, this year she felt near tears, along with the children. The same grouchy elf had arrived like the ghost of Christmas past and herded children on his assembly line. Santa was more interested in Darby than the children, even asking her for a date on his break. It was the first time she'd been asked on a date in months—and by a Santa who smelled like cigarettes.

The days and evenings flew by and Darby didn't feel any happier. She had arrived back in the States like Dorothy, clicking her heels together saying, "There's no place like home, there's no place like home." But Darby wondered about the rest of the story. Was little Dorothy content to be back in Kansas? Did she grow up, marry a farmer, and age against the rolling plains? Or did she remember that once she wore red, magic shoes—shoes that could kill a witch and possess more magic than all of Oz? Could she return home and exist with Oz in her mind? Or would dreams of yellow brick roads and an emerald city call her to return?

Darby didn't know about Dorothy, but she knew that the feeling of missing something grew with every moment.

Perhaps she'd changed too much to stay home.

⭑⇒◉⇐⭑

"I've waited long enough," Richter said. He paced the park walkway while Ingrid sat on a bench, feeding pigeons. "How can you be so calm about this? The woman went back to the States. Brant and Darby did not connect their information as you thought they would. How will we find the heirlooms now?"

Ingrid continued to drop crumbs of bread. "I said I hoped the two would connect their information. We simply don't know what exact pieces Brant knows and what this woman knows. We do know she's Celia Müller's granddaughter."

"That's another thing I want to know. How did you know she was Celia Müller's granddaughter? And how did you know for me to look for her to come to Austria?"

"There are some things I'll keep to myself, for now. I will say that I didn't know for certain she'd come. At least, not for sure. But the pull of riches lures everyone."

"Then why did she return to the States?"

"I don't know. I thought Darby Evans and Brant would discover the truth, but he is far more suspicious than I thought. Yet I know we are closer than before."

"How can you say that?" Richter wanted to take her bread crumbs and toss them away. "We have nothing, and I don't see how this plan is ever going to work. If we wait too long, the treasures will be found and claimed."

"Yes, but there's no other way."

"I can think of other ways."

"Patience, my grandson."

"I have debts that aren't waiting patiently. Perhaps you can wait a lifetime, but I can't. And I won't." A flurry of pigeons scattered to flight as Richter stalked away.

In her little free time, Darby took to driving country roads along cold irrigated pasturelands, through the rocky, oak-covered foothills and into the snowy mountains that surrounded the long valley floor. But for all her wandering, Darby was unsure what bothered her. The work she'd once tackled as a challenge now drowned her. Yet it was more than just her work. It seemed she'd become misplaced somehow, and if she didn't find out what to do, soon only a shell of herself would be left.

Every night she stayed at the studio late and began to find her way through the mess Clarise had made. Darby decided she'd never leave Clarise in full charge for that long again. She could shine in public relations, advertising, and photo shoots, but her organizational skills were lost behind the bubbly smiles she gave their clients. The office was a mess. Orders lost in stacks. Phone calls left unanswered. Darby's well-oiled machine had quickly turned to rust. As she sat in the late-night shadows, she thumbed through a stack of photos from the Redding holiday parade. She looked out the window and wondered how the streets of Salzburg appeared dressed for Christmas. What did tiny Hallstatt look like with snow covering the village and surrounding Alps? The night sky was her connection as she imagined snowflakes falling beneath those same stars, somewhere far away.

Back to work, she told herself. *You're home now. Leave it behind.*

Darby ordered Chinese food and forced herself back to the reprint orders. Yet every photo brought thoughts of her trip, along with the questions she'd never found answers to. Finally she gave up for a while and carried the white carton of sweet-and-sour chicken to her computer. While in Austria, she'd often wished for the use of the Internet in her research. Now she tried to remember what she'd wanted to find.

Their studio office had connected to cyberspace when they'd opened two years earlier, and both Darby and Clarise had been hooked on the world inside the monitor. They chatted with pen pals and other photographers and surfed for quality equipment at good prices. Clarise even found a guy for Darby on-line, certain he was her perfect match like in the movie *You've Got Mail*. He turned out to be sixty years old. The fun of cyberspace slowly faded.

Darby logged on and tried to remember how many weeks or months had passed since she'd last checked her e-mail. She scanned the advertisements and photography E-news, surprised to see her grandmother's pen name, "GramC," in the in-box. Darby hesitated before clicking the button. The date on the e-mail was near the time of Darby's trip to shoot the climbing club in the Trinity Alps. Seeing the words on the screen was like receiving words from beyond the grave.

> *Darby-girl,*
> *Old granny is feeling better today so I made it to check*
> *e-mail, of course. Can't wait to hear about your mountain*

adventure. I'm jealous, in a purely loving way. Be ready to tell me stories.

Love you with all my heart.
Gram C.

P.S. Need to talk to you about some things. Remember the Scripture I cross-stitched and have in my room? We'll talk about it when you come down.

Darby peered at the screen. What Scripture? She remembered a cross-stitched picture in the room but not what it said. Most likely her grandmother believed Darby had read the note and the Scripture when she came down to visit her. Could this Scripture be a key to Grandma's mystery—words that would have helped on her trip? Darby also hadn't thought to examine her grandmother's computer files. Grandma Celia had only purchased her computer six months before her death, but she'd worked on them at the library and taken courses for several years. Certainly she must have kept files on her search for the Lange inheritance.

Checking her watch, Darby decided not to scare her mother with a midnight phone call. But her mind tried and tried to recall the words of the picture. Darby rested her chin on her hand and read the words again. How strange to see Grandma's note so alive, like any normal day.

After several minutes, she clicked the print button, then began to use search engines for information she'd wanted in Austria. The Web site "Find-A-People" allowed specific or general searches on names. Darby typed in a variety—Bruno Weiler, Hoffman for Tatianna's family, Müller for her grandfather's, and Lange for her grandmother's family. Names appeared in discovery columns. No Bruno Weiler appeared, but many Müllers and Hoffmans. Not one looked like a good lead. She found Professor Peter Voss in Salzburg. The screen gave his address and phone number. Darby looked for her own name and found her address and phone number listed also. It was an eerie feeling to discover herself on the screen. Anyone could procure her address.

Darby joined a cyberlibrary and continued a search that would trace books, newspapers, magazine articles, and other documents. She typed and sifted through information, printing anything that could be good information. Her growing pile was transferred into a three-ring binder under different divisions—People, General Information, Mauthausen. . . . Suddenly an old newspaper from the 1950s revealed the name Bruno Weiler.

"I found you."

She printed the article as she read it. It reported a trial in the early fifties where five guards were indicted on charges of war crimes during the time they worked at Mauthausen and other camps. Bruno Weiler was one of them. They were all found guilty and sentenced to five years in a German prison. They would have been released in 1957.

Continuing to search, she found nothing more on Bruno Weiler but located a site named "Desperate Search." It recorded people looking for missing family members, friends, or wartime buddies. It shocked Darby to see so many people looking for displaced and missing people as far back as World War II. She opened one of the files: "Where is my father?" It had facts and locations of a soldier in the United States Army who had married an Italian woman, then disappeared after the war, abandoning his wife and two children. One of the children had entered "desperately seeking." She was in her fifties, but she still sought her father. Darby was tempted to return to "Find-A-People" and seek her own father, but knew she was far from ready to pursue those feelings.

Instead she added her own entry to the list: "Seeking Bruno Weiler. I am seeking information on a man named Bruno

Weiler. He was an Austrian Nazi prison guard at Mauthausen Concentration Camp. Please send any information."

Darby added searches for the Lange and Hoffman families. On impulse, she surfed to sites about coins and Empress Sissi. After an hour of looking, she began to get a picture of the value of her family inheritance and why it was so sought after by the Nazis. Anything belonging to Sissi became instantly valuable. The entire country of Austria had celebrated the one-hundredth anniversary of her death in 1998. Darby started searching for Celtic coins found in Hallstatt, but her eyes began to feel heavy. Finally she turned off the world within her computer and ate cold Chinese food alone.

Then she headed toward her car and home. At a stoplight, she remembered a dark street—an escape from peopled routes—that she'd found in Salzburg, right in the middle of town. It was quiet and ancient, opening into a peaceful plaza surrounded by buildings. Until now she'd forgotten about that place. As she got ready for bed, more memories and questions sifted through her mind. Even as she slept, she dreamed of Austria.

⊹═◉═⊹

As Darby blow-dried her hair the next morning, she still couldn't shake her questions. She thought of Tatianna, then Bruno Weiler, then the Lange inheritance, wondering about her, what happened to him, and where the treasure was. As she later parked in the lot, late for work, another question arose. Was she just convincing herself that she needed to put Austria behind her? Yet she felt it inside—not the dying slowly, but a hopeful excitement. Maybe she needed that to get her through this late-twenties crisis or whatever she was dealing with. Her logical side reminded her that her future was in the States, right at this studio.

Clarise met her at the studio door.

"Oh, Darby!" Clarise yanked her partner in so fast that the permed auburn hair almost whipped off her head. "I have the best news in the entire world. Guess what?"

"What?"

"No, guess!"

"I don't know . . . you won the lottery, you're pregnant, you have a date with Brad Pitt and Markus said you could go? I don't know, but those would be your favorite things to happen."

"You're crazy, girl. All wrong, though very good ideas. But you'll be so excited!" Clarise jumped up and down like she *had* just won the lottery. "Creative Designs Photography is closing down, and Scott offered us first opportunity to buy their clientele list, equipment, and, yes, even their shop!"

"Really? Why are they closing?"

"Scott is retiring, and no one in his family is interested in the shop. He's offering a great deal, told me that since I used to work there, he wanted to give me first shot. This is a perfect opportunity. We'd have the chance to be the top studio north of Sacramento. We'll have to hire more people, of course, but—"

"Slow down. I need some more facts. I need time to consider."

Clarise stopped, and her hands dropped to her side. "Aren't you excited about this?"

"I don't know. I think so, but I need a moment for it to sink in before I invest my life away."

"Darby, it's exactly what we've dreamed of."

Yes, she thought, *but is it what I'm dreaming of now?* "Let's get the details, then let's talk," Darby said.

"I'll do that," Clarise said as she stormed out of the room.

Clarise stayed on the phone most of the day until Darby was sure she couldn't take her partner's screech of excitement one more time. At last she couldn't and escaped to the movies alone, something she'd never done before. But a super-sized

Coke, Reese's peanut butter cup, buttery popcorn, along with a romantic comedy made her feel worse than when she'd arrived. The couple on the screen was gooey and lovey for the second half of the flick. What could be sadder than a single person watching a romantic comedy alone? Darby found out when she ran into someone she knew—her old boyfriend, Derek Hunt, and his gorgeous wife.

"You're back!" Derek called across the lobby while she was trying to sneak off unseen. He ran and hugged her. "Tell me about the trip. I couldn't believe it when I called the studio and Clarise said you were in Europe!"

Darby pulled away and smiled. Derek hadn't changed, except his thick sandy hair might have receded slightly, and his well-defined features appeared more mature. Derek's wife, Rochella, walked up slowly and smiled, but she didn't appear thrilled to see her husband's ex-girlfriend. Long, perfect hair framed her model face, and Darby instantly felt grungy in her jeans, T-shirt, and greasy hands from too much butter.

"I've been back a few weeks," she said, wiping her chin. "You called the studio?"

"Yeah, we wanted more copies of our family portrait for Christmas cards. But tell me everything. Where did you go, what were you doing there? Was it just like you imagined it to be?"

"There's a lot to tell. It's beautiful and amazing—you both should go there someday. Get matching bikes and see the countryside."

"Rochella doesn't ride." Derek glanced at his wife. "But I still want to go someday."

"You should. . . . Well, I better get going." She made a gesture that hopefully looked like she was meeting someone.

"Oh, yeah, of course. Hey, let's meet next week for lunch and catch up. I want to see your photos, which I know you've had developed since the day you got home."

Darby didn't tell him she hadn't taken any pictures. Clarise had been too busy to ask, her mother probably didn't want to see them. Everyone else she'd brushed off with a change of subject.

"See you later," Darby said. "Bye, Rochella." She waved and hurried away, making a detour to the bathroom. Waiting a sufficient time, Darby finally hurried through the parking lot, only to get a honk and wave from Derek and Rochella. They definitely knew she was alone now. Next time she'd watch a video at home—if she could get rid of Julie's weekend friends.

⋅→▭◌⫘←⋅

Darby was surprised when Derek walked into the studio the next day.

"Rochella asked me to pick up our reprints. And since I'm here, I'm taking you to lunch."

"I'm swamped with last-minute projects. Sorry," she said, glad to have an excuse. Little could be worse than lunch with Rochella and Derek. "Half of Redding had the idea to give old, reconditioned photographs as Christmas presents this year. And it was a last-minute idea too."

"You know, that old photo idea is good, and I still have a few presents to get. Maybe . . ."

"Forget it, Derek. Your parents always like the Hickory Farms packages anyway."

"Very true. Sure you don't want to grab some lunch—just you and me? Come on."

Just then, Darby heard Clarise on the phone down the hall. "Yes, we can even buy the studio," she said with a shriek of excitement for effect.

"I'll go."

❖══❖

They sat across from each other on red velvet cushions in the dungeon-dark Italian restaurant. Neither spoke for a moment. Darby squirmed while Derek stared her straight in the face and wondered why she'd come. They'd dated from the end of their senior year of high school through three years of college. They'd remained friends afterwards, both saying they'd probably get back together after college. They wanted the last year to play and date and enjoy one more year before entering the "real" world. Then Rochella entered the picture. Derek had been under a spell with the idea that a woman of class and beauty would be attracted to him. He was from a small town; she vacationed in the Caribbean. Darby and Derek's friendship drifted quickly after that, and Darby had realized how much she loved him. It took a long time to release the idea that they were meant to be together again.

At Derek's wedding, she'd met Clarise, who was a friend of a friend of Rochella's. That's where the studio idea began. Clarise's family lived in Redding and since she had the most financial backing, they'd settled the partnership there. A year later, when Derek's job transferred him to Redding, he looked Darby up. But besides their family portrait with what seemed like an added child every year, she rarely saw Derek or Rochella. Now she sat across from him, wondering what to say.

"It's really good to see you," Derek said.

"It's good to see you too."

"So it's Dorothy home from Oz."

Darby's mouth dropped. "I've been thinking that for weeks. How did you remember my love of yellow brick roads?"

"I remember everything."

"And you were the Scarecrow, right?"

"Hey, I was the lions, tigers, and bears. Remember?" He

wiggled one eyebrow and smiled the grin Darby had once thought irresistible.

"I have no recollection." She held up her hands but couldn't help smiling. "Except what about Scarecrow in need of my tutoring help and a few brains?"

"This is getting too nasty for me." His laugh made her feel warm and comfortable while emphasizing her lack of companionship even more. All her close friends were married or pursuing their own careers, and even Grandma Celia with her ever-ready ear had left her. Darby missed having someone to talk to, laugh with, and tease. She'd had that with Derek. They'd put their heads close while discussing ideas, thoughts, and dreams. Even when they were "only" friends, they'd attacked the world with passion—she with her photography and Derek with his dreams of travel and exploration. Now he worked on the ladder of success with some company he didn't have much interest in.

Darby sat back against the cushion. She'd changed since their college days, and so had he. But Darby didn't need that youthful passion now. She only wanted someone to sit close to while watching TV. She longed to play foot wars in fluffy socks and lose herself in warm kisses. At the rate she was going, it would never happen.

Then a picture of Brant Collins flashed into her mind. Did he too wish for companionship and love? What was he doing right now? She glanced at her watch and calculated the time. He'd be either at his office working late or at home, perhaps with some Austrian woman, watching TV or playing foot wars.

"Do you have somewhere to be?" Derek studied her with an expression she'd once loved, his head tilted to the side, one eyebrow up in question. "The food hasn't even come yet."

"No, just checking the time. Clarise will have a heart attack if I'm gone from the office for long."

"Then you better start talking, 'cause I want to hear all about your trip."

Someone really wants to listen? Not because he had his own motive or agenda for my life, but because he really wants to know?

Darby opened her mouth and the words seemed to tumble out—her lonely arrival in Austria, the old man with the rake—everything. Their food arrived, and they ate between discussion and story.

Derek leaned forward in rapt attention as she told about Mauthausen and the interchangeable faces of SS and victims. They discussed what drove one man to hate and another to mercy.

"I never would have thought this before my trip, but I believe every person on earth is capable of incredible hatred or incredible love. We choose what degree we'll live at."

"Are you saying we're all capable of what the Nazis did?"

"I think we are. There were evils beyond Hitler at work, and those evils remain. When we dabble in hatred, selfish pursuits, pride, and contempt for others, our minds can descend without us totally aware, until our actions mirror our mind. I think there were some seriously sick individuals who lusted and relished the evil within them, but I also think there were mostly average people—men and women—who because of many reasons, from fear to self-preservation, were swept into the rush and performed, partook, or turned away from what they normally never would have considered."

"Scary thought, indeed. We are all capable of evil?"

"We are all capable of horrible things; we see it still today. But I think, perhaps, we are also capable of great acts of love. It must be what we put into our lives."

Derek twisted his fork around a last bite of pasta. "So do you think that the things we dabble in or experiment with, be

it feelings or thoughts, be it good or bad, will most likely lead
to the action and result?"

"Grandma Celia would say you reap what you sow. Are you
still on the subject of the demise of man, or are you speaking
personally?"

"When you someday get married, Darby, marry your best
friend."

"What? Where did that come from?" She laughed, but then
noticed the sorrow in his eyes. He touched the tips of her
fingers.

"I love Rochella, but I miss my best friend. Rochella's perfect
on the outside, a showcase. But we don't laugh like you and
I did. We don't jump in the car and go skiing or cycling. We
don't do much of anything. When you get married, make sure
it's to your best friend. You were mine, and I let you go."

In shock, Darby withdrew her hand. "Derek, you can't be
serious."

"I am. I really miss you."

Even a year ago, her heart would have pounded at his touch.
"Make Rochella your best friend."

"We have nothing in common."

Darby looked at the face she thought she would always miss
and desire. But she knew him as not her own. Perhaps something or someone was out there for her, but Derek wasn't it.
Instantly Darby clearly understood that, and she almost smiled
with the relief. "Let's see, you have three children in common,
marriage vows, and how many years together? This is a
marriage slump. Derek, you need to love her, even if your
heart isn't fully on fire, or the fire goes out." She paused,
thinking of Grandma Celia, her husband Gunther, and
Tatianna. "Love is a gift that can be lost when you don't pay
attention or keep it alive."

"Is this from experience?" Derek's expression turned grim.

"No, from observing. It's pretty funny coming from me,

the loser at love. But I've seen my grandmother and what she lost. I'm learning to cling tightly to the love we're granted. Whether you have one year or a lifetime, don't forget that love is a gift. A gift to be appreciated and nurtured—for better or worse."

"It's not that easy."

"What if Rochella were taken from you right now? Let's say she was killed or kidnapped or separated from you by a war. How would you feel about her then? You'd fight for her. You'd miss her. You'd remember the million perfect moments you've had together."

Derek was silent. His eyes seemed far away, scanning images and thoughts beyond them.

"You're right." Derek leaned against his hands. "But it doesn't help with today."

"Love her like tomorrow is your last day with her."

Derek slowly smiled. "Here I am, making a pass at you, and you lead me back to my wife. You probably think I'm a jerk."

"No, I thought that long ago." Darby chuckled.

"You can be such a brat." He sighed. "So when are you going back?"

Darby looked at her watch. "I should have been back forty-five minutes ago."

"No, I mean back to Austria."

"Why do you think I'm going back?" she asked, startled.

He gave a boyish grin. "Because I know you. And I know that look in your eyes whenever you talk about it. You seem surprised, as if you don't realize it. I can't believe this. Darby Evans is in love and doesn't even know it."

"What are you talking about?" An image of Brant came to mind. "There is no way I'm in love."

"Don't give me that. I've watched you as you talked about the trip. 'When I was in Austria . . .' or 'This great place in

Austria . . .' You left your heart there. The Alps won you over,"
he said with half smirk and half accusation.

"You think so?"

"I know so. I don't know whether to be more jealous
over you getting to go back or the Alps getting to have you.
You really are a good friend, despite my wayward intentions."

"It's not just the Alps. It's Salzburg too. The old city nestled
against Mönchsberg with the fortress above. Cobblestone
streets with musicians and outdoor cafés and markets teeming
with people. You should be jealous," she teased.

"Where are the photos?"

Darby's smile left her.

"You don't have them with you at all times?" Derek said
with a laugh.

"Actually, I didn't take any pictures."

"What? You forgot Nikki at home?"

"No."

Derek leaned forward. "What's going on, Darby? You always
take Nikki everywhere. You'd drive everyone crazy with all the
pictures you'd sneak in. Why wouldn't you take pictures of
this place you fell in love with?"

"I don't know. It just didn't seem right for me."

"Do you want to talk about it?"

"There's not much to say. My grandmother talked to me
before she died. She said I needed to stop hiding behind my
camera and really see the world. Then, when I went to Austria,
it didn't feel right for me to shoot it. Maybe I needed some
time to simply be me."

"So when are you going back?"

Darby took a long breath. She bit the inside of her cheek. "I
am going back, aren't I?"

"I think it'll be soon."

The last night before she returned to her mother's house for Christmas, Darby locked the doors to the studio and paused. She peered back through the windows into the front show-room. Christmas decorations wrapped around displays of their framed work on the walls—weddings, family portraits, and children with full smiles and bright eyes. She remembered painting those walls and hanging the portraits. Their grand opening had been one of the best moments of her life—at that point. Could she leave it all behind? Her eyes trailed upward into the night sky. Beckoning stars told her to keep looking up; she'd find the right way.

As Darby entered the driveway, she noticed the lack of Christmas lights on the eaves of the yellow-and-white house and a Nativity scene on the green lawn. Grandma Celia had loved the Christmas season and lived for tradition with baking, decorating, hot cocoa instead of morning coffee, and fresh pine boughs to bring the mountain feel into the home. It worried Darby that it was only two days before Christmas and the little yellow house wasn't decorated.

"I'm home," she called, setting down her luggage in the entry.

"Darby!" Her mother hurried down the hall with outstretched arms.

"Is everything all right, Mom?"

"Oh yes. I just filled my life too full of activity, especially at the church. I've avoided a bit of this decorating, but I did start going through Grandma's room." Her mother did look better than Darby had seen her in months. "I'm going to get all the food Grandma stored in her room and give it to the church missionary cupboard."

"Food she kept stored?" Darby glanced down the hall. "In her room?"

"Oh, yes. Grandma's kept food and supplies stored in the garage and in her room for years. 'Just in case,' she'd always say."

"I knew she hid money, but not food too."

"I also found letters, newspaper clippings, old birthday and Christmas cards from years and years ago. In fact, I thought you might want to take the letters . . . if you go back. They're written in German."

Darby stared in disbelief at her mother. "If I go back?"

"I've been doing some heavy praying. If God wants you to return, then I'll support you."

"I don't know what God wants. I don't even know what I want anymore."

"You know what God wants." Carole put her hand on Darby's arm. "He wants you, Darby."

Darby felt uncomfortable beneath her mother's gentle gaze. "You *are* too busy at church, Mom," she said, trying to lighten the mood as she walked down the hall and into Grandma Celia's room. Looking around the room, she finally spotted the cross-stitched picture. It hung near the door where someone sitting in bed could read it easily, but anyone entering or standing would hardly notice. Darby stopped suddenly, reading the words.

> Greater love hath no man than this, that a man lay down his life for his friends.
>
> —John 15:13

Her mother stood in the entry. "What's wrong?"

"Grandma thought I knew before I went to Austria."

"Knew what?"

"Grandma wanted me to read that verse before the trip. I've speculated that Grandma Celia escaped from Austria to America using Tatianna's papers. And I believe Tatianna died impersonating Grandma Celia. She died instead of Grandma Celia. It has to be the truth."

Her mother turned to stare at the picture on the wall. "Wait here a minute."

Darby had wondered why Grandma had left so many vague trails for her instead of simply revealing more truths. But Grandma had expected her to know that Tatianna did die at Mauthausen under the name of Celia Müller because of this verse. The speculation gone, Darby could have concentrated earlier on finding the facts.

"I was going to give this to you for Christmas," her mother said as she returned to the room. "I think I should give it to you now."

Darby looked away from the words in the picture to see her mother holding out a wrapped package. "What is it?"

"Open it."

Darby sat on the edge of her grandmother's bed and carefully unwrapped the green-and-gold paper to find a thin box. From inside the box she lifted out a worn leather-bound Bible. It had been white leather at one time, but the years and use had worn the gold leaf from the edges and made the cover a dull gray. She ran her hand over the top and lifted it to her nose to breathe in the scent of the past. "Grandma's old Bible. I forgot about this."

"While I was cleaning in here, I found it in her bedside table." Carole sat beside her. "Grandma had several Bibles, but I remember looking at the words all in German as a child, wondering what they said. But look inside."

"Oh, Mom," Darby whispered. In faded lettering was written *Celia Rachel Lange Müller.* Below it read *Tatianna Elise Hoffman.*

"Yes. It was given to Celia by Tatianna," her mother said. "Tatianna gave Celia even more than her life. I think she may have given her faith as well."

Darby couldn't take her eyes from the Bible. All those years, Tatianna was in their lives, unknown to everyone but Grandma Celia. And had her grandmother's great faith been born from a young girl's sacrifice?

"You need to go back, don't you?" Her mother put her hand over Darby's. "When you do, know that I will support you as best I can. This is bigger than us, Darby. It's God's work still in progress after all these years."

Darby felt as if she were slowly awakening from a very long sleep. Her eyes were barely glimpsing images and distinguishing light from shadow, but still there was a lot of sleep in her eyes, drawing her back into darkness. But she was ready to awaken, finally willing to see and face what she'd long hidden from.

That night Darby talked for hours with her mother as they decorated the house "to make Grandma proud," drank hot cocoa, and watched their annual *The Grinch Who Stole Christmas* movie. She couldn't remember enjoying her mother more. And she was finally able to share all her thoughts with someone. But another part of her, the awakening part, still waited—as if she stood on a precipice, waiting for the perfect time to jump.

⋅→═◎═←⋅

Brant drove through the darkness on freshly plowed roads north of Salzburg into the town of Oberndorf. He was not alone in his Christmas Eve journey, though he didn't know any of the fellow pilgrims who crowded the streets and searched for parking places. Their license plates were from many European nations, and he was sure he'd find many more nationalities walking the icy roadways. He got out of his car and knew he was in for a long haul on the frosty night—but that's what he wanted. Time to think, time to breathe the frozen air, time to believe in Christmas again.

Brant parked on the outskirts of town and walked back toward the river. The night was hushed above the crunching of his boots on the packed snow. He crossed the bridge over the Salzach and stopped to look into the familiar waters. Maybe next time he'd drop a wooden boat from the bridge at Salzburg before driving downstream to Oberndorf. That would be a fun activity to do with Frau Halder's grandchildren instead of the soccer practice that left his shins bruised.

He crossed the river and heard a whistle blow at the train station as a bright red locomotive chugged to a stop. The cars would undoubtedly be teeming with more people who, like Brant, searched for one thing—a silent night.

Brant had never visited the birthplace of the world's most-loved Christmas carol. He'd heard "Silent Night" first at home in America. His mother would sing it every evening during the month of December as she tucked him into bed at home in Portland. First she'd sing in German, then in English. Every night he remembered asking her to tell the story behind the song.

On this Christmas Eve, he was in the place where it began. The lullaby with its message of heavenly peace would be sung in all corners of the world tonight in more than two hundred languages. The song would be heard by carolers in America, through cathedral organs in Europe, inside thatched huts in South America, and at candlelight concerts in Australia. Brant followed the growing groups of people until he arrived in front of the Silent Night Memorial Chapel, where the original church of St. Nicholas once stood. Groups of people milled quietly, almost in expectation. If they stood very still, they might find teacher Franz Xaver Grüber and priest Josef Mohr discussing what to do with a broken church organ with Christmas Eve approaching. They might then hear the strum of a guitar that commenced a chorus of "Silent Night" as on that first night in 1818.

Brant watched the people. Some closed their eyes and tilted their heads upward to the clear, dark sky. The small, white chapel could hold only a fraction of the crowd outside. On a higher section of town, the church that housed the original altars and pulpit would re-create the moment when the song was first performed along with a midnight mass. But Brant wanted to be in the place where it began.

He, too, found his eyes moving from the simple chapel into the sky of diamonds on black velvet. He imagined a heavenly host just beyond the sight of his human eyes.

God, you know I'm not good at praying. So I'm just going to talk and hope you understand. His eyes found constellations and the long spill of the Milky Way. God was there and here, he felt, and whispered from his heart. *I want to thank you for a million things, but mainly for showing me how to live the life you've given me. Thank you for Gunther being part of my life—I don't know what I'd have done without him. And thank you for second chances, and thirds and fourths. Right now, you know what Richter is doing, why he comes to Salzburg regularly now and asks to stay with me. You know his motives. So help me know what to do.*

I also keep thinking of Darby Evans. I don't know where she is right now or what's happening in her life, but I hope she is well and that she can find you as I'm finding you.

And also I must remember all those who have lived through hell on earth—give them your peace tonight.

I don't know if that's how I should pray, but amen.

From one side of the street, Brant heard a soft chorus. A gentle wave of voices joined around him, singing in more than one language the hymn that bound them all together.

Brant's voice joined the chorus, first in German, then in English.

"Silent night, holy night. All is calm, all is bright."

⊶═◉═⊷

In a flurry of hugs and noise, Maureen, John, and the five-year-old twins arrived. Any minutes of sorrow could not hold for long with the twins ready to keep everyone busy. It seemed as if a year had passed since Darby had seen them, though it had only been a few months since Grandma's funeral.

"Auntie Darby, I hope I have a Baby Alive under the tree," Kallie said as they carried presents from the car to the house. "Do you think I do?"

"Well, I don't know."

"I hope, I hope, Auntie Darby." Kallie stopped to look at the presents overflowing the tree skirt. "I weally, weally want a Baby Alive that will wet her diaper."

"Kallie," Maureen scolded as she carried a load of presents from the car. "Don't pester your aunt, and come help Daddy bring in your suitcases."

Darby grabbed the girls as they walked by and whispered, "Maybe you can open one present after the candlelight service tonight."

Two sets of eyes grew as large as silver coins. They giggled and whispered to each other out to the car.

⊶═◉═⊷

The lights were turned low in the auditorium as they entered in silence. Darby suddenly longed for Grandma Celia's hand that always reached for hers sometime during the service. The candles were lit one by one to the soft song, "What Child Is This?" Mary walked down the center aisle and the Christ child was placed in the little manger on stage.

Who were you really, little child? Darby wondered. *Who are you now?*

Instantly, it was as if Tatianna had sent a message directly through the years. It was simply the act of an old Bible that now rested in Darby's hands. Tatianna dies for her friend. Tatianna gives the legacy of life and a faith to pass down. Tatianna was pointing the way to another one who died, not for one person or family—but for all mankind.

Music rose through the sanctuary as angels entered the stage, some lowered from above, others surging from offstage. Their glittery robes sparkled in the darkness as voices raised a chorus. "O come, all ye faithful. . . ." The wise men brought their gifts and laid them at the foot of the manger. Then other people moved forward. A businessman with briefcase in hand, a woman dressed like a housewife, a young child, and a college-aged girl dressed in tight pants with several earrings in one ear. More people came of different ages, races, and professions. All walked forward and knelt before the child.

At that moment, Darby knew she didn't want to miss what God had to offer. She wanted to be part of it all, the intricate design created with the same care as life, land, wind, and rain.

Her eyes watched the infant asleep in the manger. God as man. God on earth by humble means. God dying a humiliating death. Like Tatianna's gift.

As the pastor prayed, Darby whispered her own wish. *I want the Creator of what my eyes find in the mountains. And I will give you my life. Forgive me and my wandering ways. I don't really know what this means for tomorrow, but I'm trying to believe. I think I do believe.*

The service closed with the gentle "Silent Night."

W hen she checked the computer files, Darby hoped to find more answers. All she found was the trail of Grandma Celia's search for the Lange inheritance. Her letters were to Holocaust organizations, Austrian officials. Darby even found the letter to Brant Collins saved on the hard drive. One surprise was the discovery that Grandma Celia had organized putting up the Lange memorial plaque at Mauthausen Concentration Camp. Darby had wondered why it was written in English. The letter to the camp said she wanted something her grandchildren and great-grandchildren could read to remember their heritage.

Grandma Celia would have called it a leap of faith. Darby returned to Redding after the holiday and confronted Clarise with her idea to either sell off her half of the photo lab or become an uninvolved partner. Clarise actually looked relieved.

"Two people from Creative Designs wanted to join in the partnership, and I didn't know how it would work with all of us."

"Really? Then it will work out perfectly," Darby said, feeling a weight lift. Several days of worry had been for nothing. "Let's get something worked up on paper."

While Darby knew she was taking the right step in selling off her old dream, she wondered what her future in photography would be. Derek had mentioned Darby should call their college friend Tracey Rivens. Tracey had worked her way up to an editorial position in *Travel Today,* a competitive travel destination magazine. She looked in an old issue for their company's number.

Tracey was her same friendly self, but the business was straightforward. "Read back issues, know our photos, then send me some samples."

Darby spent two days carefully studying and making notes on the back issues of the *Travel Today* magazines she'd stored in a cupboard at the studio. She noted angles and lighting, landscapes versus action, until she was ready to search her own files. The hiking and mountaineering shots comprised most of what she boxed up and FedEx-ed to Tracey.

◦—◉═◉—◦

On New Year's Eve, as Darby watched the ball drop over Times Square in New York, she leaned close to the TV screen to see what the area looked like. This had been the designated meeting place for her grandmother and grandfather—only her grandfather had never arrived. The square currently was covered with people cheering and dancing, but once, a long time ago, a young woman had searched the crowd with hopes of finding the man she loved. And later, another young woman, her mother, had searched for the father she wanted to know.

Darby welcomed in the new year, wondering what the next twelve months held. A year earlier, she had written her usual resolutions—exercise consistently, organize the back closets at the studio, do more advertising, get a pet. This year she was selling her half of the partnership with Clarise, and Hanrey and Evans was about to be no more. The world stretched out, with no way to predict what would happen.

She flipped off the cheering crowds on the television and sat in darkness. On a long gold chain around her neck, she wore Grandma's ring. Her fingers felt along the edges as she considered the near future. Once in Austria again, she hoped to prove Tatianna, not Celia Müller, died in Mauthausen. She hoped to start a new career. She hoped to find out what had happened to her family inheritance. But for once, Darby knew her life wasn't in her hands. It was both exciting and frightening at the same time.

⊷≡○⊜≡⊷

For better or worse, by late February, Darby was finally checking in her luggage at San Francisco International Airport and hugging her mother good-bye, for the second time in a year. Her belongings were in a storage unit in Sebastopol, her dream of a photography studio sold off. Darby found her plane on the Departures screen and breathed a sigh. "I hope I'm doing the right thing," she said aloud.

At 11:30 P.M. her old time, Darby's plane bounced and touched down at 9:30 A.M. in München—Munich, Germany. Soon she'd catch the connecting flight to Salzburg, Austria. She couldn't keep her eyes from the green fields of Germany as the plane slowed. She made a vow to herself: *Whatever I do or don't discover, I hope to tell my children and someday their children about this journey. You were right, Grandma. This is my story now.*

CHAPTER TWENTY-THREE

The gray sky spit wet snow against the window of the taxi. The cold wrapped around Darby's legs as she paid the driver and tugged her luggage toward the Hotel Zur Goldenen Ente on Goldgasse in the heart of the Old City. After she settled in, Darby picked up her umbrella before the urge to plop onto the bed outweighed her new travel smarts.

Snow began a soft descent, but mittens, a hat, and scarf kept her warm. She stood in the center of Domplatz and watched the long fall of snowflakes down to the cobblestone streets. Her breath froze in the air as she breathed in the good and familiar scent of aged stone. The church bells began to boom, roaring and echoing off the walls of the enclosed courtyards and streets. Darby stood transfixed by the sound, closing her eyes and then opening them again to see if it was truly real.

I'm here. I'm really here again.

Salzburg was like returning to a friend.

The Mr. Bubble Darby's mother had sent along awaited her in a hot bath that evening. With skin turned pink and fingers pruned, she bundled up in her robe and dialed the Voss home. Somehow the three months had slipped away from her, and she had not called or e-mailed the professor or Katrine even once.

"Professor Voss, this is Darby Evans."

"Hello! How are you?"

Darby smiled at the enthusiasm in his voice. "I'm very good, especially since I'm in Salzburg."

"Right now? You are back?"

"Yes." Darby felt the joy throughout her entire being. Yes, she was back.

"How wonderful that you return! With the mysteries from yesterday, you could not stay away?"

"No, I couldn't." She wrapped the robe more tightly and stretched across the bed. "I believe I'll find part of myself in some of these mysteries, if we're able to solve them."

"You are correct. We always find more of ourselves when we look to the past, especially our family past. And Darby, you come with great timing. I am attending a conference this weekend at the university. You can come with me, if you like."

"What kind of conference, and is there an English version?" Darby asked a bit wearily. "Or will you be translating for me the entire day?" she teased.

"Possibly translating, though there are some workshops in English. The seminar is called 'Holocaust Awareness in the New Millennium.' "

"It sounds great, and I'm honored to be invited. Tell me when and where, and I'll be there. And if you have time, I have more letters for you or Katrine to translate."

"With pleasure. Then, after the conference, we must meet

and see what information to seek. Do you have anything new?"

"Actually, yes. Do you remember Bruno Weiler—I mentioned him in our last conversation before you left for Dublin?"

"*Ja*, the SS guard. I wanted to contact you." Professor Voss's voice sounded excited. "I intended many times to call or e-mail because I found some information about a Bruno Weiler."

"You did?" Darby reached beside the bed into the brown leather satchel she'd bought for her return to Europe. She extracted the file labeled *B. Weiler.* "While I was at home, I found information about a trial and some prison time after the war."

"That is important news. That was after the war? I found enrollment records of a Bruno Weiler in Vienna in the late 1950s. He was attending university there. I wonder if it was the same person."

"My information said he was released in 1957. If it is the same as your Bruno Weiler, we have his next location. Was there any other information? Did he graduate?"

"He was taking graduate courses but dropped out midterm. That is all I could find from the admissions office there. But this is good work. We have become like Sherlock Holmes and his sidekick—what was his name?"

Darby laughed. "I have no idea. I was a Nancy Drew and Hardy Boys fan myself."

"Now it will bother me all night until I remember." Darby heard him sigh as she finished writing Professor Voss's information in her file. "Sherlock Holmes and . . . it has left my mind."

"I'll bring the letters when we meet for the conference. Please tell Katrine hello for me."

"Yes, and Katrine will be very pleased you returned. Before you leave, I am sure she will want some time with you. 'Girls' night out'—is that correct? How long are you staying?"

"Actually, I can stay as long as I want. I'm a free woman."

"Wonderful. Perhaps Austria is your future?"

"Perhaps."

"Watson, that is it!" he shouted.

"Excuse me?" Darby held the phone away from her ear.

"Elementary, my dear Watson. Sherlock Holmes and Dr. Watson. That was his name." Professor Voss chuckled as if he were embarrassed by his outburst. "I am really living up to an 'absent-minded professor' image, am I not?"

"I didn't know how much I'd missed you until now, Peter. I'll see you Saturday at the university, right?"

Professor Voss laughed heartily. "9:00 A.M."

The auditorium was crowded with conference attendees. As Darby searched for a seat, she recognized several languages in conversations surrounding her—French, German, and possibly Yiddish.

"Darby Evans!" a voice called from behind. Before she could turn, she felt a hearty pat on the back. People looked their way as Darby and Professor Voss had their reunion in the aisle.

"It is so good to see you again." His hazel eyes sparkled.

"And you also, Dr. Watson," Darby said with a smile.

"Excuse me, but I am Sherlock and you are my sidekick."

"Really?" They laughed together like people who'd known each other for years.

"I have a little something from America for you." Darby handed him a small, wrapped box.

"For me?" He acted like a child as he ripped open the paper. "A new Slinky! And just in time. My old one is a tangle of bent wire beyond further restoration."

"I expect a lot of help now that you have new inspiration."

"You will have it! Did you know the Slinky was invented by a man named Richard James in 1945? In fact, his wife conceived the name. Since that time it has sold over 250 million." Professor Voss opened the box and held the Slinky in his hands, passing it back and forth. "It takes over eighty feet of wire to make it."

"Very interesting. Only you would know the history of the Slinky."

"Come now, I have seats up closer. Remember, I may need to translate everything into your ear, except for the workshops in English."

"I remember. So I am the sidekick after all."

They found the seats reserved by Professor Voss's coat and beaten briefcase. They had just sat down when the conference commenced. An older professor took the stage, speaking solely in German. People laughed several times at what Darby expected to be the usual speaker jokes while Professor Voss tried to give her an overall translation of what would take place in the one-day conference. Darby decided she definitely needed some German classes, and soon. Each workshop teacher stood and gave an overview of his class. Then it was Brant Collins who rose from the front row to stand before the podium.

Brant had been in her thoughts almost daily since she'd returned to Salzburg. On one of her walks through Salzburg, she'd looked up his office, only eight blocks from her hotel. But what could she say to the man until she had some hard evidence to prove who her grandmother really was? Now here he was, standing before her.

He spoke first in German, then in English. Suddenly his eyes turned and met hers. He stumbled over his wording for a moment, then continued without glancing her way again. Brant announced that he was leading the English-speaking workshops.

Darby addressed the professor, who acted suspiciously preoccupied. "Peter, did you know Brant Collins would be here and that he'd be leading the English-speaking classes?"

"Of course I did," he said back with an innocent smile.

"Why are you smiling?"

"Me? Well, it would hurt nothing for the two of you to talk."

Darby's eyebrows lowered. "You aren't doing what I think you're doing?" She couldn't believe it, but his sly smile revealed his matchmaking intentions. "Remember that we have some major issues keeping us from being even acquaintances. Have you spoken with him at all while I've been gone?"

"No, but I think if you could tell him everything you have told me . . ."

"Is this why you invited me to the conference?" Darby whispered loudly as the room applauded the next workshop leader.

"Of course not. It just worked out that Brant was teaching all the English workshops. I thought you would find it very interesting and helpful in your quest into your past."

"My quest into my past. You make me sound so fascinating, like Jacques Cousteau searching the ocean for lost treasure."

"If you do discover the Lange inheritance, it will be as amazing as the Frenchman's discoveries."

"We have a long way to go before that happens."

Applause rippled again, and people began to rise from their seats.

"We now break into our workshops until the afternoon speaker. He is a survivor of Bergen-Belsen," Professor Voss said, standing. He winked and patted her shoulder. "I hope you enjoy your workshop."

⸗⊚⸗

Darby sat near the back of the classroom. The room filled quickly with mostly foreign attendees who would know the common language of English. Darby picked up a neat outline of Brant's workshop, "A Survivor's Continued Nightmare."

Brant entered the room, talking to a young man who took the last seat in the front row. Darby squirmed in her chair, wishing she could slide beneath it. Brant hooked a microphone to his shirt and turned the tape machine on before beginning his lecture. His face was tan with a very slight line along his temple toward the dark hair by his ears. Darby would get a similar sunglasses tan when she went snow-skiing often. Something in the way he moved sent a nervous jitter through her entire body.

Before he spoke, his deep brown eyes met Darby's. He nodded a greeting, then began to talk. The talk focused first on the lasting effects the Holocaust had on individual lives. He discussed the intense guilt many survivors felt over living while so many had died.

Brant's words made Darby recognize small signs she'd never noticed in Grandma Celia. Though her grandmother had not survived a concentration camp, she escaped Austria while many of her friends and family had not. Darby remembered Grandma's minor swings of depression over the years, especially during milestones such as the date of her wedding anniversary. Darby had known of these times, especially recalling occasional words that were out of place for the woman of strength and faith. "Have I done anything of importance with my life?" "I've never endured anything."

Hearing Brant talk about the constant, often hidden, struggles of many survivors made her wonder how much her grandmother had held inside. She wished she'd known sooner, that Grandma Celia wouldn't have had to bear her struggles alone.

As Brant moved to the next part of his talk, Darby fought against the stirring she felt inside every time he looked her way. He was more attractive than she remembered. He didn't seem as uptight, but more at ease with himself and the crowd. Darby found herself watching his hands holding the edge of the podium, or his eyes that looked above the people in the classroom to his own memories of survivor stories.

His workshop moved to the survivor today. He stressed the

importance of recording testimonies and of helping survivors and their families. Darby remembered the lists of people still seeking family and friends on the Internet site "Desperately Seeking."

"A large number of survivors have spent years in silence, unwilling to share their experiences with even their closest friends and family. Now, in their final years, many seek closure or want to record the truth of what happened. History is often twisted to fit modern times. My organization wishes to preserve the facts and lives of the Holocaust victims and survivors so future generations cannot change the truth of what happened."

A few people applauded. Brant paused awkwardly, then nodded.

"In my conclusion, I want to explain what I've only recently discovered. The Holocaust, or *Shoah,* was a horror unlike any humankind has seen. We must ensure that it does not happen again. We must uplift life by protecting those who cannot protect themselves, by rescuing and educating and loving both potential predator and victim. But since most of you here are educators, writers, journalists, politicians, or students aspiring to be one of these, I want to remind you of something I have missed until lately. Be sure to take the time to live your own life. The survivors have gone on with theirs to become statesmen, poets, diplomats, soldiers, film producers, and leaders in their communities. They have continued with life, marrying and having children."

Brant looked down for a long moment, as if he were sharing a deep secret he was unsure how to tell. He looked specifically at Darby, then at the entire class of listeners.

"Steven Spielberg, the renowned American filmmaker, received an Oscar at the Hollywood Academy Awards for best director of *Saving Private Ryan.* As Mr. Spielberg received the award, he said this: 'There is honor in looking back and respecting the past.' That is a statement to be remembered.

There is honor in looking back. We should respect the past. And yet, I must remind you, from personal experience, do not keep your eyes turned back so much that you miss your own today, and your own tomorrow. For we are each granted one life. Learn from yesterday. Heal the wounds of those around you—the pain is everywhere, in everyone. But also, live. . . . Thank you."

The room was deathly quiet until an elderly woman stood and began to clap. Others followed until every chair was empty. Brant was unhooking the microphone when people moved forward to shake his hand and ask questions. His eyes met Darby's, before the crowd blocked the way. She wanted to talk to him. His workshop had been powerful. Yet she could not deny her attraction toward this man who believed her grandmother a fraud. He had spoken with sincerity and depth in his voice. He had given the facts, but she could see how much he cared through his deep, brown eyes. He sought the crowd for under-standing. *Do you understand what these people have endured?* his eyes seemed to ask. *Don't return to your life and forget this.*

The line was long to speak with Brant, and Darby was unsure what to say. But it was clear he wasn't the coldhearted man she'd first believed him to be. However, that fact didn't change what he thought of her grandmother; and as yet, there was still no proof to change his mind. Darby didn't even know what he thought of *her*. She left the classroom, pausing in the hallway to collect her thoughts before moving toward the luncheon where she'd planned to meet Professor Voss.

⋅⊷➤═◉═⊶⋅

The afternoon passed rapidly with two more workshops. Darby had told Professor Voss about her interest in freelance photography for newspapers and magazines with some possi-ble writing in the future, and he encouraged her to attend two workshops, "Holocaust in the Modern Press" and "Preserving the Images of Yesterday," both taught by an international media giant. Darby found the classes provided headphones that translated the German into English, so Professor Voss didn't have to translate the workshops for her. The information was invaluable, giving her a renewed passion for the work she'd almost given up on. She might make a living yet, and she might love that work in a way she never had before.

As Darby left her last workshop and headed toward the main auditorium for the closing speaker, she rounded a corner and almost bumped into Brant.

"Excuse me," she said, awkward in his presence.

"How are you?" he asked.

"Good, and you?"

"Good."

"I really enjoyed your workshop this morning."

"Thank you."

"Well—," they said at the same time, then stopped. They stood in the hall with people moving by and suddenly both smiled at once.

"Do you realize how much you surprised me when I was introducing my workshop?" Brant asked, shaking his head. "I nearly lost my entire train of thought. I thought you were in the States, and there you are, sitting next to Peter."

"I was just as shocked to see *you* walk up there." Darby couldn't stop a giggle as she remembered his expression. "Now we're even, since you made me cry and nearly burst with anger on the first day we met."

"I don't always bring out the worst in people."

"No, just me." Darby tucked a strand of hair behind her ear, aware of how close they stood.

"I really did feel bad about the crying thing."

"You should have. I don't cry easily."

When Brant smiled, Darby noticed his smooth-shaved jaw and soft-looking lips.

"So you couldn't stay away from Austria?"

"Somehow it lured me back," she said.

"And . . ." Brant hesitated, as if contemplating whether to ask. "Have you found anything?"

"Herr Collins?" A young woman with a handful of papers nudged him from behind.

Brant turned to gather the papers from the petite girl. Darby was surprised she spoke in English.

"Can I do anything else to help you?" the girl asked, biting her lip.

"No, this is great. Thank you, Melissa."

"Any time." Melissa glanced back twice coyly as she walked down the hall, but only Darby noticed.

"They just surround you," Darby said.

"What?" Brant looked confused.

"Still as gullible as ever."

Brant appeared lost, then the light bulb turned on. "Not that again. She's a student from the States."

"I'm surprised you haven't been snatched up by one of these Austrian ladies," Darby said, then realized her joking had struck home, on a very personal note.

"I lose whatever charm I possess with my life revolving around work. Like I said today, I only recently learned the value of living. And look who's talking. Why, Darby Evans, are you still unmarried?"

She gulped. Their joking had turned serious, and she didn't like it aimed her way. "I suppose, much the same reason. All work and no play—you know." Darby consulted her watch. "But look at the time." He grinned as she diverted their conversation.

"Time for the general session, just in time." Brant shook his head. "I'll see you later, Darby."

⋆⇒◯⇐⋆

"Remember me?" Richter said into the cell phone. He walked away from the bright sidewalk down a darkened pathway near the river. A group of tourists passed, chattering in the cold as they turned to cross the river into the Old City.

"What do you want?" the voice replied. "I thought you were never calling us again, never coming back. We've adjusted quite nicely."

Richter clenched his fist. He needed to stay calm. He needed to get this right. "I just wanted to see how you and Mom are doing."

"That's a good one. I know you need money for your debts. But since you asked, your mom and I have never been better in the last two years. So don't try coming back into our lives. It's not going to happen."

"I've cleaned up my life, Dad," Richter said.

"I don't care, Richter. Long ago I quit having a son, so don't call again."

"When did you ever have a son?" Richter slammed the phone against the railing again and again. He cursed and hurled the phone toward the dark waters, hearing a splash a second later.

Now what would he do? His father was his last chance. Yet when had his father ever shown him any love? Richter had been sent to boarding school all year and in the summer to Gunther and Ingrid's. He was an only child, the one neither of his parents ever wanted. They had their life with rich friends and rich vacations, and a kid didn't fit into what they wanted out of life.

He cursed again and pounded his fist against the railing.

"Having problems again, Richter?" a voice said from behind.

Richter turned slowly to face a large, older man rising from a bench behind him. He looked straight at the man whose unwavering stare brought a fearful churning in Richter's stomach. His contact was not supposed to be this early, and it certainly wasn't supposed to be this man. Richter had seen him once, but only in passing. Why would he take the risk to meet Richter in person? It wasn't a good sign.

"Everything is great," Richter said, forcing a smile.

"You were given your loan in good faith. Now I suppose you're going to tell me you need more time—again."

"I told Thom about the old Lange inheritance," Richter brought up quickly. "Did he tell you?"

"It's your ticket to wealth, I suppose."

"I know it is. You don't understand the worth of the brooch alone. And the coins—there may not be another set of this kind in the world. I'll pay you back and have enough to loan you money."

The man didn't join in the joke.

"Anyway, the woman who could be my opportunity just came back to the city."

"So what are you going to do?"

"I have some plans, and you don't have to worry, I make good on my debts. I always have before."

"I'm more interested in the Lange inheritance. I'd also like to hear everything you know about this woman, Darby Evans."

Richter frowned. How did the contact know her name? "Will some of this come off my tab?"

"Just keep me informed. Not through Thom, but straight to me. I'll take care of everything else."

Frank Beck looked like any older man Darby would see at an early-bird breakfast at Denny's or walking a miniature dog in the park. He lived in Florida, golfed with his friends, attended synagogue, and drove a motor home in the summer months to destinations with cooler weather—his favorite trip had been a six-week drive to Alaska. His wife of fifty-one years liked to knit booties for their new grandbabies and great-grandbabies and to play cards with her friends. The couple especially loved morning coffee with cream-cheese danishes on the balcony of their condo. But, too often, Frank Beck returned to his previous life, sometimes during the night or when driving past an industrial smokestack or when hearing the sound of a train rumbling on its tracks. Then Frank would find himself hungry, cold, and completely terrified even as he clenched the wheel of his silver Cadillac or sweated on his Serta Perfect Sleeper mattress.

Frank spoke in English, for like Grandma Celia, he vowed never to speak German again. Coming to a German-speaking country for this conference was most difficult.

Darby watched Frank as he spoke to the captive audience. He first told of his life today, then descended into the darkness of a history that lived with every beat of his heart. "It was my job to burn bodies in the ovens. I did my job—or I'd become like them. Very quickly you are numbed to the reality, the smell, and the faces you choose not to see. But one day, right before me, I recognized a face. It was my father. We'd been separated months earlier, and I had tried to find where he was taken. Then I found him right there. I could not think of it. I put my father into the oven to burn." His words faltered.

"Some people do not understand why many survivors continue to seek compensation or the return of properties, heirlooms, and money. Yet the companies that profited from our labor continue to thrive. The banks and insurance companies that would not return monies have earned much interest and wealth from us. Imagine the insurance policy your father purchases and faithfully pays is then used to fund the Nazi regime that destroys your family and life. Then when you attempt to claim your father's insurance after the war, you are rejected, though you hold the policy in your hand." Frank held his fist in the air. "The policy the insurance company gave your father is in your hand after hiding beneath the floor of your barn for six years. There is the proof, but still you are rejected. Why? Because the Nazis didn't issue death certificates when they murdered. Insurance policies require proof of death, not just an eyewitness who saw his father's face before burning it."

He shook his head and his voice lowered. "Yet people say it is long since past. 'Frank, you have rebuilt your life. Leave it behind you.' For my wife, myself, and many others, it cannot be left behind. It is forever part of us. We had every bit of humanity stolen from us. Yes, we survived, but there are pieces that can never be reclaimed."

He paused, looking down at the podium. "And yet, I did not

come here this weekend to emphasize such things. Instead, I want to be a reminder to those who will listen and take the message outward. Again and again, we say do not forget. Simon Weisenthal writes this in his book *Justice Not Vengeance:* 'Hatred can be nurtured anywhere, idealism can be perverted into sadism anywhere. If hatred and sadism combine with modern technology, the inferno could erupt anew anywhere.' I say to each one of you, tell the stories and remember us."

With those simple words, Frank Beck left the stage. The auditorium echoed in serious applause, not a roar of jubilation, but with hands together in honor and respect. Darby could not clap, only watch the man descend the stairs.

The conference closed, and she walked slowly through the crowd toward the exit. She thought to tell Professor Voss good-bye, but he was in the midst of a crowd of colleagues. A blast of cold hit her face as she pushed open the university doors. The clouds churned in the late-afternoon sky, as if deciding whether to create a storm or move on.

She halted on the landing with her hands on the railing. A thousand sentences, words, and feelings from the seminar coursed through her mind, but what could she do with it all? One thing was clear: she'd never be the same. Her eyes had opened a little more. There was so much more to know and learn and understand, and suddenly she wanted to know so much and to pass it along to others. Perhaps her photographs would do that for others someday.

Addressing the gray-and-white clouds wrestling above the tops of the buildings, she vowed, *I'm going to share stories. Like my grandmother before me, I will be a storyteller like I was designed to be. Whether through photographs or words, I want to share with people who are like me—seeking light through the darkness.*

And as Brant had said, she wanted to live her life with all

the fullness she could find. *God, I've lived my life without you for a long time and even now forget you all the time. But I know I need your help. I need you every day.*

The door opened behind her, and several people left the building. Darby adjusted the strap on her satchel, waiting for them to pass. Then she headed back toward the city center. She had some photographs that needed to be taken.

"Darby! Wait!"

She turned to see Brant Collins jogging down the street from the university entrance. "Professor Voss asked me to walk you back to your hotel. He regrets he could not be here himself."

"I think I can manage without help." Darby knew what Professor Voss was up to, and she didn't like it.

"I go this way, anyway," he said, falling into step beside her. He pointed toward the sheer mountain cliff above the cathedral domes. "I live on the other side of Mönchsberg, through the tunnel."

Darby looked toward the mountain. She'd never gone through the tunnel to the other side. The Old City had become like home, but the rest of Salzburg was still a mystery. "As long as I'm on the way."

As they continued on, Darby remembered the first time they'd met and walked these same streets.

"What did you think of the conference?" Brant asked.

"Excellent, very moving. The last speaker was incredible."

"It's amazing to discover what man will do to man," Brant said quietly.

"I can't understand it." Darby glanced at Brant. She wondered what those eyes had seen and ears had heard. No wonder he became lost in his work, forgetting how to live. "I don't think I could hear those things all the time."

"I think you could. You'd do it because it's important to help them. It's important to record their lives and try to understand, if even in the smallest sense. They deserve at least understanding. It's amazing what takes us so long to see."

"What do you mean?" Darby asked.

"Here I am in my thirties and finally starting to see what life is supposed to be about. Not just work or myself, but well, the big picture."

Darby weighed her next words. "You mean the big, big picture. As in, God?"

She saw him hesitate, then plow forward.

"I guess I am. Here we walk with the religion of Christianity influencing most everything in this city. But to get past religion and history and look at it for yourself, the real meaning of God, Christ even, and then accept it for yourself . . . Well, I guess you didn't need to hear this."

Darby almost didn't want to admit that she understood what he meant. "Actually, I know exactly what you mean. Kind of scary, isn't it?"

Brant stopped. "You too?"

Darby could only nod. She was just discovering God on her own and couldn't quite explain without referring to the influences of Tatianna and Celia in her life. She and Brant would start talking about God and end up arguing about who her grandmother was or wasn't. But Darby did wonder, as they continued a thoughtful pace, how two people who had such obstacles between them also had reached the same place in their lives, and they seemed to be moving in the same direction.

They passed through Mozartplatz with its tall statue of Wolfgang Amadeus Mozart, then turned toward the river.

"I'm this way," she said, motioning straight ahead.

"No Cozy Hotel?"

Darby caught the raised eyebrow and small grin. "I'm at the Zur Goldenen Ente on Goldgasse."

Brant smiled. "Staying a bit more Austrian, I see."

"I try not to be too gullible," she said, lifting her head a bit.

He laughed softly as they stepped toward Residenzplatz beside a string of shops and restaurants. The streets were busier with window-shoppers and strollers crowding the sidewalks. They walked until the block of buildings opened to Goldgasse, with its gold sign fluttering above. The breeze was calm in the street that seemed more like a mysterious passageway. A single car could squeeze down the first third of the street, then it narrowed more tightly and only pedestrians could fit all the way through.

"Here I am," Darby announced when they reached the yellow Hotel Zur Goldenen Ente. A wreath of decorations lined the doorway and windows. Tables were folded against one side of the building since it was too cold even for the outdoors-loving Austrians to eat on the street.

"So here you are." Brant shuffled his feet, as if he wanted to say something. He glanced at the five-story hotel connected as one with the other buildings on the block. "I was wondering. . . . I thought I'd ask though it's kind of late notice."

Surprised to see that calm, cool, collected Brant Collins was acting nervous, Darby queried, "You thought you'd ask what?"

"An elderly couple in my last workshop gave me tickets to a dinner concert." His eyes roamed the ground, the opposite building, her shoulder, but didn't look directly at her. Suddenly, she thought she knew. Could Brant Collins be asking her for a *date?*

"I guess the couple bought the tickets but have to leave the city tonight. It's at the St. Peter Stiftkeller, a nice restaurant. You might find it interesting if you like Mozart. It's very Austrian."

"I like Mozart," she said, confused about his intentions again. "Are you giving me the tickets, or are you . . ."

"Well, yes, I could give you the tickets," he said, stumbling over his words. "They're here in my pocket." He fumbled in his black coat, pulled out the two tickets, and handed them to her.

"Or were you asking me to go with you?" she interrupted.

Brant shrugged. "It doesn't matter. You take them and enjoy."

Darby smiled. Seeing him squirm for once was quite nice. "Why don't you take one, and we'll both go? I can meet you in front, or we don't even have to sit together, unless it's reserved seating."

Brant seemed to relax. "No, it's not. But since it's easier for me to go on foot than try to find parking, I could come by and walk with you. . . . If you want me to."

"Sure," she said, trying to sound casual and unaffected by the thought of an evening together.

"I'll be by at seven-fifteen. It starts at eight, but I'd like to get there early."

"I'll see you then." Darby's mind ran in a million directions— what should she wear, what was she doing?

Brant left so quickly that she wondered if he had similar misgivings, similar butterflies. She hurried upstairs after checking her watch. What would they talk about? How could they possibly go somewhere together without bringing up the obstacle that kept them apart?

⊷⊜⊶

Darby heard the elevator doors open but waited the appropriate five seconds before opening the door to Brant's knock.

"Hello," she said, uncomfortable with her clothes and hair and shoes and everything she'd tried on and tossed and done in the last two hours. She wondered why she'd chosen the long, black skirt. Would she be able to walk in her black dress shoes? The black shirt with burgundy-and-black scarf suddenly seemed tight, and her face felt hot. She'd curled her straight hair with hot rollers and sprayed them till they barely moved. Did it look too fluffy and unlike her?

"Ready?" she said, hoping he didn't notice her blush.

"You look really great," Brant said with a smile.

That's when she noticed how good he looked, also dressed in black with turtleneck, jacket, and slacks. Her grandmother would say, "Dashing!"

"You do too—look great, I mean." Darby hurried to get her key and purse before he noticed the pile of clothing stuffed on the other side of the bed.

Salzburg was cold and the sky dark as they walked, but as usual, the city had yet to fall asleep. Beacons of light shone on the fortress above and on cathedral towers, around fountains, and from street lamps. Patches of snow glowed on Mönchsberg, but she'd been told that the city hadn't had snow in weeks. Through archways and plazas, they arrived at St. Peter Stiftkeller, nestled against Mönchsberg's sheer rock. As they entered an open-air courtyard in the center, Darby noticed the netting above that hopefully stopped any loose rocks from hitting the building. High above and beyond view, Hohensalzburg kept a watchful eye over the Old City. Dried vines hung from the sides of the netting, probably lush and beautiful in the spring and a wonderful place to eat with the open sky above for those seeking love. Darby liked the dark, wooded restaurant, but it wasn't what she'd anticipated for a Mozart Dinner Concert. She followed Brant's lead up a stairway and down a long hall. They put their coats in a small room, then entered a beautiful hall. Darby paused in the doorway. This was more than she'd hoped for. The baroque décor, chandeliers, wood floors, and tables laden with flowers and china gave the effect of stepping back into the eighteenth century. The waiters wore red jackets with white ruffled shirts, and waitresses moved around tables in full skirts and aprons.

Brant stood beside her in the doorway. "The St. Peter Stiftkeller was first mentioned by Alkuin, a court scribe, during a visit by Emperor Charlemagne in the first century. It's considered the oldest restaurant in Central Europe." He extended his arm. "Shall we, my lady?"

Darby put her arm through his. "Yes, we shall."

The tables were already filling, and they found two seats at a round table near the front of a small stage. Darby sat and scooted herself up just as she noticed that Brant had tried to push her in.

"I've obviously not dated in a while, especially someone with manners," Darby said apologetically, then laughed.

"You speak English—you sound American?" a young woman beside her asked.

"Yes, and you're an American too?"

"We're all Americans on this side of the table." Three other women about Darby's age said hello. "We also have a couple from Brazil." The man and woman nodded. The American woman continued, "Our other couple is from Hungary, but they don't speak English very well. So what about your guy?"

"He's not really my guy, I mean, not my guy at all—," Darby said, stuttering.

"I'm Austrian *and* American," Brant replied. He smiled at Darby, seeming to enjoy her very red face. "Are you ladies here together?"

"Oh, yes. We are four married women on the loose."

"That sounds dangerous. So how did you pick Salzburg?" Brant asked.

"Well, Lucee and I have always dreamed of coming to Europe." She nudged a brunette beside her who was looking at a mural on the ceiling. "Oh, my name is Cate," she said, extending her hand to them both. "Anyway, Lorna loves classical music and plays the violin—and of course, this is Mozartland. Bailey didn't care where we went; she'll travel anywhere. After a bit of research, pulling places out of a hat, finding babysitters for the mass of kids we have between us, and getting the guys to agree—well, here we are."

Lorna, the musician, joined the conversation. "We decided that if you get the chance, sometimes you just have to go for it."

"I agree," Brant said, eyeing Darby. "Why else would I invite you here tonight?"

"Really?" Darby returned wryly. "You didn't exactly invite me—at least not very well."

"We're here, aren't we?" Brant put in with a grin.

Darby shook her head at him in mock chagrin and turned back toward Cate. The woman with pale skin and green eyes studied Brant, then Darby, evidently trying to figure out their relationship.

"So this is the trip of a lifetime?" Darby asked quickly.

"Or the first of many over our lifetime," Cate said, then leaned closer. "My friends are a bit strange at times, but I'm glad to be stuck with them."

"We heard that," Bailey said from a few seats over. She pointed a long, manicured finger toward Cate. "You're stuck with us, so get used to it."

Lorna added playfully, "We need Cate for our journeys. This girl can strike up a conversation with anyone, whether they speak English or not."

At that the four women laughed as only close friends can, as if behind a simple glance were jokes and memories no one but each other could understand. This evening felt right— with a man at one side and other women who understood friendship surrounding Darby. And all this in the magical setting of Mozart's day.

A waiter arrived to take drink orders and Bailey announced, "Champagne for our entire table. This is a night to remember."

"This is the best butter I've ever had," Lucee said, taking a bite of her roll.

"And the bread and cheese," Lorna added with a bright smile. "Except Bailey and I would pay fifty dollars for a Coke with ice."

"I've been loving the ham—oh, the ham in Austria," Cate said with a sigh.

Darby bent close. "Breakfasts here are the best. I love those rolls they serve at every hotel and bakery. And the jams."

All five women noticed Brant's humored expression, and they burst into laughter.

The champagne arrived and everyone toasted together. Suddenly, as if the clink of glasses was the cue, the doors in back burst open and the musicians entered the hall. All eyes were on their entrance as they carried their instruments to the small stage in front—several violins, a cello, and a bass. They sat, adjusted music in front of them and then, like a long-awaited exhale, the first violin began to play. A second later, the other strings joined, dipping and swaying in their individual steps that combined into a perfectly choreographed dance. From the entrance, a rich voice bellowed.

In dashed a dark-haired man in a red Mozart coat, wearing a black hat with white plumage. He moved toward the front of the stage with posture straight, arms out wide, and a slight smile upon his lips. His voice boomed above the strings in an Italian song.

The American women *oohed* and *aahed* enough for all of them, though Darby too felt the exuberance of such a night. The program continued with music and opera between dinner courses: cream of lemon soup with chicken slices, braised fillet of pork on applewine-horseradish sauce served with potatoes, and dessert, *Wespenneste,* a sweet surprise with a cocoa profile of Mozart's face. Darby took in the stained-glass windows and the mural on the carved, coffered ceiling. The sophisticated ambiance was like nothing she'd experienced previously. Brant smiled at her when she looked his way. With their chairs turned during the music, Darby sometimes felt too strongly Brant's presence so near her one side. Once, when he dropped his program, his warm breath brushed the side of her neck as he bent beside her. For one night she wanted to forget their differences. It seemed they both knew without speaking a word that they disagreed greatly, but were willing to put it aside for one evening together.

The musicians returned after the last course and were joined by a couple who pranced and sang around the tables. The man would reach for the woman, and she would teasingly run away. Around and around the tables they sang and chased until at last he captured the woman, drawing her into an irresistible embrace. The room roared with applause as the song ended. The couple skipped to the front and bowed, then turned and motioned toward the musicians, who stood and bowed. The applause thundered through the room. Darby's hands hurt from clapping, but she continued to applaud as the entire entourage exited the hall.

Darby's face felt flushed as they entered the night's chill. She said good-bye to the American foursome, who laughed and chattered as they strolled away. Suddenly she was alone with Brant after one of the most remarkable evenings of her life. She who loved the song of the mountains had found love in Mozart's strings. Better yet, she could tell that Brant understood how awed she was by this night.

"Do you go to these events often?" she asked as he slid her coat around her.

"I've lived in Salzburg for years, but that's the first time I've gone there." They made their way across the small square where taxis picked up patrons.

Darby stopped after they stepped through an archway. "Thank you for taking me. I feel like a child on her first trip to Disneyland."

"You're welcome," he said, looking down at her. Brant glanced behind them and pulled her away from the street and close to him.

"A bike was coming," was all he said before the familiar

jingle of chain and metal passed by. Darby drank in his closeness, getting a quick scent of aftershave. Just as she was about to move away after the bike passed, Brant's fingers encircled hers.

They walked the cobblestoned street without speaking a word. Their hands spoke in turns, tracing palms and fingers. Their fingers folded together, then slid apart, and together again. Darby's breath was stolen, and her eyes closed at her pounding insides.

Then he stopped and drew her toward him. Darby's back touched the stucco wall, her hands fell to her side. Brant took a step toward her, their eyes locked together in the darkened corner. He lifted a hand and touched her hair, then ran a finger along her cheek and onto her lips.

He opened his mouth as if to speak, then instead bent to kiss her. He hesitated a moment before their lips gently touched. His hands rested on the wall beside her face, his body came closer until every inch of her felt his closeness and wanted him even closer. Brant kissed her softly, then longer and deeper. She felt herself melting away. Then a nagging voice spoke inside her head.

"Wait," she whispered. "Wait. Or I-I don't know what will happen to me."

Brant took a shaky breath and stepped back. He gazed at Darby tenderly, then turned away, running a hand through his hair. Neither spoke as he took her hand, and they began to walk again.

This time Darby stopped. She took both his hands.

"If you could only believe?" Darby pleaded with her eyes. He had to have some faith in her or she could not do this, or allow herself to feel this.

"I do believe—I believe you." His eyes became sad.

"But you don't believe my grandmother." Darby shook her head as he looked away.

"It's not as simple as you think," he said. "Next week I testify in a trial because I trusted without being sure. And I'm already sure about your grandmother. I don't know why you can't face the truth."

"Truth? I know the truth. Professor Voss and Katrine believe it also, so why don't you talk to them? I don't understand why you aren't willing to try—to be open to the possibility. Otherwise, everything I seek is fighting against you."

"There's so much I want to tell you, but—"

"Brant, thank you for giving me the best night of my life," she said, then fled, leaving him standing in the shadows.

⋆⚊◉⚊⋆

Brant counted the floors and saw a light turn on in Darby's room. She was right up there so close, yet so far from his reach. He stood in a darkened shop entrance across from her hotel and sagged against the doorway. He cared for Darby Evans, could even fall in love with her. But he ached for he knew she was the one person he could not have—at least, not now. Perhaps not ever.

She wanted him to believe in something he could never believe. Was he doomed to the fate of Gunther—to never have love that would last?

Brant saw a shadow pass the window. He wasn't giving up without a fight. He'd find out who Darby's grandmother really was. Once she accepted the fact, perhaps they'd have a chance. Or would she resent the truth coming from him? First he'd get the answers. She was too close to let go of now.

CHAPTER TWENTY-FIVE

Darby knew her motives weren't completely clear, but her determination was renewed after a night of very little sleep. The time had come to pull out the stops and begin digging. She needed proof of her grandmother's identity, and Darby hoped Bruno Weiler would be that proof. She had met other dead ends and the SS guard might be another, but Darby was ready to find out. If it went badly, she'd try something new.

A taxi took her to the train station, where Darby purchased a ticket for Hallstatt. As she rode the white ferry across the dark waters of Hallstattersee, the memory returned that her grandfather had driven the ferry—perhaps this very one. She gazed at the driver and tried to imagine what her grandfather had looked like. She'd never seen a photograph of him.

Darby rang the bell on the desk of Gasthaus Gerringer and heard footsteps upstairs. Sophie exclaimed as she saw Darby and rushed to hug her tightly.

"I so happy to see you again," Sophie said. "You still in Austria, I see."

"I went back to California but had to return," Darby said happily, as if they were old friends.

"I believe your same room available today." Sophie reached for a book under the counter.

"I don't need a room," Darby said, wondering what response she was about to receive. "I came to talk to your grandmother again."

"I think she will see you." Sophie's eyes sparkled, much to Darby's relief. "She is much changed since you last came. My mother and I think it because she got her past in open and she know we still love her. Please, give me moment and I will be back."

A few minutes later, Darby stood before the old woman. She looked the same as last time, except there was no *hmmp* greeting. Instead the old woman nodded at Darby's *"Grüß Gott."*

Darby sat in the chair across from Frau Gerringer. "Bruno Weiler," Darby said, watching for any changed expression. "You gave me his name, and I thank you. I've found that Herr Weiler was at Mauthausen as an SS guard, like you said. I'm asking if you will tell me everything you know about him."

Sophie spoke to her grandmother, then back to Darby. "What have you found, she asks?"

"I haven't found a lot of facts." Darby sighed and looked straightforwardly into the old woman's eyes. "I haven't found the facts I need. But I'm learning a lot about my grandmother and about myself. When I was here before, I came because my grandmother asked me to. I did not tell you that the records say my grandmother was not Celia Müller. They say Celia Müller died at Mauthausen. But I know that Tatianna Hoffman died under Celia's name, instead of her. Now I am here for myself. I want to prove what happened so I can change the memorials and give Tatianna the honor she deserves. If possible, I also want to find what happened to my family inheritance."

The old woman didn't speak for a few moments. Then Sophie translated for her. "She say you are learning many things, as even this old woman is. But your family inheritance. Many people seek such things today, but they are only objects, not lives."

"Yes. And if they are not recovered, it is God's will. But Tatianna gave up her life, and I'm alive because of it. I must at least try to do my part. If I fail, I'll know that at least I've tried."

"She will tell you what she know about Bruno Weiler."

Darby felt she'd just passed some kind of test. She relaxed against the back of her chair and thanked the old woman.

Sophie listened to her grandmother. "She say they all were in school together. Bruno was younger. He was a funny boy, always joking and laughing. But father very stern. Bruno not like to go home when father not working. He ate dinner at her family's house many times. He and younger brother were friends, also good friends with your grandmother's brother. My grandmother married young, but she still live in village and see this." Sophie paused and listened again. "Very near same time of marriage, Bruno leave for Vienna to stay with aunt. He keep in contact with her brother and visit sometime—he cut off communication with Celia's brother; Warner was his name. I'm sure because he was part Jewish. One winter, Bruno comes with Nazi youth information. He try to get village boys to join and go to Vienna, but her father not let brother."

The back-and-forth dialogue continued as Darby took quick notes. "They hear nothing for long time. Then brother get letter about Bruno's position at Mauthausen. Later, her brother join war and was killed first week in battle. They not hear from Bruno again. Then after the war, she read he was charged with crimes and sent to prison. Nothing else after that."

Darby glanced up from her paper. "I found out he went to university in Vienna after he was released from prison in 1957."

"She say his mother moved to Vienna after his father die.

She live with her sister there. Mother name was Dorthe
Schumacher Weiler and her sister was Heike Schumacher.
Heike was not married."

"When was the last time she heard anything about them?"
Darby asked.

The old woman shrugged and scratched her chin before
speaking again.

"She say it had to be around 1950 or 1955. Long time ago."

"Can you remember anything else?" Darby wrote down the
information as the old woman shook her head.

"She say that is all she know of family and of Bruno." Frau
Gerringer put a hand on Darby's arm. "She say she hope you
discover all that you seek."

Darby nodded and clasped the old woman's hand, placing
her other hand on top. "*Danke.* I hope so too."

A distant roll of thunder echoed through the mountains to
the village.

"Oh, I hear that storm coming tonight," Sophie said. She
opened the curtain, and Darby could see the rain already
beginning to fall.

"Perhaps I'll stay tonight after all," Darby said. She had
brought a duffel bag with extra clothes just in case she found
some lead to follow.

"I'll give you your room, then," Sophie said with a bright
smile. "And you will eat dinner with our family."

⋅✦⟐⟐⟐✦⋅

The mountain storm crashed in quickly, and Darby was glad
she'd decided to stay. She loved the fearful sound of thunder in
the mountains as it rolled down peaks and ridges, echoing
through crevasse and saddleback. Sophie gave her the key to
her second-story lakeside room without showing it to her,
since Darby wasn't a customer but a guest now. She came down

for dinner with the Gerringer family of three women that reminded her of her own family. Later she carried up an electric heater to use until the water radiator that was warmed by a woodstove downstairs grew hot enough to heat the rooms above. Darby fell asleep bundled within the thick feather comforter while winter howled and beat its fist against the windows.

But late in the night, something woke her. Silence. Darby wrapped a blanket around her shoulders and stepped onto the balcony. Her bare feet touched cold snow. She slipped her feet into her boots without tying the laces and returned outside. The moon through the puffy after-storm clouds had turned the lake and air and snow and trees into a deep winter blue.

Darby had never cared much for winter. The season came and stripped the land of life. It disguised itself in purest white, but destroyed all it touched.

"I'm sorry I'm a traitor," Darby whispered to the broken, limp sticks that last fall had probably held bright flowers. "But I can't hate winter tonight."

As she looked into the blue world so still and full of magic, she wondered about the winter that stole life from the land. But perhaps winter was not the end, but actually the beginning. The harsh conditions stripped away all that was hidden in the summer months. It beat and seemed nearly to destroy until the essence of all things was made visible. Both good and bad could not hide from the cutting winds and tempest storms. And only through a winter passing could life be brought to its knees in surrender and prepared for rebirth.

Darby stared into the deep winter sky.

This is your winter, she could hear Grandma say. *We all pass through times of winter. But winter will pass. And as you heal, you find yourself stronger, richer, more alive than ever before.* Darby imagined the gentle hand, pushing a strand of hair behind her ear. The sky called to her, and Grandma's voice disappeared. Instead she heard a voice from deeper within her soul, a voice she'd only begun to know: *This is your winter, Darby. Embrace it as I bring life in you again.*

CHAPTER TWENTY-SIX

We have half the letters translated," Professor Voss said as Darby's white breath was cut in two when she closed the door to the phone booth. The cold morning shone with the covering of new snow on trees and walkways, a crystal blanket of white.

"Do they offer any information?" she asked, warming her mittened hand by rubbing it against the side of the phone.

"Not really. They are all letters your grandmother wrote to your grandfather over the past sixty years. They tell what is happening in her life, how much she misses him, the life events of her daughter, and later, grandchildren."

"Why do you think they were written in German? My grandmother never spoke one word of German that I ever heard—until on her deathbed."

"I am no psychologist, but perhaps, because of her vow to never speak German, it helped to write the letters. Or maybe she held a bit of hope that she would someday find Gunther and be able to give them to him."

"It's pretty sad," Darby said.

"*Ja*, but also very inspiring. They had great love. So you are returning to Salzburg?"

"I'm going to Vienna," she said and began to shiver.

"What is happening?"

"I found out for certain that Bruno Weiler knew both my grandmother and Tatianna. His aunt and mother lived in Vienna after the war. Perhaps I'll find one of them in the city or another Weiler. Since I'm partway there, I decided I might as well see your capital before returning to Salzburg."

"You will probably find nothing, but a trip to Vienna is essential for all travelers at one time or another. There are also many places with archives in Vienna, but in German, of course. I wish I could be there to help, but I have classes all week."

"I'll make a quick trip and see what I can find." Darby's teeth chattered. "I have so many trails to follow. There is the search for the brooch and coins. This morning I asked at the museum if any Celtic coins had been discovered in Hallstatt, but they said no. Then there's finding proof about Tatianna, and I'd like to gain more information about my family, especially my grandfather."

"It seems Bruno Weiler is the key to many things now."

"Yes." Her entire body was shivering, and Darby wished for more of the warm fruit tea she'd had at breakfast. "But I'm freezing out here, so I'll call you from Vienna."

"Katrine is here and says to go to Demel's Bakery. It is the best in Vienna."

"I'll do it."

"And Darby." Professor Voss's usually cheerful voice sounded serious. "Be careful."

⊷═◉═⊷

Brant had accomplished little of his workload in the last two days with two companies pressuring him to finish his end of the work. He received notice that he would not be called as a witness after all in the Aldrich case—the duo had opted for a plea bargain. Part of him was relieved; another part longed to face the man and woman and give his testimony. But beyond the Aldrich case, much more was bothering him. He had to decide what to do about Darby. Should he simply tell her everything and see what happened? Suddenly, Brant knew. Professor Peter Voss. Darby said the professor believed her. Once Brant told him the facts, that could change, and Peter would know what to do next.

Brant consulted his desktop Rolodex and punched in the phone number.

"Peter, this is Brant. I need to talk to you."

"Well, all I must say is, it is about time."

Brant shook his head. "Then you really do believe all of this."

"Definitely. Why do you not?"

"Because it can't be true."

"Why not?"

Gunther. Gunther could not have been wrong all these years. "We need to talk. I'll be right there."

◦─◌═◐═◌─◦

Darby had ridden a train only once, and that was an antique locomotive in Mount Shasta, California, which included a staged train robbery. The trains of Europe were like moving from a Model T Ford to a modern sports car. They were a reliable way of transportation here—running on schedule, efficient and comfortable. She climbed aboard a non-smoking car and found a vacant section where the seating was divided into separate rooms. As she stored her luggage overhead, the train *whooshed* from the Hallstatt station. The Eurail pass she'd purchased in Salzburg allowed a week of travel over a four-month period. If Vienna didn't work out, Darby could board a train and go nearly anywhere in Europe. By morning she could be in Paris or Rome or Amsterdam—the thought was tempting.

Snow flurries turned to raindrops as the train journeyed from the northern mountains to the open rolling hills of Upper Austria into the Danube region. After a while near the Danube, Darby looked up from her Austrian Tours map toward the direction of Mauthausen. She was back, riding past what would forever rest on the hillside with its ghosts and ash pile.

The rolling hills and fields succumbed to dense forest—the Vienna Woods that led into the heart of the city itself. Darby grabbed her bag and waited for the doors to slide open. She quickly walked through the smoky train station toward the exit, then halted, gazing up at the buildings and bustle and feeling like Mary Tyler Moore. She breathed the city—ah, Vienna! Home for centuries to artists, musicians, culture, and coffeehouses. The imperial city was a bridge between the East and West, a mixture of cultures and ethnic groups from Viennese to Slavic heritages. These streets had seen empires rise and fall, had been the toast of the classical world and the host for Cold War conferences where surely spies met their contacts with plots of espionage.

Darby had read about the city in her guidebook like every good tourist should, but added her own notes from her grandmother's stories. For Vienna had also welcomed a newly wed couple for their honeymoon. Darby remembered her grandmother saying, "Salzburg is quaint with charm—your darling welcoming with outstretched arms. Vienna is like an enchanter who draws you with his sophistication, though you fear his power."

Darby felt small in the midst of the enchanter. The afternoon sky sprinkled snow flurries as she hurried toward a line of taxis parked along the street. Though she hadn't made hotel reservations, there was no doubt where she'd stay, despite the cost.

"Hotel Sacher, please, *bitte*," Darby said as the driver of a white Mercedes took her lone duffel bag.

"Ah," the man said with a smile. "Very good choice."

The Mercedes zipped forward, darting in and out of traffic. Darby wanted to look at the map and out the window toward the sights, but she kept her eyes on the road ahead. This was carsick travel. As a delivery truck whirled past them and then they zipped around two cars, Darby knew she'd made the right decision not to rent a car with these crazy streets and crazier drivers. They zoomed past a long park and again Darby wished she could read her guidebook and map. Unlike Salzburg, with the old city and sights in the same area, Vienna stretched out with its palaces, parliament buildings, opera houses, parks, and historical sites scattered around the huge "inner stadt" or city center. The famous Ringstraße hemmed it all into a labyrinth of connected one-way streets, with the Danube River making a flowing barrier on one end.

Darby was completely turned around, believing they should be leaving the city, when she saw the massive State Opera House. The taxi stopped on the opposite side of the street. She stepped out of the cab and looked up to a towering hotel with red banners and flags fluttering in the late afternoon breeze. Hotel Sacher.

The driver tipped his hat before speeding away. Darby stood at the red carpet entrance, staring up at the luxurious hotel. Her faded jeans, brown boots in need of polish, and brown, hip-length leather jacket didn't quite fit with the opulence of the hotel, but she eagerly walked inside anyway.

The receptionist smiled and found a single room for over two hundred and fifty United States dollars. Darby signed the paper with a twinge of guilt for spending so much. But it didn't take long to feel it was well worth the cost. She found a hall of photographs of VIP guests: Ernest Hemingway, Princess Caroline of Monaco, John F. Kennedy, Queen Elizabeth II of England, the Dalai Lama, and Thomas Mann, to name a few. She smiled at the portrait of the Bee Gees, then spotted Arnold Schwarzenegger, Austria's golden boy. All were guests of the famous Hotel Sacher, where she arrived alone with her duffel bag. The Sacher had been built in the 1870s on the site of the Kärntner Tor Theatre where Beethoven premiered his *Ninth Symphony*.

Darby took the elevator up and entered her room, feeling like a princess arriving at her royal chamber. The room was fit for royalty with chandeliers, mint green carpet, and matching bedspread and curtains. A white ornate desk and chair sat near a window, and beautiful oil paintings adorned the walls. Somewhere in this same hotel, her grandparents had spent their first nights of love together. The thought made her single bed look very lonely. Darby tugged on the gold chain and studied the ring on the end of it. She ran her finger around the edge. "You've been here before, haven't you? This time you're alone without your other half. A lot like I am."

Darby took off the necklace and settled for a luscious bubble bath before plopping on the bed and perusing the room-service menu. She called in and chose the *Wiener schnitzel* with *Sachertorte* for dessert.

The history of the hotel's famous dessert was created before the hotel was even built, a brochure read. In 1832, Franz Sacher was an apprentice chef when Prince Metternich requested a special dessert for his elite guests. The problem—the head chef was ill and sixteen-year-old Franz was assigned the task. Now the Sacher annually used one million eggs, 70 tons of sugar, 60 tons of chocolate, 35 tons of apricot marmalade, 25 tons of butter, and 30 tons of flour to create its famous tortes, which were shipped around the world.

Slipping gratefully beneath the cool sheets of her bed, Darby propped herself up and ate her food. The last bite of rich chocolate with the layer of apricot marmalade below the icing topped off her full stomach. She leaned against her pillow and flipped through channels, watching CNN and the BBC until she could move again. The quiet of the room brought thoughts of Brant. One part wished he could be with her at that very moment; another part believed it could never work. If Brant cared for her at all, why did he so easily let her go? Why did he hold so strongly to his facts on paper when she was in front of him, asking him to take a chance on her? And she didn't think they had anything in common, except their tendency toward being workaholics. When Darby did know the truth and proved it to Brant, would they be able to put it all behind them? She didn't think so. The ache inside was not as great as her anger. How could she ever care for a man who would not give her the benefit of the doubt, and over the most important thing in her life?

But before she could address that future, she needed to have the proof. Not only for Brant, but for her original purpose of returning Tatianna's name.

Darby eased from the bed and found a phone book in the desk. She spread out her papers on Bruno Weiler and searched the directory. She'd never know what the future held or didn't hold for her until she found the facts. The Ws produced no Weiler at all. Next she skimmed for the aunt under Heike Schumacher. There were many Schumacher names. Suddenly Darby sat up and stared at the name, comparing it to her notes. There it was: *Heike F. Schumacher.*

Darby checked her watch. It was already nine o'clock at night, but she dialed the numbers on the telephone anyway. Some things couldn't wait. Immediately, a young voice answered.

"Hello," Darby said. "*Sprechen Sie Englisch?*"

"*Ja.* I do," the woman's voice said.

"Good. My name is Darby Evans. I'm looking for a woman named Heike Schumacher who had a sister named Dorthe Schumacher Weiler. The woman would be quite old. Have I reached the correct residence?"

"I do not know about sister of Frau Schumacher, but she is very old—one hundred years next month. She is asleep at this time."

"Are you her daughter?" Darby asked.

"No, I care for Frau Schumacher."

Darby hesitated. Should she ask now or wait until she could speak directly to the older woman? She took the chance. "I'm actually looking for the nephew of Heike Schumacher. His name is Bruno Weiler. Do you know anything about him?"

The woman hesitated. "I think you should instead speak to Frau Schumacher about such things. I give her your name and telephone and she call you back perhaps?"

"Could you please have her call me? It is very important." Darby gave the information and the woman said good-bye so quickly Darby wasn't sure her name and phone number were actually written down.

Darby listened to the dial tone and put the phone down. She may have just ruined her best chance to find Bruno Weiler.

Brant arrived at the home of Peter and Katrine Voss ready to tell them everything. His friend needed to know why Darby's grandmother could not be Celia Müller and why he had kept the story of what he knew about the Lange inheritance to himself. But as Katrine welcomed him inside, he was first faced with the letters of Darby's grandmother.

"I am in the middle of translating a new set Darby brought from her grandmother's house," Professor Voss said. He handed Brant a pile of papers. As Brant sat at the table and examined them slowly, his entire body turned cold. He gasped when he found one paper with a copy of a ring on it.

"What is this?" he asked, his voice straining to speak.

"It is a diagram of Darby's ring—or actually the engagement half of her grandmother's wedding set."

Brant stared at the photograph. "Peter, we need to find Darby. *Now.*"

✦➤═◎═◄✦

Darby woke early to take a shower. She then waited, paced, and stared at the telephone, willing it to ring. Breakfast was room service again. Outside, the day was sunny and almost warm looking. Darby read about the Vienna sights in her *Lonely Planet Guide*, and finally at noon, dialed the number of Heike Schumacher again. No one answered.

By afternoon, she decided she must go out or go crazy. She slid on her jeans and a wool sweater, gathering her hair into a ponytail. She had packed light for what was supposed to be a quick day trip to Hallstatt, and today was her last change of clean socks and underwear. She buttoned her leather jacket and met a cold afternoon despite the sunshine.

Darby found that the Hapsburg Dynasty reign of six hundred years was evident throughout the capital. The beauty of the city displayed what it had once been—a cultural and political giant of an era gone by. Darby wanted to see everything and had enough mapped and planned for a week of sightseeing. But she barely made it through the courtyard of Hofburg, the Imperial palace, after taking a dozen photographs when the nagging wonder of a missed phone call made her decide to return to the Sacher. The wealth of shopping and the magnificence of the sights would have to wait for another day.

She waited for a bus to pass and noticed a gray sedan parked across the street. It seemed like she'd seen that car before, maybe even several times. But there were cars zipping around everywhere, and dozens of gray sedans with tinted windows. Darby continued down the street and glanced back at the license plate. It was an Austrian plate, nothing unusual.

She walked a few more blocks, down tree-lined streets to the turn of the Ringstraße. A gray sedan drove slowly by, the same license plate. When she came upon the car parked a few blocks up, on impulse, she pulled out her camera and began to click the shutter. The car sped away.

Darby suddenly realized that no one knew where she was. She'd told Professor Voss she'd call, but she hadn't yet. No one knew what hotel she was at, or that she'd made contact with the home of Heike Schumacher. Darby decided to go straight to the hotel.

She let out a sigh when she saw the bright flags waving her to safety a block away. Then a woman with bleached white hair stepped from a doorway in front of her.

"Excuse me," Darby said, stepping around.

"You seek information, do you not?" the woman said in English.

Darby turned around. The woman leaned against the building with a cigarette held loosely between two long fingers.

"Were you speaking to me?"

Darby checked to see if the woman could be talking to someone else. But few pedestrians moved along the street. The woman barely gazed at her as she took a long drag from the cigarette.

"If you want to know the answers you seek, come with me." The woman walked around her and up the street. Darby didn't know what to do. Who was she? Where did she come from?

"Darby Evans, are you coming or not?" She waited impatiently.

Darby tried not to look shocked. "How did you know my name?"

The woman smiled, but there was no warmth in the expression. "Trust me."

Darby edged several steps closer. "What do you want?"

"I want nothing—is it not you who seek answers?" The woman pointed down the alley. The gray sedan sat with the back door open. The engine was running. Through the tinted windshield, she could see a man in the driver's seat.

Darby took a step back, expecting anything. The woman dropped her cigarette and ground it into the sidewalk.

"Are you going to get in? We won't force you. But if you want answers, it will take a little cloak-and-dagger, as they say . . . but you will have your answers."

"How do you know me? Why have you been following me around the city?"

The woman shrugged. "We are only messengers sent to take you where you can find answers. Does the name *Tatianna* mean anything to you?"

"What do you know about Tatianna?"

"I know nothing. But I know who does. But you must choose to come."

Darby paused to consider the choice, her mind turning a million images. Her grandmother in her coffin, Professor Voss, Brant's face the night of the Mozart concert, her mother as Darby promised to be careful. But her need to know what had happened overthrew any mental warnings. Darby quickly stepped to the side of the car where the open door invited her into the dark interior. The woman opened the passenger door and sat in the front seat.

Darby leaned inside. "I need to tell someone where I am going."

"Get in or go your own way," the woman said, barely looking over her shoulder. The man didn't turn at all. "You have but one opportunity."

Darby sat on the leather seat. As soon as she closed the door, the sedan sped forward down Kärtnerstraße. She had been one block from her hotel. As they passed the waving flags of Hotel Sacher, Darby knew she'd made a terrible mistake.

CHAPTER TWENTY-EIGHT

"Peter, have you heard from her?" Brant asked, pacing the room with telephone in hand.

"No, she was supposed to call. We have not heard a word."

"It's been all day. I really think we should try to find her." Brant had heard the worry in Peter's voice too. "She could be anywhere, but why don't we start calling hotels?"

"I think you are right. We need to find her. She does not have a car so would probably stay near the Ring."

"Okay, hotels along the Ring. You take three stars, I'll go four. We'll just move up till we find her. I know she was looking for authentic Austrian places, so no more Cozy Hotels."

Professor Voss chuckled, then sounded serious. "She is quite a lady, Brant."

"I know. I'll call you in an hour."

Brant hung up the phone and searched for his Vienna hotel guide, hoping he wouldn't have to run to the information office before starting to call. But he found the brochure soon enough and started circling hotels. He'd been ready to fly to

Vienna last night to find her. Even with the facts firmly in his mind, Brant could hardly believe the truth. If he'd seen Gunther's ring earlier, he'd have known.

Brant picked up the phone. He must find her. But he also dreaded it. What would she think when she discovered her grandparents could have finally found each other, if only for a little while, if only Brant hadn't stood in the way? Would she ever forgive him? Could he ever forgive himself?

◦→▬◉▭←◦

No one spoke as they moved from the city. Mile after mile, Darby's panic grew. They drove south, passing signs for Graz and Klagenfurt. She knew in hours they could be in Slovenia, Italy, or Switzerland. These people could do anything to her, and she'd disappear without a trace. No amount of information was worth this. What had she been thinking? Darby decided that if they slowed, she'd try to get out. The doors were unlocked, the door handle beside her. Hours seemed to pass, though the road signs said far less.

"Where are we going?" Darby's voice sounded loud in her ears as it broke the quiet.

"Where we need to go," the woman responded without a backward glance.

"I want to go back. I don't want to know anything, I only want to go back."

The man and woman glanced at each other, but neither spoke. Darby didn't know what to do. The sun dropped low behind them as the man flipped the headlights on. Darby knew the shadows would soon consume the day.

After another half hour, the woman turned in her seat. "Time to lie down."

"You want me to lie down?"

"That's what I said."

"Why?"

"You ask so many questions. Get down." Her voice was stern. Darby did as she was told with her head toward the door and hand on the handle. The car slowed down an off-ramp, but not enough. They continued for more miles, more hours, it seemed.

The engine wound down. This could be her chance. But where was she? From her view, she hadn't seen buildings, only dense trees for a while. If she jumped now . . .

Darby paused too long. The car moved without completely stopping and steadied faster again. Dusk turned to darkness. The car turned in switchbacks, ascending higher and deeper into the woods. She was a fool. She knew her curiosity may cost her life.

"You can sit up." Finally the car ground to a halt. The headlights illuminated a tall, iron gate connecting solid block walls. The gate opened, allowing the car through. Not only did Darby not know her whereabouts, now iron gates locked her within massive walls. Gravel crunched beneath the tires as they curved through the woods. The dense trees would provide many hiding places, but the snow on the ground wasn't inviting. Around a bend, the trees opened, and a large, lit house stood in a clearing.

She could still run. But would she survive the night in this cold? Darby had no idea what direction she'd go. What if she got lost in the Alps? Or perhaps they weren't even in Austria. Darby knew she'd have to take her chances with whatever she was about to face.

The man drove the car around a circular driveway with a small fountain in the center. A walkway led to imposing double doors at the entrance to the house. The flat-fronted, two-story house was not typical Austrian with flowered windowsills. It stood straight and tall, probably intended for elegance. But against the night sky, the windows were the eyes of a creature staring at her, the doors a giant mouth ready to consume her. Darby didn't get out of the car until the driver opened her door. He propped himself against the car and lit a cigarette. Darby followed the woman toward the house.

No one greeted their arrival. The woman closed the heavy door and made her way across the hardwood-floored entry. Down the hall, their footsteps echoed through the house and up a wide, curving stairway. At a doorway, the woman motioned Darby inside, then turned and left without a word. Footsteps on hardwood floors echoed away.

Darby entered the room expecting someone or something. Only a fire crackled with long burnt logs and new wood piled crisscross above. The study had one dim lamp in the corner, and one wall was lined with books. Light danced on the volumes, a reflection from the rock fireplace on the opposite side of the room. Darby wondered where she should stand, or if she should sit in the chair in the corner or the one behind the large, wood desk. The fire beckoned, and she realized how cold she felt, from inside out.

Soon footsteps returned. Darby waited, her back to the fire, near an iron poker. A young woman who looked a lot like the woman from the car entered with a silver tray—her sister perhaps? The girl glanced at Darby curiously and set a tray with teapot, two cups and saucers, and dainty pastries onto the desk.

"Why am I here?" Darby asked the girl.

The dark-haired, dark-eyed girl only smiled at Darby, then hurried out. Her footsteps drifted away.

Darby peered suspiciously at the tray of food and drink. *If they're going to hurt me, I guess they want me comfortable first.*

A painting on the wall caught her eye. She recognized it from a book of Impressionist paintings at home. She moved closer and knew it was an original Edgar Degas painting. Whose home had she been delivered to?

Heavy footsteps would be her answer. She moved to her position by the fire, near the only weapon she could find.

He filled the doorway—large in height and weight with a presence that matched his size. Surely at least in his seventies, an old man in theory; still Darby knew instant fear. She had never seen him in her life, but she knew him to be a man of power. And her life rested in his hands.

"I knew you would come." He headed toward the tray. "Miss Darby Evans, in her persistence, could not resist." He poured two cups of tea without looking at her. "Despite the danger, you would get into a car with strangers, with no one knowing where you are or where you are going. Tonight you could disappear, and no one would ever find you. Not your mother in California. Not Brant Collins in Salzburg. Have some tea."

Shocked by the man's knowledge, Darby sputtered, "What do you want from me?"

"I have few wants from you. It is *you* who sought me." He turned toward her. "First tell me, who am I?"

The light from the fire lit his features: black eyes, thick face and lips. Darby knew. "You are Bruno Weiler."

"At one time, yes, that was my name. Good. Perhaps you should have been a detective instead of a photographer." He moved behind the desk with his cup and sat in the wide leather chair.

"How do you know so much about me?" Darby asked, not moving from her position by the fire. She glanced at the door and knew she could be out of the room before he could move from behind the desk. But what then? Who waited down the hall or outside? What would she do, and where would she go?

"I make it my business to know people who are putting my previous name on the Internet and making contact with my aunt. It can be dangerous to resurrect names that were supposed to have disappeared." He leaned forward with his elbows on the desk and motioned her to sit. "After all your seeking, tell me. Who killed the woman you seek?"

Darby slowly seated herself in a chair, feeling the eyes of this man who had once been a Nazi camp guard, who had gone to prison for his crimes. She tried to stay calm and figure out what to do next. She stared into cold eyes and cleared her throat. "Who killed Tatianna?"

"Yes. This is what I want from you. I want you to tell me who killed Tatianna Hoffman."

"I don't . . . the Nazis."

"The Nazis? Your skills are not as sharp as I expected."

"The Nazis at Mauthausen." Darby hoped that was the right answer.

"But who killed her? Tell me. Who killed Tatianna Hoffman? Who killed her at Mauthausen Concentration Camp? Who lifted the gun? Who watched her look upward, already gone, before a trigger was pulled? Who pulled the trigger? Who killed Tatianna Hoffman while Celia Müller escaped to America?"

Bruno Weiler stared hard into her eyes. Darby's mouth went dry; her hands shook. Tears built on the edges of her eyes.

"You did," she whispered.

"Yes, I did."

Bruno focused on the fire as a log bent and dropped into the flaming coals. "Yes, I killed Tatianna Hoffman. And you have entered the home of her killer."

⋆⇒◯⇐⋆

Brant dialed Darby's hotel and asked for her room for the third time. Again, no one answered. It had taken forty-five minutes of calling to find out she was staying at the Hotel Sacher. But she wasn't in her room. He imagined her splurging on the luxurious room, shopping in the city, walking around all alone, searching for an old Nazi. She had traveled the world, but somehow Brant could hardly handle the thought of her alone in Vienna. He wanted to be there with her.

He let it ring over ten times, then slammed the phone down. Where could she be?

Brant dialed the number again.

"Yes, you have a guest there, Darby Evans. Will you leave another message for her? It's urgent that I talk to her as soon as she returns. No matter what time it is."

Bruno's jaw clenched as he looked at Darby. His dark eyes beneath hooded lids told her nothing. "Now that you know, we will talk."

Her hands clung tightly to the edge of the desk as she kept her eyes on the living link she'd sought so long. Bruno Weiler was the last person to see Tatianna alive. He was also Tatianna's killer. How should she feel or think as she sat in the chair facing him? She needed to stop shaking and figure out something to do or say.

"You have questions for me. I see them in your eyes. Let me speak first. I will tell you what no one else knows. Not my children, not my ex-wives, not my colleagues. The few who ever knew are now gone."

Darby shuddered. "I don't need to know."

"But you do. You have most likely spent your whole life wondering, probably running from those questions. But somewhere inside you wanted to know. Didn't you?"

"Perhaps. But more than answers, I desire to leave this house tonight."

Bruno folded his hands and rested his chin on them. He stared at her for a long time. "I already have enough blood on my hands."

Did that mean he wouldn't hurt her, she wondered? Maybe she didn't want to know this man's secrets. He could easily change his mind or order someone else to keep her from revealing them. "Why will you tell me what no else knows? When you can't tell your own family? I'm a stranger."

He raised up heavily and walked to a glass cube on the bookshelf. He picked it up and set it on the desk next to Darby. Inside she could see a gold medal. "I received this for valor and courage. Yet I am a coward. I fear what my children will think of me. I fear their rejection."

"Then why me?"

"I have become an old man. Something about age brings the past forward. I am haunted now more than ever. I see everything with more memory than during the events. I find myself knowing more than I knew then. And you are the one living link to my past. You are the only one I can tell."

Bruno walked to the entrance of the room and closed the heavy door. It shut with a final click. He returned to his chair and again faced Darby. She felt glued to the seat, hypnotized by the truth she was about to hear.

"Few people know me as Bruno Weiler. My mother kept her name after the war, but she died many years ago. My aunt is the only contact to me. You called her home. She is ill and aged, but she knows if someone seeks information about Bruno Weiler, trouble usually lurks close behind. You left your name and hotel, but we already had been tracking you. You almost discovered that the first day you arrived in Salzburg."

"The man in my room?"

Bruno nodded.

"Why have you been tracking me? I'm only trying to prove who my grandmother really was."

"Are you? There is also the matter of your family inheritance."

"Yes, but that is not my main concern. Of course, I'd like to find out what happened to them, but lost riches are not my main goal."

"Many others would have it another way. I've known about you since you were a child. No one knows that I kept track of your grandmother over the many years, and your mother. Once, while on business in San Francisco, I drove by your home in Sebastopol. You and your sister had a tent in the front yard with dolls on a blanket. That was many years ago."

"Why? Why would you do that?"

"I wanted to see what happened with the gift of Tatianna's sacrifice."

"Then Tatianna did take my grandmother's place. I had no proof."

"Oh yes, Tatianna died as Celia Müller. She gave her life for your grandmother's and your mother's and yours. I knew this the day I saw Tatianna die."

The questions on her lips could be dangerous to ask. Darby looked at the man for the cruelty of a murderer, but instead saw weariness, and perhaps, vulnerability.

"Before you ask more," Bruno said, sensing her struggle, "I will tell you. I will tell you everything, if you are ready to hear."

She rested her hands on the table. "I'm ready."

Bruno leaned back in his chair and began his story.

"I knew your grandmother from the time we were children in Hallstatt. Her family was not rich, but well known in our village, especially with the legend of the brooch and coins. Your great-grandfather was the archaeologist who had family ties to Emperor Franz Joseph. My family was poor, my father an embarrassment to me. Today, we call it a dysfunctional family and alcohol abuse. Then, it was simply my life.

"I remember Tatianna came to our village when we were young—the girls were inseparable. Celia's younger brother and I were always good friends. We loved to bother the older girls, and especially, I remember one time: Celia's brother and I must have been around eight. The girls were around eleven. We had tried and tried to find their secret hideout."

Darby saw childhood revelry in the old man's eyes as he drifted into the past. She scooted forward, expectantly, clinging to the words that told the story of her grandmother before Darby knew her.

"After weeks of following their footprints and trying to follow the girls, we discovered their hideout deep in the woods inside the hollow of a gigantic, fallen tree. I can hear Warner saying excitedly how good it was we found it at that time, for the girls planned a secret initiation.

" 'I think it's some secret ritual or something,' Warner said. 'A girl thing for certain.'

" 'Maybe they will become blood sisters,' I said as we sneaked through their hideout filled with dolls, a tea set, and dried-flower bouquets.

" 'No way. Celia would faint if she saw her own blood. Tatianna would do it, I bet, but not my sister. I can tell it will be a big event, though. We better find a good place to hide if we're going to watch.'

" 'In those branches up there,' I suggested. 'They'll never see us from below, and then we can hear and watch them.'

"We had to go outside and around the bottom of the trunk to get into the twists of branches that overhung the girls' hideout. After settling in there, we waited for what seemed forever. Finally they came. I remember thinking how they reminded me of forest fairies with their long, white dresses and flowers in their hair. But young boys aren't supposed to think such thoughts. 'Girls, yuck,' I mouthed with a gagging motion that made Warner start to laugh. We were sure we were caught, but they didn't hear us. Instead, they ducked into their hideout and settled around a small log table. We had the perfect view.

" 'Today is one of the most important days for us,' Tatianna said.

" 'I still can't do the blood sisters thing, Tati. I'll faint.' Celia bit her bottom lip.

" 'Oh, I know. That's why I thought of something better. First, I want to ask you this, but you have to be sure of your answer.'

" 'Okay,' Celia said.

" 'Do you want to be my friend forever and ever?' Tatianna's eyes were large.

" 'Oh yes, I want to be your best friend forever and ever,' Celia said with a large smile.

" 'I just wanted to be sure. Now let's lock our baby fingers together.'

"Across the table, small hands reached. In the center they met with pinky fingers hooked as one.

" 'Celia Rachel Lange, I promise to be your best friend for my whole life. No matter what happens, how old we get, or even if one of us moves far away, I still promise this forever.'

" 'And I, Celia Rachel Lange, tell you, Tatianna Elise Hoffman, that you are my best friend and will always be. No matter what happens or how old we get. And I promise to be your friend forever.'

" 'And ever.'

" 'And ever,' they said in unison.

" 'I wish we could get matching rings or lockets, but this will have to do.' Tatianna lifted a box onto the table. She opened it and reverently took out two long, prickly stemmed roses—yellow roses. 'This will be our forever friendship flower. Whenever we see a yellow flower, especially a yellow rose, we'll remember our vow to be best friends always.'

" 'What a good idea, Tati. I love roses, and yellow is my favorite color. I'll remember today always.'

" 'Forever and . . .'

" 'Ever,' they said again.

"Warner and I stayed in our places while the girls drank pretend tea and giggled about girl things. When finally we left, we put on masks of disgust, though I think we both were a little jealous of a friendship so pure. And the image of their vow with fingers locked together came back to me so vividly when I saw Tatianna at Mauthausen."

Bruno stiffened as if the mention of that place jarred him from gentle memories.

"I want to tell you, I did not change from that boy into a killer in just a moment. It takes time. Almost so slowly you don't see that you're disappearing. I left Hallstatt as a young man to find my life in the city. I came to Linz and Vienna, ready to make my mark upon the world and break free from my family line of failures. I was full of awe and curiosity for the modern world and hoped for a new, more powerful Austria. I wanted to be part of that Austria and joined the Nazi party with its rebellion toward the old ways and passive government. The Party sought power and strength and a greater future for our weakened country. When joined with Germany, Austrians would leave a mark upon the entire world. If some individuals were trampled in the process, it was a sad product of forward movement. Many of us believed these things."

Bruno focused intently on Darby. "*I* believed these things." Then he turned away, toward the fire, and into yesterday once again. "I did not advance the way I expected. I did not at first recognize that greed, corruption, and even that old class ladder existed larger than idealism. I became SS in hopes of greater advancement and was sent as a guard to Mauthausen Concentration Camp. It insulted me. I wanted a more noble position than guard to felons, political prisoners, and Jews. I was promised my time there was a mere stepping-stone—all future officers did some dirty work. Prove yourself there, and you will advance. So I went to prove I could be the best, the smartest, the bravest. I convinced myself that the creatures in the camp deserved their punishment, and already I was a very angry man. I saw those people as criminals, animals who fed on our future, leeches on our social system—some probably innocents, but such was the cruelty of bettering mankind. It was the pathway to a future mankind and survival of the fittest. They were not like me. They did not feel or think as I did. Behaviors of greed between prisoners were only further proof—a father who killed his son for food, an instance of cannibalism, the constant undermining of authority. I didn't look at the good in them. I could not allow myself to see acts of love and chivalry.

"Many of the other guards were sadistic monsters who lusted after blood and torment. But what could I do about that? I had my advancement and own step-up to be concerned with. Though I was no innocent in it all."

Bruno again glanced at Darby's white face, then back at the fire.

"One day in early summer, I heard of a pretty girl in the jail-house. I heard her name—Celia Müller. I did not recognize the name, for I'd left Hallstatt before her marriage. Some officers were discussing her, how they hoped she would be assigned to the brothel—even though she was a Jewess. She did not look Jewish. She wasn't emaciated, for she had not come from other camps as most others had. She had been for months in prisons and under interrogation, and now she was there and looked better than the others. If only she would speak and disclose the hiding place of the Lange family inheritance, they said, perhaps she would be released to the brothel. I knew immediately—Celia Müller must be the girl from my village, Celia Lange."

Bruno's speech faltered. Darby watched him carefully as he stared, almost entranced, at the crackling fire. Somewhere a long way off, she heard the mournful sound of a train.

"There was no way for me to see her, and I did not want to. At times, a woman's cries could be heard from the prison. It became routine when a certain officer arrived at the camp that the woman would be interrogated. He visited often and was frustrated that she would not reveal it. He had thought time and interrogation would make her give them the hiding place of the inheritance—a wealth for the finder or a huge advancement in rank. A comrade assigned to the jail gave me details as he heard information. He said even Hitler knew of the Lange family inheritance—some Celtic coins, perhaps the oldest ones of our region, and a brooch from Empress Sissi. Celia's father had already died at Mauthausen before I was assigned there. I didn't even allow sorrow for Warner, though he had been my childhood friend. The SS officer had been so thoroughly angered about their death without giving any information about the inheritance that he'd sent the interrogators to the gas chambers. Then they caught Celia."

"At the Swiss border," Darby said.

"Ah, yes, that is correct. Almost got away, they said. They believed she would give them the answers."

"But she couldn't, because she didn't know."

"Correct." Bruno sighed. "I did not see her until the day I was called to execute her. And then I knew. It wasn't Celia, but Tatianna who stood before me."

He spoke with unseen layers of time and regret falling from his face. His strong expression turned vulnerable, guilty, and sympathetic at the same time.

"Some guards enjoyed adding suffering to their victims. They would wound them and then walk close to see the pain before finishing them off. I aimed straight for Tatianna's heart. She watched the sky as if waiting to leave. I pulled the trigger."

A log fell into the flames, and sparks popped in the quiet room. Darby saw the scene in Bruno's faraway gaze. She had seen one tiny passport photo of Tatianna but could picture the woman perfectly. A bullet freeing her from her torment, freeing her spirit toward life.

"So I, not anyone else, killed Tatianna Hoffman. And as I took her life, she gave me mine."

Startled, Darby asked, "What do you mean?"

"I pulled that trigger and instantly understood. I knew Tatianna had somehow given her life for her friend. Already I had begun to question my beliefs in the darkest hours of night. I performed my duties, but I felt haunted by feelings that I couldn't and wouldn't face in the daylight. Tatianna changed that. I knew so clearly, as if a veil had been taken from my eyes. I saw it all. I looked at myself and detested what I saw. It triggered my redemption from the Nazis, though always my name would be associated with them, and always my hands are stained with blood—no matter what I have tried to do."

Bruno cleared his throat. "Now you know. Now I have spoken it to someone. Not even my children know."

"What did you become? Did you stay in the camp?"

"Only a week later, I received the promotion I so desired. I took it and went to Germany. Once it was my greatest desire, but then, my greatest opportunity. I became a betrayer to the Party I had given my oath. They never knew it was me. I was even imprisoned as a Nazi war criminal, even though I spied for the other side."

"Why didn't you reveal that at your trial?"

"The Nazis hadn't disappeared. Their power was greatly injured, but not destroyed. And if I revealed my truth, it would endanger others. I fulfilled my duties as the good Nazi, and then Bruno Weiler disappeared. I moved to America for ten years, then later returned to Austria. I was given financial help from some friends I helped during the war. I received some physical alteration, then began a new life as a new man. As you can see, I have done well . . . on the outside."

Darby nodded, glancing at the Degas painting. "Yes."

Bruno looked at it also and smiled wryly. "People would call me a powerful man, but inside, all men are only men. And for me, my life will always return to Tatianna. She had a power in death I have never found. It was in her face. I heard about it once at a church service in America. There was a man who was stoned to death; Stephen was his name, if I remember correctly. They say his face shone like an angel. Tatianna's face was like that—like she was really free. I have never found what she had. The blood of others will always be with me."

Darby could see the struggle within Bruno. She wondered what she should feel for him—anger, hatred, fear? But she could find none of those for this killer of Tatianna and of others. "My grandmother would say that the blood of Jesus purchases the blood on our hands and all of our sins. His life for ours, like Tatianna, but also to save all mankind. If only we ask."

"Celia Lange said those words? Tell me, do you believe these words?"

"Me?" Darby felt her face flush as she was suddenly on the spot. It was one thing to quote her grandmother, another to state her own belief. "Well, I would have said 'no' not long ago, probably six weeks ago. But now? Yes, I do believe it. I believe God forgives us when we ask. I believe Jesus died to provide that forgiveness. His life for ours. In a very strange way, Tatianna showed me that."

"How can you, or I, know for certain?"

"I'm wondering myself. I guess that is faith."

"Would you grant me forgiveness?"

"What? You are asking me to forgive you?"

"I cannot say it to Tatianna or Celia or the others. But will you give it?"

"It is not mine to give. I would, if I could. I think that is a matter for you and God."

Bruno nodded slowly. "You don't make it easy for me."

"I will give you the forgiveness I can give. But I think that only God's will make you feel complete."

"Perhaps I will seek him and see."

Darby glanced at the fire, reduced to embers. The tea in her cup had long grown cold. She could see a swirl of what had to be snowflakes in the window behind Bruno. She put her hands in her coat pockets, and Bruno moved to the fire. He added several logs, then took the poker and stirred the embers into a tiny flame.

"Now you know." He stood by the fire, close to her. "Warm yourself, and I will get some tea." Bruno replaced the poker. "It is late, but I apologize I cannot allow you to stay tonight. The less you know about who I have become, the better."

"It must be difficult, living a new life," Darby said as she rose from her chair. Her back ached and her muscles longed for the soft bed at the Sacher. But that was a long way off. Then, with a start, she remembered that only hours ago, she wondered if she'd ever see the Hotel Sacher again, or her mother, her friends, or Brant Collins.

"It is the world I live in. Everyone has secrets. Money, power, position—they all link the good and the bad. A man must be careful, especially a man of position with my kind of tainted past. And you, my dear. Do not make the same mistakes. Remember, the family inheritance remains an interest for dangerous people. Many have been killed for much less money than the inheritance is worth."

"I'll be more cautious, I promise."

Bruno left for hot water and returned with more food and tea. She hadn't realized her hunger until she began eating. Outside, a car engine rumbled to life. On her way out, Bruno pointed the way to a bathroom down a hall. Photographs lined the wall, and Darby was shocked to see one portrayed a younger Bruno shaking hands with President Reagan. She didn't linger long.

"Time to go," Bruno said, extending both hands. As her hands were gathered into a tight embrace, they looked deeply at one another. Tears brimmed in Darby's eyes. She knew they could never meet again.

"I will have a letter delivered to you from a certain ex-Nazi, Bruno Weiler. It will tell that Tatianna Hoffman died at Mauthausen Concentration Camp, not Celia Lange Müller. It will be your proof, I will make sure of that. Then, if you do find the Lange inheritance, it will be yours. But still, be careful, Darby Evans. Remember my words, for I insist that you hear me clearly. I know of others who desire what should be yours. I cannot be there for you."

"Thank you. Know that you and your secret are safe with me."

"I do not doubt it."

Darby walked alone to the front door and glanced back toward Bruno as she stepped outside. He nodded as she closed the door. The same driver was in the car as she again sat in the back. The woman was not there. The driver only spoke when it was time for her to lay her head down and then again when she could rise. A touch of dawn lit the east as they arrived in front of Hotel Sacher. Weary in every inch of her body, Darby plodded toward the entrance. When she looked back, the gray sedan was already gone.

CHAPTER TWENTY-NINE

A desk clerk handed Darby messages from Brant, who had called throughout the night. *What could that be about,* she wondered, but was too tired to care. Plus, it was too early to call him. Darby entered her room and dropped onto the bed without taking off her clothing. She closed her eyes.

Far away an insistent sound disturbed her. She awoke to the phone ringing and ringing beside her head. The hour hand on her watch had moved only a few times.

"Hello?" she said with her eyes still closed.

"Darby, where have you been? I've been worried sick about you. Didn't you get my messages? Why didn't you call?"

"It was too early."

"Are you okay?"

"I was a few minutes ago and having a great dream—Brant, is that you?" she said, awakening a bit more.

"Where were you?"

She sat up in bed and noticed the light shining around the edges of the window shade. "I had some information to follow up."

"And it took all night?"

"Brant, is there a reason I have to tell you where I've been?"

"No, no, I've just been worried. But if you don't want to give me an explanation, that's fine."

"Why have you been worried? And wait a minute, how did you find me?"

"It's a long story. Are you sure you're all right?"

"Yes, Brant."

"Well, you aren't an experienced traveler, you could have made a naïve mistake . . . I had all sorts of images going through my head."

"Me naïve, inexperienced?" *If he only knew.* "I'm learning rapidly."

"Okay, okay. Now that I know you're safe, you must get back here right away. Or I can come get you?"

"What is so desperate it can't wait?"

"I need to speak to you in person—today. I went to . . . just get back to Salzburg."

"All right. I'm sure there's a morning train to Salzburg. I'll be on it."

"I'll be waiting."

Darby flopped against the pillow. What could be so important it couldn't wait? She imagined Brant worried and pacing in his apartment. The image made her smile. Suddenly Darby sat back up. Maybe he'd been with Professor Voss. Did that mean he believed her story?

⋆⟞◉⟝⋆

Darby wondered about it all the way back to Salzburg. She found humor in Brant's early-morning call. Mr. Serious worried about her? She could imagine his eyebrows pinched, jaw clenched, fingers anxiously punching telephone buttons. For some reason, Darby found that funny. Perhaps he had some new information? But she knew the story now, and soon she'd have proof in her hands. Darby didn't know how she would explain her source, but if Brant pushed too far she'd tell the truth—"If I tell you, I'll have to kill you." She laughed out loud, imagining Brant's expression.

One mystery remained—the inheritance. But Darby was too tired to think of that—at last, her purpose was accomplished.

Darby leaned against the headrest as the train gently rocked back and forth. She hoped to catch some sleep as the Austrian countryside whirled by and she was delivered to Brant. Whatever he felt desperate to tell her would be no surprise to her. She was about to prove the facts to him.

⊷═◉═⊷

Richter could not believe what he was hearing. "Could you say that again?" he said into the phone as he took a drag from his cigarette.

"You are freed from your debts," the voice said. "And I want you to leave Darby Evans alone."

"I don't understand. Why would you simply cancel it all?" Richter didn't know whether to be elated or suspicious. Suspicion rose higher because he knew no one simply canceled debts, especially this man.

"Just do what I said."

The phone clicked, and Richter heard the dial tone. His debt, his fear for the last six months was canceled. It didn't make sense. And why was he told to leave Darby Evans alone? Suddenly he knew. The inheritance. He tossed the phone on the couch. *She must be close. And I won't be cheated now.*

⊷═◉═⊷

The trains were punctual, but never early. Still Brant came to the Bahnhof an hour before Darby's arrival. He waited in the terminal and watched the schedule of incoming trains. Then his cell phone rang. He considered turning off the power, but wondered if it could be Peter.

"Hey, Brant! It's Richter. Where you at?"

"I'm at the train station. Is there something you need?"

"I'm just in town and thought we'd get together."

"I have plans. Next time, probably."

"Hey, I've been trying to contact that American woman."

"Why?"

"Since you weren't moving on her, I thought I'd take a shot. Where's she staying?"

Brant froze. "How did you know she was back in Austria?"

"You told me, remember?" Richter laughed. "You're too young to lose your memory."

Brant could not remember telling Richter, but perhaps he had. "I'm at the train station getting ready to pick her up. She's returning from Vienna."

"Really? Well, I can tell by your voice, I've jumped in a little too late. The two of you are finally connecting? I must be rubbing off on you."

"I need to go, Richter." A train arrived at the station, but not Darby's.

"Okay, I'll get ahold of you another time."

Brant clicked his phone off and stuffed it into his jacket. Richter was looking for Darby? Why? No matter what, Richter had better stay away from her.

⋆⇒⊙⇐⋆

"Salzburg!" The conductor called over the speaker. Darby already waited in the narrow doorway with her bag. The train's rocking slowed and the brakes screeched as the train pulled into the Bahnhof. She pushed the door lever before it opened automatically. Brant knew something, and finally she was going to discover what it was.

Darby saw him walking the length of train, searching the doorways. Their eyes met, and she felt a rush of emotion. If he opened his arms, she was sure she'd fall into them forever. Fatigue and the fear from the previous night had left her open, ready for Brant. But his hands were stuck hard into his coat. He reached only for her duffel bag, and his face held no joyous greeting.

"We need to talk." Brant's eyes spoke desperate words. "Alone."

She was tired of mysterious games. All she wanted was a few more hours of sleep. She followed Brant from the train station in pants she'd worn twice and slept in once, a shirt that had been wrinkled at the bottom of her duffel, and a jacket that smelled slightly of smoke from her adventures in train stations and car rides. Brant stopped in front of a dark-blue sports car and dumped her bag into the trunk. He hadn't said a word since they'd left the station. He unlocked her door and closed it behind her.

"Brant, I'm tired, delirious, and I've had way too much coffee on the train. See, my hands are shaking." Darby held up a hand. Brant gripped the steering wheel and didn't look her way.

"Why are you so serious? What's going on?" Then she saw that his eyebrows were creased into one, exactly as she'd imagined. She laughed. "Let me guess . . . in one day, you've decided that you can't live without me—you're crazy about me." She leaned toward him, laughing more until she noticed his expression—still looking ahead, jaw set, hands on the wheel. "You were supposed to laugh."

Brant started the car and zipped into traffic.

"Where are we going?" she asked in a whine, trying to relax against the headrest with eyes closed. After more silence from Brant, she opened her eyes and insisted, "Stop the car or talk to me or take me to my hotel. This is ridiculous."

Brant made a sharp turn and maneuvered into a parking place. He shut off the engine and faced her. "I've been trying to figure out how to say this. Where would be the perfect place? Maybe we should go to my apartment or to your hotel."

"This looks good to me. Now talk."

His eyes studied her, as if memorizing every detail. Darby felt uncomfortable under his gaze, wondering what she looked like after a night of little sleep and the early train trip.

"I believe her, Darby. I believe Celia."

His eyes watched her response, but Darby was uncertain. This was the news she'd hoped for on her return to Salzburg that morning. And did he really mean it? "You believe my grandmother really was Celia Müller?"

"Yes."

"Why? Did you read the letters? What makes you believe now?"

"Where is your grandmother's ring?"

"I'm wearing it." Darby removed the gold chain from beneath her shirt and coat.

"Can I see it?"

"Sure." She unclasped the back and handed it to Brant. What was he doing? she wondered as he slid the ring off and handed her the gold chain. This was not what she expected of him.

"Darby, I don't know where to start. I've looked at it over and over again." He ran his hand through his hair. "I didn't believe her. I mean, how could I? But now—"

"Brant. I know."

He lifted a finger to her chin, then touched her lips. Darby knew she should back away; there was too much to work out. But she couldn't move. His hand lingered against her cheek, then suddenly pulled away. Brant turned and gripped his fist on the steering wheel. What was he tormented by? Darby wondered. He straightened up as if in decision and took something from a box inside his coat pocket. It was a ring. The two slid together, and the curved settings snapped into place.

Darby froze inside. She took the rings, now one. "Where did you get the other half?"

"I told you about the mentor who changed my life? That man was Gunther Müller."

"Gunther Müller. My grandfather? My grandfather was alive after the war?"

"Darby, your grandfather is alive *now*."

CHAPTER THIRTY

My grandfather is alive. You're certain?"

"Yes. He's been very sick, has had a stroke, and wasn't supposed to survive. When I was going through his things, I found the ring."

Darby shook her head, drew her feet onto the seat, and wrapped her arms around them. Her eyes stared out at the noon traffic and shoppers as her mind fought to comprehend Brant's words. "Where is he?"

"Here, in Salzburg."

"Here!" She put her hand over her mouth.

"His stroke was last fall, and he's been at a rehab clinic in Munich for months. Then, right after Christmas, his wife moved him to a nursing home in Salzburg. He's been here ever since. I visit several times a week, but only in the last month has he made real progress with his speech."

"His wife? He remarried?"

"Darby, I take all the blame for this. If I had better investigated when your grandmother wrote me—but I had no idea.

They could have been together—your grandparents. But I sent that letter back. I didn't tell Gunther—didn't want to put him through something like that."

"No, Brant," Darby said slowly. "This isn't your fault, it's his. He never came for her. She mourned her whole life. He remarried and got on with his life while my grandmother was writing him letters every year."

"Gunther only married to help a friend of theirs. I promise you, he never got over Celia. But he truly thought she was dead. He was at the Hungarian border when he got word Celia had been caught. He stayed for months, and then the notice of death came from Mauthausen. Of course, he believed them. He paid all the money he had to try to get her body. All he received was this half of the ring, which was a miracle in itself. With that ring, he had no doubts that his wife and child were dead."

Darby's body shook, and tears fell in streams down her cheeks. Of course, it made sense. But the horror pulsed through her. The two of them could have been together—all of them could have been together. It would have changed everything, their entire lives. Her mother would have had the daddy she so longed for. Suddenly Darby was struck by the realization: her mother did have the father she sought. Gunther Müller was alive.

The questions, accusations, truths, and lies pounded in her head. "I have to see him."

"We'll go right now."

Brant immediately started the car and took off.

"Wait," Darby said. "Take me to my hotel first. I'm meeting my grandfather for the first time. I need to clean up." She turned to him. "Does he know—about me, my mom, and sister?"

"No. I haven't seen him since I saw the copy of the ring. I wanted to tell you first. Perhaps I should have prepared him. He's weak, not well. I don't know what to do."

"I don't either. We'll decide when we get there. I just need to see him." She laid her head against the side window and watched the world zip past. Somewhere in that city her grandfather lived and breathed. The missing link in the family, the missing link in her life.

⋅→⟾◉⟾←⋅

Brant sat on the edge of the bed as Darby showered. He looked at a shoe she'd left on the floor and picked it up. It was the black dress shoe with the chunky heel she'd worn the night they'd gone to the dinner concert. The side of the bed closest to the window was rumpled. So that was the side she slept on. The same one he liked. He closed his eyes and listened to the sound of the shower.

Brant shook himself. He needed to think of other things and not get himself too caught up with Darby Evans. She was in shock. But how would she feel after that shock wore off? Would she be angry at him?

And what of Gunther? He knew the old man would understand. He'd know Brant had been protecting him. But would meeting Darby be too much?

He wished Darby would hurry so they could go see his old friend.

⋅→⟾◉⟾←⋅

Darby grabbed Brant's arm. "Wait," she whispered before he opened the large oak door to the care facility. She pivoted, taking in a breath as she gazed down the cement walkway lined with landscaped trees and grass and then toward Brant's car in the parking lot.

Brant put his hand on hers. "Ready?"

She exhaled with her entire body. "I think so."

Brant opened the door and Darby entered. The white floors

looked cold and clean. Their footsteps echoed down the long hallway. She heard groans and laughter in different rooms as they walked. After a turn down a long hallway, Brant stopped at a closed door. "This is it."

"You go first."

Brant opened the door, and Darby peered over his shoulder. The bed was covered with a blue bedspread, but no one was in it. Brant entered first and checked the small bathroom.

"What does that mean?" Darby asked, her pulse pounding. "Is he all right?"

"He was starting to get around last time I was here." Brant checked his watch. "It's too early for dinner. I'm sure he's fine, or I'd have heard something."

They heard footsteps from the room next door. A cleaning woman entered, and Brant spoke to her in German.

"She said he's in the chapel."

The woman glanced at the wall clock and spoke again.

"I guess chapel is over. He's probably in the game area."

"I thought you said he wasn't well."

"He's been improving. And Gunther's a fighter, that's for sure."

Darby was about to leave the room when something caught her eye. A miniature rosebush on a small table in the corner of the room. It blossomed with yellow roses. She touched a petal the size of her fingernail.

"Yes, this must be my grandfather's room," she said quietly.

"I wanted you to find the memorial your grandfather made for Celia in Hallstatt. I hadn't seen it in years and forgot that the nameplate is covered. You have to open it to see her name. But there is a rosebush growing at the base. It blossoms yellow roses."

"My grandmother's favorite flower."

"At least once a year, under the cover of night, Gunther would take his own yellow roses from his garden to her grave. He never missed a year."

"And all the while, my grandmother was living and missing him on the other side of the world, tending her yellow roses."

Brant turned Darby toward him and drew her into his arms. "It's going to be okay. Somehow, it's going to be okay."

Darby rested against his chest for a minute, then slowly pulled away. "Let's find him."

They left the room and headed back down the hall, turning right. Above the sound of their footsteps, Darby heard a deep, steady voice speaking as they reached the doorway.

"That's Gunther," Brant said, sounding surprised as they stopped. "He sounds much better than just a week ago." Darby's eyes moved to a table with chess figures and two men sitting on opposite ends. The man speaking had his back to them.

"Wait." Darby grabbed Brant's arm. She looked at the thick, peppered-gray hair, a little in need of a comb in the back where a fuzzy piece stood up. Her eyes caressed a wool sweater over his wide back. Her grandfather. His voice was only slightly slurred, but she caught a hint of laughter within. "What is he saying?"

Brant whispered close to her ear. "He's teasing the other guy, and, as typical for Gunther, is giving the man a Bible lesson. He said that when we take communion and say we partake of Jesus' body and blood, we accept that we may face the sufferings and trials that Jesus faced. But God has conquered all things, and so we have nothing to fear. He just asked the man, 'Have you partaken? Perhaps that is why you are losing?' I can't believe he's talking so well."

"So what do we do?" Darby asked softly. "Perhaps we should have a doctor tell him. What if we set him back? What—what if . . . what if he doesn't want a granddaughter after all these years?"

"He wants you, Darby. Don't be afraid of that. I don't know what we'll tell him or not tell him. Let's meet him and go from there." Brant slid his hand around hers reassuringly. "Are you ready?"

"Yes."

"I'm with you, every step." He led her forward. "Gunther?"

"Bra-nt."

Gunther turned slowly. A smile beamed from his face and Darby noticed light blue eyes that might resemble her mother's, but there was no immediate recognition of other features. Gunther smiled at her, even raised an eyebrow at their hands, but nothing would have told them who they were to one another. She could have bumped into him anywhere and never known this man had some of her same blood.

The two men spoke German, so Darby was only able to understand a word or two that indicated Brant's surprise over Gunther's health. Then Gunther turned his attention back to her, saying something and extending a hand.

"American," Darby heard from Brant in another round of German.

"Ah, an A-merican?" Gunther said, interested. "Bend down here."

He reached for her hands, and she wondered if he'd notice her trembling within his own unsteady fingers. Darby bent down and looked up at him, extending her hands.

"You w-atch for this man. He very disturbed at times." He winked and grinned up at Brant. Darby's tears began to flow.

"Is there something wrong, my child?"

The words *my child* brought a surge of emotion. Darby saw her grandmother's dreamy eyes as she spoke of this man. She remembered the letters of love, so deep and youthful and full of tomorrow. She saw her mother, waiting and searching the Times Square crowd, hoping, hoping that he'd appear. And the ghost who haunted their family was right in front of her—alive and breathing.

A sob broke in her chest as she looked down at the floor. She heard Gunther's chess partner wheel away in his chair, and she tried to force herself to stop crying, but the tears only flowed harder. The hand holding hers tightened, and she felt a gentle pat on her back. He spoke to Brant in German and waited for an answer.

"Gunther," Brant said tenderly, "This is Darby Evans. She is your granddaughter."

The hands pulled away, and Darby heard his gasp. Her tears stopped, but she could not look up.

"Her grandmother's name was Celia Müller."

Gunther spoke hoarsely in German. Brant began an explanation in Gunther's native tongue. Brant knelt beside her, speaking upwardly, with his arm around her. Darby remained before him, unable to look up from the floor, like a child waiting for either stark rejection or arms of love. She heard Gunther exhale, long and deep like the final breath had left his lungs.

A hand touched her hair as Brant stopped speaking. The shaking fingers lifted her chin. Their eyes met, both with tears.

"My grandchild. I never had a child, never thought. . . ."

Gunther's fingers touched her cheek, a strand of hair, her forehead.

"When did she die?"

"Four months ago."

Gunther's mouth dropped, and his light eyes looked away. He put his hand upon his head and shook it slowly as if not able to believe his ears. He exhaled another long, deathly breath, and Darby could feel him shiver from deep within.

"Gunther?" Brant asked. "Are you all right?"

"No. This is worst, and best, of days." His hands shook violently, and he clasped them together.

"I think we should take you to your room."

Brant pushed the wheelchair. Gunther held Darby's hand the entire way and glanced up often, as if to be sure she was still there.

They entered behind a nurse who spoke to Gunther and

examined him closely. Gunther disagreed with the woman. Darby wished she could understand them.

"Are you sure?" Brant asked. "If you need rest, we can come back in a few hours. I don't want you having a setback."

"I don't want y-ou to go. I want you here. I want her, Darby, here. My grand-daughter. I w-aited my entire life to see her."

Brant helped Gunther into the bed and carefully removed the older man's shoes. He pushed a button to elevate the bed to a sitting position, then covered Gunther's legs with the blue bedspread. Gunther reached a hand toward her, and Darby moved a chair close.

"I still cannot understand. How?"

"Tatianna Hoffman died at Mauthausen. Somehow she took Grandma's place. My grandmother was told you were dead, and when you never came to your meeting place, she believed it."

"I believed she was dead," Gunther said, shaking his head. Suddenly, he sat up straighter. "Oh, dear Lord. She didn't. She could not have!"

"What is it?" Brant asked.

"Ingrid. Ingrid was with them."

"Who is Ingrid?" Darby asked.

"My wife. Ingrid went with Ta-tianna and Celia to Swiss border. She was with them the night the Nazis met them. Ingrid knew everything."

Brant sat in the chair beside Darby. "Ingrid knew Celia escaped and Tatianna was taken by the Nazis? And she never told you?"

"Never. She told me Ce-lia was taken."

"What did she say happened to Tatianna?" Darby asked.

"She say Tatianna was so close to border a-nd after Nazis took Celia she decided to leave Austria."

"When did she tell you all of this?"

"The night she beg me to marry her. The war had just ended, the c-ountry was mess, divided by A-mericans, British,

Soviets. Ingrid's ch-ildren were Nazi babies, and she need pro-tection. I had been in re-sistance, injured for the cause—a perfect co-ver for her. I a-asked everything about night of Celia's capture. She could have said truth. I would have g-gone to America and found Celia."

"But she needed you for her own safety." Brant stood up swiftly in anger.

"You know what?" Darby sat forward. "Grandma's letters. One was from a woman with 'I' initials. The letter was from 1942, three years before the war ended. She told Grandma Celia about Tatianna's death and also that you had died. The woman told Celia to quit writing and get on with her life in America. The woman also said she had a Nazi friend she might marry."

Brant and Gunther eyed one another. "Ingrid," Brant said.

Gunther began to shake again. "I have tried my whole life to do good. How can this happen? How?" Tears burst from his eyes. He moaned and curled onto his side. Darby jumped up and leaned over him, wishing to protect him from all he must feel. All she could do was wait.

His wide back continued to shake with years of lost sobs. Darby looked at Brant and saw the fear in his eyes.

"It's all right, Gunther," Brant said, cradling the old man in his arms. He spoke softly in German. Darby couldn't stop her own scattered tears and saw Brant wipe his face from time to time as he rocked his old mentor. Finally, Gunther's sobs slowed, and she believed he was asleep until he reached for her hand. His thick hand held hers and stroked it gently.

Brant opened a drawer on the nightstand and handed Gunther a handkerchief. The old man wiped his face and blew his nose like a trumpet sounding. He chuckled as he turned and sat up. "I m-eet my granddaughter for the fir-irst time and act like a blubbering fool. I a-apologize, my dear."

Darby sniffed. "Oh, don't be sorry. You've lost her all over again. And you've been betrayed."

"Yes. And I could have gone to my grave without ever meeting you. See, I should be thankful." His smile was weak but sincere. "Please. Will you tell me about her?"

Darby smiled at the stranger she instantly loved. "She was absolutely amazing. Learned the computer before anyone in our household. She became an American citizen before I was born and never spoke German again."

"She h-ad to leave this all behind, perhaps," Gunther said.

"On the outside, I know she did, except I grew up with tales of the Austrian Alps. So in a way, she contradicted herself. She did not speak of the difficult times to me. My mother had a long struggle, wanting her father—wanting you—so they quit speaking of you before I was born. Yet I know she didn't leave you behind. She was a brave, independent woman who loved with a full heart."

"That sounds like Cel-ia. Though I ne-ever considered her brave or inde-pendent."

"Oh, she was. She jogged in a senior citizen marathon and volunteered two days a week at the public-school kindergarten. Perhaps she had to become strong once she lost you. She also had a strong faith in God."

"Then it is God who saved us both—made us to be strong without each other."

"Yes," Darby whispered. Her eyes found Brant's dark, compassionate eyes. She could barely tear her gaze away from him as she continued to tell about her grandmother. Memories from childhood, Grandma Celia's favorite American movies and books, her to-die-for New York cheesecake. Gunther took it in like a starving man tasting food once again. Darby talked, with Gunther asking questions, until night fell around them. "Grandma has a rose garden in our backyard. Her favorite flower bush in the center of the garden—"

"Yellow roses," Gunther finished. He looked far away and infinitely sad. "I've been placing those flowers on her memorial for sixty years—and all that time she lived and breathed."

"A few nights before she died, Grandma told me how much she loved you. She said you were her Prince Charming, and she never loved a man again. She wrote you letters, one every year. I have them with me."

Darby found her long, black purse and took out the packet they'd picked up from Peter Voss before arriving at the nursing home. "We were trying to find information in them. But the last one has not been opened. It was written September 15 of last year. She died October 3."

Gunther reached for the letter and held it against his chest. "October 3. Wh-at was I doing that day? Why did I not feel her, her spirit leave? Why did I not know she lived all these years?" Gunther caressed the neat cursive words on the envelope. "I would kn-know that writing any-where."

The door to Gunther's room opened, and the nurse appeared surprised to see them still there. Brant talked to her, with Gunther adding a few words before Brant and the nurse exited the room.

"They think I'm old and need some rest," Gunther said with a smile. "I don't want you to leave yet."

"Brant will take care of it. But you could use some rest. And perhaps some time alone?" Darby motioned to the letters on the edge of the bed.

Brant returned. "They gave permission for us to stay awhile longer, maybe even the night, but only if Gunther is able to rest. They want to prepare him for bed and to eat his dinner." Gunther frowned, and long creases furrowed his forehead. "I promise to bring her back. We'll be in the cafeteria."

Darby glanced back at Gunther before she walked out. He was already opening the letter from his bride.

They made small talk as they picked up trays in the cafeteria. Both chose a meat stew with dumplings. Darby could tell something was bothering Brant. They carried their trays to a quiet, indoor garden room.

Brant stirred his food and hardly ate. Darby gobbled hers down and ate both their breads. She asked him three times if he was feeling all right. After they had cleared their trays away, they walked to the end of the glass room. The stars twinkled above in the dark, cloudless sky.

"I need to ask you, Darby," Brant said, his eyes troubled, "can you ever forgive me?"

"You have to know it wasn't your fault. You didn't lie to them. You were protecting Gunther. I'd have done the same thing."

"I've spent my career trying to help people subjected to the evils of others. And my one chance to help the person I love most . . . They could have had her last months together."

"They have eternity together."

Brant turned his head toward her. "Yes, they do. Thank you."

"No," Darby whispered. "Thank you, for giving me my grandfather."

Darby stood on her tiptoes and kissed him on the cheek. He gathered her in to his arms and she rested her face against his chest, hearing the steady beat of his heart.

"Darby, I think I'm beginning to need you in my life."

"You do need me."

He pulled away slightly and saw her smile. "Oh, really?"

"Yes. Because I think I'm beginning to need you too."

"You already need me. You need me terribly."

"Oh, really?" Inside, every part of her agreed with him. "One thing about this forgiveness . . . can I take it back the next time you infuriate me?"

"You think you'll keep seeing me in the future?"

"Well, since we love the same man, I'm sure our paths will cross."

She laughed as he drew her close again.

Someone cleared a throat, and Brant quickly dropped his arms from around Darby. A nurse stood, looking embarrassed, at the entrance to the indoor garden. Brant took Darby's hand and led her toward the older woman. They discussed Gunther, and then the woman hurried away.

"He's ready for us. But we have strict instructions."

"As long as we can stay with him."

Gunther waited in the room lit with only a small lamp. His arms were folded over a sharp line of white sheet and blanket. Suddenly Darby wanted to take him away, far away—all the way back to Grandma's home in California. He needed rest, and it showed in his eyes, though his smile was joyful at their return. But she hoped it would happen, that he could be in the house his wife had made into a home.

"We can't talk anymore, or they'll kick me out," Darby said

as she grasped outstretched hands. "You must sleep, and I'll be here when you awaken."

"I st-still find it hard to believe. My granddaughter."

"Yes, I almost fear I'll wake up to find it untrue. But you must get strong. You have a daughter—what a wonderful surprise you will be to her. She waited and hoped until it destroyed a place within her. She needs you to be strong for her. And you have another granddaughter and some energetic twin great-granddaughters."

"The family I believed to be dead. I will rest and get strong for th-them."

"Yes, so sleep. Sleep."

"Will you?" Gunther patted the bed beside him and moved over. "I've never had my child so near."

Darby glanced at Brant, who was sitting in a chair in the corner. She felt her lip twitch and nose burn. "And I've never had my grandfather so near."

The bed groaned as she moved the metal railing down. Darby remembered only months before she had rested with her grand-mother. Carefully she sat on the bed and stretched out. Her arms were awkward, looking for their place. She rested her head on the pillow, moved and squirmed until it felt right. Not long ago, Darby had circled Grandma's body. Now her grandfather cradled her tightly, her head beneath his chin, his arms on hers. She breathed medicine, age, and a hint of deep spice. He touched her hair and spoke soft words in German that needed no inter-pretation. Wet drops, not her own, fell upon the pillow. Warm breath rustled her hair. She couldn't move, afraid it wouldn't be true. There were no memories of a father's arms, no bear hugs or loving pats. That longing had never entered her conscious-ness until now. Darby moved closer yet until she heard the patter of her grandfather's heart. It wrapped around her, beating and beating like a rocking chair with gentle pats upon her back. She could stay here forever.

⊷══◉══⊶

"Darby, wake up." Someone touched her hair and cheek. Her mouth felt dry, her eyes sticky, her arms tenderly held and tangled. She turned toward the voice—Brant's.

"Darby, it's morning."

The arms were her grandfather's, and his breath continued to lull and call her back into rest. It hadn't been a dream. She had a grandfather. She couldn't wait to call her mother and sister. They'd fly there in a day or two, and their lives would be changed forever.

"I have to leave, Darby," Brant whispered.

"Why? What's wrong?" She gently untangled herself, and Brant helped her from the bed.

"My secretary called. I'm not sure how they tracked me down since I turned off my phone, but a nurse woke me and said it was important. I'll be gone until late afternoon. Unless you want to come with me now."

"No, I'll stay."

"That's what I thought." Brant took a step closer and touched her hair. "Take care of him."

"I will."

⊷══◉══⊶

Darby spent an hour dozing in Brant's chair, against the pillow he'd used. Finally Gunther stirred and woke. A morning of activity began. They ate breakfast and later lunch, played several hands of cards, and Darby pushed him in his wheelchair around the hospital and through the indoor garden. They never stopped talking until Darby worried she was letting him do too much. Brant hadn't returned by afternoon, and Darby felt a terrible need for a shower. The nurse gave strict instructions for Gunther to have an afternoon nap.

"I need to leave, but I'll be back tonight or early in the

morning," Darby said. She'd only met him the day before, but felt she'd known him a lifetime. "I need a shower, or you won't want me back."

"I will ta-ake you, even if you smell badly." He chuckled and pinched his nose. "I do-o this whe-en you come close."

Darby laughed, loving his smile and hearty chuckle. "We both have work to do. You must get better. I must give the best news to my family and make arrangements for them to come."

"Yes. Y-es." Gunther beamed. "Bring my family. But fi-irst, I must tell you one, one thing. I hid it. I hid your in-heritance. I mu-st tell you where it is."

CHAPTER THIRTY-TWO

Darby stared out the window as the taxi zipped through traffic. It seemed the world should be a different color or perhaps lost its gravitational pull overnight with all the changes she'd experienced in the last days. But people continued to walk with their feet on the same sidewalks as they had yesterday, and wisps of clouds still drifted in a blue sky.

She leaned her head against the cool window and closed her eyes. Her newfound joy mingled with gentle sorrow like oil mixed with water. One emotion would rise to the surface, then the other would bubble through. Her grandfather was alive! Her mother had a father. Her nieces a great-grandfather. Yet Grandma Celia, who had yearned a lifetime for her lost love, had missed him by only months. The smile and stories of Grandma's life had sheltered the sorrow she'd never been freed from. And her joy lived only a plane ride away. What if it had happened to Darby and her love—to her and Brant?

The taxi proceeded down tiny Goldgasse, and Darby was

struck with a wave of exhaustion. For some reason, behind closed eyelids she thought of Maureen. Her sister was tucked away asleep at home, and her life was about to be changed along with all of theirs. Darby missed her sister as she hadn't since childhood. They'd been closer then, and Darby didn't know why she'd allowed them to drift so deeply into their own lives. She vowed to turn that around. She'd also call Tristie in Montana—perhaps fly up for a visit. Her woman friendships were essential to life. She knew that not just from Tatianna and Grandma Celia, but it rang true within her. She'd missed a lot in the last years, but no more.

Darby's head remained against the window, hair cascading across her face. Her feet felt too heavy to move when the car stopped, though her mind continued its race around the discoveries of the last two days. She moved away from the window as the cab driver prepared to open the door, but he was looking somewhere else. Across the car, through the other back window, she could see a man's slacks, belt, and tucked-in shirt. It had to be Brant. She'd be able to see on his face the completion of decades of trials. She'd fall into his arms and find spring after a long winter. The heaviness upon her shoulders would lighten, even leave. Brant. The man she knew she loved, as Grandma Celia had loved Gunther Müller.

The opposite door opened.

"Darby Evans." The face was not Brant's. "Remember me? Richter Hauer. We met in a restaurant when you were with Brant." It took a second for her mind to match this man with bloodshot eyes and a few days' stubble to the arrogant man she'd met months before.

"Ah, I think so. Yes. I remember." Why was this man closing the door and the taxi driver returning to the front seat? "I'm getting out here."

"Brant called me and asked that I escort you to his office. He had a meeting he couldn't get away from." The cab driver hadn't moved. "Go ahead."

"Wait." Darby reached for the door handle. "I have some calls to make and need a shower, some rest."

"Brant said it was urgent. I tried to catch you with Gunther, but you'd left. Gunther told me you were coming here. On my word, what a shock to discover we are related in a way, right? My step-grandfather is your grandfather." He smiled at her with an incredulous look. "Miracles do still happen."

Darby hesitated. This man must have talked to Brant and Gunther to know these details.

"Go ahead!" Richter called again. The driver glanced questioningly at her in the rearview mirror, then the car moved forward down the dark street. Darby didn't speak as her thoughts tried to slog through a molasses of tiredness, facts, and suspicions. Brant didn't like Richter, she remembered. So why . . .

Darby eyed Richter as he peered anxiously behind them. His hands were grasped together strangely. Suddenly, she realized she shouldn't be with him. He looked at her quickly, and she saw danger in his eyes.

Richter grabbed her hand. "I need you to come with me. Everything will be all right. Just do as I ask." When Darby's mouth opened to cry out, he squeezed her hand in warning. "My grandmother, Ingrid, kept her lover's Lüger collection after the war. She passed them down to me." Richter forced her hand against his jacket. She could feel something . . . a gun?

Richter glanced behind them again, leaned forward to instruct the driver, then sat back. The car stopped, waiting for traffic. Darby looked back toward her hotel, where she'd been going a moment before. A moment before she had been safe, ready to call her mother and sister and then rest and see Brant and Gunther, and now. . . .

"I'm in a difficult position, Darby." His face hovered too close to hers. "I must have something that I have long sought. Only you can help me. I have no doubt that Gunther told you where he hid the Lange inheritance."

Darby's mouth opened, but she could not speak.

"Please, Darby. I have little time."

The cab turned onto Residenzplatz. Life seemed so normal. People strolled, carriages waited to give rides, artists hawked their paintings on the street. "What do you want?"

But she knew. Richter raised one eyebrow, knowing she understood. Was this why Ingrid had deceived her grand-mother so long ago? Had the greed for the Lange inheritance not only cost many lives, but also enticed deception long after the Nazis had been destroyed?

The taxi halted, and Richter tossed a bill forward. Darby realized they'd only gone a few blocks from her hotel when Richter grabbed her hand and yanked her outside. Panic raced wildly through Darby. Should she scream? Run into one of the shops? Then Richter pinned her close to him.

Richter had parked his car near the restaurant where she'd first met him, the day she'd first met Brant. The more she sought an escape the more trapped she realized she was—like a butterfly in a jar.

"Just show me where it is, and nothing will happen to you. I promise." He walked her beside a white BMW and almost dropped his keys as he unlocked the door.

"No." She planted her feet, remembering too well her fool-ish impulse to jump in the car that took her to Bruno Weiler's house. And this was different. All the television shows said to never, ever be forced into a car. "I'm not going anywhere."

"You are. Get in." He pushed her toward the open door. She tried to get away, but Richter grabbed her with a fierce hold. "I have a gun, right here in my pocket. Come with me, and you'll be safe. But I can't let you walk away."

She hesitated a minute too long so Richter pushed her inside. "Move across. You're driving. Take the keys."

"Where am I going?"

"You tell me." Richter shut his door firmly.

Darby searched the tourists and carriages and shopkeepers for anyone to help. *This can't be happening!*

"So tell me where we're going," he insisted.

Darby didn't say anything. He pulled out the gun and rested it on his lap.

It really was an antique Lüger. It appeared almost ridiculous pointing toward her instead of resting inside a museum case.

"I'll tell you where it is, and you'll let me get out."

"You tell me where it is, I'll get it, then I'll let you go." He stared at her as she carefully moved through traffic. She could see him from the corner of her eye.

"It's in Hallstatt."

"Hallstatt?" Richter thought for a moment. "You mean the grave?"

Darby nodded.

He looked surprised. "Why didn't I think of that before?"

When Richter glanced at her, Darby knew they thought the same thing. "I wish you had," she said.

⁎⚬⚬⁎

Brant had just convinced himself that he had not seen Darby with Richter in a taxi, leaving Goldgasse together. Then Richter's car had pulled from a side street down the one-way exit. Darby was driving. Brant was on his way to see her, to watch her sleep, to share her phone calls. His important meeting had been nothing—another frustrating interruption. Frau Halder didn't know who the urgent message had come from, but she'd taken it seriously. Brant sometimes had mysterious clients meet with him secretly, but this time, no one showed up at his office.

He had parked beneath a tree on one of the streets sur-rounding the plaza, then begun walking when he saw Darby inside the taxi from across the street. He wondered why she was leaving Goldgasse. Then he saw Richter beside her.

Shocks of denial pounded through him as his mind tried to decipher what he'd seen. He should have followed them when they passed in Richter's car, but he sat too long. It couldn't be.

Brant suddenly remembered the "coincidental" meeting the first day he'd met Darby. Richter had come to the restaurant by chance. Then something had happened in Vienna two days before, or someone. Darby hadn't explained why she disap-peared for the night. Was everything a lie? His mind brought up all sorts of ideas. Perhaps she wasn't even an American, but someone Richter and Ingrid had recruited to finally get the Lange inheritance while Gunther was recovering.

And this morning. He had been called away from the hospi-tal. Did it give opportunity for Darby to ask Gunther where he'd hidden it? Only Brant knew Gunther had hidden the heir-looms at all. Gunther had only withheld the location.

Brant looked back toward his car and wondered what to do, and how this could be true. But it seemed the truth was before his eyes. He'd been betrayed once again.

CHAPTER THIRTY-THREE

Daylight faded in the valley as Darby and Richter drove the north edge of Hallstatt Lake. Night would come soon. Darby noticed the last reflection of pink on the water as she drove. This man promised her safety once she revealed the hidden treasure. Could she really believe him? He'd already told her several lies. Could this be, perhaps, her final glimpse of sunlight? She checked the rearview mirror again. No one had followed them from the city. Surely Brant would wonder where she was, be searching for her maybe. But he was too far behind.

God, you can't want this to happen. Not after everything. Not after this journey you've led me on.

Had Tatianna thought those same words? What doubts and fears did she have during those last steps before death? Darby wanted to be strong, setting her jaw and holding her head high. But inside she felt weak and shaky and feared she might crumble at any moment. She prayed for strength over and over again.

Richter had been quiet the last few miles. She imagined him hatching his plan to retrieve the inheritance, and then what? Darby needed her own plan and could only think of the Gerringer home in Hallstatt. If she could somehow get to them, perhaps she'd make it.

"Take a right at the next curve," Richter said.

"That's not the way to Hallstatt," Darby said, her voice rising. This was not in her plan.

"There's something I must do first."

⊷══◉══⊷

Brant had tried roads and places in Salzburg but couldn't find Richter's car anywhere. He'd stopped by Darby's hotel, called a dozen times, driven to Richter's favorite places, and started once toward Munich and Ingrid's house. Instead, he phoned again on his return to Salzburg, but no one answered. He'd gone to Gunther's, only to leave without talking to him. For how could he break this news to the old man now? But could the old man be in danger? The police would believe none of this—it was all speculation.

Late afternoon faded quickly into night. He drove into a parking lot and hit the brakes hard. *Think, think,* he told himself. If only he'd tailed Richter and Darby immediately. Brant picked up his car phone and tried Richter's cellular but received only a recording that indicated the power was off. He called Darby's hotel again, feeling like he was repeating her trip to Vienna. Could that have only been days ago? Again, there was no answer in her room. The front desk said they hadn't seen her. Next he dialed Ingrid in Munich. The line picked up.

"Frau Müller is in Gosau today," the housekeeper said. "She's finishing work there before closing the house."

Brant hung up before saying good-bye. Gosau was over an hour away. And what if Darby wasn't there?

He squeezed the steering wheel. There were only two options he could think of. Either Darby had betrayed them and was involved with Richter and Ingrid, or Darby was in trouble. His eyes said she'd tricked them. His heart told him differently. Yet his feelings had certainly failed him before.

Brant battled back and forth. Darby had appeared in Salzburg at the same time he began to suspect Richter and Ingrid were involved in something. She'd disappeared in Vienna for an entire night and never given an explanation as to where she'd gone. Richter was looking for her when Brant picked her up at the train station. And the ring—the one piece that had convinced him. Ingrid most likely had seen it on Celia's finger years ago. She could have made a duplicate and given it to Darby. The evidence and seeing Darby drive off in Richter's car all pointed one way.

But then he remembered other things. Darby so childlike and afraid after her room was broken into. Could that have been part of the act? Was she capable of faking their night at the dinner concert and her interest at the Holocaust conference? Were her laughter and kisses only for dramatic effect? And if Darby was partnered with Ingrid and Richter, why hadn't she gone straight to Gunther for the information they sought?

Then the image of Darby asleep next to Gunther made him ignore the facts and believe in her. He'd watched them sleep so deep and safe and secure. Though they'd just met, they were not strangers, but grandfather and grandchild brought together at last.

"If she's not involved, then she's in danger," he said aloud.

Brant turned the car out of the parking lot while hitting the buttons on his phone. He didn't want to worry his old friend, but he needed to know one thing: where was the inheritance hidden?

◦─▭◦▭─◦

The sign said *Gosau*. Darby turned the car to the right. "Are we going to Ingrid and Gunther's house?"

"Just follow my instructions." His voice revealed his own conflicting thoughts. "I need a few supplies. We can't dig with our hands, now can we?"

Darby remained silent as they drove miles of twisting mountain road through dense forest and along a silver stream that caught the last lights in the sky. The car was warm and comfortable with the scent of men's aftershave, but Darby felt sick. The road rose from the forest into a long mountain valley and into tiny Gosau. Richter directed her up myriad streets to a hillside house—Gunther and Ingrid's, she assumed. The smaller house next door must have been where Brant had spent his childhood summers. She imagined him as a boy exploring forest grottos and visiting Gunther on the porch of the larger house.

A black car was parked in the driveway of the larger house.

"What will my grandmother think of you, I wonder?" Richter smiled slightly as he slid the gun back into the jacket pocket. Darby hesitated, glancing around as she got out of the car. Richter watched her every move until they were inside the house. No one greeted them. The house was empty except for a few belongings and some furniture covered with sheets. Darby heard a steady *swish* from somewhere, and Richter motioned her toward the stairway. He followed close behind.

Inside a room at the end of a hallway, a woman stood with her back toward them, sweeping the hardwood floor. Bookcases lined the walls, and a small couch sat covered with a sheet like a punished child left in the corner. French doors opened toward the second-story porch, where the lights from the village below glittered like beacons through the glass.

The woman turned quickly as they entered. With one hand

over her heart and the other on the broom handle, she scolded
Richter in rapid German. Age had changed Ingrid's beauty, but
not robbed it. She stood with straight posture, holding herself
with something of grace or pride. Her hair was pinned up for
work, but her clothing was stylish beige slacks and a clean
white-and-tan shirt. For an elderly woman, Ingrid would be
considered beautiful, and Darby felt a jealous sting that this
had been Gunther's wife for the last fifty-five years. But the
lines in Ingrid's face weren't from laughter; she seemed unable
to smile or to sing.

"Grandma, speak the English you insisted I learn. I have
brought my American friend to meet you."

Darby and Ingrid evaluated one another in silence. Then
Ingrid spoke to Richter in a hushed tone in German.

"Her name is Darby. Darby Evans."

Ingrid put her hand over her mouth and dropped the broom
with a loud clatter.

"Darby, meet Ingrid," Richter said quietly. "Your step-
grandmother."

Ingrid stalked toward Richter, speaking angrily.

"English, remember?" Richter shook his head, then grew
annoyed and defensive at Ingrid's words. "There was nothing
else I could do. We were about to lose it all. Darby told me
where it is. Gunther told her."

"You talk with Gunther?" she asked Darby, her voice
sounding strained. "Why you bring her here, Richter?"

"I needed supplies on the way to Hallstatt."

"Hallstatt?" Ingrid said, turning away.

"Yes. Right there, all these years. And we thought it was a
simple pilgrimage to his dead wife."

"It was," she said bitterly. "Why you come here? Why bring
her?"

"Everything will be fine. Darby is coming with me to get the
coins and brooch, then we'll do something. . . ."

"What?" Ingrid asked. "Did you think? What will we do with her?"

"I don't know."

Both pairs of eyes glanced her way. They started firing words back and forth in German. Darby searched the lights of the village for a way out.

"I'll be in the basement, getting supplies," Richter said.

"*Nein*. Take her with you."

"You may want to say some things to her." Richter stared for a long time at his grandmother, then at Darby. All at once Darby realized she wanted to ask Ingrid a thousand questions and accuse her of even more. "I'll be downstairs, not far away."

"Be quick about it, Richter," Ingrid said, standing tall as if trying to compose herself.

The women listened to Richter's exit, down the stairs, through a door. Darby walked toward the French doors. She peered at the railing and beyond it, wondering if she could jump the ten or twelve feet to escape. But wouldn't Ingrid immediately call for Richter? She could easily overpower Ingrid, but what would she do—hit an old woman? No other house was nearby except for Brant's old, deserted cottage.

Darby opened the doors and stepped onto the wood balcony. She glanced back to see what Ingrid did. The older woman sat on the edge of the couch, her head down in thought. The deck was high, too high, it seemed. She'd get hurt and never be able to run unless she could hide in the darkness somewhere. It may be her only chance.

Ingrid stood in the doorway and flipped on the porch light. The illumination over the older woman's head brought deep shadows below her eyes. "What did Gunther say?"

Darby leaned back against the railing and faced the woman who'd destroyed her grandmother's and grandfather's lives. "I had the letter you wrote Celia telling her that both he and Tatianna were dead."

Ingrid raised her chin and glared coldly at Darby. "I did what I had to do at that time. Your grandmother was my friend, a long time ago."

"Your friend?"

"I knew someday this would come. I don't know how, but I knew. And you could never understand."

"You're right, I could never understand." Darby wanted to tell Ingrid what the lies had done to her grandmother, her mother, and even her own life. But where would she begin? And would it matter?

"It wasn't my fault. It was the war. You can accuse me, but your grandmother would not have lived without me. She was a mess. I saved her as much as Tatianna did. We all did things we did not expect—war does that. Even Celia. She betrayed Tatianna."

"What?"

"You know so little but accuse me still."

"How did Celia betray Tatianna?" Darby's heart pounded. She'd always had one thought that she feared to consider—that her grandmother escaped by using Tatianna, betraying her. Sure, she knew her grandmother would never do that, but what about in such a treacherous time? Darby paced into a dark corner of the porch. "My grandmother was not a betrayer."

"She admitted it to me."

"Tell me."

"Tatianna and Celia made some pact or vow of friendship as young girls. When Celia's father was captured by Nazis, Celia was given information that Tatianna was the person who revealed his hiding place. Celia believed it. I believed it too. I became friends with all of them in Salzburg. Tatianna was always reading her Bible and talking about how she served a loving God. She wanted to be a missionary and use music to bring beauty into the lives of the poor. I didn't believe it—

until later. The two girls loved each other, as much as Celia and Gunther loved. Then everything began to fall apart. Her father taken, we knew Celia had to hide. The news that Tatianna was the one who told shocked Celia. Celia accused her and left with Gunther. Tatianna was devastated. But later Gunther sent for Tatianna. I volunteered to drive Celia out and Gunther arranged for Hallstatt. When I arrived, it was Celia and Tatianna who were there."

Darby sat down in the armrest of a wooden chair and glanced up into a diamond sky. At least her grandmother hadn't actually betrayed Tatianna, but instead their vow of belief.

"Then what?" Darby said it like a challenge, while listening for Richter's footsteps below. "How did it happen that Tatianna gave her life for my grandmother, and you stole what was left?"

"You make judgment so easily when you not there. I not intend what happened. Your grandmother escaped because I take her. I made difficult choices, and after war, I was in great danger—my children also. Gunther gave safety for me, and I believed he was dead when I wrote Celia that letter. I told myself that Celia rebuilt her life in America. I was sorry to find that she die last autumn."

"How did you know?"

"She contacted me last year while searching for inheritance."

"My grandmother called you? Last year?"

"Yes." Ingrid's face was shadowed as she looked away from the light.

"Why didn't you tell her the truth then, when they still had time?"

"After that many years? It was too late. I always thought Gunther knew where the inheritance was but also wondered if somehow Celia got it out of Austria. When she call, I knew for sure that Gunther must know. Celia say she sick, and I sorry for that. I call once, and your mother give me news of her death."

"And you never told her about Gunther." They had been so close. Celia and Gunther could have at least had a few months together. But again, the greed over the Lange inheritance took lives away. Darby felt an almost uncontrollable urge to slap Ingrid. She was shaking, overwhelmed that she could harbor such anger toward another person.

"I need to protect my own," Ingrid said. "And Celia dying— why then tell her about Gunther, after all the years? I have to do hard things. You not know the choices you make until in the danger. You do not understand."

"Then make me understand," Darby said firmly. She may never know if Ingrid didn't speak now. "What happened the night my grandmother escaped?"

Ingrid breathed into her hands, then wrapped her arms together. "Chaos. The world was in chaos. The plan was to take Celia out, and Gunther would be a decoy at a house in Upper Austria. He would follow later. We pretend it was great adventure—Celia's escape to America. I get Tatianna and Celia at Hallstatt. We took several days to go through the Alps—we have to take one road, then switch to another. We try to laugh a lot. But inside I know we all sad and afraid."

Ingrid folded her hands and spoke calmly, but her words took them both back to the last night together. Darby could see the three in their car, speeding toward hope and safety. . . .

The car switched back and forth down the alpine road. Tatianna hummed a tune of the Glenn Miller Band.

"One more mile," she said with her hand on Celia's. "I will miss you, my friend."

"It won't be forever," Celia said softly. "We'll return after the war, or you will both come to America. Never can we be apart."

"That's right." Tatianna spoke with a confidence Ingrid didn't understand.

The car rounded a bend and slowed. Ingrid knew it to be the last, and then they would be separated from Celia—probably forever. She hated the thought but felt envious all the same. She didn't have the money to leave, so she'd have to find her own way of survival without anyone's help. A sign for the coming Swiss border flashed by them.

"Oh, dear God," Celia said. "Dear God, help us."

"How could they be here?" Tatianna hit the brakes.

The car lurched forward as Ingrid saw a black car blocking the road, directly in front of the Austrian-Swiss border. Suddenly headlights beamed behind them.

"Where did he come from?" Tatianna held the wheel tightly. "Celia, get in the back, and both of you lie down. I'm going to ram straight through."

"No, you'll never make it!" Celia shouted.

"I'll give it my best."

"Stop!" Celia grabbed the steering wheel. "This isn't your fight!"

"Listen to her, Tatianna!" Ingrid said. "We'll all be killed if you try."

"Okay, okay." Tatianna's voice calmed, and she brought the car to a quick halt.

Celia turned in her seat and looked fearfully at Ingrid and Tatianna. The vehicle behind them stopped. Head-lights glared through the window. A man in the front car got out and opened the back door, waiting.

Celia touched her round stomach and closed her eyes for a moment. "I want you both to go home as quickly as possible. I should never have endangered you by allowing you to come—I'm sorry for that."

Tears filled Ingrid's eyes. She knew Celia was only being strong. They all knew Celia would not get away. She'd never see Gunther again, would never hold that baby in her arms. Ingrid felt tied with fear for Celia, but with just as much fear for herself. Would they come after her too?

Celia leaned close to Tatianna. "I have to ask one thing first. I'm so sorry, Tati. I didn't believe in you. After all these years together. I know you so well. I know your heart. But I lost faith anyway. When it counted most, I let you down."

"Stop," Tatianna whispered. "It's all right."

"No, it's not. Please. Will you forgive me?"

The girls stared into years of memories.

"I forgive you, my dear one."

"Thank you." Celia reached for the door handle. She winked at Ingrid and smiled at both of them. "Hey, remember, the heroine always gets away."

"Stay inside," Tatianna ordered, grabbing Celia's hands. "Listen to me. I love you like a sister, no, more than a sister. I'd do anything for you, and this is the only thing I can give. Ingrid, get up here in the driver's seat."

"Tati, you can't go to them. They simply want me. I won't endanger your lives any more than I already have."

"Stay in the car," Tatianna ordered.

Before Celia could speak or move, Tatianna was out of the car. She motioned to Ingrid and slammed the door. Ingrid climbed over the seat as Tatianna walked forward. Her shape was illuminated in their headlights, making a long shadow across the ground.

"What does she think she can say to them?" Celia asked, putting her hand on the door. "I'm going out there."

"Stay inside!" Ingrid hissed. "You have your baby to consider. Perhaps she can do something."

"Like what?"

"I don't know. Just be silent, or they'll take us all."

Celia watched as the man in SS uniform met Tatianna. She took some papers from her coat and handed them to the man. He looked them over and began to move toward the car where Ingrid and Celia waited. Tatianna blocked him, her mouth moving rapidly. Finally, the man in black uniform peered at the car for a long moment, then pointed Tatianna to his vehicle. He slammed the door as she got in.

"What is she doing?" Celia tugged at the papers in her own pocket. "Oh, dear Lord. No! She changed our papers! They think she is me!"

"Celia, don't you dare get out, or they'll kill us all!" Ingrid's terror rose, waiting for guns or men to take them too.

The vehicle behind them moved away. The black car parked before the border crossing pulled backward and slowly passed them. Celia yelled and lunged across the seat as they saw Tatianna. Tatianna waved and motioned for them to go ahead. Then she was gone.

Ingrid looked from her hands in her lap back to Darby's face. "Your grandmother would not stop crying, but I drove her across border and try to tell her not to worry. The Nazis would discover who Tatianna was and let her go, I say. I do not know if she believe me. Celia made me promise to help Tatianna. I promise, but of course, I could do nothing."

"Couldn't, or wouldn't?" Darby asked.

Ingrid was startled from her faraway thoughts. "I help save your grandmother also. She not make it across the border without me. I took her to contact location. I never see her again."

"But you heard from her."

"Yes. During war, she kept making danger for us with her letters. 'What happened to Tatianna? Her family? Of course, Gunther?'"

"So you told her they were all dead."

"I told truth about Tatianna. I heard nothing of Gunther and believed he was dead. Her letters had to stop. You don't get letters from America asking about Jews and political prisoners when you live with SS officer—you would be thought a spy and shot. You cannot understand war. I have only myself— not an escape like Celia. People were starving or murdered for nothing."

"But in the end, we know who was Celia's real friend."

Ingrid turned away and, with a start, Darby wondered where Richter was. She also wondered how much time she had left. This was no game, and she was running out of time. Darby hurried to the edge of the deck again and looked down. There could be rocks; it was hard to see in the darkness. She glanced back, but Ingrid watched in silence. She thought Ingrid's expression said, *Go. It's your one chance.*

She was about to jump when she heard a noise. In the dim light, she spotted someone in a chair below. A red glow from a cigarette illuminated his exhalation. Richter was waiting.

Darby yanked Ingrid back into the room and closed the door. "What's he going to do with me?" Darby implored Ingrid to help her. The door slammed downstairs. Richter was coming.

"No. Richter will not hurt you." But Ingrid's eyes moved away.

Perhaps Darby should run back out to the deck and jump. But as she made a move to do so, Richter walked casually into the room.

"Time to go." Ingrid would not look at him. "Come on, Darby."

"Leave her here with me," Ingrid said suddenly. "After you go to Hallstatt, pick me up. We'll leave her here. It will give us time."

Richter shook his head. "No. She's coming with me."

"Don't make this worse for us," Ingrid said, taking a step toward Darby. Her hand lifted, then dropped back to her side.

"Perhaps we'll come back here in a few hours. But I want

you to be in Munich, waiting for me. I'll take care of everything."

Richter took Darby's arm. She glanced back at Ingrid and
saw fear in the older woman's eyes.

CHAPTER THIRTY-FOUR

A glacial moon shone through icy sheets of clouds as they arrived in the small village—the village Darby loved and where her family had once lived. Richter continued to assure her of her safety, but his words were of little comfort. What *could* he do with her after he'd retrieved what he wanted?

"The scenic town of Hallstatt," Richter said. His fingers twisted on the steering wheel. He was close, very close. "Thousands of visitors walking here every year with a fortune beneath their feet." The car crept into the sleeping village. "To your right, famous Hallstattersee, perfect for diving or sailing. To your left, the Celtic museum where you can see relics from the oldest salt mine in the world. And up the hill in the cemetery, the Lange family treasure, lost, but soon found."

Darby's heart sank as they passed Gasthaus Gerringer. One light was on in the entry room, but the rest of the house was dark. They continued through the Marketplatz down to the parking lot below the lower church.

Richter nervously glanced around as he parked. Tall street-lamps lit the asphalt lot and danced in the dark waters of Hallstattersee. But no one else was around. Richter hopped out and walked around to open her door. Cool night air hit Darby's face as she left the warmth of the car. Richter handed her the keys.

"Open the trunk," he ordered.

From within the trunk, Richter grabbed a flashlight and gave Darby a small toolbox and hand shovel. She evaluated the narrow street, knowing she could run to the Gerringers' home in minutes. But would she make it two steps away from Richter?

"Remember what I have," he said, knowing her thoughts.

She nodded and felt the cold fingers of fear reach further inside her. Richter slid his arm around her waist, trying to hide the small shovel between them.

Their footsteps echoed along the dark concrete as they started up the steep road. "Talk to me."

"What do you want me to say, Richter?"

"I don't know." He stopped and turned her toward him. "I guess, I don't know."

From the road, they turned up a stairway onto a steep upward trail. Darby imagined Gunther's annual pilgrimage at this time of night. Over sixty years for nothing.

"This wasn't how I wanted it," Richter said quietly, pausing to look at her. "Don't think I'm enjoying this. I've traveled the world, gambled and played with the wealthiest men, but here I am creeping up a dark mountain, sneaking, forced to drastic means. It's not what I want."

"You chose this, Richter."

"I can't live a life in poverty, can't leave everything I know behind. I've worked hard taking care of my grandmother. My father and uncle used her money."

Darby remembered how Bruno Weiler had changed from a

youth seeking grandeur into an SS killer—all with the best of intentions. Selfish ambition, denial, conceit, and greed led downward until evil was justified as good. Bruno only saw himself by a jolt of humanity in the face of Tatianna. Was there a way to open Richter's eyes?

"I've made mistakes, and it only takes a few to mess yourself up," Richter continued.

"Why should I pay for your sins?"

He turned toward her and thought for a moment. "It's hard, I know. But doesn't someone always pay for another person's sins?"

Darby opened her mouth to speak when she heard a car approaching.

"Wait." He pulled her into a dark alcove. On the road far below them, a police car drove by. Richter cursed. "Why is he here?" They waited as the car continued down the street and out of view. "We're moving too slow. Come on, but be quiet."

They switched back and forth up mountain stairways and passages until the red lit candles behind a wooden gate bid them entrance.

Richter pushed the gate open. "Which one?" His voice was hushed and anxious as his flashlight bounced from one headstone to another.

They walked the gravel rows, though she knew the general location. On the top, near the bone house. Every moment prolonged was a moment more.

The headstones in daylight with tall, narrow roofs were symbols of lives once lived. In the cold night, the roofs were arrowhead fingers pointing from grave to sky. The flowers planted in rich soil in spring were bright and hopeful in daylight with dim, red candles flickering undying love. Night and winter brought the flowers into a matted mass, like spirits caught and tangled, unable to find escape from the ground.

The red candles were one-eyed creatures, staring and promising that soon she'd join them.

"We're wasting time." Richter squeezed her arm till it hurt.

"At the top, in the Protestant section."

They walked carefully between eyes and spirits to the upper graves. Even the few stars that broke in from the clouds peered at her coldly with no twinkle or hint of peace. The shadows no longer hovered and jeered, but waited to consume and make them her own. She saw where houses, not too far away, were swallowed in shadows. Houses that offered safety and life.

Richter dragged her along awkwardly with the shovel in one hand. The gravel ground beneath their feet; she hoped loudly enough to awaken someone. Winter snow was still piled behind the bone house and on several graves. Darby followed Gunther's instruction to the middle grave close to the upper railing. She moved from grave to grave until she stood in front of a wood and wrought-iron headstone. The wooden post had a pruned rosebush twisted around the base and up a wooden cross. Like some of the other headstones, a black plate covered the nameplate. This had to be it.

"Are you sure?" Richter whispered.

Darby knelt on the edge of a short, concrete border and opened the metal door. Inside it read *Celia Rachel Müller.*

"This is it." Richter's voice had changed, and she wished to read his expression. He handed her the shovel and flipped off the flashlight. "Dig."

Darby gathered her hair into a ball and stuck it into the back of her jacket, then she began to push the hand shovel into the cold dirt. She uprooted several bunches of flowering plants and rested them on the ground, leaving the rosebush at the top of the grave alone. With every reach of the shovel, she pushed herself closer to the end of her chances. Her hope was dwindling.

Richter had moved away. He was listening, watching, seeing

if they were followed. He was nervous. She could imagine his thoughts. *What am I going to do with her? Brant will be looking now. Gunther will tell him we've come to Hallstatt. They could come at any moment. Can I let her live? How can I?*

Darby shivered as her hands pushed the shovel into the grave. What would it be like to die, and to die tonight? She pictured her mother far away at home . . . probably having breakfast or taking a stroll with her friends. Gunther would be sleeping safely in his bed. Brant? Where was Brant right now? She wished for tomorrow and a thousand tomorrows to be with him.

Darby brushed her hands off on her pants and continued to dig. This grave devoid of a body—would it take her life? She looked down into the cold, frozen ground her hands reached into. It was the only grave here without a body.

She stopped. A quiet, comforting Voice spoke in her thoughts and she realized, *There's something here that you want me to find. There's something in the dirt of this empty grave that's for me. I'm in the valley of the shadow of death, and you are showing me something. What? That I am to meet you tonight? That the cold ground will not be my home? What?*

Suddenly her fingers touched something. Using the shovel in her right hand, Darby hit a hard object.

"Did you find it?" Richter said from over her shoulder.

"I think maybe."

She could see only his profile as he looked one way, then the other. When he faced her straight on, she saw only a black shadow.

"Hurry up!" Richter loomed over her. "Get it out."

He flipped on the light and kept it shining into the hole. Darby continued to dig and move the dirt away with the shovel and her hands. A rectangular shape was uncovered several feet down. Darby pulled and dug until the earth released it. She set the object on the concrete border.

It was a metal box wrapped in heavy plastic. Richter took out a pocketknife and cut the waterproofing. Then from somewhere surrounding them, Darby heard something. She couldn't get a direction but thought she heard footsteps. Then Richter heard it too. He flipped off the flashlight, grabbed her close to him, and crouched by the grave. His eyes pierced the darkness like a hunter seeking its prey. The noise stopped.

"Come on," Richter insisted. They crept in the night, beside bushes and around to the tall, white cylindrical building of the Bein Haus.

"Stay there." Richter pushed her against the side of the entrance wall. The stone chilled her back. Richter sat a few steps away, listening. She noticed the gun in his hand. And even then she could hardly believe it was real. Richter holding an antique gun in his hand, her on the ground of a bone house. The surreal moment should feel anything but that. It was more real than any moment of her life, for it could be the last.

Richter tried to pull open the heavy doors, then noticed the lock. Her eyes caught the image of a skull on the door as he swung the flashlight around. Above the door, Darby remembered the symbol of Alpha and Omega—the beginning and the end.

Richter found something in the toolbox as he returned the gun to his coat. He bent in front of the door. Darby was on the ground beside him, her eyes closed. She heard the sound of rapid sawing and then Richter removed the lock. The heavy door opened and a stark, musty smell billowed like ghosts loosed from their chains. Richter pulled her up and pushed her inside. She stumbled in and leaned against the corner. Darby knew a thousand empty eyes stared. Open jaws cried eternal screams. Richter again paused and listened. Then he closed the tomb door behind them.

"I need to see what we have here," he said, flipping the flashlight on. "Then we'll go."

Darby crouched in the darkness as he opened the metal box. "At last. I almost didn't believe it, but here they are." Richter held up the three coins, one at a time. He flipped them over and examined them in the light. "Amazing."

Shaking against the cold cement wall, she felt fear again. Thousands of bones circled the room and waited, waited. She wanted to be strong and have faith. *God, I'm so afraid. Why are you letting this happen?*

And then she thought of Tatianna. A woman who gave her life that others could live. Grandma had said once that death was a stepping-stone, like childhood into adulthood. But to Darby, that step terrified her.

She remembered Grandma saying, "Eternity is closer than we realize, Darby. Like a child cannot perceive the workings and thoughts of his parents, so are we children unable to see eternity all around us. For like the apostle Paul said, 'To live is Christ, but to die is gain.' "

But I want to live.

And then she saw it—in a flash of understanding. Brant had said not to forget to live. To live is Christ. To live something meant more than just believing in it. Tatianna knew it. Grandma Celia knew it. No greater love than to give up your life for a friend. And to truly live was to live for what you believed until the gain of eternity. This was what she could only find in the shadow of death. This she found in a grave empty of a body, in a house of bones without souls. Perhaps, at the last moment of her life, she was finally discovering what it was to live.

Richter snapped the lid closed on the metal box. "It's not here. Where is the brooch?"

"Gunther said he never had it."

"Why didn't you tell me!"

"The coins themselves are priceless," she stammered.

"They'll be enough. Celia's father gave the coins to Gunther, but not the brooch. He knows nothing."

"Fine," Richter said, his voice calming. "The coins will have to do."

"What happens now, Richter?"

He stared at her a long time, and she could almost hear his thoughts, searching for what to do. It all seemed to lead back to the easiest escape for him. "My options are limited." He shone the flashlight on his watch. "How did it get so late? I've got to get out of here."

He swept the flashlight around the room, revealing a mass of skulls with dark eye sockets. He ran his hand over his chin, then glanced down to where she sat against the wall. His jaw tensed as he bent and gathered the coins back into the box, then stood with the box under one arm. His eyes on the door, Richter pulled the gun from his pocket.

A sharp knock suddenly sounded.

"Quiet!" Richter hissed and flipped off the flashlight. He crouched, grabbing her tightly against him.

Darby heard shuffling footsteps outside, then another quick knock on the door. She wanted to call for help, but the gun was pushed against her ribs.

⋆═◐═⋆

Hands clenched to the wheel, Brant tackled the miles in what seemed to be slow motion. His car couldn't go faster, but it wouldn't be fast enough. He'd called the police in Salzburg and Hallstatt. But no one helped. They'd keep an eye out, but there was no evidence of a kidnapping. Brant knew he looked like a jilted lover. He dialed numbers on the car phone. It rang and rang. He was about to hang up when she answered.

"Ingrid, have you talked to Richter?"

"I haven't seen him. Why?"

"Ingrid, listen to me. I don't know everything, but I know enough. If Richter has been there with a woman, there is serious danger—I must know the truth."

Ingrid paused long enough for Brant to know she knew something.

"Did he call you? Has he been there? Tell me!"

"I do not know what you mean—"

"Listen to me, Ingrid. Gunther and I know about Celia, that you lied to her and to him. We know all of that. Now if something happens to Darby, I also know that she was last seen with Richter. You have to tell me!"

The line was silent.

"Are they in Hallstatt?" he asked.

"Yes."

"Now I know for sure. I just passed Bad Goisern and will be there in fifteen minutes."

"Brant," Ingrid said, "you'll never make it in time."

CHAPTER THIRTY-FIVE

on't say a word." Richter held the gun aimed at Darby as he let her go and crept toward the door. He was thinking, trying to decide what to do. "It's probably a priest, but maybe . . . if you call out, I'll have to kill him, and you."

Darby wrapped her arms around her chest. "I won't say a word."

"I'll be back." Richter took off his jacket, put the metal box of coins under his arm, and tucked the gun into his waistband. He shone the flashlight in her face and opened the creaking door. He stepped out and ran as the door closed her in, dooming her to complete darkness. Her heart pounded, and her eyes strained to find even a shred of light. There was none. She put her ear to the door and heard Richter's footsteps but no voices. Her eyes jumped around to see anything, but could only feel the hundreds of eyes looking her way. There was no sound beyond, no sound within. And no escape anywhere.

Sudden noises outside made Darby scurry backwards. She hit the stacks of bones hard. Skulls fell from the shelving, rolling onto the floor. She screamed as one landed in her lap.

Then the door opened, and she saw a lighter darkness from the crack. Her hand found the shovel nearby. She waited in the corner, heart convulsing, eyes frozen on the doorway, waiting. No one entered.

On hands and knees, still clutching the hand shovel, she moved toward the side of the door. Any second she expected Richter to jump inside. She heard more noises—muffled voices that seemed to disappear among the headstones outside. Minutes later, car doors slammed—perhaps a trunk, too. Then tires screeched away.

It crossed her mind that perhaps someone had gotten Richter. The police? Brant? But why hadn't they called out to her? Seconds were hours. At last she pulled the door inward and carefully peered outside. If she could make it to the hillside behind the white tower, she could hide there. She took a few breaths, said a quick prayer, and dashed from the building. No one stopped her. She ran in blindness, red candle eyes staring as her legs scraped against concrete graves. The dark shadows against the mountain would give her safe harbor. Almost there. Then her feet hit something and she sprawled forward. Gravel cut into her hands and chin. She'd tripped over the metal box and scattered the coins. Her hands wildly gathered the coins, picked up the box, and she moved on. She jumped over a stone fence and up the steep incline of forest above. Her feet stumbled. Silent noises and spirits were behind each step. Not until she had buried herself deep into branches and forest did she pause. No one had followed. No one was there.

Through the trees and down below, she saw lights and heard noises. Then footsteps moved toward her. Darby was near the wooden stairway that went up the mountain, and the footsteps were coming up. She crouched against a tree trunk, feeling as if her body must be illuminated in the darkness. Her legs felt too long, her breath too visible, and she wondered which way to bend her head. The footsteps stopped nearby.

Darby held her breath. *God, help me. If you don't want me to die, help me live—truly live!*

Voices shouted below and lights danced around the cemetery. The footsteps sounded again, moving up and past her. Wooden stairs creaked as the figure climbed higher; then the weight transferred to the earthen pathway and disappeared.

"Darby!"

She froze in place in shock, wishing to close the gap between herself and the voice calling her name.

"Darby! Darby! Where are you?"

"Brant," she whispered. "Brant." Her voice wouldn't reach him. "Brant!"

A light sifted the mountainside. She got up and began to push toward its source. The light swiveled toward her.

"Darby!" He jumped the small fence and ran through brush and branches. "Thank you, God!" He drew her into a swift and gentle embrace. The flashlight fell and rolled down the hill as he held her in his arms.

As Brant picked her up, her head fell against his chest. His heartbeat became her lullaby. She was safe.

CHAPTER THIRTY-SIX

Darby didn't need an English translation to know that Brant was growing angry with the Austrian officers. She didn't have any more answers. Richter was not to be found, though the police were sure he wasn't the man Darby had heard run up the mountain. They'd traced Richter's footprints back down the mountain. Even more amazing, he'd left the coins behind.

Darby told the police about the sound of a car and voices. Yet Richter's car was still in the parking lot, and Ingrid had been found still in Gosau—alone. It almost seemed like someone had taken Richter and left the coins behind for Darby—but who, and especially, why?

Darby sat on the cold picnic table, a blanket around her shoulders, as morning began to shine over the tall mountain. Darby could tell the pieces she knew—Richter's plans and motives. But no citizen came forward to tell what had happened. Muddy footprints had been found on the wooden steps, but the trail ended through the woods and back at the parking lot.

"I'm taking you home." Brant touched her forehead tenderly. "The police can talk to you more this afternoon." He gathered the blanket more tightly around her shoulders. "I'll tell them we're leaving."

A single tear slid down Darby's cheek. Brant's finger caught it as he hugged her and pressed his lips against her forehead.

"You're safe now," he said.

Her gaze lifted over Brant's shoulder toward a hunched old man watching the scene. It was the elderly man with the rake. As he turned away and took painful steps back toward his home, Darby saw a generation limping away with the stories and memories departing with them. Grandma Celia had told her much, but left out even more. It would all be lost soon. The pages closed. The book shelved. Darby wanted to keep it alive as much as she could. To tell the story as she knew it, and keep the words of life alive.

Brant kissed her forehead again before crossing the street to a group of officers. Darby's eyes closed in utter exhaustion, though a peace grew in her soul. God wasn't ready for her to leave quite yet. And she was ready to truly live for him.

A vehicle passed, and the police angrily motioned it to continue. She glanced up. The gray sedan moved by, then stopped. Darby stood up. A man emerged from the crowd of curious onlookers and walked to the car. Before opening the passenger door, he stared directly at Darby. He looked familiar somehow. As he ducked inside the car, she noticed mud caked on his shoes. Darby's own feet felt frozen in place. She knew the car was the same one that had taken her to Bruno Weiler. Had the man who took Tatianna's life now saved hers?

Brant walked toward her and stopped when he saw her expression. The tinted glass made it impossible to see in, but as the car started past, the backseat window rolled down.

"Is everything okay, Darby?"

A puff of smoke streamed from the window, and then Darby saw Bruno Weiler.

"What is he doing in Hallstatt?" Brant asked.

"You know who he is?"

"Of course. He's Minister Johansen—one of the most powerful men in Austria."

Darby glanced up at Brant, then back to the car.

Bruno tipped his hat at them, and the gray sedan pulled away.

D

arby sat wedged between Aunt Helen and Uncle Marc as the New York cabbie drove through traffic.

"Slow down," Aunt Helen squawked. "You'll kill us all."

Darby smiled as they pulled to the curb. She'd become quite accustomed to crazy taxi drivers. Her mother hesitated in the front seat before getting out. The noise of the city surrounded them as the doors opened. Another cab halted behind them, and the door burst open.

"Auntie Darby," her niece called and hurried toward them. "Kallie's Baby Alive wet Daddy's leg." She covered her mouth as she laughed.

Darby saw her sister's family fuss inside the cab as Kallie slowly got out, and Maureen looked for baby wipes. Darby then noticed her mother. She stood on the sidewalk, oblivious to the cars zipping past or the flashing lights and signs of downtown New York. Waiting like a frightened child, her eyes searched the crowd. Darby walked close with camera bag and tripod in one arm and put the other arm around her mother.

"What if he doesn't show up?" Carole asked.

"He will."

"I've done this before. I've waited here—many times. Right in this noisy place, I've searched the crowd. He never came on the promised date."

"He didn't know. He knows now."

Darby looked at the elongated triangle of Times Square. It was nothing like the quaint European plazas. It bustled with traffic zooming around what she'd have thought to be a large road divider. Tourism had come to Times Square with shops, Disney stores, Good Morning America, and billboard advertisements flashing from tall buildings. It smelled like city streets and some other smell coming from the hot dog vendors—not the scent of a juicy dog, but the stringent smell of a warming element inside the vendor machine. That smell with exhaust fumes was Times Square. Not the place for a romantic meeting as Celia and Gunther had imagined, but Gunther had told his young bride to meet him at the only place in America he had heard of in 1939, except for Ellis Island. So this had been the designated plaza. Over sixty years later, the reunion would finally take place—on the April 3 wedding anniversary of Gunther and Celia.

Darby had spoken with Brant the night before while he was still in London waiting for his delayed plane to take off. They'd take the red-eye and be here as scheduled. Darby prayed it would be true, especially as she looked again at her mother's face.

Kallie and Kellie ran to Darby and hung on her jacket. "Auntie Darby, Kellie said I'll have to leave Baby Alive at home now because of what happened on Dad's leg."

"Girls, come here and stay close," Maureen called. They scurried to their mother, who bent down and whispered in their ears. John was still wiping at his leg.

"Let's make a deal," Darby said to her mother. "You look at

that giant TV screen, and I'll search the crowd. I told them to meet near the ticket booth. They'll come. But I'll tell you when I see them, and then you can look."

"That might be best. My heart jumps at every young man I see, thinking it could be your Brant."

Maureen now walked up to Darby. "John is taking the twins to get a hot dog, and Aunt Helen and Uncle Marc are joining them. So where are they?" She bit her fingernail.

"They'll be here," Darby said. She gave her sister's hand a reassuring squeeze, though her own anxiety began to rise. What if, what if, what if. Then, across the square, she saw them. In flashes through the crowds, she saw Brant's dark hair. He was pushing Gunther in a wheelchair through the people.

"Mom," Darby said. Gunther searched the crowd, and suddenly their eyes locked. He put up his hand and Brant stopped. Then Gunther struggled to rise from the chair.

Carole gasped, her hands over her mouth. Instant tears streamed down her cheek as she took a few steps forward. Darby and Maureen waited behind.

They moved toward each other as if in slow motion, then stopped a foot away. Darby felt wetness on her own cheeks as Gunther reached out and gathered Carole into his arms. At last, father and daughter were meeting for the first time.

Maureen wiped away tears too. "This is their moment. I'll go find John and the girls and be back in a little while."

"Are you sure?" Darby asked, seeing the emotional struggle in her sister's face.

Maureen nodded and backed away.

Brant helped Gunther onto a park bench, then headed toward Darby.

"You made it," she said softly. In the busyness of plans and her return to America, they'd found little time to be alone in weeks. Now they were closing one chapter of their lives. What would the next one bring?

"We couldn't miss this day." Brant extracted an envelope from his coat. "I brought a letter from the museum in Hallstatt. They wanted to thank your family for donating the coins. I also have the final papers on the memorial for Tatianna at Mauthausen."

"All in German, I suppose?"

"Of course. You know, it's time you start learning your own German."

"I was waiting to see where I lived before I enrolled in classes."

"Professor Voss and Katrine already found a course in Salzburg for you. They are anxious for your return."

Darby smiled. "It's.something we'll have to discuss."

"Among other things." Brant reached his fingers around hers.

"So what do you think happened to Empress Sissi's brooch?" Darby asked.

"You're very good at changing the subject," Brant said, shaking his head. "If Gunther never had the brooch, it could be anywhere. Perhaps some Swiss bank or vault in Argentina. Guess that's for another day. Right now, there's only one mystery I'm concerned about."

"And what is that?"

Brant turned her toward him and held both hands. "What happens tomorrow, and the day after that."

Darby's eyes swiveled toward her mother and Gunther. They were in a world alone, unknowing of what occurred around them. They talked with heads close and tears flowing. Darby wiped her own cheek again. Then, through the noise and bustle, Darby sensed a presence like a lost memory recalled.

She couldn't see her face, but instantly knew—Tatianna. The girl waited in a jail cell—one of the ones Darby had seen in Mauthausen. She stared at the morning light growing through her cell window. Then, Tatianna stood as the door opened, and took the long walk between guards across cobblestone roads, past barracks and fearful eyes. They led her to a line of others. Her eyes saw a man beside her, a man with nail holes through his bare feet. She looked upward and saw a bird conquer the sky with outstretched wings.

Darby turned back to Brant and smiled. "We may even have the day after that."

The trail was steep and the air crisp as I hiked toward the empty wooden bench above Hallstatt, Austria. I'd been there only five months earlier, wondering if I'd ever return. After all, it had taken eighteen years of European dreams to get me there the first time.

I can still see the map on the floor as my cousin and I plotted our someday Europe trip. I was ten; she was fourteen. Later, in French class, my friends and I researched foreign exchange programs that would make our dreams come true. After I got married, I bought a *Europe on $50 a Day*, certain we'd go in a year or two. But it took longer than my plans. And through the waiting I discovered that dreams are never truly fulfilled on your own.

My husband and I at last touched European soil when I was researching *Winter Passing*, my first novel. We flew to Amsterdam, then headed to Austria via train. Every day passed in a flurry of wonder. We walked Vienna streets and palaces at midnight and wore mining clothes during a salt mine tour. Suddenly we were home again, and I wondered if I'd conjured the story during a long sleep.

Austria haunted me as I worked on *Winter Passing*. Just as Darby had to return, I felt I must also. But was that my dream, or God's plan? And then, amazingly, I was in Austria again.

This time three friends from high school—Katie, Jenna, and Shelley—stopped their lives to explore Austria with me. They waited below in a café as I climbed the steps above Hallstatt and found that bench as evening shadows descended. It was Easter Sunday. I'd recalled this view so often in the past months that it felt as familiar as an old friend. I took it in, breathed the memory, and realized clearly how God was working in the smallest details of my life.

On this trip, I glimpsed God's view again . . . in an elderly man raking leaves in Hallstatt, an elderly couple watering flowers in the cemetery, and a woman telling of her Nazi grandfather who saved his best friend's Jewish wife from almost-certain death, going to prison himself instead. I stood with three friends in Salzburg as midnight bells boomed the glory of God. My feet walked Mauthausen and Dachau—where people like me had seen the ashes of their dreams destroyed, along with their lives. I wondered how to live with their stories and sorrow breathing within me as I left those towers behind.

I'm home again, in Northern California. But in my mind's eye, I often look out my window and see green hillsides and sharp peaks. I see cobblestone pathways and hear church bells ring. While I know where my home is, and I get glimpses of trails ahead, I also have an empty wooden bench thousands of miles away that holds special words just for me. For that place in Hallstatt was more than a bench along a trail. It's a place I recall now as I continue my upward climb. I look back and remember what I engraved in memory: *Cindy, you glimpsed God's face today. Don't forget this when you leave it behind.*

And as for you, my stranger-friends who read this book, I wonder who you are. I wonder about your times of winter and your long-held dreams. I prayed for you that day on my bench. My prayer then, and now, is that God will give you a view you've never seen—whether it's from your back porch, a rock by the sea, or perhaps even in Hallstatt, Austria.

Seasons of change, busyness, joy, and fear come as surely as the autumn leaves next October. But we can continue upward when our breath has been stolen by the steepness of the climb. We discover God's strength through a winter and find ourselves more closely linked to him as springtime comes. And along the way God fulfills dreams—some we didn't even know to consider. And as we journey together with him, we find *he* is the true dream, holding the smaller ones in his hand. That's what our benchmarks truly tell us.

I hope we carry our benchmark words together. And we return there often.

ACKNOWLEDGMENTS

All I am, have, or do is because of God—Alpha and Omega.

I must thank my uncles (John, Chris, and Andy) for stories, laughter, and dreams.

Grandma and Ron—years of love, postcards that stay with me. Michelle Ower, Alanna Ramsey, Laurie Williams, Kim Shaw, also Sherie Silva, Marian Morgan Hunt, and Christi Harrington for friendships that last. Jon Walker and Tracey Bumpus, writing encouragement and much more. To my Martinusen extended family I send appreciation and love (Mom Martinusen and all), and also to Shawn Harman.

Specifically in helping *Winter Passing* come to life:

David—you give so much and ask so little. Everything (sharing dreams, our babies, first trip to Europe, morning coffee, and every day) has been with you.

Cody, Maddie, and Weston—my gifts from heaven, each so unique, each such joy.

Dad and Mom—for giving more than I'll ever know. I wish I could write what you both mean to me.

Jen—from pine nuts and forts through many seasons together— both blood and heart sisters.

Tricia Goyer—recall our first Mount Hermon Writer's Conference and laugh out loud. Thank you for every call across these one thousand miles, and for honesty in my writing (even when I didn't like it).

Katie Martinusen (from third grade to infinity and beyond), Shelley Chittim, and Jenna Shelby—friendships that go the miles—be it jogging in the rain, all-night chats, or an adventure to Austria!

My One Heart sisters—oh, for prayers, praises, and encouragement when all courage was gone.

Janet Kobobel Grant—your wisdom, love, and friendship—and you're an amazing agent too.

Curtis Lundgren and Ramona Cramer Tucker—editors and friends.

Tyndale staff—you make me feel at home, and what a great group you are (Anne, Ken, Travis, Sue, Lorie, Becky, Ron, Justin with your great cover, and all the rest).

Anne de Graaf—for a good-bye in Hoek van Holland that said so much.

Robin Jones Gunn—you've mentored by example on friendship, motherhood, writing, and more.

Wendy Lee Nentwig—our friendship across such distances.

Marlo Schalesky—honesty and lessons we've learned together.

Joe Evich—writing socks, conference gifts, and dear friendship over the years.

The Wagnleitners' (Reinhold, Elisabeth, and Anna)—Salzburg and Mondsee tours, Maroni, Reinhold's patience despite my many questions, and especially for open Austrian arms. I know we'll meet again.

Chittims (Shawn, Shelley, Mike, and Deb) and Joe Gazzigli for weekends at the Mount Shasta house—I'd still be typing without that time on the mountain.

Thanks to Rudi Haunschmied and Martha Gammer of the Mauthausen/Gusen Web site in Austria.

Cathy Snider—that electric coffee-cup warmer meant so much, really. You kept my eyes open on many late nights and tired afternoons.

AUHS District Office—I missed you all when the book was done. Thanks for letting me drop into your world for a while.

Shelly Gates—for old days of maps and stories that started this all.

To my friends at church, Bible study, and that wonderful writer's group (Maxine Cambra and all) who have encouraged and supported with prayers. I could write another book to thank the many people who have touched and influenced my life. I hope each of you already know how important you are to me. This small work could not have been done without each one of you. I can only say I gave my best for all you've given.

Suggestions for Further Reading

Non-fiction:

Coca-Colonization and the Cold War: The Cultural Mission of the United States in Austria After the Second World War by Reinhold Wagnleitner

The Night Trilogy: Night Dawn the Accident; All Rivers Run to the Sea: Memoirs by Elie Wiesel

The Celts: The People Who Came Out of the Darkness by Gerhard Herm

Schindler's Legacy: True Stories of the List Survivors by Elinor J. Brecher

The Holocaust: A History of the Jews of Europe During the Second World War by Martin Gilbert

Why History Matters: Life and Thought by Gerda Lerner

Fiction:

The Zion Chronicles series; the Zion Covenant series; *Twilight of Courage*; all by Brock and Bodie Thoene

Web sites:

Many Web sites have information about the Holocaust, Austria, and World War II. These sites also provide archives, testimonies, and other links. Here are a few from my research:

Austrian Press and Information, Washington, D.C. — *http://www.austria.org*

Mauthausen/Gusen Information Pages— *http://linz.orf.at/orf/gusen*

Mauthausen Memorial (English version)—
http://www.mauthausen-memorial.gv.at/engl/index.html
Holocaust/Shoah Research Resources—
http://www.igc.org/ddickerson/holocaust.html
United States Holocaust Museum—
http://www.ushmm.org
Austria Tourism—*http://austria-tourism.at/*
City of Salzburg (English version)—
http://www.salzburg.com/engl/

blue night

Cindy McCormick Martinusen

TYNDALE HOUSE PUBLISHERS, INC. | WHEATON, ILLINOIS

I will repay you for the years the locusts have eaten—
. . . and you will praise the name of the Lord your God,
who has worked wonders for you.

JOEL 2:25-26, NIV

AUSTRIA
November 28, 1944

Lukas Johansen didn't deserve her. He knew this. Yet he must ask anyway.

She'd say yes. He knew that, too, though he feared she shouldn't.

His breath was a long stream of white as he leaned against the cold bark of the black oak. He glanced behind him and then relaxed, allowing his mind to anticipate her arrival. It was a wonder they could grow love in the desperate world surrounding them.

His eyes strained against the glare, searching for movement where the rough trail disappeared over the hillside. Susanne's sun-white hair would appear first; then her soft gait would bring her head in and out of view until he'd see her forehead and face. Finally all of her would be framed against the horizon. She'd be smiling as she wound around rocks and mud in her hurried pace to meet him. Her easy grin and quick laughter were addictive. Lukas couldn't get enough of the life that poured from her.

He stared toward the hillside where deep blue mountains rose sharply above the trail. Below, thin plumes of smoke rose from chalets dotting the valley floor. Late-afternoon light was falling slowly to evening; then it would move swiftly into night. Lukas' impatience grew. As soon as Susanne reached him, he would ask.

The words were not practiced. Lukas had no clue what he'd say. No getting on one knee—he wanted to look her straight in the face. He'd probably find himself trying to talk her out of saying yes. "You should not marry me. I do not deserve what you give. If you knew who I was, you would hate me. My past could destroy our future."

He worried he'd be too convincing.

Yet the guilt always remained behind him like a hound after its prey. Justice meant he should suffer—all the days of his life. The frayed patches of his present work could never fully cover his past sins. But Lukas would ask her. And Susanne would say yes. They might both regret it.

Where was she? He pulled out his watch and checked the time again. Perhaps she didn't get his letter after all. She could be home wondering why he hadn't written as promised. It had been several days since he'd seen her—too many days for him. He wished she didn't have to take the morning train away from him at the beginning of every week. He knew good work required sacrifice these days, if work could even be found. But the first three days of every week were empty without her. He knew it bothered her, too. But she said they had to be thankful she didn't have to work away from the village every day like others did. Susanne could always find something good in the world. Soon he would take her away from this place of insanity. *Soon,* he would promise her.

Lukas glanced over his shoulder again. His hidden life compelled frequent looks behind. No place possessed complete safety. Not a large oak in the crook of two hillsides. Not even the mountain peaks above. Security was found in the moment past. If you were alive tomorrow, then today had been safe. He longed for that to end.

He reached for his gold pocket watch but then couldn't wait any longer. His feet moved faster into a jog and then a run on the soggy ground of the alpine trail. A sudden urgency pushed him. He stopped only before the last rise to her house. He bent down, trying to calm his breath and burning lungs. At last he took a long, deep breath and moved ahead.

His eyes swept the yard and then the house. She wasn't hanging white sheets on the line or tending geraniums in the window boxes. The front door was ajar. There was no lazy smoke from the chimney. His step quickened. The cows in the field behind the cottage stretched their necks between the wooden poles and moaned. Lukas stopped at the open gateway. Boot prints—of more than one person—smeared mud across the stone walkway. Lukas pivoted, awaiting the trap. Then he saw them: red dots and splotches bright against a lasting pile of snow by the porch. Turning quickly, his eyes caught more splotches and smears along the porch, doorjamb, wooden siding, and posts as he rushed inside.

Dishes lay broken on the kitchen floor; specks of red splattered the table. The pine cupboard's contents had been yanked out and shattered across the counters, sink, and floor. It appeared as if a starving beast had ripped the room apart except for a distinct heel print near a pool of blood beneath a wooden chair.

Lukas stared at the dark red pool that streamed along the ridges of the pine floor planking. He'd seen such pools before—always beneath chairs or tables or walls where someone had been held and hurt for a long while.

"Susanne!" His voice echoed up, frantic, against the beamed ceiling.

Through each silent room, he searched upstairs and down. The door to Susanne's grandmother's room was the only one closed. He pushed it open—afraid of what he'd find, yet urgent to know. No one was there. He turned to leave and heard a noise like the whimper of a small animal. Lukas followed the sound behind the door toward a darkened corner. Susanne's grandmother was on the floor, her back to the corner like a punished child. The woman was hunched over, her skirt bunched around her knees. She clutched something against her chest.

"Frau Olsen?"

The whimper became a sob as his footsteps creaked against the wood floor. She gazed up at him, tears streaming from her red-rimmed eyes. Terror cried from her worn eyes even while her mouth continued its sob.

He knelt in front of her and noticed what she held against her chest—Susanne's childhood rag doll in the gingham dress.

"Where is she? Where is Susanne?" Lukas asked softly.

He touched her bowed shoulder. She wrenched away, letting out a wail that echoed through the house. Lukas left her there, even more desperate to find Susanne. Had she been taken? There must still be hope. He stood in the kitchen, telling himself to think, and think wisely. He could save her if he kept his head. She might be at the police station in town being interrogated. If they knew who he was, they'd want him instead. But how could he barter with them and exchange himself for her freedom?

His eyes roamed the room and his mind sought the first step. Then he realized there was a trail to follow. A blood trail. It led outside. He ran out the door, along the porch, and down the steps to where the snow displayed blood in crystals of red light. At the corner of the house he slipped and fell on a patch of ice. He rose slowly, the roof dripping water from long icicles next to him. His feet walked almost woodenly over the slush.

She was facedown, her arms straight at her sides. The beautiful sun-white hair had come undone. It lay twisted in the snow and around her back.

"God, please, no," he could only whisper. Carefully he turned her over and cradled her head in his lap. He tried to wipe the blood from her face but smeared it across her cheek.

Lukas looked wildly around for someone who could help. It couldn't be too late. How could he love her and yet not have known what was happening to her? Why hadn't he come sooner?

He held and rocked her back and forth, hoping somehow that God would change his mind. Waiting in numbed silence, he gazed above the mountain peaks. But a prayer would not come to his lips. Still he hoped for a miracle. That God would realize he'd made a mistake. That today was not the day of death for Susanne Olsen. That God would say to her as she stood in front of him, "You are too early." Then he'd turn to the Death Angel. "Return her. The world yet needs her."

The cows stared from the corral. One bawled mournfully. A breath of wind swept through the trees. From the house he heard the old woman's continual wail. Stillness closed around him, suffocating him.

And night pressed in. As it slowly consumed the light, Lukas studied her face. He'd hoped to see the peaceful gaze of an angel, not the look of death he beheld.

"I came to ask you to marry me. I want to be with you always." Her expression remained unmoved, a resolute statue, not Susanne at all. "You cannot leave me yet. What will I do now?"

There was no answer.

Lukas knew that at last justice had reached him. But Susanne had paid the price.

⁂

VENICE, ITALY
Spring, Three Years Ago

Kate Porter walked along the edge of a wide canal. Water lapped gently against its side. In her life a place like this was a postcard-sized thought or a setting in a romantic movie. But the world had suddenly grown smaller. Today she stopped and stood before tall, flat-fronted buildings and awakening shops.

Her husband awaited her return to their hotel room, not far down a winding alleyway. They had stepped inside the postcard. They were vacationing before Jack's conference within the frames of a movie scene. A passport and a United Airlines ticket, and Kate had awakened to stroll along the streets of Venice to buy espresso and brioche from an Italian café.

Venice. A city built upon water with the width and breadth of lives and dreams divided by vaporettos, gondolas, and cool breezes. Little wonder that artists and writers had been drawn to this city for centuries. Kate had never thought she'd see it for herself. After all, her spot on earth was a simple home in a simple American town. The history, culture, and ambience of this place reached beyond that. It was overwhelming, but she also loved it and wanted to see everything this world could offer.

Kate walked slowly to memorize each step along the Riva del Vin toward the towering Rialto Bridge. The bridge appeared above a low mist, an ancient arch spanning the waters. Its curved rail, trimmed in stone balustrades, carried the echo of centuries-old footsteps. Once the only means of crossing the widest canal in Venice, the Rialto now provided a center-stage view of the Grand Canal, where morning travelers already passed through the dark waters in black gondolas and touring boats.

She couldn't wait to share all this with Jack. It would be the best business/pleasure trip of their lives. A part of her wished they had brought their daughter. How Abbie would love this place. When Kate passed a row of wooden posts, rising like sentries from the canal water's edge, she decided the three of them must come back sometime soon.

It was good for her to be alone this morning, to brave the foreign soil she once thought she'd fear. That was the real reason she'd left the hotel in search of food. And she'd passed her own test. The girl who had never felt the need to leave the United States was now conquering a Venetian walkway.

But the unexplored would have to wait just a little longer. The pastry warmed through the bag she carried and the espresso cooled with every step.

Jack had better be awake.

"I'll be back in just a little while," she whispered to the city, pausing at the entrance to their hotel. Leaving the morning breezes for the stale indoors, Kate made a mental schedule of the day ahead as she climbed the stairs. They had several days before Jack's archaeological conference began. The wafts of pastry made her stomach yearn for the Italian treat.

The door was locked. When Kate tapped with her elbow, a flick of paint cascaded to the ground. Only in Italy would they pay such a price for a "quaint" hotel room with faded walls and worn carpets. Jack must be asleep or in the shower. Kate balanced breakfast and extracted her room key from her pocket.

"You should be proud of me," she said, pushing the door open.

The shower water was running.

Setting the pastry and espresso on the tiny table, Kate dug into her carry-on bag for her travel guide. They must try gelato after lunch and Italian espresso after visiting the Basilica di San Marco. She bit off a piece of pastry as she paged through the guidebook.

If Jack would just get out of the shower.

Perhaps she should pull one of their evil cold-water tricks. Kate sneaked toward the bathroom, but the door's creak ruined any chance of surprise. Then she noticed the shower curtain. It was scrunched open against the wall, and a puddle had pooled on the floor from the spray.

No one was there.

She turned off the faucet.

"Jack?" She peeked behind the door, already knowing he couldn't fit there. "Okay, where are you? You know I hate these kinds of surprises."

Her gaze moved around the bathroom, then back into their room. The wardrobe doors were open. Jack's suitcase was still zipped shut. She had opened their dual shaving and cosmetic case.

Perhaps he'd gone to find her. But his clothes were on the floor.

The bed was a mess of sheets and covers. The pillow she'd used was flat and off center. But Jack's pillow looked as if it had been fluffed and adjusted just right.

And there was something on the pillow.

Shaking off the beads of water from the shower, Kate walked toward the bed as if in slow motion. On the pillow was a piece of broken blue ceramic.

She had never seen it before.

But it was here. And Jack was gone.

part *one*

Hours continuing long, sore and heavy-hearted,

Hours of dusk, when I withdrew to a lonesome and
unfrequented spot, seating myself,
leaning my face in my hands;

Hours sleepless, deep in the night, when I go forth,
speeding swiftly the country roads, or through the city
streets, or pacing miles and miles, stifling plaintive cries;

Hours discouraged, distracted—for the one
I cannot content myself without.

Hours when I am forgotten (O weeks and months are
passing, but I believe I am never to forget!) . . .

—WALT WHITMAN, *Leaves of Grass*

CHAPTER ONE

Kate Porter could feel a distant urging. It nagged at her like a light tap on the shoulder or a drip of water from a faucet she couldn't see. She cast it aside as always and let her thoughts drift with the slow creak of the porch swing and the flow of dark clouds rolling across the moonlight. Such nights had the power to quiet the distant highway or even the wind in the trees. Once they would have bred dreams and plans for tomorrow. It was no longer so.

Yet even this dreamy night could not calm the uneasiness that moved in her—like the first hint that a season was changing. She tucked the flannel blanket around her crossed legs and leaned her head against the chain of the swing.

Tonight felt different somehow. Kate wondered about it, listened to the night sounds. Life had continued on one consistent plane for so long. A gentle night like this had not been allowed. Instead it prodded her to search harder, try more, scour her thoughts again and again for an answer. That day in Venice had changed who Kate had always been. Like clay spun in the hands of a potter, she had been shaped, molded; then suddenly something had gone wrong. The wheel continued to spin with her there, awkward and misshapen, abandoned on the wheel.

Kate had become accustomed to it.

Yet the distant tapping seemed to say she'd forgotten something that morning three years earlier, something that was essential for her now.

Remember. Remember.

She tried. What was it? What else had she lost that day, besides everything? Kate kept circling that nagging something, but she always ran without finding the answer.

When the French door scraped open behind her, Kate realized she'd been ignoring her daughter's call—without really knowing it.

"There you are, Mom. Look what I found." Her daughter's bare feet padded across the wood-planked deck.

"What is it?" Kate asked, her eyes blinded by the light from the windows. She tried not to feel annoyed at the interruption as she adjusted a pillow in the empty place beside her.

"Daddy wore this shirt on our daddy/daughter night." Abbie spread a beige shirt over Kate's lap. "See my milk shake's still on his sleeve."

"Yes, I see. And I remember." Kate wondered why her daughter had been in the walk-in closet looking at her daddy's clothing. It was becoming a regular habit.

Abbie hopped up beside her. Her thin legs dangled, but not straight out like when she was smaller, when the bend of her knee didn't reach the edge of the swing. Abbie had always gone to bed easier if she spent a short time on the swing with Kate or Jack or all three of them together. It had been a long time, longer than Kate realized, since they'd been on the swing together.

Abbie pulled the shirt around her shoulders and rested her head against her mother. They rocked back and forth with the distant sound of cars and crickets and bullfrogs. Kate glanced at her daughter engulfed in Jack's shirt. How that represented their life. Jack so clearly with them, in everything they did. Yet now he was only an empty shirt with no arms inside to give them strength or warmth. Kate slid her own arm over the shirt and around Abbie's shoulder.

"Mom, will he ever come back?" Abbie met her mother's gaze. She wanted the truth. It was the same question Kate asked every day.

Kate placed her feet down to stop their rocking. She touched the tip of Abbie's chin and wished she could take back the last three years—for both their sakes. The old life of family time, dance recitals, and church involvement had been shattered into police interviews, unsuccessful searches, and a mixture of hope and loss. Now confusion, fear, and nightmares were as normal as car payments, shopping, and the growing pile of unopened gifts to Daddy. That Jack Porter had vanished without a trace was a fact. But how? Why? Would he return?

"I don't know. If he was coming . . ." Kate paused, not sure she wanted to admit this even to herself. "If Daddy was coming back, I think he would have been here by now."

Abbie nestled her head against Kate again and gathered Jack's shirt more tightly against her thin frame. "God can bring him back."

Kate pushed her feet from the deck into a soft swing. How could she argue with the faith of a child?

"Mommy?" Abbie hadn't called her Mommy in years.

"What, my girl?"

"The sky looks blue."

"Yes, it's a blue night. You don't see them often. The moon behind the clouds and I don't know what else, perhaps the season. It makes the night blue."

"I like it."

"I do too."

"It's God's way of telling us Daddy is okay, and he's coming back."

Kate wanted to give her a long explanation why that wasn't true. Why tomorrow's dawn would start a new day for both of them, another new day without Jack. She only held Abbie tighter. Sometimes a child's faith was really a futile wish. Perhaps that was what faith had always been.

⊷═◉═⊶

For two and a half years, Abbie had slept in Kate's room. It was mutual need. For six months now her daughter had decided to sleep in her own bed. Kate missed her presence and would welcome her back, but it must be a good sign for Abbie to not fear sleeping alone. If only Kate could reach that place.

Kate stood in Abbie's doorway. The antique bedroom set would need restoring soon, she thought, chiding herself for paying too much for it. Kate knew better with owning her own antique shop. But when the set had come onto the auction block, she couldn't resist. The carved walnut headboard with a tiny light built into the center matched the dresser and bedside table. It was perfect in here.

"Tell me again about the day Daddy disappeared." Abbie tugged the purple, flowered bedspread up over her head and held the lace edge with her fingers.

When Kate didn't move or answer, she peeked out from under the covers. "Mom? Are you going to tuck me in?" She pulled the covers over her head again.

"You wouldn't let me forget," Kate said with a smile. While lifting Abbie's arms, Kate pulled the covers neatly over her daughter's lap. The blankets tucked perfectly beneath her.

"Well?" Abbie asked.

"Well, what?"

"Tell me again."

"I've told you too many times. And we were supposed to start *The Voyage of the 'Dawn Treader'* tonight. In this book, we'll see what it's like at the end of their world."

"You and Daddy were in Italy," Abbie said with a determined look. Kate couldn't distract her daughter so easily anymore. "You went to get pastries in the morning and you came back and he was gone. All that was left was a little broken piece of blue tile or something. And we've never found him."

Kate brushed Abbie's bangs back and kissed her forehead. She wished a seven-year-old—*her* seven-year-old—didn't know such a story. But there was no protection from the truth.

"Let's start a new story." Kate meant the C. S. Lewis book on Abbie's nightstand, but then she realized: *they* needed a new story for their lives. It seemed they awoke each day to the same page and repeated it again and again. Time was passing, but they were stuck trying to change the past or at least mend it. If they didn't move on, was there any chance for a future?

"Okay. I wonder how they will get into Narnia this time," Abbie said. Her eyes were already blinking heavily.

Kate noticed it was an hour past her bedtime. "Let's start tomorrow. I had no idea it was so late. We spent too much time on the porch swing."

Abbie gave a long groan. "Well, then, will you sleep in my bed tonight, Mommy?"

Abbie's eyes pleaded and another "Mommy" worked a knot inside Kate's middle. "It's too small for both of us. You could sleep with me."

"No, I should stay here."

"I'll snuggle till you fall asleep."

"Good." Abbie moved over and opened the covers.

It took another fifteen minutes for Abbie to stop smiling and asking little questions and finally allow her body to drift into slumber. She turned and curled with her back toward Kate. It was the same sleeping process since she was a toddler. Her eyes would start to droop, she'd give one last attempt to stay awake, then she'd turn to face the wall and sleep would come.

As Kate watched the back of her daughter's cotton night-gown move in slumbered breath, her own thoughts rummaged back through Abbie's questions. Kate still couldn't shake the feeling that she'd forgotten something. That day in Italy was a wrinkled page of paper she'd clutched so long her fingers had worn through it. It still amazed her how entire lives were destroyed by a single rift in time. She'd sought every detail or any phrase spoken strangely. But had she missed something?

Few mornings could compare with that morning. Certainly, the first dawn of their honeymoon when they kept calling each other "husband" and "wife"—just to hear the sound of it. Or the hours after Abbie's birth when Jack held their infant daughter to the window and introduced her to the world. But their morning in Venice would have been listed soon after those other memories.

The city of dreamers, painters, and lovers had been a long way from Oregon rain, new buildings, and short history. . . .

Kate awoke gently as if she'd simply taken a breath of fresh air. Light through thin curtains warmed the room, reflected light that had first danced from ancient walls and frescoes and then discovered the play of their room. They were on a quiet street with only the footsteps of morning travelers and an occasional slap of an oar in the canal nearby. The walls were soft yellow, and terra-cotta pots of red geraniums were arranged on the floor and table. Bright paintings of Tuscany's vineyards and coastlines brought the feel of Italy indoors.

Jack faced away from her, his breathing heavy and deep. Blankets and sheets were twisted and pulled over them in odd directions like legs and arms entwined together.

Kate tugged on the blankets and slid herself against the length of Jack's warm body. His breathing moved against her chest.

"Jack."

He didn't move.

"Remember where we are?" She rose up, propping one elbow on the bed, and stroked his earlobe.

He grumbled; she smiled.

"Jack, we're in Venice."

He rolled toward her, stretching and rubbing his eyes. He always awoke like this, though Kate hadn't taken the time to watch in quite a while. Back home, mornings were alarm clocks, coffee, day planners, and lists. But this is what they'd have. It started now.

"We don't have to hurry this morning," she whispered. Although his eyes remained closed, she could see half his smile.

"But you want me to wake up now."

"We don't have to go anywhere."

"But you want us to go everywhere, right?"

"Yes," Kate said, kicking the covers away and getting out of bed. She couldn't wait to see what last night's darkness had hidden from view. She pushed aside the curtains and fully opened the creaking windows. Several stories down, a storekeeper arranged a display. Ripples of light reflected from the canal waters. What kind of world waited beyond their window?

Kate turned and could feel Jack watching her. Did he think she was beautiful standing in front of the window, light haloed around her dark hair? The look on his face said he did.

She moved slowly toward him, then hopped on the bed, bouncing up and down while he tried to grab her. "Get up, get up! We have to see Piazza San Marco, Museo Correr,

Basilica di San Marco—do you like my Italian accent? I
don't care how expensive it is to ride that gondola; we're
doing it. Magnifico!" She jumped, acting like she would
land on him as their laughter mixed together.

"Your guidebook is going to disappear." His threat dissi-
pated into a gasp as she landed on his chest. "Jet lag. Doesn't
that count for anything?"

"I think it's more than that," she said, kissing his chin.

"Another night like last night and we may only see these
four walls."

She jabbed her fingers below his ribs. "I'll tickle you
awake."

"Okay, okay!" He grabbed her hands. "Should we call
home and check on Abbie?"

"Don't try to distract me. Anyway, it's midnight at home."

"No wonder I'm so tired."

Kate studied his smile, which was more of a half grin, and
tried to memorize the moment. They'd talk about this morning when they were an old couple walking in their garden.
She'd remember his face, slightly tanned after his last dig;
his sleepy gray-green eyes and dark messed-up hair; the
small scar beneath his left eye. His hand behind his head as
he watched her watch him. She'd never forget this.

"The day has begun," she whispered.

"It's midnight, remember?" He tried a fake yawn.

Kate got off the bed and opened her suitcase. "Okay, I'll
go to the bakery, get some Italian pastries and an American
paper, if it can be found, while you hop in the shower."

"You shower first; you're the slow one." He sat up, twisting his fists into his eyes.

"I'm hungry now. Can't you smell fresh-baked pastries
through the window? Besides, I'll be showered and dressed
by the time you've read your paper. Unless you can skip one
or two sections this morning."

Kate rummaged through her suitcase and dressed quickly. She brushed her teeth in the bathroom, then put on some lipstick and tucked her hair into a clip. "Full European makeover when I get back. You won't recognize me."

"That doesn't sound good," he said, smiling. "I kind of like you the way you are."

"Be back soon. The bakery is only two or three doors down." She leaned close to kiss his forehead, nose, lips, and chin.

Jack grabbed her arms and pulled her toward him. "Look at you in bed again," he said. "We're in Italy! We have a million things to do and see. Unless you'd rather have break-fast in bed." He grinned wickedly.

"Go take your shower and be awake when I get back." She grabbed her jacket and their room key and opened the door.

"Be careful," he said as he sat up. "And could you get me some coffee? I think I'll need it."

Kate would hear those words again and again. Simple morning words and requests. They were the last she'd hear Jack say.

The wind chime outside Abbie's window softly woke Kate from her thoughts. The night-light cast a soft halo around the room and on the top of Abbie's light brown hair. And suddenly, there it was. Like a gentle whisper in her ear, she knew it. Kate sat up and stared at her daughter. What—or rather whom—Kate had forgotten was right beside her. Kate had been physically present every day. But while Abbie was growing up, Kate had focused her energy on finding their old life.

I didn't forget Abbie, she told herself. But tonight she seemed able to look at the last three years more clearly. On the outside, she'd performed her motherly duties—bedtime stories and kisses—but Abbie had not been fooled. She had clung to her mother at first, trying to draw her back. But the years had brought Kate further away, and Abbie had become accustomed to it. They'd given their full effort in trying to find Jack, and in doing so, Kate had become a part-time spectator in Abbie's life—not the mother she'd once been and always hoped to be.

That morning in Venice, Jack had asked if they should call Abbie. How she wished they had, even if it had been midnight. Perhaps it would have stopped what happened. Jack had thought of Abbie at first dawn. The days since that morning had slowly torn Kate from keeping her daughter at the dawn of her thoughts. Finding Jack—whether he was dead or alive— had been her goal. Yet suddenly she knew what he would want—for her to be there for Abbie first.

Kate tucked the covers once again around her little girl. Sliding Jack's shirt from under Abbie's pillow, she held the fabric against her face, hoping to find some scent of his after-shave. There was none. Too many years had passed.

"Abbie, I promise to be a better mother," Kate said tenderly to her sleeping child. "We're going to get through this and put it behind us."

The book on the nightstand caught her eye. The time had come for a new story. They'd waited for Jack long enough.

But had she missed anything else?

CHAPTER TWO

T he vow was breaking.

Lukas Johansen didn't know if he was ready.

After nearly six decades, they would not only speak but also meet once again.

Long ago, five men had vowed their loyalty: Karl as their leader, Jantes who would die too young, Oskar the intellect, Edmund with his serious loyalty, and Lukas himself. They had fought side by side, watched one die in their arms, and discovered together that victory would not bring the peace they'd hoped for. The war ended. And these men who'd survived as one were forced into another vow—to never meet again.

If ever they crossed paths, passed on the street, attended the same gallery opening or political event, there was to be no acknowledgment that they'd ever known one another. Not one of them could attend Edmund's funeral, which dropped their original group of five—then four when Jantes died—down to three. They might know what was happening in the others' lives, but only through individual investigating. Spouses knew little. Children even less. So why meet now? Why threaten the secrecy and break the silence?

Lukas felt the descent of the plane in the dizzying drop of altitude he always disliked.

"We'll be arriving at Phoenix International Airport at our scheduled time in about fifteen minutes." Lukas ignored the rest of the pilot's words as he clicked his seat belt in place. He glanced out the small window and blinked his eyes wearily to the inaudible sound resonating in his ears. It was the sound of waiting.

Waiting was a noise that drew a person into reminiscent places, away from where he stood in a line or stared at a telephone willing it to ring, or as he checked his watch for the tenth time. Dread, anticipation, anxiety, expectation—all fell under the wing of waiting. Lukas didn't hear it with his ears but with every part of his being. Waiting was like a rodent, or a hundred rodents, with sharp, tiny teeth that gnawed from the inside out.

On the Lufthansa 747 bound for Phoenix, Arizona, United States of America, staring from his first-class window seat, Lukas realized he had been waiting. He'd waited for this day for over fifty-five years, hoping he'd escape into the grave instead. A reunion brought people together who sought to see one another, though there was no reason Lukas should not desire to see these men. He'd say he loved them if asked, though he wasn't sure he actually did. These men had been his world when the rest of the world had been destroyed. He'd survived on them as much as he survived on food and water. But without word or contact in so many decades, now they were strangers with ties closer than brothers. They were also the past he wished left behind. What images and emotions would arise when their eyes met once again? Would they even know each other now? More than their faces had changed from youth to old age. The days when five men fought one

CINDY McCORMICK MARTINUSEN

enemy now seemed like a movie he'd once seen, even played a part in.

Minutes and seconds fell away as the plane touched ground, wheels bouncing and screeching. He watched the pavement and ground whirl past; then they slowed the way he always imagined the last seconds of life would be like. Time would slow, slow until one second was an hour and then eternity loomed ahead.

Lukas would have to go through customs first. An ache always formed in his stomach whenever he crossed a border or passed through customs. His ulcer, he'd told himself, until he realized it always happened at borders. He knew there was nothing to fear. But that nothing tensed through him, though in his life he had walked through customs over a hundred times. He wore a tailored suit and carried expensive luggage. There was nothing suspicious in his manner. He was respected, a retired diplomat no less.

The plane maneuvered toward the gate. Beyond the tarmac, the gates, and customs agents, two men waited. Maybe they sat side by side, stood at the window watching the plane taxi in, or bought coffee from the airport McDonald's. Surely neither had digressed to wimpy Starbucks. Men like them drank coffee dark and strong and would not be seen at a trendy coffee-house. Things changed, but not some things or some people. At least, that was his hope—or perhaps his fear.

Lukas remembered their vow made long ago, in another dimension: "I promise to keep this pledge. We each vow loyalty to one another. I become a brother to these men."

Five men had repeated those words that now sounded so idealistic and unnatural in the world he lived. Lukas had first met the entire group in the hidden room beneath Karl's home on the night of their pledge. They didn't trust Lukas at first; he was the newcomer to the group. But they trusted their leader, Karl. And Lukas would prove whom he served again and again. At that time, it was the only way to survive. And with the memory of those men came other memories—memories he wished to leave buried.

Susanne. Her name was right on his lips. He had not spoken her name in decades except for once, when one of his ex-wives said he called to her in his sleep.

"Who is Susanne?" came the morning scrutiny. Thinking back, he recalled that it was Bernadette who had asked, since Vera would not have cared. But Bernadette would take it as an insult to her own beauty that he could possibly call for another. Lukas could never explain who Susanne was, despite the argument it caused.

"Susanne was brave and valiant," Karl, her brother, had recalled on the night the five men gathered. "She believed in an Austria free from Fascism and Nazi terror. We will continue the work she believed in. And we will avenge her death."

Karl's past words rang oddly in his ears as the pilot thanked the passengers in both English and German for choosing his airline. Loyalty and brotherhood didn't fit the time and place now. Lukas Johansen was a powerful man. His grandchildren watched MTV and surfed the Internet for Hollywood movie stars. Words like *loyalty* and *brotherhood* were either as old-fashioned as phonographs and switchboard operators, or they alluded to some secret cult or neo-Nazi clan. The average man wasn't called to such words anymore—at least not in today's world.

Time changed the world.

Lukas already longed for this meeting to end. It would be only two days, he told himself. He should be able to endure that and would insist on sleeping in a hotel. Yet memories he thought exorcised now arose like ghosts haunting his mind. Perhaps they would tell new stories? Or simply laugh at the antics of comrades now gone? He hoped, how he hoped, that they wouldn't talk about the losses and those things that caused them to depart from each other's lives. He hoped this was simply his old friends' desire to meet war buddies before age took them all.

Yet something inside told him otherwise. There had to be a greater reason behind this reunion.

Did he have the strength to face it?

⋆⇥⊜⇤⋆

Lukas felt inward relief as the customs agent stamped his book and nodded him forward. In all the times he'd passed through a crossing, he'd never shown what he felt inside, even long ago when he'd had real reason to fear the sight of a uniformed guard at a national border.

A large family flowed around him, hurrying to the baggage claim. He'd brought only a carry-on, so he followed the exits to the departure area. His walk was always slow now, but today even more hesitant. He began to scan the groups of people.

Then he saw them.

Karl Olsen and Dr. Oskar Gogl waited against a wall. They stood next to each other without smiling. A surge of emotion built within Lukas' chest, surprising him by his lack of control. The years had worn against their bodies, though Karl remained a tower of a man with wide shoulders and a belly that had grown with time. Oskar stood straight, his inquisitive eyes reminding Lukas of a harmless schoolboy you'd ask to help with your homework. Their age surprised him, but he'd know those faces anywhere.

Lukas suddenly wished for the hugs and tears he'd criticized earlier. He walked toward them in a steady pace, pulling his suitcase behind. They walked toward him—Oskar's smile growing wide and Karl giving a nod of great approval. Lukas felt a tinge in his sinuses up to his eyes that he feared he could not control. Everything he'd achieved—the power and success—these men were the reason. Yet he'd forgotten his roots. Each of them had vowed to forget. They were brothers, long lost and nearly forsaken.

"Lukas," Karl said, his voice catching.

Lukas stopped in front of them, completing the triangle. Never had he realized how much he missed them until their flesh joined in vibrant handshakes. The stir and noise of the airport with its sounds of many air conditioners and muffled movement and voices faded around them. They would soon laugh and reminisce and tell about life so many years ago. Yet those stories wouldn't sound true even to the teller's ear, for time seemed to have slipped those years into a dream. All that was real were the years of war together and the moments ahead.

Suddenly Lukas knew that some vows were *meant* to be broken.

Clouds of gray and white danced and whirled like a portrait van Gogh would have painted. A few raindrops, tapping against her window, were like fingers drawing her attention.

"Showers likely today in Corvalis with a high of seventy-one degrees," the weatherman had forecast that morning.

Kate paused from her work and gazed out the window. Her backyard flowers called to her to come and play. Her geraniums had done well through the winter, and green shoots poked from the rich soil where she'd planted bulbs last autumn. The dark sky above promised a drink to the bordered plants and lawn.

Rain was healing to Kate, and Oregon provided much therapy. Yet the same rain detracted her from the task at hand. Instead of doing paperwork or profit-loss charts, she yearned to be in her workshop, where the steady rhythm of the rain would beat on the tin roof. She'd gladly trade in her paperwork for the smell of wood stain and the feel of sanding an antique bureau and offering it a second chance. But there was a business side to owning Restorations, and that was her downfall. If she merely had to varnish and paint, take the old and restore, add new pegs, or strengthen a brace, Kate would be wealthy.

She forced her focus back to the pile of papers that had grown beyond ignoring in the past weeks. Discipline was needed even on a cloudy day, even with raindrops pleading— at least until Abbie's return from school. Kate put a stack of receipts in an envelope and noticed one of the files in her in-box.

It was Jack's file. Once Jack was the man she'd stood beside on a cloudy day at the beach and promised her life to. Now Jack Kenton Porter was a manila folder of information. Or, rather, many folders. She'd kept a section for each year within the cabinet beside her. Jack had his own cabinet. Inside those files were missing persons' information, other disappearances in Europe, Italy, and Venice itself. She had photographs available to send to police stations and phone numbers of people she'd called and called, who now only took messages through their secretaries. The first-year section was crammed with papers and folders organized and labeled. She had packets of information from Amnesty International, Missing Persons Bureau, and on and on.

The next year's section was a little sparser, the following even more. The current year was one folder thick and kept in her in-box. She'd noted the retirement of a local FBI agent she once called regularly, a new missing-persons Web site she'd yet to contact, and other odds and ends. Kate had begun clipping articles on tragic and mysterious occurrences. They bore no relation to Jack—an article about organized crime in Eastern Europe, a bite-sized sidebar on violence statistics in American small towns, a newspaper reporting the trial of a Chilean leader for human rights violations.

Perhaps she put such items within Jack's file to add something to the emptiness. They were the only things she could add to her life with Jack. The rest of their marriage was frozen in a moment of time while the world kept moving.

Quickly, before she lost her courage, Kate opened a cabinet and put the current world of Jack Kenton Porter inside. She closed the cabinet hard enough to rock it slightly. The files were reminiscent of her last few years. At first so full of activity. Friends and family calling, helping, supporting. Other people were against her and wrote letters of accusation: "We know you did something to him."

She'd been determined and full of faith and hope, sure that truth would prevail. Now few people besides her closest friends and family called. She'd wished for in-laws to share the struggle—people who'd known Jack since birth and loved him as much as she did. But both his parents had passed away—his father when Jack was young and his mother the first year they were married. Jack's brother worked on a fishing boat in Alaska and rarely visited.

Life had moved on, and they didn't know what to say. Kate reminded some people of their own fears about the unfairness of life. God didn't keep anyone from the scars of living, no matter how involved in church you were. If it happened to the Porter family, it could happen to anyone. Their name had gone from one of the upstanding, Christian families to a tragic and unthinkable mystery. What do you say to that?

Kate could still see suspicion in some eyes. "What *did* happen to Jack Porter?" She heard their silent questions when they kept their children from staying the night or were always "just so busy" to follow through on setting an actual date to get together.

Something *had* happened to Jack.

The people who knew Kate best assumed he was a low-life creep who abandoned her or perhaps had somehow fallen into one of those Venetian canals that ran murky water through the city. A body could stay under forever or wash right out to sea.

Then there were those who knew Jack better. Jack could make a friend anywhere. These people knew he was strong. Jack couldn't slip and die in some canal when he'd done dozens of dives and underwater explorations. And he wouldn't abandon his family. So they questioned Kate's motives.

Family and neighbors who weren't "religious," as they called Jack and Kate, held mixed opinions. Everyone had an idea behind her back. One cousin was sure Jack had been taken by aliens. An outspoken neighbor once announced too loudly in the grocery store about those "hypocrites in the church who have worse problems than normal people." Everyone had a theory, but the answer would probably never be known.

A long raindrop ran in a stream down her window.

It was time to move on.

The decision itself was difficult enough, but to actually put it into action seemed nearly impossible. Kate was stuck in quicksand. Even though she now reached for a branch to escape, it didn't mean she'd make it out alive. How did she say good-bye to someone who wasn't there? A grave or a jar of ashes would have provided a focal point—something to grasp or shed tears upon. And what if—what if she'd missed something?

Kate rested her head in her hands, her elbows on the stacks of papers covering her desk. There was also a pressing fear she'd ignored for three years. Without her husband, without the world they'd built together, without the search and the dedication to prove her innocence to every doubtful person— without all that, who was she? When all alone, with everything stripped away, who was she?

Be strong. Don't search too deep. Take one day at a time.

Remember you have a daughter who needs you back. Get your work done.

Kate returned to the file of invoices. This was part of her renewed focus on Abbie. She must consider their financial future, when instead she only wished to drift away. There were no insurance settlements or social security to help those with a missing husband. But Restorations was doing well, considering its rough start and the competition of online auctions. With the small shop as her sole income, Kate had barely kept them afloat for several years. Garage sales, budget shopping, and a loan from her family helped. Kate had refused to sell the house—what if Jack called or came home one day? How would he find them? Now the shop was on its feet after gaining a good name and regular customers, and their debts were getting paid off. They were going to be all right. Kate needed to work at organization and the taxes she was behind on. Someday there'd be insurance money when enough years passed for the courts to pronounce Jack dead. It would provide Abbie with a college fund, a first car, a nice wedding.

But what of her own future? That appeared cloudy. The fog would someday lift from her life. Perhaps she should make a few small goals, something just for her that didn't ride on answers to the questions of the past.

Her wall clock down the hall sounded the half hour. Kate straightened and realized she was actually looking toward the future. Wasn't that progress? Survival had been the game for so long. Now the years ahead were opening before her eyes.

She studied the drops of water gathered on the hydrangea blossoms outside the window. There might yet be someone inside her. She needed time to get to know herself again. Time to feel really alive, to be able to give Abbie spontaneous and unmasked love like she used to. They should do something together, something fun and carefree. Perhaps a short trip, such as to an indoor swimming pool. Their family had always loved the water. Jack and Kate had taught Abbie to swim as a very young child; it had been one of their favorite pastimes. Boating or snorkeling, anything water related. Kate hadn't done those in so long. She tried to recall the last time. It had been before Jack disappeared—that she knew. It was before her love of water had turned to fear. All because of the words of an Italian *poliziotto* three years ago. "Your husband is floating in that water, isn't he?" The image of Jack under some canal had never left her, even as time passed.

She remembered the officer spoke terrible English, and she could barely understand him. Kate tried but continually had to ask him to repeat his words. Finally, they waited for an interpreter. All the while Kate fought panic and the shock that Jack could not be found. She was alone in a foreign country with its unknown procedures and was suddenly the object of suspicion. She was sweating and shaking at the same time.

"You must know something," the *poliziotto* said. His eyes bore through her in a way that made her wonder if she actually could be somehow involved. Was she going insane? Did she know something more? But she didn't; there was nothing. Jack was simply gone when she returned.

"Was your relationship volatile?"

"Whose idea was it to come to Venice?"

"Where did the grant funding for the conference come from?"

"Do you have the information for this archaeological conference?"

"We will contact the conference director to confirm your story."

"What happened last night?"

"Did you go to a restaurant?"

"Was there an argument?"

"Did you make love?"

"Tell us again what happened. Start at the beginning."

She had answered again and again, feeling dirty and fearful and frantic. The translator grew tired. Officers came and went, continuing to ask her questions. Some had been kind, the one brutally suspicious. She continued to answer. No, they weren't politically involved. She was a mom and owned a small antique shop. He was an archaeologist and taught at the local university. No arguments. Yes, a late dinner at a café. Yes, they had made love. No, no argument.

They checked every source.

The conference was real, the grant legitimate.

They had a daughter at home.

In October, they would be married nine years.

"Something is not right with this story. A man cannot just disappear," the officer had insisted.

"I know that!" Kate had cried, tears spilling down her cheeks. "He was there. I went out for just a few minutes, and all his things are still in the room. Where could he have gone?"

Kate had called her family and could barely speak when she heard her father's voice. He called the American consulate. Hours of terror, hours more with Jack still gone. What if she'd known then that three years later she'd have no more information? It would have driven her mad.

The rain was still falling in long streams against the window. The papers continued to wait and wouldn't organize themselves. Kate turned away from the window, away from yesterday, and propelled herself into today.

Yet sometimes, though she'd feel guilty afterward, she wished it had been her who was lost beneath the murky water's edge.

⋆⇒◉⇐⋆

Karl drove a gray Buick with leather seats and an air conditioner that already fought the Arizona spring heat wave. Lukas was surprised to see where his old friend had made permanent residence. Karl, the man of the mountains, full of might and vengeance, now lived with sidewalks and coordinating landscapes surrounding every home and business. Perhaps there was safety in anonymity. Or perhaps he had gotten a good bargain for the place.

"Welcome to American suburbia," Karl said as he pulled into the driveway of a midsize, gray-and-white home—a cookie-cutter replica of the ones around it. There were scrubs and sage in the hills above them and droopy, transplanted poplars in the middle of every lawn. Karl had loved trees.

"How do you like it here?" Oskar asked Lukas' unspoken question.

"I have learned to golf." The garage door rumbled upward and then closed behind them as they drove inside.

"I have an air-conditioned work area," Karl said, as if to convince them. Lukas spotted the wooden bench set up with table saw and a neat row of tools pegged to the wall. He thought of his own estate with wooded acres and manicured grounds. He had a woodshop the size of Karl's house, though he rarely took time to work in it. Was this Karl's only option?

Karl's wife, Marta, was waiting with old Austrian hospitality. Platters of cheese, fruit, and bread waited beneath plastic wrap for their arrival. Lukas had always liked Marta and her spunky personality. She was small in stature but had never been afraid to take on anyone. She was an old woman now, moving in careful strides but smiling as broadly as ever. She snapped the kitchen cloth at Karl when he popped a slice of boiled egg into his mouth. Lukas was assured she had lost none of the attitude he'd admired.

They ate and laughed while reminiscing. "Remember when" was the most-used phrase, though they avoided what all of them remembered most—death, struggle, sorrow. They recalled mistakes in the field and drinking until nearly blind and almost being caught by Gestapo agents because of their stupidity. They chided Karl for forgetting some of the native German they all spoke while within the walls of Karl and Marta's home. Lukas felt at home with them again, even in such a foreign place. It had grown dark outside, and remnants of food and coffee surrounded them despite Marta's continued straightening up.

Then, right in the middle of their laughter, Lukas was reminded. There was something more to this gathering. More than a reunion of brothers. He didn't know why he suddenly knew it. The more they talked and laughed, the more Lukas grew uncomfortable. Something wasn't right.

Lukas caught Marta staring at him too long. "You know, don't you?" she asked.

Abruptly, the room went silent.

"What?" Oskar asked, chewing a bite of bread.

Lukas could not escape the hold of Marta's gaze. She nodded gently and smiled. "You are wondering why we asked you to come. You know this is not just a reunion of old friends."

"We contemplate this for many months. Why should I resurrect what is dead a long time?" Karl rested a hand over Marta's. "It was Marta's idea actually."

"We did agree to never meet again," Lukas said. "There had to be a reason for this. Are you in trouble, Karl?"

"Could you slow down for a moment," Oskar said. He pushed up his glasses and looked around the room.

"We all are in a precarious position. Only Marta and I have been the ones to know it," Karl stated flatly.

"Explain," Lukas said.

"We should have met sooner. I cannot describe what it means to see you both. Too many years have passed, and we were brothers."

"But it was necessary for us to survive," Lukas said.

"*Ja*, but do you know that even the Waffen SS and all German divisions have reunions? How can they and we cannot?" Karl said.

"Because they are no longer suspects of crimes—at least not many of them. We could be put on trial, even now," Lukas stated. "You could be deported, Karl."

"This is true. The guilty often flourish the most, but innocents such as ourselves could be accused." Karl shook his head.

Lukas shifted uncomfortably. He had done much worse than Karl even knew. Yet he was the one who'd found success, power, and sizable wealth, while Karl lived in middle-class America. Karl would say that he'd paid for his sins, but Lukas knew that some things could never be righted.

"We cannot undo these years we've lost together, though Karl and I believe we would have done it all differently," Marta said. "But there is something we can do for those years past."

"Something we can do now? What could this be?" Oskar asked, leaning forward.

"I do not know how you will take this news. Marta and I came to the United States and settled in Arizona twenty-eight years ago. We wanted to blend in with the world and hide from the past. But we were unsuccessful. Either I awoke from a nightmare at least once a week, or she did—and this is absolutely nothing compared to what our Jewish friends endured in the camps. Perhaps God hounded us so we would hide no longer. Ten years ago we began to make a search."

Karl paused and eyed each one of them. "During the war, the five of us were given one final mission. Our goal was to find SS officer Wolfram Meizer. Wolfram Meizer was involved in Nazi death squads that murdered thousands of people in the Baltic states. We also knew his reputation as one of the more vicious guards in several camps. As you know, our orders were to find this man and discover exactly what kind of armament was being produced in personal knowledge of Wolfram. Because we were en route to your escape from the Occupied areas, Oskar never knew the reason you were brought in, Lukas."

"I mind my own business. Did then, and I still do." Oskar sipped his coffee. "But what does this have to do with our reunion?"

"Wolfram Meizer killed my sister, Susanne. Neither of you knew that she was working as Meizer's housekeeper several days a week. That led to her death by his hand. I do not need to repeat our old mission or the failure in losing Susanne and Jantes. We almost had Wolfram. We should have investigated his death further. At the time, we believed the records and testimonies."

"What are you saying?" A coldness Lukas recognized from long ago seized him, spreading through him as if his blood were freezing within his veins.

"We now believe Wolfram Meizer survived the war."

Something deep and sharp sliced through Lukas. All he was and had become began to crumble into tiny shards. The idea that Wolfram Meizer could be alive during all these years insulted his very existence. His entire life's work seemed null and void with the thought that his greatest enemy had been free to live and grow old as he had.

"What are we going to do?" Oskar asked.

"We will find him," Lukas said.

"We believe we have." Karl folded his hands as if to pray. "And here lies the danger. We may know his location. But he may also know ours."

Kate knelt to inspect the underside of a dusty table-and-chair set. Pairs of feet walked past as she examined it for damage or cracks in the wood. The auction was getting crowded already. She got up and sat in one of the chairs and wrote the table number in her notebook, running her hand along the carved edging. It appeared in disrepair and would be missed by many buyers, but she was familiar with this builder whose business was destroyed by the Civil War. Kate had been looking for a Charles Buchanen table for a long time. She tried to think how she could keep the oak claw-foot table for herself instead of reselling it at her shop. First she'd have to win the bid.

"I made it!" Kate turned to see her friend Connie O'Brien balancing two capped Styrofoam cups in her hands. "Only an hour late," she said wryly, as her purse strap slid off her shoulder.

"Would you like some help?" Kate asked. She took one of the cups of coffee.

Connie plopped into the chair across from Kate with a sigh. "Can we stay here for four or five hours so I can unwind and not hear the ringing of children's voices in my ears?"

"That chair will probably get a higher bid with you in it. With a little help, this set could be beautiful once again."

"I think mucho help would be required to make *me* feel beautiful again," said the harried-looking, slightly overweight mom.

"Wasn't it you who was sure you could balance book-keeping with day care? My home is my sanctuary—yours is the local zoo."

"Was that me? I absolutely don't recall. My mind was snatched by two-year-old T-Rex Randy, who thinks it's his job to bite every dino-child on the playground. Look at my wounds." Connie pushed up her sweatshirt sleeve and pointed, but Kate couldn't see anything except her friend's soft, freckled arm.

"I think we should find a better place to sit," Kate said, motioning toward the auction manager. He'd glanced their way twice.

They moved through the warehouse labyrinth of antique furniture to a snack bar that served only donuts and coffee.

"So how did you escape?" Kate asked as they sat across from one another.

"We only had three kids today since the flu bug landed. My aide is watching them while I take an hour to myself." Connie took a long sip from her cup. "This caffeine fix should help me function as an adult again."

"That would take more than a coffee." Kate smiled.

"Okay, okay. So tell me, *Kathryn*," she said, emphasizing the word like an antiquated Englishwoman would, "how *are* you?"

Kate smiled, recalling their long-standing joke. Connie had once started counting how many people asked Kate, "How are you?" during a single church service. She broke them into categories of whether the *how* or the *are* or the *you* was accentuated. The winner was the "how *are* you?" Connie wanted to enter Kate into the *Guinness Book of World Records* for the most-asked phrase, sure that her friend would win. Kate had often dreaded the pastor's closing prayer, knowing she'd soon be assaulted with the question. Worse, still, was when people stopped asking and returned to the usual "how are you?" After three years, she was just anybody else with another tragedy behind her. So it was nice to hear Connie ask, however jovially she put it.

"I am *just* fine. How *are* you?"

"Settling nicely into this chair, thank you for asking." Connie took another sip of coffee and sized Kate up with her gaze. "Is everything all right? You look exactly how I feel—tired."

"Thanks. Perhaps you need to cut back a little."

"I think you're changing the subject. What's up?"

Kate continued to drink her coffee. She wasn't sure she was ready to face this. Today was about escaping from the world of decisions that plagued her; it was her chance to search the auction for pieces to bid on. Her shop was small, but furniture moved quickly. Her customers especially liked that she always had something new and interesting.

Yet, Kate mused, Connie was never easily daunted. Perhaps if she verbalized her thoughts to another, it would make them real. "Okay," she finally admitted. "Abbie and I need to move ahead with our lives. But I'm not sure how to do that."

Connie's eyebrows rose. She quickly wiped cinnamon-specked whipped cream from her upper lip. "This is something. Waiter, bring us some champagne! Let's sound the church bells!"

"All right, Connie. Don't hesitate to embarrass us."

"When have I ever been afraid to embarrass you? But wait; hold on. These words of yours sound somewhat familiar. Oh yes, they're the very words I've been repeating to you for the last six months. Imagine that!"

"If I didn't love you so much, you would really get on my nerves."

"I know. I'm irresistible." Connie puckered her lips and blew a kiss. Her expression softened. "I can be too pushy. And I was a bit obvious when I went through that phase of giving you those self-help books."

"Ah yes. *Who Moved My Cheese?* and *Severing Your Spirit Hang-Ups* weren't high points in your support."

"I already apologized a million times. But some of the inspirational quotes I e-mailed were good, right?"

Kate nodded with little commitment. Quotes and books and advice from Connie and other friends had been water through her fingers. The gestures were appreciated, but the words did little.

"This hasn't been easy for me either. You don't know how hard it is to see your best friend go through a catastrophe. I want to fix everything for you."

"Some things aren't supposed to be fixed," Kate said and smiled.

"They have to be healed," they said together, repeating one of their pastor's favorite lines, the cause of much laughter between them—however true the words.

"I'm proud of you, Kate. Deciding to move on with your life. But what does this mean exactly?"

"I told you; I'm still trying to figure out that part."

They both sat in silence for a moment.

Then Connie shook her finger as an idea formed. "This is *The Empire Strikes Back*."

Kate rested her chin in both hands, watching her friend with amusement. Life often mirrored a scene from a movie in Connie's world.

"Remember the part when Han, Luke, and Princess Leia

escaped down a wall panel and fell into that trash compactor room? There's all that garbage and dirty water and an underwater snake that I think Han shoots after it almost eats Luke. Oh, Chewie was there too, 'cause I remember his fur getting wet, and I thought he probably smelled like a wet dog. I hate that smell."

"Are you coming to some point? And by the way, that scene was in *Star Wars,* not *The Empire Strikes Back.*"

"Are you sure?"

"Remember Princess Leia had her hair like two cinnamon rolls on the sides of her head? She only wore her hair that way in *Star Wars.* Anyway, your point?"

"Well, the walls started closing in and they couldn't do anything to get them to stop. Luke was on his walkie-talkie thing trying to get R2-D2 to reprogram them. It gave me the creeps imagining all of them smashed together like when I use my trash compactor and even a green-bean can squishes flat. Can't you just see them all smashed together—Chewie with his wet hair—"

"Connie, return to Earth, please."

"Okay, okay. At last, you realize you need to get out of the garbage heap. And I know you didn't want to get in the garbage cylinder of the Death Star. I know you needed to search the garbage to see if Jack was there, but he's not. He's not. And now the walls are closing around you, and you can't find out how to get out. So you need some help from the outside." Connie smiled as if all should be clear to Kate.

Kate stared at her friend for a long time. "If we hadn't been friends for so long, Connie—"

"Don't you get it? You need a friend to help you get out. So I'm helping you get out."

"How are you doing that?"

"I'm ordering you to get away with Abbie. You need to help her realize that you are both moving on. Take something symbolic to mark the end of that old life and the beginning of the new—I don't know what, but something. I wish those Italian police would have given you that piece of ceramic you found on the pillow."

Kate had wished that too. It was the lone item that could remind her that the nightmare was real. But it was across the sea, locked away as evidence.

"You could have thrown the ceramic into the ocean!" Connie demonstrated for her. "I'm very serious about this. You need something to let Jack go. He's gone, and you need to say good-bye."

Kate recalled similar thoughts she'd had, both about the good-bye and something special for her and Abbie.

"Then you can move on with your life."

"You've never said it out loud before," Kate said in a low voice. "That Jack was really gone."

"I know. I wanted you to say it first. But I wouldn't have pushed you. Even if I did drop some hints the wrong way, I wouldn't have pushed for you to make this decision if I thought there was any chance of Jack coming back. I knew Jack. I loved him too. But I especially know how much he loved you. The two of you were what fairy tales are made of. If Jack were alive, he would have come back by now. If Jack is alive, it destroys everything I believe about love. Kate, Jack is gone."

Kate nodded slowly. Finally she could hear these words and believe them. Finally she knew that Jack was gone forever.

⊷⊜⊶

Perhaps they'd always known it. Somewhere inside, when the doubts arose, they had stuffed them away. When they'd been finally free of the weight of a nation and a war that destroyed great cities and many lives, it had been too heavy to pick up again. When a fight has lasted long and leaves the body and spirit downtrodden, when victory is announced, the enemy defeated—quiet doubts can be ignored.

Wolfram's death had been too easy. They'd found Jantes. Jantes, the one who tried to make Lukas laugh because the others believed it impossible. He'd finally succeeded by telling a story so ridiculous that the owls in the trees must have chuckled. Then, the next morning, Jantes had moved ahead to scout the area. Wolfram had been waiting and had assured a slow death for the young man whose only dream was to farm his father's land again. Lukas had found him first. He had held Jantes in his arms and looked into eyes glazed with pain. Jantes' tongue had been cut from his mouth and his stomach sliced with agonizing mortal wounds.

Jantes died in that muddy ditch with Oskar, Karl, Lukas, and Edmund surrounding him in a circle, his blood covering each of them. After that, the remaining four pursued Wolfram with a vengeance despite their actual orders. One thought consumed them—*find Wolfram*. It was pure revenge that drove them. And then they had reached the camp. . . .

They had been silent for several moments now as Karl retrieved documents from his office. The refrigerator hummed from the other room. Marta rose and moved to the kitchen, returning with the percolator to once again fill cups littered around the room. Karl returned, carrying a large cardboard box he set on the floor. Lukas caught Oskar's odd, puzzled expression. It had been a long time since Lukas had seen that look. Oskar had always adopted odd facial movements in difficult situations, as if he didn't know what was happening. But the truth was, Oskar was the most intelligent of them all.

"So, tell me. Was Wolfram helped? Or did he convince the Americans he'd make a good spy against the Russians? Or the other way around?" Oskar's voice actually trembled as he spoke.

"How can you be certain?" Lukas asked. He buttoned his sweater up the front, still feeling cold inside.

"I didn't want to believe it either." Karl leaned against the couch and crossed his arms. "This man killed my sister and Jantes. But let us look at the evidence. None of us actually saw his body. We didn't push to do so, because of what we saw in the camp."

They were silent once again.

The camp had been the final blow. Each remembered and could still feel the skeleton fingers clinging to their wool pants; they saw hollow-eyed skulls who smiled and cheered as they walked among the living dead. The stench of death had permeated their clothing, even their own skin. It caused them to retch and brought madness to their minds. Different from the grief of losing Susanne and Jantes was seeing what mankind could do to mankind. Lukas had known already.

"I want to know—how can you be certain?" Lukas asked again. He wanted to banish the thoughts of yesterday. All this was getting too close and he feared what the memories would do to him. Wolfram's body was supposed to be long decayed. The American soldiers swore they'd seen his shredded body after the camp inmates reached him.

"Look at the photographs," Karl said. He passed several enlarged black-and-whites toward Lukas. Oskar moved to sit beside him. The first photo was old and the man in it was walking away from the camera. Lukas didn't want to believe it. Not until the third photo did he and Oskar feel convinced.

"These were all taken in Argentina in 1956," Karl continued.

"How did you get them?" Oskar asked.

"I have made connections with a group of Nazi hunters."

"Ah, really?" Oskar said, adopting that puzzled look again. "How did this begin?"

"It began with our contacts during the war. I have kept in

touch with the others from the Austrian Resistance. And my role in the underground gave me connections with the Allied army, especially the American army. Those contacts have remained, but of course, I pulled back considerably when the crimes began involving the blue tile pieces. We believed then that it was essential to be clear of any suspicions that would link us to those murders. Now I see that this was Wolfram's doing.

"Marta began to read more about the Blue Tile Crimes. She studied the locations—"

"Stop," Oskar interrupted. "I have not been kept aware of these things you call Blue Tile Crimes. I knew of one murder when you contacted each of us to no longer keep our group together, but I did not know of more."

"I have a file," Karl said. He found a manila folder and dropped it on the coffee table. "We have at least six murders, several of them high-ranking officials. But let us cover that information soon. Oskar, you look through the file and it will connect with what has led us to this gathering. But to return to Wolfram, it was in the records of war crimes trials where Marta found the first testimony about Wolfram. The officer on trial told of an event that took place several days after Wolfram was supposed to have been killed. We first believed it a mistake."

Lukas glanced at Marta and wondered if she'd read the testimonies from his trial also. It had been long ago, and only a few people, including Karl, knew about his time in prison. Had Karl told her? Lukas had had a different name then and had spent those years trying to pay back his old sins. It wasn't so easy.

"I wasn't ready to hear it, and I became quite angry about her prodding. But when Edmund died in the late eighties, I realized that my life would not last forever. Could I go to the grave with such a truth? So we began to dig. Most of my loyal contacts were retired and had time to help. No one knew of our group's connection with the blue tiles, and because we vowed to stay apart, we ensured no one would find out. The Nazi hunters already had Wolfram on their list. That's when we obtained these photographs. But I wanted to tell you something else. Since working on this, I wrote to Edmund's widow, asking if she had found a piece of broken blue tile. She told me that she had seen it years earlier, but that she didn't find it in Edmund's things."

"Are you saying you believe Wolfram was involved in Edmund's death and that he took the blue tile from him?" Lukas asked.

"It is only a suspicion."

"You have known these things and you have not contacted us?" Lukas asked.

"There was little reason in the beginning," Karl said. He lit a wooden pipe that had rested beside his chair. "Lukas, you were still very much a political figure at the time. The last thing you needed was old comrades returning, especially with the problems we faced after the war. Oskar had buried himself in research and lectures. And we didn't know where Wolfram was at the time. It seemed frivolous to contact you with nothing. But let us start with some background."

"Karl has been learning the computer. He made this summary of Wolfram." Marta gave them each a folder with information inside. They had prepared for this reunion well.

Lukas read over the first page, though he knew all the information already. A young Wolfram Meizer had joined the Nazi Party in 1931 while living in Munich, Germany. During the war, he became an SS Death's Head member and later a guard at several death camps, including Dachau and Mauthausen. At the close of the war, he worked at Ebensee in Upper Austria— a subcamp of Mauthausen. The words spoke of knowledge gained firsthand.

"We have a report from one of the survivors who witnessed Wolfram in action," Marta said. Then she read aloud: "'Wolfram Meizer was one of the cruelest officers. He would kill for any purpose. If he was in a good mood, he would kill. If angered, he would kill. Drunk, celebrating, or sick—it did not matter. I was working in the field when Meizer walked by. He tripped over a rock and hurt his ankle. He was furious and pulled out his gun, though none of us looked at him or said a word. He shouted for someone to come to him. None of us moved. He pointed to the young man beside me. The boy begged and cried, but Meizer shot him in the face. He did this to three other men and then left the field. This was one of many instances.'

"A report from another SS member. This took place in what was formerly Yugoslavia. 'We lined them up; they were all women. Meizer shot them in the neck one at a time. I believe there were at least fifty.'"

"And there was also Jantes and Susanne," Oskar said softly.

"What has Wolfram been doing since the war?" Lukas asked.

"He escaped Europe, probably using a false Italian passport. He went to Paraguay and Argentina, where he owned various businesses and two houses, one by the ocean and one in the mountains. In the late 1960s, he even lived in the United States for several years before returning to South America. It was only in the mid-1990s that he disappeared. At first, we feared he had died. But now we believe we have located him once again, using a name—perhaps even several—different from the one he used after the war back in Europe."

"You *feared* he had died?" Oskar took a sip of cold coffee.

"Yes," Karl said firmly. "We want him alive. We want him to pay in this world for what he has done. Marta believes he will get justice in the next life, and I hope that also. God's justice should be even worse since the cries of the innocent are in his ears even more than ours. But I still want justice."

"Why would he change his name now?" Lukas asked as he sifted through the papers in the folder. His thumbing stopped at the copies of the photographs. In one, Wolfram stared from the page straight into his eyes.

"Because he has an important reason for returning."

"Which is what?"

"That is something we do not know. There are several possibilities and locations. I believe he is after something that was left behind."

"As in something the Nazis left behind? Another Nazi treasure hunt, I suppose." Oskar chuckled as he said it. "And what exactly will we do once we find him? What is this justice you speak of? Remember, we are all old men. Our days of revenge are over. Perhaps I am speaking for myself here, but if you have not seen a mirror lately, well, friends, you are old men now."

Karl laughed. "Unfortunately, I do not need a mirror. But there is something we can do. We'll expose him. There are still dedicated war-crimes investigators, also the media if need be. I hope he will stand trial and have prying reporters hound his last days. He has known too many years of freedom."

Oskar scratched his chin, thinking. "You know he will get lawyers to say he is unfit for trial. The other recent trials have gone that way often enough."

Lukas listened to the dialogue around him and read over the papers. He stopped when he found a photograph of a young woman that seemed to have been printed from the Internet. "Who is this?" he asked, holding up the copy.

"Ah yes, this is a delicate matter." Karl glanced at Marta and then back at them. "I need to tell you about a woman who lives here in the States. She may be a link to Wolfram."

Lukas looked at the photograph again.

"Her name is Kate Porter."

He never slept well in someone else's home. A hotel worked because no one's life was there. But to sleep in the house where a family or individual lived meant breathing their air and memories. Lukas should have gone to his hotel as planned. Oskar, snoring from the couch, was evidently not bothered by his displacement. Everyone except Lukas had voted for their staying the night, since the evening had worn into the late hours.

Perhaps he felt so troubled because of the months he'd spent hiding in the homes of strangers—strangers entrusted with his life. He never wanted that dependence again. Or perhaps it was the flood of this information—something he didn't want to face so late in life. Wolfram Meizer alive. Memories and questions about Susanne. An American woman with a missing husband who somehow tied into their lives, though he believed there was more to that than Karl had yet revealed.

Lukas turned in the bed and straightened the covers. He heard muted conversation and a stifled laugh in the room beyond the wall. Karl and Marta were awake also. They were probably discussing their reactions to seeing wartime friends turned old. Did Marta laugh at how Oskar's nose now looked like a bumpy gourd and that Lukas' own forehead now revealed a gathering of age spots?

He turned onto his back and stared at the ceiling. There was much to process and more to come. They'd finally given up for the night. It was like a maze trying to follow Meizer's path and figure out what he was now seeking.

Another muffled laugh worked through the wall. Suddenly he wondered what it would be like to love and be loved like Marta and Karl loved each other. Did Oskar feel that strongly about his wife also? Lukas' thoughts went to Susanne. But this brought back the questions that haunted him. Had she really loved him as he had loved her, or had she been gaining his trust to discover the truth of his loyalties, whether for the Allies or the Nazis? He'd never known of her involvement in the Resistance until after her death. Did that change what they'd shared?

Lukas' thoughts should focus on the present. His fear that the past would flood over him if he came to Phoenix had come to pass. He considered getting up again. He could look through Karl's information and gain more information on this woman Kate Porter and Wolfram's investments and . . . he should think about those things. But sleep at last began to fall over him, bringing images of Jantes in the mud, the breathing corpses of the camp, and as always, Susanne.

⤝══◍══⤞

Kate woke early but waited to get out of bed. Not for the same reasons that had kept her there in days past, when it had taken tremendous strength to move back the down comforter, when her feet had felt tender and unprepared for walking and her energy had seeped into the padding of the Sleeper Queen mattress.

With the light growing through the windows, Kate savored this new feeling.

Connie had told her, "Wake up to a new day. You are putting the past behind and moving forward. Tomorrow is that first day." Then Connie had described a movie, which Kate hadn't listened to; she was too busy telling herself to do it. To make tomorrow new.

And it was.

Unlike other mornings that seemed to be a continuation of pain that ached from morning through night into the next dawn, this dawn brought a great sigh of hope. She was caught up on bills, her house was mostly clean, and she and Abbie were going on a road trip—a trip to tell Jack good-bye.

Kate kicked back the vanilla-colored comforter, got up, and hurried to make coffee and waffles. A new day it was. She couldn't wait to tell Abbie about their four-day minivacation a week away. Perhaps she'd let Abbie choose their destination. And sometime between breakfast and next Friday, Kate would help her daughter see the essential need to tuck Daddy away in their hearts and move on. Together they would find the strength to do what only three years' absence made possible. The time had come.

"I want to visit the aunties," Abbie said later between syrup-soaked bites of waffle.

Kate's fork slipped from her fingers and clattered against the plate. Her weathered spinster aunts, wonderful as they were, weren't her idea of time away.

"You said we can't go more than five hours away," Abbie begged. "That means we can't go to Europe to find Daddy or to Grandpa and Grandma's for a visit. I choose Auntie Hannah and Auntie Geraldine, especially since Grandma says that the aunties are going to die someday and I add a lot of sunshine to their lives."

Kate hadn't yet picked up her fork. Her child with heart-shaped face and clear blue eyes appeared innocent of the world around her. Then she unloaded casual statements across waffles that spoke what her thoughts really held. Kate closed the open map of the great Northwest she'd placed on the table. When Abbie smiled at her sweetly, Kate wondered what this seven-year-old knew about manipulation.

Once she'd caught Abbie reading one of the "change your life" books Connie had dropped off. Kate had looked at the book, a guide to management, and had tried to decipher the message Connie was sending within the pages of *Who Moved My Cheese?*

"Rick's boss passed these out to all the employees at Software Visions," Connie had said. "It's more for businesspeople but it also addresses a lot of life issues."

Kate had skimmed the book and laughed again and again. What kind of management book was written using mice as the example characters? The short chapters covered the choices of mice as they sought their cheese. Either they adapted to the changes of their cheese being moved, or they eventually croaked. The story was supposed to help employees better adapt to change ("they keep moving the cheese") and to be proactive in their work by anticipating change ("get ready for the cheese to move").

"My cheese didn't just move; it disappeared," Kate had told Connie the next time they met. "And my cheese is not coming back. What does a little mouse do?" She was half amused and half annoyed by Connie's gift.

"But Jack wasn't your cheese; your *life* is your cheese." It was as if Connie had prepared for this discussion. "Or your cheese is more accurately your future and your present situation."

Kate wasn't ready to hear it. Perhaps she was the mouse in the book who was shriveled in the corner, weak from lack of cheese. Kate turned to joking about whether her life was Gouda or more likely Swiss, with holes pressed through it. Connie had sighed and joined in the debate over cheese varieties, adding in movies that included famous "cheese" scenes.

When Kate found Abbie reading *Who Moved My Cheese?* she worried. It was bad enough that her daughter had had few friends in the years since Jack's disappearance. Abbie didn't fit in with little-girl ways and had little patience for what she called "the silly and mean behavior" of many of the girls in her class. Now she was reading a management book for entertainment.

Abbie continued to eat her waffles. Perhaps, Kate thought, her child knew exactly how to get her cheese no matter where it moved.

"Okay, my daughter." Kate paused, wondering what to address first. She went for the reference to Jack. "You want to go to Europe to find your daddy? Is that what you're trying to say?"

Abbie's expression shifted from cherub to surprise. She hesitated, then asked, "Can we?"

"Come here and sit on my lap."

Abbie slowly put down her fork and came to her.

Kate twisted a strand of Abbie's honey-colored hair. She could see highlights of auburn as her fingers pulled through. Was this the moment to make Abbie understand that her daddy was either dead or certainly not coming back? Kate wanted to keep the momentum of her new day, but Abbie's yearnings were too raw to ignore.

"I know you aren't quite ready to say good-bye to Daddy. I don't want to either. If a million prayers would bring him home, he'd be here. The police in Italy, even the FBI and many other people, have tried and tried." Kate touched her daughter's chin. "But you have to understand."

"I don't want to talk about this," Abbie said, jumping from her lap. "Do we get to go see the aunties or not? Can I start packing my stuff?"

Kate's hesitancy produced a long "pleeease" from her daughter, and then Abbie disappeared down the hall at Kate's slight nod. Kate was failing as a mother, right before her eyes. She didn't know what else to do. Abbie could close up her feelings like a door slammed and locked, with a smile covering the pain. Kate often had to search for some hint in Abbie's words or actions to find out how her daughter really felt—and Kate had done little of that in the last few years. Jack had been better at drawing Abbie out. When another child had hurt Abbie's feelings in preschool, Kate knew nothing about it when she picked her daughter up. That evening Abbie broke down on Jack's shoulder and immediately told him the story.

Kate sat in the quiet of the breakfast nook and wondered what to do. "The aunties?" she said aloud. Of all the places to choose. The purpose she'd assigned this trip had just shifted from a farewell to more of a challenge. Kate wished to leave now while her resolve was still strong. But Abbie's school and the antique shop pulled her to that curse of adulthood—responsibility. It turned even worse when she called Aunt Gerdie with the news of their visit. Gerdie suggested that Kate pick them up and then drive all of them to California to see Kate's parents. Abbie was on the other line, cheering for the plan.

"Aunt Gerdie, I only have four days," Kate put in, trying to bring some reason to the situation.

"Where's your sense of adventure?" Aunt Gerdie responded jovially. "And did you realize that's Mother's Day weekend? Your mom would be thrilled, and all of us women, mothers or not, can be together. This is perfect."

"Yeah, perfect, huh, Mom?"

"Perfect," Kate muttered.

"It's an hour and a half to our house and seven hours more to your parents'—not bad for a young woman like you. I once drove for three days straight to see my best friend before she left for the mission field—"

"Okay, we'll do it," Kate said in surrender. The entire plan was hatched by Aunt Gerdie. Kate felt as if a hurricane had come and destroyed her vacation in one swift blow.

The trip was complicated, exactly what she'd hoped to escape. Days later complications increased. Mason called.

Lukas let the warmth of the shower pour over him as the bathroom filled with steam. Once, travel never phased him—now, every muscle complained. The beds in even the best hotels didn't compare to his at home. Chairs were uncomfortable, and several days of leaning over papers at Karl's house had taken its toll on his neck and shoulders. How had he ever slept beneath trees and stars on cold, rocky ground?

For two days, they'd discussed and reminisced. Lukas insisted he sleep at the local Sheraton the second night. Only in America would a hotel offer a shopping and entertainment center with a 166-foot water slide. Children and adults in bathing suits roamed the halls. Brochures boasted of the amenities he didn't require.

Lukas needed to return home. An important election was approaching, and though it hardly affected him since his retirement, there was always the media in need of opinions and party responses. His retirement had not taken away his influence in the government.

And now he needed to be strong for another reason. The discovery that Wolfram was alive would give him something to work toward. There would be little peace now that he knew the man was in Europe—exactly how close to home, Lukas would find out.

The message light was flashing on the hotel phone when Lukas left the bathroom. He still needed to pack and his flight was only three hours away. It was probably Oskar or Karl calling for a final good-bye. He checked the time and realized that Oskar would already be at the airport.

It amazed him that the days had passed so quickly. He would be glad to leave this arid land. Glad to get back to his mountains. The three men and Marta would meet next month at his home in Austria after each of them worked in his or her assigned area. It would be good to welcome them back. Neither Karl nor Marta had been home in nearly thirty years.

And so much had happened during that time. Lukas examined his sagging chest above the paunch of his stomach. Once he'd been lean and fit. Would this body be strong enough to carry out what lay ahead? Not that he needed physical strength. Using the good sense of three men and a woman, they had laid the plans, keeping in mind their limitations. This would not be like the old days of sneaking through the woods, killing sentries in the dark, infiltrating enemy zones—this would be a battle of will and mind. It would mean finding the enemy first and destroying him in ways he would not expect.

Lukas was an old man and not in body alone. He suddenly wondered if it would be worth it. Would he feel any satisfaction bringing down an old enemy—even one he'd hated for so long? If not for the protection of his life and his friends', he would actually consider leaving revenge in God's hands. He'd thought Wolfram was dead once before; it had been little comfort. Why would it be different a second time?

He picked up the phone and pushed the message button while sucking in his stomach and pushing back his shoulders.

"Lukas." Karl's voice on the recording held a steady urgency. "Return this call. I need your help."

Karl knew Lukas' flight schedule. He wouldn't call unless essential. Lukas picked up the phone with a great sense of foreboding.

The line was busy.

CHAPTER SIX

There are mysterious connections between people. Something unexplainable that draws two people together like an instinct uncontrolled. The connection doesn't consist of love or simple attraction, though it could grow into friendship, passion, and later love. Kate would sometimes analyze it: Where did it come from? Was it always mutual? What was its purpose?

Her thoughts wandered the old path of these questions when she felt that connection stir at the sound of Mason's voice on the phone. She was comfortable with the feeling, like a fluffy afghan tucked up to her chin on a chilly day.

"What are you doing right now?" he asked without saying hello.

She smiled and sat in her overstuffed chair by the French doors. Abbie was outside, playing school with Whiskers, the calico cat.

"I'm making plans for a four-day escape from my house and shop."

"How did you work that one?"

"Trudy wanted extra hours, so I'm giving them to her."

"Isn't your daughter in school? You aren't teaching her to play hooky this early in her education, are you?"

"Teacher training Friday and Monday. Worked perfectly, didn't it?"

"I could get envious. Where are you going?"

"To pick up the aunts and drive to my parents.'"

"Let me renege on the jealousy statement. I thought you said something about an escape?"

"I'd had something else in mind, but Abbie made the choice with some help from Aunt Gerdie."

"That explains it. What did *you* have in mind?"

"The open road perhaps. What I really miss is the water—scuba diving or snorkeling, even swimming would do. I've been thinking of water quite a bit lately."

"Not exactly what I had in mind."

"What did you have in mind?"

"Dinner, the two of us."

Kate didn't speak for a moment. Mason always invited both her and Abbie whenever they did something. "Is everything all right?"

"I'm not the best swimmer. And I'd like to talk to you, alone."

And there it was. Kate didn't know what gave it away—the fluctuation in his voice or something more instinctive. She'd wondered with a mixture of dread and anticipation when or if this day would come. She'd always felt a strong drawing toward Mason. It was an attraction that made her want to be near him, to hear his voice and laugh with him. She felt guilty about it often enough, while also wondering if he felt the same. Kate had been alone for a long time. Sometimes her skin yearned to be touched, while her mind turned fearful at the actual thought. She missed being loved and loving someone in return. But the decision to put Jack behind her needed to be with pure motives, not with any thoughts concerning Mason.

Kate and Jack had known Mason for years. Jack and Mason played golf from time to time. They were in the same men's group at church. Mason's insurance company was doing well and kept him busy, so they would invite him to dinner regularly. They'd double-dated when Mason had a girlfriend. When Jack disappeared, Mason was one of the few friends who didn't abandon her. Instead, he checked on her and Abbie, cleaned the gutters in the spring, and did odd jobs around the house. He'd take them out for pizza or Italian. But this was different.

"So, when?" she asked almost fearfully.

"As soon as possible."

⊷═◉═⊷

Lukas sat on the sofa, his hands folded, elbows resting on his knees. Blue and red flashes from the police lights out the window washed across his face. He lifted his head as if it weighed a hundred pounds to look again through the open door where men in uniforms took notes and photographs with their eyes turned downward. He could see the bottom of two gray-stockinged feet oddly twisted and uneven.

After Karl's urgent message, Lukas had called back.

It had taken three tries before he heard Karl's voice. "You have a plane to catch, but I need you to stop by. It is hard to explain." Karl talked like someone afraid of being overheard.

"I will come over."

"Marta is gone this morning with the car. She was dropping off Oskar at the airport. You must take a taxi."

"I will be there in less than an hour."

"Be careful."

These last words told him a lot now. Karl had known danger was near. Lukas had changed his departure and kept his room at the Sheraton for another night. When he arrived at Karl's, it was like replaying an old memory. The door was ajar, though he saw no blood at first.

Karl's desk chair was overturned. Lukas saw legs turned awkwardly and then the large frame of his friend on the floor. A small pool of blood soaked into papers that had fallen beside him. The wound looked minor, possibly caused from his fall to the floor. There were no other injuries he could see. Karl's eyes were closed, but there was no pulse.

Lukas hurried to the kitchen for the telephone, a towel, or something, anything. Karl could still be alive. He cursed his legs that wouldn't move fast enough, as if quicksand pulled at his every movement. He was searching the counter for the phone when he heard a car pull into the driveway. He hurried to the door; Marta met him there. She froze with a bag of groceries in her arm. She didn't seem surprised to see Lukas but instantly knew something was wrong. He tried to stop her, but she pushed by, dropping the groceries in the entry. They were still there. Eggs splattered across the welcome mat.

And on the desk above Karl's body, Lukas had found a fragment of blue ceramic. A blue tile. It was in his pocket now.

The coroner arrived and took Karl away. The police began to leave. After Karl's body was taken, Marta was led away toward her room. A sob cut through the low voices still there as if electricity flashed through the house. Then Marta screamed for Karl. Lukas remembered a scream like that from long ago. It sounded almost familiar, since he'd heard it often in his sleep. Lukas' first instinct, crazy at it was, was to find Karl. His wife needed him. After all they'd endured together, this was how their marriage ended. They'd made their home in a subdivision where kids rode by and teenagers cruised too fast. There were fast-food restaurants and video stores a mile away. An old man could not be killed in such a place.

"Lukas!" Marta's plea was heard from the master bedroom.

He hurried down the hall and found her standing beside the bed. An elderly woman was trying to sit her down. Marta's face looked panicked, but she steadied when she saw him. "Everybody out." Marta's voice was strong, though tears flowed freely down her face. "I must speak to Lukas."

The elderly woman hurried from the room. A policewoman hesitated, then left also. Marta closed the door and leaned against it, as if thinking. Lukas waited.

She paced across the room and stopped in front of him. "He is gone, Lukas. My Karl is gone."

A sudden sob dissolved her against his chest, her arms around his middle. She hit her fist against his back once and regained her composure slowly. He patted her back awkwardly until she looked up at him. He could see that she might dissolve again at any moment.

"I must be strong, be strong," she said and set her jaw. "I know who you were."

Lukas felt his eyebrows drop slightly. She nodded as if he'd spoken.

"I've known since the war. Your real name is Bruno Weiler. Once you were a Nazi, an SS even. You worked at a concentration camp. You were our enemy before you were our friend. But something made you betray the Nazis—I never knew what. I didn't trust you, but I trusted Karl. And you proved whom you served."

She paced the room and wiped her face.

"After the war, those years you disappeared, you were in prison for crimes you did as Bruno Weiler. Karl and I were the only ones who knew; Oskar and Edmund thought you were lost in the aftermath of war. You could have called on many people to save you. Karl told me some of the people you helped while betraying the Nazis. They were powerful families who could have helped. But you faced those ghosts. And when you were free, Lukas Johansen was alive, that other man gone forever."

His expression didn't change, but inside he was surprised, even fearful. He also wondered if he would ever be free from those ghosts.

"Wolfram, he did not know you as Lukas Johansen. Karl and I know the families you helped during the war. You saved them from certain deportation to the camps. And they helped you after your time in prison. We heard how you fought going into politics because of your past. But your past was too far buried—that was made certain. Until now. Wolfram knew you during the war before you betrayed him. Perhaps you even believed that Susanne was killed because Wolfram knew you were with us. He didn't. Wolfram didn't know you were part of our group. You were brought to our house to help us find Wolfram. You were told that our place was just another safe house. Karl was instructed to be certain of your loyalties before you joined our group."

"Was Karl instructed to ascertain my loyalty, or was Susanne?"

"No. Never. She loved you, Lukas. That was not part of it. I promise you; she loved you. But listen to me. These are things in the past. It is today that you must be wary of. You see, Wolfram might have known about your time in prison, but then Bruno disappeared after several years. No one except a very few have known that Lukas Johansen was ever Bruno Weiler. But now you've come to our house. We did not know he was so close. Otherwise, we would not have brought you here. And we know—" she gestured toward the living room, and tears rolled again even as she clenched her jaw—"this was Wolfram."

"Yes." Lukas took the piece of blue tile from his pocket and handed it to her.

She held it in her open palm. "Do you understand? You and

Oskar are not safe. Especially you. Wolfram knew that Bruno Weiler betrayed him. If he could locate Karl, then he will know that former Austrian minister Lukas Johansen was visiting here. He will know that Lukas Johansen is his betrayer, Bruno Weiler."

It shocked Lukas to realize that the identity he had maintained for nearly sixty years was now compromised. His two ex-wives had not known, nor any of his children—only once did he speak of his past to another. He must not think of this now. Karl was dead, and Marta needed him.

"I am safe for this moment. Wolfram will not move yet. In fact, I am certain this could not be his direct work. Remember, he is an old man also. Perhaps he will wait for me to come to him." Lukas actually had no idea what Wolfram thought or what he would do. But the words seemed to comfort Marta. The reality that Wolfram could have come here and done this without help was impossible. "I will stay with you."

Tears raced over the lines in her cheeks in a continuous stream. "How will I live without him?"

"Let us get through today. We will think of tomorrow when it comes."

The Phoenix Coroner's Office would most likely give a natural cause of death, he assumed. The gash in Karl's head was a result of a fall from a heart attack. Lukas wouldn't object. They need not know what he knew. This was his fight now.

Lukas suddenly felt he'd lived a hundred lives. He was tired of living and getting over tragedies. Old people were supposed to get rest, retirement, peace. He had none of that. And now he must watch his back again. For decades no one but a handful of people knew who he really was. Now Karl was dead. What kind of world stole the life of a man such as this? Lukas knew he shouldn't ask himself, for as soon as he thought it, a hundred faces of good men and women returned—faces of death. How weary he was of hatred and grief and especially of the memories. If he wasn't careful it would all wrap around him and drag him straight into oblivion. But Lukas knew no other path.

CHAPTER SEVEN

The memorial service was held two days after Karl's death. Few people attended. Karl and Marta had no children. They had only a small group of friends in the community, because the past left many fears about growing new friendships. Lukas knew from experience. The service was graveside, short and simple. Then it was over. His friend was beneath the ground.

Though she claimed to be fine, he knew Marta needed him. She cried at night, then upheld her usual strength to any neighbors or acquaintances who stopped by during the day. Oskar stayed at the house with them, taking the first flight back to Arizona from Maine after Lukas had phoned him with the news. But Oskar could not stay long since his wife had just received the news that she had early stages of cancer. Whenever Marta left the room, they discussed what really happened and what to do. Lukas knew he wouldn't have Oskar's help in the months ahead.

The morning after the funeral Marta joined him and Oskar

for coffee. Her eyes were red, but she was dressed, with makeup on and hair in its usual pulled-up style. Lukas and Oskar were discussing the blue tile when she entered the room.

"What do we do now?" she asked.

"We would like access to Karl's office," Oskar said thoughtfully.

"Yes, of course. I'll open the safe also."

Lukas watched her walk with great effort, as if her legs now carried the weight of a thousand years. He admired Karl's widow. He envied what they'd shared—everything. Lukas' ex-wives had known only sketches he revealed during a nightmare or in a moment when he forgot himself. Once while sitting with his second wife as they watched their girls play soccer, he had remarked on his love of playing soccer in his tiny yard in Hallstatt and how the ball always ended up in the lake. Vera had looked at him strangely and said, "I thought you were born in Vienna." But Vera didn't probe because she didn't want to know. Her world was peaceful, and that's what mattered.

Perhaps it would have been different if he'd shared with someone what he'd endured and what he'd done. The one time he *had* told his story—to a young woman not long ago—he'd felt freer somehow. She'd told him about the forgiveness only God could grant. But still he couldn't seem to find it.

Lukas followed Oskar into the office. Marta had opened a cabinet door, revealing a built-in safe. She turned the lock this way and that until they heard the soft click.

"Here's the file on Meizer," Oskar said. He flipped through the papers as Lukas searched the small safe.

"This looks like all the information Karl already shared with us. But it will help."

"What is this?" Lukas asked as he looked at a small cardboard box with address and paid postage but no recipient name.

"Should we open it?"

Marta didn't hesitate. "No, we must mail it. I forgot Karl told me. I asked him why he has this package with paid-for postage. He said it wasn't time yet, but that it must be mailed."

"Should we first look inside?" Oskar asked.

"We mail it, just as it is," Marta spoke firmly. "Karl said this, 'If something happens, mail the package.'"

"You do not know what is inside?" Lukas asked, turning the box over.

"I trust Karl with that."

"Then we'll mail it," Oskar said. He was spreading other papers around the desk, though Lukas could see they were all the same documents they'd explored the first day of their reunion.

"I will make some sandwiches," Marta said in a tired voice. She shuffled away with her shoulders slightly hunched. Lukas wondered if she'd survive this.

They sat around the kitchen table and ate in silence. Marta moved quietly around them, cleaning the counters. After brushing the crumbs from his whiskers, Oskar moved to the couch for his usual afternoon nap.

Perhaps they were all too old for the task before them. If a day searching files and planning the next move was this diffi-cult, how would they ever find Wolfram Meizer's location? Karl's absence was felt in everything. He'd been their leader—now it was up to Lukas to take his place. He knew his position but did not desire it. Too many thoughts moved through Lukas' mind, keeping him from rest. He needed to think—think and breathe fresh air, even if it was Arizona air.

Marta stopped him at the door. "Would you mail this down by the park, a few blocks away?"

"You are sure?"

"I promised I would."

Lukas considered opening it as he left the walkway of Karl's house. It could be important, provide better answers. Without a name on the front, would the package arrive at its destination? The inner wrapping was too tight for him to know what it contained. He could open it and repackage it without Oskar or Marta knowing. Lukas played the thoughts in his head until he stopped in front of the blue mailbox. In the end, he dropped it in after repeating the address over in his mind several times. He hoped they wouldn't regret it.

The subdivision had a small park for neighborhood children. As Lukas walked the two blocks, beads of sweat soaked into his collar though the day had turned unseasonably cool for an Arizona May. He found a bench that faced yellow plastic slides and chain-link swings. A group of young children climbed and shouted while their mothers chatted on the other side of the playground. One mother would get up to break up a squabble or help a child get the gravel from his shoes. Strollers and snacks in Tupperware containers, boxed drinks and sticky faces, birds chirping, and the sun warming the wool hat he'd brought from his closet at home.

What a bizarre and obscure line between this, an average American day, and where he'd been earlier—within the intrigue and spy stories that were as real as these sunscreen-lathered children before him. How did the two worlds coexist without either ever knowing of the other? Chubby smiles and carefree days just blocks from secret packages and a dead comrade. Lukas felt jerked both ways.

He walked by the blue mailbox on his way back and already regretted the mailing. It bothered him that he still clung to such old futility as fulfilling a dead man's request. Nothing would have been harmed if they'd checked the package. Nothing at all. He took a receipt from his wallet and a pen from his pocket to jot down the address before he forgot it. His memory wasn't what it used to be. The more he thought about it, the more Lukas realized how essential it was for him to find where the package was going.

⋆═◉═⋆

Welcome
Restorations—Old & New

Kate turned the sign so it could be read from outside the window. Painted by an artist friend, it was the subject of new customer comments.

"What a lovely sign," the older patrons would say.

Restorations—she was embarking on a restoration of her own. Now that she and Abbie were getting away, it was difficult waiting for the day to arrive.

Kate peered through the front window, surrounded with vines and mini white lights, for any smudges she needed to clean, then walked through room settings of antiques—living room, kitchen, dining room, and bedrooms. She dusted and straightened as she moved to the back section of antique books. It was a peaceful Monday morning with the light rain pattering overhead. A gas fireplace hummed from her living room section, warming the narrow shop that really did feel more like a cozy house than a store. Some of her regulars came and enjoyed sitting in the library area and sipping the variety of teas Kate made available. She was still considering an espresso machine because of all the requests she had received.

Restorations had been her line of survival in more ways than one. Many mornings the shop forced Kate from bed when all she wanted was to hide forever beneath the covers. But she knew that if the shop failed, she would be forced to sell the house, perhaps move, further disrupting both Abbie's and her life.

The shop also gave Kate a place to explore her creativity and provided a short escape from Jack—Jack's search, Jack's disappearance, and memories of Jack. But sometimes she felt she'd leave it all behind for something else, something she'd yet to know or find. It was only an inkling she had from time to time—an inkling she'd pack inside under the heading "Stop looking for greener grass when you have a struggling lawn that needs you."

Now with a short trip ahead, Kate longed even more for the time away. Just a few more days, she told herself throughout the day when her mind kept drifting away from work. She quoted the wrong date on a late-1700s rocking chair and the customer corrected her, frowning as if Kate knew nothing about antiques. Later, Trudy, her only employee, discovered the teapot had been filled with a mixture of Orange Spice and Mint Green teas. Kate had wondered why no one had drunk any.

"You're nervous about tonight," Trudy said with a smirk on her face.

"Why would I be nervous?" Kate wondered how Trudy had heard about her dinner plans with Mason.

"Jane told our Bible study so we could pray for you."

Kate stared at Trudy for a moment. Because of Connie's weekly family night, Kate had gone to her next choice for a baby-sitter—Jane. Jane was Ms. Professional Christian. She traveled often and spoke at retreats. Kate liked the woman and, though Jane was always a flurry of productive activity, she had cared enough to check on Kate and Abbie when few still did. For Christmas the year before, she'd given Kate a coupon book for five nights of baby-sitting. Whenever they saw each other at church—which wasn't often because of Jane's involvement, the large congregation, and Kate's inability to get there on time since Jack had disappeared—Jane would remind her that she still had those baby-sitting coupons to redeem.

So Kate had called and Jane was thrilled, even though she had to switch some things around to be able to do it. "It's all right though—ministry is ministry." Kate didn't know what she thought about a night baby-sitting Abbie being considered "ministry." Sometimes Kate saw glimpses of her own future in

Jane's schedule-dominated life, if her own had not been interrupted. And that scared her to death.

Trudy was explaining how the women's group thought it was a good sign that Kate was dating again. "It has been such a long time."

Kate didn't want to be the subject of Bible study gossip and thought she should explain that dinner with Mason was far from hitting the dating scene.

The phone interrupted.

"Mrs. Porter, this is Mrs. McDonald at Corvalis Elementary. Abbie's teacher brought her to the office a few minutes ago. She doesn't seem to be feeling very well today."

"I'll come pick her up. Is she all right?"

"Well, Mrs. Konner is here and . . . why don't I let you talk to her?"

"All right."

"Hi, Kate. I'm not sure what is wrong, but Abbie just hasn't seemed herself all day. At recess I had her stay behind so I could talk to her and she started crying. When I asked what was wrong, she wouldn't tell me, so I thought you might pick her up or come talk to her."

"I'm coming right now."

Abbie looked small and fragile sitting on the couch in the office area. Her head was bent, and she watched the tips of her brown shoes bobbing up and down. She spotted Kate and quickly covered a fake-sounding cough with her fist. "Hi, Mom," she said with another forced cough. "I don't feel good."

Kate crouched in front of her, looking intently into her face. "Let's take you home, all right?"

Abbie nodded and Kate noticed tiny tears in the corners of her eyes. She put an arm around her daughter and told the office secretary they were going home. They were silent as they walked outside; Abbie leaned close against her as if to hide her face from the students they passed.

"Abbie?" Kate began when they were both belted inside the car and she had put the key in the ignition.

Abbie turned toward the outside window. "Mom, I just don't want to talk about it. Is that okay?"

Kate thought for a few moments. "I can't help if you don't talk to me."

"Remember those times when you said you didn't want to talk? You were crying and I asked you why, but you couldn't say why. Now I know what you mean. You just can't talk about it yet." A tear careened down her cheek and she wiped it away quickly. "Maybe it's just my time of the month."

Kate had to stifle a laugh. Abbie was still looking out the window in deep contemplation. Obviously she was repeating a Connie line, not even knowing what it meant. Connie often used the phrase in her descriptions of woes, "and it isn't even my time of the month," or "of course, it would have to be my time of the month so I completely broke down crying."

Kate placed her hand over Abbie's for a slight squeeze and then turned the key in the ignition. At home, Kate made hot cocoa and they rocked together in the porch swing. While Abbie was cheerful again, she didn't approach the subject of her tears. Kate tried different tactics, but Abbie was good at moving around them.

Later Kate walked by Abbie's bedroom, where the door was open only a crack. She was carrying a laundry basket and had come in search of stray socks or clothing when she heard Abbie playing.

"And that's why I must leave forever," Abbie said in a deep voice.

"Daddy, please don't go. I missed you. I want you back." The voice was of a little girl.

"I came home and no one missed me," the deep voice said.

"I did, Daddy. I promise. Take me with you."

Kate knocked lightly on the door as she pushed it open.

Abbie's expression held the word *guilty*. "Hi, Mom," she said quickly, lining up the stuffed animals she was playing with.

"We need to talk."

Abbie shook her head.

"I'm not leaving until you talk to me." Kate sat on the bed next to her.

"I like things the way they were. Now you want to know everything about me."

Kate was taken aback. "I only want us to be close. I want to be a good mom. I want you to tell me what's bothering you." She reached to pull Abbie toward her, but her daughter scooted away. For all Kate's reassuring thoughts over the years that Abbie was coming through the loss of Jack fairly unscathed, it hurt to realize that she hadn't really peered beneath Abbie's smile to what her daughter really felt and thought.

"When will Miss Jane be here?"

"I'm going to call her because I don't need her to come tonight."

"Why? Because of me? Mom, Miss Jane promised to teach me how to cook ginger cookies, and Grandma wants me to make some for Christmas this year. If Miss Jane doesn't come, how will I learn?"

"When did you talk to Grandma?"

"At e-mail lab today. Please, Mom."

"You e-mail Grandma?" Her daughter had a whole life she didn't even know about.

"And Grandpa and Reece. Sometimes Aunt Gerdie, too, when she has time to visit her friends and use their computers. So can Miss Jane still come over?"

Kate nodded, though she didn't want to go. Abbie had moved into her "everything's great" attitude, and Kate suddenly knew that this was the biggest disguise of all. The only way to reach

Abbie was if her daughter learned to trust her enough to share her struggles. It wasn't going to happen overnight.

Abbie continued to weigh on her mind as she stood in front of her closet later and realized she hadn't gone shopping like she'd hoped before this dinner with Mason. Once inside the walk-in closet with its racks of pants, shirts, coats, and the smell of cedar and musty shoes, Kate wished she could slide into a warm corner and hide from the outside paths awaiting her decisions.

Her fingers trailed the fabrics of her clothes that had changed little in the last few years and then moved toward Jack's section. She'd promised herself a dozen times that she'd box his things away. She felt the cottons and acrylic mixes and denim from Jack's Dockers for the university, his khakis for fieldwork, jeans for home and play—they all hung waiting to be picked from their hangers and worn again. With the touch of each fabric came the return of a related memory. The black tie and jacket was their last Christmas party together. Work boots with mud cemented to the edges was a dig she'd worked at with Jack. The gray shirt was a night to a suspenseful movie—her makeup had smeared on the collar where she'd buried her face. The days of their marriage were lined up here in neat rows. She had often tried to reach into the past and live them again. But they were past, she reminded herself now.

Kate returned to her clothing and chose the only outfit she still liked—a black skirt and burgundy blouse. The rest of her hanging clothes were church outfits or scarves, shirts, and pants for the antique shop—all of which she was completely bored with.

Jane arrived at Kate's door that evening with one arm covered in clothing. Jane was in her early fifties, but she always had more energy than anyone Kate knew. "When you said that you didn't get to go shopping, I decided to bring a few of my things in case you felt like something new. Oh, but you already look nice."

Kate followed Jane's quick steps down the hall to her bedroom and surveyed the outfits. On their hangers they looked like professional women who'd gone limp after a long week on Wall Street. The feeling that tonight was a big mistake kept getting stronger.

"Mason is such a great guy. We've tried to find him some-one for years. The church's most eligible bachelor, that's for sure. We should have made you an appointment at the salon—manicure, massage, facial, highlighting."

"You're making way too much of this."

"Oh no. This is an important step for you, Kate. I know we didn't meet until after what happened, to your husband, I mean. But it's been horrible for you—we all know that. We can't even imagine it. Tonight is your night."

Kate wished she felt as excited. It interested her that Jane kept sliding into forms of *we* as if the Bible study group or the pastoral staff were such a part of Jane that she had become pluralized instead of a single individual.

"Mom? You're going on a date? With Mason?" Abbie stood in the doorway and stared at the carnage of clothing as if she'd interrupted great plans of betrayal mapped around the room.

"Yes," Jane said with a wide grin. "Do you want to help make Mommy pretty?"

Abbie turned quickly and hurried from the room. Kate found her beneath a sheet she'd earlier spread from Abbie's bed to her dresser to kitchen chairs forming her newest fort. She was curled in the farthest corner with her head on a small lacy pillow. Kate sat on the floor and put the sheet over her head so she was inside the fort too.

"I think I have the flu." Abbie sank her face into the pillow with a groan.

"You were all right a minute ago."

"But now I feel sick. Maybe I have hyper-thernia."

"Hypothermia?"

"Yeah, that."

"You only get hypothermia from being in the cold too long." Kate reached across stuffed animals and books to touch Abbie's arm softly. "Why don't you come out of here?"

Abbie slowly sat up but didn't crawl from beneath the fort. She picked up her sticker collection book and thumbed through it without looking at Kate. "Why didn't you tell me where you were going?"

"It's only dinner with Mason."

"You didn't tell me."

"I should have. We haven't been talking as well as I'd like so it was easier for me not to tell you. And I was worried about what you would think. I'm sorry, Abbie. I think it would be best after today to just cancel."

"Are you in love with him?"

"No!" she said too quickly. "Not at all. I like Mason, and he's been a really good friend. He's been your friend, too, like a real uncle."

"Why didn't he ask me this time?"

"I'm not sure, but he said he wanted to talk to me tonight."

Abbie finally looked at Kate, searching for any additional answers. "Okay, then. You should go."

"I don't feel like it now."

"No, you should go. And I need to learn to make those special cookies with Miss Jane."

"You'll have a good time with her?" Kate made a face that looked like Jane's pert expression.

Abbie giggled. "Yeah, she's pretty nice."

"I rented *Anne of Green Gables* for you."

"Really?" Abbie crawled past her. She hurried into the other room in search of the movie. Kate stayed on the floor and gazed around the disastrous room.

Jane peered into the room and then came in. "She'll be fine."

Kate sighed and nodded. Jane put out a hand to pull her up.

"She has school tomorrow, so bedtime is 8:30." They walked toward the living room. "If she gets her reading homework done, you can let her stay up till 8:45."

"I did finish my reading," Abbie said from the couch.

"Abbie, no inventions without Miss Jane's approval—like when you made the whipped-cream-and-chocolate-syrup sandwiches when Connie watched you."

Abbie frowned. "Okay, but we are making the cookies, aren't we?"

"Definitely," said Jane and winked at Abbie. "We'll have fun without disasters."

"I left the restaurant phone and my cell number on the fridge." Kate leaned over the back of the couch and gave Abbie a kiss on the cheek. "I love you."

"You promise you won't fall in love?" Abbie's eyes scrutinized her. "What would happen to Daddy?"

Kate glanced at Jane, who winced with a this-is-out-of-my-league expression. "We'll talk in the morning, Abbie."

"Kate," Jane said, stopping her in the entry, "you look very pretty." Kate glanced at her reflection in a mirror by the front door and found that she, too, was pleased with her appearance. "I hope you enjoy your evening."

Kate left the house quickly before she changed her mind. As she drove toward the restaurant with the sun fading in the western sky, Kate had a strong sense that she was betraying both Abbie and Jack.

CHAPTER EIGHT

A couple walked ahead of her through the restaurant doors. The man held the door for Kate but then was drawn close to the woman again, like two magnets pulled together. Kate couldn't help but glance at them a few times, though they were oblivious to her presence. It only increased her loneliness.

She turned to search for Mason Phillips. She was late, and she'd seen his car already in the parking lot. Through the open patio door, she could see him. Their eyes caught, and she waved at his smile. Kate wound through the candlelit tables, low voices, and chink of silverware and glasses, her eyes on Mason's the entire time. He watched her with an admiring smile, more admiring than she remembered. Kate found him more attractive than she ever had and knew he thought her beautiful at that moment.

But instead of enjoying the gaze that drew them toward one another, she was jolted back to that morning in Venice when she'd wondered if Jack thought her beautiful. She could see his face vividly in that moment. With effort, she blinked away his image, but Mason's expression showed that he'd noticed the intrusion of something between them.

"Hi," she said timidly.

He stood, and his presence had a powerful effect. "Hello," he said and pulled her chair from the table.

Kate felt awkward as he scooted her in. The evening was warm, and the sky had cleared as the last remnants of evening hung on the horizon. The trees had opened their green wings and white, potted impatiens dressed the open patio.

"Remember this table?" Mason asked, sitting across from her. His dark eyes prodded her to remember. He was handsome with his warm smile and neat, dark hair that receded slightly at his temples.

"We came here for my birthday with Abbie a few years ago. I'd forgotten that. We sat here?"

"Yes. Your thirty-second birthday. Connie was sick and your friend Jane was out of town. You didn't want to do anything, but I made you."

"You have a better memory than I do."

"Are you ready for your trip?"

"Yes. It should give me time to really think about things."

"Time to think? What is churning inside that head of yours now?"

Kate realized she'd just opened the door to a serious conversation, one she wasn't sure she wanted to share with him. She paused for a moment, gazing over the wrought-iron fence toward the shadows of flowers and scrubs.

"It's been a hard three years," she said.

"Yes." He reached and took her hand. His touch stirred something she'd nearly forgotten. Kate looked at his smooth jaw and then at his mouth. She hadn't been touched in a very long time.

"I'm trying to be patient," he said without moving his eyes from her face.

"Trying?"

"For a very long time."

"You've never said so before."

"Didn't you know?"

Kate realized she had. There was mutual attraction between them; yes, she had known that. But that he actually wanted to move past friendship? She imagined she had known even while she ignored the idea. Now it was out in the open between them, and he was awaiting her response.

He sensed her hesitation and turned her hand over. "What do you feel?"

"Mason, I'm not really sure."

"Do you feel anything?"

"Yes," she whispered.

He smiled and looked at their hands. Kate liked his smile; she always had—the way it gave his face more character and life. His touch sent slow tingles up her arm and brought thoughts she didn't know how to cope with. She'd shut down these feelings for so long, and it terrified her to have them awakening again.

"If I only knew what happened to Jack . . ."

His fingers paused their journey over hers. The waiter stopped by and took their drink orders.

When he departed, Mason spoke. "Jack is always with us."

"Yes." She pulled away and stared into the candlelight between them. "I always thought that true love would endure anything, and if two people pledged their lives and hearts, something almost magical took place. Surely I should have some kind of feeling that should tell me what happened to him, whether he's alive or dead. Though I just can't imagine him alive any longer. But there's nothing solid that I can say I know for certain. No answer from God or any intuition. Nothing."

Mason watched her as she spoke. He always listened, but tonight he didn't appear as interested. There was impatience in his face. "Then what do you believe happened? And can we ever get past it?"

Kate twisted the linen napkin in her hand without looking at him. "A few weeks ago I watched a television special called *Disappeared*. The woman they interviewed believed her husband had been murdered." She glanced at him and noticed his interest. "The man's office was ransacked and they found traces of his blood in the room—but no body. For eight years she assumed the worst, until he was arrested in a different state for faking his death and stealing a new wife's money. The women were crying in the interview. Both said they had no idea their husband could do such a thing. As I watched, I wondered if I could be interviewed for that show. I can't believe Jack would do that to me or to Abbie. But those families would have said the same. It scared me. I mean, who can you trust if not someone like Jack?"

Kate didn't mean the words to hit a target.

"I guess it would be hard for you to trust again," he said, though she knew what he was really asking.

"I don't know if I can." She realized the truth as she spoke the words. Mason was a good man, but Jack had been too. A battle raged within her. One part wanted Mason to love her, wanted him deeply, with cheesy soap-opera music in the background. Then the image of a trial appeared in her thoughts, with judge and jury pronouncing her guilty, guilty, guilty. Another voice told her how ordinary it all felt. She'd thought she'd wanted the ordinary again. Dinners with her husband as they leaned over flickering candlelight, family charades and laughter, man-sized socks in the laundry always turned inside out, church on Sundays and Wednesday nights—she had wanted the life she'd had with Jack.

Mason seemed to be offering her an ordinary life again. Yet the pages couldn't be turned back and Jack be replaced by someone new.

Kate shook her head to clear away the thoughts.

"I'll wait for you, Kate. If you aren't ready, I'll wait till you are. I'll wait forever."

"Forever is much longer than you think."

He seemed to search every one of those words. "All right then, I can't say forever. But I have endurance—I've breezed through three years. But I need to ask you to be willing to try also. Could you at least try to let me get close? We will move slowly, a bit at a time. If you need space, we'll back up. And we'll see what happens. Kate, can you give me that much?"

She nodded but felt a growing sickness in her stomach. She'd assured Abbie she wouldn't walk near this path with Mason. She'd told herself the same.

Kate had occasions of great strength. She could make a decision and move toward it fiercely. Mountains would begin to move. But it was the passage of time that gave her trouble. Her resolves weakened; obstacles made her question the path. But none of that strength was with her now. She'd made promises to Abbie and to herself. Now she was making another one to Mason. They were promises that contradicted each other and would surely bring sorrow to someone.

⋄⇥▅◑▅⇤⋄

Kate didn't want to go in. Jane would be waiting and wanting a report. But Jane was asleep on the couch with her briefcase open on the floor beside her. Papers were in her hands and on the floor. Kate touched her shoulder.

Jane groaned as she sat up. "How was it?" She yawned and

straightened her blouse, then pressed her hands around her short hair to straighten any wayward strands.

"Good," Kate said.

"Mason is a great guy."

"Yes, he is." Kate felt suddenly tired. "Thanks for staying with Abbie. Was she all right?"

"Sure. We made whipped cream–cookie sandwiches after our cooking lesson. She was a happy camper."

Kate smiled. "She gets her way with another baby-sitter. Would you like to stay over?"

"What time is it?"

"Ten-thirty."

"That's it? I can't believe I fell asleep." Jane closed her leather briefcase and blew a sleepy kiss good-bye. "I'll call for more details later. Oh, you have several phone messages I left on the counter."

Kate closed the door behind Jane and leaned against it. The house was quiet and lit only by the living-room lamp. Kate saw the list of messages on the table but didn't reach for it. Instead she shuffled through the mail and carried a few bills that still read "Mr. & Mrs. Jack Porter" to the couch. She could tell that Abbie had already gone through it. Abbie loved to get the mail. Kate had ordered several magazines for her so she could find something with her name on it. The highlight was always a package from Uncle Chris. Her single uncle liked to treat Abbie to anything from a boxing mummy to a cuddly teddy bear.

Kate opened the bills and set them beside her. Loneliness swept into the room like a fog. One of the hardest parts of losing Jack was the loneliness she'd never considered before. After being with someone every day and every night and then losing them, the silence became an enemy and an accuser.

Jack, why can't you tell me what happened? God, why can't I have peace?

Kate noticed a paper partway under the couch. She pulled it out and looked at Jane's typed letter to all the Sunday school teachers about a meeting they were required to attend. Kate read the letter again and again. It was her old life on that sheet. She'd written such letters to the women's group or to the parents of her Sunday school class.

Were her faith and religion as basic as that? They had been more like her career or hobby than the foundation of her life. Kate knew she'd been sincere in her beliefs, but now that she examined her old life from a distance, those beliefs had turned cold as she immersed herself in work. Did she truly love God as she professed? Kate didn't know anymore.

Weariness overtook her. She stretched out on the couch, turned on the TV, and flipped through the channels of infomercials and low-budget movies. Hours later she awoke, stiff and uncomfortable, to a group of exercisers bouncing across the television screen. The clock read 3:30 A.M. She turned off the TV and trudged down the hall, Abbie's night-light leading the way to her bedroom. She shed her nylons and tossed them to the overstuffed chair, where a gathering of discarded clothing already rested. Taking a step toward her bed, she raised her blouse to pull it off when something caught her eye in the dim light.

Something small rested on her pillow, right in the center. She could see its darkness against the cream-colored pillow-case. Kate picked up the small object and, though it had been years, she was shocked at the recognition of it in her hand. It was cool to her touch but felt red-hot, as if she couldn't let go but wanted desperately to be rid of it.

Her other hand reached for the lamp to be sure. And there she stared at the piece of broken blue ceramic that returned her to that room in Venice. Blinding fear coursed through her.

Abbie!

She raced down the hall in fear with the broken ceramic in

her hand. Why hadn't she checked on Abbie when she'd come home? With one hesitant pause, she flipped the switch. Her daughter was there, lying on her back. Her closed lids flinched in the blinding light, but she stayed asleep. She was there.

Kate turned off the light and knelt by Abbie's bedside. Then the house closed around her. The darkness and any creak seemed to possess another presence. Someone had put the broken ceramic on her pillow. Someone had been in her house. Had it been while she slept on the couch? And what if that person was still here?

CHAPTER NINE

The television screen cast white flashes on the walls—the only light in the hotel room. Abbie's head rested against the pillow, facing the TV. She was asleep at last. Kate flipped on a lamp and found the remote to turn off the cartoon. She glanced again at the locked door. After numerous shakings, Abbie had awakened and found it exciting that they were going to a hotel in their own city in the middle of the night, and that they were acting mysterious in the process. Kate tried to make it seem fun, like a surprise party for two.

They were safe here, Kate hoped. Her nerves felt jittery, as if she'd drunk too much caffeine. Now that she was locked within The Corvalis Inn and wasn't required to portray the fun-mommy role, the questions assaulted her. How did the ceramic piece get in the house? What did it mean? When had it been placed there? Kate thought of calling Jane to find out what she knew. Perhaps she'd call her parents, though she tossed that idea, knowing the futile worry it would cause them. She should call the police or the FBI, but every time she picked up the phone she stopped herself.

Kate had habitually called an officer friend in the months after her return from Venice. Until one visit to the station. Adam had been both her and Jack's friend—someone she could count on, someone with connections, even if all the assurance she received was "I'll keep searching." Six months after Jack's disappearance, Adam sat down with her. She thought it odd he'd asked her to come to the station, odder still when he brought her into one of the interrogation rooms—for privacy, he said. But once there, she knew something was wrong. He wasn't acting like himself. Adam went over the months and phone calls and all that he'd done. He asked her why *she* thought there were no leads, none of any kind.

"Jack's photograph and information has been sent around the world. We've had experts in international kidnapping and ransoms, political killings, missing persons, but there's nothing—no ransom note, no terrorist group claiming responsibility, no contact with his relatives or old friends, no sighting of him with another woman, no body washed on shore or found by fishermen. These are the facts, Kate. You have to tell me if there's something we don't know."

Kate was transported to her last experience in an interrogation room. Then she knew: Adam suspected *her*. After months of no information, even Adam was suspicious. He kept her there for several hours, finally admitting that sometimes people tried to cover their guilt by seeming to be overly concerned. He'd let her go, saying that he believed her—though she knew he wasn't fully convinced. From then on, she questioned herself constantly and feared every inquiry and move, asking herself if it made her appear guilty. Added to her already anxious feelings was now the fear of how others saw her. Excessive concern might be construed as guilt. Too little concern could be interpreted the same way. If she did everything or nothing at all—someone would suspect her motives.

Kate picked up the phone, glanced at the curtains covering every inch of the window and at the dead bolt over the door-knob. She couldn't stay here forever. She dialed Connie's number.

"If this is another telemarketer, get your time zones right," Connie grumbled after several rings.

"It's Kate." She heard a rustling on the phone as if Connie quickly sat up.

"What's wrong?" Sleep had raced from Connie's voice and was now replaced by calm fear.

"It's a long story, but I'm at a hotel in town. I could use you right now."

"Kate, what happened? You have to tell me something."

"I found a piece of broken ceramic—exactly like the one in Venice. It was in my house, on my pillow."

"How did it get there? Dumb question, I know. Where are you?"

"Corvalis Inn. Room 253."

"I'm on my way."

Kate slouched into a chair beside a small table. She took the broken triangular shape from her pocket. It looked exactly like the one she'd found in Italy and clutched until the Venetian police had taken it away and locked it away in their evidence room. Any analyses had turned up nothing. Only its presence on the pillow was suspicious.

The room was silent and warm, contradicting the unrest she felt inside. Within fifteen minutes Connie knocked on the door. Kate peeked at the distorted head through the peephole. She opened the door to her friend with disheveled hair and mismatched clothes—flannel sweats and her husband's T-shirt.

Connie hugged Kate immediately and held her for a long moment. Then she pulled away and peered inside the room. "Let me see it."

Kate pointed to the coffee table and bolted the door behind them.

"So this is it? Is it the exact same one?" Connie held the ceramic to the lamp as Kate walked past the bed to sit in the chair.

"I don't know. I didn't have the first one for very long. But it looks like it."

"Maybe it was stolen from the police in Italy, or maybe that jerk officer was really in on this and now he's after you, or maybe this is some kind of a test to see how you react to prove your innocence."

"Connie, this is real." Kate had the feeling her friend was reverting into some fantasy world. Connie's expression cleared and they both glanced at Abbie, who now slept on her side.

"I'm sorry. You must have been terrified."

Kate didn't respond.

"And you didn't call the police?"

"No."

"But this is big. This is important."

"I know it is. And I know I should call. Every time I pick up the phone, I ask myself what it would look like from their end. I mean, who found the piece of ceramic? I did. Is there anyone else who could have put it there? No. Two people were in the house all night. How could someone break in, and why would they? I've touched it so my fingerprints will be all over it. Will there be any others—besides yours? Good chance not. I could see it as an evening news story. Think about it—the disappearance of Jack Porter is still a mystery. Who's suspect number one?"

"You're right." Connie set down the ceramic and began pacing the room.

"I am?" Kate had been prepared for Connie to disagree.

"We need to pray." Connie's face was serious. Kate's mouth dropped. She had expected other suggestions to come from her friend first. That Connie immediately suggested prayer meant she understood the mess Kate was in.

"Well, pray then."

"Mom?" Abbie was sitting up in bed. "Hi, Miss Connie."

Connie waved at her, but she was back to pacing, and the movement of her lips showed that she was already praying.

"Honey, try to go back to sleep, okay?"

"I'm thirsty." Her eyes closed even though she was sitting up.

Kate found a plastic-covered cup in the bathroom, struggled with the wrap, then filled the cup with water. Abbie had fallen back against the pillow but reached for the cup.

"Sit up or it will spill all over you." She helped Abbie take a few sips, then gently laid her back against the pillow.

Connie had stopped pacing. "I'm sorry about all this," she said, her eyes red and hazy. "I pushed you to put Jack behind you. And when you try to, all this happens."

"It's not your fault."

"What is God doing? I could sure use some help here."

"Maybe God doesn't want me to live a normal life. I wish I could understand him even slightly."

Connie didn't respond. They'd discussed long ago how Kate hated to hear the pat Christian responses she'd received when Jack first disappeared: "God works all things for good. The Lord has a plan." Even if the words were true, people used them as a way to shirk off her pain and excuse themselves from any real help or involvement. How could they vaguely understand what it was like to lose half of yourself and not know where it was?

"We'll do it different this time," Connie said firmly.

"What?"

"We need to be stronger, more persistent."

Kate stretched out on the bed beside Abbie and closed her

eyes. The world was suddenly moving too fast, and she had no strength left.

"I saw this show once . . ." Connie paused as Kate shook her head. "No, this was a true report about a woman searching for her missing daughter. She knew her husband had taken her to his homeland in Bolivia, or was it Quebec, or maybe Saudi Arabia? I don't know. . . . But this woman began doing her own searches and hired an international private investigator. Eventually, she got her daughter back—even though she did have to kidnap her illegally."

"Are you saying you think Jack is alive?" Kate stared at Connie.

"I've lost all opinion now. Do *you* think he is?"

Kate leaned on one elbow. She saw a soft glow around the edges of the thick curtains. Dawn was coming. The idea of Jack's being alive—breathing, sleeping, eating, dreaming— even more terrible. "I almost hope not. If Jack is alive, he was not the man I thought I knew."

"But someone put that thing on your pillow. Someone of flesh and blood did that. I think it's time, so let's start making a game plan. Maybe we should get—"

Abbie stirred. "Mom?"

"It's still too early to wake up, Abbie. Try to sleep longer. We'll be quieter."

"For some reason, God's not finished with this in your life yet." Connie sat at the table and held the ceramic fragment again.

"Mom?"

"Connie and I are talking."

"But, Mom . . ."

"I'll turn on cartoons or something. I'll take you to the pool in a little while."

"But, Mom, I have to tell you something."

"What is it?" Kate's patience was weakening.

"I put the tile on your pillow."

Kate stiffened. Her neck turned slowly as if on a creaky hinge. Abbie stared back with a worried, am-I-in-trouble look.

"*You* put it on my pillow?" Kate's face paled. She sat up on the bed. Her stomach churned, and a million thoughts coursed through her. Had Abbie been in danger? Had someone given it to her daughter while she was out enjoying the night with Mason? "This is very important," she said, trying to keep her voice calm. "Where did you find it? And why did you put it on my pillow?"

"Well, I put it there 'cause I remember that's where you found the other one. I was going to tell you, but I fell asleep before you got home. Miss Jane had to make some important phone calls before we could watch the first part of *Anne of Green Gables,* so I went and got the mail. There was a small box, and I thought it was from Uncle Chris—no one's name was on the front part. So I opened it. It scared me to see what was inside, and I didn't know what to do. I thought Miss Jane might get mad at me for opening the mail so I just hid it in my room."

"And when did you put it on my pillow?"

"After Miss Jane put me to bed. I tried to sleep but couldn't. I thought you'd be mad, and I didn't want Miss Jane to be mad at me too. So I went in your room and put in on your pillow so you'd see it. I tried to stay awake, but before I knew it, I was waking up and you were taking me to the hotel. I forgot all about it." Tears rolled down Abbie's cheeks.

"It's okay, Abbie. This isn't your fault," Kate whispered, touching a tear before it streamed off her chin. "Miss Jane never knew about the box?"

"No."

"And it came in the mail?"

"Yes, it was there with just the bills. I didn't have any mail, but I was so excited—"

"Where is the box now?"

"I threw it in the trash, way down at the bottom when I thought I'd get in trouble."

"We need that package." Kate stood. Connie was already handing Kate her purse and keys. "Abbie, you aren't in trouble. This is not your fault at all. I just hope Jane didn't take out the trash."

"Should we all come with you?"

"No, this will be better. Now that I won't envision some prowler creeping through the house, I'll be fine."

Connie's eyes assured Kate she'd make sure Abbie was okay.

"What movie is this from? And does it have a happy ending?" Kate asked Connie as she put on her coat.

"I wish I knew." Connie sat on the bed. "Where are your shoes?"

"I left so quickly I didn't get them."

"How did you check into the hotel—oh, I'll just sit here and imagine it."

"I'm glad you find it amusing."

She opened the door and Abbie ran to hug her legs. Tears burst from Abbie's eyes. Kate bent low and embraced her tightly. Her hair smelled of dried whipped cream and watermelon shampoo.

"It's okay, Abbie girl. You did nothing wrong. No one is upset with you."

"O-okay," she managed between sniffles.

Kate leaned back and looked deep into Abbie's glittering eyes. "You are a very special girl, do you know that?"

Abbie nodded and smiled slightly.

"I promise I'll see you soon."

As Kate closed the door, she remembered saying similar words to Jack when she'd left their hotel in Venice. It always came back to that day.

CHAPTER TEN

Her house appeared unusually shadowed as Kate pulled into the driveway. Perhaps because she never saw the outside this early in the morning, with the sun just emerging from behind the eastern mountains. On the way over, she'd wondered at every corner if someone would grab her.

The hall was still lit. Kate had flipped on the light in her hurried and terrified escape with Abbie. Now it seemed loudly silent as she walked through the entryway.

The overflowing trash can was sticky with the whipped cream can and chocolate-coated paper plates she pushed aside in her search. A butter wrapper glued itself to her hand, and the burgundy edge of her sleeve landed in something brown and gooey.

Then she saw the box. Kate extracted it from the rest of the garbage and set it on the counter. There was nothing distinctive on the outside; it was simply an average postal box. Kate wiped it clean with paper towels, closed the flaps, and searched inside the trash until she found all the pieces of the label. There was Poly-Fil inside the box and a Ziploc bag. There was no return address, like Abbie had said, but even more strange was that though her address was printed neatly in blue ink, her name was not on it. The postage label was smeared from the trash contents, but it looked like it was post-marked a few days before. Kate made out a few letters until she had the origin—Phoenix, Arizona.

Phoenix meant nothing to her. Kate had never been there, and she didn't know anyone from there. She had a cousin in Kingman, Arizona, but that had nothing to do with this.

She turned more lights on and carried the box to the couch. Her thoughts went through every possibility as to why the ceramic had been sent, by whom, and what Arizona had to do with it. The time had come to call the police—Adam, probably. She had spoken to him only a few times since that day in the police interrogation room. Kate dreaded the thought of going back there and putting herself in the center of suspicion. She remembered what Connie had said about international private investigators. Perhaps that should be her first move instead.

Connie brought Abbie home a few hours later. They'd picked up fresh bagels, and Kate pretended everything was great for Abbie's sake. They were supposed to leave in two days for their four days away. Abbie told Connie about Grandpa's horses and how Grandma was teaching her how to play card games. Connie said she'd stay the day and had already told her husband and called a substitute to come to her house for day care. Kate was on the couch, having stowed the box and tile in her closet. Abbie and Connie were in the kitchen, their voices distant, as if they were swallowed by a thick fog.

"Let's leave your mom alone for a little bit," she heard Connie say. "Kate, you didn't sleep last night. We'll make plans in a few hours, but rest awhile so you can think clearly."

Kate's thoughts protested, but her body didn't. She went to

her room and stared for a moment at her pillow with the slight indention where the tile had been. She could feel the old, consuming weariness moving over her. She fought it, but she'd forgotten how strong its hold was. She'd struggled with it for so long, some days succumbing and awakening to a lost day. It was a depression or sorrow, or perhaps fear so strong that it made her want to drift away, to go insane and feel nothing. Maybe insanity was really the greatest escape of all—not a fearsome affliction but a respite from a world of pain.

Kate was determined to fight it. She'd sleep and be strong again. For the past three years it had been Abbie and the antique shop that had kept her from falling too deeply—this time it was for herself also. Kate would face this and find the answers—at least enough answers to move on.

Hours later she awoke. It had been good sleep. She was on Jack's side of the bed with her pillow nestled against her. The phone rang, but she didn't reach for it.

A few minutes later Connie tapped on the door and peeked in. "Are you all right?" She looked worried but put on a smile. "Perhaps we should call the doc for some Prozac injections?"

"Why not an IV?"

"This woman has already called twice." She opened the door wider and pointed to the cordless phone she had pressed to her chest. "She's an older lady, I can tell, doesn't quite get the message that you shouldn't be disturbed. Says it's very important. I can get rid of her again."

"I'll talk. I feel better, much better. Thanks, Connie." Kate sat up and reached for the phone. Connie closed the door as she left.

"Mrs. Porter?" The slight vibration in the woman's voice indicated her age.

"Yes?"

"Very good. I have tried to reach you. I tried calling last night also."

Kate sat up straighter, trying to recognize the voice with its strong accent. "Who is this?"

"Please, if you will listen. You will receive some mail soon. There will be no return address or sender's name. But—"

"I received it last night. Who is this?"

"It arrived already? That was very fast indeed. Did you open it?"

"Yes." Kate was standing now. "But who . . ."

"Then it is very important that we meet and discuss what was inside. I do not want to discuss it on the telephone."

"Who *is* this?" Kate demanded.

"A friend. I am someone who cares."

"Why can't you tell me who you are? Why did you send it to me?"

"If we could talk in person it would be much better than over a phone."

"You know where I live?" Kate queried, instantly wary.

"I have the address, yes. We are currently in Portland."

"We?"

"Please, Mrs. Porter. I know my telephone call and the package must make you very afraid. But we can meet in a public place that you choose. We want to help you."

Kate was suspicious, afraid, curious, and she wanted to know something—anything—after having nothing for so long. She felt herself fading into the person she'd been in the first years of Jack's disappearance—weak and frightened. She had to find a way out.

"I'll meet you."

"Very good. It is important that you trust me and not tell others. There is nothing to fear. I have some information you will want."

Kate turned toward her door as it creaked open. Connie peered inside. "I'll come to Portland. Tomorrow. Give me your number, and I will call on my way."

"Yes, That will work."

Kate pulled out drawers in her bedside table until she had a scrap of paper. She found a green crayon to write the number of the Portland Sheraton.

Connie was standing in the doorway. "I'm going with you," she said after Kate hung up the phone.

"Where is Abbie?" Kate asked. "Did she hear any of this?"

"She's teaching Whiskers the waltz. Who was that?"

"I don't know. Someone who sent the ceramic piece or at least knows who did. The woman says they have my address, name, and phone number—which is not a great feeling."

"You're meeting them tomorrow?"

"Yes."

"Let's call the police." Connie's face looked sorrowful as she said it. She understood what it would mean for Kate.

"This won't be dangerous. I get to choose the place we'll meet."

"I'll wait in the car then."

"Abbie needs to go to school and have someone pick her up. She already missed today."

"What if they're terrorists or want some money? I'm calling Mason to go with you."

"No. It wouldn't be a good idea. Mason can't be involved in this."

"Whatever you say, Agent Scully."

"Who?" Kate had to laugh, knowing it would be some bizarre Connie-thing.

"You know, *The X-Files*."

"Has anyone ever told you that you watch way too much TV?"

"I might have heard that before."

Connie sat on the bed. Kate plopped down beside her. They stared at one another.

"I don't know how to survive this again," Kate whispered. "Everyone says, 'Oh, you will, you will. We'll help you. You're going to make it—just have faith and God will see you through.' They say it must be a comfort to have Abbie with you. Just yesterday I thought I *was* going to make this."

Connie touched her hand. "I don't know how or if you'll survive this. But I'm with you all the way. I can promise you that."

"Only a true friend would be so honest." Kate closed her eyes. Then a thought struck her. Had the box contained only the tile? Abbie always ripped open Uncle Chris' packages to see what they contained before she read the card he sent.

"Where are you going?" Connie asked as Kate suddenly hopped up.

"Agent Kate has an idea."

Connie followed her to the trash can. Abbie was still outside with Whiskers so Kate carefully sifted through the contents again. Down near the bottom, she found an envelope that had escaped her earlier search. Her name was on the front.

"Amazing," Connie said in a hushed voice. "Open it."

> *Dear Mrs. Porter,*
>
> *I try again and again to write this letter to you. I am sorry about what happened to your husband. In some ways, I feel responsible. My hope was to meet with you and tell you everything I know. However, the arrival of this package means this is not possible. You will be contacted soon by others who will know how to help. I have entrusted my blue tile as proof of my sincerity. Please guard it well until you meet the others.*
>
> *Be careful and keep this confidential. It is of the utmost importance.*
>
> *Sincerely,*
> *Karl Olsen*

"Kate, there's your proof."

Kate nodded and read it again. "Yes. Finally, something real."

CHAPTER ELEVEN

Lukas sat on the small couch by the window. He flipped through the *London Telegraph* with swift movements, annoyed that this was the only international press he'd found downstairs.

"What is wrong?" Marta asked. She sat on the couch at the other side of the suite. The phone was beside her.

"Why did you say we have information for her?"

"I didn't think she would come without a reason. And we do have information for her, the poor woman."

"You should have let me call."

"You would have scared her straight to the police, if she has not already been there."

Lukas slapped the paper down in annoyance. He was irritated at Marta and upset because of it. She was Karl's widow—the once beautiful young woman who had endured terrorizing events and yet survived to be kind and concerned for others. It drove him crazy. Her worry for Kate Porter had cost them information they needed. She had not confirmed what was actually inside the package, though both of them felt fairly certain. If Marta had let him open the box before mailing it, they would not be in this position at all.

Lukas realized his irritation ran deep. It went back to his arrival in America. He should be home or at least on a plane right now. He'd be in the middle of a midmorning snack or already watching the first movie of the international flight. Thoughts would be turned toward home and his daughters and grandchildren. He'd be dreading the thought of returning to the business and politics of government. Was the euro holding against other world currencies? What scandal was about to rock which official? Would the election preparations swing the current polls? Questions that had once been essential and urgent and pressing.

Yet since the graveside ceremony of his longtime friend and the deep night tears shed by Marta, Lukas thought a government agenda sounded like the squabbles of schoolchildren. That knowledge bothered him. He should want to close his days with banal worries and political issues. He'd yet to truly commit to this search for Wolfram, even though the unanswered questions had pushed him to come to Portland and pursue the lead of Kate Porter. But he still fought it, wanting to slide into the oblivion he'd had before this reunion. What was wrong with him? Had he lost his will to fight for the life of a friend?

"I tried to say as little as possible. What if the phone is being listened to?" she reasoned.

That's when he realized that Marta knew he was grouchy because of her, or partly because of her. She'd thought over her words before speaking. It was wise of her to consider phone tapping, but he doubted such lengths had been taken. Yet what did he know?

"Are we going to eat out or get room service?" Marta asked.

"I have never been to this city. Perhaps we should eat in the hotel restaurant."

"You are a creature of habit, aren't you?"

"What do you mean?"

"You like your paper, your coffee, your safe hotel."

"I am an old man. I need my few comforts."

Her laugh sounded good. It was the first time since Karl had died that Lukas had heard anything of the usual Marta in her voice. His annoyance cleared, and her laugh made him smile.

The Cup O' Day Café was in downtown Portland. A group of regulars already sat at outdoor tables. From hidden speakers funky music played. It sounded composed in a tropical third-world country, with lots of bongos and ukuleles. The café smelled of rich espresso and spicy herbs that antagonized Lukas' nose. He detested trendy coffeehouses. West Coast America believed themselves the inventors of a new fad, while the Viennese had been gathering young and old to their coffeehouses for centuries.

"She was smart to pick a place like this," Marta said as they found a table.

"The coffee is probably terrible, and we will need to go to the counter for our order. No service in America." Lukas cursed in German, drawing a long look from Marta. No, he had not forgotten their decision to speak English while here. "Some words must be spoken in your own language."

Marta clucked softly but grinned. Her expression soothed his anxieties in a way that surprised him. A waiter stopped by for their order, and Lukas checked his watch. They were still early.

"She will come," Marta said.

He didn't doubt it, only dreaded it. He wanted to make this quick—get the tile fragment and any information on her husband's disappearance and then leave before this woman learned too much about them. Lukas now longed for home with a depth he'd only known as a young boy when his mother was very ill and he'd had to stay with his aunt for a month. These American smells and feelings were all wrong. He needed home.

Then he saw her through the large windows. She was younger than he'd imagined—closer to one of his daughter's age. Kate Porter walked inside, pausing at the door. She held her brown purse in her hand like a shield and glanced around the shop. She wore a skirt and blouse—at least she wasn't as casually dressed as most Americans.

Their eyes met. Lukas could see relief in her face. What had she expected?

They shook hands and introduced themselves. Marta had convinced him to give accurate details. Marta had convinced him of a lot of things.

"Did you bring the package?" Lukas asked before they had returned to their seats.

"No."

"We would like the item returned." He knew his voice sounded harsh, but he wanted to get the tile and end this connection. Marta should have told her to bring it. He again wondered why Karl had brought this woman into their lives. He must have known this meeting would have to take place.

"I didn't plan to give it to you." She seemed shaken by his abruptness, and Lukas was glad of it. She must not think they were an elderly couple for her to pat and cajole like children.

"It was a mistake that you received it."

"Did Karl mail it?"

Marta glanced at him.

"I did," Lukas said. There was no need explaining everything to this woman. Something about her rubbed him wrong.
She sat there trying to figure him out and gain answers he
would not give. "What do you know about Karl?"

"Were you involved in my husband's disappearance?"

Lukas could see this would go even worse than he'd
expected. "No, I was not."

"Do you know what happened to him?"

"We know he disappeared three years ago. Perhaps you
could give us those details."

"You must know something more, or why would you send
me the package? And where is Karl if he didn't send the package?"

"Excuse me," Marta said. "We must slow down and talk
first. Gain some trust all around. Mrs. Porter, would you like
to order something?"

Her eyes flicked briefly to Marta, then back to Lukas. She
was afraid of him, but not as much as he wanted. This would
not be as easy as he had hoped.

Kate hadn't anticipated such an elderly couple. Except for
their heavy European accents, they appeared to be any old
couple walking in any Portland park on a Sunday afternoon.
He would be a cantankerous, old man, and she the kind,
grandmotherly type. What Kate had expected, she wasn't sure.
Perhaps people who leaned more toward spy-movie characters—the chain-smoking woman and the dark, probing eyes of
the intelligence director, though she felt that this man noted
her every word. Yet looks could be deceiving, and she found it
true once they started talking. The couple wasn't even a

couple. The woman lived in Arizona—the man didn't say. There seemed as much espionage possible between these two as between the couple on *All in the Family*.

"Lukas has three daughters, but I have no children. Do you have children?"

Lukas did not speak, as the woman did all the pleasantries. He kept glancing around with a look of distaste, especially when the beat of bongos increased into a rich South American song. Kate knew he wanted to get to the reason for this meeting as much as she did. For a moment, she had the sense that this was all a joke. Could she really be sitting with two people who were her first link to Jack? Perhaps they knew nothing. But finally she had proof in front of her eyes that all of this had happened, that she hadn't lost her mind—and Jack in the process. The events were real. Jack's disappearance was real. In some ways, Kate wished she had followed one of Connie's fantastic plans to wear a hidden microphone, have the police drag these people in, or videotape the meeting from a hidden location. But it was Karl Olsen's letter that changed her mind. He trusted her with the tile, so she would trust him, wherever he was.

"I have a daughter," Kate said. "She's seven years old. But could we talk about the piece of ceramic now?"

"Ceramic?" the woman asked, glancing at Lukas as if she couldn't understand. Kate couldn't remember her name. She had wanted to write them down, ask for the spelling, and then try to find out who they really were. Perhaps that was some of Connie's influence.

"The object in the package. Did you know what was inside?"

"It is not ceramic," Lukas said. "It is an antique tile."

"Like the tiles in flooring?"

"Decorative tiles are used differently," Lukas grumbled, as if any kind of explanation annoyed him. "They can be found all over the world in palaces, churches, mosques—some are very old; others are found in the average kitchen."

"I am familiar with decorative tiles. Where did this one come from?" Kate put her elbows on the table and leaned closer. She had many questions to ask, and the letter was tucked in her purse. The most important questions she'd ask soon; first she'd gain the woman's trust, maybe even the man's by some miracle, and then seek the truth.

Marta glanced at Lukas as if to question how much she should say. Kate wondered about their relationship, how long they'd known one another, what brought them here.

"During World War II, that tile was broken into five pieces," Marta said. "One piece was given to each of five men who were part of the Resistance in—"

"Marta," Lukas said. He didn't have to say more, because it was clear that Marta didn't like the reprimand. She acted as if she hadn't understood his silent message.

"One of the fragments is in a police locker in Italy, and I have another," Kate said. "Where are the other three pieces? And how do you know all of this?"

"You are wrong," Lukas said. "The tile you found in Venice was not an original piece, but only a copy."

"How did you know I found the ceramic—the tile—in Venice?" She suddenly wondered how much they knew about her. "And it wasn't an original?"

"No, it was not." Marta said. "One of the original tiles was stolen in 1945 by a German named Wolfram Meizer. The tile you found matched the shape of the piece that used to belong to Jantes—a friend of ours."

"But how do you know what my tile was shaped like?"

"Marta's husband, Karl, gathered the information about the tile you found in Italy. He had a photograph of it." Lukas and Marta glanced at one another.

"Where is he?"

There was a pause and Marta spoke. "Karl died recently."

Kate and Marta stared at one another for a moment before Kate turned away. Now she better understood Karl's letter. "Do you mind telling me what happened?"

"We believe he was killed, or he died in the process of . . . his heart was not so strong."

"I'm sorry." Kate said the words, then stopped. She didn't want to say that because she had disliked it when people said those two words to her. What did they have to be sorry for? Now she'd spoken the dreaded words.

"Your husband included a letter with the blue tile." Kate opened her purse and set the letter in front of Marta.

Evidently surprised, Marta appeared to fight to contain her emotions. She picked it up. Lukas leaned over and read it to himself.

"How is my husband connected?" Kate asked after several minutes of listening to bongos change into a CD of Mediterranean guitar.

"That is what we are not certain of," Marta said. "Karl knew more, but he did not tell me."

"Why did you send the tile?" She spoke to Lukas. "It seems obvious that you don't want me involved in this."

"That is the way of Lukas," Marta said. "It is a complicated story as to why Lukas mailed the box. He didn't know the contents at the time."

"How are you involved in this blue tile—" The waiter arrived with coffee and pastries for the couple. Kate noticed Lukas peer skeptically into his cup. She ordered a vanilla mocha and caught his frown. The woman said this was Lukas' way, but she felt dissected beneath his gaze.

"These five men who each received a piece of the tile—" Kate leaned back in her chair and watched Lukas—"were you one of the members of the blue tile group?"

He glanced at her with a hint of surprise; then anger over-shadowed his face.

"I want the tile," he said, as if releasing each word as calmly as possible. "It was a mistake for Karl to involve you."

"How can you say that?" Marta said before Kate could respond. "Karl had a reason for this. He said in the letter he felt somewhat responsible for her husband's disappearance. There is more than you know, Lukas. Do not speak of him that way again."

Her words quenched Lukas' anger like a flood of water over fire.

"Kate—" Marta put her hand over Kate's. It shook, but Kate couldn't tell if it was because of emotion or age. "We hope to have some answers about your husband as we do our own investigating."

"Are you working with some kind of police or investigators?"

"We do not work with those agencies," Lukas said solemnly.

"I want to be involved." She said the words quickly, tossing herself in without gauging the warning signs. Kate thought she perceived a slight smile from the woman.

Lukas Johansen's reaction was quite the opposite. "That is out of the question."

"Why?"

"This is about something that happened long ago. These are things you can't even understand."

"Make me understand."

"How can you comprehend something beyond your life and years? This began even before the war. What do you even know about our war? Let me speculate. You took a semester at university? Or you read a novel? You went to the movies and watched *Schindler's List* with popcorn and Coca-Cola?"

Kate didn't answer.

"Lukas," the older woman chastised.

"This is about me. And my husband. Tell me what happened to him, and I will go away," Kate insisted.

Lukas folded his arms across his chest. "I do not know."

"We might know something," Marta said. They both turned to her quickly—Kate in hope and Lukas with an unspoken warning. Marta ignored him and leaned toward Kate. "This is about my husband also. The man responsible for my husband's death is probably the same one for your husband. We do not have evidence yet—we pursue that cause. Yet before you commit to this, you must know what it will cost you."

"I don't know if I can go on with my life without knowing."

Lukas was shaking his head. "To become involved could risk your life. Did you not say that you have a daughter? And probably a comfortable life here in America? Are you willing to risk what you have for the knowledge of what happened? I suggest you think about that. Marta's husband, my comrade, is in the grave because of our search for answers. It is too high a price to pay for answers, even for revenge. This is what you must decide."

Lukas pushed his chair back loudly and left them at the table. Kate watched him glance around the room and storm toward the bathroom. The room was suddenly too noisy, Marta's eyes too inquisitive.

Kate lost her courage again. "I need a little time."

"That is expected."

The two women's eyes met, and they seemed to understand one another.

"Do you think my husband could be alive?" Kate asked.

Marta gently churned her hands and stared at the table. "Wolfram has left a trail of deaths where he has been. I tell you that because I would not want to hope my husband was alive when he was not. But I cannot say for certain. If you are a praying woman, I would pray. This could be the most important decision for you. We will be returning to Europe—Italy and Austria."

"I cannot go to Europe. I have a child, a business."

"I want you to know what could be necessary. Nothing is impossible, but if I had been granted a child, I would be as hesitant—you are a good mother. Take some time. We would ask for the tile if you choose not to help."

"Give me a week?" Kate couldn't believe she was even considering it.

"Of course."

Kate hardly breathed until she was a block away from the old couple inside Cup O' Day. For a moment she leaned against a building to catch her breath. Marta had given her a number to call. She wanted an answer within a week, whether Kate would join in the search or release the tile fragment.

Kate had a decision to make—the most important one of her life.

The taxi pushed through traffic and onto the highway. The rain clouds of the Northwest had pattered toward the east, leaving the sky a brilliant blue. Lukas wanted to find fault in the region, but arrow-topped pines bent over lush meadows tugged at his favor. He wondered why Karl and Marta had not chosen an area that resembled their homeland more closely than did the arid desert of Arizona. Perhaps they thought they'd forget for a while. Strange how he had stayed and learned to live with the past behind him, for the most part, while the Olsens had escaped the land but the ghosts of yesterday drew them back. Karl Olsen was dead because of it.

Lukas stared at the whirl of trees and hillsides along I-205 as they sped toward the Portland Airport Sheraton. Marta was silent beside him.

The taxi driver tapped the steering wheel to the beat of a song that he played too loudly for Lukas' taste. A dispatch came through his radio, and he turned it down, though his left hand never missed a beat. Marta stared out her window. The yellow cab swept past a puttering Volkswagen painted to look like a strawberry, and Lukas noticed that RVs seemed to rumble off and on exits in every direction. RVs with white-haired drivers were everywhere in America.

"The West," he spat.

Marta turned toward him. "You are a bitter old man." It was the first time she'd spoken since they'd left the coffeehouse.

"We can speak at the hotel."

"Why? Do you fear you will hurt my feelings?"

"Perhaps." He kept his eyes out the window and glanced from time to time to check the meter on the front dash. "And other reasons."

"I am not weak, and you are not my master, Lukas Johansen." He realized she was furious at him, especially when she switched to German. "I will not have you speak for me or tell me what to say or not say."

He, too, switched to German, even though the driver glanced at them a few times. "You are angry because of the meeting? I should be the one angry."

"And you are."

He turned away to see the crooked peak of Mt. Hood rising in solitude into the sky. That was another strange thing about the mountains of this region. The tallest peaks rose alone from valleys or lower ridges, unlike the massive chains of peaks and ridges at home.

"You are angry, and I am angry," she said. "If I had less respect for you and myself, I would have told you . . . well, my mother's instruction is still in this old woman. But you will not silence me again."

Lukas stared at her profile since she wasn't looking his way. He could only shake his head.

"Kate Porter will choose whether to work with us or give up the tile."

"That was not offered," he said too loudly. The cabbie's eyes appeared in the mirror again. "I walked away for a moment, and she believes she has this choice."

"We are old, Lukas. Do you know that?"

"I know that very well. But this woman cannot help with that."

"We are old and she is already involved. You are recognizable throughout Europe."

"And an American will not stir up notice?"

"Wolfram did something to her husband—most likely his body will never be found. I would want to know. And Karl wanted her involved. He knew we needed her. He also felt responsible—I want to know why."

"So he did keep some secrets."

"We shared our lives. He would have shared this with me at the right time. I was not threatened by things that would worry me. Eventually Karl always told me. Eventually he would have."

"What do you think this is about?" He lowered his voice. "We can't form some secret group like the old days. Those days are gone. But suppose we did—we would never bring in an American mother who knows absolutely nothing about this. It is insanity."

"I decided to offer Kate Porter the chance to help. I would want the same offer. Now, Lukas, I grant you the same choice. Do you want to help me find Wolfram Meizer?"

"What are you talking about? This is up to me."

"No. Karl and I have been searching for more than a decade. This man took my husband. He most likely took this woman's husband also. Perhaps the two of us will work together. I know that you have not committed in your heart. You feel it is your duty because I am Karl's widow and because of old vows and Susanne's death. But we are too old for that. We must seek Wolfram Meizer because we want justice, not revenge. We must commit all of our energy, perhaps the last energy we will give to something in this life. Just as I spoke to Kate Porter, I speak to you. Be certain for yourself and not anyone else."

Marta spoke without looking at his face. Her eyes now turned to probe him, as if she could understand thoughts even he wasn't familiar with.

"You have not been near me in all these years, Marta. Yet you believe to know me so well?"

"I know you. I know both the good and the bad," she insisted.

He shook his head. "You don't."

"I know why you don't like her."

"Who? Kate Porter? I have feelings neither for nor against."

"That is not true." She spoke with confidence, and he hated that this time she was right. He didn't like Kate Porter, though he couldn't say why.

"We can trust her," Marta said, then paused as if considering her words. "She reminds you of Susanne."

Instant anger welled inside him. Marta's eyes were compassionate, but his face burned as if slapped. "How could you speak such words? That woman is nothing like Susanne."

"They do not look alike, and she is older than Susanne was when she died."

"When she was murdered," he corrected.

"Yes. But I find a spirit and a kind of . . . is it innocence to the world? Not innocence, for this woman has endured pain. But she is brave without knowing it."

"You should have written great works of fiction, Marta."

"I knew Susanne. She was my sister-in-law and the only true friend I ever had. I know some qualities of Susanne when I see them. Think about it and you shall see also."

Lukas had begun to pull at a small tear in the vinyl seat when he noticed it and stopped. It bothered him that Susanne was no longer a clear image in his mind. He knew he had loved her laugh and her soft hands with their slight lines of dirt under her nails from the work she did on her grand-mother's farm. He could still make out the pieces of her that he loved, but lately her entire image had eluded him.

Marta's hand on his surprised him, and she softly squeezed. It had been a long time since someone had touched him so gently.

"She was true and honest and good. And she loved you, Lukas. You have wondered that, haven't you? Karl did not believe me, but I knew you were troubled when you learned Susanne was part of the Resistance. She wanted to tell you but thought you would not trust her love. I wanted to tell you, but everything happened so fast in the end." She sighed and moved closer. "She did not want to love you at the beginning because of your past. In the end she loved you despite your past."

Great emotion flooded through Lukas. He turned back toward the window and pressed hard to keep everything locked inside. The taxi had exited the freeway and was cruising toward the airport hotel. He felt as if a valve had been opened and unwanted feelings surged through him. His chin twisted and his muscles tensed. For over fifty-five years he had wondered. Now in a taxi in America with some strange funk music playing and Marta beside him, he had learned the truth.

"Lukas?" Her voice was quiet. "Are you all right?"

He cleared his throat. "Justice instead of revenge. I will have to get used to such an idea."

The tile had been in her car, tucked in the glove compartment in a Ziploc bag filled with cotton.

Holding it in her hand now, Kate propped it against the driver's side window. No light showed through. She examined its ridged pattern of cobalt and wondered about its origin. It wasn't the blue and white of Dutch delftware, but the ridged pattern reminded her of something European. Lukas and Marta wanted this back if she decided not to be involved in their search—their search for some enemy from WWII. It all seemed preposterous as she sat in the driveway with her engine running.

Abbie was at Connie's, where Kate should have picked her up, but she wanted to see her little house first. She sat for a while and gazed at familiarity—the brick walkway and flower beds under the cottage-style windows. She always intended to cut the grass that grew inside the long crack in the driveway, but whenever she approached it, she'd notice how the grass clung desperately to its source of soil, surrounded by cold cement. And she'd leave it there. Sometimes in the summer she even sprayed water its way.

Now as she stared at and searched the familiar, everything seemed changed. Again.

Three years ago Kate had flown back from Venice alone. Her parents had returned a few days earlier to bring Abbie back to Oregon. Kate had held out, hoping for some word. Those were the loneliest days of her life. She'd stayed near the airport, where it felt cold and impersonal but allowed her to blend in with the travelers, families, and lovers. Then she had gone home and left Jack somewhere behind.

Mason had met her at the airport while her family prepared for her arrival. She remembered the first glimpse of her cozy home and how instantly foreign it appeared. She didn't have a moment to really think about it for weeks. Then Kate began to be alone—family and friends had to move on with their lives and she insisted they go.

On her first trip home from the supermarket with her backseat loaded with groceries, she'd stopped right here with the engine running. The front tree had been smaller then and the lawn recently mowed by a helpful church member. The house had appeared the same as it had before she'd left with Jack—yet it wasn't. It was the first time she realized that the house she loved would survive and continue without Jack, without her. It wasn't hers to own. She was here for a season, and then the house would hold other lives. She'd still clung to hope and prayers, but a part of her had known that Jack's voice wouldn't be on the answering machine when she walked inside. Jack wouldn't eat the food inside the white plastic bags. Jack wouldn't be able to make this okay.

Kate saw that again now as she sat with the blue tile on the dashboard and the heater humming. Everything felt instantly empty and hopeless. Days before she'd been moving toward a new life, a future, a tomorrow not tethered by yesterday's sorrow. Now this tile, these people, this unreal story of Nazis and Allied resistance was crashing into her world and knocking it out of orbit—just as she'd thought it was back in control. Kate had to make a decision. This time the decision would be hers.

An hour later she was at Connie's. Kate's smiles and actions felt like drying clay that could easily crack under pressure or rapid movement. She found Abbie and Connie on the computer, working on the Connie and Tim O'Brien homepage. Connie updated her family news and photos weekly for relatives and friends. Kate gave Connie a brief summary with her asking, "What are you going to do?" But Abbie interrupted, excited about their trip the next morning. So Kate took Abbie home without any resolution.

Later Connie called several times to see if Kate was going to see her family, what she'd decided, whether she should search the Web for an international private investigator. Finally Kate quit answering the phone and didn't pick up when Mason called either.

Kate had to force her excitement about the trip. So much

hung over them to whisk away for four days. But Abbie fluttered around, getting her things in order. She filled Whiskers' food bowl and cleaned his water dish, then went to the neighbors to make sure they knew where his toys were located— she'd forgotten to tell them those things when she'd asked them to watch Whiskers.

"Mom, you have to read to me," Abbie called from the bedroom.

Kate relented beneath Abbie's "pleases." *The Voyage of the "Dawn Treader"* was perched on Abbie's covers. They had read little in the last week. The book had fallen behind Abbie's bed and was lost for several days. Kate began with chapter 2. The young king of the enchanted land of Narnia was explaining why he was sailing toward the world's end:

"'With Aslan's approval, I swore an oath that, if once I established peace in Narnia, I would sail east myself for a year and a day to find my father's friends or to learn of their deaths and avenge them if I could.'"

The words stopped her from reading, and Abbie curiously looked up from her pillow. Kate had read the Chronicles of Narnia as a young girl, but she'd forgotten that Caspian's journey into the unknown seas was for the purpose of finding people.

"Mom?" Abbie asked.

Kate started reading again as an unknown sea stretched before her and Abbie's lives. Did she dare sail where maps were not yet drawn? If only she could peek ahead to the last page and see that she and Abbie would be safe and better for taking the journey. But real life didn't always include happy endings.

In fact, it rarely did.

CHAPTER FOURTEEN

A mother and daughter in a silver SUV cruised down a winding road toward Crocker Valley. Kate didn't have the energy for this journey to pick up her elderly great-aunts and drive hours to her parents'. She didn't want to hear the aunties bickering, or be the responsible driver, or keep the secret of the last few days from her family members. There was much to decide and this felt like running away.

"Mom!"

Kate's heart jumped as she looked for something ahead in the road, then over at Abbie. "What is it?"

"Nothing," Abbie said, but her expression spoke, *You weren't listening to me again.* That expression was too common. Kate didn't know how often she'd blocked out a conversation or answered on autoresponse. During those moments Abbie could have asked, "Can I join the Charles Manson fan club?" and Kate would have answered, "Sure, honey."

"Do you think they'll notice how tall you've grown?" Kate asked lightly as an apology.

"Probably," Abbie mumbled. "Aunt Hannah will try to make me like fig jelly again."

"It finally worked on me," Kate said with a grimace.

"You like fig jelly?" Abbie groaned as Kate nodded. "That's why she's convinced I will get used to it. You gave in."

They laughed and were brought together, discussing the most awful Aunt Hannah creations, from liver-and-bell-pepper soup to lard butter. Soon Abbie decided they should sing. So Kate put in a bluegrass band CD that Jack had bought after hearing the group perform at an antique expo in Washington State. Abbie loved the CD and cranked the music. They sang loudly to the songs that reminded them of Jack while Kate tried to cast aside thoughts of broken blue tiles and life-changing decisions. For the past three years she'd acted out the role of a normal mother with her thoughts somewhere else. Now Kate determined to focus on the present, on this trip. It would take time to gain back what they'd lost. They needed laughter and smiles with Kate's thoughts and heart fully there. The decision sounded logical, but the battle had begun again.

"Let's listen to that one more time!" Abbie said, smiling as a song ended. She flipped the CD back and they sang even louder.

The miles clicked away. The farther from home Kate drove, the more distance she wanted from the blue tile, an elderly couple who wanted her decision, and even Jack Porter. This trip might provide the right perspective. She was pulled between two worlds. She couldn't survive there for long. Abbie grinned at her while singing a song. Kate knew one path would be chosen and the other forsaken.

Aunt Gerdie's baby blue luggage waited on the front porch. Aunt Hannah was in the garden, tending her plants with pink gardening gloves covering her hands and a wide straw hat covering her head like a mushroom cap. Upon their arrival, she immediately left the garden and hugged them both. Then she began to list all the reasons why travel did not go with old age.

"The last thing I want is hours in a cramped car so I can sleep in a bed that isn't mine. I never sleep well in strange places. And I don't like using the powder room at those rest stops, especially after we cross the California border—you know those California criminals are just waiting to catch someone unprepared. I'll have to bring my pepper spray. I've never understood why Kerby raised all of you in that state—it caused me many hours of worry and prayer."

"Hello, girls," Aunt Gerdie called from the porch, carrying a travel pillow. "Are you ready to hit the road?"

Aunt Hannah sighed long and heavy. "I better pack my liquid fiber."

After a short break in the house with Aunt Hannah trying to convince Abbie to try fig jelly on her scone and last-minute trips to the bathroom, they loaded in the car once again. Aunt Hannah insisted they each wear a straw hat to keep the road glare from their faces. "It's bad for your eyes, and skin cancer is always a worry." Kate knew all four of them looked ridiculous with their wide-brimmed hats. Abbie's kept falling over her eyes as they left Crocker Valley and turned back toward the highway. Aunt Hannah sat in the passenger seat with the large travel pillow tucked around her neck because she got carsick and had neck problems.

Aunt Gerdie, who was reading the *Crocker Valley Post*, leaned forward. "Aunt Hannah, did you know Henry Kronley died?" Kate remembered Jack had always chuckled at the way the sisters called one another "aunt."

"No, I certainly didn't," the older sister said, raising her head from the neck pillow in concern. "What could have happened?"

Aunt Gerdie held the paper in front of her, hitting Kate in the back of the head as she straightened the pages. "'Henry Kronley, age 86, died at his residence after a long illness.' Were you aware that he had a long illness?"

"He certainly looked fine the last time I saw him," Hannah said.

"I thought the same. I wonder what happened."

Kate glanced back at Abbie, who gave her a partial wink of humor. Kate didn't think the aunts had missed one morning of reading the obituaries. Even while out of town, when they wouldn't know the deceased, the aunts read the obits. Kate was sure it was the main reason for their daily newspaper subscription.

"We should send a card to the family." Aunt Gerdie plunked back in her seat. "I could hardly believe what my eyes were telling me. Isn't that such a shame, such a shame?"

"Aunt Gerdie, we're all dying fast at this age." Aunt Hannah tried to turn in her seat with the pillow stuck to her neck. "Abbie dear, your great-great-aunt is having a late-life crisis. You wouldn't know what that is, but it's a pain in the hind end, that's what it is. I've been quite content getting old and enjoying my garden. Now she suddenly wants to do all kinds of strange things."

"Like what?" Kate asked with a smile. She could just see her aunt getting the urge to skydive or something. The image of round Aunt Gerdie flying through the air with her short kinky hair flapping around her face brought a laugh to her lips.

"I'd like to go skydiving," Aunt Gerdie said.

"What?" Kate and Aunt Hannah asked in unison.

"I read about a woman in her seventies who did it and survived. I may be older than that, but why couldn't I?"

"So nice that she survived," Aunt Hannah said in disbelief.

"I've seen photos, and there is usually a handsome young

man strapped to you for safety. That was my favorite part of the idea."

Kate laughed, but Aunt Hannah's frown deepened.

"Or I thought about parasailing or a cruise—something to get me out of Crocker Valley before I end up in the obituaries."

"Aunt Gerdie, what is going on with you?" Kate asked as she left the small winding freeway and entered wide Interstate 5 South.

"She's going through a late-life crisis, I'm telling you." Aunt Hannah crossed her arms over her chest. "She wanted to buy a sports car last week and cruise the coastline with scarves around our heads and Jackie O. sunglasses. The woman is going to break a hip, I just know it. Some old people get Alzheimer's; some just go insane."

"We'll sing 'Born to Be Wild' and look for cute old men," Aunt Gerdie put in.

In the rearview mirror, Kate saw Abbie shaking her head like Aunt Hannah, but with a smile on her face.

"Getting old is for the birds, I tell you. You have to fight it with everything in you," Aunt Gerdie said determinedly.

"I'd rather enjoy my old age," Aunt Hannah said.

"Let me tell you something, young lady." Aunt Gerdie touched Kate's head. "Do all you can in this life. When you wonder what to do and you ask God to answer and he does, then you do it. Don't be some old woman and wish you'd crossed bridges or walked roads that looked scary at the time. Those are the ones with the best destinations. Are you hearing me say this?"

"Yes, Aunt Gerdie. I'm listening." Kate wondered what the words meant to her right now. Was it coincidence that her ancient great-aunt was giving this advice at this time?

"I hope you are listening. Life passes quickly, and we spend our time on a lot of insignificant things. We let fear keep us from some of God's greatest plans."

"Will you leave the poor dear alone?" Aunt Hannah tugged the brim of her hat down a little. "We want to enjoy ourselves, not get a course in life philosophy from an old woman. All us old folks have regrets and lost wishes—it comes with age."

Then they were quiet as they sped down the road with the other vehicles all moving toward their own destinations. Kate wondered if she'd someday be an old woman regretting great parts of her life.

CHAPTER FIFTEEN

By midafternoon Kate was the only one awake. Aunt Hannah expulsed small snorts from her passenger-side perch. Abbie's and Gerdie's faces pressed against pillows on windows in the back. Kate sped down I-5 South, crossing the Oregon-California border, where Aunt Hannah would begin carrying her pepper spray even if there was more wildlife than people in this part of California.

Kate enjoyed having the peace of the road to herself. A highway was a different experience when taking a road trip. The same soft whine sounded in her tires and mileage fell away at the usual pace, yet there was a whisper of excitement that could never be felt when driving on a usual errand or to a short destination. A journey was a blank canvas. Kate wished she and Abbie hadn't set a destination but had allowed the road to lead them. She'd done that once with two girlfriends the summer before their sophomore year of college. They'd packed maps, pillows, and junk food, then flipped a coin at major intersections and ended up in Austin, Texas.

Whenever she left for a trip, Kate would get that same tingle of excitement. She became aware of road noise—rumbling big rigs and the zip of cars. Suddenly she felt owed something— as if people should move aside because her car was spanning distances and claiming a chunk of America beneath its tires.

The enjoyment of the road wore off when her passengers awoke. Aunt Hannah needed the "powder room" every thirty miles from then on. Kate expected the drive from the aunts' house to northern California to take seven hours more or less. But with lunch, a snack, and powder-room stops, it took over ten hours before they descended from the mountains around Shasta Lake to dip into the top end of the Sacramento Valley.

Kate left the highway and drove familiar back roads. The towns of Anderson, Olinda, and Happy Valley were nuzzled in spring green. A line of hazy blue mountains surrounded them on three sides, watching with a lazy gaze toward the inhabitants below. Plateaus and open fields covered in green velvet would soon turn yellow beneath the scorching summer sun. Kate loved the month of May in her hometown, for grass colored the fields and the sky was crisp and clear after a rain. Oaks dotted the edges of fields, with gangly Digger pines clumped along seasonal streams. They followed roads Kate remembered like old friends. She saw the red metal roofs of Cottonwood High and remembered with a bittersweet feeling the graduation that tossed classmates from high school into the world.

"Abbie, that's my old high school."

Her daughter craned her neck to look out the window past Aunt Gerdie. "Is that where you played volleyball?"

"Yes," Kate said, as they passed the large gym.

The school looked new with its fresh paint and trimmed lawns, as if it were still the school she'd attended in the eighties, though improvements and new additions disturbed those memories. How many graduates had passed through those rooms since then? Where had all those people gone? The entire world had been spread before her as she'd sat on those concrete steps with friends, perusing college catalogs and dreaming of who they'd become. She'd felt able to do anything.

Memories flooded her: stubborn tears after breaking up with a guy she'd thought was "forever"; a failed trigonometry test; an argument with her best friend; cutting class and prom preparations; laughter in the hallways; a smashed bumper in her friend's classic Corvette. The years had been a tumult of good and bad as she had begun to shed the skin of youth and tried to imagine college and life as an adult. And here she was in that old play, trying to discover herself again.

"To be young again," Aunt Gerdie said from behind Kate. "I would do everything different."

"Are we near God's Point?" Abbie asked as Kate accelerated and left the school behind.

"How did you know about that?" Kate asked. "Did Grandpa tell you?"

"Yes. He said it's an important place where he once talked to God. He said pretty soon I'd be old enough to go."

"That's just like Grandpa. Look straight ahead at that line of ridge. We'll see it better from Grandma and Grandpa's, but that is where God's Point is located."

Within minutes they were turning down Old Oak Lane. Kate drove slowly up the gravel driveway. The trees in the yard and the small orchard seemed to have grown by feet since her last visit the week before Thanksgiving. Perhaps it was the leaves that gave them more height, or perhaps she hadn't really seen them in a long time.

"I think my hind end has fallen to sleep," Aunt Hannah said as they pulled to a stop.

The flowers bloomed in barrels by the porch and old Walton wagged his tail from his spot on the walkway. Kate had come home.

Kate's mom opened the front door, and her father came in from the corrals.

"Grandpa and Grandma Golden!" Abbie hopped from the car without closing her door.

They bundled into groups, dipping and turning to greet one another. Aunt Gerdie asked, "Were you surprised that we could get Kate to do this?" Aunt Hannah hurried inside to use the bathroom.

Her mother hugged her and said, "Kate, this is wonderful, and for Mother's Day weekend too. Cottonwood is ready with all the usual festivities."

"This will be Abbie's first Cottonwood Parade," Kate said.

"Well, it's about time." Her mother winked and turned to welcome Aunt Gerdie.

Kate felt a tap on her shoulder and turned to meet the face of her father. He put his hands on her shoulders and looked long into her eyes before hugging her. "Let's bring in your goods."

It took several trips before they dumped Kate's luggage into her old room and the aunts' into her brother's.

"Katie, this means a lot," her father said when they finished. She felt instantly guilty for it not being her idea. Now that she was here, it seemed so easy to come, except for Aunt Hannah.

Again her father gazed at her. "It's always good to have you," he said. But in those few words he'd really spoken much more: how much he missed her, how good it was for her to come, that he knew she had something on her mind, and he wanted her to tell him when she was ready.

Dinner and talk filled the evening. They sat on the back porch after dinner, and Kate realized where her love of outdoor evenings originated. Abbie explained all about the Narnian travels they were reading—of Lucy, Edmund, King Caspian, furry Reepicheep the warrior mouse, and the difficult boy named Eustace.

"They just landed at this island, and Eustace was complaining like usual. Do you want to know what happened, or are you going to read the book?"

"Go ahead and tell me," Kate's mother, Paula, said with interest.

"A pirate kidnapped them and put them on a slave ship."

"That's awful," Paula said.

"Mom, can we read some more?"

"The book is under one of the seats in the car. Why don't we read another story tonight?"

Abbie appeared disappointed for a moment, then smiled as if a lightbulb had lit an idea in her head. "Maybe Grandma could read one of her stories. I always like the one about the bread that rises out of the oven and all through the house, and the boy hides in the woods because he thinks he'll be in trouble for trying to make bread on his own."

"Give kisses and let's go find it," Kate's mother said.

Abbie made her rounds and followed Grandma inside the house.

"That girl is a storyteller," Kate's father, Kerby, said.

"She remembers much more than I realized." Then Kate worried—what if Abbie told Kate's mother about the blue tile in the package?

"Kerby?" Aunt Gerdie asked from the doorway with the paper in her hand. "Do you know a Walter Wundermeyer of Anderson? He died yesterday in a motorcycle accident."

"Still reading the obituaries, Gerdie?" he asked with a grin.

"Until I'm in one of them." She pointed a tired finger to the page.

"No, I don't know him."

"He was only sixty-seven. What a shame. At least he was enjoying life when it happened."

"Is she all right?" her father asked as Aunt Gerdie drifted back inside the house.

"Aunt Hannah says it's a late-life crisis."

"A few days away from Crocker Valley will help—it'll give her something new to share with the ladies at the library."

A chorus of crickets sounded from the thicket of flower beds and trees in the backyard. Somewhere a dog barked and a bug light zapped. Soft yellow faded to gray to black from the horizon to the top of the sky.

"It's beautiful this time of year. I could never fully enjoy spring because I knew the heat was coming soon to destroy the green hillsides," Kate said. "I wish it could stay this way."

Her father took a sip of coffee, thinking about her words. "Sometimes the best things don't last very long. If we had flowers and green every season, we wouldn't see their value."

Kate nodded. They were words well spoken, though she wished it wasn't so.

Night fell around them and they moved inside. Kate settled into her old spot on the couch with her feet on the coffee table and watched her father's favorite show on the History Network.

Only her childhood home could help her make her decision, Kate suddenly believed. Yet there was something more to gain. She didn't know what it was, but she was glad she'd come.

CHAPTER SIXTEEN

Except for the aunts, they all left early to park her dad's old truck along the parade route. Hannah was road weary, and Gerdie wanted to walk over and visit a "cute, old widower," as she called him, who lived down the street.

Kate, Abbie, and Kate's folks ate breakfast at the little restaurant on Front Street. The country-style eatery was crowded with costumed kids and adults. After omelets, hash browns, and Abbie's silver-dollar pancakes, they paid seventy-five cents at the Little League stand for steaming cocoa and carried the Styrofoam cups back to the truck.

The Cottonwood Parade brought the whole town to the streets. Abbie set up her lawn chair along the curb next to Grandma's and Grandpa's, while Kate sat on the tailgate. They waited for movement down the street—Abbie and Grandpa planning how she should ride his horse in the parade next year. An idea formed in Kate's mind as she watched them talk. *What would it be like to move back?*

In her childhood Kate had loved to roam the fields and wide, shallow waters of Cottonwood Creek. But as a teen she couldn't wait to leave small-town living behind. In college her visits had brought contempt for rural life and ways. But today she wanted it back. She wanted to bank, grocery shop, and grab an ice cream within a mile of each other. She wanted to take walks along the country roads of her youth and have Abbie attend her old schools. As if she had discovered a beloved childhood toy that had been stuffed away and forgotten, Kate knew she loved this place.

Looking around, Kate saw people she remembered along the parade route and at the different booths. Mother's Day weekend in Cottonwood was when families dusted off their cowboy hats, whether worn only once a year or daily. The Thursday kickoff barbecue started the four-day event with the Rodeo Queen being announced. Two days of rodeo and community activities brought together locals and tourists alike.

"There's something to be said for putting down roots," Kate whispered.

"Kate Bait!" Tayler, her brother, rounded her father's old Ford with two chairs in his hands. He tossed them in the back of the truck and grabbed her in a tight hug, kissing the top of her head. "It's about time you came for a visit."

"I had an old aunt practically drag me here," she said.

"Yeah, so I hear. That makes us feel good. I knew you should never have gone to Oregon for college—we could never get you back."

Kate punched him lightly on the arm. "Where's your wife?"

"Sarah's with Reece on the kindergarten float. Gotta keep those kids from falling off."

"That would be a good idea," she said with a laugh.

From down the street a marching band began to play. People young and old strained from the backs of trucks and along the streets for the first view of the Cottonwood Jr. High band that opened the parade every year.

"It takes you back, doesn't it?" Tayler said as they climbed in the back of their father's truck. He set up the rusty lawn chairs for them.

Kate noticed the soft lines that formed around his eyes as he squinted against the morning sun. Her brother had her father's looks—strong jaw and cheekbones, gray eyes, and sandy brown hair. His thirties had broadened his shoulders, finally making him look like a man and not the tall, thin kid he'd appeared for years.

The band came into view, and the flutes played a refrain before the rest joined in.

"There you were," Tayler said, pointing to the clarinet section. "Remember those shiny braces that would cut your lips?"

"Well, at least I didn't have to wear headgear at night like someone I know."

"At least I didn't—"

"Are you two being good up there?" Paula Golden was giving them "the look" from her perch below.

"Sorry, Mom," they said while elbowing each other. They were twelve and fourteen for a moment again.

"Did we have many dreams as kids?" she asked. A horse-drawn carriage carted a family of clowns past them.

"We didn't have great aspirations, but we sure had fun and great imaginations, if I do say so myself. With Mom reading so many classics and all that poetry to us, we didn't have much choice. Remember playing Moby Dick after lightning downed that oak in the front pasture?"

"I forgot about that," she said, laughing at the image of a young Tayler jabbing homemade spears into the tree trunk as if it were the whale. "Remember when we dug out that cave and used the dry creek bed for *Journey to the Center of the Earth*? We always had to play your favorite stories like *Captains Courageous* or *The Time Machine*."

"There was no way I'd let you hoist me up a tree as Peter Pan. I wasn't that stupid."

"Here come Reece and Sarah!" her mother called.

They both stood up and waved. Tayler and Sarah's son, Reece, wore a painted, cardboard pig snout and ears. He waved wildly at Abbie when he spotted her. Sarah was busy watching children and sent only a quick smile and wave when she heard their calls.

"Hey, pretty lady!" Tayler shouted, and Sarah blew him a kiss.

Kate smiled, happy his voice betrayed none of the strain of the last several years after Sarah's miscarriages and failed pregnancy attempts. Her brother did well on the small ranch he had always wanted, where he could watch things grow and the seasons change. But the difficulty of a marriage surrounded by grief and frustration had been his greatest challenge. Kate knew her brother struggled with not helping her more after Jack's disappearance. Tayler wanted to fix the world, but he couldn't mend his wife or his sister.

"Have I told you that I love you, big brother?" she said lightly, with her arm flung over his shoulder. Her lawn chair tipped and creaked beneath her.

Tayler's face was serious when he turned toward her. "Thank you, Sis. I love you too."

The afternoon brought Tayler, Sarah, and Reece to the Golden home for a family gathering. Kate's mother made stew and bread-machine sourdough while the other adults watched the kids on the swing set. With Kate's worries over Abbie's lack of friends, it was good to see Abbie run and play with Reece like any normal child. After a late lunch, Tayler pulled a box of old kites from the garage rafters. Everyone went to work rigging up a workable kite. The afternoon turned cool with slight breezes carrying high white clouds overhead. Soon colorful diamonds reached to touch the cottony sky.

Kate watched from outside the front pasture fence. Her

jacket sleeves covered the sharp barbs as she leaned against it. She'd felt detached from everyone for so long. Now she paused to watch her family. Life had continued on in spite of her three frozen years. Her nephew had grown taller and lived without memories of Uncle Jack. The seasons had passed over her hometown and the lives of the people in it. Her old dog had aged, and her father's horses now needed dental work.

While the world moved on, Kate had been stuck as if she'd fallen in some ancient bog with mud sucking her down. She wanted out, wanted to run, but always the questions, the hope that was dashed again and again, the faith that didn't conquer all—these things grabbed at her progress. A woman who'd spoken about losing a child had described it well: "You can't do anything. If I made a goal to do my dishes in a day and I actually did it, then I felt proud of myself. I was unable to pull myself out."

Kate watched bandaged kites flutter into the sky. Abbie ran with her hand clutching the string behind her, but her kite skidded and scraped the ground. All able hands were busy with their own clusters of bobbing kites.

She bent through the barbed-wire fence and jogged across the freshly cut field, feeling her hair bounce lightly onto her shoulders. Abbie was now tangled in the string. Kate's hands reached for Abbie just as Abbie's small shoulders slumped in defeat.

"Do you know how many times the Wright brothers tried to fly before they ever left the ground?"

"How many?"

"Oh, sure, ask for the exact facts." Kate cupped her daughter's chin. "I don't know, but they had to try a lot. And they needed each other to do it."

"Will you help me?" It was strange to hear her daughter ask such a basic question and seem unsure of the answer.

"Of course. I used to be a pretty good kite flyer in my day."

"Okay." Abbie's voice rose an octave. "Do you want string or tail? That's what Grandpa says."

"Whatever you don't want."

"I'll take the tail and run. You hold the string, okay?"

"I'm ready."

Abbie adjusted the red-and-white kite she'd covered with flower stickers and patched with silver duct tape. Then they ran.

The little kite fluttered and bobbed as Abbie let it go, climbing higher and higher. Kate let out the line, gauging the height and wind current. Abbie ran and jumped beneath the kite as if she could suddenly fly up and catch it. Above a field where they stepped over horse dung, the little kites, dipping and soaring, colored the sky. They worked hard to keep flying, to get higher into that sky.

Kate remembered that once she could fly. There had been a young girl not so long ago who carried a sheet onto the roof of her house on a very windy day. Tayler had mocked her idea, which only spurred her determination. Their mother was gone to town for an hour and the wind was right. A gust filled the sheet, then died away. From his perch in the mulberry tree, Tayler said she was crazy. She ignored him and concentrated. The trees began a soft swirl, then harder—the sheet billowed. She jumped. And hit the ground.

But she'd believe in flight again when the wind whipped hard against her face, bringing the hope of a time when she'd certainly soar. Little kites tied to the earth by a string but flying with all their might.

It's not over for me. I can still fly. In that moment she again believed in human flight.

Then the wind died down. *So much for wings,* Kate thought as the kites bobbed, struggled, and finally tumbled to the ground. It seemed that just as she'd made a breakthrough, God pushed her right back down.

"This is the best Mother's Day I've had since you and Tayler lived at home," Kate's mother said as they walked in from the field. "Remember this? 'Come to me, O ye children! And whisper in my ear, what the birds and the winds are singing in your sunny atmosphere. For what are all our contrivings, and the wisdom of our books, when compared with your caresses, and the gladness of your looks? Ye are better than all the ballads that ever were sung or said; for—'" she turned and put her arms out like a conductor and all the adults finished with her—"'for ye are living poems, and all the rest are dead.'"

"Longfellow," Tayler said. The children gazed in surprise. "Longfellow is Grandma's favorite poet, and that poem is the most recited one, as you can tell."

They began discussing different poets, but Kate felt the words of Longfellow's poem walk with her. She'd forgotten about that—how her mother would call her and Tayler "my living poems." Kate had called Abbie that as an infant. But she'd forgotten.

Kate worked daily among furniture and objects old and dead. Here was a life before her, not in need of restoration, but fresh and new and filled with the life only a child possessed. Kate watched her daughter run with Reece, their kites in hand. She realized in that moment how deeply she loved her child. The frozen places of her heart thawed, and she loved with a wonder she'd forgotten.

"Abbie!" she called. "Would you like to see my secret tree?"

"Can Reece come too?"

"Why don't we take Reece a little later and just you and I go?"

"All right."

The others went inside for hot cocoa. Kate touched the top of her daughter's honey hair that had turned stringy and smelled of wind. They walked hand in hand down the road along the side of the house, past the horse corrals and across a wild field.

"You have a secret tree?" Abbie asked.

"It's not such a secret anymore. I used to climb into the highest branches and watch Tayler come try to scare me. He couldn't find me until I started laughing. It's over there in that grove of oaks."

An overgrown path meandered through the green field toward a stand of wide, old oaks that had once been Kate's secret wonderland. The thicket of many-leafed branches kept the green grass from turning brown and was a place she could always find shade from the summer heat. There were at least twenty trees in the grove, with massive and moss-covered trunks decaying on the ground. Tayler and Kate had imagined the trees were felled by a tribe of Native Americans who surely had loved this place as much as they did. Silence was strong within the ring of trees, as if even the birds and insects knew this was a magical place. It smelled of moss and decaying wood and leaves.

"This looks like the Wood Between Worlds."

Kate smiled, realizing how much her daughter remembered from their readings of the Narnia Chronicles and also how true her observation was.

"I never thought of that. If there were pools of water beneath the trees, we could hop into them and try to reach another world."

"Don't you wish we could?" Abbie's eyes sparkled with imagination as she tipped her head toward the umbrella of branches and leaves overhead. "We could pop in and out of different worlds and maybe somewhere we'd find Daddy."

Somehow Kate had guessed Abbie was thinking of her father before she spoke his name. "Where do you think Daddy is?" Kate stopped at a downed log and sat down.

"I don't know." But Abbie said it in a way that made Kate wonder.

"Please tell me. I won't laugh at your thoughts."

The sun shone in soft patches through the overhead branches like light through stained glass.

Finally Abbie spoke. "In kindergarten, I told my friends Daddy was on a special mission that only very important people do. The kids believed me, and I believed it too. But now the kids at school don't believe it anymore. They say Daddy left us like Jeffrey's father. One boy said maybe you killed him and put him in a box in the ocean."

Kate tried not to react outwardly. "And what did you say?"

"I told him he watched too much TV."

They both smiled.

"I've thought of lots of reasons why he hasn't come back. What if he was shipwrecked on a deserted island like on *Swiss Family Robinson?* Or what if he discovered something really bad, and the bad guys aren't letting him go because of it. I wrote down thirty-one things that could have happened in my diary. When I grow up, I'm going to go look for him. And I don't think you should give up either."

Kate wondered what to say to that, though this time she wasn't worried. She knew they were making progress—Abbie's confession was proof. Maybe with their shared honesty they might find peace over the loss of Jack someday.

"Abbie, I'm glad you told me that. We'll stick close together from now on and tell each other what we feel. I know we're going to be all right."

When Abbie's hand reached for hers, Kate knew they'd made a promise. They stood and Kate wound through the grove, holding Abbie's hand and stepping over branches. Finally she stopped.

"This was my tree. I'd climb up there and feel bigger than

the world. Sometimes I'd bring my book; other times I'd sit there to think and escape my brother."

The wooden boards she'd nailed into the trunk were loose and some missing. Kate estimated the tree must be over forty feet tall, though it had seemed even taller as a young girl. The thick branches forked heavenward. She could see the remnant of one of her "rooms"—a scrap of plywood her father had given her when he built the saddle shed.

"Can we climb up?" Abbie asked excitedly.

"I'm not sure, but let's try."

Kate tested a board and it popped from the rough bark. Abbie laughed as it flung her backwards.

"Guess we'll try another way."

Kate tried boosting Abbie up, but then an old rope remnant unwound and broke. It looked impossible until Kate saw a fallen log with spiked branches poking out. Together they dragged and hoisted the log up against the bark. Kate scratched her legs and arms, climbing and helping Abbie until they made it. Once in the tree they climbed higher and settled in a branch intersection.

"We did it, Mom!"

They laughed together at the memory made and then gazed through the other branches toward Kate's old home, the fields, and fences. They spied old Walton, tail wagging, walking slowly toward the front porch and the horses eating new grass in the side field.

"From here you can see that ridge." Kate pointed to the long crest of a hillside that Cottonwood Creek had cut. "That's God's Point."

"Oh," she gasped. "Why did Grandpa first go there?"

"Well, his mother died in a car accident. She had prayed for him for many years, and he was feeling very sad about losing her. So he climbed up there and decided to wait until God talked to him."

"Did God talk to him?"

"Grandpa said God came in a soft, gentle breeze, and the words were spoken on his heart."

"What did God say?"

"He said, 'I am with you always, even to the end of the age.' "

"Wow. I want to go up there someday."

"When you're a little bigger."

"I can't wait to grow up."

Abbie's words surprised Kate, as they sat on different branches above her childhood grounds.

"Enjoy your childhood, Abbie. Don't spend too much time looking forward, because we adults spend quite a lot of time looking back. We need to enjoy the season we're in." She paused, considering her own words. "I think I'm beginning to learn that lesson after many lost years."

They sat in the tree, with Kate shifting now and then, realizing that branches weren't as comfortable for adults as for children. She told Abbie some of her old adventures in the grove and wondered why she'd never shared them before.

"Didn't you and Uncle Tayler have a secret treasure spot?"

"How do you know so much?"

"Grandma and Grandpa e-mail me."

Kate laughed at the idea. As a child in this tree, could she have ever imagined such a thing as e-mail and that her parents would be doing such a thing with her child?

"Yes, yes, we had a secret treasure spot. Instead of buried gold and jewels, we put our own treasures inside."

"Like what?"

"Let me remember—I had my favorite fake pearl beads, a feather I found that I was sure had come from a bald eagle, a postcard from Hawaii when the aunts went there, a silver dollar my grandfather gave me. What else?" Kate tried to envision the metal box they had painted gold and their ceremonial placing of treasures inside. "Tayler put a four-leaf clover that he pressed, a bunch of his favorite rocks which made the chest—as we called it—really heavy, and some other things like that. But after the first time we buried it, we'd dig it up all the time, put new things in, and take other stuff out. I needed those pearls for a slumber party."

"I can understand that," Abbie said in a grown-up voice that caused her to giggle at herself.

"We even made a map from a brown paper bag and burned the edges to give it that old look. Maybe we should do that for you at home."

"Is your treasure still there?"

"I don't think so. We'd move it around for a while until we found a hollow tree trunk to hide it in. But I seem to remember Tayler digging it up when he was home from college."

"Can we look? Please?"

Kate looked at the shadowed woods below and wondered if the treasure could really be down there somewhere.

"I guess we could—if we can get out of this tree." The climb down was harder than the climb up. When they finally reached the ground, the soft light from the overcast sky had fallen a shade darker. But it had been well worth the scratches and work to make the climb. Kate couldn't remember the last time she'd sat above the world in the arms of a tree. It should be mandatory for all adults—to remind them of the simplicity of childhood.

"We better hurry." Kate brushed bark from her hair. "My stomach is hungry, and night comes quickly within the grove."

"Where to?" Abbie asked like an adventurer on a quest.

"This way!"

Off they ran among trunks and fallen logs down a small slope to a giant tangle of roots that rose high above them with the giant tree stretched out in eternal slumber.

"We had a bad storm once when I was a little older than

you. This was the tallest tree in the grove then, its massive branches reaching above all the others. After the storm, Tayler noticed the branches weren't there. It was top-heavy and that storm had tumbled it right over, ripping the roots from the ground and leaving this pit at its base. We were sad about the tree; it was so beautiful. But it made a great place to play and hide treasure. I'm sure our treasure box is gone by now."

They hopped into the pit, now not as deep of a crevice because of years of leaves and decay. Kate couldn't see inside the tangle of roots. She reached her hand into the cavity with great care, afraid of what she'd feel. Her fingers touched something cold and metal.

"It's here," Kate said in surprise.

"It is?" Abbie's face shone with excitement.

Dirt and wood showered her arm as Kate pulled out the old metal box. They climbed out of the pit and set the box on a tree stump. The chest was rusted through on one corner, dirty from years in and out of the ground, with most of the gold paint worn off and the original silver metal showing through.

Kate was hesitant to open it. Once Tayler had hidden a pack of cigarettes in there when he was twelve. She didn't know what else was later hidden there during high school, since she had stopped coming to the grove by then. The lid creaked open and Kate tried to make a quick assessment, but Abbie was just as quick. Instead of old cigarettes, she found candy wrappers with tiny holes eaten through and some plastic toys.

"Look, a Tootsie Roll wrapper." Abbie held it up, but nothing was left inside.

"This is strange," Kate said as they carefully went through the contents that reminded her of the inside of a piñata instead of her old treasure box.

"Mom, this has my name on it," Abbie said, holding a yellowed envelope.

"Let me see that." Kate knew the handwriting even though the last letters in *Abigail Rose* were water damaged.

They were words from the past.

"Can I open it?"

Kate hesitated too long—Abbie was already lifting the tab with careful strokes.

"There's money and a note!" She showed Kate a ten-dollar bill and then handed Kate the note. "Mom, will you read it?"

Kate took the worn paper from her hand. She read it and read it again.

"Out loud, Mom."

> *"Surprise, Abbie. Here is some spending money while we are gone. Grandpa really likes Rocky Road ice cream so maybe you could treat him. Mommy and I will miss you while we're in Italy, but it won't be long until we return. I want you to always know how much your mom and I love you. We'll bring you back a surprise—it will be better than that huckleberry bubble bath I bought you in Montana. Oh, that smelled! We'll have to put some in Mom's bathwater because of that evil cold-water trick she pulled. I love you more than string cheese."*

Abbie and Kate stared at one another as if they had truly heard Jack's voice.

"I remember that, the 'I love you more than string cheese,'" Abbie said in a whisper. "Daddy told me to try string cheese when I was a little girl, and I didn't want to. He said that he loved string cheese, and I asked if he loved it more than me."

Kate nodded, staring again at the letter in her hand.

"Mom, God does answer," Abbie said softly. "Remember we prayed? Now we get a letter from Daddy."

"It just doesn't work that way," Kate said in shock, shaking her head. "This must be a mistake. We need to find Uncle Tayler."

He had found something. Lukas went through the papers again to confirm what he'd already read. The same facts remained on the page.

It was deep night—later than he wanted to know. He sat in Karl's study and stared at the packet of documents he'd discovered stuffed in the back of a file cabinet.

Lukas and Marta had left Portland right after their talk with Kate. And, though the call of home tugged heavily at him, he'd returned to Arizona for a few more days to help Marta. Again Lukas had gone through the files and papers in case he'd missed anything on Wolfram Meizer. It had taken Lukas a long time, for Karl's study was unorganized and filled with fishing, golfing, and community magazines that he'd saved for years—Lukas had located a stack from the eighties. Karl seemed to collect papers, canceled checks, payment receipts, comic strips, and e-mail funnies.

Then Lukas had found the white, oversized envelope.

Now he knew that Karl had had more information than he

originally revealed. Not only that, but Karl appeared to be involved in areas that cast the light of suspicion directly at him. Did Marta know about this? Lukas believed they'd shared everything. Perhaps she wasn't as trustworthy as he had assumed.

He rubbed his eyes and glanced at his watch, inwardly groaning at the time. He must be reading the documents wrong. The late hour caused his mind to work sluggishly, and stress fought against him. Yet there was the proof before him. Lukas glanced toward the open doorway. Down the hall, in the room she'd shared with Karl for years, Marta now slept. Did she know, or was this a secret kept from her also? He wanted to wake her and ask at that moment. But first, he must rest. He'd need sleep and strength before confronting her in the morning. If the words were correct, Karl seemed involved not only in Wolfram's work but also in the disappearance of Jack Porter.

Lukas would wait until morning.

◆━◉⊂━◆

Tayler held the paper. His mouth twisted downward in what Kate knew was worry.

"I remember this." He nodded as the memory returned. "Jack helped me prepare the treasure box for a kind of cousins' fun night. We were going to do it while you and he were gone. Jack was worried about Abbie being left for that long. We put candy and toys in there, and Sarah and I were going to lead a scavenger hunt. I think you, Sarah, and Mom had gone to Chico that day—yeah, that was where you were because Sarah bought . . . that doesn't matter. But I remember now he put a note inside the box."

"How could you forget this?" Kate tried not to blame him, but her hands still shook from the shock of seeing Jack so alive on the page.

"It was one of many kid things we'd planned, like a three-legged race and stuff Mom was working on. You and Jack had made those envelopes for Abbie to read each morning of your trip. Remember?"

Kate remembered. They'd stayed up late the night before their drive to Cottonwood. They were delirious to the point of laughter after packing, and Kate had heard of this great idea of a daily letter. Jack had drawn a smiley face on each of her fingertips in the process of trying to write the notes. Their laughter and pranks made the process twice as long. But she remembered the letters:

Day One—We fly from California to Italy today. Draw us a picture and we'll bring you home some airplane wings.

Day Two—When you wake up, it will be nighttime for us on our first day in Venice. We'll miss you.

Kate knew this was as far as the notes had been opened. After Jack's disappearance, her parents had flown to Italy after getting emergency passports and were with her for a week. Abbie stayed behind with Tayler and Sarah. Kate wanted to be the one to tell Abbie what had happened, but she didn't want her expecting to see both her parents get off the airplane, only to be shocked by the news. So with Sarah's help Tayler had done his best to explain. But it wasn't until Kate arrived back in Corvalis alone that all of them felt the reality. The memory of Abbie's face, so pale and solemn when they first saw one another, was a stark contrast to the rosy-cheeked excitement she now wore as she talked in the other room with Grandma.

Kate took the note from Tayler and set it on the kitchen counter. The rest of the family discussed in hushed voices in the living room. She sought Jack's words again and again. They seemed the words of a man who loved his daughter and looked forward to returning. But what was certain anymore? If he'd only given the slightest clue—something like, "Abbie, I have to go away for a few years, but I promise to return. Don't give up." Or "God's work is nearly done for me, but we will be together someday." Even, "Abbie, I love you but I still must leave. I'm very sorry, but I won't be back." The worst possibilities were better than silence.

"I need to get Abbie to sleep," Kate said. "She's sure this is an answer to her prayers."

"Kate," Tayler said with his hand on her arm, "maybe it is."

"How can you say something like that?" Anger spread through Kate.

Her sister-in-law glanced up.

"Let's go outside," Tayler said, taking Kate's arm. He opened the sliding-glass door, and the cool of night touched her face. "Mom will get Abbie to sleep and give good words of wisdom."

Kate hesitated, but her mother had heard Tayler and nodded for her to follow him. Kate closed the door behind her and waited for her eyes to adjust to the darkness.

"I once knew all these constellations," Tayler said as they leaned against the porch railing. It was an expected move of her brother's to divert them from the subject at hand.

"I don't fall for your tricks any longer, Brother. And besides, you never knew any constellations besides the Big and Little Dippers, except for the ones you made up."

"And I've forgotten all the ones I made up," he said. Then he turned to her. "I don't know how to help you, Kate. I can't bail you out. This is strange for me to say, since we never were good at talking about spiritual stuff. But I know that God is still with you and Abbie. I think you'll be able to see that someday."

"One part of me believes that. I only wish I could see it now."

"I'm not through with my questions for the Big Guy—questions like, why can't Sarah and I have more children? Or why were *we* born in American luxury while another man lives his life in poverty? Things like that. I have just begun to see that God's love is greater than I can imagine and his ways are a mystery. I guess I should focus on God's and my relationship and not on all his dealings with the whole world. But enough of my musings. . . . To find this letter now, after so much time has passed . . . I don't know what to think. But maybe God is doing something in your life. . . . Oh, what does a rancher from Cottonwood know?"

"A lot, I would say."

"Really? Because I've wanted to ask you . . ." Tayler pulled up a metal love seat with vinyl cushions, the legs scraping across the wooden deck. He sat down and his face fell into the shadows. "Kate, did something happen?"

His question threw her off balance—from stars and God to this sudden directness. "What do you mean?"

"You tell me. I've noticed something different in you. I mean, of course you've been changed since Jack disappeared, but on this visit, there's something else. I asked Dad about it, and he said you'd tell us when you were ready." Tayler scooted over so Kate could join him. Both propped their feet upon the railing. "Or are my musings getting the best of me?"

Kate weighed what it meant to tell Tayler about the blue tile fragment and her meeting with Lukas and Marta. Telling required accountability. If she chose to get involved, her family would worry. If she chose to put the past behind, the fewer people who knew she'd passed up this opportunity, the better. She stared at the sky, but it gave no answer. It only sparkled with myriad stars in the night, unchanged by earth's problems.

Then she made a sudden decision. "Something happened. A few weeks ago I decided to put Jack behind Abbie and me and start a new life—or try to. Being here has made me consider coming home."

"Now I see why Jack's letter would upset you so much."

"That's not all of it. Less than a week ago I discovered new information that could change . . . well, I'll just say it. I found a blue tile—like the one I found in Venice."

Tayler's legs dropped from the railing and he sat up. "You found a blue tile—where?"

"In my house. It was mailed to me. And the people who mailed it contacted me right before I left for this trip."

"Kate, start at the beginning and tell me everything."

A pebble, even the smallest, dropped into a lake could not hide the ripples that spread and widened across the smooth surface. Tayler insisted that Kate tell the story to their parents and Sarah. Kate was at least relieved to have the aunties and Abbie already asleep. She told of finding the tile, of meeting Lukas and Marta, and then felt the impact of the story as if she'd been whisked away from a catastrophe. Seeing it now from a distance, she realized further the magnitude of what had happened by the reactions of the others. It seemed like a fantasy as they sat in her old living room and discussed a group of Resistance fighters who carried fragments of a broken antique tile.

"And you've kept this to yourself? Abbie too?" Her mother asked.

"I'm surprised she kept the secret—and a little concerned. Abbie thought she'd done something wrong by opening the package and putting the tile on my pillow. And I didn't want to tell anyone because it seemed futile to cause worry at this point."

"You need us more than you know," her father said, and Kate instantly recognized the truth.

They talked and strategized with coffee cups filled and refilled into the late hours. Her father led prayer several times for direction. Kate wanted answers, then and there, but there were none. No one told her what to do, though she knew they would support her decision.

"I see what this weekend at home is all about," her father said. "It's about coming home."

Kate turned to her father, expecting to see a smile and hear about her moving home so they could help more.

Her father's face was unwavering in its intensity as he spoke. "Sometimes a person needs to come home to face the world again. I don't mean Cottonwood. There's a place within us where we find who we really are and who made us. Once you've come home, then you can do what God put you here to do. We want our own path, and we tend to look over at the plans of others to make our list of wants. But God's path is the one to follow. It's going to be rocky and hard, Kate. But it's worth the destination."

Her father's words were many for him. And they were truth. Two roads stretched before her, and Kate stood at the fork—unsure, taking one step down, then back-stepping quickly.

"What is God telling you?" her father asked.

"I don't know. I can't hear him."

"He will answer if you really listen. And I know where you can find him."

Lukas had not fallen asleep until the time he usually awoke. The smell of bacon and coffee had stirred him from slumber. He now leaned over the breakfast Marta had made—bacon, crepes, fruit—and wondered how to talk to her.

His fork scraped the plate loudly as he cut the crepe. The bacon was cooked exactly the way he liked it—a little crispy but not burned. Marta refilled his coffee cup and he thanked her.

"What is it?" she asked, sitting down across the table with her own breakfast.

This was his opportunity. "Nothing," he said.

"Did you sleep well?"

"Fine." He took a bite of bacon with his eyes on his plate.

"Are you feeling all right?"

"Yes." He gulped down his coffee.

"Then what is it? What's wrong?"

Lukas left the room and returned to drop the white packet on the table. "I found this."

Marta paused a second before taking another bite of food.

"Do you know what this is?"

"Yes," she said.

"Then you lied to me."

"No, I didn't—and neither did Karl. This was not relevant to our search."

"How can you say this is not relevant or that you did not lie? For one, you and Karl told me you had not been back to Austria."

"I said that *I* had not been back. Karl went and I stayed behind."

"Explain this to me now," his voice boomed.

"Calm down and I will," she said, her voice rising in a challenge.

Lukas held his tongue and settled back in his chair. They stared one another down with him losing. Her hands were shaking more than usual, and he felt sick at the thought that she'd known about the packet and hadn't told him. He wondered if it was truth she'd now speak.

"You know what is inside then," she said, tapping the envelope. "I will make it simple if that is possible. Karl believed he knew what Wolfram was seeking—an area where the Nazis had hidden something. He did not know the exact location since there were three possibilities. He also did not know what was hidden. I believe this began in 1994, but all the years blur together anymore.

"Karl never told me the exact details. But he found someone who knew Wolfram in South America—the wife of an exiled Nazi. Her husband was approached by Wolfram about a partnership. They had made other business ventures together. Then he died. She believed Wolfram poisoned him and collected the profits from their companies—she was shocked to discover she was not a beneficiary. But she was smart in one way—she made copies of all her husband's dealings without him knowing it. When Karl returned from Argentina, he came back with the information in that packet."

"Why would this woman give Karl the maps and German documents?"

Karl paid for this information. "It took a substantial portion of our savings and retirement. The woman wasn't married to an exiled Nazi for nothing—she knew how to get what she needed. After Karl obtained the map of the three locations, he contacted a diving specialist, an expert who had done underwater discoveries of ships and airplanes, things such as that. They were going over the three areas where we believed Wolfram was attempting to return."

"Was Karl trying to find Wolfram or this hidden stash?"

"He wanted both. I know what you are thinking—that we were in search of lost Nazi gold. You should know we were not interested in wealth. Other than gold, there is Nazi technology and records of companies that collaborated with them that have never been recovered. There are also hopes that documents will still be found giving families proof of their stolen artwork, bank accounts, and land holdings. You know the Nazis' attention to paperwork. They were almost fanatical about accurate information."

"Yes, I know."

She paused, apparently realizing her mistake. Of course Lukas knew, because once he himself had been a Nazi.

He spoke before she fully recovered. "Karl could have joined a Holocaust group to recover this lost information. Do you believe it is some of the lost Jewish treasure?"

"That is what we have assumed. But Karl could not join another group because of Wolfram. A major expedition could not be kept secret. Wolfram would disappear again. Karl's first goal was to find Wolfram. Karl believed that if we found Wolfram first, then we would hand over any information we found to the proper authorities."

"What happened after he met with this diver?"

"Karl came home for the winter. He kept in contact with the diver—his name was Rudy Blessing. Then in late winter, Karl could not reach him. He tried to e-mail again and again and phone him. Karl finally went to find him, but Rudy had disappeared months earlier. Karl found another piece of blue tile at Rudy's residence."

Lukas wanted to believe this and the pieces of tile fit together. "So that is how Jack Porter comes into this," he said in deep thought.

"What do you mean?"

"Rudy Blessing and Jack Porter worked together in 1989 in the Mediterranean. It is in these papers. Jack Porter worked on a dive to a ship that Blessing discovered."

"I did not know that." Marta paused, thinking. "But this explains why Karl sent Kate Porter the tile. After Rudy Blessing's disappearance, Karl shut down the search because he felt responsible for the man's death—we, of course, assumed that Rudy died as one of Wolfram's victims. Karl felt terrible and would rarely talk to me about it. He had really liked the man. It was the last straw for him. A few years later, everything changed. Karl wanted to start the search again. Now that I see the dates, that was the time when Jack Porter disappeared. And Karl must have wanted to help Kate because he felt responsible for her husband's death just as he did for Rudy."

"Supposed death. We do not know for certain."

"Well, yes, I guess that is correct. I have wondered about the Kate Porter factor and did not know the link. I believed Karl was helping someone linked to Wolfram, though I thought it strange—sometimes a wife from the old ways does not feel right asking everything. Now I understand. Karl was tortured over what happened. And that is why he called the reunion together. He had given up the search for Wolfram until Jack Porter. Then Karl said to me, 'How many lives will it take?'

Right after that we started searching for Wolfram again. He knew Wolfram had to be stopped."

"And he soon knew he needed us to help," Lukas said.

"Yes," she said softly.

"You should have told me earlier."

"It did not change the facts. You already had the map of the three locations, and you basically had the information, except—"

"You should have told me."

She nodded and placed her hand over his. "I am sorry. You know everything now."

Lukas turned his hand over and wrapped his fingers through hers. He was surprised by the great relief he felt at her touch and her words. Her face softened, though even in her anger he thought she was beautiful in a way only age and grace could be. Lukas didn't allow himself dependence on people, but he was getting very comfortable with Marta to the point of need. Enjoyment and fear were equal partners. But with the coming battle and after Karl's recent death, Lukas knew he was risking more than he should.

CHAPTER NINETEEN

Kate couldn't sleep. The clock read 4 A.M. She still had hours before they piled into the car and headed north, enduring the inevitable powder-room stops. She needed rest for the journey, but it would not come.

Kate rolled over carefully, not wanting to awaken Abbie on the other side of the double bed. In the night-light's glow, she could see the keys to her father's 1947 Willys jeep. He'd given them to her before bed. She knew what he was suggesting. Her family could give their opinions and advice, but only God could give a true direction. Her father knew where to meet him—God's Point.

Throughout the night Kate had wrestled with the thought of meeting God on the mountain. What if he wasn't to be found the way her father had found him there? Even more frightening, what if God actually *was* there, waiting?

Snatches of sleep carried dreams she couldn't remember and allowed little rest. Finally, she gave in and got dressed. There was a morning chill as the horizon grew light. She grabbed her father's jacket from the coat hook in the hallway and her mother's knit gloves, knowing it would be even colder on the ridge. The jeep took a few tries before it rumbled to life. She turned on the heater, knowing the old jeep would take half the drive to start warming up.

Kate turned down the driveway with the canvas top flapping in the wind. Kerby Golden now made the journey to the ridge an annual event. He'd make a day of it, sometimes bringing Kate's mom or anyone who wanted to go. When each of his children turned fourteen, he brought them there. They sat on an outcropping of rocks, gazing across the view of country and mountains all the way to portions of civilization. When Kate's turn had come, they'd gone in the evening. There her father had told her, in his few words, how much God meant to him and how man couldn't find true peace without a right relationship with the Creator. Kate had believed it then, though it was her only trip to God's Point. It seemed simple and clear up there above the world. Life wasn't so simple now.

She drove the paved road until it turned to gravel, then across a dirt road that cut through an alfalfa field.

Her father's annual pilgrimage had begun on the day after his mother's funeral. He was a young man then, newly married, with a baby on the way. He had been close to his mother. She had prayed for him for years. She'd spent a long time telling him about the peace only God could give and how life could not fulfill him without the love of Christ. As much as he had loved and respected her, he didn't need God. He didn't even know if he believed in one. His life was great as it was and much too busy to seek matters of philosophy. Days before she was hit by a car while walking along a country road, his mother had said the words that would haunt him. "Whatever it takes, I hope you find God. Life is meaningless without him." In his grief, he'd climbed the ridge of mountains and found the place he'd later call God's Point.

The road turned downward into the creek bed. An echo resounded up the canyon as tires clattered against creek rock. Kate sought the place where the river ran wide and shallow. She leaned over the steering wheel, making sure the winter rains had tapered off enough to cross. Dark cliffs rose above the opposite side of the creek, making a climb seem impossible. Kate knew the way toward the dry spring that transformed from a winter runoff into a trail up the mountain during the remaining months of the year.

The cool of the creek bed rose from the water and chilled her nose and cheeks. She turned up the collar of her jacket, thankful her hair hung long enough to warm her neck. Her feet had warmed beneath the slow heater. Kate drove between brush and trees until the trail grew too narrow. She parked and opened the canvas door. Kate felt uneasy about the woods still shadowed in the early morning light. It felt strange to be among the tall trees. Her father would say she'd lived too long in town. She headed up the trail. Twice she stopped and considered turning back, but in fifteen minutes she pressed up the last incline. Her air came in sharp, painful breaths.

Kate stood on the side of a small rocky clearing, not daring to step out any farther. Her father had cut a bench from a fallen trunk; it reminded her of a church pew. Yet, instead of resting beneath a cathedral's dome, the rough-hewn pew gazed up into the artwork of God. This was holy ground, she believed. It took several moments to feel brave enough to walk near the edge of the cliff and sit on the bench. The morning light grew in a soft, horizontal line as the sun spread its arms across the open, rolling country, miles to the east. Far below the creek, from which she heard gentle ripplings, lay unseen in the darkened canyon.

Feeling small, she wished for her father's presence beside her. This was his place. Her eyes closed for a moment as she took in the fresh morning scent. The world seemed to wait, but she didn't have the words to begin. It would be awkward speaking to God as if he were right beside her, all around her, or in the view before her. God was too large—it would be like conversing with a mountain as you stared upward from its base.

This was who she was. A girl from Cottonwood—against the vast world. She hadn't dreamt of being anyone great or exotic—she'd just wanted sunrises and sunsets with happiness in between. She wanted to give her best to whatever she did. She'd passionately loved both her husband and her child. She'd tried to love others and God most of all.

In this crazed world, why would God require more?

"Why?" she whispered.

Nothing.

No wind or sounds or words.

Then, *What do you want from me?*

A cold chill crept through her, and the bench seemed unnaturally hard. This was foolish. Everyone would be awake by the time she returned, and they'd have expectations. They'd know where she'd gone and wonder if God had met her there. She'd have nothing to tell them.

Kate rose to leave. He didn't stop her, this God whom people loved and devoted their lives to. He didn't stop her from leaving or chase after her with words of truth. She—who wanted to leave the mountain with a glow like Moses when he climbed down from Sinai with stone tablets in his arms— carried nothing.

This was not her place, not her God's Point. Perhaps there was nothing of the sort for people like her. She'd never received visions or heard God's voice. She didn't have dreams that set her course or miracles that changed her life.

Kate stumbled along the trail. It was much rougher going down. Ridicule followed and mocked her for coming all this way. Finally she could see the outline of the jeep against the cliff and the dry spring below the next turn. She took her eyes from the trail and missed seeing some loose rocks. Her feet slipped, and Kate reached for something to stop her fall. She landed hard, feeling the sting of rocks and hard dirt.

Her hands burned, and one knee pounded where a patch of blood oozed through her jeans. Limping the last steps to the jeep, she sat on its rough vinyl seat. She failed to pull her pant leg high enough to see her scrape. But then the pain eased, and she knew what it was—just a skinned knee like she'd had a hundred times as a child.

Below her the creek shone like a pathway of pure silver. And tears began to fall, gently and without direction. Kate wanted them to stop, angry at her weakness and at God's silence. Why couldn't he meet her on a mountaintop? How could the One who set the intrinsic balance of life and creation not be there to find her?

"A Christian isn't supposed to feel this way," she said aloud to herself. "A Christian is supposed to feel joy and peace, not turmoil and loneliness."

Then she thought of Jesus. Had he escaped turmoil, loneliness, rejection, and pain? What made her immune? Perhaps her faith was not that the sun would always shine, but that God would be with her when it didn't. Kate saw her old self before Jack had disappeared. They had been happy and safe. But when her bubble had been popped and her heart punctured, she'd been lost. She hadn't even known she'd built a fool's paradise around herself until it all fell apart. Then she hadn't known what to do.

Had God been with her? Kate remembered past times when he'd seemed as real as her own life. Had memory and those moments been only a fantastic illusion? She recalled those times—youth church camp, her wedding day, a long night when Abbie had a very high fever, and even the day Jack disappeared—when she had felt moments of God in her life.

She studied those memories for some falsehood. Then Kate

moved over the last few years of silence. And suddenly she realized he had not always been as silent as she'd thought. God had been speaking in his small, still voice through others, circumstances, and things she called "coincidence." The words had been spoken, but she hadn't listened.

Kate leaned against the steering wheel with its rough edges and closed her eyes in surrender. Words came to her: *You are not hidden from my eyes.*

She looked up. The canyon grew lighter as the sun neared the horizon.

"You aren't trying to knock me down, are you, God?" she pleaded. "I've been fighting you, when you only want to walk with me. You want us to do this together. Show me the way I should go. Show me how to be a mother to Abbie. And give me strength to walk the path you have ahead."

Kate returned to the house. Her father sat on the front porch waiting. Kate felt instantly sheepish at the question in his eyes as he approached her.

"I have an idea," he said, giving her his hand as if she stepped from a carriage.

"What kind of an idea?"

"I think you should start with that blue tile. Find its origin and age—you're in the right business for that."

Kate paused to examine his face. He wanted to ask her about her journey to the mountaintop but loved her enough not to. Yet, without asking, he knew what she had to do.

"Start with the blue tile. That's a good idea." Kate sighed. "Dad, I think I'll be going back—to Europe, I mean. I'm not sure how it will work with the shop and Abbie and everything. I never wanted to return there. It's been one of my fears."

"What is another fear?"

"Well, I'm a little afraid of finding out what happened to Jack."

"And what's your greatest?"

"Not ever knowing what happened."

"Then you must go to Europe. Even if nothing is found, you'll know you tried everything." He put his arm over her shoulder.

"I know."

They turned toward the front walkway.

"How did the jeep run?" he asked.

"It took me where I needed to go," Kate said. They smiled together and walked toward the house.

He leaned against the headrest and closed his eyes. The first rush of wheels as they lifted from the ground brought a sigh of relief. He was leaving the United States. Home awaited when the wheels touched earth again. The flight home had always brought relief despite the country he returned from—but this flight brought a longing stronger than he'd felt before.

People around him began to converse and order drinks. Lukas reached across to the seat beside him and found Marta's hand. She clutched his with a quick strength that made him look at her face. There were silent tears in the lines down her cheeks, and she did not look his way. While he found comfort on this flight at the thought of home, Marta was leaving everything familiar behind and returning to the place her plight had first begun. And Karl was not with her. Lukas tugged at a corner of his handkerchief until it pulled free from his pocket. She took it with her other hand.

Lukas turned toward the window as the plane passed

through the clouds. He thought of home and the journey ahead. This final chapter of his life would not be what he'd anticipated. Earlier that year he'd been approached to write a book and to lecture at the universities. He'd always planned his retirement to include many days at his mountain estate, enjoying a good pipe and readings in the Germanic literature he'd long wanted to study. Perhaps he'd get to know his grandchildren better, even his own daughters. And that would end his life, the last page closed.

Now this would not be his way. Life had rarely taken him where he wanted to go. Every vision of his future had been changed. The sins of his youth were never recompensed, no matter how hard he'd tried. And now he must find Wolfram—who once told him why he should join the Nazi Party, then ridiculed his struggle with the moral issues of the cause. Later he had become Lukas' enemy. They thought he had died, but now Wolfram was back to haunt him. Lukas had to remind himself that Wolfram Meizer was only flesh and blood, and a man who had taken much from him. Life had not brought justice to Wolfram. And so Lukas would bring it with swift revenge. He could now feel the hatred that would give him the strength. He would allow it to consume him enough to destroy the man who made Marta cry and who helped destroy his own life also.

The plan had begun to formulate. Marta was convinced Kate Porter would decide to join them in Europe. Lukas hoped not. But regardless, he would think every step through and move in ways Wolfram would not expect. It would begin with a letter, written by his hand. The words were already memorized. Somehow Lukas would find the right channels to contact, the letter would reach Wolfram, and there would be no turning back.

He wrote the words in his thoughts again:

> *Wolfram Meizer,*
> *Do you remember me? Do you remember I betrayed you*

long ago? Has that kept you wondering what happened to me—the one you could not reach?

I remember you. I remember Susanne in the snow. I remember the muddy ditch where you left Jantes—did you know his name? And I remember Karl. We are left—you and I. Age burdens us and carries us near to the grave. Who in the end will still be standing?

Time will give the answer.

Until then,

Bruno Weiler

. . . Is he too as I am now? Does he still rise in the morning, dejected, thinking who is lost to him? And at night, awakening, think who is lost?

Does he see himself reflected in me? In these hours, does he see the face of his hours reflected?

—Walt Whitman, *Leaves of Grass*

part *two*

"Our system is so terrible that no one
in the world will believe it to be possible."

—THE KOMMANDANT OF AUSCHWITZ

CHAPTER TWENTY-ONE

Usually the man looked westward in this coldest hour of the night. He'd send a prayer in that direction, allowing the briefest moment of hope.

But this time, he paused at the doorway to stare at the mountains to the east—there was a thin line of light separating the ridge and the sky. The sight was mesmerizing, and he yearned to see all the colors of dawn. He could not recall when he'd last seen the dawn, and he didn't try to remember. The thought played through with the rising of the great sun, the sun he'd not see today or any day soon. With profound effort, he turned his face away.

The block building was dark and cold—colder, it seemed, than outside. Passing the red blink of the cameras mounted at every corner and the padlocked doors, his footsteps echoed in the stairway as he descended to the concrete floor of another hallway. Entering his room, he closed the heavy metal door without pulling the light chain above. His feet knew the steps to the edge of his simple cot, most likely an army-surplus item. Darkness surrounded him like a heavy fog, but it comforted more than imitation light. Fake light would be a mockery after staring toward the first inklings of dawn only moments before.

The way the pale blue in the east had reflected across the black waters would not leave his thoughts and that bothered him. He ached for daylight with almost a hunger, something he had not allowed for a long time. The routine he had established for survival was simply to function, making him a mechanical, subservient human, with few reminders of humanity. To confirm that he remained among the living, he retained a strange friendship, rare laughter, and his writings. The rest of what he had been was carefully placed in his inner locked storage, and someday he hoped to recover it.

He was nocturnal now. Perceiving in darkness came naturally to him like it did to other creatures of the night—a bat or raccoon, or perhaps a wise owl. At first he'd fought the change because it would be his surrender to them. During most of the day he'd stay awake with the knowledge that sunlight warmed the world somewhere above him, beyond his sight. But the change had come. To do the work required rest, so his body betrayed his will. He hated his weakness—especially when the light of this dawn revealed that he had succumbed to his captivity.

He walked the few steps to the tiny sink and touched the corners, already knowing his toothbrush had not been returned since the week it disappeared. They'd played their game with no rules again. It was always the smallest things to demean him, remind him who was in control. The toothbrush and eating utensils were their favorites. Sometimes only a butter knife came with his meal or a fork for his soup or nothing at all. He imagined them watching and laughing. Tonight there had been no meal waiting at his door.

Cold water felt good against his face, and he took long drinks bent over the sink. It didn't fill his hunger but helped.

His muscles ached after the full night. The coming summer months granted less hours of night and thus increased their workload. There seemed a greater urgency than before. He knew he would awaken to a decent meal—they needed him now and, though the game brought them pleasure, he must have energy to do their work. He found satisfaction in that.

Beneath his bed he found the lump of wood he'd been carving beside the ones he'd already completed and saved until he could give them as gifts. They were lined up, showing the progression of his time as the figures improved. The first one appeared to be a bumpy, misshapen horse, but the newest figures were smooth and detailed. A cat, an elephant, a flower with a stem, and a smiling girl—these were his gifts for the birthdays and Christmases he'd missed. Holding the wood in his hands, he considered flipping on the bulb. Instead he let memories carry him.

Somehow he must get out. They were smart and they knew his weaknesses. They'd found a way to keep him captive. It didn't require locks on his doors. It forced him to live in darkness and artificial light—either from fluorescent tubes or from the bulb dangling in the center of the room. But they hadn't destroyed him in the process. Somehow they still needed him. *That must be the way for this madness to end,* he thought. He must find their weakness.

Jack Porter had been trying for three years.

⋆⟞◉⟝⋆

Jack awoke with a start. He could always hear footsteps before they reached the upper stairway. Though every muscle tensed, he didn't move from the bed. The sound proceeded down the stairway to the lower entrance, but he was unsure who it was until the weight and pace could be gauged along the concrete floor.

The locks to his door had already been turned. For the past week this had been the new routine after his return from the mountain. He wondered why they didn't trust their own mind games to keep him inside anymore.

The footsteps stopped, all four locks flipped one by one, and the door groaned open. He had to shield his face from the hallway light spilling inside.

"Your package is early this time." Ian set the envelope on the table.

"*Danke,*" Jack said. It brought a slight smile to Ian's face.

Jack waited until Ian left and turned all the locks before he rose from the bed. He wasn't sure he wanted to see what was inside. Again he wondered why the routine had been broken. Perhaps they knew he'd deciphered their method of bizarre deprivations—the missing toothbrush, a razor and soap one week and none the next. He'd thought he could predict an irrational pattern. But this was unexpected.

He would need the light, but they'd be watching. Jack tried to sleep instead, refusing to give them the satisfaction of seeing his eagerness to open the package. He couldn't do it for long. This was his one link to the outside, to his old life. These bi-annual arrivals had kept him from insanity, even the consideration of suicide. But the photographs crumbled away the protective armor he fought to wear, leaving him naked and unprotected. His ultimate weakness—they knew it as well as he did.

In one quick surge he jumped up and pulled the chain. The light flickered and burned into the room, chasing the shadows to the corners. As he turned over the manila envelope, he noted, as usual, that there was nothing to give him a clue. Then he pulled out the photos—all printed copies from a computer. Glancing toward the camera eye that stared at him from above, Jack arranged the three photos in a row.

No outside reaction, he told himself. His hands shook from

the effort as he held each photo to believe more fully what he'd already seen.

If Jack had died three years ago, he'd have wanted his wife to move on with her life. He would have said that and believed it. But that was with the condition that death was as he'd envisioned. Jack had never gone for that white and cloudy vision of heaven. If the Creator of this world was somewhere beyond the wall of the universe preparing a place for his children, it would not be colored fuzzy white. In his musings, Jack leaned toward the vision of a vibrant heaven. Meadows, valleys, hillsides of dark greens—open spaces that rolled and stretched for hundreds of years. Towering plateaus like he'd seen in New Mexico and Utah with their red towers of rock stretching for leagues and worlds. A thousand years could be spent exploring the surface of steep ridges and peaks, deeply cut valleys, islands covered with pines, and others with exotic flowers and crystal seas. In the details of life he saw on earth—the complexities, intricate design, and balance—how much more eternity would be.

Jack's musings went long. He'd had plenty of time for them.

But what if he was wrong? he thought as he stared into the face of his wife and then of his child. What if heaven or hell or mortality was to be suspended between life and death? Wasn't the lake of fire what he felt now—the pain of being banished from life and love? Could hell be worse than this? It was hell to look into the face of your wife and see that she could be happy without you. Hell was watching your daughter mature without your hand to touch her.

Kate was laughing. His old friend Mason leaned close beside her, grinning. This was the first laugh, smile even, that he'd seen on his wife's face in three years. Mason's hand was over Kate's and their cheeks touched slightly. Jack had seen other photos with Mason in the background or with his arms draped around Abbie and Kate. Suddenly the meaning of the photos clicked together and Jack understood.

The photo of Abbie showed the complete loss of baby roundness in her cheeks. She was swinging on their porch swing with long, gangly legs hanging over—a Band-Aid on one knee. He didn't know about the scrape beneath her Band-Aid. He didn't know the many bumps and bruises the years had brought his daughter, when once he knew every detail. Her hair was a shade darker—from wheat to honey—and cut shoulder length in an older style. Did her hair still smell like the watermelon shampoo she liked so much? Abbie was only seven, soon to be eight—still a young girl—but it would not take long. The years they'd been apart, agonizing as they were, had actually swept by quickly, he realized as he looked into his daughter's face.

Jack moved to the third photo, of Kate alone in her garden. Sunlight shone around her hair. Though her face was shaded because of the glare from behind, he could see a gentle smile on her lips, as if she'd found peace among the dirt and flowers. Her hair had changed slightly, similar to Abbie's shoulder-length cut—one side tucked behind her ear with a section fallen against her cheek. He imagined they'd gone to get matching haircuts—a girls' day out. Kate watched him, look-ing deeply into his eyes, oblivious to how her gaze ripped into him. A part of Jack accused her for being happy, even envied that she could smell their daughter's watermelon hair and put Band-Aids on her scraped knees. It wasn't her fault, he reminded himself. She didn't know he was here, staring at her, yearning to pull them from two-dimensional. She didn't know she stared into his face. But mostly Kate didn't know he missed them so deeply it scared him.

Jack didn't understand the message in these photos. The others he'd received, now hidden beneath his cot, had warned him that they could reach his family whenever they wanted.

His thoughts of escape were destroyed by those images. Who did Kate and Abbie trust behind the camera lens? Who was that close that he could never reach them first?

That was the old message. But these photos spoke something new: "They don't need you anymore. Your family has moved on." He held the first one. Mason was turning toward Kate and making her laugh.

Kate and Abbie had moved on.

If Jack had died, he would have wanted it. But it was different to still be alive.

He must discover why he'd been given these photos and what worth there was in life without the hope of returning to Kate and Abbie.

Wolfram Meizer didn't need a mirror to know he was old. He felt it when his eyes opened and as he rose from bed in a body that groaned and creaked with every movement. Yet a glance in a mirror still startled him. Perhaps it was because he looked in one so rarely; inside he believed himself the man he once was. Age was the only thing he'd still to master. But he hadn't given up on that yet.

Papers were overrunning his office. On the television across the room CNN International reported a recent African uprising. The sound was turned low enough for him to ignore, but high enough in case anything of importance came on. It rarely did—unemployment in Russia, secret cloning operations, Britain's AIDS findings—nothing particularly relevant to him. Still he must always watch. Wolfram wished for a secretary in that moment, though he would never trust someone among his things. At least, never again.

He stretched in his chair, leaning far back while scanning the four televisions mounted inside a long open cabinet near the ceiling. Two screens showed complete darkness—one, the lit hallway; and another, Ian studying charts and smoking a cigarette. He must remind Ian to be sure to watch the screens of the dark rooms from time to time also—he'd become a bit lazy about that. With his mental memo in place, Wolfram returned to the screen of his laptop as he went through e-mails and made several phone calls.

Wolfram stood and raised his hands toward the ceiling; his back ached from the office work. He'd left the castle grounds for a few weeks only and returned to mounds of work—it never ceased to require his attention. He walked along the bookcase, and his eyes caught the book about Otto Skorzeny. It made him angry every time he saw it. So why did he keep it? As a reminder of what had been stolen from him and also to remember that men like Skorzeny were dead now. Skorzeny the officer, the German hero, the admired legend to neo-Nazis after the war. Yet all his stunts and books and freedom after the war didn't save him from death. With his death, his fame receded year by year. Perhaps such men didn't have to flee Europe after the war. They weren't hunted and didn't live in fear in those early years. But the youth of the world didn't remember the deeds of Scarface Skorzeny now—how he'd saved Mussolini from death by parachuting into the mountain villa where Mussolini was held. They didn't remember his postwar work with the American government or that his friends were the elite of the world. Few knew of such stories now.

Wolfram had outlasted most of them, and he had no intention of going anytime soon. There were many such things to comfort him, even if he was spending so much time hidden away in this secluded place. It would be worth it in the end.

With a flip of a remote, the cabinet above him closed, shutting away the tubular rooms. He thought again about what comforted him now. The work had grown old, but progress drew close to completion—he was sure of it. He'd push them a little more and finish it by autumn's foliage. Then he'd finally be justified, his work ensuring his name would be remembered. Soon he would have what he always deserved.

Wolfram Meizer enjoyed being *kommandant* of his world.

Wolfram pounded his fist against the table. A splash of steaming coffee spilled over, dampening one of the three newspapers he read every morning. The sunshine reflected from the drops on the patio table. Meizer's eyes stayed on the black words and images before him. He had heard the news, but seeing the printed version shocked him further. Not Otto Kauls—it seemed impossible. He read the words again.

> *Survivors and their families gathered outside the Latvian courthouse today after the indictment of Otto Kauls. Dr. Kauls is accused of war crimes and crimes against humanity after allegedly participating in the murder of several hundred Latvian Jews and other civilians during the summer of 1943. Lawyers for the 84-year-old doctor claimed that he was unfit to stand trial. The judge decided otherwise.*

Further down Wolfram read statements from the witnesses—a local civilian, the daughter of an alleged victim, and others. They had a tight case against him.

> *"I was in the woods and heard the shooting, many rounds, then a pause and more rounds. I crawled through the brush and watched Dr. Kauls walk among the bodies and shoot anyone still alive. One was an infant held in the dead mother's arms. There were bodies and blood all over the ground, old women and men, children and families. Those images never leave me."*
>
> *"My mother was used as a human guinea pig. Otto Kauls*

*is no doctor; he is a monster. It is possible that my mother's
brain and body parts are sealed in jars in that private collection he still possesses today."*

*Dr. Kauls lived in South America from 1945 to 1988
before he returned to Europe. He was found in the Lithua-
nian village where he had been living for the past ten years.*

"Idiot!" Wolfram hit the table again.

The photograph captured a dejected and weak man, not the
old friend he remembered as tan and strong, smiling across a
table laden with Caribbean lobster, smoked salmon, and Banks
beer.

Otto had not been a fool like some of the others. Nearly
every month Wolfram found reports of Holocaust survivor
settlements, another deported ex-Nazi, or a pro-Fascist group
as the target of propaganda. It shouldn't surprise him.
Decades and decades could pass and they'd still lord it over
the world because they'd won. Groups with free thought who
were aware of the underlying plots would forever receive
constant attacks—even old men near their deaths could not
find peace.

Footsteps sounded from the graveled garden path.

"Ian!" Wolfram stormed, rising from the chair.

The steps quickened and Ian emerged from the forest.
"What is it?" he asked in a voice that betrayed his annoyance.

"Do you know about this?" He held the paper up as Ian
approached.

Ian's eyes flickered slightly and Wolfram knew the answer.
"I read it this morning."

"Do you remember him?"

Ian shook his head slowly, as if trying to conjure up the
memory.

"When you had a terrible cough, this man took care of you.
You were too small to remember." Wolfram paced the rock

patio. He stopped when he noticed Ian watching him. He told his body to calm and control the stirring rage.

"Sit with me." The metal chairs screeched as they pulled them across the stone. Wolfram motioned for Ian to have some of the coffee in the carafe, but Ian refused. "What did you think of the report?"

"I think it is typical."

"Typical? That is all you can say? It is an injustice to rob an old man of his last days. Will they prosecute any Russians or Americans for wartime activities?"

"No," Ian said. "Only the Nazis or those who are against their beliefs."

"Yes."

"Our civilized nations try to say they do not believe in God, that evolution has been man's path, yet they are hypocrites." Ian—with his light, wavy hair and dark eyes that didn't move from Wolfram's—spoke so calmly and with so little expression that Wolfram nearly admired him.

"And why are they hypocrites?" Wolfram asked, taking the bait with pleasure. It interested him that Ian had come so far without his realizing it. This boy had initiative and thought for himself.

"They cling to moral laws and ethics when, without a God, there is no need for forced rights and wrongs. The strong will survive. The weak will not. When the governments realize this, our world will finally be free. Until then we will have these ridiculous trials."

"You do understand then."

"Yes."

"This—" Wolfram touched the page—"is from ignorance. This man was a doctor and scientist. Medical advancements are progressive because of men like Otto. Our world condemns how he obtained his knowledge, but his research is used in their modern science."

Wolfram leaned back in his chair and stared down the sloping grounds. He saw images of twisted bodies and crying German women. The Americans and British had murdered thousands of civilians during the war. They dropped bombs on Dresden and Hamburg—cities all over Germany. And what had they done to the innocent people of Japan? It was justified as "war necessity." The Nazis believed the same. If the Allies had lost, perhaps they'd be up for war crimes. The ironies never failed to anger him. If he were younger, if only he were younger . . . Ian, silent across from him, was evidently thinking his own thoughts. That's when Wolfram caught the black ink eyes of his old friend in the newspaper and knew just how careful he must be. A part of him wanted to get out of Europe—go to the Middle East or back to South America and leave this work for Ian.

"I walked up for a reason," Ian said.

"Wait," Wolfram said, lifting his hand. "Let me drink my coffee."

His cup was almost empty. He filled it again and stirred some milk into the dark brew. Opening the paper, he began to read through it slowly. Ian remained seated, seemingly unconcerned by Wolfram's demands.

Wolfram skimmed the business page, but his thoughts bounced back to the idea of leaving. He knew he couldn't do it; age and comforts kept him planted. And soon the castle grounds would be finished. But even sooner, Wolfram hoped, the original operation that had brought him back would at last be complete. It was his final goal. As much as he'd tried for years to stay away, he was drawn like some gravitational force that wouldn't release him. It had pulled him during his wandering years when he'd trekked the Andes, feeling at home as he stopped in the small hotel of another exiled German. He'd had women, alcohol, every pleasure he craved. Still, the calling of something stolen from him, something that should have been his, worked and wore against him. It was the one thing he couldn't have.

When he'd done all he wanted and gained more than he'd imagined possible, he gave in to that call to discover what he would have had if the war had lasted another week, perhaps even a few more days. If he hadn't been forced to leave Europe. If he'd had a little more time. Wolfram would see it before he died, or this quest would kill him. He would not end his days like his old friend Otto Kauls.

Wolfram pried his eyes from the newspaper to the brightness of the morning, ignoring Ian's finger tapping the table. There was surprising comfort in the laws of nature; as Ian had said, only the strong would survive. Wolfram watched the silver threads of a spider's web that stretched wide across the tips of a green thicket. Suddenly a fly flew straight into the snare. It stuck and struggled. In a quick swoop, a black-and-gray spider flew across the silk and began a furious spin around its prey. Wolfram smiled and took a sip of nearly cold coffee.

"We must speak," Ian insisted.

Wolfram let the interruption pass this time. Ian had been up all night after all. "Then speak." Wolfram's eyes remained on the long legs of the spider as it twisted and turned its victim.

"I received a message about a man in the States. His name was Karl Olsen."

Wolfram turned toward Ian. He had gone to the city for one day only and had missed the call—this was business he had planned to keep from Ian. "Yes?"

"The message was that Karl Olsen is dead."

Wolfram savored the words like the first taste of fine wine. Unable to keep the smile from his lips, he stood.

"Then we are nearly finished."

CHAPTER TWENTY-THREE

Jack dreaded the instant shock of cold water creeping around the edges of his wet suit and sliding inside the worn cuffs. He'd soon warm; his body heat against the neoprene lining would raise the temperature and he'd lose the chill. At their depth the water would always be dark, even if it wasn't the middle of the night.

They'd spent an hour with their lights beaming against the particles and staring into the eyes of pike and whitefish that gazed with wonder before turning and sliding into the night. Jack knew this area along the steep wall of the lake well. There was only a slight slope from mountaintop to water's edge to lake floor. Jack could locate each deep gouge where underwater missiles had been tested during the Nazi era. He'd checked thoroughly to assure that the indentations had not formed cracks that would cause breakage or landslides above. Tonight he checked again. With their movement within the mountain—the months of drilling within the old salt mine— damage beneath them must be gauged regularly.

Jack turned to check Ian's location. Through the haze he could see Ian's light move against an area where the slope jutted outward. Jack knew there were other reasons for Ian's interest in the dive. He'd always come in the past when Rudy was well enough to dive too. Jack and Rudy both believed Ian had other reasons besides rock crackage for his dives. He was looking for something, and Jack had his theories. These lakes were full of mystery, but if Ian sought lost treasure, it would be found too deep for divers. It must be something else.

Jack moved away from Ian toward an area below the docks of the castle grounds. Jack had explored this area only once, checking for rock movement in a lower outcropping of rock. It took time to find it. Holding his light in front of him, he kicked smoothly through the water. This area had the greatest slope. He could follow the lake wall straight up to where it shallowed to the shore of the castle grounds. It was the only shoreline on this end of the lake with the sides surrounded by sheer mountains. Across the lake was a large shoreline where Jack had seen a distant village with lights that shone like beacons, reminding him of life outside the alpine prison.

On their most recent dive, Jack had found the long crack in the rock deep beneath the dock and upper grounds. If the crack grew and created an underwater avalanche, the estate could possibly be in jeopardy. It was a thought Jack had begun to consider.

He thought of it again as he reached the area and checked his gauges and waterproof watch for the time. Ian would expect him back in ten minutes or less. He had little geological experience and had wished for more on countless occasions, since they had been working him outside his field of expertise. The great "they" didn't seem to understand that he was an archaeologist, not a miner or geologist, when they brought him here. Yet Jack wouldn't give them reason to doubt it now—he needed them to need him. It ensured his safety as well as his family's.

He knew these people were serious. The first six months of confinement, with their taunting and photos, were proof enough. The following year and a half, he'd been moved around and then brought to Ian. Ian was who he saw now, their fore-man or puppet—he wasn't sure. They'd worked at another site for some time before they'd settled here a year ago.

But two plans had begun to formulate in Jack's mind. If he could fake an accident, make Ian believe he had been pulled down by rocks and drowned, he might have a chance to escape. He'd put a reserve tank outside the boat and use it to cross the lake beneath the water. The danger should be removed from his family with his supposed death. Then he'd reach authorities and get help out to Rudy.

The other plan—the avalanche and possible destruction of the castle grounds—put his life in jeopardy. Since the most recent photographs had arrived, he'd considered this plan more than once. What did he have to return to? What did he have to look forward to?

Jack moved through the water, remembering the night he lost himself to a panicked need to escape. He'd had no plan, only pure desperation. Straight across the lake he swam, while Rudy and Ian worked along the wall. It took his logic only an eighth of the way across the lake to kick in and turn him back. The risk was too high. Someone very close took those pictures of his family. It would be nothing for them to reach Abbie and Kate.

In Jack's first months of captivity, they'd given him countless photos of victims—charred bodies, a headline of a family murdered while they slept, a black man hanging from a tree, a little girl shot with a doll in her hand. Those images turned him around. He wasn't here because of some amateurs—they had an essential reason for keeping him here. They'd worked too hard and long, taken too great a risk by kidnapping an American. There was something very important about these diggings.

Halfway back from his attempted escape, he had surfaced. Already Ian had lights skimming the water's surface. Jack waved his arms, feeling defeat spread over him at the loss of freedom so close yet too costly. When he boarded the boat, he made an excuse about going too far, though he knew Ian never really bought it.

The accident idea might work, he now thought as he recognized an outcropping of rock. He found the crack and noticed how it had widened by half an inch more and appeared to have cut deep. Jack turned downward to follow it, though he knew he couldn't go far. The pressure increased with the depth, and his equipment was too old to push far. He often feared a hose would break, so he kept careful watch. The crack in the rock widened as the light's beam followed its jagged line. Then Jack saw a large hole in the rock wall. He held the light with one hand and grasped the ledge with the other. A few rocks came loose and floated downward. He needed to be careful or the accident he wanted to fake could actually happen. The light beam sought the sides and then disappeared into the darkness of the gouge.

Jack swam downward and inside, just a bit. Then he realized that this was not the underside of an outcropping as he'd first believed. It was an underwater cave. The lipped ridge of rocks above the opening had kept the mouth of the cave from view on previous dives. Or perhaps some of their digging inside the cave had broken loose any blockage. The light gave no answer to its length. Jack backed out and examined the edges. The ridges in the rock indicated man-made qualities, as if the walls had been chiseled and widened. But he believed the cave was natural in origin. As he followed the wall down, he remembered to check his watch. It was time to get back.

Jack found Ian moving in his direction, no longer investigating the rock wall. When Ian caught him in his light, he gave him a thumbs-up. Jack checked his compass, and they swam until they saw the lights along the hull of the boat. Slowly they surfaced, following the line of bubbles from their masks.

Rudy waited beside the ladder, grabbing up the tanks, belts, and gear. Water streamed from their sleek bodies as they climbed from the weightless world of water into the boat. Jack peeled away the wet suit, and the chilly night air stung his skin.

Rudy tossed Jack a towel and then one to Ian. "It's not right for me to be left up here," Rudy said, rubbing his mitten-covered hands.

"Get well and you can come with us," Jack said.

"I'm trying; you know I'm trying." A cough burst from his lips as if to contradict his words.

"Get where it's warm, right now," Jack scolded.

Rudy nodded between coughs and descended the cabin stairway. Ian was putting away equipment. Jack knew he should help, but this time he sat in the stillness of the boat, breathing the cold mountain air. For a moment he stared across the water to the lights along the opposite shore. People had normal lives over there—eating in restaurants, watching television, laughing, singing, loving. He was separated by mountains and water, though much more than that.

"The locals wanted to know about our nighttime activities." Ian was watching him. "Remember the boats coming round a few months ago?"

"And what are we doing? Really?" Jack asked it like a challenge.

He knew the reason they'd brought him here—they believed he had knowledge that would help them. And they believed his archaeological skills were essential, though geological skills were more necessary. They couldn't hire another professional who could share their work with the world. Jack and Rudy had worked as a team in the past: Rudy was experienced in underwater archaeology, and Jack had worked at Native American caves in Montana. They were the perfect choice. What he didn't know was what exactly this group wanted him to find. Jack still didn't know after three years.

"We are remodeling the grounds of an old castle," Ian said with his usual serious expression. "Often at night we enjoy studying fish."

"If I knew what fish to look for, I might help find it." Jack said it casually as he pulled the towel over his head and rubbed the water droplets from his hair. He didn't want to see Ian's eyes probing his face or hear the lies in Ian's responses. In a twisted way, he liked Ian. Ian was part of the group who kept him here, though Jack had yet to sway the young man's allegiance or move him to some compassion. That had been one of his original plans. He'd worked little by little toward friendship but had fallen prey to his own game. The fact that Jack could actually like Ian—the person, the man—was proof of how warped this life in captivity had made him.

"Some knowledge can destroy you, Jack."

"How can my life be more destroyed?" Their eyes locked, and Jack noticed a slight flicker in Ian's expression before he turned away. He wondered if Ian ever imagined the life they had stolen. Ian knew about Abbie and Kate. But did he consider what it felt like? What had Ian's life been like before this assignment or project or whatever this was for him?

Tall and quiet, Ian ran his hand through his hair, sleeking it straight back. What thoughts moved through his head? He never revealed any beliefs or past or reason for his presence here. Ian only expressed what was expected in the moment.

He finished putting away equipment and turned back to Jack. "Let's go over the maps. You can show me what you found."

"What I found?" he asked, wondering if Ian already knew about the cave.

"I'm sure there are changes from our last dive. I found a few cracks that had deepened. Didn't you find anything?" Again his eyes did their probing.

"A few. I'll record the changes."

They descended the steps into the boat's tiny cabin. Ian flipped on a light over the table as they scooted around the booth seat. Rudy had made coffee and poured it into gray tin cups. Strange how much freedom Jack felt when on a dive or in the boat, as if this were a normal underwater expedition. Out here he was nearly an equal with Ian, and Jack enjoyed the luxury of real conversation with Rudy instead of their fragmented talks through the heating vents and their coded taps through the cement wall. These dives were rare now, something Jack actually looked forward to. Unlike his previous work in the soot and recycled air of the tunnel, these dives brought a dread of the night's end. The boat had a faint musty scent that Jack loved. It was the smell of mold and rope, closed-up cabins, and open waters.

Ian unrolled the map and set his cup, a compass, and a can of chili on three corners of the paper to hold it down. The renderings showed the lake from different angles. There were figures indicating depth levels around the lake, the widths at various points, previous dive locations, and sketches of the mountain ranges with marked areas of digs and blastings. One drawing depicted the joining of two mountains, where a spring began and flowed into a stream that cut to the slope of the old castle grounds that had been Jack's home for the past year.

Jack studied the map with Ian beside him.

Rudy sat in a chair and flipped through an Austrian newspaper that he'd found crunched under the table when he sat down. "Says here that Charles Schulz died. You know, the Peanuts cartoon guy."

"Snoopy was one of my favorites," Jack said.

"Everyone loved Charlie Brown. My favorite was when he gets that terrible little Christmas tree—"

"How old is that newspaper?" Ian asked.

Rudy looked and didn't respond. Jack could tell it must be old news.

"I found nothing changed here or here." Ian touched points they'd previously marked on the map. "It did not appear that the digging inside the mountain had protruded through the lake wall."

Rudy folded the paper and leaned toward the light. "Then the water we hit in Tunnel 8 could come from an underground lake or spring, though the solidity and depth of the rock makes that theory doubtful."

"What did you find, Jack?" Ian asked.

Jack studied the map. He could see where he had marked the crack he'd reinvestigated tonight, but there was nothing of the underwater cave. Ian again watched him.

"This area could perhaps have impact damage. There was approximately a three-quarter-inch widening in the crack and several inches' depth change. Something to watch in the future." Jack spoke casually as if it held little importance. He turned their focus to a structure area a hundred meters from the cave. "Ian, if you didn't find any damage to these areas and this is directly beneath the internal digging within the old salt mine, then I agree with Rudy—we did not reach the lake, but some other water source."

"Why can we never make progress here? Your calculations inside the mine must be wrong." Ian's voice had a harsh ring to it, enough for Rudy to put his coffee down.

"I've gone over them again and again," Jack explained. "Rudy has double-checked me. We aren't far enough to have reached the lake—tonight only confirms what I already believed. And if you blew out the wall of the lake from the inside, the water would fill the tunnel before anyone could get out. The water we cut into must be a spring."

"Unless we tapped into an underwater cavern," Rudy suggested. Jack wished he hadn't thought of it.

"Explain," Ian said.

"If there was already a cavern or a spring that ran into the lake beneath the rock, we may have broken through the top of it. The water didn't rush into the tunnel for one reason—we were digging downward. It also didn't have the pressure because there is some other outlet for it."

Ian nodded. "We must dive lower. Or we must go into the water from inside the tunnel."

Jack now suspected that Ian did know something about the cave. Or perhaps it was what they'd been seeking all along.

Rudy continued. "We don't have the equipment. I've read about teams cave diving. It can be very dangerous work. We'd need a diving bell, and if we go too far inside, then it won't be enough to have twenty to thirty minutes to decompress. Some deep cave dives require hours of decompression, so we'd need a chamber to transfer into after each dive. Beneath that kind of surface, every second is more valuable than in any other dive we've ever done. We'd need underwater scooters, lights, a wall mapper that fires sonar to find our way, along with a trailing cord to help us get back out. There's no room for error in this. This three-man team can't do it, especially with this equipment we're patching up after every dive."

"We'll get the equipment," Ian said.

Neither Rudy nor Jack spoke. They knew such equipment wouldn't be found on a black-market order form.

"There is little enthusiasm. Perhaps there are things you don't tell me, information you withhold, plans of sabotage? Do you want to leave this place? Until this is finished, you have no hope," said Ian.

Jack guessed that Ian was getting pressure. But it also

angered him that Ian again referred to their freedom, dangling it like a carrot before their faces. Jack knew it was a hope they'd never fulfill.

"*Will* we be freed, Ian?" Jack asked. "We've been here too long and know too much to be allowed to walk away. You know this group better than we do. What will they do when our work is done?"

Ian's face took on an expression of surprise. It brought fear to Jack and Rudy to see that Ian had believed the same lie that they had believed. But now Ian recognized the truth. Of course they would not be allowed to go home, even if their homes were still waiting—which for Jack it wasn't. The risk was too high for their captors to allow their freedom. In that second Ian knew it also.

Ian left the map and climbed the stairs from the boat's cabin.

Neither Jack nor Rudy spoke for a long time. Jack continued to stare at the map. "Why don't we blow this entire place up?" he said in a low whisper. It was an exhilarating thought. "We have access to the dynamite."

"You know why we don't. I have a nephew, and you have a family who are safe as long as we do what they say."

"If we could get enough sticks in the perfect places, there'd be no one to harm them."

"I know you aren't serious, Jack. But in case a part of you is, remember that these people are more than the few here. I've been with them longer."

"Who are they?"

"My guess is that they are linked with neo-Nazi organizations, perhaps even other fanatic groups," Rudy answered. "They must have connections in the States. Possibly the operation is smaller than we guess, but sometimes I feel it's larger than I imagine."

"We're getting close to what they want. Ian showed

emotions tonight—he's getting pressure and a lot of it. But we need to find what we can do."

"We wait."

"You've been here too long, Rudy. Don't lose your fight. They say inmates in prison reach a point when they don't want to leave anymore because those walls mean safety to them. That can't happen to us."

"It won't."

"Then what can we do?"

"We can pray," suggested Rudy.

Jack leaned back with his hands behind his head. He should have expected such a response, but hearing it now made him teeter between humor and anger. When Jack had known Rudy Blessing years earlier, their roles had been reversed. Rudy, a Catholic by family, not faith, had attended mass a few times a year and had his mother's rosary beads in the instrument drawer of the boat he lived on. Jack was honored to spend a summer doing underwater diving with the Blessing team in the Mediterranean. He'd been full of youth and spiritual faith back then, unafraid to share his beliefs with anyone interested, including an only slightly curious Rudy.

"Sometimes God wants action," Jack countered. "Prayer alone has taken us nowhere."

"Prayer has probably done much more than we know," Rudy said with a look that reminded Jack of the countless times God had helped him survive another day. Rudy's friendship alone had been an answer when Jack thought he'd go insane from his solitary confinement.

"Sometimes I think you like it here," Jack grumbled.

"No. I want freedom. It often amazes me, the strength of that desire—how God designed us to require it. But I can also see the great good in our time here."

"What great good?"

"I've come to truly understand. All pretense, obsession,

desires, possessions—it's all been taken from me. I had many dark moments before you came. My fight was with God even more than with them. It almost killed me. Finally I surrendered to God in sheer desperation. They kept me in this filthy basement for months—a place that would bring a man either to God or to insanity."

"I know that basement," Jack said, wishing to erase the memory of his six months there.

Wondering where Ian had gone, Jack looked up the stairway but saw no one. Another pot of coffee percolated on the stove, but he could still feel the stifling air of that basement. He remembered scratching his tallied days beneath the scrawls of other captives who had been there before. His marks would reach one hundred seventy-three, while one person had marked over four hundred. Had that been Rudy? They'd never talked about the means that had brought them together.

"I began to pray in that basement. I prayed for someone to talk to and, though it took almost a year, you came," said Rudy.

"So this is *your* fault?"

"I hope not," Rudy said with a laugh. "You had great faith when they brought us together. You came right when I was losing it again."

"I would not have survived without you." Jack took a quick drink of his coffee while his thoughts returned to a night he'd sunk so low that life hadn't seemed worth living anymore. It had been Rudy's words that saved him: "Think of this moment, then the next moment. You'll go insane if you wonder what your family is doing right now, what they are thinking. Get through tonight. Save a bit of food every meal in case the next one doesn't come. Hide something that will give you something they don't own. And do something for your family—write letters and poems or bring rocks from the diggings to someday give your daughter."

Jack had not told Rudy about the latest photos of his family—the evidence of their life without him. If he ever gave Abbie the wooden animals he'd learned to carve or Kate the letters he'd written, it would only be salt in their healing wounds. *What now, Rudy? What keeps me going?*

"Can you see the good that God does in the midst of bad?" Rudy put his elbows on the table and rested his chin on his folded hands. "When everything was taken, I could see what was important. I gained a greater view of life and death, even eternity. I know this is just a moment in eternity. This is my work right now. God doesn't want men to oppress men. But man's free choice affects even the innocent. One person sins and another pays the price. It's not fair—but a world that doesn't follow God will never be just or fair or happily ever after."

"And we're the ones paying for another's sins."

"God doesn't promise a 401(k), nice house, perfect family. He promises to never leave us or forsake us. *You* told me that a long time ago."

"That seems like a different man. I know I still believe, but sometimes it doesn't feel like enough."

"Have you ever been to a museum or an exhibit of a great artist, Jack?"

"Sure. I spent a week in Florence."

"Then you'll understand this. My favorite painter has always been Picasso—don't ask me why. There was this exhibit in Paris—I must have gone five or six times in a month. I liked to stand very, very close to a painting—as close as I could without making security too nervous. I'd stare at a small section. One painting included this awful pea green color within the outline of a woman's lips, and the strokes looked terrible from close up. But the farther I walked away, the more beautiful the painting became. The entire picture was revealed."

"So this is the awful pea green of our life painting?"

"Of our eternal painting, perhaps." Rudy stood and poured more coffee into Jack's cup. "Do you know what Oswald Chambers writes about prayer?"

"More Oswald?"

"I have his book in my room."

"How? I can hardly get paper and ink."

"I prayed and I asked. They must have ordered it from South America. The box said Amazon something."

"Amazon.com?"

"Yes, that's it. I still have the box."

"That's an online bookstore. A store on the Internet where you can order books with one push of a button."

"The Internet, yes. Interesting."

"No, unbelievable. They ordered you a book from Amazon."

"Ask and ye shall receive."

Jack shook his head in disbelief. "Just tell me what Oswald says about prayer."

"He says that prayer is absurd."

"I didn't expect that. But lately, I'd almost agree."

"Oswald writes that prayer is not practical but absurd. We should understand that prayer is stupid from the common-sense point of view. It feels like doing nothing. Haven't we heard a thousand times, 'All we can do now is pray,' as if that's the last resort or the worst-case scenario? Isn't the *prayer* word used in all kinds of absurd situations, like when we don't want to help someone or don't have anything else to say? 'I'll pray for you.' And yet prayer is the greatest mystery of all. It is faith. When we do truly pray, we are acting on the faith that the words we throw to the air are doing something. And prayer does. It breaks barriers and changes the nature of life."

"My mind would agree, but what I feel is different. I haven't seen barriers broken and life changed in a very long time. I don't even hear God as I once did."

"He has entrusted you with silence."

"Great—what a gift."

"Oswald writes: 'God is working for His highest ends until His purpose and man's purpose become one.' The best thing to remember is that we should live this life to fulfill God's purpose, not our own. For God's purpose will eventually be greater by far than our own, if we can only believe and allow him to move and change us."

"Trust in the Picasso?"

"It'll be even better than a Picasso in the end."

Both men were quiet, each lost in his own thoughts. Jack heard a slight creak overhead and then footsteps. Ian must be above them. Returning to the maps and sketches they'd charted again and again, Jack spotted the place where he'd found the cave and again decided not to mention its location, not even to Rudy. Until Jack knew more, he would let this be his own little secret.

CHAPTER TWENTY-FOUR

Wolfram closed the wooden blinds on the French doors and turned the lights low. The television in the corner was on mute but flashed from across the room.

He'd moved his favorite birds back into the office. Whenever he left the castle grounds, the cages were moved. No one entered his office while he was gone. The slight light calmed the birds, and they chirped softly. He hit the remote to open his surveillance cabinet. Wolfram switched a button that showed the security room with the lone guard watching monitors and reading a book. He listened for movement in the house—nothing. Rudy's room was dark, Jack had a light on and was carving wood at the table in his room, Ian had fallen asleep while leaning way back in his chair. The hallway to the barrack was empty.

The wheels of Wolfram's chair squeaked as he sat before the antique desk. With one hard pull and his other hand holding a latch, the front panel of his desk opened to reveal a red metal safe. He turned the dial and heard the click of the lock. Behind several stacks of currency—American and euro—he found a white handkerchief folded and held in place by a green rubber band. Wolfram withdrew the handkerchief and set it on the desk where the lamp shone a circle of light.

It annoyed him how his hands shook constantly. He noticed it when drinking his coffee and sipping soup and now as he pulled the rubber band away.

The two tile fragments in the handkerchief differed in size and did not fit together. Whoever cut them had not gone for form or precision. Three pieces were missing that would join his two, and soon he'd have one of those fragments. Wolfram wondered which one it would be. He knew what he hoped. Then only two pieces would be left, and he may not even need them, though he would want them eventually. This whole tile had almost been his once—before it had been broken into five pieces. The betrayal of a woman had stolen that from him.

Wolfram remembered that Susanne Olsen had been Karl's sister, bringing a chuckle to his lips. Karl Olsen was dead now too. He remembered the giant of a man he'd seen only once, through the scope of his rifle. Karl had been moving through the forest steadily and with great care. Wolfram's view was perfect, like watching a cat sneak up on a lion. He was the lion watching from above. His finger rested on the trigger when he heard something behind him. Climbing the back of the ridge was another of their Resistance comrades. This one was not so lucky as Karl Olsen. The following years would prove his mistake in not killing Olsen first. The man had caused him much trouble, keeping his name on watch lists around the world. Bounty hunters came after him, investment required partnerships, and he was forced to monitor every move he made—it grew tiring.

Wolfram moved the tile fragments, arranging them in different ways. He'd had one piece for over fifty years, since he found it wrapped in cording around that kid's neck. Wolfram had been stunned to see it there. The boy didn't talk easily, but it took little time for him to reveal that his team members each had a piece. Wolfram thought he'd have the pieces back within the week, that he'd get each one of the four remaining men. But he couldn't predict the war's end or his need to escape without the chance to get them all back. It took decades to get the second tile fragment.

He picked up the telephone, though it was the middle of the night in America. He wasn't even sure what time zone the western states were in and he didn't care. The voice that answered didn't sound groggy but alert. Perhaps they'd been awaiting this return call.

"You should speak to me only," Wolfram said without introduction. He knew he would be recognized.

"Of course. I gave little information to Ian, enough to receive your return call quickly."

"Next time only speak with me. Now I want details." Wolfram hated the man's accented German, but Wolfram's English was even worse.

"We had two men in Arizona for several months. I decided I should be there for the actual confrontation. We watched for a few days. Our subject brought two men to his home. I will send you the information we found on them. One will be of particular interest."

"Would these be older men, his age?"

"Yes."

Wolfram nearly smiled. The remaining two tile fragments. "And do you have photographs?"

"We will send the files at once."

"Good."

"The two men were not there when you met with Olsen? Olsen had a wife also."

"They were all gone when we met the old man."

"Did he know who you were?" Wolfram wished he could

have seen Karl's face and heard his words. Had he known those were his last moments alive?

"Yes. He mentioned your name."

"Good. How did it occur?"

"Without much assistance."

"I do not understand."

"He was old. We threatened him, pushed hard to get the item—it was too much, I suppose."

"And you left behind the object that I asked?"

"Yes."

"And the item—"

"I must first ask you. When will we have what you promised?"

"I am working on that." Wolfram leaned back in his chair. "Old secrets can be hard to find."

"You've been working on it for a while. There is a lot of pressure here, and it's difficult keeping the wayward ones in line. They have little patience."

"Precision is key. Impatience will destroy the cause."

"But we need something to keep them satisfied. Some proof, perhaps, that this is worth waiting for, as you have promised. Our men respect you greatly and do not doubt your word—I do not mean to imply that. But it would help the restlessness if there was something definite to show them."

Wolfram drummed his fingers on the desk as he listened. He nodded slowly, then a bit faster. "I understand. I will send a copy. It is a document from October 1944 that I stole from top secret Gestapo files. It describes plans for the greatest weapon that would make their work in atom splitting—"

"Do not tell too much on the line."

"And now, when will I have what you took from Karl?" Wolfram looked at the missing spaces between the two tiles.

There was a long pause. "We did not get it."

Wolfram pulled the phone away; he could feel the anger rise

within him. "Franklin, you had better explain," he said through clenched teeth.

"You said we would not use names."

"You have other things to worry about right now."

"We believed Olsen had given the piece to us. But after our leave, I realized it was the exact piece I had left in his office—it was one of the copies. It's a delay—we'll get the original." Franklin spoke as if it would be simple.

"Yes, you will." Wolfram's hand slammed over the tile pieces. "If you knew how long I've waited for that." Wolfram regained his composure. "Keep searching. And there are two others. This is essential to what you request of me."

"We will get them," the voice said with confidence.

"Send those photographs of the men at Karl's."

"They will be there within the half hour."

Wolfram slammed the phone. His left hand remained over the fragments. He needed at least three pieces of the tile map to complete what he'd begun—without them he searched aimlessly. Fool Americans could not get the job done, as he'd always suspected. They could talk big, but the results proved their inefficiency.

Wolfram sat in the dull light of the room. The birds were now quiet. There was a new set of maps he should look through, but the warmth of the room and comfort of his chair kept him reclined. Wolfram glanced at the clear, plastic case on the corner of his desk. It had rested in that place for so long that he rarely saw it there. It looked like a paperweight with a small speck in the center. The speck was a tiny, glass capsule. That capsule had been his companion for almost ten years before he had confined it in the clear case. Many had used theirs, biting through the glass while in a cell awaiting trial or at the moment of capture. Instant death was their escape as cyanide exploded through their system. Wolfram had never needed it. Close at times, perhaps. But here it remained at his side, a testimony to his endurance and destiny.

He reminded himself of this as he mulled over the last thoughts of Karl Olsen. They were not as he had hoped. Instead of fear, Karl had felt contempt. He had given the fake tile fragment, believing he'd taken another jab at his opponent. Wolfram closed his eyes and breathed slowly. Karl was dead. Karl was in the grave. Karl would soon turn to rot. Wolfram thought of the many bodies he'd seen—twisted limbs, mouths gaping, eyes wide with surprise or more often with nothingness inside. That was Karl Olsen.

A ding sounded on his computer, breaking the stale air. Wolfram clicked a button and watched the file download. He printed the file and waited. It took only moments for the faces to come through. Wolfram set the papers beneath the lamplight. The first showed three men meeting at an airport. Three old men who looked nothing like the soldiers they'd once been. And then he knew what Franklin had meant about being surprised. One man in the photo was tall and burly, smaller than Karl Olsen, but a large presence anyway. He carried a briefcase, and a carry-on bag was beside him. The expensive suit looked comfortable on him, even after his flight. This man was conditioned to traveling and dressing well.

And Wolfram knew that face.

"Former finance minister Lukas Johansen. Why do you greet Karl and Oskar as if you are old friends?" Wolfram leaned close to the faces. He pulled back with a sharp intake of breath as the knowledge hit him. "Bruno Weiler, you old, betraying fool. You have been here all along."

⋅⇒◉⇐⋅

The gravel under his tires crunched louder than the high-pitched whine of his golf cart. Wolfram knew he looked ridiculous to his employees, motoring around in his buggy to investigate the progress around the grounds. They could laugh when he wheeled away, but they would never dare laugh to his face.

He stopped suddenly and backed up a foot away from a young boy. The engine idled, and he remained on the cushioned bench. The apprentice gardener glanced up with a potted plant in his hand.

"What kind of plant is that?" Wolfram asked in German. A blank expression etched his features. The boy didn't understand. Wolfram leaned over and smacked the boy in the face with his leather gloves. The boy didn't move, only stared with fear in his eyes.

Wolfram turned the wheel and drove toward the house. A better system was required for him to get the work from these men. Ian would calmly explain that Wolfram himself had requested workers who did not speak German. Wolfram wasn't even sure where these men had come from—Romania, Bosnia, Turkey perhaps. He hadn't cared at the time. All he wanted was men who would do the work for enough pay to mind their own business, not be able to talk to locals if they ever left the grounds, and could return without ever knowing the exact location of the castle. The money brought them and did its work. Wolfram knew he should be understanding—but if he wanted to know what kind of plant was stuck into his soil, he deserved an answer.

He drove around a wide stairway dressed with overflowing potted geraniums to the upper level and entrance of his house. Storming down the hallway, he intended to put some fear into his housekeepers. He loved the fear he saw in their eyes. They might complain and make threats about quitting behind his back, but they would do what he asked. Why? Because Wolfram had money. And money made people shut up and do what he asked.

As he passed the aviary built into one side of the hallway, Wolfram stopped to a gathering of chirping. The birds fluttered and hopped from the branches of the potted trees. Their water was full, but the food wasn't. He hadn't fed them yesterday.

"You need me, don't you?" he said in German. "I will feed you when I want."

He walked into his office. The room was warm and smelled of bird feces. The four cages in the corner sprung to life as he closed the door. These birds had water and food—he'd checked earlier that morning. Wolfram walked around his desk and sat in the overstuffed leather chair. He leaned his head back and rocked. As his mind sought possibilities for a better operation, he opened his eyes to stare at the birds.

Something about caged birds drew his fascination. He could watch the four cages, each of different height and volume, for hours. The largest cage held his newest recruit—one he'd watched and chosen from the larger aviary in the hall. The finches were in constant motion, chirping as they hopped and skipped from nest to perch to swing. He liked to see the progress of their movements from the small cage to the larger ones. Could birds be jealous? Did they watch the lone bird in the largest cage and want what it had? Did they peer at Wolfram with black, beady eyes and desire his freedom? He watched to discover—he'd been studying different species for years.

A psychoanalyst friend in Quito, Ecuador, found Wolfram's view on jealousy fascinating. Their discussions in smoky cafés were often long. But Wolfram believed the man was really more interested in the workings of Wolfram's mind than in the conversations about bird behavior. The friend once said, "Jealousy is never satisfied," as if to warn Wolfram. Wolfram agreed on the surface, but underneath he knew that nothing in life brought satisfaction, except in the pursuit of it. Jealousy fed his life; he'd admit it to anyone. But not his own jealousies.

Wolfram loved to pursue what others wanted. The birds wanted what he had; he knew by the way they watched him now.

He'd first discovered the power of jealousy long ago, and all because of Paris. Wolfram had never been to a city away from his own country other than Vienna. When he received the orders with Paris as his destination, he immediately wrote to his mother, telling her in words only she could understand. "Mother, you know the place you've dreamed of going—I will be there next week." It was a short assignment escorting a midlevel officer, but he'd be in Paris and at such a time. The grand city was no longer France's Paris, but Deutschland's. Germany's Paris. They had conquered their great rival.

Wolfram had had an afternoon to himself—the officer demanded privacy after meeting with a Frenchwoman of great beauty. Wolfram walked the Rue de Rivoli toward the narrow point of the Obelisk where he glimpsed the Eiffel Tower beyond. A surge of adrenaline pumped through him as he crossed the busy streets and then stood at the Place de la Concorde. The twenty-acre square with cars, cyclists, and German military driving round the outskirts was the heart of Paris. He turned a full circle—Eiffel Tower, Seine River with the Parliament rising over the bridge, gardens, and Musée de l'Orangerie containing Monet's treasures, the columns of La Madeleine. In the center island stood the shining gold-plated, 3,200-year-old Obelisk that had once adorned Luxor in Egypt before its gifting to France.

Wolfram breathed the autumn air that day in 1940. It amazed him to think that Napoleon had marched where his feet now walked. King Louis XVI had ordered the beheading of Austrian-born Marie Antoinette, along with a thousand others, at this place. Wolfram imagined the blood in the square stone grooves. This site was the pulse of France and her history. And Paris' heart, history, and future now belonged to the Nazis.

Wolfram peered down the long Champs-Elysées. It was not as busy as usual. People were afraid. At the far end of the long street was the boxy frame of the Arc de Triomphe. Parisian architects had designed the city well, with sweeping gardens that rose to meet monuments and framed entrances to palaces. Nazi banners waved everywhere. The French flag was nowhere in sight. Swastikas fluttered in the morning breeze to remind all Parisians that now they were German property.

Later he had explored the streets. He noticed an older woman wearing a scarf that reminded him of the one his mother wore when she went to market or to the theatre with his father. She claimed it was from Paris. She yearned for Paris and its fashion and must be quite envious of his journey here. Wolfram would buy her a new scarf and enjoy the questions she'd ask, trying to act like a doting mother rather than coveting every detail all to herself. She'd brag to her friends and display the scarf, but the jealous part of her would never forgive him for achieving her dream—something she'd never have.

Paris changed him. Wolfram knew that even as he explored the city. He saw what it meant to conquer and own what belonged to another and to have what someone else wanted. Never before had he possessed something in such a way. Germany possessed France. He was Germany. His mother's wish to see Paris—he possessed that too. It filled him with a strange yet great power. Later in the day, he had found his own Frenchwoman and had taken what he wanted from her.

Wolfram's return home did not give him the satisfaction he'd imagined. When he arrived with the scarf and postcards, his mother wasn't there. His father waited at the hospital, and the black-and-red scarf would soon be placed in her coffin. A mixture of alcohol with some medicines she was taking, they said. But Wolfram had discovered the truth. The Jewish doctor he'd forbidden his mother to see had killed her. The man must have given her the medicine before his deportation. He couldn't believe that someone as proud and strong as his mother could have made such a mistake. It was murder—it had to be. Wolfram was determined to find his mother's killer, even transferring his post to be a guard at Mauthausen, where he believed the doctor was sent. It had taken months to discover that the old man had died in the cattle car en route from Dachau to Mauthausen.

Wolfram inspected the precision neatness of his office—everything had a place now. The birds chattered, perhaps plotting a way to reach the larger cage or freedom itself.

Wolfram was meant to possess. That time in Paris had been the catalyst for what had lain dormant since his creation. Some were born to own, while others were born to be owned. It was part of the line of evolution. The strongest knocked the lowest from existence. It was how the human race had grown and survived. No cave dwellers remained—there was proof that the human animals must be destroyed. Hitler had seen it, though his greed had made him impatient for too much too soon, destroying what should have been the Germans. There would be new changes—very soon. Evolution was now in their hands—to choose what should be created or destroyed. The natural world had ordained it. Mankind would make it happen.

Wolfram looked outside. The gardens that swept in a straight line to the house must be completed.

And Lukas Johansen must be found.

Chapter Twenty-Five

Jack walked the path his feet knew by heart. Every night he left his barrack home in darkness and returned in darkness. Tonight he slowly walked back with the dust of a mountain coating his clothes, skin, and throat, and clogging his ears.

Palov, the most outgoing member of the small manual-labor crew, shouted a good-bye. Jack had at first assumed he and the rest of the crew were locals, before he realized they spoke a Slavic language. He still didn't know if they'd been hired legally or if they'd been stolen from other salt mines. None of them spoke English or German, so Jack lifted his hand as their paths parted. Usually Palov made hand motions, asking Jack to drink beer with them as the shift ended. But Jack always had to smile and wave them on. It was clear they still didn't know he was captive here. Most likely they believed he was partners with Ian and free to quit the job and move on.

But tonight all the crew was tired. So Palov and the other three men plodded away toward their temporary housing in the crook of the mountain.

Jack was weary too. His back ached, and the holes in his boots kept filling with dirt and rocks. Jack imagined a hot shower, a sharp razor, and clean sheets to find rest in. It was maddening to think that he, Jack Porter, was actually being held prisoner. He worked and lived in a nighttime mountain paradise with the same constellations over his head that had been there all his life. When he remembered his prior world, it seemed impossible—surreal even—that this was happening to him. It was easier to surrender to the knowledge while inside his concrete room. Out here and during the hours of his workday, it was hard to comprehend that he could never go with Palov and the others, that he couldn't get on a boat and go home.

And yet it was so. The mountains and water became his jail cell, his family the lock that kept him inside.

Jack reached the barracks and entered the main hallway. Ian's door was open, and a light burned inside.

Ian met him as he passed. "Would you like a shower?"

Jack nodded, partially resenting that he must have permission, the other part thankful to not wait the four days until the weekly luxury. Ian unlocked the bathroom several rooms down and closed the door when Jack entered. The water was cold, the soap rough, and he couldn't stay under long. But he was clean.

Jack dried the hair that dripped down his back. The towel was thin and stuck to his body—it didn't smell fresh either. Several months had passed since Ian last granted a razor and scissors to him and Rudy. Jack dried his face and the short beard that was ever his annoyance and dressed in the same worn clothes he'd had beneath his work coveralls. A few raps at the locked door brought Ian back.

"We aren't making the necessary progress," Ian said when Jack emerged. A shiver ran down Jack's spine, and he longed for the wool blanket on his bed. He envied the thick red jacket Ian wore.

"We are doing everything we can," he said.

"It may not be enough." Ian disappeared into his room. Jack heard a television and had the strong urge to see it. Instead he turned toward the hall and basement stairs.

The light blared a one-hundred-watt glow over his head. Jack was cold all the way through and now regretted the shower. He wrapped himself in the blanket and sat at the small wooden table, hoping the bulb would add some heat to the room. He glanced at the vent in the bottom corner of the room and wondered how Rudy fared beyond the cement-block wall. Rudy's health was improving too slowly. Jack hoped summer would get rid of the plaguing cough and allow him to gain weight and strength before another winter.

"Now I'm making plans for my future here," he whispered in disgust. His voice sounded strange in the room, as if the walls muffled the words as soon as they were spoken.

From beneath his bed, Jack brought out a pen and paper. He stared at the paper. A week had passed since he'd last written— since the day the photographs had arrived. He had returned to those images each morning he awoke as a reminder of the reality he'd now entered. Tonight he would write again. The blank pages awaited his words.

The first page should be easy to write. It was the throwaway page that would be read while he worked. Jack had discovered the way to keep his supply of paper and pens from being taken. If his letters were amusing or if his readers thought he'd reveal something, they would allow him to write, providing ink pens and soft, onionskin paper. They believed he didn't know. Jack always left a single hair on the stack of fake letters. It was often gone upon his return. Jack had begun to play their game, even though their rules changed often.

He couldn't think of the words he would leave to be read. Instead he went straight to the ones he could only be rid of once they were there on the page. His pen touched the paper, paused, and then moved quickly.

I have lost count of the days, but I think it is toward the end of May. I will ask Rudy the date next time we speak; he never loses a day. I have not written you for a while. There is little left for me to say. My writings to you have given me strength and hope to continue. Now I know I am only a shadow of what I once was. Once I was a man with definitions and characteristics I could describe. This place has taken that away.

Now I know that I wanted you to wait for me, even if I was only bones in the ground. I wanted to be the lone thought in your head. I wanted what we shared to be strong enough to bring us together again. This is the part of me so filled with self. It shames me to admit, but I want you to long for me as I long for you. I have labored over the possibilities and tried to turn time back. If only I would have gone with you that morning in Venice. I won't say those words again. Right now you are sleeping, somewhere around the world. You do not know that I am alive or that I write you as I once would explain my day after Abbie had fallen asleep. I wish I could hear of your days again. But now I write my last letter to you. My own desire for you must be released. I must love you enough.

God perhaps will choose to use us as individuals now. We must believe in him instead of the love we once shared. Our love is only strong through him. And I will love you forever. But I must be free from you as you are free from me. Perhaps then I will find a way out. Good-bye, Kate.

He leaned back in the chair and decided he would destroy this letter. The writing of it was necessary, but he would not want to see it again.

"Jack," came a whisper mixed with a round of muffled coughs.

He flipped off the light and crawled to the vent in the wall. "I'm here," he whispered.

"How did it go tonight?"

Jack laid the blanket on the floor and stretched over it with his ear close to the ridges of the vent. "Not great, according to Ian. We could use you."

"It's bad when I miss the tunnels. This room is driving me crazy. Any thoughts of another dive for you and Ian?"

"Possibly. Get better and we'll talk about it."

"I'm trying." Rudy paused. His voice sounded different when he spoke again. "I've been thinking that, in a sense, this is my fault. Jack, they chose you because of me. They found a recommendation I wrote about you, and they made contact."

"I can't believe you'd say that."

"But the correspondence was what convinced them that you were the one. We would work well together, and your family would keep you here."

"You've been in that room too long. It's my turn to encourage *you*, I see."

"I don't need encouragement. What I want to ask is that you'll forgive me."

"There's nothing to forgive."

"It would give me peace just to know."

"Then I forgive you." Jack leaned his head against the vent. "Now, good rest."

"Good rest."

Back on his cot, Jack considered Ian's words. The operation was a failure so far. But Jack suddenly knew what they sought. It *was* the underwater cave that he'd found. They believed it was inside the mountain—their molelike diggings were in hopes of finding it. The salt mine had produced little—Palov and his men worked in a field they did not know. It was all for show, while Ian, Jack, and sometimes Rudy worked in the tunnels forbidden to the other men. Jack spent his nights mapping and searching old tunnels for anything left behind by the previous occupants. Ian would study those maps and the few objects Jack had found. The greatest excitement had come when they found the underground spring.

He bolted upright. It wasn't an underground spring as he suspected. They had reached a section of the cave. Jack tossed off the blanket and began to pace. If this was true, then the cave went deeper than he'd imagined. He could hold the key to what these men wanted. It could be his chance out.

⋆━◉◠━⋆

The sun sought to scorch the skin on his face and neck as he stood on the end of the dock, staring across the waters pocked with waves. Wolfram lowered his hat over his face to shade his eyes. Two boats secured to the dock knocked gently against the bumpers. Wolfram would enjoy a ride in the large cruiser back to civilization. He'd been secluded too long and missed the outside world of noise and constant activity. The quiet of mountains and lakes brought too many voices from the past sliding into his thoughts.

It won't be long, he promised himself. The castle grounds were nearly complete. The remodeling of buildings and the castle expansion were nearly finished. If the other work could be completed, he would be free from this place and his future secured.

"I want to own a mountain," his father had once said. A young Wolfram had watched from the slight crack in the cupboard, where he'd crept to escape his father's unpredictable rage. The boy watched in both fear and awe as his father settled himself into the chair—his legs spread wide and hands behind his head. Wolfram's mother had given him a cup of coffee on a silver tray with a silver milk server. She never lacked in detail. He watched his father pull at his mother's dress and wrap his hand around her thin leg.

"What would you do with a mountain?" his mother asked, slapping his hand.

"I would own something great," he said, and with one swoop he swept Wolfram's mother onto his lap, toppling the silver tray. She was angry and he laughed as she cleaned up the mess. But his father would never own a mountain or anything else for very long. He would end his life a pauper with every investment gone wrong.

A crisp wind blew from the water, and Wolfram walked from the wooden dock with steps slow and heavy. What made him remember that moment from his past? He had many memories from within that hideaway where he had found safety and could spy without being found. But only that one memory when his father put his claim on a mountain came to mind now. Wolfram had forgotten that. He usually kept those memories locked away. He was no longer that weak and timid child. He was no longer the son of a man whose anger destroyed his own life.

"Father, I *do* own a mountain," Wolfram whispered.

On the side of one mountain was the entrance to what had once been a salt mine. The one thing he'd never owned now waited somewhere in that mountain or in one of the surrounding ones. Though he was close, he knew patience was required. Yet it ground at his nerves that after so many years, he was this close but not close enough.

At least no one else knew the secret that only the highest-ranking Nazis had long ago ordained. Wolfram had made a careful examination of that fact in the last decades. Ernst, the one man Wolfram had tracked in Argentina, a Nazi in hiding as he was, had worked in the operations offices. He had the maps of three locations but was unsure which one had finally been chosen as the top secret location. Wolfram promised they would work together and build a Fourth Reich. But Ernst proved himself not as loyal as he claimed. In the end, Wolfram had the maps without the use of a trustworthy partner. At first he had thought he could find the location without the blue tile. He now knew this was the site, the other two locations distractions, but a year here had proven his need for the five pieces that made up the tile.

If not for that witch, he would have succeeded long ago. Wolfram had planned everything with precision. He'd bargained with one camp inmate at a time—food for information. They had eagerly told their stories, not only for survival but for a chance to betray the officers and guards who held them. His work paid off, and he found the inmate who would be used in the delivery of goods to the secret location in the Alps.

Wolfram could find pleasure in the memories of his work. His commanding officers had never suspected him of having intelligence beyond working as a guard. As the war ended, he saw the need to use extreme caution in everything he did. The time had come for such precision planning again.

He reached the white golf cart and paused to gaze above the gardens, beyond the castle and past the groves of pines and birches. Hidden behind the trees was the flat roof of the barrack. They were sleeping now—Rudy and Jack. He would work them harder. He'd find Lukas Johansen and Oskar Gogl.

This time he would succeed.

CHAPTER TWENTY-SIX

Jack's eyes could not adjust even though he stood in the shadows. They had grown stronger in the darkness, but full sunshine pierced even his squinted lids. Ian waited beside him as Jack rubbed his eyes and tried to think why he was leaving the bunker during the daytime hours and where he could be going.

The diggings had yielded little. Over the past year, he'd progressed through a cave, found objects both from the WWII era and others possibly of Roman and Celtic origin. Yet everything was quickly taken away, making an analysis impossible. Had he failed and was now to face the wrath of those who held him? Ian gave no warning, but he never did. Jack thought of ways to make himself and Rudy valuable—that was the key to survival.

Ian checked his watch and motioned for Jack to follow. Jack could barely open his eyes once he left the afternoon shadows. How ironic that the sunlight he'd longed for now killed his eyes. With every step along the wooded path, Jack's foreboding grew. He recalled well his first six months of imprisonment. Would he meet those two men again—the only two men he had depended upon for life? They had enjoyed their role as gods, taunting him and promising every harm imaginable. They knew about Kate and Abbie and liked to tell stories of women and children they'd met and abused. Jack knew they were mostly stories and that the photographs were probably archives, but the words and images worked at him despite his own logic.

Jack stopped along the stone pathway beneath the shade of a birch tree. He waited for Ian to turn toward him. "What is this, Ian?"

"Come."

"What should I expect?"

Ian said nothing, which concerned him even more. Perhaps they knew about the underwater cave. Or could they have done something to Kate or Abbie? Jack could feel his strength drain and panic spring into the empty spaces.

"God, help me," he whispered to himself. With these words, peace fell over him—an actual, true peace even in this moment. Jack realized this could be his walk to death, his last moments in the sunshine. Fear tried to inject its sting, but something stronger took it away. He was no longer afraid of leaving this world.

The woods opened and the curved path joined a wide walkway flanked by gardens all the way to the water's edge on his left. They moved upward, with the dock and shoreline behind them, toward a large white mansion remodeled from the framework of a castle. He'd seen only glimpses of the house through the trees, its roofline from the mountain entrance above, its dark outline during the midnight dives. Now he could see where the original structure, a stone turret and walls, joined the remodeled section. It was huge and grand, forcing him to realize the monetary resources of those who kept him here. Money such as this meant power.

They ascended stone stairs, headed across a cobbled square and then up another set of stairs through the front double doors. Jack walked with his shoulders straight. They would not destroy his spirit today. The door creaked, long and loud, as it opened. Jack heard the birds before he saw them. The long hallway, with its tall ceiling and magnificent rooms opening through different doorways, seemed designed for the giant at the top of a beanstalk—he was definitely Jack. Everything was bigger than necessary, yet the rooms were silent.

As they passed a mirror, Jack caught the reflection of a stranger walking with Ian. A haunted man with circles beneath his eyes and chin and cheekbones narrowed from weight loss stared back. His hair had more gray, and he appeared nearly fifty when he'd yet to hit forty. This man was not the Jack Porter he once greeted in the morning mirror. The sight of himself stole some of his confidence. Waiting at the end of the hallway, Ian motioned for Jack, knocked lightly on the door, then opened it.

Jack's eyes had weathered the full brightness of day and then the dull light of the hall. Now he entered a study where sunshine streamed through the open French doors at the opposite end. As they walked through the room, Jack took in a few details until the television caught his eye. He recognized Larry King on CNN—the first news he'd seen besides scraps of outdated papers in three years. Jack smiled as he passed it, somehow believing that God had given him that glimpse as encouragement.

Through the open doors, they approached a man sitting at a white patio table. Even from the back, Jack could tell he was old and was surprised by his age. As they moved around, he studied the face that perused a newspaper. He must be over seventy, perhaps even eighty. But there was pride and strength about him in his straight posture and air of royalty about his large head. His hair, thick and brushed straight back, was dyed black, and he had large sideburns. A tailored suit fit well over his large frame, the tie smooth beneath a dinner jacket. They were at a secluded estate, yet this man dressed impeccably for his afternoon soup. Obviously his polished shoes had not walked in the dust or the gravel outside. As he leaned forward to sip his soup, he touched his tie.

Jack had expected a compound of terrorists, neo-Nazis, or anti-American forces. He'd spent hours trying to discover who these people were and what they were after. Yet he had seen no one along the paths outside or in the rooms within the house. Jack peered back into the room and around the private garden for the faces he expected. There was no two-way mirror or camera with an eye on him. Could he really have been kept here all this time, not by the great "them" he had imagined, but by this "him"?

Jack knew there had been at least three men who'd entered his hotel room in Venice. In seconds they were inside, and he was unconscious from some object to the head. There had been other men when he was transferred to different locations. Where were these men now? An old man sipping his soup brought an absurdity to his struggle.

Jack fought the instant shame. This man, this old and crumbling man, could not have destroyed his life, caused his family and himself immense pain, forced him to live in the night and work within the walls of a mountain. He could not be held captive by the desire of this lone man. Could he?

Without acknowledging Jack's presence, the man took a long drink. As he drank, his long earlobes moved. The man leaned back and stared for a long time. Another drink, another stare. How could older people stare as if seeing something behind their own eyes? Was that how great plots were discovered? Perhaps that was why they kept him at exhaustion level—so as not to drift into the places where the mind made most anything possible.

At last the old man spoke, but in German. The reason for Ian became clear. He was the interpreter. "Come forward," he said through Ian.

Jack moved in front of him. The dark eyes that studied him made him self-conscious. He realized this was part of the game. The loss of every small convenience cut into his human dignity. This crotchety old man enjoyed a sunny afternoon and used Jack as a pawn. Yet Jack felt no fear, none at all. He felt stronger than he had in a long time.

The man spoke and waited for the translation, then continued. "Your work here is almost done. You will want to go home then."

Jack tried to ignore the tinge of hope that stirred. There was no home to go to, he reminded himself. It had all changed. This man had done his work well. He'd fed Jack hope until the end came near; then reality was his destruction. His family had moved on, so there was nothing else for him but this. That was what this man wanted him to believe. Without Jack's faith beyond understanding or logic, this man would have succeeded.

God, give me strength. Tell me what to do and say. I need the will to fight and be strong for whatever future you have for me.

"My name is Wolfram Meizer," he said through Ian, then waited for a reaction. "I am your captor, your king, if you will." As he motioned for Jack to sit across from him, he smiled.

"Why did you bring me here, Wolfram Meizer?" Jack sat in the chair while Ian remained standing.

"You are here to be my hands. To do as I tell you and move where I want you to go."

"No, why am I here at this table right now?"

"I wanted to see you in person. I want to tell you how

important it is for your work to succeed—and soon. Your work must get finished, Jack Porter. I wonder if I can trust your work."

"What will happen to me after I finish your work? And to Rudy?"

"Rudy does not get better and cannot work. What good is he to me now?"

"Rudy is essential," Jack said, anxiety rising. He would need to protect Rudy. "I am unable to work without Rudy."

"If you neglect your work, Rudy may be neglected also."

"What if I find it?"

"It?"

"The secret I'm supposed to find without knowing what it is."

"You will have freedom."

"I do not believe you."

It took a moment for Wolfram to get the translation. It made him laugh. "You do not have to believe me," Wolfram said in English.

"I have no choice, you mean."

"*Ja, ja, das ist* it. No choice."

Yet Jack *did* have some power over this man who sat with such confidence. He now knew the discovery of the cave was the best thing that had happened to him in three years.

◦━◉◓◦

It became the new routine. Jack would work through the night in the salt mine, return to the bunker and sleep, to be later awakened and brought to the house. Wolfram would be in his office or his smoking room or on the patio with his afternoon meal. He always sipped his soup from the same white bowl and drank his coffee from the same white cup, with saucers under each. Every day he ignored Jack's presence for the first several minutes, then he would wave him forward at a given time. Jack would sit down and Wolfram would stare into other places. Jack had the feeling Wolfram precisely planned not just each and every moment of his own life, but of Jack's and Rudy's lives also.

On Jack's fourth visit, when Wolfram turned his attention his way, Jack said boldly, "I would like a Bible."

"In English, I suppose."

"Yes." Jack nodded.

Wolfram spoke to Ian, who left the patio for the office. He returned a few moments later with a thick, leather-bound Bible in English and handed it to Jack. Why would he have such an item? Jack wondered.

"Anything else?"

Jack paused, a bit taken back. "Oswald Chambers' book *My Utmost for His Highest* and a John Grisham novel—one of his most recent ones. And a razor." Jack then realized what he should be asking for. "Most of all, some antibiotics for Rudy, if not a doctor to see him."

Wolfram spoke and Ian responded, "He wants you to write it down. He says you are good at writing." Wolfram gave a sly smile. Jack relished the fact that Wolfram thought he had surprised him, as if Jack didn't already know about the letters.

The next day Jack brought the paper with his requests. He'd added pears and oranges to his list for both himself and Rudy. Rudy had once said how much he missed eating pears to the point that he prayed every night for some. Jack had smiled as he wrote *pears* on the list. God did have mysterious ways.

Fatigue was becoming a great enemy. Wolfram seemed to forget Jack needed rest, especially with the increased pressure to finish the project. Ian's weekly work schedule pushed the diggings beyond dangerous. They used explosives more often. Jack made plans to smuggle some into the barracks, but Ian inventoried them after every shift.

Despite the weariness he fought, Jack looked forward to his time with Wolfram. The old man seemed to find pleasure in talking to Jack. Sometimes he'd speak about nothing of importance: his annoyance about an area of his gardens where pansies had died from an unexpected frost, or the overload of advertisements on television. But mixed within these mostly one-sided conversations were bits and pieces of the Wolfram Meizer Jack was interested in deciphering.

As evening fell, Jack would return to the barrack and record Wolfram's words. Every day he tabulated the little phrases. He hid these pages inside a ripped part of the lining beneath the cot—something he could do against his captor. Through the bits of conversations, day after day, Jack discovered who held him and why. He scanned the record of their conversations and began to understand the mind of Wolfram Meizer.

May 31

Wolfram talked and stared, and I wondered if he sometimes forgets I'm there. He'd comment on something on CNN, and I realized how he uses it to work on his English. Often he gets the news story completely wrong. It's strange having Ian speak his words for him. I often wonder why Wolfram repeats some things. Some of his words today: "Man must be of value or there is no value of him living."

There was a CNN story on former Yugoslavia that sparked his interest. He said, "We almost won, you know. The tunnels were being dug, and we needed a little more time. Did you know the technology we were gaining?"

June 1

Nothing of importance today. We sat in his smoking room. The newly remodeled walls are already tinged with the scent of smoke. He puffed on his cigar and wanted to hear about my work in the States.

June 2

Wolfram said, "In Gusen, a camp near the Danube River, we had planes built. And all underground."

June 3

There is more than I can remember from my conversation with Wolfram today. I'll write what I can recall. It was like getting a whole view inside his mind. I don't believe Ian had heard Wolfram speak about these things before. That in itself is a concern. Does Ian wonder why Wolfram gives me so much? I wonder.

We were in his office, and CNN showed a refugee camp in former Yugoslavia. The video made Wolfram lean forward in his chair.

After a lengthy stare, he spoke. "If we had one cold night, they died like rodents eating poison. They were animals, licking soup that dripped onto the filthy floor. They broke every rule and deserved punishment. It is their fault we lost the war. Did you know that?"

I asked who he spoke of.

"The Jews, Italians, Poles, criminals, and weaklings."

"Weren't they starving?"

"You should see what people do when they don't have food."

"I can understand a little."

He ignored my comment and continued. "We must look toward the larger picture. I once had a commanding officer with this great career who became obsessed with finding a family heirloom. It was some coins and a brooch that belonged to the Austrian Empress Sissi. He would not give up when he could have saved himself at the end of the war. Instead of making preparations to leave Europe, he kept searching. Ridiculous. Many people were killed because he couldn't get it."

"He never found this heirloom?" I asked.

"No. One part was found by the family not long ago, but the brooch is still missing. I saw one woman die at a camp over that brooch, and there were others also. Even the officer died in his pursuit."

There were other comments that I'll try to remember and add later.

June 5

It's strange how these years around Ian—though he usually speaks perfect English, and I think he speaks several languages fluently—and with Rudy's bits of German, now I can sometimes understand Wolfram before Ian translates. Ian did not come for me until it was time to work again. The rest was needed. But Wolfram said nothing of importance to record, except I did see the video screens of our rooms in a cabinet when we passed through the office. The door hadn't been closed all the way, but I pretended not to see.

June 6

Wolfram was full of thoughts today. "Hitler lost his genius to gluttony. He gobbled too much and it destroyed us. It will be different the next time."

I didn't respond, so he looked me in the eyes when he said, "The armies prepare around the world. You must know where to align. The hatred of men as well as their loves can be used to make them do nearly anything."

June 7

Today I asked if Wolfram had ever let any of his birds free. He stared at them in their bizarre, different-shaped cages—with one bird in the largest cage, and four in the smallest. He said, "Once I let a little bird go to see what it would do. But it didn't know how to fly anymore. I let the cat inside. It would have died anyway."

June 8

For the first time I saw true fear in Wolfram's face. He was talking about the Jews, trying to convince me of the truth of an international plot. He said, "They are not human. They just look like it on the outside. Don't ever let them fool you."

Suddenly he faced me as if he was looking at me for the first time. "You not Juden?"

I wanted to say yes just to give him a scare, see him choke on his soup.

Ian spoke before I could decide. "Nein, Papa."

I did not know if I'd heard Ian correctly. I asked, "He is your father?"

"Yes. He is my father."

Now much more is clear about Ian.

I'm writing what even seems of small significance. Perhaps this will be for a purpose I don't yet know. Tomorrow I'm to get a tour of the remodeled castle. Rudy confirms that this is good—it's giving us knowledge that will be useful. I keep wondering why. Why is this happening now? I think it is perhaps a bored Wolfram who likes to play with our minds. But I also think he is getting quite desperate to find what is in the mountain. I pray before I leave my room and hope these bizarre meetings will produce a way to escape.

CHAPTER TWENTY-SEVEN

Wolfram went through the plans one final time. The last phase of the grounds' development was days away from completion. His contacts in the States had located Oskar Gogl living comfortably in Maine. Lukas Johansen would not be difficult to track down.

He stretched and checked his watch again. There were several hours before Jack Porter would arrive. The hours with the man were amusing. Jack continually tried to understand him and seek a way to freedom. The young man could find no peace in his position. And Jack wasn't telling the entire truth about his explorations; Wolfram had that feeling the more they spoke. There was not enough fear in Jack Porter's eyes— that was the proof.

Wolfram walked to the kitchen to see what his housekeeper was preparing. He rarely saw the older woman. Hilde was paid well and needed little time away. She adhered to his stringent rules, and he'd never caught her in even the smallest infraction. She had been well trained long ago.

Hilde looked up, surprised to see him in the kitchen. His feet thundered over the stone floor.

"Grüß Gott," she said softly as she kneaded some bread dough. Her arms were thin and her sleeves pulled up.

"Grüß Gott," Wolfram replied. He noted that Ian had brought a white bag of medicines, pears, and oranges from his morning trip to town, which brought a smile to his face. That made him wonder about the mail, so he left the kitchen and walked to the sideboard by the front door. Wolfram went through the bills and catalogs. Then he saw a large envelope with a return address from an acquaintance in Vienna. Inside he found a note from the man and an unopened letter. The letter had been sent to Wolfram in care of this man, who had forwarded it on to his village mailbox.

Intrigued, he opened the letter and met the words of Bruno Weiler. His hands began to shake. The memories returned with the rising of his rage. In a mad swoop he cast the mail onto the floor and slammed his hand through the mirror on the wall. Blood gushed from the wound as he crumpled the page in his fist.

Bruno—or Lukas—his old betrayer wanted a fight. And Bruno Weiler would get his desire.

> Never say you've come to the end of the way,
> Though leaden skies blot out the light of the day.
> The hour we all long for will surely appear—
> Our steps will thunder with the words: We are here!
>
> In blood this song was written, and not with pen or quill,
> Not from a songbird freely flying as he will.
> Sung by a people crushed by falling wall—
> Sung with guns in hand, by those whom freedom calls!
>
> From "Zog Nit Keyn Mol" ("Never Say")
> Written by Hirsh Glick in the Vilno Ghetto of Poland (April 1943)

part *three*

Some call this island the World's End,
for though you can sail further,
this is the beginning of the end. . . .

—C. S. Lewis, *The Voyage of the "Dawn Treader"*

Chapter Twenty-Eight

Rain streamed down the car windows like so many tears Kate had yet to cry. She'd held the tears inside, not shedding one in the weeks of May and June as she prepared to leave her world behind. Her cottage home was now behind her, awaiting the couple who would house-sit for the summer.

She was going to Europe. Suddenly, in a confusing flurry, the time had come. Abbie was quiet as they left Corvalis, Oregon, and headed for California, where Kate would leave her daughter with her parents and catch her flight. The idea of parting had caused them both much anxiety.

"Do you think Reece understands I'm not going to Australia?" Kate asked.

Abbie smiled bravely and even giggled. "I don't think so. A few days before school ended I had my last e-mail lab. There was a note from Reece. He wants you to get him a postcard of a koala bear and a kangaroo."

"I'll get an atlas out and show him where Austria is."

"I know—like the bologna between the bread of Germany and Italy—that's what Grandpa told me."

"Grandpa is very wise."

Kate guided her SUV from Highway 34 to join the flow of faster traffic on Interstate 5 South. Connie called Kate on the cell phone three times with questions about her trip. What she really was trying to say was finally said on the last call.

"Okay, it's just that I won't know what to do without you. I'm joining this summer Bible study and I wanted you to do it too. And summer swim club and everything. But then I'm also so proud of you and excited and—I mean, Europe for the summer! This is amazing! But, of course, I won't say a word to anyone. I love you, my friend."

Kate said the same and they hung up—again. For the thousandth time she wondered if this was a mistake. It helped to have her family's support and also Marta's, who called a few times a week with new thoughts about Kate's trip.

Kate's realization weeks ago in Cottonwood had started a domino effect that made this trip possible. Abbie was out of school by the beginning of June. Kate's most faithful customer, Mrs. Charles, bought several pieces Kate had previously refused to part with, providing the money for the summer in Europe. Kate's father would manage Restorations from afar, with Connie as his contact and bookkeeper after she decided to close her in-home day care—the smashed marshmallows under their pillows had been the last straw. Trudy had asked for more summer hours before Kate could even approach her. It all worked out—and this time Kate didn't write it off as coincidence.

Marta warned Kate to keep her destination a secret from all but her closest friends. Kate had anticipated that, yet many people's suspicions would mount unless she planned something. She could hear the rumors otherwise: "She's spending

the summer in Europe? I thought she struggled financially."
Or, "Always expected to see something suspicious from her."

Kate wanted to divert attention without lies. If the need
arose, Kate would say she needed to get away, and Abbie
wanted to spend time with her grandparents. She'd said it a
few times and then hurried away or changed the subject. Time
moved so quickly that few people had asked.

Then Mason had arrived at her doorstep a few days ago.
"You've been vague on the telephone when you actually do
return my calls. Every weekend you've been busy, and now I
hear from Jane that your mom is ill and you're moving there
for the summer, possibly for good, and Connie might take
over the shop. Kate, what's going on?"

She invited him inside, but he didn't move so she came out
on the porch.

"Is there any truth to this?"

"Not much. But I am leaving for a month or so. I meant to
tell you, but it just never seemed right. So I've avoided you."

"At least you're honest." He wore a grim expression she'd
rarely seen. "You're still searching for him."

"I have some things to get together in my life."

"What happened to us?"

The words they'd spoken at the restaurant seemed long
ago—before finding the blue tile, before meeting Lukas and
Marta, before going to California, where she'd found the
strength to seek Jack one more time. Kate hadn't forgotten that
she and Mason were supposed to be testing the waters to see if
a relationship was possible between them. She'd just avoided
it—and him. Now she knew how unfair that had been.

"I'm sorry. But it was too soon."

He looked at the ground. "So where are you going?"

She bit her thumbnail, and he waited for her answer.
"Europe," she said. "I met some people who are helping me
find out what happened."

Mason shook his head. "Kate, when will you understand? He wasn't the man you've turned him into."

"What do you mean? Tell me that you saw him with another woman or that he behaved differently behind my back. If you can say that, then perhaps I can believe you. Perhaps it will change my mind."

"I can't say those things. But you've made him into a saint by this memory you cling to. He wasn't a saint or some hero. He was a man, just like I am. Life is worth living, Kate. You can't live forever in the past."

"I need to know. I've prayed for answers, and now this opportunity has come."

"It tells me a lot that you didn't come to me."

"You aren't a part of this." He was hurt by her words, but Kate knew it was the truth. This was her path to be taken without him. She studied his face and the hand that rubbed his chin. Kate realized Mason didn't have the rough hands she often yearned to hold her; his were long and soft and beautiful hands, but they weren't the ones she longed for. She needed Jack.

"I'll be here when you return," he said gently.

"Don't wait for me any longer."

"There's nothing else I can do," he said, forcing the words through his teeth.

"That isn't true."

"Do you care for me?"

"Very much." She reached for him, then pulled her hand away. "I think . . . I mean, I believe we could have loved one another if our lives weren't these lives. Does that make sense?"

"No. It makes no sense at all."

"You don't want it to. I think you've known it all along."

He nodded after a few moments. "Good-bye, Kate. I'll be here when you return."

"Mason, don't wait for me. I can't say what tomorrow will bring, and you need to walk your own path."

Kate had watched him until his car disappeared down the street. He was behind her now, left with everything else she'd known for so long. She'd settled into a life sans Jack and was just getting familiar, even comfortable, with the prospect of a future. Now Kate had chosen to cast it aside for a great unknown. But she wasn't alone. God would be with her every step and mile and continent ahead.

‹‐⟐⟐‐›

Kate had one full day before she left her family and child behind. She could tell that her mother worried, but both her parents supported her decision. Her brother wanted to come with her, but Kate wouldn't take him from his own family. She'd call if help was required, and Tayler had already applied for a passport just in case.

While everyone else in the house was tucked into their beds, Kate sat on the bed and opened her Bible beneath the round glow of the butterfly lamp that had been hers as a kid. She started turning to the book of Colossians, but her eye was caught by words in the Old Testament book of 2 Samuel. She read of King David and the death of his infant son. David had been heartbroken, but one of his statements echoed through Kate again and again: *"I will go to him one day, but he cannot return to me."* She realized that whatever had happened to Jack, he could not come to her. But she would go to him—be it on earth or in heaven.

Abbie rolled toward her and mumbled something in her sleep. She smacked her mouth softly, then was still again. Kate watched her daughter, with her hands folded beneath her cheek, and knew that she couldn't leave her behind.

It would be morning in Austria, Kate calculated, so she

grabbed the address book from her purse. Kate tramped to the darkened kitchen for the phone and punched in the long series of numbers before she could talk herself out of it.

A woman whose voice she didn't recognize answered the phone in a flurry of German. Kate asked for Marta and the woman grumbled something else, then set the phone down with a clatter. Moments passed before Marta came to the phone.

"I have to bring Abbie," Kate said quickly. "We'll rent a bungalow or whatever you have over there."

Marta chuckled. "It will be wonderful to have a little girl in this house. We could all use it."

"Lukas won't be so welcoming. He isn't happy with me, so how will he handle a child? If he isn't nice to her—"

"Don't worry, Kate. I will prepare Lukas. You make the arrangements. Does she have a passport?"

"Yes. We got her one after Jack—in case he was ever found and we needed to come over. I brought it to my parents' with me."

"You have known this for a while then?"

"No, though I guess I hoped. Could it be dangerous for her?"

"I do not believe it any more dangerous than leaving her there. We are safe in Lukas' home. We have made few plans and will make the rest when you arrive. But she will stay here with me if you need to go anywhere we have concerns. Or you will stay here. Or perhaps you fly her home if it is difficult. Anyway, bring the girl, and we will establish the details after your arrival."

"Thank you, Marta."

Hours passed without sleep. Kate read her Bible and then a new novel that she'd bought for the plane ride, though she should be reading more about WWII and the Nazis. She turned off the light, but her mind wouldn't relax. Doubts came with the darkness. Should she take Abbie? What would it be like to return to Europe? Kate considered calling Mason in the morning to say good-bye. She'd certainly call Connie. What should she bring for Abbie on the plane? Her daughter's birthday was coming—should they come home or celebrate it without family? What was Kate thinking? This entire trip was pure insanity. Her entire life was being disrupted, and for what? Possible answers?

Kate wrestled with her thoughts, something she'd done often but did even more so tonight. At last she gave up and remembered to pray. She prayed for herself and for tomorrow. Then she went through the list of her family and friends, trying hard to remember what each was experiencing. It made her realize how consumed she'd been with her own life. But she continued to pray for even the unknown in their lives. For Aunt Gerdie's late-life crisis and Mason's future and on through the rows of faces she saw in the darkness. And sleep finally came.

Lukas had settled into his old routine at home. Messages, appointments, and mail had awaited former minister Lukas Johansen. He worked through them, feeling needed and productive again. Marta spent hours on the computer, making arrangements to sell her Arizona house and get her mostly boxed-up possessions into storage. She also organized for Kate's arrival.

He could feel the tension in his daughter Anni at the idea of having a stranger with free decision-making power in the house. Anni had become quite comfortable in the house she'd never lived in as a child. It had been three years since he had allowed her to move in. Marta was sensitive to the young woman, but Anni had never been easy to manage, and Lukas had never been good at talking to any of his daughters, especially Anni. But in all, he was happy to be home. Home was like a nice slow pipe after a hectic day. And the weeks in the States had been more than hectic.

Back in his element, Lukas had decisions to make. He had

invitations to teach at several universities—Innsbruck was closest. The publisher for his book deal had left several messages. His retirement years were supposed to be this way. Years ago the political buzz had pointed toward his appointment as chancellor of Austria. After all, he had worked well under Chancellor Kreisky's administration from 1970 to the early 1980s. Austria had experienced years of growth despite the scandals that never fled political life. Jewish Chancellor Kreisky was criticized for appointing wartime Nazis into his cabinet, but no one in government knew Lukas could be counted among their ranks. Lukas understood Kreisky's desire to unify Austria and to put the past behind, though Lukas also found it intriguing that, decades earlier, Kreisky had been forced to flee Austria because of the men he appointed as cabinet members. Sometimes Lukas would gaze around at his colleagues and realize he was sitting in a room of former enemies. They would have killed Kreisky under orders of the Third Reich. At the beginning of the war, Lukas guarded men like Kreisky; and by the end of the war, he would have killed these ex-Nazis. Now they worked together for the good of a new Austria—whatever that meant to each of them.

The political climate shifted away from Lukas when the Social Democrats lost a majority and a coalition government formed. It didn't bother him because politics were his life now, but he wouldn't accept the position of chancellor, not with his past. Though his secrets were well covered, he'd seen skeletons escape closets that had seemed to be shut tight. Someone in that position would be very carefully scrutinized, especially after the President Waldheim scandal. Waldheim had claimed he had no knowledge of his unit's atrocities, but few believed him. Lukas quietly backed those who wanted him brought up on war crimes. The Waldheim case deserved to be looked at. Lukas knew colleagues who had an old Nazi Party badge—most everyone joined during the late 1930s when *Nazi* meant being the political favorite. Later a Party number was practically necessary for survival. But this wasn't simple politics or even service in the German army. Waldheim was an Austrian president who had been a Nazi SS in the Death's Head Division—and the members of Death's Head served their name well. Waldheim's and Austria's images were tarnished in the eyes of the world. For Austria, it wouldn't be the first time or the last.

But Lukas always stepped back when the scandals came. Sometimes he expected a bony finger to point at him. His benefactors who helped after his prison time had instructed him carefully, even paid for minor facial alterations. But Lukas would still feel fear rise when an unexpected camera appeared in his face. Why he was spared, he didn't know. His work in the Austrian Resistance perhaps helped, or maybe his skeletons were truly buried deep.

Lukas was out of the political arena now. He missed Vienna enough to still travel there often. Marta had been to Vienna only a few times as a teenager. They'd go for a week soon and he'd show her everything.

He made mental plans in front of the fire one evening. The Kunsthistorisches Museum, home to some of the world's finest art, would be high on the list and the Hofburg Palace, where once the imperial Habsburgs ruled the Austro-Hungarian Empire. Some summer festivals had started already, performing his favorite operas at the renowned Vienna Music Festival that drew the world's wealthiest and most influential guests. Soon enough he would show Marta everything.

Kate Porter was due to arrive in a few days. Lukas wished they'd already taken one trip to Vienna. Once the American woman came, it would be time to concentrate on what he'd been avoiding since his return.

A fire blazed in the living-room fireplace. Lukas sat in his wing-backed chair and sipped the coffee Marta brought him.

She sat in a chair beside him, staring into the flames. He wanted to ask how she was doing, but instead he tried to watch and gauge her progress. Her adaptation appeared to be going well. Marta hadn't known how much she'd missed the Alps, she said. Now Lukas found little jars of wildflowers around the house, though he'd yet to catch her in the act. One morning he'd found the flowers outside his door.

From the corner of his eye he saw that she was still deep in thought. In their short time together, he was amazed at how comfortable he felt talking to her, even if their discussions led to disagreements. There'd been no one in his life like that. Perhaps he trusted her because Karl had trusted her, or because she'd always been faithful through the years. He only lost courage in asking how she was doing. Did she still cry over Karl at night?

Marta sipped her tea delicately, her lips gently touching the cup. He wondered how she pulled her long hair into the soft curls around her head. She nodded to herself as if deciding something, then turned to face him. He was about to smile when he noticed her determined look.

"What?" he asked.

"I want you to welcome Kate and Abigail in a generous manner when they come."

"I am allowing them to stay at my own house. That seems like a generous manner, especially when there is a child involved." Lukas was irritated to no end about the child coming. There would be toys to avoid and no rest from the noise.

"We need children around us. This place may be beautiful, but it can be very cold. Your daughter does not like me here."

Lukas didn't like that Marta had felt an empty coldness to his house. He wanted her to feel welcome. "Anni does not like anyone."

"She reminds me of her father."

"You are not correct. I like you very much, Marta Olsen." He hoped to get a smile from her, but she ignored him.

"Your heart is not in this search for Wolfram. You do not wish to do this?"

"What I wish is not relevant. I wish to be a much younger man. I wish for a little peace. There is little choice in this matter."

"You are home in your mountain haven. Nothing can touch you here."

"I do not fear for my life, Marta. I believed we were pursuing Wolfram for revenge."

"I am tired of revenge. Justice, not revenge, remember? Nothing will make it all right. Nothing will bring back those years we've lost or return Karl to me. Don't you yearn for peace?"

Lukas shifted in his chair and felt her study his profile. "Peace is something I have never known except for brief moments. But I do long for it."

They watched the silent flames consume the oak logs with only an occasional snap of surrender. Lukas thought back to the beginning. When he'd first dreamt of belonging to something great. He'd believed the Nazi Party was that—it promised a future and development for a better tomorrow. The controversial aspects had seemed minor compared to his thoughts of a greater good, until these issues had become reality and he had been faced with the guilt of being swept up without using his mind or his conscience.

He sighed. "I wish someone could have told me that the decisions of youth haunt even your dying days. We talk of justice and revenge—should I be exempt from them?"

"You went to prison for your crimes," she said. "Lukas, what exactly happened in those years before you came to us?"

The images were never far from his mind's eye. Once he had confessed those sins in this very house to a young American woman named Darby Evans. It had been months since he'd last checked on her, now living in Salzburg. She was the only one to hear his words, the only one it made sense to tell. But he wanted to tell it again. He kept waiting for someone to condemn him, to call him the murderer he was and confirm his own words.

"I killed a young woman."

Nothing changed in Marta's expression—not a twitch or movement in the lines of her face.

"Tatianna Hoffman was her name. She died to save her best friend." He folded his hands together and rested his elbows on the arms of the leather chair. "I knew both Tatianna and her friend during our childhood—we grew up in the same village. It was my first firing squad." Lukas could see his victims as clearly as the fire before him. Tatianna so thin and changed from the carefree village girl he once knew.

"There were others in the line against the wall. But I killed Tatianna. I could have chosen one of the men, or I think there was a child there, but I suddenly cared for her. I aimed true so she would not suffer. It was the first time I had cared in a very long while."

Marta watched the fire, and he wondered if she had heard him.

"Her best friend survived the war by fleeing to America and had a child—a daughter who later had a daughter of her own. I met that young woman this past year. She told me about God's forgiveness. And I actually saved this woman's life."

"You saved the granddaughter's life—of the friend who escaped the war? Recently?"

"Yes," he said in a whisper. "Was this God giving me another chance to make right what happened with Tatianna?"

"Perhaps." She nodded. "*Ja*, perhaps."

"It brought me closest to peace, the closest I have been since childhood. Then I went to a reunion in America to see my old comrades."

Marta was wiping away a tear. Lukas hadn't seen her cry in weeks.

"Why this?" he asked, wanting to reach across the gulf of space between them to touch her cheek.

"I do not know."

"You do not cry for me?"

"Yes, I cry for you, Lukas. I cry for your heart and life and that we brought you into this when you were at last leaving the past behind. I cry for your unshed tears."

He wondered how she knew about the tears that never found him.

"You need not cry for me. Redemption may not be so easy as I hoped, but I do not deserve your tears. Cry for Karl or Jantes or Susanne. Even cry for Tatianna and now this woman Kate Porter, who has lost her husband. Look how God forever faces me with young women—and this Kate brings a girl child. I even have three daughters. Could God not give me sons? Women haunt me since Tatianna."

"I think that is part of your peace. Let them comfort you, not make you afraid. Do your daughters know this story?"

"No. Three daughters who know nothing of what their father has done, or even his birth-given name."

"Perhaps it is time to tell them."

Lukas turned quickly toward her. "How can you say such a thing? They must never know. Am I not already haunted enough without seeing my own children hate me? They think I am a leader who fights for his beliefs. How do I tell them that once I was the enemy I have fought so long against? Never say that again. There is one last danger, and that is Wolfram. We must focus on him. If I do not seek him, he will seek me."

"Wolfram will leave you alone. Karl was seeking him so he—" Marta stopped, and Lukas realized that perhaps she wished they'd stayed far from Wolfram. He had not told Marta of the letter he sent, sure it would eventually make it to Wolfram's hands. He could not hide now.

"He will not leave us alone," Lukas said. "I've been wondering about the tile pieces. We will look at Karl's piece when Kate Porter returns it. Wolfram may want more than just an old revenge."

"Then we have work to do before your death. I believe in the end, you will find your peace."

"I hope you are right." Lukas thought of Karl on the floor of his house. There had been no peace for his friend. He deserved it even less.

⟶━◉━◦⟵

All that was familiar had been pushed behind her.

Flights were on schedule. Kate and Abbie had a barely manageable amount of luggage. They had left Redding, California, before the sun rose and changed planes in San Francisco and again in Frankfurt, Germany, to their final destination of Innsbruck, Austria. Abbie loved flying and saved her packet of pretzels as a souvenir. She watched the Disney Channel on the trans-Atlantic Boeing 777 and followed the digital map on her monitor that showed their present position and point of destination. When they flew over England, Abbie enjoyed picturing the children from the Chronicles of Narnia and the queen of England below them.

Kate and Abbie both peered through the plane's small window on the last flight. The snow-covered Alps shone like panes of cut glass, reflecting light at differing angles. The peaks looked like a dozen ranges that had collided together, stretching in every direction along the horizon. Kate had never imagined the white-capped domes to be so imposing. Villages and winding strips of roadway could be distinguished within deep valleys as the plane descended toward the skiing village of Innsbruck.

Kate's airport instructions were simple—after baggage claim and customs, look for Lukas' daughter Anni, who would pick them up. She was there—a thin woman in her thirties with bleached blonde hair. There was no welcome in her eyes. She casually held a sign in one hand that said "Porter," while holding a cigarette in the other.

"I'm Kate Porter. And this is Abbie."

The woman nodded. A man rose from a bench and helped with their luggage.

"I am Anni Johansen," the woman said in a thick accent. Clearly she did not enjoy her assignment as chauffeur. "This is an employee of my father's."

The airport was small, so in minutes they were riding in a gray sedan, with the couple in front and Abbie and Kate in back. Neither the woman nor the man said much to them. The soft leather seats and gentle rumble of the vehicle rocked Abbie to sleep, her head against Kate's shoulder.

"How long until we reach Lukas and Marta?" Kate asked, leaning forward.

Anni glanced first at the man who was driving before answering. "In one hour we arrive at my father's estate," she said, with a half turn her way. "How many days do you and the child and Marta stay with us?"

Anni's tone indicated what she thought of company in her house.

"At least a few weeks," Kate said.

Anni said nothing else for the rest of the drive.

Kate watched the world outside the speeding vehicle. Pines grew from the mountain slopes to the rim of livestock-dotted fields. The colors shimmered with an energy all their own here. Just yesterday she'd left Cottonwood with its already heat-washed landscape, where the color was slowly being sucked from trees and fields, even the sky—like water drained from the thirsty land. But Austria's colors had awakened from the winter's nap with new greens, the bluest skies, and mountains that chose their own tints throughout the day—whether borrowed from the lakes below or the shades of sunset.

As the sun dipped behind the mass of mountains above the valley road, it dawned on Kate that she was really in Europe again. Though this was a much different Europe from the water-locked streets of Venice, she'd actually come to a place she'd never wanted to return to. And she wasn't afraid.

Iron gates opened wide for their arrival when the driver hit a digital switch on the car's console. Through tall pines the house shone in the shadows, illuminated by miniature lights along pathways and in the surrounding gardens. Unlike the quaint Austrian homes Kate had admired on the drive in, with decorative trimmings on the gables and wooden flower boxes bursting from every window, the Johansen residence was reminiscent of the old imperial Austro-Hungarian Empire with its air of sophistication and grandeur. She assessed the house at over a hundred years old, though it appeared spotless and new. The winding lawns were shaved short like a cut carpet, and a fountain bubbled in the center of the circular driveway.

"It looks like a place for a princess," Abbie said, rubbing her eyes as the car stopped. The man got out quickly and opened Kate's door.

Marta walked down the steps and embraced Kate at the car. Lukas stood in the entrance at the massive double doors.

"You must be Abigail," Marta said, bending to see her.

Abbie's sleepy smile brightened when she noticed the fountain. "The water looks pink."

"Yes, a special color for our special guest. You will see the dancing fairies in the morning. We need to get you out of the chill."

"Welcome," Lukas said without a smile. He reached to shake Kate's hand.

"Danke schön," Kate replied, which earned her an approving nod.

Marta had made dinner and done much to prepare for their arrival. She'd set up a playroom in an upstairs bedroom with a children's kitchen set and TV and VCR, where Abbie could also sleep if she chose. Abbie could hardly be pulled away from the room to come to dinner—dumplings and a beef dish with thick burgundy gravy. Neither Anni nor the man in the car joined their meal. Lukas spoke little while they ate, but he asked Abbie if she liked her room. Marta claimed it had been Lukas' idea, though he brushed it away as untrue. Kate knew Marta must be able to work miracles on him.

The tiring day and jet lag caused Kate's eyes to burn as Lukas and Marta drank another glass of red wine. Kate noticed Abbie's curiosity. Her daughter's past exposure to drinking had been a rare holiday toast or Jack's brother, who came to town every few years carting a twelve-pack of beer. Kate would have to explain to her that in Europe drinking wine was as common as drinking Pepsi was at home.

Marta noticed Kate's weariness and ushered them both upstairs. The room was neat, though a bit chilly. Two thick down comforters folded sideways on the bed would warm them. Kate couldn't wait to slide beneath the folds of the clean sheets and comforter. Yet when she lay in bed waiting for Abbie to return from the bathroom, sleep would not come. Nothing here was hers or had the scent of home. As Abbie came bounding in with her toothbrush in hand, Kate realized there was one thing that reminded her of home—her daughter. And if God had ever been near her, she prayed he'd be here with them now.

Kate showered and dressed in their room, then left Abbie still asleep in bed. At nine-thirty the others would be awake. She heard someone in the breakfast nook.

"Good morning," Kate said, hoping to see someone other than Anni in the room.

"*Guten Morgen,*" Anni replied in a cool tone, returning her gaze to the newspaper in front of her.

"That's right, *Guten Morgen.*" Kate glanced around, feeling awkward.

"Do you want coffee or tea?" Anni didn't look up from the paper.

"Coffee would be nice. Where are the cups?"

Anni pushed her chair from the table with a loud scrape and retrieved Kate a cup of coffee. She motioned to the cream and sugar on the table. Before Kate could even thank her, she'd left the room.

"I see you met Anni once again," Marta said as she entered the nook.

"Yes."

"She is Lukas' middle daughter. The oldest lives in Germany with her husband and three children. His youngest is at university in Paris."

"I don't think Anni likes having company."

"She treats me the same. But you will not see her often." Marta motioned toward a small hallway leading to an area of the house Kate hadn't seen. "Lukas waits for us. Did you sleep well?"

"Yes, very well." Kate's stomach grumbled. But she was at the mercy of this family. Kate liked her independence and didn't know if she could stay in the house for long.

Lukas' study was a few doors down the hallway. Marta knocked on the closed door before entering, though she didn't wait for an answer. It could have been a study for someone like Ernest Hemingway, Kate thought. A great place to write novels in, with its oversized leather furniture, rock fireplace, and bookcases along the wall. A beautiful antique desk dominated one side of the room and was surrounded by boxes of files. Pinned to one wall were maps and photos that didn't match the neatly framed art on the other walls. Lukas sat behind the desk, also lined with stacks of files.

"Good. I want to get started. We will have breakfast soon. The girl has not awakened yet?"

"Abbie," Kate said, looking at him directly. "The girl's name is Abbie, or you may call her Abigail."

Lukas grimaced and stood up, moving toward the map on the wall behind him. Marta sat in a leather chair near the fireplace.

"Did you bring the tile?" Lukas asked.

"Yes."

"I will ask to see it a little later."

"I ask that you be honest with me," Kate put in. "If you don't feel I need to know every detail of this—" her hands swept the room—"I understand. But I want to trust everything that is said here."

"Yes, it is agreed," he returned thoughtfully. He glanced at Marta, who nodded for him to continue. "We seek a man named Wolfram Meizer. I told you about him in Portland."

"Yes. I did some research on him. He was a guard at several camps and part of the SS Death's Head Unit, the Topenkopf—is that how you say it?"

"Good enough. Where did you find this information?"

"In a book about the men in the camps. It detailed many of the guards with their marital status, religion, the camps they served, and other descriptions. But if I found the right person, the book said he died in 1945."

"Do you have this book with you?"

"Yes, along with other papers I found."

"Very good. We will use that to search for other guards from Meizer's unit who may still be alive. Until recently, we believed he died in 1945. Now we know he is alive, and we have three locations to search. At one of these places, we believe we will find Wolfram Meizer."

"If we find him, how will that help us know what happened to my husband? We can't walk up and ask."

"What do you say—we will cross the bridge when it comes?"

Lukas' words didn't encourage her.

"When we find Wolfram, there are many options to be decided upon," Marta said. "It is something we should discuss. We can contact a Holocaust group or the Austrian government to press criminal charges against him."

"Let us find him first. Come, Kate, see the locations we will be searching."

She moved around the desk and stood beside him. The map of Europe had red pins stuck in three locations.

"Wolfram took this map from a Nazi in Argentina. This

man's wife provided Marta's husband, Karl, with a copy. The three locations were possible hiding spots for Nazi loot."

Marta leaned against the desk behind them. "There are priceless artworks, gold bullion, documents, and other valuables that have never been found since the war's end. Austria had paintings and sketches from the famous painter Gustav Klimt inside one of the most famous museums in Vienna. These were either stolen from the museum or taken by forced sales from Austrian Jews. Many paintings around the world have been proven to be stolen works yet have not been returned to the families of survivors and Holocaust victims. But then there are the works and gold never recovered. Some were lost in unreachable Swiss banks, and others perhaps locked in caches around the world."

"You believe one of these sites is one such hiding place?"

"It is possible."

"Why would he wait so long?" Kate studied the three points on the map—two in Austria and one in Italy.

"My husband believed Wolfram could not return because Nazi hunters sought him. Wolfram was also rumored to have murdered an exiled Nazi in South America."

"Let us not cover too much information too soon," Lukas said. "Let us return to the map. The first location is Schloss Weiss, a castle in northern Italy."

Kate compared the red pin near the Austrian border and its relation to Venice, Italy. The distance wasn't far. She'd spent hours studying maps of this area and surmising the routes for a kidnapping. Within a few hours Jack could have been taken to Switzerland, Austria, Germany, or France. It would take even less time for a fast boat to cross the Adriatic Sea and reach Slovenia or Croatia, even Bosnia or Herzegovina, where terrorists could demand a ransom. But none ever came. Later she had studied the water currents and made inquiries at coastal villages for any John Doe, or whatever they called an unidentified body in Italy.

The map brought back those memories she'd tried to push away. Nights of hopeless tears when she agonized over where on earth her husband lived or his body rested. He was somewhere. Kate never thought it would take this long or that she'd be in an Austrian estate looking at a map again.

Lukas was watching her when Kate turned from the map. "The castle dates to the thirteenth century, during a time when there was a regional feudal war. Apparently many passageways were built. These were convenient during the close of WWII as one spot in the ratline," Lukas explained.

"What exactly is the ratline?"

Lukas glanced at Marta as if to say, "She doesn't know anything."

Marta spoke quickly. "It was the line of places that Nazis used to escape from the Third Reich nations down through Italy and on to South America. A group called ODESSA organized it, and such points as the Schloss Weiss would keep these men and women along the journey."

"I've heard of ODESSA. The group consisted of SS members who formed a network to escape Europe during the war. I just did not know the term *ratline*."

"Now you do. ODESSA and the ratline have been used in Hollywood movies and much fiction, but the group and the route did exist. We'll talk about this information later. Marta's husband found testimony from a man captured in 1947 and accused of wartime atrocities. He named Wolfram Meizer as one of others who stayed at Schloss Weiss in 1945 before Wolfram escaped to South America.

"Locations *zwei und drei*—two and three." Lukas pointed to another red pin close to the third in upper Austria, not far from the German border. "This is the Salzkammergut area of Austria—the lake district. Our last two points on the map are both in this region. The believed Austrian Redoubt would have occurred here. The Redoubt was—"

"An area in Upper Austria where the Allies believed Hitler would make his last stand at the end of the war. They thought he would hide within the Alps with his top officers and military and keep the war from ending."

"Good," Lukas said, raising his eyebrow. Marta smiled. "I was raised in the Salzkammergut region. The lakes are deep and mountains rugged, much like here. There are also many salt mines and tunnels within the mountains. The Nazis had underground armament factories built by concentration camp inmates, where they built airplanes and weapons beyond the eyes of the Allies."

"Sounds like a perfect place to hide something after the war. But then, so did those secret passageways inside the castle in Italy."

"Yes," said Marta, "but we have ruled out the pin up there labeled *drei*."

"That is correct," Lukas said, sitting on the edge of the desk. "Wolfram will not be found at Toplitzsee, or Lake Toplitz."

"How can you be so certain?" Kate asked. The lake was small, elongated, and near another larger lake.

"There is one building on the lake—a restaurant. It has become a tourist site, with tours from around the region taking visitors on a Nazi treasure hunt. This lake is famous for legends of Nazi gold. They are certainly true stories. Eyewitnesses tell of SS officers dropping wooden crates into the water. Many divers have tried to discover what is inside the crates, but the lake is deep and dangerous."

"Karl and I watched a program about the lake."

"Yes. An American television network was a part of funding an exploration with Simon Wiesenthal Foundation. It was popular news in Austria for some time. Scotland has its monster in the lake, and we have our missing Nazi treasures."

"Did they find anything?" Kate asked.

"Yes. They used special equipment—what are they called in English?"

"Minisubmarines," Marta helped.

"That is correct. The crates were broken, but they recovered counterfeit British notes." Lukas sighed and sat in the leather desk chair. "There is much to explain."

"We will do a little at a time," Marta said. She brought a fold-up chair from the corner for Kate to sit in. "I will take a turn. Kate, you know who Heinrich Himmler was?"

"One of Hitler's top men," Kate said. Her father's History Network collector's tapes saved the day.

"Himmler headed Operation Bernhard, which would flood the economy with counterfeit currency. First the British pound and then the American dollar. They used artists, bookbinders, engravers, and printers in concentration camps to do the work of making the templates. They planned to murder the workers when the project was complete."

Lukas leaned an elbow on the desk and looked at the map. "It is said the war would have had a different outcome if they had begun the project earlier. A survivor of the project said they perfected the American hundred-dollar bill and prepared to print a million dollars a day. But the war was ending too quickly, and the project relocated."

"Now it ties into our two locations in the Salzkammergut region," Marta said. She rounded the desk to stand before the map. "Some of the counterfeit money ended up in Lake Toplitz. The inmates were kept alive—perhaps Hitler or Himmler believed they had time enough for the operation to save the war. The inmates were moved from camp to camp until they came here." She pointed from the lake to a town north and over a range of mountains. The third red pin was stuck on the blue outline of a lake within the range of mountains. "This is Ebensee. On the outskirts of the village was a subcamp of the larger Mauthausen Concentration Camp. Inmates were used to dig tunnels into the mountain for underground armament factories. The Operation Bernhard inmates were secluded from the other prisoners. And Wolfram Meizer was a guard at KZ Ebensee during the last six months of the war."

"It does tie together." Kate nodded. It was fascinating, something her father would be greatly intrigued by. But this was also very real for the present. "Yet the counterfeit money would mean nothing now."

"Correct. But this region became a kind of draining pot for those fleeing the greater Reich. Goods were shipped from Berlin to be hidden, and inmates were moved into Bavaria and Austria. Hitler had a mountain fortress outside of Salzburg. We don't know exactly what Wolfram discovered, but we believe it happened while he was at KZ Ebensee."

"The second pin in the Salzkammergut region is between Ebensee and Lake Toplitz."

"It is Waldsee—*see* means "lake." And *wald* means "forest." Lukas and I do not have much information about it. We began to organize everything this last week."

There was a knock on the open door. Anni looked at them in front of the large map and then at the papers and boxes with a mixture of annoyance and curiosity. "The child is awake," she said to her father.

"Thank you," Kate said, quickly moving around Marta and to the door.

"She is in the kitchen," Anni said as Kate passed her.

Kate's feet echoed down the hallway as she turned the corner to where Abbie sat on a stool, sipping something in a teacup. Her hair was tousled and she still wore her nightgown.

"Good morning, Abbie."

"I called you," she said with a small pout.

"I'm sorry. I didn't hear you. I should have come and checked."

"It's all right. The lady who picked us up at the airport yesterday made me some tea. She gave me these yummy things to put in it instead of sugar. One popped into my mouth too." Abbie giggled and pointed to the pink dish with brown crystal squares inside. Kate picked one up and took a small test— brown sugar and molasses. With a wink to Abbie, she popped one in her mouth just as Marta entered the room. Kate acted as if she were caught red-handed, which brought a good laugh to Abbie.

"This is the room I want to be in," Marta said, glancing at Kate, who swallowed the candy quickly. She smiled at Abbie. "Do you remember me from last night?"

Abbie nodded.

"Would you like some breakfast? You and I can make it for everyone."

"I want to stay with my mom," she said shyly.

"We can all cook," Kate said with a wink that brought another smile to Abbie's face.

As they boiled eggs and Abbie arranged meat and cheese on a plate, Marta said quietly to Kate, "Lukas must still be talking to Anni. This either will make things worse or we could see improvement. I do not hold my breath."

⊷⟞◉⟝⊶

Jack had folded the blanket twice before stretching out in front of the vent on the floor. He was cold as always and wondered if he'd ever again be completely warm for more than a few hours. His time with Wolfram Meizer would thaw him to the bone, only to be returned to the basement and on to the tunnels. If he survived this, he'd go to the Hawaiian Islands for a year and never be cold.

Rudy was trying a new experiment through his side of the vent. Jack waited in the darkness with his fingers pressed on the metal grate.

"Well?" Rudy's whisper echoed through the vent.

"Nothing so far."

Jack enjoyed the nights when they weren't too exhausted to stretch near their vents. He imagined them as young boys who lived separated by an alley, so they'd send flashlight signals back and forth. It made him smile to think of Rudy stretched on the cold concrete on the other side, now trying to find a way to pass a note across the span of a few feet between vent covers. He wondered what kind of arm Rudy had invented to push paper through—a wire arm made from collected paper clips or a contraption made of eating utensils. Jack liked to tell Rudy he was MacGyver in disguise and that if they only had a stick of bubble gum they could be free and safe with their families in only minutes. Rudy had never seen the television show, so he couldn't appreciate Jack's humor.

Jack felt a light touch against his fingertip. "I feel it." He scooted up and tried to reach through. The paper disappeared, then was there again, but not close enough. It hit the ridge and crumpled.

"A little more. I got it." Jack had to remember to whisper. He could hear Rudy's hushed celebration mixed with the deep-lung coughs that stayed with him.

"Now we have a new way to communicate if necessary."

"It's even fun," Jack said with a chuckle.

"I have some news," Rudy said in a serious tone. "I borrowed some books from Ian."

"Ian would do anything for you, Rudy. Have you ever asked him if he'd help us escape?"

"Actually, I did. But he said no."

Jack laughed quietly, imagining Ian's deadpan expression. "So what news did you find?"

"One book was about this region. It's in German, but I'm getting pretty good at reading German now—all those old newspapers and such have helped. Well, if I'm reading correctly, then it seems that a dam was built on the village end of the lake over fifty years ago. Want to guess the exact date?"

Jack leaned close to the vent, thinking. "Maybe early 1945?"

"You just made the winning answer."

"What do I win?"

"A trip for two into a scenic underground tunnel system."

"Thanks. So the dam was complete just prior to the end of WWII. Anything else?"

"Not really, but I did find that a bit of a coincidence. Maybe what these people are seeking is really inside that dam."

Jack was in thought. "Did the lake level rise at all when they constructed the dam?"

"Ah, *that's* what it was saying. I couldn't figure out a few words. But I think it rose something like ten meters once spring melted the mountain snow and filled the lake. By then the war was already over. The village had to restructure, and homes were torn down during the dam construction to make way for the rise in the lake level—I'm sure that was unpopular, but citizens didn't argue with the Nazis by then. They knew what would happen. I thought you'd find that bit of our lake history interesting."

"Yes, I do," he said. Now Jack knew how the cave opening had the man-made markings. The lake had been low enough for divers to work there, so perhaps the cave hadn't even been under the water at all at one time. Ten meters was around thirty feet.

Jack wanted to tell Rudy about his discovery, but the vents couldn't be trusted with that knowledge. Perhaps their new note system? Rudy was saying good-night and Jack was glad he was off the floor. The cold quickly went through the wool blanket and into his skin.

He later looked at the paper Rudy sent through and laughed, knowing Rudy also thought of them as boys passing secret notes. It read "Will you tell Melissa that I like her?" There were three boxes marked: *yes, no,* and *maybe.*

But those were the same choices he gave himself when he thought of telling Rudy about the cave. He decided that somehow soon he must tell his friend. The new knowledge might give Rudy the energy to fight this illness he couldn't conquer. Jack decided they needed another night on the lake. He'd tell Ian he was concerned about more cracking.

The cave was waiting to reveal its secrets.

ukas wanted to ignore what he saw happening before his eyes. He'd done it many times before, believing everything would work out. But Marta had asked him to talk to his daughter. Anni was the hardest of his children to speak with, perhaps because she was the most like him.

She had paused after Marta left the room, then turned to leave also.

"Anni, please come inside," he said. It was a relief to speak German again after talking with Kate and Marta in English.

"A game of chess?" she asked, nodding toward the chess stand in the corner with hand-carved marble pieces lined for battle. "I remember when you taught me long ago."

"You had come for the summer and were bored to death."

"This fortress can be dull for a fifteen-year-old."

"I suppose," Lukas said. He recalled how different his childhood had been with a father who enjoyed the tavern more than home. At fifteen he had run away several times, hiding at his friend's house until his aunt in Vienna volunteered to take him in. Life was better for a time, until his wandering met the idealism of the Nazi Youth. Immediately he'd been drawn in with promises of position, honor, and duty. He'd once had a friend who was half Jewish and that posed the greatest problem in his new beliefs. But the more propaganda he read—the scientific facts about the degenerate traits of the Jews and the reports of their plots to control the government—the more his anger grew. At one rally, he found himself shouting and chanting with all the others, and it scared him to hear his father's voice from his own lips.

"You don't seem interested in chess with your daughter."

Lukas turned to Anni. She had always worn her anger on the outside, in her body language and tone of voice. He recalled his vow to be a different father to his children than the one he'd been born with. Lukas' daughters had gone to the best schools, had money and position, and he never once had yelled at them. But all that hadn't brought his children closer to him.

"Is there something you want to say?" he asked Anni.

The challenge came swiftly. "Why did you bring these women here?"

"Kate's husband is missing. We may be able to help." Lukas rarely told Anni anything of his business besides what she needed to do. He felt like her employer instead of her father. There was little warmth between them, and he didn't know how to break the wall that had grown so high.

"You are a home for refugees? Last month we gain the older woman and now this one and her child. On every trip, Father, you return with more women."

There was pain mixed in her sarcasm. Lukas was sure of it. Anni rarely showed emotion other than anger. Anni's mother was constantly frustrated by her middle child. Vera was the quintessential Viennese woman—hospitable, charming, never ruffled, full of pride in herself and family. If one of his affairs had not been such a public embarrassment, Vera would never have left him. Once her pride was tarnished in the eyes of society, she would never return to him. Lukas missed the sound of his daughters in the house, but he didn't fight for them. It was Vera's place to raise them.

Lukas recalled how Anni had called him late one night several years back. He'd never heard her voice sound helpless before. He had driven to Vienna to pick her up, and Lukas was stunned to see her so sick and vulnerable. He took her straight to the hospital, where she was treated for a drug overdose. They later drove from the hospital to a rehab center, where she stayed three months. Lukas visited once a week though they rarely talked. Their way of growing close was through a game of chess. He hated to lose. And he had started to lose regularly the last weeks before she checked out. Lukas had offered her a place to live and a job. This hadn't been her first trip to rehab—only the first time she'd called him. He knew that without a place away from her old life, she would be calling again. Anni had accepted his offer.

"You have made it clear you don't like this," he said carefully. He wondered if Anni knew she was a special case, not just one of many women he liked to help. Marta and Kate weren't here for that reason. It just happened. Did Anni understand this and know how much he enjoyed her living at the estate? "I would appreciate it if you were polite with my guests. They are guests for a while and then they will leave." Did Anni know she was more than a guest?

"If that kid gets into my stuff or is too noisy, I don't know how much I can take."

"But you will try?" Lukas realized he was saying the same words Marta had said to him.

"I suppose." As she rose to leave, she glanced at the map.

He should tell her everything. Anni had helped him before in his business matters, which were sometimes bordering on illegal, proving herself loyal countless times without questions or the need for answers. But he wouldn't risk her being involved in this. The danger that lurked on the edges was too great. Lukas couldn't lose his daughter to the battle begun long ago. Wolfram Meizer had already taken enough.

⟡

After a short nap for Kate and a quick tour of the estate grounds for all of them, Lukas deemed it time to work once again. Marta had established right away that they would talk about their mission only within the walls of Lukas' office, not when they were eating, on a walk, or in front of Abbie. Kate found it humorous that Marta called the search a "mission." Two senior citizens, Kate, and Abbie were members of a secret mission. Who would have thought?

Kate brought her tile to Lukas' office, where a fire crackled in the rock fireplace and the lamps were turned on. Marta had opened the shades to the one window in the room, though afternoon brought little light in.

Abbie was upstairs, playing in her new room after discovering a dollhouse that she might have claimed to be too old to play with at home. But she was arranging the rooms and dressing the small people when Kate returned downstairs.

They stared down at the four tile pieces: Karl's larger triangle, the copy made from Jantes' original that they'd found in Karl's office, the smaller piece Oskar had sent by courier, and Lukas' squared section. By now Kate had heard about Oskar Gogl, who hoped to join them soon. But with his wife's medical problems, he wasn't sure when. Only one portion of the square tile was missing.

"What do you think?" Marta asked Lukas.

"I don't see anything special about it."

"Do you know where the tile came from?" Kate said. "What is its origin?"

Lukas and Marta looked at one another before Marta spoke.

"Karl's sister was part of the Resistance group before Lukas joined us. She brought the tile to a drop point with instructions for Karl to divide it into five pieces—one for each team member—and to bring it to the next meeting." Kate caught the solemn way Marta's eyes flipped toward Lukas, then back to her. "Susanne was killed before the next meeting, so the full reason was never discovered. Everything was terrible in those last months of war, and we never thought the tile was the real key. But this is what Lukas has begun to question. We wanted to see the pieces together to decide."

The tile drew their attention again. The copied tile was slightly different from the others, with its darker color and grainy edges crumbling easily. The other three were a bright cobalt blue with a raised pattern; their broken edges exposed a white, grainy texture.

"I did some research on this," offered Kate.

"Really?" Lukas said, moving around to sit behind his desk. Kate noticed that he seemed tired tonight.

"I'm an antique dealer, remember? I may specialize in more early American pieces, but I have resources."

"And what did you learn?" Lukas asked.

"I think most important to know is that this is not an antique."

"How do you know?"

Kate picked up information she had brought from home and reviewed what she'd learned. "I won't read everything, but first of all I never realized the great history in tiles and the many varieties. Victorian encaustic tiles, Dutch and English tin-glazed tiles, European stove tiles, medieval floor tiles, Italian, and on and on. It was the thickness of the tile that gave me the first clue. Different centuries have different characteristics of thickness and hardness of their tiles, along with the actual process of making them. But twentieth-century tiles tend to be the thinnest of all. This tile fit that model."

She picked up a piece and turned it around in her fingers. "There are other characteristics to determine the time period of a tile. For example, eighteenth-century tiles usually were chamfered to slope inward so they would abut neatly with the others. Or some seventeenth- to early eighteenth-century Dutch and English tiles had two opposing nail holes in the corners.

"The blue color probably came from a metallic oxide from cobalt. The majolica painting technique used variations of color and tone—see how the blue had darker shades in areas. The raised edge was probably pressed into it, or the clay was poured into a mold."

"Would this have to be made in a factory?" Lukas picked up one of the fragments.

"Single potters were capable of doing such work."

"What are you thinking?" Marta asked.

"I am not sure," Lukas said. "If it is not valuable by age and it obviously has nothing buried within the clay—I often wondered if that was why Susanne told Karl to divide it. She may have thought there was something inside, an SS intelligence note perhaps? I am just giving ideas here. If we knew the answers behind the tile, we could better predict what Wolfram would do." He leaned far back in the chair, staring at the ceiling. "*Vas*, I mean, *what* is your conclusion on the age?"

"After I read everything, my guess would be no later than the early 1900s. I'll leave these descriptions for you both to go over, but that's my thought."

"This is good," Lukas said.

Kate enjoyed his rare approval while it lasted. She picked up a file with a list of questions stapled to the inside flap. "How could I forget?" she said, looking at the name on the page. "Rudy Blessing."

"The other missing victim," Lukas said, unconcerned. "Tell us about their connection. Let us get comfortable here."

"I will make some coffee and tea," Marta said. She left the room, and Kate was instantly intimidated by Lukas' presence. His dark eyes examined her beneath hooded lids. She plunged on as if her advocate, Marta, was still there.

"Before Jack and I were married and he was still in college, he went on a summer internship with Rudy Blessing's diving expedition. Jack spent the summer with Rudy's team on an underwater archaeological search."

"This is interesting," Lukas said. "We have a definite link. The two locations both have lakes, no oceans nearby. But with underwater archaeologists, lakes, wooden crates dumped into Lake Toplitz, and other lakes in the Salzkammergut region from which German armament and objects have been recovered, we have a pattern."

"The castle in Italy has a lake nearby also?"

"Yes."

Kate felt the question stirring, the one that had taunted and kept her from life for three years. She wanted to ask Marta, not Lukas. But she couldn't wait. "Lukas, please, I need to know one way or the other. Do you think Jack could be alive?"

His fingers were laced together as he rocked in his chair. He seemed in great consideration. "I will say this raises us one notch closer to that possibility."

⋆≓◎⊂≓⋆

It was past midnight, and it seemed they'd covered a hundred subjects. But Kate still had more on her list of questions. Dinner was long behind them, Abbie was sleeping, and they were all tired. They discussed the Blue Tile Crimes. There were a series of crimes in South America and one in Germany during the early to mid-1950s—a well-known doctor, several political figures, even a man named Ernst, a suspected Nazi in Argentina. All were murdered, and a blue tile fragment was left at the scene of each crime. Every piece was the same shape and pattern as the one Kate found on Jack's pillow.

It was Marta's idea to trace the raised design on the tile onto a piece of paper. Kate placed the paper on top of the tile and gently rubbed with a charcoal pencil until the pattern appeared. They examined it for a long time. The design that wrapped around the tile was neither congruent nor clear. If it had been art it leaned toward a cubist or perhaps a surrealist image depicted in a pattern of lines and shapes. Perhaps the shapes and design would have meant something to Wolfram Meizer, but it didn't reveal anything to them. Maybe the final piece would make the pattern clear.

"That tile belonged to Jantes," Marta said softly, picking up the copied piece.

"Jantes was the funny one in the group. He made us laugh until we cried. A handsome young man also—the village girls were at his mercy."

"Wolfram took Jantes' tile when he killed him and used it as a pattern for fake tiles he left behind at the crime scenes." No emotion showed in his face as Lukas rose to add another log to the fire.

"Why would Wolfram do these crimes?"

"Quite an intelligent twist if you think about it," Lukas said.

"I do not like to agree, but it is true." Marta folded her hands on her lap. "We believe Wolfram committed these crimes for his personal reasons—perhaps he was trying to get information or revenge. He would leave the tile piece to divert blame away from a single individual and make it appear to be the activity of a terrorist group—our group. I am sure you have heard of bombings or other crimes where a group then claims responsibility. Wolfram was doing that, but casting blame upon us. Perhaps we should have come forward, but we'd moved on in our lives. We did not want the suspicion, especially since we did not know who could be doing such crimes. Were there more tiles? Why did Susanne ask us to divide the tile? These and other questions kept us unwilling to come forward."

"But it also kept our group from reuniting and hunting Wolfram down. What is the best way to discredit something?" Lukas asked Kate.

"I'm not sure."

"You are a Protestant or Evangelical?"

"Something like that," she said. "I believe in the Bible."

"Good enough. Now when the Nazis murdered the Jews in the name of Christ or because they say Christ was murdered by the Jews, what does that do to your religion?"

"Besides making me angry, it makes Christianity look bad to those who don't understand it. Christ was a Jew himself, and the foundation of my beliefs stands against everything the Nazis did."

"Explain the foundation," Lukas continued.

"Jesus said to love God with all your heart, soul, and mind and to love your neighbor as yourself."

"But if no one tells these words to the victim who is hurt in Christ's name, what do they believe?"

"That Christ would ordain such a thing," answered Kate.

"Yes. This is not a great example, but you can understand how Wolfram used our group's name to do his evil, which in turn harms us very much. I think he thought if we were prosecuted or the press found the story, he could locate us quickly and get the missing tiles. Those tile pieces, and I am sure revenge, are very important to him. But we may never know for certain why he did this."

"Kate, do you feel like you've entered a spy movie?" Marta asked with a chuckle.

"That would make me a very old Bond, James Bond," Lukas

said, and Kate realized he'd made a joke. He even smiled slightly to himself.

"I was thinking *Mission Impossible*," Marta said. "Will my instructions disintegrate in five seconds?"

"They might," Lukas said, stretching his arms. "We must rest, but this is what I believe we should do in the next few days. I will go to Schloss Weiss to see if I can pick up Wolfram's trail from there. Kate, I know about someone you can speak to. I cannot go with you. My former position in government makes it difficult to interview people about such matters. The news could raise a lot of suspicion—or get straight to Wolfram. There will be things you must do on your own."

"I understood that before I came," Kate said. The fire had died down, and a chill moved through the room.

"This man lives in Italy. He was in several camps and knew Wolfram Meizer. Karl had his name listed in the files. I found some information on him. His name is Francis Moore. He is a survivor of the camps, speaks excellent English, and has authored several books. He was at Ebensee at the end of the war."

"Where in Italy?"

"Venice, I believe."

"Venice?" Marta asked. She looked at Kate in shock.

"Yes," Lukas said, in a voice that questioned her reaction. "Kate has been there, so transportation will not be a problem."

"She shouldn't have to go there," Marta said.

Kate listened to them go back and forth, as if she were outside looking through the window. Her comfort in the idea of returning to Europe came from knowing she wouldn't be returning to Venice. Now she felt like God had tricked her in a way. Or had he only taken her a step at a time? How far was she willing to go from what made her feel comfortable to get the answers, to possibly get Jack himself?

"I don't know what to do about Abbie."

"Marta can stay with her here."

"I won't leave her."

"Then take her with you."

"No, I don't want to take her to that place," Kate said.

"You can do the trip in one day. It will be a long day."

"Lukas," Marta said, "she should not do this. Do you not understand this?"

"Do we want Wolfram? Does she want to know about her husband? This is not easy work, and we do not wait for perfect conditions. Wolfram does not sit and do nothing because his men might get afraid. I must go to Schloss Weiss and see what I find there. Kate does not know Italian or German—she would get nothing. Francis Moore speaks perfect English and has shared his story again and again. If you are too afraid of Venice, then I will go myself later or get someone, but it—"

"I will go," Kate said, "but only for one day."

"This is only the first step," Lukas said. "Do you know what we have begun? This will not be comfortable or nice all the time. This is a battle. This could be a battle for our lives."

CHAPTER THIRTY-TWO

Marta quickly became Abbie's adopted grandmother. Kate enjoyed time with her daughter and Marta outside the estate walls. The Alps were like Kate's tiny magical tree world in Cottonwood magnified a thousand times. They followed trails and collected handfuls of wildflowers. When Kate told Abbie she would be gone for a day, Abbie didn't seem to mind as long as Kate was back at bedtime for *The Voyage of the "Dawn Treader."*

"We still haven't finished it yet," Abbie said.

It eased Kate's mind to know Abbie would be happy for the day. The arrangements had been made by Anni, which made Kate a little nervous. She'd probably have train tickets to Siberia instead of Italy.

"I don't want to return to that city," she confided in Marta the day before she was to leave; they were walking from a mountain trail to the wide paths of the estate.

"I understand. We will wait until Lukas is feeling better and then I will go with him. Or I will go and speak with this Francis Moore instead of you."

"What's wrong with Lukas?"

"He is old, and he refuses to see a doctor."

"You can convince him of anything; don't you know that?"

"I lose my power when it comes to doctors," Marta said regretfully. "I did not think it wise for you to return to Venice."

"I didn't either. But I've prayed and thought about it. It will be good for me to go back and contribute to our group. You and Lukas can't do everything, even if sometimes I want to be a child like Abbie and have someone take care of me—for just a few moments."

"I know the feeling. We are strong women, you and I. We have to be. But even strong women need a shoulder sometimes. Let us care for each other until another shoulder comes along."

Kate nodded and patted Marta's back. She noticed gentle tears in the older woman's eyes.

◦→➁═⊙═⊂←◦

Marta drove her to meet the midnight train. Kate was glad for a cheerful driver this time. She'd chosen that mode of transportation to avoid another Anni chauffeuring experience and to skip a day of frequent plane changes. Marta stayed long enough to give her a quick lesson in rail travel, then waved good-bye so she could get back before Abbie woke up. Kate was alone with a few other travelers at the tiny station along the railroad track. She could see her breath as she waited where she hoped the first-class nonsmoking car would arrive. As the chill creeped through her taupe panty hose, Kate wished she'd worn slacks instead of her straight black dress. Then the track began to hum and the flat-fronted red train zinged toward them, coming to a quick stop.

Kate picked up her bag, noticing how fast the other passengers hopped on. She had to take the nearest open door—second-class smoking. The doors slid closed immediately behind her and before Kate left the loading and unloading area, the train was whizzing along the track again. The cars had the stench of years of smoke layered like paint over the walls, seats, and any patrons who stayed for long. Kate kept walking through cars until she reached the empty nonsmoking section. Settling into a seat with a small table in front of it, she realized that this was it—her return to Venice.

Inside her black leather bag she'd packed her Bible. Kate turned straight to Psalms and read the verses she had underlined the night before. God was her strength, her refuge, her deliverer, her shield, her song—she kept reading those verses throughout the journey. The word *refuge,* in particular, stood out. Years earlier, Kate would have thought a refuge was a place of escape. But it wasn't so. Refuge was a place God kept her as the storm waged and as life continued. It wasn't a transported hiding place, but a peace in the midst of life. Only now could she understand that.

The day awoke gradually as she traveled and changed trains several times. The distance changed the landscape. White, flat-fronted buildings with brown window boxes and gabled roofs dotted the hillsides and villages in Austria. Across the Italian border, the scenery slowly gave way to red-tile roofs and sweeping vineyard hillsides the farther into northern Italy she rode. As the train left the mountains and rolling countryside behind to cross more cities, the colors seemed a shade less vibrant.

Francis Moore, the man she was going to see, had recently been admitted into long-term care in Venice. Lukas had contacted Moore's wife, who volunteered to meet Kate at the Santa Lucia Station at the west end of the Grand Canal. The smoky station was bustling with movement by the time Kate disembarked. Moving toward the main entrance where Marie Moore would be waiting, Kate paused. A wave of panic tried to overtake her. This was too real: the smoke, the voices surrounding her, and something slightly familiar she couldn't describe. Then she realized what it was—the scent of a city on water. And Kate knew that she should never have returned.

=◉=

Lukas rubbed his eyes as he leaned against the headrest in the back of the gray sedan. His usual driver and handyman, Rey, was at the wheel, but they had spoken little since their morning departure toward the south. Lukas' energy would not return, and a day in bed due to Marta's insistence had probably made it worse.

He hated being old. It made him grouchy.

Kate would be in Venice by now, he calculated. He wondered how she fared. Marta had given him a long lecture on his insensitivity in that situation. It had seemed a logical decision to him. Kate had been to Venice before so the city would be manageable. Francis Moore's English made him accessible to the young woman. Marta asked why he didn't give *her* the assignment. Lukas had tried to think fast and brush it aside as Kate needing to feel like an essential part of the group. This trip would be her contribution. Marta always had a comeback. She said Kate had assisted with her research on the tiles and her studies to know something about the war before she'd come. Lukas grew tired of the banter. He wasn't going to tell her why he hadn't asked Marta to go to Venice. He hadn't thought of it—that was all. She wouldn't have believed him.

But the deeper truth he'd keep to himself: he worried about Marta. She acted so strong on the outside, but he saw little signs of her grieving. And she had become attached too quickly to Kate and Abbie. He didn't want her hurt when they went their separate ways. Sometimes he worried that he had become too attached to Marta. When he imagined her gone from the house, he felt not sorrow but fear. Could he live without her? Could he live without wildflowers in little jars, without her kind rebukes, without her presence?

Lukas realized they'd crossed the open border into Italy. He needed to concentrate on this Schloss Weiss. But he'd keep Marta near the estate as much as he could. Until Wolfram Meizer was found.

·—≡◎⫘—·

Marie Moore spoke only broken English, which didn't help Kate's anxieties about this trip. But at least they didn't travel to the area where Kate and Jack had stayed. When Marie and Kate arrived at Francis' long-term-care nursing home, Kate took in the Mediterranean-style gardens and arched breezeways. She had never seen such a comforting medical facility.

Marie accompanied Kate to the doorway of Francis' room. "A bad day for him today. This come sometime. He be old Francis tomorrow or next day. *Mi* man is strong." Marie smiled. "Come tomorrow?"

"No, I can't. I have to return to Austria," Kate tried to talk slowly so Marie could understand.

A frown replaced her smile. "Small time. Small time." Kate assumed that meant she had a short time with him.

The room had an overpowering smell of menthol and medicine. Francis Moore appeared tiny and frail against the white of his hospital bed. An IV ran to his bruised hand. Smiling, he motioned Kate to come inside.

When Marie spoke to him in rapid Italian, he answered simply, "*Si,*" and she left the room.

"Very good, she will leave us. My wife gets too concerned."

"It is the job of a wife."

"*Si, si.* And this husband will do as she asks. We will talk a short time. She is retrieving my book, an English version, from the hospital library for you to take. It is my memoir."

"Thank you," Kate said. Francis knew she had questions about his time at Ebensee. He wanted to talk while he could—that was what his wife had told Lukas. But now in his presence, Kate didn't know quite where to begin.

"You are Kate Porter, and I am Francis Moore." He pushed a button that raised the bed up straighter. His hair was pure white and his brown skin wrinkled, as if he'd spent all his days in the sun.

"I apologize for not introducing myself."

"It is fine. Now I am told this is about KZ Ebensee and Wolfram Meizer."

"That is correct. Would you mind sharing your story with me?"

"He is still alive, isn't he? Wolfram Meizer is alive?"

"We believe he is. We are trying to find exactly where."

"Why do you seek him?"

"He may know what happened to my husband."

Francis considered her words instead of asking for more details. He shook his head as he stared at her for a long time, examining words and memories in her eyes. "I do not need to know everything," he said. "But I want you to seek Wolfram for other reasons also."

Kate gazed into the man's eyes. A cold gray, they reminded her of an ancient star that fought hard to keep bearing light. Francis Moore had done a lot with his life since the war's end in 1945. He'd moved the world to remember and take a good look at itself and its future. But there was deep pain buried inside, pain Kate could recognize but never comprehend. Its vastness was too great.

"I understand," she whispered, because she did. He wanted her to seek Wolfram for him and for the others who could not.

"Have you been to Ebensee?"

"Not yet."

"There is a good museum by the Catholic church. The

Resistance Museum with good people who can help you. You should also see the camp location. It will help in your search to understand this man you seek." Francis closed his eyes in weariness.

"Is there anything you can tell me?"

"It is in my book. I put as much as words can say in those pages. It is a photograph, but only those who were there can truly understand." He closed those steel gray eyes. "I am too tired to tell it myself. You tell our stories when we are gone, all right?" With these words he opened his eyes and looked at her intently.

"I will try," she said, nervous about what this would mean to her. "I don't know how, but I will try."

"That is all we require."

Marie Moore returned Kate to the train station. She had come a long way for fifteen minutes with Francis Moore and his book. But somehow it was worth it. Outside the station, Kate ate lunch at a café beneath a red-and-white umbrella. She used the phone Lukas had loaned her to call the estate. Anni answered in a tone that told Kate she was interrupting. Quickly Anni informed her that Abbie and Marta had gone flower collecting or animal tracking or something like that; then she hung up.

Kate relaxed for a moment, watching a line of people who waited at a landing along the waters of the Grand Canal. Then with a sudden purpose, Kate paid her bill and went to the ticket booth. She watched the light wind ripple the waters as she carried the ticket to the now-loading group heading for the Piazza San Marco.

Plaster peeled from walls, flowers bloomed fully, and tourists and couples strolled the bordered walkways as the boat cruised the canal toward the wide mouth of the Grand Canal. Kate marveled at the ancient city once again.

With the jacket she'd needed in Austria tucked beneath her arm, Kate disembarked after passing beneath the stone-carved mass of the covered Rialto Bridge. The sunshine heated the pavement and warmed her fair arms and face. Within minutes, Kate reached her destination.

Venice was much more crowded than she remembered; tourists and voices in many languages swirled around her. But she was back. Her feet moved and stopped in the exact same places until she stood in front of the hotel where she and Jack had stayed.

It hadn't changed in the years since she'd carried the paper bag of warm pastry upstairs. Time hadn't worn on these walls like it did on the people who walked in and out of the arched, wooden door. Kate thought of who she'd been then. Nearly four years ago now. She'd stood here with excitement for the day ahead, not knowing that inside her room her husband was gone. She never could have expected what had transpired between that day and this one.

Kate stepped back to the edge of the canal until she looked up and found their window. The doors were pushed open, and white lace curtains fluttered in the soft breeze.

And Kate felt peace. Whatever happened next, she was going to be all right. This place had not stolen God's presence from her life, though it had taken her a long time to see that. God would repay what had been stolen—not necessarily Jack, but a life and a future. She never wanted to endure such pain again. But with the perspective of this sunny day in Venice, Kate could see that as an individual, she was better and stronger for all she'd endured. Pain and sorrow had brought a greater compassion into her life. The experience had wrenched her from the walled world she'd enclosed around herself.

With one last glance, Kate said good-bye to the place that had begun her new life. And she suddenly found that she wasn't afraid anymore.

CHAPTER THIRTY-THREE

"Mom, look what I made." Abbie plopped on the end of the bed with a straight line of a crocheted chain. Kate sat up and looked at the clock. It was past nine, and she could tell that Abbie had been up awhile. The soft, white comforter had kept her trapped in slumber after her long, tiring journey to and from Venice.

"You're doing a great job," Kate said encouragingly. "You told me on the phone you were learning to embroider."

"I started learning that yesterday."

"Mrs. Olsen has spoiled you."

"Mom, she's Frau Olsen."

"Yes, she is."

"Yesterday we had a tea party in the woods, and I helped make all the meals. Do you know how to embroider?"

"Not really," Kate said, a funny frown on her face.

"We'll learn from Frau Olsen together. I like doing things with my ole mom too."

"Your *ole* mom? Hey, little lady!" Kate grabbed her daughter and started tickling.

"Okay, okay, my young mom!"

"And don't you forget it," Kate said, touching the end of Abbie's button nose.

"Frau Olsen said she's going to make me an apron for my birthday."

"You told her your birthday is coming soon?" Kate stretched and sat up higher in bed.

"Yes. She said if we're still here, we can have a party."

"That sounds great, honey. But I think we'll be home by then." The thought of home made Kate realize that she hadn't called her parents or Connie since the first few days. Her best friend had probably found some movie script to match her life here and was dying to share it. Kate missed the way Connie made her laugh and how she seemed to barely hold her own life together, but then accomplished more than most people she knew. Kate hadn't even sent postcards yet.

"Come downstairs and I'll make you some tea, okay?" Abbie hopped from the bed and was gone from the room before Kate replied. She heard small footsteps pad down the hallway and stairs.

As Kate rolled over, Francis Moore's book fell to the floor with a clunk. She had read some on the train and planned to read more in bed, but the late hour and long journey brought sleep with only the introduction finished.

Kate now began to read. Within fifteen minutes she was hurrying down the stairs in her pajamas with the book in hand. She passed Marta and Abbie in the kitchen. "Where is he?" she asked.

"In the sunroom," Marta replied with a wondering look on her face.

"Abbie, I'll be back for tea in a few minutes, all right?" Kate was already out of the doorway when Abbie said okay.

Lukas appeared to be part of his chair with his back pressed in and his arms along the chair's arms. A plume of smoke rose gingerly from a pipe in his hand. The morning sunlight poured into the room. Kate had almost forgotten how his presence could intimidate her, and she suddenly remembered she was still in her pajamas and she'd not brushed her hair or put on any makeup.

"I found something," she said, hurrying toward him.

"I found some things also."

"Great. At the castle?" Her heart was pounding.

"Yes, but—"

"First, you must read this." She came closer.

He straightened and nodded to the chair beside his. "This must be Francis Moore's book. I have meant to read it for years."

"You will wish you had. Read this part here." Kate handed the open book to him and scooted the other chair close. She reread the words from beside him, so anxious that she could barely keep still.

> We had known something was suspicious with Theo. He worked on special assignments. The officers usually kept him separated from us. But Meizer also would take him for work details. Some believed he was spying on us to Meizer.
>
> You could see that Meizer was in a rage when the door first flew open. He stormed into the printing room and searched every face. Then he saw Theo.
>
> "Did you save the template?"
>
> "You told me to destroy it," Theo said. "What happened? I gave it to the girl. She said you wanted me to give it to her."
>
> "Do you know the coordinates in your mind?"
>
> "I can try. But I destroyed everything. You told me to." Theo was already begging.
>
> Wolfram turned into a crazed man as I had seen many times. He grabbed his gun and hit Theo in the face. Theo fell,

and Meizer went mad, hitting him with the butt of his pistol until it was covered in blood. Theo was dead.

Lukas was silent.

Kate took the book from his hands and turned the pages back. "Look what Theo did before the war."

Lukas read the words and nodded. "Theo Mochlmann was a tile maker."

"Now read this." Kate was excited. "It's Susanne."

A young woman had come to the camp. She had come twice before, I was sure, because we all moved to the fence to watch her. We did not care that this might anger Meizer. This girl was like seeing a stream in the desert. She was all we dared not hope for—her youth and innocence. She was afraid to enter; we could see that when she looked at us—a mixture of sympathy and disgust in her expression. We did not blame her, for we knew we must appear as filthy skeletons. One inmate claimed she had touched his hand gently and told him to hang on, that soon help would come. We wanted to believe in an angel at the time.

We talked about the girl and tried to find out more about her. Someone discovered she was Meizer's housekeeper and that she came to the camp to bring Meizer fresh bread and eggs for his morning breakfast. Of course we all speculated more. The houseboy relayed that she was not his mistress, though Meizer had that intention. Once when she came and he was drunk, he had proposed to her and tried to take her in his arms. She had blushed and pushed away. That is what the houseboy told us, but he knew we wanted to believe in our angel. So I never knew if what he said was true or not.

After Meizer murdered Theo before our eyes, he left the camp. The kommandant was angry because Meizer left without permission. We all believed he was going after our angel—that she was the girl Theo had talked about. We were afraid for her. I think even the atheist in our small group began to pray. But we never knew what happened to this girl because she never came to the camp again.

Hope was lost, but liberation was just around the corner. I believe that some of us would not have survived if not for our angel giving us hope.

"Susanne," Lukas said, closing the book.

"Isn't it amazing? Karl's sister was their angel. She convinced Theo to give her the tile that she brought to the drop point Marta told me about. You were right about Wolfram wanting the tile; he wanted the tile in 1945. He didn't find it—" Kate paused as she realized it—"but Wolfram did find her."

"Please leave me now." His voice was strained, and it surprised her to see his expression. He held the book against his chest, crinkling his forehead as if in pain.

"Of course," Kate said solemnly, turning to go.

Then his voice stopped her. "Kate, get dressed."

"Why?" she asked.

"We are going to Ebensee."

"Mom, don't feel bad if you have to leave me." Abbie read her thoughts as they sat drinking tea. Kate was drinking quickly, and she noticed her knee bouncing up and down. She kept listening for Lukas to come into the kitchen. She sighed deeply and wondered again if she should have left Abbie in the States with her parents. But they had enjoyed many moments together since coming here—cherished moments, and now guilty moments.

"I just have these things I need to do," Kate explained.

Abbie sat across from her with a too-large flowered apron over her clothes. "I don't mind. I like Frau Olsen a lot. She doesn't have a granddaughter—she doesn't have any children at all."

"That's true," Kate agreed.

Abbie hopped from her chair and came toward her. Kate pulled her onto her lap. Her daughter's head was almost level with her own. Kate touched Abbie's braided hair.

"Mom, I need to talk." Abbie turned sideways to look at her.

"What would you like to talk to me about?"

"We talked before we came about why you were coming here. I was so happy when I got to come too. So I decided that you can't feel bad about going places. I know you are going places to find Daddy."

"You know it may not happen the way we want. Abbie, I must be truthful with you. We may never know what happened. We may not get him back."

"I know. But I keep praying and praying. If Daddy did die—" Abbie bit her lip—"then we will have to be strong and get through it."

Tears built in Kate's eyes as she hugged her daughter, whose words were bigger than she was.

The emotion continued to escalate as Lukas and Kate prepared to leave. Marta had confided in her about Lukas' love for the girl Susanne. Now she understood his strange mood when they'd read Francis Moore's book. And though Abbie's words gave her strength, Kate continued to feel guilty about leaving, even if it was only for the day—again. So it was with questions and sorrow that she departed for a concentration subcamp with Lukas.

Kate pivoted in her seat to wave at Marta, Abbie, and Lukas' usual driver, Rey, who seemed surprised that Lukas was taking the car without him. The massive gates opened as they approached, and Kate turned to watch them close her daughter safely inside.

Please, God, protect her when I'm there and when I'm gone. Protect us all and guide everything we do.

After a long silence, they began to talk.

"You didn't tell me what you found at Schloss Weiss," Kate said.

"That is correct. I nearly forgot. It is a hotel now. The owners were friendly and enjoyed visitors who like to talk. They tell me that a man of Wolfram's age rented the entire place for six months. The couple spent the winter in Greece with the money, and they suggested it was a sizeable amount. But then Wolfram abruptly broke the six-month lease and left. They seemed happy about it because they were concerned about closing the hotel during the summer."

"Do you think Wolfram was there to see if it was the location of the Nazi secret?"

"Exactly. I do not think Wolfram knew the location because he did not have the tile. While we are gone today, Marta is going to further examine the tile pieces for clues of why they're so important to Wolfram. Tonight we will do that together."

"Why would that inmate Theo help Wolfram by making the tile and showing him where the Nazi treasure was?"

"To survive, most likely. Wolfram probably promised freedom or food for the location of where the officers were hiding Nazi loot."

"What will Ebensee show us?" Kate asked, admiring the green meadows and tall mountain peaks surrounding them.

"I do not know if that place was the beginning, or the beginning of the end. But it will show us where this all began, and it will lead us to the end."

CHAPTER THIRTY-FOUR

I t was all changed. Lukas recognized the landscape if he looked up at the way the towering mountains were
shaped at this place in the narrow valley. But now the road
was lined with houses. He remembered fewer trees and army
vehicles that had dug deep ruts into parts of the road.

Neither he nor Kate had spoken since they left the main
roadway to follow the KZ Ebensee signs. They were driving
along a residential street when he saw the stone arch that had
once been the gateway into the camp. He stopped in front of it.
Instead of barracks and mud and U.S. Army personnel, there
were homes and yards and children playing.

Lukas could not decide if that was good or bad. Who could
live with such ground beneath them? with ashes and blood
fertilizing their flower bushes? But then, why not have life
grow from death and make laughter and love where blood and
tears had fallen?

Kate wanted to read the gold-colored plaque on the stone
arch. Lukas didn't get out of the car when she walked to it and
snapped a photo. It had been his idea to bring the camera, to

document everything in case something held a clue. Lukas wanted as much evidence as possible against Wolfram Meizer when the day came for the authorities to bring him before his victims. But Lukas also couldn't help feeling his own guilt. He knew that the ugliness that had burned within him had never been exorcised from his soul. It could never be.

"The plaque was placed there in 1995. A bit late, it seems," Kate said once she returned to the car.

"That was the fiftieth anniversary of the liberation. Some things take a long time to remember—and to admit."

"This is so strange," she said. "How could people live here?"

He had to follow the signs to find the cemetery parking lot that was shaded beneath trees. First he noticed the monuments behind the low stone fence—he'd seen photographs of the larger ones at Mauthausen. The monuments were erected by the countries of the world who had lost citizens to the Nazis. This smaller camp was obscure in comparison to the well-known camps like Dachau, Auschwitz, Belsen, and on and on. Yet this subcamp, which didn't even earn full camp status, had dozens of country monuments within the stone border.

Kate was already waiting outside the car, but Lukas' legs wouldn't move. Finally he got out, leaving the door open. He followed Kate to the iron gate, where they entered the place of the dead.

Now he remembered, though everything seemed put in its wrong place. Across the courtyard he saw the row of black ovens surrounded by bricks and plaques for the dead. He remembered the sign that hung over the crematorium. He'd memorized it after reading the words again and again. It was a dying man's last breath of dignity.

> Not ugly worms
> Must in the future be nourished by my body!
> The clean flame should eat me up.

I always loved the warmth and the light
Therefore burn my body and do not bury me.

"I've been here before," he whispered.

"Marta told me a little," she said softly, lacing her arm through his. It bothered him for an instant and he almost pulled away. He had only slowly come to like her, even respect her. But he knew she reached for him out of her own need also. And he suddenly needed her arm as he walked this ground again.

"I grew up just over a few ranges of mountains in Hallstatt. After Susanne died, we followed Wolfram's trail for months, not knowing he had returned here. We arrived at this place just after the camp had been liberated by your U.S. Army."

They walked toward a large white sign near one wall. It gave a short history of the camp with descriptions of where the barracks had been located. Lukas looked at it closely, getting the perspective of the camp right in his mind.

Kate read a section aloud. "'Ebensee was a subcamp of Mauthausen Concentration Camp. It was built on November 18, 1943, as a labor camp to construct a system of tunnels into the mountain for a rocket-research factory. Most of the prisoners arrived from Mauthausen or other satellite camps.'"

Lukas remembered. He remembered every detail of the day he had arrived. It was sunny and warm for early May. He'd forgotten how beautiful Salzkammergut was—when raised as a child in such magnificence one quickly forgot to really see. And the war had helped blind his vision to beauty. The Americans had arrived just a day earlier. Local Resistance groups had already been in contact with them, but Lukas, Karl, Edmund, and Oskar came quickly to find Wolfram and exact their revenge. Jantes' blood stained their clothing, and his agonizing death rang in their ears.

The corpses.

Lukas could see them now, and he abruptly yanked away

from Kate. He closed his eyes and opened them again. They disappeared for a minute, then returned. Pure white bodies, naked and disfigured, were stacked like firewood or just left beside a pathway. Living corpses reached for him. The stench of disease and death made them cover their noses. But many skeletal faces smiled—they smiled and cheered from stretchers—some half dressed, some not at all. Their feet were black from frostbite and wrapped with any bit of dirty cloth. Their teeth were missing and their eyes so sunken he wondered how they saw. And they smiled for him.

Lukas remembered meandering through the camp. Karl had given them the news they wouldn't believe at first: Inmates had killed the guard Wolfram the night before. They all wanted proof, but the body had already been burned. Karl argued with them, wanting more, when Lukas had walked away. He wandered without destination through the sickness and odor. Some of the German POWs were dragging bodies and piling them in heaps. Their shoulders were hunched and uniforms dirty, not the proud Nazis they'd once been—like *he* had been.

An American trooper was telling a liberation story to several other soldiers as Lukas passed. He heard the young man tell of an inmate looking through his kit bag and emptying a tube of toothpaste into his mouth, then kissing his hand and asking for an autograph.

"Most beautiful place in Europe," the blond-haired young man said. "If this area isn't paradise on earth, I don't know what is. But then we find this. We hear there are camps like this dotted all over the place—I never would have imagined one place so terrible on God's earth."

Lukas' time as SS *Unterscharführer* Bruno Weiler at Mauthausen flooded over him. It had been liberated also. If he had stayed with the Nazis, he would have been dragging bodies along a path. If Tatianna had not come and his eyes not been opened, he would have continued for five more years into the

darkness of evil—an evil seeping upon stolen lives like
fermenting wine. Five more years he would have partaken of
that cup. Would he have become like those men—too drunk
with the wine of darkness to truly see what they'd done?

The American soldiers were disgusted and angry. Battle
tough, they were brought to tears at what they saw. The SS did
not fear the Americans as much as they feared the prisoners.
Revenge was allowed. Guards not protected by the troops were
literally torn to pieces. Lukas remembered stopping in front of
something twisted and strange on the ground. He'd stared at it
for a while until he realized it was an arm, the arm of an SS officer—he could see a portion of the swastika armband in the dirt.

Then he had been recognized.

The inmate had been following him. Lukas saw the man
walk boldly toward him with an American GI, when Lukas
had paused in his dazed walking. Their eyes met, but Lukas
didn't know the inmate.

He spoke a fragment of English. "He, he. He guard at
Mauthausen." The man's finger shook as he pointed. Eyes
from everywhere turned toward Lukas.

That's when Lukas had looked back, realizing he'd walked a
long way. Karl and the others were nowhere in sight. And he
knew it was his fate. He should be punished. Perhaps that
would take away the disgust of this place, of his fellow Austrians, of himself. Not only the disgust but the guilt. Guilt so
heavy and piercing, he didn't care if he lived or died.

"Come with me," the American said. "We'll ask you some
questions at headquarters."

Lukas didn't resist. In that place, this place he stood once
again, he didn't really care. The inmate had called him Bruno
Weiler and, before they reached headquarters, Lukas had
destroyed his papers stating his name as Lukas Johansen. Karl
would eventually find him and try to free him, but Lukas didn't

want it. He swore Karl to secrecy until he served what justice demanded.

But Lukas would never feel the relief and freedom, even when he walked from the prison years later. He'd admitted his guilt and gone to prison. There was no finger the size of a twig pointing and accusing him now. But the guilt would never leave him.

"Read more," he said to Kate, as if the sign were the prosecuting attorney.

"'In April alone, 4,547 died. There were too many for the crematorium. A thousand dead bodies were found when the Americans liberated the camp. The ovens could burn 8 bodies at once. They were kept working 24 hours a day and could not keep up.' Herr Johansen? Lukas?"

He looked her way. His eyes felt glassy until he blinked.

"You saved some of them. Marta told me. You saved some families and gave information that helped the Allies. You saved lives." Her voice was soft, but her words angered him. How dare she speak anything about that time when she knew nothing at all?

He said nothing, lest he regret what anger brought to his lips. He turned away from her and again saw the line of black ovens encased in brick, some with their doors open.

How many had he saved from the flames? Never enough.

⋆═◎═⋆

Kate watched Lukas sit on a concrete curb and lean into his hands. There were noises around—the cars on the distant highway, a saw cutting wood for a remodeling job within view of the graves. But the cemetery itself seemed to hold a silence all its own. Like the eye of a storm, it rested. Countries from around the world had brought their offerings of flowers— mostly silk and plastic arrangements—but some were fresh. This place had not been forgotten.

She walked around the manicured lawns surrounded by raised, bordered squares. A lone headstone rested in the center of the green grass. Kate realized the number etched into the stone was the number of bodies resting beneath. Who were they? It was easy to see just numbers and nearly pass by a smaller mass grave. Oh, only 208 in this grave compared with 1,377 in the last one. Or what about a large camp, where millions had died? But in this one grave were 208 lives. Each unique individual was born into the world with a cry and left the world the same way. Who had they been?

"Let us go," Lukas said, joining her, his steps slowing over the gravel. He followed her without speaking until they were inside the car and the engine running. He stared over the stone fence. "I thank you for your words. I know you mean well."

Kate nodded, wishing she could find something to say to help him. But silence seemed best.

"I cannot go to the museum today. This is enough. We will stop at the tunnels for a few moments, then return home."

Kate looked again toward the area where 208 people rested.

The sign was like a trailhead marker beside the road. Lukas stayed in the car while Kate hurried up the path to the entrance of the underground tunnels. A group of people were there, listening to a soft-spoken, handsome young man who described the background of the Ebensee subterranean "gallery." Kate blended in with the group and listened.

"One military agenda of the National Socialist Party toward the end of the war was to improve its missile industry. The Allies bombed many factories and so an underground facility was established. The A4, also known as the V-2 bomb, was under development here.

"Five hundred prisoners from Mauthausen were brought here in November 1943 to build the camp. It was extremely difficult work, digging into the mountain. If prisoners became ill or unable to work, most were returned to Mauthausen, where they died from exhaustion, illness, or murder. By the end of 1944, nine thousand prisoners were interned at Ebensee."

Instead of moving inside with the group, Kate stayed at the entrance. There was nothing else there but history now. Tours were given here every day during the summer months and on weekends during the off-season. Tours to remember and tell the story. But this wasn't where Wolfram Meizer was to be found.

Lukas was talking on the cellular phone when she returned to the car. She closed the door after getting into the leather seat, and then she noticed the look on Lukas' face. "What happened?" she asked, fearing the worst possibilities.

"I have been asked to the invitation-only opening of Garten Wald."

Kate was perplexed.

"It is our second location, a restored castle grounds located on Waldsee—Forest Lake, not far from here. The host is unnamed, except for being its honored proprietor."

"It's Wolfram Meizer. Why would he invite you to this?" Kate asked, stunned.

"He believes himself smarter than we are. Another surprise move on his part."

"But you can't go," she said.

He set his jaw. "Of course I will attend."

Kate was silent as the car rumbled to life. She tried to picture this Garten Wald—"Garden Woods" was its translation. It would rest on the lakeshore of Waldsee, similar to the alpine lakes she'd seen so many of, probably secluded but not uninhabited. It seemed completely impossible, but what if Jack was at Garten Wald?

"We found Wolfram," she whispered.

"No. He found us."

CHAPTER THIRTY-FIVE

Jack and Rudy had perfected their system of passing information through the vent between their rooms. Rudy passed through a "wire arm," as he called the contraption that carried their notes. Through that process, Jack was able to get Rudy's information about the building of the dam on Waldsee in the 1940s. Rudy was also good at drawing cartoons. He'd leave one for Jack when he returned from the tunnels. Jack gave reports of each night's expansion in a coded message, in case they were ever caught. Then he told Rudy about his discovery of the cave. Rudy confirmed Jack's suspicions—Wolfram was searching for a cave or tunnel the Nazis had used during the war to hide something of great importance. Rudy had figured that out from bits of conversation over the years.

"Why do you think he asks me to the castle every day?" Jack asked Rudy through the vent.

"When Wolfram gets bored of watching his birds in their outside aviaries, he brings a few inside. He likes to put some of his birds in bigger cages to see how they react and how the other birds react to their position. Then those birds are moved to the smallest cage of all."

Jack thought about Rudy's words. "So when were you his favored guest? And why were you demoted to the small cage?"

"It has been many years. We weren't on Waldsee then. And I believe Wolfram grew bored of me. I think he suspects that you know something you don't tell him. So he attempts to sneak information from you."

"You mean the way I attempt to sneak information from him?"

"He tells you exactly what he wants you to know. Though he must be getting old by now, and his brain isn't always as sharp."

"It's amazing that Ian is his son," Jack said, folding part of his blanket to make a flat pillow.

"I'm praying for that boy's soul. Let's not get into a debate over him again. Ian sees more than we know—we think we fool him all the time. He's probably saved our behinds from Wolfram a time or two."

"Maybe, but I think the *Mein Kampf* doctrine is tattooed into his brain tissue," Jack said.

"Some things only come about by prayer and fasting—that's what the Bible says."

"Fasting? If we fasted, we'd die."

"There are many ways to fast besides abstaining from food, my friend."

"Our entire lives are a fast—an involuntary one."

"That doesn't count. Quiet a moment," Rudy said in a firm voice. "Someone's coming."

Jack heard the footsteps also and crawled quickly to his bunk. He distinguished two sets of footsteps as they approached. They stopped at his door and the locks clicked open. Instead of Ian's tall, narrow frame, nearly all the hallway light was covered by the presence of Wolfram Meizer in his doorway.

When the chain was pulled, harsh light flooded the darkness. Wolfram walked inside and examined the room. Ian entered behind him and stood near the small table.

Wolfram spoke to Jack, but Ian did not translate. They both waited and looked at Ian. The old man was expectant, eager to receive a response. He turned to Ian and spoke what Jack understood as "Tell him."

"What is it, Ian?" Jack asked. It took another moment for Ian to take his eyes from Wolfram. But instead of translating, he spoke to Wolfram, who laughed heartily, saying, *"Nein, nein."*

"Ian, what is it?" Jack was trying to think of the small cage he was about to be placed inside.

"He said your wife is here."

"Who?" The word was his, but the voice sounded strange in his ears. He couldn't say her name in this place. Had Wolfram brought her to this prison? "She is here? The estate?"

"That is what I asked," Ian said. "But she is not here. She is in Austria. Your wife has been here for several weeks."

Wolfram seemed satisfied by Jack's stunned emotions. He picked up a wooden kitten, Jack's best carving yet, and scrutinized it closely. As Jack looked out the open door, his sudden urge was to race outside and lock Ian and Wolfram inside. But Wolfram was too quick. As if he had read Jack's mind, Wolfram headed for the door himself, the carved kitten in his hand.

Ian and Jack stared at one another for a minute; then Ian left him and locked the door as he went.

"She is here," Jack whispered to himself. "Kate is here."

⋆⇒◎⇐⋆

The days passed in rapid succession, moving them toward the date of the gala event at Garten Wald. Marta was angry that

Lukas was going to attend and wanted to go with him. He refused. Kate had kept her distance for a few days and let them work it out. It was time well spent with Abbie. Lunches in hand, they would follow pathways dotted with wildflowers and studied maps that showed routes to the Naturfreundehaus huts that extended all the way across the Alps. Kate's legs were sore every day for a week. They took photographs in fields of flowers and brought back specimens to press and frame when they got home.

At night Kate used the Internet to gain more information. Marta and Lukas reached a peace settlement and joined her again. They began tracking Wolfram Meizer's past activities. The same maps of Austria that Kate and Abbie used to plan their future cross-country trek were used to study Waldsee and the surrounding mountains.

Lukas made contact with departments in Vienna and the Salzkammergut and found descriptions of the property Wolfram had bought on the secluded end of the lake. It took time to track, since Wolfram had used false names and corporations to shield the true ownership, but using Lukas' contacts and some assumptions on their part—the activities of Wolfram Meizer began to unfold. One report told of the ruins of a castle and an abandoned salt mine that Wolfram had purchased in the late nineties at an enormous price. Mountains towered around the lake except where the village rested on the western edge. The rest of the lake sloped straight up, making it impossible to travel the circumference of the lake on foot. The restored Garten Wald resting in the flattened joint of two mountain ranges could only be reached by boat. Lukas also obtained an old diagram of the original tunnels of the salt mine before Wolfram had bought it.

Every day Kate fought the urge to rent a car and drive to Waldsee herself. But it couldn't be risked. She kept herself busy with Abbie. They called home and Cottonwood several times.

Connie was excited to hear from her and reported that Whiskers had a surprise for them when they came home—three new kittens. Kate, Abbie, and Marta shopped at the local village; Lukas insisted on going with them, though he sat on a bench in the small park and smoked his pipe. Kate and Abbie finally sent off a few postcards—to the only people who knew where they really were. Kate had debated about sending Mason one. In the end, she decided not to and told herself she'd call him tomorrow. She'd been saying that for weeks now.

The morning of the Garten Wald gala arrived. It had been decided that Kate would go along and stay at the village across the lake. If Lukas didn't return by the scheduled time, Kate would call the local police. Lukas wanted Anni, Marta, and Rey to remain at the estate. He hired extra security for the grounds, which relieved Kate's worry about Abbie's safety. Wolfram Meizer had a plan, and they had yet to discover what that plan was, besides drawing Lukas into his lair.

She would be away only one night, Kate thought as she loaded her suitcase into the car. She saw Anni peer from a window and then disappear inside. The young woman was consistently in a bad mood.

Once in the car, Lukas began to pull from the driveway. Kate turned in the seat for her usual backward wave to Abbie and Marta.

"Lukas, stop!" she said suddenly. Kate could see Abbie running down the road after the car. She got out quickly, before Lukas had completely stopped. "What's wrong?"

Tears streamed down Abbie's cheeks as she tumbled into Kate's arms.

"Abbie, are you hurt? What is it?" Panic streaked through Kate. She held Abbie back to look for blood.

"I didn't tell you. I almost forgot."

"What?"

"I love you, Mom."

"I love you too." Kate's face was level with Abbie's as she wiped away the tears. "You don't have to cry, honey."

"And, Mom, please, please come back."

Kate put her hand over her mouth. "I'll come back," she said quickly. Then she realized that it wasn't something she could promise. "I will always do everything in my power to come back to you."

Tears poured from Abbie's eyes. "Bring Daddy back too."

⟶⇒●⇐⟵

Wolfram Meizer buttoned the jacket over his stomach and gazed into the mirror. The snow-white shirt and black tuxedo fit his shape to perfection. He strolled through the house, his castle, where every light in every room was turned on, except in his office, of course. Stopping before the floor-to-ceiling windows in the master parlor, he gazed outside.

The musicians were set up on the front terrace, the caterers had candles ready to light on the decorated tables, and food was prepared in his kitchen. Tiny lights lit the pathway along the wide entrance from the boat dock to the terrace and the castle doorway. Tonight the world would meet him. He had started well-placed rumors that the mystery host was a wealthy German businessman relocated from South America—the truth was often the best deceiver. Didn't everyone want to see the grand reconstruction of Garten Wald and meet the mad owner no one knew much about?

Wolfram had selected his guest list carefully: cabinet leaders, members of the Viennese upper class, old money moguls, Party leaders. The choices would seem random, thus making it suspicious in an intriguing way. The rumors of intrigue would bring the ones on the list hurrying to the village. Others would ask themselves, "Why was that one invited and not me?" "How can I get on that guest list?" the intentionally uninvited would ask. Yet others would think, *There is a plot of some kind brewing.*

Wolfram took a deep breath to prepare for the night ahead. It would prove to be one of the best of his life. And there was one guest on his list he had waited decades to meet again.

Jack had tried to rest, tried to figure out a plan, tried to understand why he wasn't brought to Wolfram's office any longer, and why no one was allowed to do the nighttime work. Rudy had been no help. They talked for a short time through the vent, but then Rudy grew tired and needed rest. Jack could tell that Rudy didn't understand the desperation of the situation.

Jack had tried to discover Kate's location, when she had come, and what she was doing in Austria. He'd found out nothing. But tonight something was happening, and Jack was willing to do the impossible.

He went to the door and began pounding until he heard footsteps. Suddenly, the door opened, and Ian stood in the doorway.

"Ian, have I ever asked you for anything for myself?"

"No."

"I must ask tonight. Have I ever given you reason not to trust my word?"

"No."

"Then trust me."

Their eyes locked, each evaluating the many months they'd spent together and what it had meant. Had friendship developed over that time? Had the friendship fostered trust? Had trust grown strong enough for each man to risk his own life in the other's hands?

"What do you ask?"

"That you help me find my wife."

"I know already."

"Where is she?"

"At the village tonight."

Jack was stunned at the thought of Kate—his Kate—across the lake where the lights called to him. "I must see her. And I need your help."

CHAPTER THIRTY-SIX

Three boats had been chartered for the occasion. A string quartet played softly as Lukas walked to the boarding station. His invitation was carefully examined while a reporter talked in front of a camera, pointing to where the lights of Garten Wald shown across the water.

Lukas was welcomed aboard the wide, flat boat. Drinks and hors d'oeuvres were offered on the open bow by waiters in black-and-white uniforms. Other guests lounged along the railing and the glass-sided cabin, holding drinks and tiny plates. Flags crackled gently in the evening breeze—Austrian, European Union, and another gray-and-red flag with the letters *GW* within double diamonds. Lukas wondered if some-where in the design the letters *SS* or *NAZI* or a swastika could be hidden from first glance.

Lukas stood along the railing, facing the water. In no mood for small talk, he had already tried to avoid several familiar faces and a member of the press he remembered from Parlia-ment. But he couldn't enjoy solitude for long without seeming surly, so soon he was engaged in conversation with a small group of people he'd known in Vienna. They discussed a new proposal of speed limits, then debated the origin of the wine they drank.

Lukas remembered that a king once said of his wealth, "Meaningless, meaningless. It was all chasing after the wind." What did Lukas really have? His daughters did not know him. He owned properties, several businesses, a casino, and investments in a hospital. As time passed, his work in the government now seemed irrelevant. It was all really worthless.

But Wolfram was building more than an estate in the side of a mountain. There was too much at stake here, and he had too much help. It was a legacy for the future. A legacy Lukas would stand against; yet he was walking right into its headquarters.

The boat landed along a dock. As Lukas and the other guests disembarked, he noticed the woods growing down to the edge of bordered gardens. Flowers arranged in intricate designs lined the wide, cobblestone path and stairways leading up to the castle. Wolfram had prepared an elegant first impression. Lukas distanced himself from the other guests he recognized and assessed the grounds as they moved toward the main terrace, where he could hear a violin playing. The entrance to the salt mine was dark but visible in a cutout section above them. Lukas also glimpsed the flat roof of a structure beyond the wooded area behind the castle and farther up. Would Wolfram dare have Rudy Blessing and Jack Porter locked in one of those buildings? He would believe anything of Wolfram. His old enemy was an intelligent and devious man. And when suspicions arose, Wolfram welcomed his critics with open arms.

The remodeled castle had a white turret on one end with a GW flag waving from its cylindrical roof. Lukas saw three floors of lit windows, and he estimated the house to be twice the size of his own. The group climbed the steps to the castle, where earlier guests talked in circles. More guests were arriving at the docks below.

Lukas made his rounds of the groups he was familiar with along the terrace. Trays laden with an assortment of foods covered a table at one end opposite the orchestra stage. Candlelit tables drew groups while others wandered through the house. Most people were interested in meeting their mysterious host. One rumor said he'd returned from Africa after making a fortune in the sapphire industry, another that he had connections in Hollywood. Rumors always ran wild.

Lukas decided to go inside, when someone spoke from a microphone on the stage. "Welcome, my guests. I am greatly pleased to greet all of you."

Applause filled the terrace. Many stood in the presence of their host. If a hundred years had passed, Lukas would have known this man. His nose was larger and his jowls now hung like a bulldog's. He'd gained weight upon his once-trim physique. He still wore his jet black hair slicked straight back. Wolfram was the aged version of the man he'd long known.

Wolfram had been a reckless youth, but he now stood and spoke with an air of royalty. "I am Wolfram, though that is not the name given to me at birth."

Although his name would not be recognized, a stir of voices questioned one another in curiosity.

"I invited you here to enjoy an evening, explore the grounds, and discover the magic of Garten Wald. New friendships will be established here tonight as Garten Wald opens officially. I envision a place for you and other dignitaries to come and enjoy Austria, be it for business or for pleasure. At one time, rival peoples met here under the neutral invitation of the castle lord. Peace was found between the two peoples. May this again be the purpose of Garten Wald."

Light applause followed. Someone behind Lukas whispered,

"What does he believe—that peace accords will be formed on the grounds?"

Wolfram continued. "I have a humble token to show my sincerity for peace and unity among party members, peoples, and the nations. Please, if you will."

A large display covered with red velvet was rolled onto the terrace. The television crew's cameras pivoted immediately to cover the event.

"I invited you here for something more than a mere party. I also want to share my journey. It is not a past I am proud of. Perhaps some will understand it as their own; others will find it difficult to understand, but tonight it must be spoken at last."

Chairs had been moved and wineglasses set down as every face turned, captured by Wolfram's words.

"I spent my childhood days in a village not far from here. My home was not a happy place, and I grew to be a young man seeking something to believe in."

Lukas knew that now the lies had begun. Wolfram had been raised in Germany, not Austria.

"My story is not unlike many Austrian stories. We found the Nazi Party to give us hope for a new beginning. Yes, they spouted their anti-Semitic and racist views along with the message of a greater vision. But anti-Semitic views were already ingrained in much of our culture since the time of the great Crusades or even the Roman age. The fear and misunderstanding of different peoples have always bred hatred. It is not right, but it is fact. And so, as a young man seeking something to believe in, I found the Nazi Party."

Across the crowd and beneath the small white lights, Wolfram's gaze met Lukas'. They had not stared into each other's eyes in decades, and yet it was all there between them—the memories and hatred alike.

"I had a different name at that time."

A cold sensation, quick and consuming, passed through Lukas. With a sudden light of realization, Lukas knew Wolfram's words even before he spoke them.

"My name was Bruno Weiler."

No one reacted to the name or noticed the flash of a smirk Lukas perceived as Wolfram glanced his way again. Wolfram continued with Lukas' story of joining the Nazi youth and of the Anschluss, when Austria was joined with the German Third Reich, and Hitler marched across their border to the cheers of many, including himself. Lukas had moved back involuntarily toward the shadows, away from Wolfram's sight and the eye of the camera. Wolfram was telling Lukas' history and claiming it as his own. It was not a past Lukas liked to remember, but it was his nonetheless. That Wolfram would claim to be Bruno was a twist of mad genius that Lukas didn't fully understand. It brought more fear than anger.

"In 1941, I was assigned the position of guard at Mauthausen Konzentrationslager. Finally, I understood what Hitler and his party were about. But it was too late. No one dared disobey the orders, or he would soon wear the uniform of an inmate. I participated in a firing squad where a woman from my own village was killed."

How did he know about Tatianna? Lukas wondered. He'd never spoken of the girl whose death opened his eyes to what he was doing and who he'd become.

"I cannot say what changed me, but I knew I must help stop this madness. I began to keep records on weapon-making sites and military secrets that I eventually gave to the Allies. I also worked with the Austrian Resistance. At long last, the war ended. But the past came back when I was arrested for Nazi crimes. My comrades could have helped me, but I chose not to fight the charges since I continued to feel terrible guilt. I could have escaped judgment by revealing that I had worked with the Allies and the Austrian Resistance, but I felt the sins of my time at Mauthausen deserved more than a few years in prison.

"Some will say I betrayed Austria. Others that my sins can never be forgiven. I understand both lines of thought. I can only walk the path I believe is right."

No one spoke as Wolfram lowered his head, then raised it to study his audience.

"So now I offer another small token as proof of my repentance." Wolfram gestured toward the velvet-covered display. "I was in South America in 1992 and bought a small art collection. This past year I discovered the collection's original owner was a Jewish family. The paintings were stolen from them during the war. Tonight I proudly return the works to the family. The Neumann family was informed of my gift and sent the grandson of Holocaust victims as a representative. David Neumann, would you please step forward?"

Lukas watched a middle-aged man walk from the audience. Unsmiling, he joined Wolfram on the stage. Wolfram took the edge of the velvet covering and tugged it down. There were gasps and applause as the distinct form of a Klimt painting was revealed.

"I hope this is yet another link in the reparation of peoples in this nation. The rest of the collection is inside, available for you to see. This is a special event. No one has seen this collection in its entirety since the late 1930s. Thank you all for coming."

Loud applause and cheers continued as Wolfram and David Neumann shook hands. People around Lukas talked. One commented, "Political walls are hard to break down, but men like that can do it."

Groups began to move close while others already sauntered toward the house. Lukas waited on the outskirts, talking to people he'd seen at dinner parties in the past. He was composed as always on the outside, but his eyes kept glancing in Wolfram's direction. Wanting to leave, he tried to consider what Wolfram would expect from him. There was a handful of people still alive who knew Lukas' old identity. But none, least of all himself, would want to refute Wolfram's claim. It would be messy and jeopardize everything. Yet how could he allow this man to take his identity? Lukas felt like the door to a very small cage had just been closed around him. Worst of all, he didn't know what Wolfram fully intended to do.

Lukas stayed with the chatter of men and women he'd known for years, though really knew nothing about. They were diverse in backgrounds and politics but all intrigued by the man who had invited them here tonight. The crowd lessened as music and dessert were offered in the water gardens. He scanned the patio in quick darts of movement, but Wolfram was not to be found.

With feigned interest in the painting, he made his way forward. The work reminded him of another Klimt painting, with the woman's long drawn face, dark colors, and mosaic design in her flowing robe.

If Wolfram meant to assay the suspicion in his countrymen, the revelation of a piece of artwork like this would certainly give the answer. It would be widely disputed where he obtained the piece. The usual Nazi rumors were unneeded because Wolfram had actually admitted his past in public. Wolfram knew how to gamble. The gift of the art collection to a wealthy Jewish family could be considered generous retribution, as well as the fact he'd already gone to prison for his crimes. Disgust and anger pulsed through Lukas. He recalled the bodies of Susanne, Jantes, and the white corpses with open eyes and cold fingers at Ebensee.

"Former minister Lukas Johansen," a voice said behind him. Lukas had felt the man's presence before he spoke a word. He turned to face Wolfram Meizer.

"It has been many years," Wolfram said.

"Not enough." They stared coldly at each other, like a challenge. "Bruno Weiler, is it?"

Wolfram laughed. "I believed you would find that interesting."

"What makes you want to be Bruno Weiler?"

Wolfram's gaze did not waver. "Let us talk first."

"After so many years, now you return to Austria."

"The world cannot compare to Europe."

"Especially when you want something." Lukas spoke in a low, precise tone.

"Some desires grow with age."

"But what exactly did you lose so long ago that you seek again?" Lukas gazed toward the dark mountains, knowing Wolfram watched every movement.

"Only solitude and peace in my native country," Wolfram answered.

"You will be returning to Germany?"

"You remember everything, Bruno—I mean, Lukas. Germany may be my birthplace, but Austria is home."

"I find that interesting."

"I think my confession interested you, or angered you? I also remember a young woman who once interested you. I believe her name was Susanne Olsen?" Wolfram taunted.

This is where it is leading, Lukas thought. Wolfram would strive for his weakest point to drive home the dagger, but Lukas was prepared to deflect it.

Wolfram leaned close as a group passed; a few people glanced their way curiously. "I did not realize it until Karl. My contacts discovered that Lukas Johansen is meeting Oskar Gogl at Karl Olsen's home. I wondered why a former Austrian minister would do such a thing. Lukas Johansen could not be my old comrade Bruno Weiler. He could not be the betrayer of my confidence and *der Führer.* How could I have missed that all these years? Was it your facial changes or my stupidity?

Bruno Weiler would not simply disappear in the labyrinth of postwar chaos. I allowed my own situation to keep me from pursuing him fully."

"I am sure your exile to South America did not make it easy," Lukas said, seeking Wolfram's own weakest place. Once he had known this man to fail beneath the lure of drink and a beautiful woman, but the older version of that man would most likely find pride his greatest failing. "Why were you forced to flee Europe when many others stayed, even worked for government agencies? Did you not have aspirations in the Party—want to be *kommandant* of a subcamp, king of your own little world? Ah, I forgot. You were demoted down to camp guard. It is not wise for an officer to get drunk with one of his men and not realize secret military plans were stolen from beneath his nose. Did this not happen to you more than once, and you did not know until I was far away? You led me to the Party, and I walked out with your future as an officer."

Wolfram took a step closer, his face now a sneer. A young man walked toward them with a tray of wineglasses. "Not now!" Wolfram said loudly. He regained his composure, even smiled. "She called for you. Susanne."

Lukas did not say a word as Wolfram laughed.

"As she died, she called for a man named Lukas. I wondered who that could be but never knew until recently."

"And is it not ironic that because of my betrayal of you, I was brought into Susanne's life?" Lukas said in an even tone. "She cared for me, not you. She called for me."

Again Lukas took the smile from Wolfram's face. Yes, pride was his weakness now.

"Men do not take from me. Not even you. Susanne was a temporary fancy. I enjoyed her more seeing her die."

He would not hear it, Lukas told himself. He would not see the body in the snow or the way she turned his way as they walked together. *Keep her out, or you will not be strong enough.*

Lukas realized he had long since clenched his fists at his side. He wished for a weapon so he could destroy this man with pleasure. But first he needed to see all the cards Wolfram held.

Feeling sick and full of adrenaline, Lukas paused before speaking again. "What about Jack Porter?"

"I have no idea what you speak of." There was not even a glimmer of fear on that self-confident face.

"What of the pieces of broken tile?"

Wolfram's manner turned serious. "That interests me."

"I will trade the tiles for Jack Porter," Lukas said quickly. "You can find your treasure with the complete set, isn't that right?"

"Jack will not go without his comrade, I'm afraid."

"Then trade the tiles for both men."

"I need the men and the tiles, and I don't think you trust me with both." Wolfram reached around Lukas and slapped his back hard.

"You will be exposed, Wolfram."

"Did you not hear my grand confession? I am Bruno Weiler, who paid for my Nazi crimes after the war. I make the world right even further by returning Jewish heirlooms to prove my change of heart and alliance."

"There are others who know you are not Bruno Weiler."

"*Ja*. The other guards from Mauthausen who are still alive. Old men who will not refute me or reveal their own past. It is worth the risk. For what can be exposed—that I am not Bruno Weiler? Then who is the real Bruno Weiler? Former minister Johansen may have a very ugly skeleton in his closet. We have some members of the press here tonight. And I have a nice microphone. Is there anything you would like to say? You should hope and pray no one begins to search my background. Only your own will be in jeopardy."

Wolfram laughed heartily, bringing many eyes their way.

"You do not see it, do you? We are very much alike, you and I. Very few attributes separate us. We started out the same, our families, our beliefs—we were even friends. But you lost the vision of a greater world. You scratch away at idealisms that are completely meaningless. Ah, you do not like that word, do you? We are equal men, Lukas Johansen. But I am free from what burdens you. Will you ever be free from your guilt? Men like you never are. So you help me or you will have more guilt upon your soul—Jack Porter's life is in your hands. And do your daughters know who their father really is?"

⋆━◉⟨⟩⋆

They moved quickly along the edge of the woods, watching for guests while passing the dinner party. Jack followed Ian closely, barely seeing the people through the thick brush they stayed behind. They reached the water, and Jack spotted the tiny dinghy pulled onto shore. There were a flashlight and an extra gas can in the boat.

"Remember the arrangement," Ian said. Jack nodded and shook Ian's hand. He would keep the promise no matter how hard it would be to return to the barrack. His word had been given, and Rudy's life depended on it.

"Jack," Ian said, "I will help you and Rudy survive this. When we make the find, you will be freed. I give you my word."

"As I have given mine," he said.

"You must look better than that," he said, pointing at Jack. Ian tossed him a bag he carried. Jack unzipped it to find a set of clothing and a pair of shoes. He had wondered what to do about his appearance once he arrived at the village in rags. It wasn't what he'd envisioned for meeting Kate, and he'd hoped to borrow someone's laundry hanging from a clothesline.

"Thank you, Ian. Thank you for everything."

Jack used the oars for the first fifteen minutes on the lake, then tugged the string to the outboard engine, guiding the rudder carefully along the rugged shore toward the village lights shining in the darkness. The night was still and the water smooth. Only the urgency pounding within him interrupted the late hour. The boat's motor echoed too loudly, and he couldn't stop looking back, half expecting to be trailed. Instead he saw the casual journey of a well-lit boat leaving Wolfram's dock.

He turned the motor down to a slow, trolling speed. It seemed like hours, but Jack's watch said it was only one when he approached the town along the water's edge. He could distinguish the lights now from their sources on doorposts, streetlamps, and walkways.

Civilization. There were people strolling along a cement walkway in the cool of a summer night. From the darkness beyond the realm of town lights, he sat and watched them. There was little time to waste, but the sight of these people— of lives so close and so far away—mesmerized him as if he were a boy seeing a candy shop for the first time.

The boat putt-putted quietly as Jack sought an inlet along the rocky shoreline. He turned the motor off and coasted toward the shore. When the aluminum hull grazed the shore, he stepped over the edge. Water pressed against the rubber of his high rain boots as he dragged the bow onto shore and tied it off to a tree. He washed his face and arms in the cold lake water, then crouched in the darkness for what felt a long while before grabbing the duffel bag and pushing through the dense undergrowth. If someone stole the boat—he couldn't think of that now.

After Jack had changed his clothing in the brush, he found a dirt trail up a rise and through the trees. The shoes were a little loose and the pants baggy, but there were no holes or stains. It seemed that eyes stared at his every move from the darkness. A twig broke beneath his foot and he stopped to listen. No one was following. No one knew he was here. Jack told himself this again, realizing the wide gulf between captivity and freedom.

The trail turned from dirt to stone and light shone ahead. Then Jack entered the light. It felt both magnificent and terrifying to walk like any other man in the world. He didn't have to stay on one pathway from the barrack to the tunnels to the castle to the barrack. He could run all over, even ride in a car somewhere. It was the oddest sensation to be free, even if that freedom was for a very short time. No one understood it. The woman he saw through a window, the couple strolling along the street. He saw people here and there as he came to the village square. They took little notice of him, though he nearly expected applause and cheers at his arrival. Jack loved the tiny village. It looked so quaint and cozy even at night. He would love to explore it with Kate on his arm. And now she was only minutes away.

Jack followed the directions in his mind, reciting what Ian had told him as he made each turn, until he stood before the sign that read *Zimmer frei*. Ian had explained this was similar to a bed-and-breakfast in the States but less expensive and very homey. Kate was in room 10. She was up there now; Ian had come that day and confirmed it. His wife didn't know he was coming. He didn't know what she'd say, though he'd spent hundreds of hours imagining this moment. He kept feeling fear instead of joy. It was too overpowering, so Jack sat on a bench outside the hotel.

The time had come. But could he really go inside?

⟶⟨⟩⟵

Kate had never seen Lukas like this. He paced her room and explained the details of his encounter with Wolfram Meizer. She was stunned to realize that Jack was truly alive. He was alive!

"Marta would want us to call the police."

"But we know it would be too dangerous for your husband right now."

"Will you give Wolfram the tiles?"

"I do not know. He told me under his breath that he will kill Jack unless we bring the tile pieces to him in three days. He wanted the pieces now, but I said Oskar's was in the United States. I must go to Vienna tonight. There is something I must decide and people to meet with about it. You will come with me. I will get you a room there."

"Why Vienna? Shouldn't we get back to the estate?"

"I need more help than Marta right now. But I must get Anni to meet me in Vienna. It is time for me to talk to my daughters."

Kate knew what he was saying and saw the turmoil in his face. "I will stay here and take the train in the morning."

"No." He shook his head.

Kate put her hand on his arm. "Lukas, I will be safe here— Wolfram is too busy tonight. Go do what you must. Tell your daughters and be free of it. I will meet you tomorrow at the estate."

He nodded and put his hand over hers. "Thank you."

⤙⬤⤚

Lukas had left only fifteen minutes earlier, but Kate already regretted not going with him. She stood at the window and looked down at the street where he had gone. Even at this late hour people walked in the square and sat on benches. She closed the curtains so that not even an inch of window showed through. The room was cramped with a twin bed, table, antique wardrobe, and bathroom.

The walls began to close around her. She was alone. Jack was alone, but he was alive. Lukas believed he was just across the water. Earlier, on their drive to the bed-and-breakfast, Lukas had pointed out the lights of that castle. Now Kate had the overwhelming desire to see those lights again—the lights of the place where she now knew Jack could be living. But Lukas had told her to stay in the hotel, for her own safety.

Kate undressed and put on the white cotton shorts and shirt pajamas she'd brought. All the while she dreamed of how she could get to Jack. Perhaps she could somehow get aboard or rent a boat and do her own investigating. If he couldn't come to her, she'd go to him. If not for Abbie, Kate would have taken the risk. But she kept seeing her daughter's tears and feeling those slim arms clinging to her.

Kate was looking for her toothbrush when someone knocked on the door.

The door creaked open and, instead of Lukas, a stranger stood before her. Kate tried to shut the door when he said her name.

"Kate."

She paused, trying to see his face. The light in the hall cast shadows over his unkempt hair and scruffy beard.

"Kate, it's me."

It was Jack's voice; she'd almost forgotten the sound. She knew the recorded voice of her husband from watching home videos over and over again. But this real voice was brought from memory to reality. She'd recognize it anywhere. He stood there, waiting for her. But Kate couldn't move. Her hands were shaking and her feet unable to take a step.

He was here. Jack. But he was more than a stranger; he was a ghost. Kate wanted to run or slam the door in his face. She'd longed for him just seconds before, but now Kate knew— worse than losing Jack was to have him suddenly back and not be the Jack she knew.

His expression read the fear in her eyes. He appeared hurt.

"Jack!" was all she could say.

He nodded, and the light from her room fell on his face as she released the doorjamb and it creaked an inch wider. His eyes were Jack's eyes. They were red and rimmed with tears.

"Jack," she heard herself say again, softly. But she couldn't move toward him.

"Katie, I have a million things I want to say to you." He took one step and then another. The distance closed between them. His arms reached for her. His embrace was awkward, and his touch felt foreign and cold against her skin. She tried to hug him back but couldn't.

"You're here. This is really you."

"Yes, frightening sight that I am," he said with a chuckle. He quickly closed the door and turned on a lamp. He glanced around as if someone might be there. This Jack looked older and beyond tired; he was haggard. The beard changed him completely—he'd only once grown out beyond stubble.

"Please, tell me about Abbie. Tell me everything." He grabbed her arm, reminding her of a starving man in desperate need of nourishment. It frightened her, but she considered how she would feel if she'd been the one taken from family and friends for so long. "Kate, I wish I had time to hear about every day. You can't imagine—"

"Abbie," she whispered, wondering what her daughter would think when she saw him. "Abbie will be so happy. How . . . how did you get here? Wait, we need to get out of here, back to Lukas'." Kate was stunned that at last she had Jack— the goal she'd worked for for more than three years. It was over. Jack was here.

"No, Kate. I can't. I only have a few hours."

"What are you talking about?"

"I promised I'd return. That was the only way for me to do this. I gave my word."

"Go back? To Wolfram?"

"Yes. There is a man there, my friend. If I don't return, they'll kill him."

"Rudy Blessing."

"Yes. Then you know about everything—why I've been here?"

"A little, yes."

"What did you believe? Did they leave you a note, or was there blood to make it look like I died?"

"I didn't know you were alive until tonight. All this time I knew nothing."

He grabbed her and embraced her for a long time. This time it didn't feel as awkward. Her hands clasped his back and his breath grazed her neck.

"I'm sorry, Kate. I tried to find a way to get back to you."

"You can't leave again," she said. Her emotions were tied up. "I know you had no choice before, but let's leave now. Abbie has to see you."

He sat on the edge of her bed, his face in his hands. Moments ticked by as Kate studied him—his shoulders were hunched, and his hands weren't the rugged ones she'd known. These were cut and callused, as if they'd worked a hundred years.

"We don't have much time," he mumbled, then stared at her. "I forgot how you looked. No, I didn't forget, but I didn't remember what it was like to be in a room with you. I have to stay focused—we must make a plan."

He wanted to plan, and she still had a hundred questions. How did he get here tonight? Why couldn't he have gotten word to them earlier? Why would he come only to leave again?

"Jack, what happened that day?" she asked.

"Can that wait? There is much I want to talk about. I must hear about Abbie. There are so many things."

"Start at the beginning and tell me everything."

"We don't have time. If I asked you the questions that have been killing me for days and weeks and years—like why are you here? Why are you in Austria?"

"I came to find you, to try one last time." She saw the great emotion in his expression. "Please, Jack, I need to know what happened."

"You mean that morning in Venice?"

"Yes," she whispered, feeling as if she were talking about two other people. That couple could not be her and this Jack. What put this great gulf between them?

"It was easy for them," he said. "They knocked on the door not long after you left. I thought you'd forgotten something. When I opened the door, they hit me. I remember little of the next few weeks and didn't know I'd lost weeks of time. The first six or so months were like that—a dark haze of solitude. I was moved around after that and finally began to do what they chose me for—to find the location of some Nazi loot. We were in Italy at a castle there for a while."

"Schloss Weiss," she said, trying to imagine him in these places while she had waited and sought him from home.

"It was all planned. Remember the grant I was awarded to attend the conference? It was Wolfram's doing, though he went through several organizations. He's a powerful man with links to neo-Nazi groups in the States and Europe. He pays them to do most of his work. He's a man who enjoys playing with others' lives. They chose me because I'd worked with Rudy that summer. They e-mailed me, pretending to be him, telling me about a grant to go to this conference. We e-mailed back and forth in the months before our trip."

She watched his hands. Those hands she'd once known well.

"I'm sorry, Kate. I can't imagine what you've gone through."

"And you," she whispered, looking at him again. This time he didn't seem so much a stranger. She could see more of the Jack she'd once known. They talked quickly, hearing the time tick away in their heads. Kate tried to think of ways to keep him from leaving. He kept asking about Abbie, their families, friends, what people thought had happened, and her life without him.

She hadn't noticed the worn brown bag he'd brought. Jack opened it and handed her something. "This is important. Who took them?"

"How did you get these?" she asked as she flipped through the stack of photographs.

"Wolfram."

"How did he get them?"

"Kate, who took these pictures?"

"Connie. But—"

"Connie, your best friend, movie buff Connie? Does she know you are here?"

"Yes."

"That's how Wolfram knows about you being here."

"You think Connie could be involved—with this?"

"I have been receiving these photographs since after my first six months. You're certain she took them?"

"I'm sure. I remember all of these. She has a digital video camera and tapes everything—not just us. But these photos, I remember. We had a barbecue last summer at her house." Kate realized how awful that sounded. They'd had a barbecue and he'd been imprisoned. Then she stopped at the one with Mason's arm around her and the next one with them laughing and another with Mason. She wondered what he'd felt when given those. The progression of Abbie's age was a surprise, reminding her how long he'd been gone.

They sat in the quiet, knowing the time wouldn't last long.

"What time is it?" he asked, then saw the clock. "I must get back soon, but I'm getting Rudy out with me. In one week."

"No, we don't have that much time. Wolfram wants the tile pieces—you may not know what those are—but the tiles probably show the location of the treasure Wolfram seeks. We believe that he'll use you to retrieve it once he knows where it is."

"I already know the location."

"Of the treasure?"

"I found a cave on our last dive. I'm sure it's what Wolfram had us looking for."

"Then the cave is underwater? If this is it—unbelievable. Did you know that Wolfram has been seeking this treasure since the war?"

"I've known very little, though they've sent me underwater, inside mountains, and exploring the remains of buildings, castle foundations—whatever they led me to. I was never told what I was actually looking for. How do you know all of this?" Jack asked.

"I'm working with two people who were part of the Austrian Resistance and sought Wolfram during World War II when he was a Nazi guard. They thought he was dead until recently. It's a long story, but this could change everything." Kate was beginning to find hope in the idea of Jack going back. "If we could retrieve this treasure—"

"No, you couldn't do it without someone seeing you—and in such a short amount of time." Jack thought for a moment. "Tomorrow night. Let's do this fast and get it done. I'll insist on Rudy going on the dive. I think I can manage that much. Do you think you can get a boat and wait alongshore, let's say, two hundred yards away?"

Kate nodded at his determined look. They discussed the impossible—a simple plan to end their three years of separation. Kate realized as they talked that if the plan didn't work, if this was the only moment granted them by God, the moment she'd begged for, they'd lost much of that time discussing tomorrow night's plan. But it had to be done.

"Tell me more about Abbie," Jack said, as if also realizing

the passing of their precious time together. "Is sparkly pink still her favorite color?"

Kate smiled, remembering how Abbie's eyes had grown large at anything that sparkled, especially pink. "She likes purple now, but she collects sparkly stickers."

"Do her eyelids still have those soft blue veins when she sleeps?"

"Not really. But she still does that turn toward the wall right before she finally falls asleep, and remember how she used to smile and laugh in the middle of the night? She did that again last week for the first time since—well, you know."

He nodded. "What's her favorite ice cream?"

As Jack went through his list of questions, Kate felt as if he'd come home from a very long trip, hungry for all the news.

"Abbie has never stopped believing we'd find you, Jack. She's the only one who still believed." Kate wanted to admit her own guilt and say how sorry she was for giving up.

He put his hand over hers. "I didn't believe either. If you knew how many times I prayed for a night like tonight. And now it's gone and I never said all I wanted to say. Kate, I understand that you had to move on. Tomorrow could be the beginning of another struggle, learning where we all fit into each other's lives again." He was looking at their hands, touching her fingertips one at a time. "I don't expect you to feel the way you once did. I'm not the man you married. I know that."

"Jack, come back to us tomorrow. We can work that out later. Just come back to us."

Kate walked to the dock with him. They stood in the shadows. The air was cold now, as night was turning toward dawn.

It was time for him to leave.

Would she see him again? Would this be the good-bye she'd once thought she wanted? Perhaps the pain of a good-bye was greater than not having the chance to say it.

He took her hand as they stood there. Everything would

move fast now. It would be over by the next dawn, for better or worse.

"I'm going to walk away and tell you that we'll see each other tomorrow. I can't stand good-byes."

"I remember."

Jack looked up at the sky. Kate knew he was searching for a sign of dawn on the horizon. It would come soon enough. Then his eyes turned toward the moon, high in the sky. "It's a blue night," he said. "Do you remember that?"

"Yes." She noticed the way the night seemed washed in a blue haze. "The first night of our honeymoon."

Jack smiled broadly, and she glimpsed the husband she once knew. She suddenly wanted to rest within his arms, close her eyes, and never move from the warmth she knew she'd find there.

Instead she simply said, "Abbie says a blue night means her daddy is coming back."

"I believe she's right. God gave us tonight."

"Jack, I don't want you to go." She stared at the ground and his worn shoes. "I understand why you must, but I don't want you to go. This isn't enough time."

He reached for her hand and pressed it to his lips. He kissed each finger and she felt tears on her skin. "If you knew how good you feel to me. If you only knew. God must give me the strength. God, give me enough strength to leave you."

"Jack. Jack, look at me." Kate turned his chin to face her. "This hasn't been enough. I'm not ready to let you go. I've missed you so . . . but I know you must do this."

He kissed the palm of her hand and took several steps away. "I left some things in my bag in your room. Something for Abbie also. If anything goes wrong, give it to her. But I plan to do so myself."

"You must give it to her." Kate said, already hating the

distance between them—the distance that would continue to grow until he was gone once again.

Jack took several steps backwards, then turned and walked into the shadows of the trees.

"Wait," she called, hurrying into the dark to find him. He waited and then pulled her tenderly against him. His hands touched her hair and shoulders and grasped her hands.

"I still love you, Jack."

"I will always love you," he whispered fiercely, then met her lips with his own. The kiss was fierce, and passion ignited within her.

But before Kate could take a breath, he was gone.

CHAPTER THIRTY-SEVEN

In two hours Lukas entered Vienna. He'd been on the phone all the way there. He'd talked to several advisors and friends about his options. Though they grumbled about the hour of his call, they knew Lukas well enough to set up the meetings for the next day. Lukas found his usual hotel on the Ringstraße, with its view of the Stadt Park. Anni would be here in a few hours. He settled into his suite and felt a great weariness pour over him. It was impossible for him to pull all-nighters anymore. Once he could go days without sleep.

Those nights of meetings that lasted until sunrise, the flights from city to city—everything he had given his life for since the war's end was for nothing now. His reputation was about to be destroyed. He would be labeled, and that would follow him and his family forever. He would see it in the faces of old colleagues and friends. That he loved his country, his children, and the freedom of men everywhere would not matter. Because he had been a Nazi, he would be considered "anti-Semitic, guilty, a murderer and a torturer." All the good he'd done would be lost beneath this name of what he'd fought against.

In addition, he would have to prove he was Bruno Weiler, which could be tricky but not impossible, and the inevitable scandal. In telling the truth, Lukas knew he risked losing everything. Wolfram knew it also and counted on his cowardice to keep his silence.

Yet Lukas felt a sense of peace, even with the coming storm of a shambled life and career and with others' lives hanging by a thread. Wasn't it a tinge of peace because at last he'd be free of his horrible past? There was comfort even in the worst circumstances when a man stood up for what was true and good and right. That's what he'd seen in Tatianna's eyes before he'd pulled the trigger and ended her life. That was the peace he'd heard in Susanne's laugh and observed in Abbie as she played.

Lukas thought of an idea. What if he traded his life for Jack and Rudy? Wolfram wanted him dead and wanted to see his face as he died. Lukas knew Wolfram. He remembered how Wolfram thrived off the suffering of others. It was adrenaline and power and nearly joy to him. To have free will at killing Lukas might give Wolfram more satisfaction than finding the treasure. Perhaps Lukas could do one final thing to redeem the past.

God, are you a God who could forgive what I've done? Would you forgive a man like me?

Lukas awoke in a chair to the sound of knocking. He quickly tucked in his shirt and buttoned the top button. In the next few hours he had three daughters to face. He'd chosen the toughest one first.

Anni came inside and stared at him with concern. Then she glanced around the room to see if anyone else was there. "Your entourage of women is missing," she said wryly. "I am not used to seeing you without them."

"Anni, come sit down. There are things I must tell you. I have wanted to tell you for a very long time."

"This should be interesting. I had to drive almost till dawn—is this some dark family secret? I'm not really your daughter—something like that?" Her expression challenged him. This child of his was so like him. Lukas didn't know how to figure out his own thoughts—how could he ever perceive hers?

She followed him into a breakfast nook area of the suite. They sat in chairs opposite each other, and Lukas struggled to think how to begin.

"So what is it? Some borderline illegal activities?" Her tone was sarcastically comical. She had been part of some of his shady dealings, and he knew she'd wondered when he'd suddenly cut off business associates in the last year. She said he'd found his conscience.

"What do you know about my time during the war?"

"The war? I know nothing. You don't talk to *me* of such things."

He knew she alluded to long conversations with Marta and now with Kate Porter. He realized that she was deeply angry and jealous.

"You do seem to have an affinity for women," she threw in. "Except for me."

"Anni, let me speak. You are my daughter. I have not been the father I could have been, and I know that now. But you are my daughter. There is nothing in the world like your flesh and blood in human form. When I first saw you and your sisters— so unique and delicate." Lukas stopped. When speaking to his daughters, he always lost his words. Why were the walls so much higher when it came to the ones he loved? He knew with great certainty how deep his love for Anni was, even as she sat across from him popping a cigarette from her case and lighting up as if she cared for nothing and no one. He feared the love he felt for her, seeing her suddenly as the fragile-hearted girl she'd once been. His love for her and her sisters was the only thing that could completely destroy him.

"I must tell you about my past."

"Does it really matter, Father?"

"Do you already know?" He hoped she did.

"I know very little about who you are today, let alone who you were before I was born. Mother never spoke to us about anything besides etiquette and how we should behave in public. Any serious questions were rerouted." Anni took a long drag from her cigarette.

"August 11, 1941, I was part of a firing squad. I killed one of them. A young woman named Tatianna."

Anni slumped in her chair.

"After that day, though it was not instantaneous, my allegiance changed."

"Your allegiance to whom?"

"I was an SS guard at Mauthausen Concentration Camp."

"So we have a President Waldheim scandal in the works? That is what this is about? Well, you are no longer in office so that will help. It will be bad for Austria, but it's not like the country hasn't survived other scandals."

"My main concern is not the scandal. It is for my children. You are not surprised? You do not hate who I am? Tomorrow it will be in the news, and this will not be an easy time. I have much to explain. Though I am a former minister, there will be a lot of controversy, tabloids, rumors, hate mail, support mail that I will not want. You will not leave me?"

"Father, I cannot judge you. Perhaps I would have worked for you then, as I work for you now."

A heaviness descended upon Lukas. What had happened to his daughter? Where had he gone so incredibly wrong that she could not perceive the difference between light and darkness? He had chosen the name *Anni*. It sounded innocent and pure—full of imagination and adventure. Yet she was none of those things. He had destroyed her somewhere between the day of her birth and this moment when she sat in her chair smoking.

"You are not ashamed?"

"I don't care what you did decades ago."

She wasn't bothered that the word *Nazi* would be forever remembered with her family name.

"Anni, you should. You must care!"

"But, Father, I don't."

Kate didn't think she had slept at all, but how could those hours have gone without a few snatches of rest? And now the cell phone was ringing. Kate jumped from bed and dug into her jacket lying over a chair for the phone. It was Marta.

"First, where is Abbie?" Kate couldn't wait to tell Marta what had happened. Even now it didn't seem real. She had seen Jack. Jack really was alive. A carved horse and a pile of papers rolled inside a rubber band lay on the table as proof. Kate had opened Jack's letters but couldn't read them. It was too much, too soon. And it wasn't time to tell her daughter. Not until she could bring Abbie's father home.

"She is making tea for us and wants to read the end of a book you two have been reading."

"A book? Yes, *The Voyage of the 'Dawn Treader'*. I forgot about it."

"Would you like me to finish it with her?"

"No, it's something I want to finish as much as Abbie."

"And you received some mail."

"From who?"

"A woman named Connie—Abbie said she is your friend."

Kate sat on the edge of the bed. "This is important. Open the letter and tell me what it says."

"Just a moment."

Kate got up, put her jacket around her, and turned the dial up on the radiator in the corner. She opened the curtains and morning light flooded the room.

"You want me to read the whole thing?"

"Yes," she said.

"It says, 'Dear Kate and Abbie. I finally found the movie that fits your journey to Austria—it's *Clear and Present Danger*, except that it's Jack who is missing instead of Harrison Ford's wife; they were in Paris, while you were in Venice and now you're in Austria; and it's terrorists who have the wife in the movie, but that could be true with Jack, you never know. Wait, maybe that was *Patriot Games*, not *Clear and Present Danger*. And I think the wife was kidnapped in London, not Paris. Well, I don't know, but this is a quick note as I rush out the door. I actually had a stamp and an envelope and your address handy, so what a miracle—I sent a letter! I'm really writing to remind you to call me or e-mail me or even a letter will do! I put some new photos on the Web site, too, if you have a computer over there to check them out. You should see what Trudy did to Restorations—you'll like it, I promise. Well, I hope. Ta-ta for now! CALL!'"

The letter sounded strange in Marta's accented English as she struggled with Connie's expressions. But as the letter ended, Kate suddenly understood. It was impossible to believe that Connie could be involved with Wolfram. And she wasn't. At the bottom of Connie's stationery and business cards were the words, "Check out our fabulous Web site with family and friend photos, movie reviews, and a lot of interesting stuff about us!"

"That's it!" Kate said. Connie's second love was her Web site. She'd put the entire disk from her digital camera right on the site for anyone to click through and see. All the photos given to Jack had to have come from there.

"What is wrong?" Marta asked as a beep sounded through the line. "Wait one moment. I must get the other call, and I always have trouble seeing the buttons . . . ," she muttered until the line switched over. In a couple of seconds she was back. "Lukas said to hang up. He will connect us to a three-person call."

Kate hung up, nearly laughing and crying at the same time. Connie's obsession with photos, movies, and the Internet had given Wolfram or his connected group ample opportunities to threaten her husband. There was no photographer hiding in the woods, or spy who had worked herself into their lives, or best friend who brought mochas while plotting espionage tactics. It was so simple it was preposterous. Wolfram must have discovered her presence in Austria by other means—not Connie.

"This is Lukas, and Marta is on the line from the estate."

"Great, I have so much to tell you both."

"Listen for a moment. Kate, I do not want you to go back to the estate. I already met with two of my daughters and the third is flying in any minute. I have appointments in the next couple hours for an exclusive interview. I will tell this journalist about my past from being a young guard at Mauthausen to the Resistance and Ebensee. It will air on the news at noon."

"What?" Kate said in horror. "You can't do this! Not now!"

"Tell us why you do this," Marta said calmly.

"Wolfram gave us an ultimatum. Three days to deliver the tiles. The press will be at the estate after this, so you and Abbie will be even safer there. And this is a move Wolfram will not expect. It is social and political suicide on my part; he would never expect me to do that. I have worried about the effects on our country. The world will label us again—"

"Lukas, you don't understand." Kate stood, glancing at the

stack of letters and the carved wooden horse that Jack had left behind. "I saw Jack last night."

"Last night? Where is he now?" Lukas demanded. Kate could hear the surprise in his voice. Kate quickly explained their meeting and why he had to return.

"What is your plan of escape?"

"Jack found an underwater cavern—it's what Wolfram has been looking for. Jack is going back to reveal the location to Wolfram's son. Jack trusts Ian—he's the one who helped Jack come to see me. I didn't like this idea at all. But Jack says it's the only way."

"It will not work," Lukas said quietly. "If Wolfram finds out, it is finished. He needs the men and the tiles to retrieve his treasure. Now he will not need the tiles. Once he has what he wants—I know this man—he will not let them go free. He cannot."

Everyone was silent.

"Did you find out why he needs the tile?" Marta asked, her voice shaking more than usual.

"I am certain that once together, the pieces reveal the location of this treasure Wolfram seeks," answered Lukas.

"It is time to get help," Marta said and flew into a stream of German directed toward Lukas.

"*Nein!* Marta, *nein!*" Lukas kept saying.

"English, please!" Kate said. "Marta, we don't have time. If I go to the police, it will take too long for them to believe me, especially since I am a suspect in Jack's disappearance. How long until a search warrant—do you even have search warrants? It doesn't matter. We have no concrete evidence! We have nothing that will bring immediate action."

"My hands are tied now. I will be followed and watched because of this scandal and many old friends will disappear," Lukas said.

Kate stood before the open window now, trying to think of a way. The line crackled when she moved.

"I know," Lukas said finally. "I am going to tell Wolfram's true story to the media. They will barrage him, and not even the castle will be secluded enough. It will distract him and give us more time if we need it. If this Ian can be trusted, they might succeed without Wolfram knowing. Marta, if this doesn't work in a day or two, we will go to the authorities."

"But what will stop Wolfram from getting nervous and . . . and destroying the evidence?" Kate asked.

"Kate, I assure you, Wolfram wants that treasure—he has waited nearly sixty years. And he wants me. He is not going to destroy his chances too soon."

"I hope you are right." She bit her lip and sat on the edge of the bed.

"Lukas, are you sure about all of this?" Marta said. "Your reputation, all these years of your work—it will all be ruined. You know that?"

"Yes. There is no other way. And it is time to tell it."

"We are here for you. I am always here for you," Marta said it softly, and Kate felt like she was intruding between them.

Kate cleared her throat. "I'm bringing a boat and waiting by the shore tonight as Jack and I planned. I'll do it alone if I have to. After their dive, I'll pick Jack up."

"I will send someone to help and delay my interview a day. But this now depends on Jack. And I hope this son of Wolfram Meizer can be trusted."

CHAPTER THIRTY-EIGHT

Jack returned before daylight. He hated to change back into the coveralls and rubber boots. He wanted to turn around and return to Kate. There was too much to mend between Kate and him in just a few hours. And how he longed to see Abbie! But he was determined to carry out his plan to save Rudy. Soon enough they'd all be together.

Ian wasn't by the shore when Jack returned. So he left the boat as he'd found it and crept back to the barrack. He peered toward the house as he passed, seeing the remnants of the party in garbage bags lined up at the edge of the terrace. A few lights were still on.

He didn't find Ian when he reached the barrack, and Rudy's door was closed as he passed to enter his own room. He shut the door. The darkness no longer comforted him. The room smelled and was dirtier than he remembered. It was cold and empty, and again he questioned why he'd returned. He knew the answer—he could never live knowing he'd deserted his friend. But what if that cost him everything—even his own life?

Jack bent down to listen into the vent. Perhaps Rudy had heard him arrive. There was no noise, but he felt a crumpled paper sticking just inside the ridges of the vent. He pulled his end of the wire arm and took the note. The only catch in their letter exchange was that they had to read them in the light. Jack found his stack of blank paper and put Rudy's note under the second page, then turned on the light. He sat on the bed, leaning against the wall. Then Jack realized his mistake. He'd entered the barrack as he always did on the nights he worked the tunnels. But last night he was supposed to be in his room all night.

Jack glanced up at the camera, its red eye always watching. He hoped Ian had thought of it. Jack didn't know the working of the security or how much Wolfram really watched, but that too was in Ian's hands. And where was Ian? Jack needed to talk to him. They had much to plan while the daylight hours gave them time. Tonight they needed to dive.

He looked down at the blank paper and flipped it over to Rudy's note.

I always laughed when people claimed to have prophetic dreams. But I hope the one I had last night was just that. It was the strangest dream. I was in the darkness and you were with me. I heard a voice calling my name, but it wasn't you, and you couldn't hear it. It kept calling, and I felt this great anxiety and asked, "Why can't you hear it?" You said maybe it was only for me. So I shouted, "What do you want?" The voice stopped calling my name but then said, "It is time for you to come home." Then I woke up.

This could be my own subconscious at work. But the strangest part is that when I woke up, I didn't feel cold, at least not for a while. I think I'm getting well at last. I don't

like to say God spoke to me, but let us hope he did. Maybe
we're going home.
    I'll talk to you soon.
    Always,
    Rudy (aka MacGyver)

Jack smiled at the letter, especially the MacGyver part. He'd
have to watch reruns of the show with Rudy when they got
home. As he began composing a letter to Rudy, he heard the
sound of footsteps.

It was Ian.

⋅➤═◉═◄⋅

Wolfram stretched in his bed. It was a massive four-poster that
rested in the very center of the large room with tall ceilings
and oversized, hand-carved furniture. Light poured through
the curtains in long dusty streams. He recalled last night and
his successful dinner party. It would be in the papers today—
front page in Austria, perhaps an inside article in the international papers.

The phone rang.

"Yes," he said. Already they reached him.

"You better watch the news this afternoon. It will interest
you greatly."

Wolfram recognized his ally from Vienna—a government
insider who kept him informed.

"Is it good?" He wondered if the lights had made him look
younger last night.

"You must get prepared. The rumor is that Lukas Johansen
is about to share some secrets."

Kicking the covers away, he stood with a thud against the
rock floor. "He wouldn't dare. It will destroy him."

"I think he knows that. But destroying you may be more
important to him."

Ian had pulled all the equipment they had, so they checked hoses and batteries in the equipment shed. They should go through every piece—test it, review safety precautions and function. Technology had changed equipment dramatically in the fifteen years since Jack had interned with Rudy's team. Jack had done dives after that time, but this was an expedition, not a simple dive. They would have to be thorough with the time they had.

Jack mapped the cavern entrance and made sketches to where it reached the opening in Tunnel 8. He didn't know if the cavern went straight into the mountain—they knew nothing. This would be dangerous work, perhaps the most dangerous work he'd ever done. Both his and Rudy's life could depend upon tonight—that is, if Jack made it out of the cave alive. If they went too far, they'd try for the tunnel, though Jack didn't like this idea. Kate would be waiting on the lake. She'd be worried if it took too long.

Jack stopped for a minute to recall that he'd really seen her. After so many days of agony and times begging God for just one more moment with her, he'd actually been with her, touched her skin, and heard her voice. If they could just get through one more day apart.

Ian had agreed to most of the plan. He'd been stunned to learn that the cavern they'd sought inside the mountain had been right below them all along. Their dives had missed the mouth of the cave disguised beneath the outcropping of rocks.

Jack and Ian went over the plan. They'd make the dive, retrieve whatever they could, then Jack and Rudy would be free. Unless there was too much to recover. Unless they didn't find it tonight. There were many factors working against them.

And then Jack heard the worst news of all. Rudy would not be diving with them. He wouldn't be in the boat either. Jack's quick plan constructed with Kate in her room was falling apart before it began.

"Where is Rudy?" Jack asked.

"He's sick again," Ian said.

Jack almost said he knew Rudy wasn't sick. Rudy was getting better; he'd said so in his letter. But now his trust in Ian was crumbling. "I want to see Rudy."

"We can see him after the dive," Ian said. He stood up and walked outside the shed, leaving the door open. Jack could see the dock through the trees. One of the boats was missing—Wolfram's cruiser. He wondered why.

They waited until the evening shadows were long over the water. Jack knew Kate wouldn't be waiting along the shore yet. But within hours, they might be together. Then there'd be no more good-byes.

The water seemed forever unchanging. Jack loved the world beneath the surface, where swimming was like flying; it was a place of wonder for him. He couldn't move too quickly, voices couldn't shout, and everything seemed slow and defined. At times he'd felt guilty enjoying the dives—it was such a contrast to the dirty work in the tunnels.

Jack and Ian carried everything to the dock. Jack passed Wolfram's boat, realizing that he had returned sometime during the day. Ian seemed unconcerned as he climbed aboard the older fishing boat. He flipped on the lights beneath the hull, and they beamed into the water just like on any other dive. There would be no need to take the boat out since the cave's mouth was right below them. There was no need for Rudy to be in the boat.

Jack stopped. No need for Rudy . . . "Where is he?" Jack grabbed Ian's arm and swung him around. "I'm not doing this if you don't let me see him."

"He is fine. This time, trust me," Ian said. His gaze was

unwavering, and Jack had little choice. Jack believed that Ian really thought Wolfram would let him and Rudy free after this. But Jack knew otherwise. He'd compiled enough Wolfram quotes to understand that the man had no intention of letting them go. The only birds he'd released were killed by the cat—that said it all to Jack.

They dived into the water and for a second Jack's worries disappeared. He couldn't deny that this fascinated him. If this had been a legitimate expedition, he would have volunteered for such a dive in a heartbeat. They were diving where no man had gone in nearly sixty years. They were seeking what Wolfram had spent his life trying to discover. The Nazis had gone to a lot of work to hide this place.

Ian followed Jack; both wore backpacks and waist bags of supplies—they barely needed weight belts. The only sound was the whirl of their two pieced-together scooters that resembled handlebars with a small engine and had a light to lead the way. Rudy had built them before Jack's involuntary recruitment. They moved along the lake floor for twenty feet until it plunged downward. He'd guessed it was about thirty feet from the surface to the cave's mouth. Jack's light found the widening crack in the rock face. Then they reached it.

The whirl of engines stopped. They examined the entrance. Jack pointed out areas he'd earlier described to Ian as to why he believed the cave was natural but had been widened by man-made means. Ian nodded slowly, then pointed inside. Jack took a steel stake and hammer from a belt bag and, with Ian's help for leverage, drove the stake into the rock wall. Rock crumbled and fell away, but the stake was secured. Ian clipped the latch end of the cable he carried to the stake. Jack took the other end and hooked it to his belt. The lead line might prove their only way out again. They checked their watches. Jack didn't like the time—they were attempting too much for one dive.

Jack went first. The darkness was different inside the cave—

not wide and expansive beyond the beam of light, but black and cold and eerily silent. He moved with the scooter in front of him for light, but with the engine still off. The rock was smoothly cut at the opening, shored up by concrete reinforcement arches. Their lights searched the cavern floor for any evidence of the cavern's secrets. Soon they reached the rough, natural walls that narrowed rapidly as they went. When Jack felt a tug on the cable, he turned to see Ian unraveling a kink in the line. Jack began to realize they'd never make it.

Almost immediately, Jack noticed that the bubbles from his tank no longer streamed behind him as he swam but rose straight upward. Checking his watch for the time and direction on the compass, Jack motioned to Ian. There was a steel ladder attached to the rock. They swam upward, sometimes with a hand on the ladder rungs to move them along.

Above him, the light appeared strange, as if the beam narrowed. Jack was about to check the bulb when his head broke through the surface into air. Ian popped up beside him, looking surprised. Streams of water ran over their masks. Ian tested the air and pulled out his breathing apparatus. They removed their tanks, masks, and flippers and turned off the valves on their oxygen tanks. Water dripped softly, echoing through the cavern. Jack unhooked the latch of the cable and attached it to a rung of the ladder, then climbed the last few feet to a flat area of the cavern floor. The air was cold and musty.

"This is amazing," Jack said with a long whistle. "We're in the attic room of a cave."

"One intentionally designed," Ian said as he stepped over the water from the ladder to stand beside him. "Unless there is some kind of air vent, we'll use up the oxygen and have to go to our tanks."

Jack picked up his light, shining it on an object a few yards ahead. Crates stacked against the rock wall bore the faded red emblem of the swastika. "This is it," he said.

They walked carefully over the rough floor in their rubbery wet-suit stockings. Their lights illuminated the small room. They examined overhead to check for weakness or breakage and down a narrow corridor. The ink-thick darkness dissolved the rays, making it difficult to see anything ahead.

"Let's see what's in the crates first," Ian said, his voice betraying his excitement. Jack fought his own—this could be the most significant find of his life. Yet what he was about to discover would soon be in the hands of an insane old man.

"What are we looking for? Can you tell me now?" Jack asked.

"My father saw top secret documents in 1944." Ian paused, looking over the first crates. His hand touched the top as if it were sacred. "He was never supposed to see this information— it was only for the highest-ranking officers and ordained by Himmler himself."

"What did the documents say?" Jack moved to the other side and tugged at the wood, holding a flashlight on the box. Even after so many years, the nails held strong.

"They described a tunnel system built to hold as much treasure from the incarcerates as possible. That is the best English translation I can give."

"Treasure looted from Jewish victims." Jack stared at the crate again.

With his large pocketknife open, Ian worked at the edges. "Exactly. The cavern was supposed to also hold the plans of the worst weapon to be used against the Nazis. It was a weapon that could annihilate the Third Reich."

"Something that would destroy them? Why wouldn't they use it against the world?"

"My father believes their discovery of this weapon came too late in the war for them to build it, but that if the plans were ever revealed, it would end the future of another rise in the Nazi Party. They would wait until Germany could rebuild and then recover the plans for this weapon. But the few men and inmates working on it all died or were killed long ago."

"And this was all in these papers?"

"Nazi Party leaders were fanatical over precise paperwork. Their obsession to detail incriminated them after the war with what they'd done. They believed words like *final solution* instead of *mass genocide of the Jewish population* or *resettlement* instead of *shipping to the gas chambers* would be adequate—"

The sound of wood breaking stopped them both. Jack held the light as Ian pried up the corner. The wood cracked and snapped until the lid pulled away. They both peered inside.

There was an inner cover and then two metal boxes side by side. They each took a handle on the ends of one box and lifted. It was heavy and awkward and thudded to the floor, sending an echo through the chamber. Ian lifted the lid with a creak of the hinge.

Their lights didn't reflect gold bars or jewels, but yellowed crinkled paper. Ian took out a handful of moisture-damaged pages. He read them over as Jack picked up his own stack. The papers were in German. There were names and numbers in the columns and rows with stamped words at the top and bottom.

"What is this?" Jack asked.

"Some of that Nazi obsession to paperwork I was speaking about. These papers are records of the people sent to the camps." Ian looked at Jack's set and pointed out the columns. "You have names, dates, country and city origins, family members. And look, here is what was taken from them. Two fur coats, one gold tooth, a ring—that was one woman. When the camps closed, these documents were supposed to be destroyed. I didn't know they kept this much detail. Many camps succeeded in destroying the evidence, while other camps were caught off guard when the Allies moved in faster than expected."

Ian thumbed through the papers quickly. Then, working together, they lifted out the second metal box.

"It's all the same." Ian stood, staring at Jack in awe. "What if they made copies of everything? What if this is the complete record of all the victims? Let's open these other crates."

Quickly they opened every crate. They all contained metal boxes full of documents. After the last crate had been opened, Ian leaned back against the rock wall. Jack watched him. It amazed him that here they were deep inside the mountain with a treasury of information before them. This was not what Wolfram had wanted to find.

Then Ian began to laugh. He laughed harder and deeper until tears beaded at the corners of his eyes. He said something in German and laughed again. Jack had rarely seen emotion of any kind in Ian—this was stunning.

"*Treasury of the incarcerates* was referring to their information. Don't you see? We have made the most significant discovery since the war, what Jewish and Holocaust organizations have been searching for. This will help survivors and their families—they'll know the fate of family members and what was stolen from each individual. Look at this! An account number for a bank account with the monetary amount!"

"Swiss banks opened."

"And not only Swiss, but all over Eastern Europe."

"And no secret weapon?" Jack said it quietly, not knowing what reaction he'd get from Ian. He glanced at his watch and realized they'd been inside far too long.

"No secret weapon. The greatest one of all!" Ian said. "These papers are the weapon. These people are witness to the world—their final act of justice. It's proof and testimony of the Nazi deeds and the Holocaust."

Jack suddenly understood it all. More valuable than treasure, these documents were the complete record of what man was capable of doing to man. What did Ian intend to do with these records? Immediately Jack knew he needed to protect these documents. He must protect them with his life, if necessary.

"I thought the typical neo-Nazi didn't believe the Holocaust ever happened."

"Not all believe that, and there is none who is typical. And I don't recall telling you I was a neo-Nazi."

Jack didn't know what to say. Did he really know anything about this man he'd spent several years with?

"My father will not be happy," Ian said. "We won't get them out tonight. These crates will break apart if we try to use the boat winch to extract them through the tunnel."

Jack was facing Ian, but Ian was moving toward the back of the cavern. "What do you intend to do with the papers once you get them out?"

"There's another turn here," Ian said. "What is this?"

A moment later Jack heard Ian cry out and then the sound of sliding and a splash of water. He raced to the back with his flashlight. Though he couldn't see Ian anywhere, there was a gaping hole under a ledge of rock. Jack lay on his stomach and slid to the edge, using his legs as wedges against the rock. He shone his light straight down. He saw what looked like a rock slide down to the water. The water wasn't calm and stationary. It moved from one side of the hole and disappeared under the other. An underground river.

It was the perfect garbage can. Anything dropped down the rocky tube would eventually be buried within the mountain or emptied into the lake. Jack knew Ian could never hold his breath long enough and there would be no oxygen all the way through. Then Jack saw two hands grabbing the rock edge and Ian struggling to hold on.

"There's a current!" Ian shouted. "I can't hang on—!"

Jack slid over the edge a little farther. If he could get a rope to Ian . . . then a thought quickly flashed through his mind: *If he didn't reach Ian, he could escape, save the documents, be with his family, get Rudy away.*

But Jack couldn't do it.

He leaned over just an inch farther . . . and then Jack began to slide too. Reaching desperately for the sides, he tried to turn. His wet suit on the slippery rock didn't hold, and Jack plummeted into the water. He slammed into Ian, who barely kept his grip.

"It's a river!" Ian shouted. "We aren't going to make it!"

"Yes, we are!" Jack shouted back. He flailed his arm, trying to find a better grip. The rock cut his hands, and Jack knew they wouldn't last long. He wished for the oxygen tanks left above them in the cavern attic. Then he remembered the tunnel. It must have tapped into this stream; it was right in this area or perhaps above them. But were they already past it? There was no way to tell.

"Hold your breath and swim!" Jack yelled, then turned around. "Ian!" he shouted, not seeing him. Jack's fingers were sliding, and he couldn't hold. Taking one last breath, he dived beneath the rock and into the churning river.

CHAPTER THIRTY-NINE

The boat had a small cabin and an outside deck—hardly room for the three people it held. The couple had met Kate at the lake at dusk. She had expected Anni or Rey to be the "help" Lukas had promised. Instead this man and woman introduced themselves as Brant Collins and Darby Evans. He had rented a boat from the village, and together they boarded it, dressed as if they were out for an evening cruise. Kate was afraid to trust these people she didn't know, but she had little choice. They were Americans, she learned— or Brant was half—and they lived in Salzburg right now. They talked little past the introductions.

Once night fell, they changed into black clothing in the cabin and turned out the lights on the boat. Brant drove at a snail's pace, moving closer to the castle grounds, where they could see Wolfram's boats tied to the dock. Lukas must have filled them in on the story, which was a relief for her. Kate could barely speak without emotion. Inside her bag she'd packed the letters Jack had given her. If this didn't work out, they were all she'd have left of him.

Kate looked through the night-vision binoculars. She could make out equipment on the stern of the fishing boat and the lights, so Jack, Rudy, and Ian were already in the water. Kate checked her watch, but they were on time. She didn't know how long they could stay under. Was it twenty minutes? two hours? Brant and Darby didn't know either. She searched the water for Jack and Rudy to surface. That had been the plan—she'd have a boat and Jack and Rudy would simply swim the two hundred yards to meet her. Jack had several optional plans for himself in case Rudy wasn't able to dive, but her only instructions were to wait near the shore until dawn, if necessary.

Darby sat beside Kate. Her presence was comforting. "How long have you been married?" Darby asked softly.

"Almost twelve years." Kate's eyes stayed on the water, searching for movement. They may not get much time to reach Jack and Rudy when they did surface. Kate wondered if the plan was still as they'd established it. Jack had a lot to do in a very short time. She'd stay here until dawn and return every night until she knew one way or the other.

Brant brought a thermos from the cabin and sat beside them. He poured cups of coffee, then rested his arm around Darby's shoulders. They weren't married, Kate knew, but a glance at Darby's hand showed a ring. Engaged. They could understand a little how she felt.

"You must owe Lukas a big favor to be out here like this," Kate whispered. It seemed they should whisper.

Brant and Darby looked at one another.

"We do," Darby said. "But we want to be here too. Lukas should have called earlier."

Their eyes met, and Kate's stomach trembled with fear. *Should have* were words she didn't want them to say in recalling this night.

Kate stared across the rippling water. No one had appeared. It was taking too long.

Darby descended the stairs into the cabin while Brant sat near the bow and watched the water, checking through the binoculars from time to time. "Let's take turns for a while. I'll watch first. Kate, I'm sure you don't want to sleep, but it might be good to try."

She thought of the little sleep she'd had and knew it was good advice, but it seemed impossible. Yet there was one thing she wanted to do. Kate opened her bag for the pack of letters.

Beneath the outline of the mountain and a million stars in the sky, she began to read by the glow of a tiny flashlight. She flipped through the letters, reading snatches of the days they'd spent apart—the moments of Jack's despair, the simple times he'd recorded as if to remind himself that he still lived and breathed, the days when hope shone through. And within the words, Kate met her husband again.

> *They've moved me again, and I've kept track of the days by cutting marks in my shoes. I must know the exact days that I'm away from you. Today is 107. Can I make it to another?*

> *What do they want from me? What could this be for? They won't tell me and I say it's a mistake. I say that till my voice is hoarse. They don't want me. Not me. This isn't for me!*

> *Today I believe I will die in this place. My body will be crushed beneath the earth in a landslide, lost beneath tons of granite and stone. Or my will to live might fail in just one moment as I walk that trail from the mines—my body giving up, my spirit escaping this prison. I've sought insanity and death at times, wishing it was simply a decision.*

> *Five hundred days I have spent away from you. Five hundred days I have not touched you or spoken where you could hear me or I could hear you. It does not seem possible.*

I wanted to write every day. I am surprised to see the pile of letters that has grown over these days and years. But I wanted to share my every day just as I long to know your every moment. But there are too many now. You will never remember them all. And I must save my paper; I do not know when more will be granted. Maybe if I do a trick they'll reward me—roll over, sit up, fetch a treasure within the earth. And I think, why should I write to say the same words again and again? I can't shout the words that I'm shouting right now. "I'm here. I'm alive. Hear my voice and don't forget me!"

Are these words to you or to God? I know nothing. The anger has me tonight. And I don't care to fight it.

I want to smell your hair and touch your skin for just a moment, though a moment would never be enough. I feel desperate to get back to you. I believe I could kill a man to do it. With my own hands, I could do it.

Kate, I'm a weak man. I can't breathe without you. I can't do this any longer. Seven hundred and thirty-two days.

Kate became anxious to know all his words, but at the same time, they were more than she could take. Jack had been with her for the briefest time. Now she knew what it meant to him; now she knew who he was. But he was out of reach once again.

She continued to read, moving in and out of Jack's world. The tower of mountains above her became familiar as Jack described them as the prison walls he loved to watch. The crisp mountain air was breathed into her lungs, the same air Jack wrote that he loved and resented at the same time. Light caught on the ripples of the lake, and the lap of tiny waves against the hull of the boat only brought Kate further to this world where Jack had lived apart from her. This land and water had become a part of him—they brought him peace in his later writings as he found peace with God.

> *Kate, I can't fully explain this. Call it my change on the mountain. But at last, I see God—even here, even now. It's what I should have seen a long time ago. Perhaps I knew it in my head, but not within me as it is now. I not only understand my need for God more than life, even more than I need you and Abbie. I believe it, feel it, and it fills me with the knowledge and peace of understanding. God is here with me. I can't deny that my anger continues to rise at times, but it's no longer out of control. I find myself marveling at the intricate design of it all. If this mountain can be so alive and balanced to bring summer flowers and winter's cleansing snows, then the One who made it can keep my life, even if I never leave this place alive.*
>
> *I think of Paul in prison, in chains. He wrote that to live is Christ, but to die is gain. I'm not ready to give up on life; I continue to want you and Abbie. But I know that God holds the design beyond what we can see.*
>
> *Almost three years—1,094 days. Even in this place today, my freedom stolen, my love for you and Abbie denied, I have found peace. I even find laughter and thankfulness. Was I ever this thankful for the love we shared? I had more than most people have in a lifetime. For that, I am grateful.*

Kate realized she was crying and had been crying for some time. She read one last portion of Jack's letters before folding them away.

> *Abbie, if ever you can read this, I love you more than string cheese, more than life itself. I'll see you again in every starry sky and every blue night.*

Jack was blind under the black water; he'd lost the light when he first fell into the underground river. As he pushed through the rough water-filled cavern, his hands stung from cold and open wounds. The river moved quickly, and he tried to move even faster while seeking the roof for an opening. He found pockets of air he couldn't breathe, knowing they would be toxic with no oxygen content. His lungs ached now and he still hadn't found Ian.

And then he knew—he wasn't going to make it. Jack knew that. And it was all right. He had been close—so close. He'd seen Kate. He'd had what he'd asked of God, another chance to see her. She had his letters. Abbie would have her gift. It was more than he'd had days ago. He could die knowing that.

Jack closed his eyes; there was no need to try and see. A few deep breaths and the water would fill his lungs. It would take only moments. He'd be truly free, and the cavern would keep its secrets.

His lips parted when suddenly he saw Rudy in the darkness. Jack opened his eyes. Yes, he saw Rudy's face staring down at him. He saw Rudy's hand reaching. Jack reached, and a firm grasp pulled at him. His body twisted and was dragged in the current. He kicked with his legs and sought another handhold. His face burst from the water and air filled his lungs. But it was Ian's face straining and Ian's hands holding his arm. Finally, Jack was free and pulled onto the platform inside Tunnel 8.

They lay on the ground, trying to breathe, rejoicing in breath.

"Where's Rudy?" Jack gasped.

Ian rolled from his back to his stomach. "What—what are you talking about?"

Jack shook his head and couldn't speak. It didn't matter. He'd see Rudy soon enough.

The sun would be up soon. It would rise through the window-panes and above the trees of his yard. Lukas sat in the cold room of his home with the telephone beside him and a lone lamp lit in the corner. Kate should be calling. She should call and say it was over.

But no one had called.

He wanted to help, but soon a television van would be parked outside the estate gates for his afternoon interview. And tonight he'd surely see old friends and ex-wives on the news giving their stories. "I always suspected," they'd say. There would be more in the coming days, especially after he revealed he was Bruno Weiler. Then Wolfram's castle would be mauled by media and paparazzi seeking answers, especially since Wolfram had claimed to be Bruno Weiler. But they must have Jack Porter and his friend free from harm first. It was a delicate matter, giving bits of information without too much and trying to discern the mind of his enemy.

At least his daughters would forgive him. Magda was the angriest, but she was also the youngest. Regina, the wise, oldest sister, seemed relieved to know the cause of his aloof-ness all her life. She cried as he told her the story and hugged him before leaving. Despite their different responses, they both promised to come to the estate the next weekend after the first full announcement settled. Anni had returned with him from Vienna. She drove and he slept. She continued to not care.

Lukas packed his old pipe and lit it, taking a long puff. It didn't relax him as he hoped.

"I thought smoking was not allowed inside the house." It was Anni, standing in the shadows behind him in the doorway to the sunroom.

"Why are you awake?"

"I couldn't sleep."

"Come in, then," he said. Her feet moved softly along the floor. She wore fuzzy, blue slippers and a robe. He had not seen her like this since childhood. Anni was always perfectly dressed, with makeup and hair in order whenever he saw her.

"Have you been drinking, Father?"

"I considered it."

"You are concerned about Kate Porter."

"Yes." He watched her sit in the chair beside him. She seemed much younger in this light. "I have other things on my mind also. I have you on my mind."

"Why is that?"

"I fear for you. You are who I once was. You seek something that is not visible but is easily found."

Anni did not speak, only stared at him as if finally realizing he truly could see her. How long had she thought she was invisible to him?

"My daughter, I fear what it will take for your eyes to open. Do you know what it took me? Oh, if you knew what I saw. Anni, if you could see my nightmares that come not from imagination but from memory."

He bent his head over his hands and began to sob. He didn't know where it all came from, but the tears, so deep and agonizing, tore through him and released their hold as they left. He couldn't stop it and didn't want to. At last what felt like a thousand years of agony and sorrow made their departure from Lukas Johansen.

Then Anni was on her knees in front of him, touching his head and hands. "Father, I will listen to your story this time. Tell me again. Tell me until I understand."

⊷══◉══⊷

"It's always coldest before dawn," Darby said. She put a blanket around Kate's shoulders, and Kate realized she was shivering. Gray had grown against the black horizon. Kate had never known a dawn to approach this fast.

"It's been too long," she whispered. "I know it's been too long."

"What do you want us to do?" Darby asked.

"I don't know."

They waited and Kate knew it was her call. "He's been down there too long. We'll go to the police at the village. Then my daughter will need me." Kate heard her voice as if it played on a tape recorder in another room. It wasn't her voice saying these words, not after all of this. Was being this close to Jack, having one last night with him, a gift or a torment?

"Let's wait a short time longer," Brant said from the stairs of the cabin. "It's the eleventh hour. Sometimes we think it's the thirteenth or fourteenth, but it's only the eleventh. We'll wait until all hope is gone."

I t felt strange to walk. Moments before they had been clinging to life. Now Jack and Ian walked through the tunnel, injured and wet, but alive.

They both shivered—their wet suits left behind and their bodies bruised and fighting the cold in their wet swimsuits. Though they knew the route to the entrance well, they followed the small emergency lights on the rocky floor. They both had to push on the door, hitting it with their shoulders. It opened to the gray, early morning light.

"We must hurry," Ian said.

Despite the pain, they ran down the path, watching for rocks on the ground and movement around them.

When they reached the barrack, Ian went through the doorway. "Get dressed and ready. I'll be back very soon." But Jack couldn't go inside. What if they returned him to the life he'd lived so long?

Jack needed clothes, and he needed Rudy. Ian had saved his life minutes ago, so he must be trusted now. He pushed past

Ian and ran by the cameras in the hallway, down the stairs to the basement and to Rudy's door. It was unlocked.

"Rudy!" he called as he opened the door. The light from the hall revealed the room, but Rudy wasn't there.

Jack went to his room. No one was there either. No note in the vent. Jack found the clothes Ian had loaned him the day before—had that only been yesterday?

Kate, he thought. She probably thought he was dead. But they'd take one of Wolfram's boats. He'd find her again. As he dressed quickly, he let his eyes sweep across the room. This would be his home no longer.

Jack searched Rudy's room for any evidence of where he'd gone. He walked slowly around the room where Rudy had been working on inventions and drawn huge diagrams and figures on the walls. The bedcovers were a mess, some kicked to the ground. Rudy's room contained clothes, pinecones, a bird's nest, pieces of wood and wire, nuts and bolts. Jack couldn't believe he'd been allowed such things. And there, stacked neatly beneath his bed were a well-used Bible and his favorite Oswald Chambers book, *My Utmost for His Highest.*

Jack had never been in here before. It was Rudy, every last mismatched set of tools and objects in the room. But Rudy was missing.

Jack raced back up to the entrance. No one stopped him. The cameras couldn't touch him now. He turned toward the woods, where he'd wait until he could search all the buildings.

"Jack, stop!"

He turned, afraid of what he'd see. They didn't need him now. But Ian wasn't holding the loaded gun Jack had expected. Ian stood there in his red coat with his hands pushed into his jeans pockets in the relaxed pose Jack had seen a hundred times before. But it was Ian's expression that put icy fear inside him. Ian was breathing hard. He'd just come from the castle. On his face were sadness, deep and troubled—and anger?

"Where is he?"

"I took him to the castle two nights ago—when you left to see your wife. Rudy was cold and covered in sweat, so I moved him to the house, where the housekeeper could care for him. Wolfram did not know. The doctor is in the village, but there was no boat because you used it. Wolfram would notice one of his boats missing."

"What are you trying to tell me?"

"I could not go for a doctor in the daylight, so I planned to go tonight, but then all of this. I told Wolfram. I told him Rudy was sick and must get help. He refused. I told him that I'd tell him where the treasure was if he helped Rudy."

"What happened?" Jack demanded.

He realized Ian was crying. "Rudy died last night."

"I don't believe you." Jack shook his head. This couldn't be true—fatigue was destroying his mind.

"Wolfram promised. My father promised he would take Rudy to a doctor. Before we left last night, his boat was gone so I believed him. But he didn't take Rudy. The housekeeper stayed with him, but she didn't know anything."

Tears ran down Jack's face. He remembered Rudy's letter. It *had* been God's voice calling Rudy home. And in the dream, Rudy had said Jack couldn't hear the call. Only Rudy heard his name.

"There was a look on his face. It was peace," Ian continued.

"I saw him in the water tonight. It is Wolfram I want to see. Now."

Surprise flashed across Ian's face. Then he nodded. "Yes. We will go see Wolfram."

⊹≡◎⊂≡⊹

They found Wolfram sleeping beneath a thick comforter in a massive bed that dominated the entire room. The door creaked on its ancient hinges and brought Wolfram rising upward like Dracula from his casket. He didn't jump from the bed, only pulled the chain of the lamp and adjusted his eyes to see who had entered.

"Ian, *wer ist das?*" he boomed.

Ian's steps thudded across the floor. He stopped at the foot of the bed while Jack stayed in the doorway.

Wolfram was trying to see him. "*Ist das* Jack?"

"You let him die," Ian accused.

Wolfram yawned, stretching his arms above his head. His words were casual and surprised sounding.

Ian translated. "He says that he did not know Rudy would die. He is sorry. I will tell him what we found in the cavern."

Ian spoke slowly, holding Wolfram's interest. The old man rose from the bed to wrap a robe around his large waist. Jack had never seen Ian this way, so intriguing and explanatory. He moved his hands as if in a play, describing every detail. And then Jack could see the moment Ian dealt the blow. Wolfram's face turned white; he grabbed his hair and began to shake.

"You did not need the tiles that took many lives. Jack found the cave without the tile. And the treasure you sought is what condemns you." Ian laughed with tears falling from his cheeks. Jack knew he was speaking more to himself than to Wolfram. Ian took a few steps toward his father.

"*Nein. Nicht mein sohn.* You not take my son," Wolfram yelled to Jack as Jack turned to leave.

"He is not taking me. I am leaving you." Ian followed Jack out the bedroom door.

Wolfram's angered voice carried after them all the way down the hall.

"I loved him, you know," Ian said as they went toward the sound of morning birds singing in their cages.

"I understand. He is your father."

"I have tried to love my father. My life has been to do his

will, to make him happy, to say what he wanted. I did not know the difference until I met Rudy. That is what I meant. I loved Rudy. I wanted you to know."

CHAPTER FORTY-ONE

I t was beyond the "eleventh hour" as Brant had called it. Past the time for Jack to surface. But neither Brant nor Darby said a word to Kate. They stayed below in the cabin, often bringing her more coffee.

The light of dawn rose across the waters, and the birds began to sing. Kate's nose and cheeks felt like ice as she watched a mist drift and play upon the water. She'd never seen a more peaceful morning. It would be perfect if not for her great sense of loss. But this time was different. There was no panic, only a terrible grief that filled her until she was unable to move. Yet, below the sorrow, and as new as this day, came peace. It came from deep within, growing and moving through her.

She stood and dropped the blanket from her shoulders. Brant and Darby came up from the cabin and peered at Kate, their sleepy eyes showing their worry.

"It's time to go," she said, and the weight of grief nearly crumbled her strength. It wouldn't take long to break her to pieces, but for this moment she stayed strong.

Brant rose from the cushioned bench and stood beside her on deck. Jack's diving equipment remained on the dock like abandoned possessions awaiting a return. Kate now wished she'd called for help hours ago. Had Jack drowned below this boat while she sat back and read his letters? The horror of that thought gripped her.

"Let's go now," she said in a voice that moved Brant toward the captain's chair.

Kate glanced once more toward the water. Brant saw it at the same time. He pointed and Kate hurried to the edge. There was movement, not on the water but on shore.

Then she saw him. "Hurry!" she shouted.

The engine roared to life, the wind flew against her face. At any second she expected to see men chasing after them or for something else to go wrong. Jack was now on the dock with another man beside him. Brant pulled alongside them, and Jack reached for the rope as their wake bumped the boat against the dock. Jack immediately hopped over the railing and into the boat, with the other man following.

Brant didn't hesitate—he turned the boat away from the dock as soon as they were aboard. The wind whipped hard as Kate's eyes sought the castle grounds for movement or light.

Then Jack moved along the deck toward her. He reached for her and the gulf between them closed at last.

Wolfram Meizer sat in his office, dressed in his gray suit with the jacket buttoned at the front. His hair was combed back and he'd found a flower for his lapel. The TV was turned off, the video screens hidden behind the cabinet.

His birds were all gone, the cage doors propped open, and the French doors let cold air rush inside the room. The aviary was empty too. All his little birds gone loose into a world that would destroy them. Jack had taken Ian, and Ian had taken his birds.

He sat and sat. Suddenly he could hear them coming back. Their wings flapped with such a beating that Wolfram believed every bird he owned was now returning to him. He remained seated, waiting for them to peck their beaks furiously against the windows and find the open door. They had eyes like searchlights, bobbing and seeking the windows in his estate. Soon his grounds would be covered, the lawns trampled, and flowers smashed. The perfect design disrupted. They could not see what progress required. They were afraid to see it and tried

so desperately to stop what nature needed. Birds had no intelligence; they couldn't even know envy as men could.

Then the flaps of wings turned mechanical and the cries
turned human. Wolfram sipped cold coffee and sighed, long
and heavy. With great care, he rose from the chair and walked
to the plastic case on his desk. He opened the lid and held the
capsule between two fingers.

They would destroy so great a future.

And so it came to this.

◆▬◉◖▬◆

Three months later

Many lives had crossed the pathway of Lukas' years. They were
lives that would never leave him, and Lukas no longer wanted
them gone. The faces didn't haunt him now; they were reflec-
tions of himself. Their blood no longer stained his hands but
had blended with his own. They were part of him. And as
such, he could share the stories of Jantes, Karl, the girl at
Mauthausen—Tatianna—the others, and always, Susanne.

Autumn winds moved through the mountains, sweeping
leaves from the long arms of trees to scurry end over end along
the trail. Lukas walked his favorite path that morning, partly
because the house was too silent, partly to feel the cold wind
on his face, but mostly to return to the place he rarely went
and now longed to be. He moved with purpose through the
thick grove of tall pines so dark and damp, then stopped at the
edging where the thicket paused into a hillside clearing. There
Lukas stood in the shadows of trees. The view opened to a
velvet green hillside with a crossroad trail worn through it.
The sky brought filtered light through the black, rolling
clouds.

He stepped from the trees and paused at the crossroad. The

descending trail led to the village below, the opposite path moved upward to span the alpine range, while the one ahead led across the clearing, past a tree stump, and disappeared over the ridge. He took that one.

As the wind gusted, Lukas slid his hands into the pockets of his wool jacket. Winter was coming quickly. He had much to do in the months ahead before the Porters returned to Austria. Lukas had given his help and checkbook to the small museum in Ebensee. Soon a new exhibit would open, telling a story that had taken decades to conclude. There, all five pieces of the blue tile would find their final rest among photographs and possessions from their group. How strange to see their things beneath museum glass. How strange, yet how essential was the need he felt to tell their stories and his own—even what he had done for both good and evil. It could change another life.

Another gust tugged his wool hat. Lukas pulled it down and closed the top button of his coat around his neck. The pathway felt familiar beneath his feet, though the time was great between the young man who used to race over these trails and the old man with slow steps that he now was. The old oak had given out years earlier when a storm pressed too hard against its roots. It had been enough to bring the tree to the ground. Lukas' groundskeeper had cut the tree for firewood, though the wood had never been burned.

The stump of the tree remained. He sat there with the wind around him and memories persistent in his thoughts. His eyes followed the path where it disappeared over the ridge. The trail would lead to Susanne's grandmother's house, where another family now lived.

It now felt right that Susanne was gone. He could not see her as an old woman, only as the girl she once was—brave and full of a love that would bring him sorrow. But it wasn't his fault. His sins had not caused her death, and she would be waiting for him—he could believe that now. Lukas remembered that last day when he waited at this tree to see her instant smile and the late-afternoon sunshine in her hair. He'd been waiting for her long after the year of her death. He sat a long while, knowing he would wait no longer after this.

The cold finally reached his bones though the contentment of the hike did him good. He turned back toward the trees and trail where he had restored the grounds of this old estate. A warm fire and a good pipe were in his thoughts as he journeyed back. Anni waited at the front walkway. He nodded a greeting and she nodded one back. His daughter looked young in her stocking hat, with a black scarf tight beneath her chin. Her cheeks and nose were pink with cold.

He thought of young Abbie and wondered how much she'd changed since he had last seen her. It would be late night on the West Coast of America; the girl he'd tried hard to dislike at first because of her youth and innocence would be sleeping, with her mother and father in the next room. Abbie had been granted a new life with her father. And the indomitable Kate, who had lived through so much these past few years, at last had her husband back and the mystery solved. Smiling to himself, Lukas thought that maybe some things did turn out all right after all. That's what Marta reminded him every day.

"We could get snow," Anni said, concern in her eyes as she watched his approach.

"*Ja,* the air feels right," Lukas said. They had spoken little since their world had changed. The media hounds, death threats, book deals, and the recovery of the lost documents beneath Garten Wald had all kept them from a serious talk. He offered his elbow and Anni accepted by sliding her arm through his.

"A game of chess by the fire perhaps?"

She smiled in her slight way and nodded. It brought a smile

to his lips also. Perhaps they'd all been granted new life, Lukas thought. These were the words he would tell his daughter. They were too long unspoken.

> . . . No one . . . doubted that they were seeing beyond the end of the world. . . .
>
> —C. S. Lewis, *The Voyage of the "Dawn Treader"*

I wish I could remember the moment I was first drawn toward the World War II era and the details of the Holocaust. What caused my deep need to read and reread these stories, to attempt to make sense of what can never be understood or explained? It began before high school, and certainly stories like Anne Frank's *The Diary of a Young Girl* and Corrie ten Boom's *The Hiding Place* were part of those earlier years.

But for me, writing on such a subject has been a difficult journey. Often I've felt unworthy to write about events and times that do not belong to my heritage. These people's stories do not belong to me. Writers are often told, "Write what you know." I've found that, instead, we must write about what moves us, what won't leave us alone, what keeps us up at night, and what we can't make sense of. That's why my first novels are about this spot in history that will never leave our world alone—and should never.

In October 2000, I returned to Europe for the third time. The first week was a whirlwind that took two friends and myself from Amsterdam to Vienna through six countries. It was a road trip with Anne de Graaf at the wheel and Tricia Goyer with her CD selections and ready camera. Trish and I would brave the Metro in Paris for the first time, two young women who were once nervous to meet real authors at our first writers conference. Anne drove from Paris to Prague in a day, and the three of us walked St. Charles Bridge that magical night of gentle rain. In quite another adventure, we sought the one last open crossing on the Czech/Austrian border (this involved protestors with farm tractors blocking the roadway, a very small ferry, and some shoddy directions). The trip held multitudes of laughter and moments we knew to be designed by the One who designed everything.

Yet not everything was picturesque. We passed several clusters of women along a Czech country road who, with the freedom of democracy, have become bound to the prostitution trade. We met Jewish siblings, young and friendly, but with the latest Israeli conflict heavy on their minds as the eighteen-year-old girl would begin her required service for the Israeli army. We also faced two days visiting three sites of Nazi atrocities—Lidice, Czech Republic, and Mauthausen and Gusen Camps in Austria.

Tricia had flown home when Anne and I came to the Salzkammergut lakes region of Austria. Near a quaint village, Anne and I walked among the monuments, ovens, and mass graves of KZ Ebensee Memorial. Through research, I met the dead in the ghetto song of a poet, in photographs of a woman and her infant who appear to be sleeping as I have slept with each of my children. I found them again at Ebensee as I stood above a mass grave and read the plaques surrounding the ovens. I wondered who these people beneath the earth were. Who were the individuals not granted their own resting place? What were their childhoods like, and what did they envision for the future?

Then I realized this site was not memory. It is our future. Ebensee Memorial will remain for generations. But at the same time, new monuments, mass graves, and memorials will be found in the lands of our world, including African countries, former Yugoslavia, and many more. This is not past us.

Cottonwood is my place of familiar roads, streams, mountain views, and people I've known since childhood. I talk to Tricia on the phone with the miles separating us and send

e-mails to Anne across the pond to Holland. My husband and I
set goals, go to the movies, or talk late into the night. My kids
and I study Eastern Europe, them for home school and me for
my next novel. And always, I daydream about Europe.

How does such a journey and a place like Ebensee change
life for me in Cottonwood, California? Sometimes I feel too
comfortable, too happy, too unaffected. But I also have been
deeply changed—in the way I view people all over the world,
what I want my children to understand, and this need to share
stories I often feel unworthy to write.

So this is my prayer for you—that your vision expand and
that God would take you on a life-changing journey as you
seek him first, because the vision is greater than yourself. My
first two trips to Europe were dreams. This last one brought a
greater vision. I'm not sure what God will do with it. I'm not
sure when or if I'll return to those lands I often daydream
about, but I know God works through all of our lives when we
allow him to be mapmaker and guide.

May your vision be clear and your journey sweet.

ACKNOWLEDGMENTS

My name appears on the cover, but this book is certainly a collaborative work. Janet Kobobel Grant, you are my agent, friend, and advice-giver in all areas of life. I thank Tyndale House Publishers for seeing my vision, for your amazing support, and for lending me the time and energies of Ramona Cramer Tucker and Lorie Popp—extraordinary editors who put much more than just a polish to this book.

In Austria:

Professor Reinhold and Elisabeth Wagnleitner—again, invaluable for me to glimpse life in Austria. Your assistance and friendship bring great gratitude.

Martha Gammer—abundant thanks for a personal visit to Gusen Memorial, the museum, a meal in your home, and finding us a place to sleep. You were a true gift.

Ebensee Museum—Dr. Wolfgang Quatember, Gabriela Eidinger, and Andreas Schmoller, for allowing me time and freedom in your archives, answering questions, and even bringing me coffee. My greatest memory was seeing Austrian schoolchildren learn about the Holocaust through the Anne Frank exhibit. You are doing a great work.

Research and Development:

Tricia Goyer—research assistance, manuscript reviewing, and just being you.

Katie Martinusen—manuscript review and the prayers that carried me.

Christy Harrington—manuscript review and honesty tempered with friendship.

Jeff and Becky Davis—information on decorative tiles.

Shelley Chittim—research on decorative tiles (and friendship).

Shawn Chittim, Shelley Chittim, Mike Chittim, and Joe Gazzigli—again, the Mount Shasta house was a perfect place to write. Thank you.

Dan Elliott—archaeology research.

Melissa Karlen—research about women in the Holocaust.

Neal Schiff of the FBI—suggestions and information on FBI and police procedure.

Todd Budde—information on insurance claims.

In addition to and including the above mentioned, both personal and professional help came from family and friends in a multitude of ways—from consistent prayer to deep friendships. I cannot name you all, so I hope you already know.

Cody, Madelyn, and Weston—my children who grant me such love and joy in all your unique and amazing ways. I am so thankful for you.

Richard McCormick—I'm proud to use the McCormick name, all because of you. You're a wonderful father. Gail McCormick—mother, friend, example. I agree we could use your maiden name too, but Guillemin McCormick Martinusen just gets a bit too long.

My sister, Jennifer Harman, gives support, encouragement, and love in a multitude of ways. Eleanor Martinusen, Teresa Price, Laurie Williams, and Lisa Peasha took great care of my children those afternoons so I could work. And, Lisa, your encouraging cards have meant a lot. Kim Shaw, we appreciated our substitute home school teacher while I went to Europe, among other things you've done. Jenna Benton, Michelle Ower, Robin Gunn, Marlo Schalesky, One Heart Sisters, Tammy Martinusen—friendship and much needed prayer. A huge appreciation to Anne de Graaf and Tricia Goyer—for that amazing European journey (and thanks to Erik de Graaf, John Goyer, David Martinusen, the husbands who stayed behind). Maxine Cambra and the NorCal Writer's Group (keep writing everyone!). Norita Brinton—for a dear gift when I needed it. Teresa Martin—dinner for my family when we all needed it and your kind notes. The Elegant Bean in Cottonwood— Janelle Pierson, Piney Adams, and Linda Finken for those MANY single shot, grande mochas with nonfat milk (sometimes), whipped cream (always), and light chocolate—but then you knew that, didn't you? You know I'll always be back.

Another appreciation (I have a lot to be thankful for!) goes to the communities of Cottonwood, Anderson, and Redding, and to the readers who've shared their own lives with me. The release of my first book, *Winter Passing,* has brought such amazing support from friends, acquaintances, libraries, local churches (my own especially), and local bookstores (Redding Christian Supply and Barnes & Noble). I cannot express my gratitude enough.

This book could not have been done without my husband, David, allowing me silence, especially as the deadline arrived; making dinners; tucking in children; and being my supporter and encourager every day of my life—thank you.

As Paul wrote to the Philippian church, "I thank my God every time I remember you" (Phil. 1:3, NIV). That goes to all of you. I echo King David's words in the psalms: "I will give thanks to the Lord"; "My soul finds rest in God alone" (Pss. 7:17; 62:1, NIV).

For more information on Ebensee Concentration Camp
Memorial and the Museum of Contemporary History, or if
you, a family member, or a friend is a survivor of KZ Ebensee,
please contact the following address:
Concentration Camp Memorial Ebensee
Museum of Contemporary History
Kirchengasse 5
A-4802 Ebensee
Austria

The Voyage of the "Dawn Treader" by C. S. Lewis

My Utmost for His Highest by Oswald Chambers

From World War to Waldheim: Culture and Politics in Austria and the United States (Austrian History, Culture, & Society, Vol. 2) edited by David F. Good and Ruth Wodak

Here, There, and Everywhere: The Foreign Politics of American Popular Culture by Reinhold Wagnleitner

Coca-Colonization and the Cold War: The Cultural Mission of the United States in Austria After the Second World War by Reinhold Wagnleitner

The Camp Men: The SS Officers Who Ran the Nazi Concentration Camp System by French L. MacLean

Concentration Camp Ebensee, Subcamp of Mauthausen by Florian Freund

A History of Decorative Tiles by Noel Riley

An Illustrated History of the Gestapo by Rupert Butler

Hitler's Silent Partners by Isabel Vincent

Piercing the Reich: The Penetration of Nazi Germany by American Secret Agents During World War II by Joseph E. Persico

Yes, We Sang!: Songs of the Ghettos and Concentration Camps by Shoshana Kalisch with Barbara Meister

The Holocaust Chronicle: A History in Words and Pictures— Publications International, Ltd.

WEB SITES

Toplitz Lake—read about the recovery of artifacts from the Nazi era—*http://www.toplitzsee.at*

The Forgotten Camps—*http://www.jewishgen.org/ForgottenCamps/*

Simon Wiesenthal Center—*http://motlc.wiesenthal.com/index.html*

Austrian Press and Information, Washington, D.C.—*http://www.austria.org*

Mauthausen/Gusen Information Pages—*http://linz.orf.at/orf/gusen*

Mauthausen Memorial (English version)—*http://www.mauthausen-memorial.gv.at/engl/index.html*

Holocaust/Shoah Research Resources—*http://www.igc.org/ddickerson/holocaust.html*

United States Holocaust Museum—*http://www.ushmm.org*

Austria Tourism—*http://austria-tourism.at/*

City of Salzburg (English version)—*http://www.salzburg.com/engl/*

Cindy McCormick Martinusen lives in her hometown of
Cottonwood, California, with her husband, David, and their
three children. They enjoy travel, camping, art and music,
snow skiing, air-hockey competitions, and books. (The Chronicles of Narnia are their favorites.) The family is also currently
homeschooling.

Cindy is an avid reader; loves the mountains and the sea;
and enjoys a variety of sports, especially skiing and playing
softball on a team with longtime friends, her sister, and a
coach she's known since third grade.

Her writing background includes the publication of articles,
short stories, and a play. However, fiction is her great writing
love. *Blue Night* is the sequel to her first novel, *Winter Passing*.

Cindy welcomes letters written to her in care of Tyndale House
Author Relations, P.O. Box 80, Wheaton, IL 60189-0080.

Christian Jr./Sr High School
2100 Greenfield Dr
El Cajon, CA 92019